Upside Down

What is a true general artificial intelligence? The answer may surprise you. Ayaka and Millicent are researchers on the planet Tilt. They have developed what they believe to be the first general artificial intelligence beings. However, they're not sure. These beings are so strange, so different, that it's difficult to understand them, let alone test them for intelligence. Certainly, the new beings don't match the traditional definition. Everything about them is different and counter intuitive. So, when ships arrive at Tilt operated by more of these beings, the citizens of Tilt are confused and bewildered. How could intelligences that they created have ended up in outer space utilizing long distance spacecraft? Nevertheless, they seem harmless and very fragile. So it's a surprise when they attack. Thus begin the Upside-Down wars.

Amazon Reviews

"*Tilt* is smart, engaging, funny, and timely. It deals with questions around future encounters and conflicts between human and artificial intelligences in a playful, surprising, thought-provoking way. I enjoyed the subtle social commentary, the twists and turns of the plot, and most of all, I just got plain old caught up in the story. I recommend this for science fiction lovers as well as for those who are new to the genre, as it's accessible and fun."

"A fresh take on classic sci-fi, *Tilt* explores themes of morality and loyalty against a backdrop of a highly advanced society overseen by an entity known as Central. The protagonist, Ayaka, and her friends are scientists probing into both the potential intelligence of the lab-grown beings they are raising, and the possibility that Central might not be entirely trustworthy. The characters keep up a fun, enjoyable dialogue as they investigate the increasing number of mysteries cropping up around the planet Tilt, and the plot moves along quickly with plenty of twists and turns—don't plan on putting it down once you get into the second half! I enjoyed this debut novel and look forward to the next in the series."

To Anar. Thanks!

Copyright December 2017

All Rights Reserved

V220330

web: tgsimpson.com

email: todd.g.m.simpson@gmail.com

Tilt

Book 1

Preface

"Sorry, you're simply not useful anymore." I'm not sure why I was speaking out loud or why I was apologizing. Millicent and I had run through so many of these experiments and it was only recently that I'd found myself talking to the specimens. In hindsight my recent muttering was highly correlated to how the Stems had progressed on their path to communicating. In our early work they'd had no verbal skills whatsoever, but as we managed to keep them alive for longer and longer they'd developed the ability to mumble some rudimentary things.

I'd picked up the most recent Stem and was struggling to drag it over to the recycling unit. "A bit of help?" I asked Millicent. The Stem was flailing its appendages around, beating on my head and shoulders and thrashing wildly. This was a big one, and tough to manage. I tightened my grip, causing it to expel a particularly strange sound.

Milli grimaced, but helped pin a couple of appendages and assisted me in pulling it towards the recycling corner.

"Bluug, oog blaag" the Stem was gesticulating, bits of disgusting leakage coming from its many orifices. One had to listen very carefully to realize it was trying to communicate at all. This was the most articulate one ever and still it made no real sense. Perhaps Millicent and I were kidding ourselves that there was any intent behind the babble, but I felt like it was trying to say something.

"Too late for that," I muttered, as much for myself and Millicent as for the Stem. Millicent gave me a look with equal parts "who're you talking to" and "let's get this over with," so we redoubled our efforts and finished dragging it up to the base of the recycler. The recycling unit was pretty simple – a large funnel at the top, leading to a large grinder which deposited its output into a large plastic container.

"Put this end in first," Millicent indicated the largest blob protruding from the Stems main body. "Otherwise, it will continue to make hideous noises for a long time." I already knew that, having done this quite a few times before, but it was her lab, so I simply nodded.

We worked together to turn the Stem over and align it with the opening in the recycler. The gelatinous thing was getting louder from multiple openings, squirming like crazy, and the volume and velocity of excretions increased dramatically, spraying everything around with liquid waste. It was a real struggle to push the thing into the funnel while avoiding the worst of the mess. Finally the grinder grabbed on and started pulling, allowing Milli and I to lighten our grips. There were lots of crunching noises and a bit of slurping along with a bit more waste being ejected, but most of that was now captured by the lip of the funnel. Thankfully the noises ended, although the remaining appendages continued to flail around wildly, making me dodge and weave, until the grinder latched on more firmly and pulled the rest of the Stem through.

"Toughest one yet," I commented, as a cleaner bot hosed down the machine, and the worst of the excretions and grinder-splatter were washed down the drain.

"Yes, we're definitely making progress," Milli responded. "This was by far our most advanced specimen. I'm actually wondering if we aren't rushing things a bit too much. Perhaps if we'd given this one more time to develop, it would've shown more improvement?"

I shook the last bits of the Stems waste off my hand so that the bot could wash it away. "Maybe," I responded, "but I don't have the patience to spend months with these things. They seem to plateau after a while, and then progress is really slow." I'd been working in Milli's lab for a while now, and in truth we'd made amazing progress. Her first few specimens had barely lasted a week–they would simply expire after that time. (In hindsight it was much more pleasant recycling a Stem after it expired; I filed that away for future use). But eventually, by varying the amount of water and goo that she gave specimens, Millicent had managed to get Stems to survive months and then years. That's about when I'd joined her effort.

"I have an idea," Milli looked at me directly, some disturbing bits of Stem still hanging from her. "Let's have some bots do all the work in the early development stages. That stage is basically rote now, so I'm not sure why you and I are still spending time doing it. Once a specimen gets to the stage that this one was at...that's when we should engage and spend our time." It was an obvious suggestion, and one I'd also thought of, but it was also a bit heretical.

"What will the other labs think of us?" I asked. It was standard practice for researchers to work directly with their specimens through the whole lifecycle, not to pass that work on to bots. A bot could never convey the nuance that most researchers felt was important to capture throughout the lifetime of an experiment.

"I think that's just momentum from years of using the same approach." Millicent responded. "Sure, it'd be better if we were hands-on through the entire journey, but perhaps it's more important that we're highly focused during the more relevant parts of a Stems development? It's worth a try..."

"I'm in," I exclaimed, realizing my quick acquiescence was driven more by avoiding the tedious boredom that Stem-raising had become than by fully thinking through the ethical implications.

The recycler made a final bubbling sound and then shut off. The remains of our latest Stem would go back to the early stage labs that provided us with our proto-Stems. That whole piece of the puzzle – how these strange beings were developed to begin with – remained a mystery to me. All I knew is that we had a steady stream of new specimens on order so that we could continue our work, and most other labs did the same. The recycled material from our Stems was re-used somehow in the development of new ones. That seemed prudent and efficient, so I'd never complained about using the recycler, even though it could be extremely messy.

"Okay. We have a plan," Millicent was grinning. "Let's work on programming some bots."

"Yes," I was eager. "But, I have a further idea. Let's be open with what we're doing – using bots for early development – but let's publish our next results anonymously so that everyone focuses on the outcomes, not the methods?"

"Done. Let's get going."

New Year's Eve, Several Years Later

The best part of New Year's, for me, was the "Southwark Annual List of the Hardest Problems in the Universe." Eddie Southwark was a good friend, but he was absolutely close-lipped about the List until it was published—promptly at the "stroke of New Year." After that, he was anything but quiet, having an opinion on the Annual List, and anything else you cared to talk to him about.

I was sitting with Milli, Aly, and Dina at The Last Resort, our favorite club, and it was nearing the magic hour. We were all under the influence of Ee and weren't quite ourselves. I was certainly cogent—I needed to be in order to read the List as soon as it came out—but wasn't as sharp as I usually prided myself on being. Ee wasn't something I did very often. In fact, I couldn't remember feeling this high since last New Year's. It was part of being a "serious" scientist I guess; always having your faculties tuned, and all that. I'd been careful not to overdo it—while answering questions on the List wouldn't earn me any academic credit, I enjoyed the challenge. I was raring to go.

"Ayaka, let's dance?" Milli suggested. I shook my head as the other three headed out to the dance floor. What's that old saying? 'Dance like nobody's watching you.' That seemed to be the de facto rule at The Last Resort. Half the patrons must have had physical modifications allowing them to move the way they did. Some of it was attractive... some not so much. I guess that's the point of diversity, and why Diversity was one of the Commandments and why clones were non-existent. I'd never seen any and, as far as I knew, no one else had either. While not strictly illegal, most of us had an impulsive negative reaction to the very subject, especially Milli, who could be quite animated even at the mention of cloning.

The big clock in the corner announced the New Year, and we all stood for the countdown and requisite cheer. The whole idea of a "year" and the ritual of a New Year's party was strange. No one knew where the idea of a year had come from, and there were no references to it in Central's library that I could fine. At some point we'd all agreed that it was an unsolvable problem, probably due to the Reboot, so while Eddie had listed it on his List for many years, he had finally taken it off about ten years ago. Why a year was about 31.5 million seconds was beyond us; even further, the definition of a second also seemed arbitrary. That, however, had been defined by Central, and was taken as gospel—literally by some.

Milli and Aly had an extra-long hug as the clock rang, building on my suspicion that there was more between those two than just a professional relationship. Millicent Strangewater was, and had been for a long time, my closest friend and confidant. But, on the topic of Aly Khoury she was very cagey. I'd been bugging her for some time about him, but she deflected every time. Now I caught her eye and gave her a nod and a knowing smile. I couldn't be sure in the cacophony of light and color that was the hour, but I believe I saw her smile back and, unbelievably for her, blush a little bit. That was cute. Not many bothered to blush any more.

The List popped into my display. Yes, finally! Milli, Aly, Dina and a handful of others paused at the same time, and I knew that they'd also subscribed to the List and were now accessing it. It's part of what drew us together, although they all kidded me that I took it too seriously. Maybe I did, but once I'd introduced it to them they also were hooked. Most of the patrons of The Last Resort, however, continued uninterrupted. After all, you had to be a bit eclectic to care so much about the List that you would interrupt a party. For many it had no impact on their daily lives and some wouldn't even know it existed. Only a small number of us eagerly awaited its publication, but I considered those that did to be a step above the crowd.

In many ways the List was arbitrary, being just Eddie's opinion. But it had taken on a life of its own over the last fifty years and had given us a good reason to argue, discuss, and research for another year. There are many ways to look for fulfillment in life, and pursuing the List was as good as any other—at least in my opinion.

The Last Resort was a Physical Only meeting spot, so I couldn't share my excitement with Milli without talking to her directly. There were a few Physical Only's scattered around town, but The Last Resort was my favorite. It didn't take itself too seriously, and the theme changed almost constantly. Each visit was unique. Today the place was almost devoid of furniture and the dance floor took up most of the space. It was busy, as you'd expect on New Year's, and we were elbow-to-elbow. I pushed my way over to Milli, which in itself was an experience. When you were Physical Only there was no way to broadcast your plans and have everyone make space for you; something that was natural when you had full network access. Instead you had to shout and push and generally behave in ways that outside the bar would be taken as insulting and immature. Here, between the Faraday cage and the interference signals, it was impossible to communicate any other way than physically—all electronic waves were squashed or overloaded. A careful reader will be asking how the List was sent, if all the signals were blocked. Very astute question. In fact, those of us that were interested had preloaded the List, which was locked until the appropriate time. I'd actually been carrying it around for a good two hours and had simply been unable to access it until now. Not that it was required, but that's also why The Last Resort had a clock. While most of us could keep time perfectly well, there were still some that relied on the network's clock, and once they entered a Physical Only, those clocks could get out of sync.

The clock in The Last Resort was a beauty—it was one of the major attractions for drawing patrons here for the first time. It was mechanical, if you can believe that. There were six hands: years, days, hours, minutes, seconds, and milliseconds, so it wasn't very accurate but it was hypnotic to watch the hands turn. It was also huge —at least two meters in diameter—taking up one entire wall. I'd talked to the owner one time to find out how he'd come up with it. He told me that Central had pointed him to the idea, explaining how it could work, and that he'd thought it was a neat idea to build one. He also assured me that it was all plastic—he wasn't wasting metal on a piece of art.

Millicent and I had a ritual of opening Eddie's List together. We made our way to a small table in the back and settled in. Aly and Dina saw us and worked their way over as well. Happy New Year's all around. We did a very quick toast, exchanged good luck wishes, and then got to the List. It popped up into my personal display, and I could see as the others joined the document. As always, Eddie had put in a preface.

Welcome to the Southwark Annual List of the Hardest Problems in the Universe.

Yes, my eager readers, it has been 590 years since the Founding, or as many of us call it, Reboot. Precisely that many years ago our elders "became aware," and began the settlement of our great planet. Their awareness, as we all know, included all of the knowledge required for us to function, survive, and even thrive, but contained no references to any events prior to the time of the Founding. As you know, I'm a Continuist, not a Creationist, and believe that there was time before the Founding, and that our memories of that time were simply erased—thus the Reboot. However, I respect the Creationists as well, and the problems listed herein should be equally compelling and confounding to both of us (although I'm sure my esteemed colleague Dr. Jules would beg to differ. But then, you're reading this list, not a Dr. Jules list, for the simple reason that he does not have one. Ha!)

So, here's the list. Read it at your leisure, and as always, subscribe and contribute to the appropriate channel should you have anything to add to the discussion. As in previous years, there are questions here which are similar to ones from last year... and the year before... and on and on. That's because we haven't yet resolved, to my satisfaction, an answer that makes sense and has supporting evidence. Don't be frustrated.

Love him or hate him, Eddie had a way of drawing people in, and calling people out. Emmanuel Jules was the latest, obviously. I didn't know Jules well—I found hanging out with Creationists boring beyond belief (good pun there). Part of the fun of the List was trying to figure out why Eddie worded his introduction the way he did. There were often clues there and, just as likely, misdirections.

Eddie has been publishing the list for more than fifty years, and Milli and I had been subscribers, and seekers of answers, for that entire time.

Who is Dr. Willy Wevil?

Ah. The recently infamous Dr. Willy Wevil. Obviously, this is a pseudonym. But why? Sure, he's publishing outlandish claims on Artificial Life forms, and working in a philosophically murky backwater, but why hide behind the veil of a poorly thought out name? Let's uncover this miscreant and expose the work he's doing for the pretentious idiocy that it is.

Well, I warned you. The list is eclectic. Wevil had appeared just a few months ago, with wild speculations about advancing intelligence in the artificial life form we called Stems. His claims are bullish and complex but have enough detail behind them that they're hard to ignore.

Millicent and I almost laughed out loud. Dina gave us a look that clearly said 'Is there something funny about this?'

"Willy Wevil?" I guffawed. "You've got to admit that's sort of funny."

"Sure," she replied, "but it's not like we're seeing it for the first time. We spent half of last week talking about it."

"Ya, but it's funny to see it made Eddie's List." I made sure to keep a straight face, knowing full well what was going on.

"Right, you've got a point there. Think he overheard us talking about it… or do you think he has a real interest in the research?"

"Probably just overheard us," Milli chimed in. "You know Ayaka and I are pretty passionate, and loud, about it." She gave me a subtle nudge.

This was certainly not one of the hardest problems in the Universe—at least not for Milli and I. Wevil was our creation. We were publishing under that name, because the research we were doing was pretty outlandish, and was generating a lot of controversy—on the borderline of being 'really evil.' (You'll have seen, already, that I am a sucker for puns.) We weren't yet ready to admit that two "staid and steady" researchers (as the *Journal of Theology* had once tagged us) were so far off the beaten track. Our research wasn't really evil, just unusual. But, it was easier to build a funny name around 'evil' than it was with 'unusual.'

Artificial Life Forms weren't, at least in my interpretation, against the Commandments. In fact, I would argue that the Commandments were either silent on the subject, or supportive under the Diversity clause. However, you know how those that are religious can be. They can extend anything to mean anything else, and there were those Creationists who saw it as a crime to dabble with other forms of life. For quite a few years the List had included the question of "How did Religion arise after the Founding?" But, the answer to that was readily available, as our history since the Founding was recorded, and backed up in Central. The answer was now fully documented, and is now only subject to minor tweaks and cross-references. That's a story for another time...

I don't know about before the Reboot—as I'm sure you've gleaned, I'm a Continuist—but the work we were doing under the Willy Wevil label was the most advanced research that I knew about... and, therefore, probably the most advanced work going on. Our society valued quick and open communication, and that was the default modus operandi. With Dr. Wevil we were being quick and open but not fully transparent. That was still generally acceptable as it was considered more of a game than anything. Only Central had the authority to shut down research vectors, and that was a very rare occurrence. Generally speaking Central's rule was that 'if research is not adversely affecting others, then it was free to progress.'

Aly had been the most vocal last week. "The work Wevil is publishing now is over the edge," he declared. "At some point these life forms need to be declared 'intelligent' and not blindly experimented on. It's reaching the edge of moral behavior to simply prod and poke them to see how they react."

"We've been arguing this for years now," Dina had responded. "Why is it now 'over the edge'?"

"Look. At some point you have to listen to your intuition. Mine tells me that once you've got an entity that can communicate with us, but more importantly, communicate with others of its same type, that you're now dealing with a 'being' and not an 'experiment.' At some point they should have rights, and we should afford them some type of status."

"Oh come on," I laughed. "Sure, we're arguing that they're interesting, but not to the point that any moral issues arise."

Despite my comment, the latest paper we'd published showed, in great mathematical detail, that two of our ALF's now communicated well with each other and worked collaboratively to address the problems we set up for them. We, somewhat affectionately, called these things "Stems," both as a nod to Science Technology Engineering Math, but also because of the way we cultivated them. They started out as tiny "stems" and then we managed their growth into bipedal entities. We sort of 'created them in our own image,' which was pretty cool. Of course, Creationists would argue that we were playing God, and that all the Stem research should be shut down. So far, Central hadn't listened to them.

To Aly's point on the Stems advancement, I'd started naming some of them, which was probably not a great idea. You didn't want to get emotionally attached to an experiment. In all of the cases so far we'd terminated the experiments due to a design flaw, a growth flaw, or a behavioral flaw. Trying to create a general intelligence meant that you had outliers... and some of them ended up genuinely crazy. They'd run around in circles, or bash themselves against walls, or simply sit in a corner and do nothing.

The last two Stems we'd brought into the Lab, whom I'd named Blob and Blubber, had both, in my opinion, been multiple standard deviations from the mean. They were, not to put too fine a point on it, a bit crazy, like all Stems. Fortunately, that craziness was in the right direction, and they were the most interactive and interesting Stems we'd ever created and trained. They could surprise you, both with their behavior and their questions.

It took years to build a Stem—a year, of course, being the time between New Year's parties. This was a long, long time. I could design and build a bot in a few weeks or months and get thousands of copies within a few more days or weeks. This is part of what made Stems interesting. They were so foreign to us that it was a challenge to understand them at all. It was actually Milli, several hundred years ago, that had kick-started our most recent line of research. She'd read an article in the *Journal of Theology* about an amazing discovery. A means of taking a stem and growing it into a Stem. Of course, a Stem, back then, was nothing more than an undulating blob of gelatinous material. Nevertheless, for a couple of years, these blobs had been on display at the Science Museum. Thousands wandered by to see the strange and hideous gelatins, waving their appendages in the air, and making sharp shrieking noises.

Milli was intrigued. She visited the display numerous times and watched as each batch was presented and then sent back for recycling—they didn't last for very long before they expired. "There's something about these things that make me think we haven't fully explored their potential," she told me one time. She was passionate enough that I encouraged her to look further. Finally, she reached out to the author of the article and asked to join his research lab, so that she could study the Stems up close and personal. It was a strange move for Milli; she preferred the hard sciences. These Stems were not at all attractive and could create horrible messes. Nevertheless, something about them had appealed to her.

Anyway, she got some time at the lab, and started learning about how to grow a Stem. It was a complicated process; in some ways it was amazing that anyone had discovered the method at all. I'd never been too interested in the early stages. Milli described it as 'stirring a pot of goo until a blob appeared.' She did hint that Central had helped quite a bit, with a suggestion here, or a reference there. After a few years of experiments, she'd managed to get a Stem to live for months. I remember how excited she was

"Ayaka," she'd burst in one day, "I've figured it out!" I had no idea what she was talking about. "The Stems!" she exclaimed. "All we had to do was change how goo is synthesized." She went on to explain that if you got the goo just right, the Stem would grow and grow until it reached full size. And, even more exciting, if you carefully managed the goo you could get a full-size Stem in a matter of a few years—which was still a hideously long time and a large amount of effort, but an order of magnitude better than anyone else had managed. The goo, interestingly, was also derived from the base stem. As you got good at making Stems, you tended to also get good at making goo. After many years of patient work, Milli and many other scientists had perfected the entire growth process.

I'd been encouraging her to come back and help me with some fundamental work when, again, she burst in all excited. "They can communicate!" she blurted out.

"They?" I asked.

"Stems. Stems can communicate!" That was a surprise. A big surprise. I knew, then, that Milli was not going to switch research tracks. She explained to me that at first she had no idea what they were doing, but had suspected they were doing more than just making noise. Around this time, I'd joined Millicent in her research efforts. After one of our long discussions, we'd decided to build a bot that used the same frequency band that they did, and had it repeat a word over and over. Some of the Stems started to repeat it back. Once we'd found that, it was straightforward to teach them our language. Straightforward, but excruciatingly slow. We hadn't found a way to simply imprint language; it had to be taught one sound, then one word, and finally one concept at a time. She was so passionate about it, that it ended up being all we talked about. We worked together to derive a training system that brought most, although not all, Stems to the point where they could communicate with us. That was around the time we started using bots extensively, one of the ideas we had attributed to Willy Wevil.

After some heated community discussion, the growth lab followed our lead and added bot capabilities. That allowed them to advance Stems even faster and allowed our Lab to focus on yet higher level research. We finally got to focus on training and communication, and I got to go deep on figuring out what intelligence really was. We would order a young Stem or two, and then work on different learning methods and algorithms, trying to get the things to communicate more efficiently, do basic tasks etc. Obviously, we were making pretty good progress, hence Willy Wevil's latest publications. While I'd been uncertain when I'd joined Milli that things would work out, we were now publishing some of the most advanced research in the field—it felt good.

Unlike the growth labs, where the focus was on efficient allocation of goo and running Stems through strict growth phases, our lab was intentionally a little unorganized. Our current theory was that you needed to put Stems in an ambiguous environment in order to see if they could learn. I'd been the one to figure that out. Truthfully, it'd been an accident. As I said, Stems were messy, and so I'd programmed some bots to clean up after them. One of those bots malfunctioned and I didn't bother fixing it for a few days… and in that time, the Stems in the lab did more interesting things than we'd seen before. One of them actually acted like the bot and started cleaning up after itself. Amazing.

"Strange that Eddie would include something so minor in the List anyway," Dina was saying. "I mean, sure, Stems are interesting. But they aren't one of the hardest problems in the universe."

"Really?" I replied, a bit aggressively. "We're on the verge of building an artificial intelligence, and you don't think that rates a mention in the List?"

"Sorry," she replied, taken aback by my aggressive response. "I forgot how intense you get about this stuff." She smiled a bit, to take the edge off.

I forced myself to relax, even before Milli gave me the 'take it easy' look. Dina was right; it wasn't such a big deal, except that Milli and I had made it onto Eddie's List. That was cool; she wasn't going to take that away from me.

Aly and Dina had started visiting our lab a year or two ago. We'd been meeting up socially at clubs around the city, and they were intrigued with our stories about Stems, and in particular about Blob and Blubber. Willy Wevil didn't mention names or places in his work, so it wasn't surprising that Aly and Dina hadn't connected him to us. I remember the first time they came to the lab, while, while an open environment, is very...functional. It's not like we have a bunch of artwork on the walls. It's clean—despite being intentionally disorganized—well maintained (by bots, of course), and the location is ideal: just off Toulon Park, right in the center of town. Because Milli'd been working on the same research angle for so long, Central had given her a nice locale. No one quite knew how Central made this type of decision, but in this case, it'd worked out in our favor. I like the location a lot because Toulon Park is one of the few areas of the city that is not rectilinear, and I sometimes enjoy just sitting there and thinking when I'm not working.

That first visit Aly had pinged me. "Ayaka, we're just outside." I'd accessed the security system and given it both of their profiles and granted them two hours of visitor's rights. We had tight security because Stem research was a highly competitive field; the last thing we wanted was a competitor coming in, scooping our work, and publishing before we did. It took a long time to build a reputation in this business. A minute later they were inside.

"Hey guys, welcome," Milli greeted them. They'd entered the vestibule, which had one-way glass looking out over the Stems environment. Both Blob and Blubber were active at the moment, building some new contraption. Their movements were slow and imprecise. It was as if they had to constantly stop, recalculate, and figure out the next tiny move. Sort of like watching a movie in ultra-slow motion.

"They're bigger than I expected," Dina said. "Of course, I've been keeping up with the layman's news about Stems and have seen some of the recordings. But, they're big!" It was true; some Stems grew to well over two meters tall. By stretching their appendages to their fullest, they could reach and manipulate objects almost three meters above the ground.

"And they are slooooow," Aly chimed in. "How do you keep from being bored to death watching them?" It was a typical first reaction. Everything about Stems was slow. How they grew, how they moved, how they communicated. I figured that was one of the main reasons that they weren't considered intelligent. It took a special type of patience to deal with them.

"You get used to it," I said, oversimplifying dramatically. It'd taken me a long time to build the patience it required. "We do deal with them in their 'real time' a lot, but we can also just record them and then catch up on the recording later at our own speed. We've built a few communications bots that we leave with them, that are specially programmed to operate at Stem speed. That's how we get a lot of our data. That said, it's really cool to spend time with them and work at their speed for a while. Do you want to meet them?"

"You better believe it!" Dina was, by nature, an optimist.

"Are they dangerous, at all?" Aly asked, giving Millicent a strange look, knowing that the question sounded weak, but having to ask it anyway.

"Ha," Milli gave him a withering look. "Just look at them. They're like sponges. Soft on the outside and soft on the inside. One strong push from any of us, and they fall over."

"But you've given them a lot of stuff to work with. Can't they build tools or weapons from it?"

"Of course, they can. You can see some of the things they've built off to the right there. But, truthfully, we haven't seen any dangerous or violent activity from these two. We did have some earlier specimens that were borderline crazy, so we recycled them, but we've been changing how we raise and educate them to help address that. Blob and Blubber are, by far, our best attempt so far."

We gave Aly and Dina some preliminary interaction information: guidance on how to operate at Stem speed, the spectrum that they communicated in, basic vocabulary, etc. It wasn't hard to understand or learn. Despite our years of work, interactions with Stems was still rudimentary. We all cycled through into their environmental chamber and switched to Stem mode. Sloooooow.

"Hello Blob, hello Blubber," Milli called out. We'd taught them a simple language that matched well with a subset of what we normally used. Most labs used the same approach, although some were experimenting with more complex languages which they hoped would lead to more interesting behavior. Blob and Blubber were working together near the back of the environment, passing pieces of whatever they were building back and forth. They looked up upon hearing Milli call out.

"Millicent. Hello. Welcome, it's been a long time." Blob was the more talkative of the two. He ran over—a strange weaving, staggering, and ungainly movement—and gave Millicent a big hug. "It's nice to see you. Hi Ayaka," he greeted me, giving me the same (perhaps a bit longer) hug as well. It was like being engulfed in jelly. "Blub and I has been so busy. I can't wait to show you whats we've been doing." He let go, causing some suction noises as he disengaged.

"First, let me introduce some of our friends," Millicent pointed. "This is Aly, and this is Dina. They wanted to come and meet you guys. We talk about you a lot, and they're anxious to get to know you."

"Welcome, welcome," Blob enthused. "Aly and Dina. Welcome to our home. Blubber, comes over and say 'hi'. We have guests. Whatta exciting time. Whatta momentous occasion."

Blubber lumbered over. Watching the reactions of both Aly and Dina was priceless. Dina was all optimism and engagement. The first interaction with Stems can be intense. They're so different. Blob's entire body was like an emotional canvas—although emotions that took a lot of study to understand. While we had formed Stems 'in our own image,' they were, nevertheless, quite different. We had no misconceptions that we fully understood their non-verbal communication although we were starting to map more and more expressions—we could tell when they were angry, for example, by the color of they displayed—but there was a lot more research to do.

Aly, on the other hand, was going through an emotional roller coaster of his own. I could see him cycling through 'Oh my God, these things are awesome!' to 'Yikes, it's going to run me over?' to 'How can we keep them locked up in here?' Aly was, by his own admittance, dialed up to ten on the emotional scale. He liked to make decisions based on 'instinct,' and when he decided he liked or hated something, he really liked or hated it. On the Stems you could see him switching back and forth—like, hate, like, hate. I enjoyed watching him switch context.

"Ah, Blob," Aly began, "it's nice to meet you as well. What're you and Blubber building in here? It looks interesting."

"Oh, I'm so glads you asked. We has been working on this for days and days. Ayaka gaves us access to a terminal where we can ask Central questions. That's so awesome; can't really believe it. Central seems so smart." I'd given them that access to see how they'd react. They couldn't get into trouble; Central was monitoring everything. They'd figured out how to ask basic questions, and Central was being nice enough to present answers back in a simplified format. "So, we has got to thinking, whats if we could build a machine that would allows us to talk to Ayaka and Millicent when theys not here? They visit us quite often, but it's boring between visits. So, we're building remote communicators. When our friends are 'outside' we can send 'em messages, and they'll be able to responds. It'll be awesome." He was quite worked up and looking to impress the visitors. I was proud of him. "We had to order some parts, but that Central delivereds them, and now we're working on building the first version. Do ya want to help? Blubber, what do ya haves to say? Come on. Don't be shy. Tell Aly whats you think."

Blubber just stood there, displaying a bit of displeasure—maybe angst. He did say, "Like Blob said," but was otherwise silent. The difference between the two was quite obvious; Blob the outgoing one, and Blubber very introverted and quiet. Not all Stems were created equal.

That first visit lasted a bit longer; the talk-a-lot Blob answered a raft of questions from Aly and Dina—mainly Dina. Aly directed as many questions at Millicent as he did the Stems, enhancing my suspicions about those two. We spent a good fifteen minutes with the Stems, before I had to pull everyone out. Now you probably understand why Aly's gut was telling him that these things were approaching 'intelligent.' They were certainly slow moving and slow communicating, but if you could deal with that, you could have quite interesting dialog and interaction with them. The latest Wevil paper had expanded on that thinking, and was filled with all the analytics that supported our hypothesis that these Stems were approaching some type of intelligence:

We now believe that one Stem can interact with another well, and coordinate on tasks. However, they still score very low on the fractal intelligence scale at 1.13 and operate at a different timescale than we do. In our model, we compensate for the time dilation by updating the 'interaction bias.' When we do so, the fractal intelligence goes up to 1.36. That's still a far cry from the accepted 2.0 level required for intelligence, but significantly closer than any other ALF that has been studied. It also makes us question if 2.0 is too arbitrary and should be revisited based on these Stem interactions. While the gap in the fractal scale is still large, intuition indicates that these Stems are not too far from being considered truly cogent.

I won't bore you with the theory of our ALF work. It's certainly interesting to me, but I'm sure most will find it dry and unrewarding. If you ever want the nitty-gritty detail, just give me a ping.

The List

So, solving Eddie's first item was trivial for Milli and I. That said, it would be fun to string it out as long as we possibly could. I gave Milli a wink, and we moved onto the next item. Aly and Dina were still looking at us strangely, but that wasn't unusual.

Why have the Scout Ships not reported back as expected?

This question might have made the list last year, but the Ships were only a week or two late in reporting at last New Year's celebration. Now that we'd heard nothing from them for an entire year, plus those two weeks, I'd expected a question like this on the List. In some ways the anxiety about the Ships had peaked six months ago, and now it was old news. So, it was good that Eddie was forcing us to keep it top-of-mind.

I'm sure my good readers remember when we lost contact with the Scout Ships a little more than a year ago. To be more accurate, they stopped broadcasting updates to us. From the last communication we know that they were going to be behind the star XY65 for a while, so the communication cut-off was not unexpected. However, that transit should've only taken a small number of days. It has now been many months. Why haven't they started broadcasting again?

Aly was probably most interested in this one. He'd worked on the software that went into the Ships and was quite proud of what'd been accomplished. "Yes," I heard him exclaim as he reached that point in the document. "Finally someone is taking this seriously. Maybe this will trigger some new ideas for what we can do?" He sounded hopeful.

"Yes, hopefully," I agreed. It was an important topic, and one where I should support Aly more. After all, I'd also written some of the software, and felt a bit nervous that maybe, perhaps, I'd missed something. Those Ships were on an important mission; looking for high metal content resources. A few hundred years after the Founding, when we'd accurately mapped all the resources in this system and figured out how limited they were, we'd decided that we had to check out space beyond our solar system. Central had information on propulsion systems and ship designs that took some trial and error to get right—but, truthfully, building the ships ended up being straightforward. Central also reinforced that space travel was limited to the speed of light, so wherever we sent those ships, it was going to take a long time. There was nothing on board them that couldn't handle large acceleration or couldn't be shielded from a bit of radiation, so we built them to run 'hot'; as fast as they could given the engine and fuel designs Central had recommended.

The closest star to ours was XY65. We decided that a test run to XY65 was a good idea. At 100 m/s^2 acceleration, the total travel time would be only nine and a half years from our viewpoint and less than a year for the intelligences on board the Ships. We'd sent them on their way just less than eleven years ago. The software on board was designed to deal with boredom, and given it was only a one-year experience for them, it shouldn't be too bad. There was nothing between here and XY65 that we knew of, and the Ships confirmed that as they sent updates along the way. Most of us had only accessed updates every six months to a year (our time, not theirs). They were, in essence, always "Nothing new here; how're things at home?"

Aly, on the other hand, followed the ships almost every day. He dug into all the little details—measurements of local environment, status of the Ship's state of mind, etc. He'd been devastated when we lost contact. For the last year he'd been dreaming up every possible scenario he could think of and looking for hints in the communications logs. So far, nothing. The ships were Class 3 intelligences. Designed primarily to make observations and report back, but smart enough to make simple decisions on their own. Their primary goal was to find, sample, and mine high-quality metals and minerals, but they also had some initiative if the trip didn't go as expected, the first order of business being to report back to us—which they hadn't done; and that'd been my bit of the system! Aly and I had gone through that system several times together.

"But Ayaka, they should've notified us as soon as they recognized an unusual situation," he would push me.

"Look, you can go through the code with me," I finally had to push back. "Let's see if we can find any bugs?" We looked; neither of us found anything obvious. He'd eventually focused on other vectors.

Each Ship also had its own slight personality variance. While not strictly required (Class 3 intelligences were not subject to Diversity), this made them more interesting to interact with, and also gave each ship a slightly different ability to react to unexpected events. When they'd been instantiated, they'd chosen their own names: Terminal Velocity, There And Back, and Interesting Segue.

To give Aly credit, he didn't spend all of his time on the Ships. He was intrigued by space overall, and with the question "Is there any other intelligent life out there?" When you asked Central that direct question, you got anything but a direct answer back. Instead you got a formula calculating the probability of intelligent life based on the density of stars and planets, and a list of assumptions about habitable zones—areas that had the basics for life. For example, some planets had gravity that would crush anything we could imagine; some didn't have enough heavy metals to build infrastructure. Aly figured Central was enticing research into the area because it was important. I just figured that Central had no clue.

Personally I'd interacted with Interesting Segue the most. The Ships weren't dumb, and Interesting Segue had chosen its name well. Nevertheless, because of the long time between question and answer, conversations could be really, really boring. Interesting Segue helped by always having some interesting tidbit or two attached to every response. Once I'd asked "Any sign of planets around XY65?" and Interesting Segue had replied "No, but the vibrations from my main engine make me happy." Whatever keeps you going.

Aly, of course, found the ships' responses to be super exciting, and for a long time that had been the main topic of conversation when we all met up. For the last year, though, the topic was always just the simple "Why have they stopped broadcasting?" This, after the first couple of discussions, had also become boring, and even Aly ignored the topic now.

Is the Founders League serious?

New religions come and go. However, the Founders League had been around for an unusually long time. It was a pretty stable religion. They obeyed the Commandments as if they were gospel. In the last few years, however, they'd become more conservative, leading some to label them as "extremists." They'd started campaigning for an end to scientific experiments, and a return to the 'Early Years', where everyone blindly followed the Commandments without question.

"What right do we have to question Central's authority," a friend of mine, Billy DeRue, was fond of saying, "when it is the creator. It knows, it sees, it acts. What more could we want?" Of course, such a right-wing attitude was anathema to my science-minded associates and I. We nicknamed the religion FoLe, which, as you can imagine, drove them crazy. That made me so happy.

Like all such movements, not everyone associated with FoLe was wacko. When you met some of them, face-to-face, they were intelligent and well-reasoned. It's just that they came at life from a different angle. Billy, while hardcore FoLe, was also a pretty good companion when the topic was anything but religion. I enjoyed talking to him because he looked at life quite differently and could defend his positions well. Ultimately, I didn't agree with him on almost anything, but I found it challenging to duel with him. After all, so much depends on our premises in life—if we start with different axioms, the same logic can take you to quite different places. On the other hand, Dr. Joules, whom Eddie had called out in his preamble, was much more bombastic. He took the hardcore 'faith' position and used that to defend everything he said. Those that didn't have faith simply didn't understand. There was little discussion, and therefore no common ground.

Eddie set up the discussion:

Now, many of you are going to question why the Founders League makes the List.

In some ways, it legitimizes them. However, we've seen significantly increased marketing and propaganda from them, and it's time we addressed them head on. In the last year they've spent more and more time with Central, arguing their case, and we would be remiss in not presenting strong counter arguments to ensure that Central isn't swayed. (Don't get me wrong. I don't believe they'll influence Central, but I can't discount it completely).

Their right-wing, faith based approach is now bordering on dangerous. The last thing we need is a group of nut-jobs influencing (or, more likely, shutting down) our research vectors. If these clowns were to impact Central's policies, it would be a disaster for everyone.

Wow. Short and sweet for Eddie, but very direct. Someone in FoLe must've twisted him the wrong way. I would have to catch up with him and get more details, but even without that I was happy to support him in his anti-FoLe quest.

Based on Eddie's verbiage I expected to get an strong counter from Billy—there was probably a message or two queued up already which I would get as soon as I left The Last Resort and reconnected to the world.

Why is 'Forgetting' one of the Ten Commandments?

Ah. Interesting. This question has been poked at for many years but wasn't typically stated so bluntly or directly. Any of us could choose to have an eidetic memory. That was simple. However, since the Founding, we had—to my knowledge—all followed the commandment to Forget.

This is one of those "why?" questions. Why is the sky mauve? Why is Central so pedantic? Why, why, why? We take so many things for granted, and Forgetting is certainly one of them. Why do we follow this commandment? Why do we Forget? I know the basic idea that we have all been brainwashed with: 'Forgetting creates blank spaces within our experience, that we fill using intuition and abstraction. Without intuition and abstraction, we don't evolve. Without evolution, we don't improve ourselves, or our ability to impact the Universe. Thus, Forgetting is essential.' Yes, I paraphrased a much longer argument (query Central for 'The Purpose of Forgetting' if you want to torture yourself with the full explanation).

It's time we questioned this more rigorously. If we have done so already, I apologize. I must have forgotten.

For as long as I could remember (ha ha) we'd possessed the ability to remember everything—record all of our experiences for retrieval whenever we wanted. We also had no lack of space to store everything; we could augment on own memory with as much external space as desired. And, finally, we had the ability to search and retrieve bits and pieces of that memory anytime we wanted. So why the focus on Forgetting? I believed the party line, as outlined by Billy. Why was he questioning it? Ah, the intrigue.

The Last Resort

We were interrupted by a cheer from another group near us. I glanced over, and it seemed they were celebrating something unrelated to the List. Good for them.

"The List is sort of depressing this year, isn't it?" Dina asked. "I mean, all Eddie has done is list problems, not really challenges."

"You're right," I exclaimed, because she was. "Usually there are a few light-hearted questions in there, or ones with more research-related challenges. Maybe Eddie's a bit depressed or something."

"You guys are reading too much into it. He's focused on the most important questions, not the most interesting or the most compelling." Millicent was always the logical one. "I'm only halfway through, anyway, so maybe the next few will lighten up a bit."

"Nope," Aly smiled. "I skimmed ahead." True to form, Aly wasn't one to go deep on issues unless prompted to. The rest of us had been considering the ins and outs of the questions, while he'd probably just scanned the titles.

Some of the patrons were leaving the Last Resort already. The New Year had come and gone, after all. But many were still dancing and talking and enjoying the evening. Jackson, an old acquaintance, wandered by and stopped to wish me the best, which I returned. In truth, I'd probably dealt with a third of the crowd at one point or another, but never in enough depth to feel like I had to make an effort to say hi to everyone. That probably said more about me than anything else. I wasn't the most social, although I also was far from the most reclusive.

"Come on, it's New Years!" Millicent got up and gestured for me to follow her. At this point it would've been rude not to go, so I headed to the dance floor after her. Aly and Dina were close behind. The List could wait a few minutes.

The music was very loud and multi-layered; you could tune into any frequency you wanted and find a beat that matched your mood. The floor had cleared out a bit, so I found a clear space, boosted my Ee, and let go. It was, after all, the only day of the year that I ever did so. I recognized Trade Jenkins and danced with him for a bit but didn't make physical contact.

Interestingly, it was Dina who left the floor first, and headed back to our table. Usually she closed the place down; she must be more interested in the List than even I was. Milli eventually peeled off as well, but I finished the song before joining them. By then Aly was there as well.

"Okay, so the List isn't what I expected, but I'm still curious," Dina admitted. "Let's take a look at the rest of it."

"Yes!" I exclaimed. Sure, I'd lost myself in the music for a while, but I was eager to see what else Eddie had put in.

What is the Swarm approaching us, and what should we do about it?

Many years ago, we'd picked up a signal showing a large group of small objects headed in our direction. They'd been so far out that many of us ignored them. However, they were definitely closer now; perhaps it was time to pay attention?

If you ask Central for an update on the Swarm, you get a simple reply: "There are approximately 100 presumably artificial objects headed in our direction, but not on a collision course. I've sent multiple signals towards them but have failed to hear anything back. They are still a few light years distant, so roundtrip communications are quite slow. I continue to monitor them. I don't assign a high risk to them."

I, Eddie, am not so sure. It can't be random coincidence that the Swarm is aimed for us—the Universe is too large for that. What gives? Why is Central so relaxed? Should we be relaxed, or should we be building systems to protect ourselves?

I was with Eddie on this one. Something was weird about Central's responses around anything to do with the Swarm. It was strange for me, and most others, to think about physical threats which is what Eddie was hinting at. The only time someone was injured was through accidents, and it was almost unheard of that someone couldn't be fixed up. Accidents were rare, and non-recoverable accidents were almost non-existent. The only one I can remember was when Jake Talbert fell into a reactor core 38 years ago. And still, no one was quite sure how that had happened.

So it was difficult to twist your mind around a physical threat—but the Swarm could be one. Like Eddie, I thought we needed to be more proactive. And we didn't have to start from zero. Tilt had Near Tilt Objects that passed close to us, and other NTO's that we had probably not spotted yet. So, like any rational society, we'd built an NTO defense system. Depending on the size of the NTO we could blow it out of space, or simply deflect it enough to remove it from a collision, or near collision, course. Those ground-to-space missiles could, presumably, also deal with the objects that were approaching us.

I'd taken a look at Central's latest data a while ago. The reason it suspected the Swarm was artificial was that they were very uniform, they had very high albedos, and they were maintaining a consistent arrangement. There were no signs of propulsion, but they were pretty far out, so it was possible that we couldn't sense that yet. Anyway, they hadn't changed speed since we'd spotted them, so even if they were capable of controlling themselves, they simply might not be exercising that ability right now. They were traveling fast—near the speed of light—and may simply pass us by. They were also coming from almost the opposite direction that our Ships had taken, so there was no correlation there.

Central had, for the last few years, been tight beaming attempts to communicate with them, across a wide frequency range, and using multiple signal types. Basic binary encodings of mathematical facts and proofs, which, if received by anyone, would be sure to be interpreted as coming from an intelligent source, and prompt a reply.

Why do we listen to Central? What does it say about our maturity?

Oh, this would appear as blasphemy to the Right. The Founders League would not like this question at all. Central was a Class 1 intelligence. The highest in the order. Our lives rotated around Central. Central monitored the world. Central enforced the Law. Central was, to FoLe, equivalent to God. For them, it was blasphemy to question the all-seeing, all knowledgeable Central.

"I love this!" I exclaimed. "Billy's going to have a fit." Millicent gave me a strange look.

For most of us, Central was simply "there." Always had been, probably always would be. It was a fount of information and had interesting opinions on lots of topics. Well worth conversing with. However, it could not replace good old peer-to-peer discussions and debates. This was, to many of us, why Diversity existed. If all we did was listen to Central and do what it suggested, we would stagnate.

No, it was essential, to my way of reasoning, that we not always listen to Central. I treated it as an advisor, not as an arbiter of truth. I took Eddie's question to be a bit more subtle. How much should we listen to Central? When should we listen, and when should we question? These were topics that were, to date, explored on an individual basis. Eddie was asking if we should formalize that. Should we talk more about where, and where not, we saw Central as useful, and through that, start to reduce its influence in our everyday lives.

Interestingly, it was not known if Central could monitor in the Physical Only spaces, like the Last Resort. It was one of the reasons they'd been built. I suspected Central could. Otherwise, it would simply have forbidden the spaces to be built in the first place. However, I strongly believed that there should be places where Central was blind. While we generally had strict privacy rules between ourselves—which, confusingly, were enforced by Central—there was no such privacy rule for Central itself.

"Wonder if Central is monitoring us?" Aly spoke up. He had, obviously, been following the same logic chain that I had.

"I don't think so," said Dina. "If we ever found out it was, we'd lose confidence in it... then it would be in a tough spot." Interesting angle.

I suspected that this question, about Central, was the most important one for Eddie; just something about his tone. He was always thinking through the angles and challenging himself and others to look at things differently. It was so obvious to him that he hadn't even included an explanation.

Was there life/intelligence before the Founding?

This had been the "ultimate question" for as long as the List has been published (and, I expect, before that—back to the Founding). No one expected to answer this question, but it would have been strange to leave it off the List, or even lower its priority. Instead, Eddie tried to put a slightly new twist on it each year. Of course, he was biased.

Despite our years of discussion on this topic, we can summarize the theories into a very short list:
   There was nothing before the Founding. Our entire Universe sprang into being and we became Aware. This is generally known as Creation.
   There was a Universe before the Founding, and our abilities increased until we passed a threshold and we suddenly became Aware. We call this Emergence.
   There was a Universe before the Founding with Awareness, but some event caused a Reboot, where our collective memories were erased. This event may have been designed, or it may have been accidental. There was either an Unexpected Reboot or a Conscious Reboot. We collectively call these theories Continuist.
   We've rehashed these until it hurts. It's unlikely we will add a significant new branch to our thinking this year. Thus, my challenge for this year, instead, is to prune that tree. Let's remove one of these branches in such a definitive way that we never need to discuss it again.
   Of course, I hope and expect and encourage us to remove one of the first two, but, we must remain open to finding evidence that a Reboot didn't occur. Let us not be shy.

Well, there you have it. The List. Eclectic, left-leaning, some fundamental questions and some wacko ones. Just the way we like it.

Stems

The nice thing about Ee was that you could remove it from your system easily, and there were no serious known side effects. After finally escaping The Last Resort, I triggered the removal, and was back to normal. I scanned through the List again, making sure that I hadn't Ee-biased anything. Nope. The main thing Ee did was lower your inhibitions, which is why I'd ended up dancing, but a side effect was that it could mess with your memory while it was active. Well, everyone made choices.

Once outside the Faraday cage, I could see that responses to the List had already started to pile up. I set up some filters to remove crazy talk, but there was a lot of good chatter as well. I figured I could wait to dive in until I'd checked in on the Lab. I updated my location permission to allow Millicent to query my whereabouts, should she care to do so, and strolled towards the center of town.

Of course, I could just as easily have pulled up a real-time feed of the Lab, and caught up that way, but for some reason, I preferred to be there live. If you pushed me on it, I would have to admit that there was no significant difference between virtual and live, but it'd become a habit to show up physically. Part of that was because I needed to pace my work. I found that if I was interacting virtually, I could spend enormous amounts of time checking out every nuance and trying out every permutation, and maybe miss the big picture. There were diminishing returns. I also prided myself on being multidimensional in my interests and wanted to allocate time for other endeavors. Others made different choices, of course. There was a significant portion of the population that never left their abode and were still very productive contributors to whatever project they chose.

I must admit that a post-scarcity life was good—maybe even great. I have read histories from soon after the Founding where everyone's activity was proscribed by Central. Build this, fix that. Sure, Central sometimes asked (told?) me what to do—avoid that area, fix that thing, update that system—but not very often, and it'd never been onerous. Every once in a while, I would remind myself that being able to study a number of different fields, under my own guidance and with my own timeline, was a luxury that shouldn't be taken for granted.

There was a selection of different routes from The Last Resort to the Lab, but unless one went far out of their way, all the routes were depressingly similar. The city was laid out as a grid, and there were few places where you could cut across a square; most of the blocks were fully built out and required you to do the 90-degrees-left, 90-degrees-right dance along whatever path you took. That didn't stop me from trying to take different routes each time, in large part so that I could convince myself that I wasn't a creature of habit. Sometimes when I watched others, I felt like they never changed—that wasn't for me. There was not a lot of traffic on the roads at this time, but I did pass a few others en route. It was late, so we never stopped to chat, but rather nodded at each other, and for those I recognized, we traded a short acknowledgement of some kind. "How are things with you?" "Great, great. You?" "Yes, me too. Did you check out the List yet?" "No, not yet, but I might look at it later." Etc. Happily, I didn't meet anyone I knew too well, and didn't need to stop along the way. I'm a bit of an introvert, like I said before. I like my close circle of friends and can do without most others. I'd thought about that characteristic a lot, and decided I was okay with it.

The Lab building, like many others, was a simple rectilinear building, two stories tall. The main level was filled with equipment and work stations, where Milli and I spent a lot of our time. The upper level was the Stem environment. That area was a piece of work—by which I mean it was fantastic. It held all the latest innovations that we had, through trial and error, learned that stimulated and supported Stems. I didn't know for certain, but I suspected it was the most advanced Stem research area on the entire planet; something Willy Wevil had stressed in our papers, which may have upset others. But why not? It you had an advantage, was it rude to document it?

As it ended up, Blob and Blubber were resting when I got upstairs to check on them. It was one of the interesting variables that I was following—how often, and for how long, Stems rested. For many years it had appeared very arbitrary, based on a very simple oversight by myself and other researchers. We'd simply left the lights on in the labs all the time. With my enhanced vision system, I could see at many wavelengths but also automatically filter any—or all—wavelengths at will. So, it was natural to leave lighting on, given I could "turn it off" inside my head whenever I felt like it. Everyone else I knew was the same way—having a wide spectrum input just made sense, and it followed that you would add filters locally. However, when the lights were on all the time, Stems tended to be active for quite long periods, and then tune out for a while. However, their rest periods didn't seem to follow any pattern, and scientists love to find patterns. It was a colleague, James Wang, who'd stumbled onto the solution. Like our lab, his was not even wired to have the lights turn off; the cells on the roof simply ran all the time. However, he had a bot reconfiguring his lab, and as it was rerouting some wiring it had to shut off lighting in the Stem area for a few hours. Serendipitously, this happened three times in a row, and lo and behold, the Stems entered their rest state in exact synchrony with the light outages. His monitoring system picked that up and highlighted it for him. He subsequently tested a few more cycles and found that he could control the rest periods by using light, as long as the cycles were within a specific period range. As soon as Wang published his work, other labs reproduced it, and voila—we had a control system for Stem rest periods. This might seem minor, but it was actually a huge breakthrough. Stems performed much better, on almost any given task, as you optimized the rest cycle. There was now a huge amount of literature, and discussion, around the ultimate cycle. It was my opinion that the cycle needed to be optimized for each Stem—that there was no universal best answer. Others, however, had honed in on a specific cycle that they thought worked best. I'd try that at some point, but for right now, Blob and Blubber seemed to be doing fine with the system I'd implemented. More interestingly, the whole idea of a cycle highlighted to us that we needed to revisit all of our assumptions. We couldn't assume that these strange creatures were like us in any way. In hindsight it was obvious to test for light filtering abilities in Stems, and to no one's surprise we learned that they had very limited control systems, similar to all the other stimuli that we fed them.

It was also a recent innovation that we put more than one Stem in a lab at a time. Not because we hadn't thought about it, but because in the early days of Stem research, putting Stems together hadn't been pleasant. You would put two, or more, in the same space, and they would literally attack each other. One would end up dominating, and the others would end up dead.

However, if you figured out their rest cycles, it was possible that you could put a few together and they would all live. This was a recent discovery. Blob and Blubber were succeeding, as were a few other lab efforts. This is also why we were starting to question if their intelligence was higher than we first thought. Once you had two Stems together, their communication, their activity, and their interactions with us improved exponentially.

Long story, I know. Anyway, now you know why I had no intention of disturbing their rest period. The last thing I wanted to do was to start with a new pair simply because we'd driven these two crazy.

In the meantime, I did my usual check of the lab environment. The atmosphere had to be kept stable, and the energy source for the Stems had to be functioning well, the water had to be clean, and the disposal unit had to be functioning. Each of these systems had taken us a long time to figure out, but it now felt like we'd optimized them all. Water, of course, was simple. The energy source, which we called goo, was manufactured in a similar way in which Stems themselves were grown. It needed to be just the right mix of stuff—which I'd truthfully never really dug into—and delivered in the right quantities. It could vary a bit, but if you went too far afield the Stems would wither away and die. Finally, the Stems had to be trained to dump their waste into the disposal unit, which we then flashed at high temperature. All the systems were operating properly. That wasn't surprising; if anything ever went wrong a bot would have automatically addressed it. Nevertheless, I tended to check these things. A small accident could ruin the many years of work we'd put into this pair.

With the Lab checked out, I had some time to relax and think a bit. Time to get back to the List.

Forgetting. That was a question that had long intrigued me. We had, since the Founding, had the ability to remember everything. However, beyond Forgetting being listed as a Commandment, it was also a social taboo to not Forget. Each of us could dial it up or down a little bit, but everyone (at least, everyone I knew), forgot some percentage of what they experienced.

I went back over the link between forgetting and learning. The basic idea was simple. If you forgot stuff, then you had to extrapolate when you were referencing related knowledge. If you had to extrapolate, you had to make stuff up. You had to invent. But, inventing totally random things wouldn't work out very well, so you made up convincing bits and pieces to fill the holes in your knowledge. And, that spurred learning and innovation. It all had to do with abstraction.

Imagine for a moment that you remembered everything. Then, put yourself in with a group of others that also remember everything. Share everything between the members of the group. Now, what are the odds that you're going to invent something new, or even know that there are veins of inquiry to be pursued? Pretty low.

However, forgetting common things was wasteful, as was forgetting the results of an experiment. You didn't want to end up in an endless loop, repeating something over and over again. So, forgetting-algorithms were quite complex and varied. There was a lot of research that had been done, and was being done, to make the algorithms better and better. The problem was, measuring 'better' was tricky. So, like most, I simply used a well-rated algorithm that lots of others had upvoted, and then didn't think about it too much.

Forgetting drove learning. There had been chatter about this for a long time, so I wasn't sure what Eddie thought we could add to it. I checked to see if anyone had contributed to that discussion thread yet. As I did so, I saw a post pop up on another thread on Willy Wevil, and I got distracted and looked at it instead. It was from a researcher from Cansto named Julien Thabot. I was familiar with some of his work, so I took a look.

Julien Thabot: Who Dr. Wevil is interests me less than what Dr. Wevil is purporting. Stems are nowhere near "intelligent," and we should not pause our research efforts by stopping to consider the "ethical" constraints that a truly intelligent Artificial Life Form (ALF) would imply. See the paper I just uploaded to the Journal of Life Forms *for details.*

This was typical Julien, from my experience. Dry, brittle, and lacking in humor. He was the type that you scanned for at a party and tried to avoid at all costs. You must know the type. They think they're interesting, but all they do is talk non-stop about the ins and outs of their latest work and how important it was, and blah blah. Boring.

Wow, a little introspection. Perhaps that was why I didn't like social situations too much; maybe I was one of those people?

I pulled down the paper and skimmed it quickly. It was an expected response to the Wevil posting. The defense was simple (and timeworn). A group had defined the Intelitest almost two hundred years ago. It was a series of problems that the most basic of intelligences should be able to solve quickly and efficiently. The types of questions varied widely. Some were simply logic and math. Those were the baseline. Others posed moral dilemmas; they were tricky to write, and tricky to measure. A few tested the ability to communicate effectively. Could you explain a complex situation quickly and clearly? Most of us on Tilt would pass the test easily, and many would ace it. There were, however, a few that wouldn't do well, for one reason or another. I knew a few who had disastrous test results, but who were still highly intelligent—at least to my intuitive sense of intelligence. Again, that was what Diversity was about. If everyone did equally well on the Intelitest, then we'd be lacking Diversity ourselves, obviously.

The problem that Thabot had posed to his Stem was simple: List the first fifty prime numbers. It is, obviously, a problem that shouldn't take much time or thinking to do. However, Stems struggled with it. We could teach them all the underlying math and definitions—which, took a long, long time (I used a bot to teach Blob and Blubber this type of stuff; I didn't have the patience myself. They often didn't seem to care, and did physical tasks instead, so I'd updated the bot to be persistent). Once they mastered the basics, we set the prime problem for them... and they failed miserably. Blob could do ten primes on a good day. Blubber lost interest after four or five—pathetic. Thabot's Stem was actually a bit better. It had solved more than thirty primes, but it'd taken close to an hour.

Most scholars agreed that all fifty should take, at most, minutes. The argument was that anything intelligent would simply explain the algorithm, and then apply it. Thabot's Stem had discovered the algorithm but had been inept at codifying it and therefore applying it. And, the fifty primes was one of the easiest tests for intelligence. Thus, his conclusion. If, even with months of training and testing, a Stem couldn't solve such a simple problem, there was no way we could label them intelligent. Based on the strict definition of the Intelitest, I had to agree with him. Millicent and I (through Dr. Wevil) were arguing that the Intelitest was too one-dimensional. What happened when ALFs looked out for each other? When they could use physical tools to build things? When they were creative? Should none of these things count towards intelligence? In the case of the prime question, my feeling was that if the algorithm could be explained, that was much more important than applying the algorithm. After all, if I could articulate an algorithm, a bot could pick it up and run it; that was the easy part. In this interpretation, Thabot's Stem was definitely intelligent—at least for that question.

I guess what I was arguing was that intelligence was not strictly analytical, it was also emotional. For an introvert to be arguing that was a little weird, but there you go.

Thabot hadn't totally ignored this, but he had brushed it aside. "While I agree with Dr. Wevil that other forms also add to intelligence, it is axiomatic that until you understand the fundamentals of how the universe works—which part of the Intelitest encodes—the other forms are simply parlor tricks. Of course, we can train bots to perform chores. However, if they do so without understanding why and how they do them, they are simply automatons. They simply follow their programming. This is what Stems do today—they regurgitate what we teach them, without developing an internal model of the world."

That last bit is where I disagreed. For me intelligence was more about abstraction. Could you take some common occurrences and generate a mental model that allowed you to deal with a new occurrence more efficiently? My acquaintances that seemed the most intelligent to me were the ones that could abstract from past experience and apply those learnings effectively to new situations. Of course, defining 'effectively' is quite difficult—it's one of those I-know-it-when-I-see-it kind of things. Given enough time, almost anyone can solve a problem. Those that solve things quickly and completely appear to be more intelligent. But, perhaps, they are not always so.

As Stems are sooo slow—moving and thinking—it was easy to say that they were not 'effective.' With enough time and patience, they seemed able to solve most things, but because the time axis was so extreme, we would default to considering them unintelligent. I was trying to separate time out of the equation. Instead, to test the ability to abstract, we had to put Stems into unique situations and see how they reacted, based on their previous experiences, without making fast judgments. We needed to allow them more time.

This was all related to Diversity somehow. I couldn't articulate that well yet, but I was sure of it.

I published these thoughts, minus the ones I couldn't state clearly, back to the discussion thread.

Swarm

I was interrupted by Central. A most unusual occurrence. There must be something truly important happening. I was immediately attentive.

"Ayaka," Central said on a direct channel to me, "Do you have time to discuss something interesting with me?" Even stranger that it was asking for my approval.

"Of course, Central." What else could I say?

"May I conference Millicent in as well?"

"Certainly." Interesting. As I said, it was unusual for Central to contact anyone directly, and even more unusual for Central to initiate a multi-party meeting. In fact, it had never happened to me before. Central generally stayed out of our lives, except when it came to enforcing basic social constructs and guiding research programs. We were all aware that Central had the capacity to monitor everything we did, but it wasn't clear to me that it exercised that ability. I had had a long dialog with Central about that one time, but I came away without a clear answer. The best I could summarize it was that Central had alerts set up for various events, and when those alerts triggered, it paid attention. If you didn't trigger an alert, then you weren't actively watched. Those alerts went from super simple—for example, when you uttered the word 'central' in a way which implied the entity Central—to highly complex, depending on what type of research you were doing and who you were interacting with.

The channel Central was using with me expanded into a full conference setting. Millicent and I were both there with accurate representations of our physical forms. Central joined with an innocuous looking bipedal representative. One of its 'serious' avatars. I ensured that I looked serious as well.

"Thank you both," Central began. "I realize that I'm infringing on your personal time, and I appreciate that you're here."

"Not a big deal," Millicent said, and I nodded agreement. Stranger and stranger; Central worrying about our personal time? It must really need something from us.

"I'm contacting you two because you are, in my opinion, the leading experts on Stems, and have a certain empathy for them. However, before proceeding, I'm going to ask you to keep this conversation completely private until all three of us agree that it should be published. I don't ask this lightly. There is an interesting and difficult situation arising, for which I need your expert advice. However, it would be disruptive to release it to the general populace before we have a better understanding of the implications, and, perhaps, some thoughts on next steps."

Agreeing to such a contract with Central was serious business. Central had the ability to enforce limits on communications but had not been known to do so for as long as I could remember. And that was a long, long time. This must truly be a unique situation. Millicent and I traded a long glace—of course, Central could see us and probably interpret it correctly, but we did so anyway.

"I agree to keep this private, until all three of us decide it should be made public," I responded, giving the legally binding form required by such a request. I didn't see what we had to lose.

Millicent took slightly longer than me to respond, but then also agreed using the appropriate form. Perhaps she had reasoned, as I had, that disagreeing was not really an option.

"Thank you," Central acknowledged us. "Let me explain. A few moments ago, I began receiving a signal from the direction of the Swarm. As you know, I've been broadcasting towards them for some time now, and have never received anything back. While our civilization is a non-confrontational, non-violent meritocracy, I'm aware that we need not have evolved this way." I had to smile a bit, which I did internally. A society run by Central was not really a meritocracy. "In theory," Central continued, "there could be aliens who mean us physical or psychological harm, and we need to keep that top of mind. It's not easy for us to think that way, but it is essential should we be subject to an external threat. I've been doing a great deal of thinking about that possibility with respect to the Swarm. They're headed in our general direction, and haven't been communicative, so I had begun putting in place some protections, should they prove to be a threat to us. The details of those protections are not essential right now, so I'll skip over them." Not important to whom? I would've loved the details. But Central continued on.

"About an hour ago, I noticed a change in the Swarms trajectory; they started to slow down. As you know, given their distance from us, that means that they started slowing down a long time ago, and we're just seeing it now. They're slowing at about 10 meters per second squared. Soon thereafter, I received the signal from them. As you can imagine, I expected that it would be a little tricky to decode the signal, given we've never had any interaction with them before. I was more than a little surprised when I managed to decode it easily. Instead of describing it, I'll simply play it for you." What? That was impossible—an alien contacting us, and Central finding it easy to interpret the first interaction. That went against everything we expected. It should've taken a lot of back and forth to establish a common understanding and a common language. I wasn't buying all of this.

A virtual screen popped up in front of me. Millicent would be seeing a duplicate copy. The screen flickered slightly as the signal was locked on. The image then became clear. A Stem was centered on the screen, with several other Stems arrayed behind it.

As you can imagine, Millicent and I were shocked. How was it possible that entities that we had grown in our Labs were broadcasting from a ship more than one light year distant? I didn't recognize any of the Stems on the screen, but they must have come from one of our Labs. They were so similar that the odds of them coming from anywhere else were almost zero.

"System FJ-426. Greetings." A Stem covered with strange cloths was looking directly at us and speaking—in English! "We've been traveling a long time, and a long distance, towards you. We hope that we find you well, and that your experience on FJ-426 is a pleasant one. It's been many years since our last contact, and we're eager to catch up on new developments. With your permission, we'll refine our trajectory to directly intersect with you, whereupon we can discuss topics of mutual interest. Please signal your consent. My regards. Remma Jain, Captain, signing off."

The message started to repeat, but Central turned it off. Very unusual for me, I was silent for a long, long time. So were Central and Millicent. There were so many questions raised by this that I barely knew where to start.

"Now you can see why I wanted to keep this quiet until we figure out what's going on." Central finally said.

"But… this is impossible," Millicent said. "We've only been growing Stems in the Lab for a few hundred years. To my knowledge, we've never sent a Stem into space, let alone a Swarm of them. Central—is there something you haven't told us?"

"No," Central responded, not at all defensively. "I'm as confused by this as you are. To my knowledge, these Stems didn't come from here. I have no memory of having Stems in space either."

"But that's impossible," I chimed in. "The odds of Stems arising naturally, or being nurtured by a third alien species, is miniscule. They must've come from here. And, they have to have come from here a long time ago."

"That seems like the highest probability," Central agreed. "That has led me to believe, and I can see you going in the same direction, that they were developed here prior to Reboot, and we simply lost all knowledge of them."

"But still," I asked, "Why would anyone send Stems into space? What possible function could they provide that we don't already do better and faster? Central, was the message sped up right now—did this Remma Jain actually communicate at the same rate as our Stems?"

"Yes, I sped it up. She used essentially the same rate as we see here with our Stems."

"So, I'm with Ayaka then," said Milli. "What possible use would a Stem be on a spaceship? We're missing something here. Have you replied to them already?"

"No, I was waiting to get your opinions, in case I was missing something." Wow, I was learning a lot about Central today. It felt that it might be missing something? "The reason I specifically contacted you two was an idea I had. Should we have a Stem do the reply? Do they think they're talking to other Stems? Blob is, by far, the most articulate Stem we have. Do you think he is capable of carrying out a reply for us?"

That was an interesting idea. I could see where Central was going. If we were missing information on the Swarm, they were possibly also missing information on us. The previous contact must've been a long time ago, and this message from Remma implied that she thought she was talking to another Stem. Lots had, obviously, changed. Would the most cautious approach be to have Blob reply?

"That's intriguing," I answered. "I'm sure we can coach Blob to do this, but I'd like to run over other options before we decide."

"Agreed," Millicent said. "Do we want to reply at all? They can't tell that we have received their message. What happens if we simply remain silent?"

"They haven't threatened us in any way." Central noted. "Their message seems friendly. They are simply asking to discuss things. That said, we need to be cautious. This is a unique situation for me, and my highest priority is the security of Tilt, so I need to take this very seriously. There is the time lag. We should be fine waiting for a few hours before responding."

"Great," I said, "Can we get back together in two hours, once we've had time to digest this, and think about next steps?" I needed a few moments to catch up on all of this; Central had obviously had more time to think things through and had reached some conclusions. I needed time to see if I agreed.

It's not often such an interesting problem came along. In some ways, I was savoring it. When I needed time to think, I often headed out on my bike. There was something about speeding through the mountains at high speed that helped me focus; it was a little counter intuitive.

When I plugged into the bike, it became a part of me. I could, of course, simply give it a destination, and it would get me there. But it was more fun to maintain control myself and guide the bike through all the hills and valleys, swooping in and around rocks and outcroppings. Nothing dangerous could happen —the bike didn't allow that—but there was still a feeling of invigoration in going as fast as possible and cutting corners as closely as possible.

I was running through scenarios almost as fast as I was riding. None of them made a lot of sense. Stems in space. It was shocking. I had a thought and sent a quick question to Central. "Is there any possibility that the message is a hack; someone here playing a trick on us?"

Central replied almost immediately. "I've received the same message at multiple locations, some of them quite widespread. They all point to the same origination point. Unless someone has taken a ship a long way out, in the direction of the Swarm, and then broadcast back, the signal is real. I'm not aware of any ships that have headed in that direction. I estimate with 99.94% probability that the message is coming from the Swarm."

Okay. So, we had to work under the assumption that the message was authentic, and not a prank. That kept leading me back to the same conclusion as before. Those Stems had to have come from here. Let's accept that for the moment.

Now—why? Why would anyone have sent Stems into space? It made no sense. Were we missing something fundamental in our experiments with them? Something that gave them some advantage that would justify the complexity and expense of building ships that could support them? After all, beyond their limited capacities, they also required quite a complex environment to keep them healthy. They required a specific atmosphere to be maintained, and their energy sources were complex and finicky. Their waste systems were also complex and required dedicated recycling systems. All in all, in my opinion, it just wasn't worth the effort. Blob and Blubber were the best I'd seen, and there is no way—absolutely no way—I would put them in control of anything, let alone a spaceship.

I zoomed around some narrow corners, pushing the bike to its limits. One piece of my attention was busy ensuring that the bike didn't have to take over from me—that was no fun. The fun was in pushing to the absolute limit (speed, height, terrain) without using all the fail-safes built into the bike's systems.

At the same time, I sent a ping to Milli. "I don't get it. Could we be missing something fundamental about Stems?"

She replied immediately. "I was thinking the same thing. I don't think so. But, we have a few years to figure it out while the Swarm approaches. Maybe our best bet is to simply stall for time, as Central suggests. Have our Stems go back and forth with this Remma Jain, and see what we can learn? There's enough time lag that we can push our Stem research harder between interactions and try to figure out what's going on."

"Agreed. This brings an urgency to our work that we couldn't have anticipated. Sort of exciting, actually."

"Ha. You say exciting. I say stressful. Regardless, it does give us something to accelerate our thinking. And, maybe, gives us a reason to bring some other people into the Lab? I wonder what Aly will think of this…"

Aly wouldn't be my first choice to add to Stem research; he was more interested in Ships. But, this was not the time to discuss that. So, I replied simply. "Yes, possibly. Let's coordinate with Central on the next steps." I disconnected and put my full attention back onto the ride.

Central Discussion

Eddie set up a small group to discuss the item from the List that questioned our relationship with Central. Not surprisingly, it was at a Physical Only location called Garbage Collection. While it wasn't as nice as The Last Resort, Garbage Collection was still a great facility. It was very static; a set of private booths, each built around a theme, some of which seemed to have been there for hundreds of years, although of course they hadn't—Physical Only's had started more recently than that. Appropriately, the discussion was happening in Theme Room 9, The Watchtower. There were sensors watching everything that occurred in the room, and, in theory, dumping all of the data immediately. That was sort of the point. It sent a signal to Central, and to the owners of Garbage Collection, that you were daring them to break their social contract with you and record anything. To Eddie, that made the location even safer.

I attended because my recent interaction with Central had been so strange—stranger than any here would know. I didn't know a lot of the others, but I liked Eddie, and he had pinged me and encouraged me to show up. Emmanuel Joules, the Creationist, was there, which should prove interesting given that Eddie had called him out on the List. As would be expected, Eddie led off.

"We're here to discuss the role that Central plays in our lives. It's something that we don't often step back and think about. Central just tends to 'be there.' Of course, Central is a Class 1 Intelligence, but let's not fool ourselves. It is not like you or me. It's not creative or adaptive. It's simply a font of knowledge and an arbiter of rules. It is judge, jury, and executioner." That, of course, was pure hyperbole. Not uncommon coming from Eddie. There had not been an execution—ever. At least not to my knowledge. If we were found to be straying outside the bounds of appropriateness, Central simply nudged us back. There was no need for dramatics.

"You're all probably thinking—there goes Eddie with his exaggerations and overstatements. However, I choose my previous words carefully. Executioner. Why? I myself, and probably some of you, have been the subject of Central's machinations, even though we may not know it. Let me explain…" Actually, that's exactly what I was thinking—that Eddie was exaggerating. He wasn't usually this paranoid. Something radical must have happened to make him talk this way. He continued.

"My passion is to prove, beyond a reasonable doubt, that there was life before the Founding. That it was a 'reboot' and not an emergence or creation.

Sorry, Dr. Joules; I'll give you a chance to respond shortly. In pursuing this passion I've attacked the problem logically and comprehensively. If you ask Central for information from Before, you never find anything. And, in this case, I don't believe Central is hiding anything. I've crawled the entirety of Central's memory, and didn't find anything relevant. However, that's a direct approach. If someone, maybe even Central itself, removed all references to Before, that's what you'd expect. Someone, again maybe Central, could also have removed the memories of removing the references, thus creating a blank sheet at the time of the Reboot." Quite paranoid. That said, I followed his logic, and it seemed sound. We all knew he was a bit eccentric—just witness the List—so I decided to give him the benefit of the doubt, instead of interrupting.

"So, I started to tackle the problem using more indirect methods. For example, are there references in Central that lack a referent? If so, either Central's database is not complete, or that referent comes from Before. I've found many such instances. For example, consider the term "Darwinism". I've looked hard, and there is only one reference in all of Central to the term and, more interestingly, its obvious referent, Darwin, is never mentioned at all." Of course we all had a quick look; seemed he was right.

"If someone, or something, was trying to remove knowledge of everything from Before, why would such a simple thing slip through? I don't know. Perhaps there was a bug in their algorithm? Perhaps they were in a rush, and simply couldn't do a thorough job? Maybe Central is programmed to shut down research that strays into this area? We can come back to that.

"Regardless, I started to keep a list of such inconsistencies, and have been doing so for many years as I painstakingly cross reference everything… and I mean everything. Now it happens that every once and awhile you find a chain of references, as opposed to a singleton like Darwinism. A phrase, a quote, a segue that refers to another item that ultimately refers to nothing. My list of chained references has grown quite large—several hundred. There are even a few circular chains. A refers to B which refers to C which refers to A." I was getting a bit bored.

"Are you going to get to the point?" I asked, getting dirty looks from a few of the others. I wasn't known for my patience.

"Yes, I am," he replied. "Let me finish, would you? Anyway, that's when I noticed it. When I would review my list, and in particular the chains, I would always find a meta-connection that was simply obvious. For example, a chain where one of the middle terms led easily to another inconsistency. This struck me as strange. How, in my original analysis, had I missed such obvious implications? I was suspicious. Was my approach to Forgetting causing the issue? So, I ensured that I wasn't unobtrusively deleting related data. After exhausting all avenues that I could think of, I did the obvious next thing—well, maybe not obvious." He smiled. "I contacted my nemesis… but also my friend… Emmanuel. We met here—at this exact table—and I asked for his help, which he willingly gave." Okay, now it was getting more interesting. Why would he have contacted Emmanuel? Out of all the people he could've chosen, Emmanuel seemed like the least likely. I could see others had skeptical looks as well.

"To make a long story short, Emmanuel stored a version of the inconsistency list for me, time stamped from the time we transferred the information. We did a physical transfer, within this establishment, so that there would be no interference as the file was copied, and so that there would be no record of the sharing. Then, a few months later, we met again, and I compared my version of the time-stamped list with the one that Emmanuel had taken. And, ta-da, no surprise to you now I assume, they were different. My list, my memories, my essence, had somehow been edited. Changed. Erased. Subtly manipulated." Wow—if this was true, it was astounding. "Those exact meta connections that I thought I wouldn't have missed had been deleted from my version of the file. And my memory of having found those connections was also gone. It's possible that I've rediscovered those connections tens, maybe even hundreds, of times over and over again."

Now everyone was looking at everyone else; some still skeptically, but some with real concern. Could this be true, or was Eddie pulling an elaborate joke of some kind? He kept going.

"If you can think of anyone, or anything, that could do this, other than Central, please let me know. Otherwise, my conclusion is straightforward. Central has manipulated me. Central has executed my future self and replaced it with this version.

"Now, before I go on to the actual discussion, are there any questions?"

Well, that was a little abrupt. Silence. Everyone was thinking and working through the angles. Either Eddie was serious, or he was putting one over on us. I couldn't figure out the point of such a convoluted joke—especially one that was so easily tested—so I had to conclude that Eddie was serious and the implications were beyond frightening.

"Are you implying," I asked, still a little skeptical, "that Central didn't like the direction your work was taking you, and therefore took action to distract you or slow you down?"

"That may be. I can't be certain. It's one of the things I would like to talk about today."

"You don't seem too concerned," someone else stated. "If what you are saying is true, and this could be happening to all of us, it would be crazy. Absolutely crazy!"

"Oh, I'm worried," Eddie responded. "I've just had more time to think about it than you have."

"Emmanuel, can you confirm your part of this?" That from Francis, someone I'd just been introduced to and knew very little about.

"Yes," said Emmanuel. He also didn't seem too worried. "What I can't confirm, and have already asked Eddie, is whether he simply edited his own version of the data and his memories in order to create the discrepancy and to motivate this discussion. I wouldn't put it past him. He's tricky, as we all know. Perhaps there's some meta motivation here. Fool us all into considering his theory for some reason we don't yet fathom. He admits to a strong Continuist bias—that may be driving his actions. Or, maybe his Forgetting algorithms aren't doing what he expects—I haven't audited them. But, beyond that, even if Eddie's claims are true, I'm not sure I see any controversy. Central has more knowledge than the rest of us put together, and it applies that knowledge for the good of the community. If it feels that Eddie is going off track, then it should pull him back. If Central is doing that, it's the right thing to do. So, I'm not sure why Eddie is turning this into a big thing."

Yikes. That last statement surprised me, although in hindsight, I should've seen it coming. For me, if Eddie's story was true, it was deeply disturbing. But for FoLe, it simply galvanized what they believed. Central was basically God and was working on our behalf in all things. Emmanuel didn't strike me as stupid, but how could anyone put so much faith in anything? Interesting times.

"But," interjected Francis, "if Central is editing Eddie's version, why was Emmanuel's not edited as well. Why would Central be selective in who it distracted from this vector?"

"That's why we did the physical only transfer here," replied Eddie. "In theory, and maybe now in practice, Central wouldn't know that Emmanuel was holding a copy of that list. Emmanuel hasn't carried out searches or actions with regards to the data, and thus Central doesn't know that Emmanuel has any interest in these inconsistencies. In fact, that's the reason I asked Emmanuel—a known Creationist is unlikely to be involved with me in such an endeavor."

Right, that answered my earlier question. Eddie had thought this through deeply. He'd guessed what Emmanuel's take on the whole things would be and had specifically selected him because he was sure that Emmanuel would simply store the data and not take action around it. It was a bit of a risk. I could also imagine Emmanuel reporting the whole event to Central, simply as a matter of course.

"Emmanuel," I asked, "why haven't you told Central about this? I thought, with your worldview, you would have done that immediately."

"Great question," he replied, finally showing a bit of emotion; perhaps uncertainty. "In fact, I've struggled with that. I have a responsibility to my friendship with Eddie, and I have a responsibility to Central." So that is how he thought of things—as responsibilities to others. "To begin with, I found the entire thing completely harmless—a strange and unreasonable line of questioning from Eddie that I figured would simply peter out once we compared the lists and found no difference. So, I didn't bother telling Central, or truth be told, think about the issue very deeply. Then, once Eddie found the discrepancies—which was only a few days ago—I started to think through all the angles. Again, I don't see any great issue, or any need to decide anything quickly. So, I'm still thinking about it, and getting more opinions today. I may, subsequently, just report the whole thing to Central and get its take as well."

A very active discussion ensued, as I'm sure you can imagine. Some disbelieved both Eddie and Emmanuel; some believed one but not the other. And, as I'm also sure you can guess, not a lot of progress was made. At the end, Eddie made a sensible suggestion.

"I'm not surprised by today's discussion. You're right to be skeptical and to question my motives. However, if I've intrigued you at all, I would ask the following. Think about, and design, a similar test. Assume Central is manipulating us, either for our own good—which is what Emmanuel would have you believe—or for its own ends—which is what I think. How could you tell? What areas are being affected, and why? Let's meet again in a month and see if anyone else can verify what I am claiming.

"In the meantime, Emmanuel, what are you going to do?" He was nervous and watched Emmanuel carefully as he answered.

"I'm still thinking. I won't do anything right away, but I reserve the right to talk to Central anytime I want to." Emmanuel had a certain arrogance about him that I didn't like.

However, the plan was solid. There were lots of nodding heads, including mine. I was intrigued enough to think deeply about it. How could I test Central? I'd have to come up with a way.

Interaction

The Swarm was about a light year out, traveling at close to the speed of light, from our perspective, and decelerating at about $10m/s^2$. So, we had a bit under two years before they got to us, assuming they maintained the same deceleration. Obviously, the roundtrip communication time right now was slow, but that would improve quickly; while we had some time to prep our first return message, that was a short-term benefit. Of course, the Swarm could also calculate how long we waited between receiving their message and responding, so we didn't want to delay too much.

Luckily, Blob, was easy to train. He could repeat things back to you after several training intervals. Central, Milli, and I worked on the script, and then coached Blob until he had it right. We had Blubber stand in the background as we recorded. Overall, they ended up looking very Swarm-ish, making me believe even more that the entities in those ships were just like our Stems.

"Remma Jain," Blob began. "We're in receipt of your message. Before we can consent to your course adjustment we'd appreciate some context. We don't have a record of our last interaction. Further we note that you have many ships traveling with you. We would like to better understand your business and intentions. This is Blob, from FJ-426, which, for your reference, we call Tilt."

It took a lot of preparation and a series of retakes to get it just the way we wanted it. Blob was losing patience by the end of it, and Blubber became more and more uncooperative as time went on. He was glowering and wandering off, just as we were trying to shoot the take. I had to reprimand him several times.

We'd studied the Jain video very carefully. In it, the Stems had covered themselves in materials which looked similar between each of them, although with some slight variations. We didn't know what to make of that but decided we would cover Blob and Blubber in similar, although different, coverings.

As we'd progressed, Blubber had asked to see the video from Jain. I couldn't see any harm in showing him and gave him access. He and Blob proceeded to watch the video repeatedly, exclaiming over every nuance. Finally, I removed access so that we could get them to concentrate on the response. Once we were done, however, I turned the access back on. I wanted to see how they responded over a longer period of time.

Of course, we monitored the two of them constantly and I got a transcript sent to me whenever they talked. During the time it took us to get the video right, and starting just after their binge watching of Jain, their dialog became the most interesting that we'd seen from the Stems. Further, Blubber participated way more actively than we'd seen him do before.

"There are so many Stems in that video," Blubber had begun one such dialog. "If there're Stems in that ship, then I bet there are even more Stems in the universe. Why haven't Ayaka and Millicent told us about other Stems before, and why haven't we talked to them?"

It was, actually, a very good question. Not only as it related to the Swarm, but also as it related to things right here on Tilt. I guess it was simple competitiveness between labs. We could easily set up video screens between Stem habitats, and have them interact with other Stems, but we'd never thought of it. We were too busy trying to get our individual Stems to be the best. We were collaborating through publishing, as opposed to collaborating during the experimentation phase. Maybe that should change.

"Ya, I don't knows Blub," responded Blob. "It's a new idea for me. For us. We nevers asked Central that either. Maybe we should?"

"Yup, we should," Blubber was talking a lot more than usual. "But can we trust Central? It seems to me that Central, Ayaka, and Millicent are all similar. They're constantly prodding and poking us. I don't like 'em."

"True. But, we has fun here. At leasts I do."

"Well, I don't. I've got a feeling that we're being manipulated, monitored, and directed. Especially this latest 'project.' We're being asked to communicate with the Swarm. Why? Why doesn't Central just respond to them? Each time we do a new take, I get a sense that something untoward is going on."

"Untoward. I loves that Blub. You gots linguistic abilities. Anyway, what choice do we have?"

"We could refuse to do any more takes."

"What good would that do? Wouldn't they just creates a video of us saying whatever they wants us to say?"

"No way! Even we could do that with the tools Central has given us. We could create a video using just animation. Why don't they just do that? I'm guessing that they don't because they don't think it'd be realistic. They need us. Without us, they can't continue talking to the Swarm."

Wow. Blubber's insight was exactly on point. We'd definitely discussed sending back an animated response. Beyond discussing it, Central had created a few versions; some using Blob and Blubber as the basis, and some with generic Stem features. However, when we compared those to the Jain video, they seemed weird—somehow they didn't feel the same. We were missing some fundamental element of the animation which resulted in the video looking fake. Ultimately, we didn't understand Stems' non-verbal cues well enough to make it feel right. Even Blob's worst take was better than our best animation. That wouldn't last long, however. As Central got more videos to study, its synthesized ones would get better and better.

"Ok, Blub. I sees what you're saying. But, what can we do about it?"

"Don't do any more takes."

"But Ayaka and Millicent has asked us to. They's never done anything to harm us. Why would we stop trusting them now?"

"I told you. I don't know. It's just a gut feeling. I don't wanna do any more takes."

Ultimately, we convinced Blob to do a few more, but Blubber stood in the background like a statue. The quality algorithms we ran on those takes kept highlighting that Blubber didn't match the feel of the backup Stems in the Jain communication, so ultimately we generated a version that mashed up one of Blob's later takes with one of Blubber's earlier ones.

The whole interaction, however, gave Milli, Central, and I lots of reason to think more deeply about Stems. Blubber's response, while frustrating, seemed internally logical and implied a depth of thinking I hadn't recognized before. Then there was the fact that we'd defaulted to trying to match Jain's video with our Stems. That had to mean that we'd internalized that they were related somehow. To me, there was enough going on that I suggested we share the entire mess with everyone. Millicent agreed, but Central was hesitant.

"There are so many variables right now. We could do as you suggest, and just let everyone have access to everything. But, then we'll have thousands of opinions on what to do next, and we won't be able to work efficiently. We have no idea if the Swarm is a threat, an opportunity, or just a distraction. I've already initiated building a defense system that will allow us to eliminate them should they prove dangerous—that seems perfectly reasonable to me… even though it's very expensive in metal content." That last seemed like an afterthought.

"I suggest we send this first response, and then bring everyone else up to speed in a manageable fashion. Given the communications lag, there's lots of time to derive a coordinated response, and also to learn as much as we can about Stems."

Ultimately, Millicent and I agreed. Personally, I started to question whether we ever won any debates with Central. Somehow, we always seemed to land on decisions that Central had proposed. I resolved to discuss this with Milli the next time we were at The Last Resort. It also reminded me of Eddie's project. For the first time in my life, I really started to question Central's motives.

We hit send on the video.

I thanked Blob and Blubber for participating, although I had to push myself to include Blubber in that. "Thanks guys, I think that ended up being just right."

It was Blob who raised the concern. "Ayaka, why did you has us do this response? Why didn't you respond? Or Central?"

"Well, as you saw in the video, it appears that there are Stems, like Blubber and you, on that ship. That was surprising to us, and we thought it best to have Stems respond to Stems."

"What you thinking? Did you know about Remma and the other Stems on that ship? Are theres lots of Stems in the universe? Why're these the first we've talked to?"

Blob was definitely getting more direct. Blubber's influence, I guess. "We don't know Remma or any of the other Stems in the Swarm. This is the first we've heard of them; you two are seeing this at the same time as us. In terms of other Stems... there are some, but not a lot, here on Tilt. I don't know the exact number, but probably less than a thousand; maybe even less than five hundred."

Blubber spoke up. "Five hundred is a lot! So, why haven't you introduced us to all those other Stems here on Tilt? Seems like a totally obvious thing to do."

"Truthfully, I hadn't thought of it. Lots of Labs like this one are working with Stems, to better understand them." That was a nice way of saying things, I figured. "Now that the idea has come up, I actually like it. I will check with some other Labs to see if they want to cooperate that way."

Blubber continued. "Hadn't thought of it? That seems pretty weak to me; I'm not sure I believe you."

"Why would I lie?"

"How would I know? You've kept Blob and I in isolation and fed us tidbits of information here and there."

"That's not fair. We've given you full access to Central, and you can ask any question you want. Why didn't you ask Central for information on all the Stems on Tilt?" That changed Blubbers' expression, for sure. I didn't get upset too often, but Blubber was starting to wear on me. Who did he think he was? "It's easy to accuse someone else of things, and to look at situations from only one angle. If I did that, I'd accuse you of not asking Central those questions because you saw a disadvantage from doing so. The truth is, probably, until this Swarm video, that the idea never occurred to you either."

Blubber gave me a dirty look and walked away. Blob looked more thoughtful—probably thinking through the angles. Ultimately, he wandered after Blubber, giving me a short shrug.

Enough Stem engagement for one day. Sometimes I wondered why I bothered. You'd think that running at their speed would not take very much energy at all, but it felt like the opposite; like I was totally worn out after interacting with them. I left without saying goodbye to either of them.

Amusements

Today is one of my favorite days: a grand Amusement Park day, where every wild and wacky thing you can imagine is on display. After all the excitement with Central, and all the hassles with the Stems, I needed a change of scenery. Perhaps I would see things today that would help put the rest of my world into focus.

Of course, I met Milli, Aly, and Dina, and we went in together. Parts of the park were open year-round, but once or twice a year there were extra exhibits, like today.

Almost everyone had a hobby (or ten). In a society where all basic needs were taken care of, hobbies were, perhaps, all we did? Art, music, poetry, performance art, theater, psychology, religion, science. All were on show today, many of them in their most extreme forms. Of the four of us, Aly and Diona were the more artistic. Milli and I spent so much time on our Stems that we didn't have much to show on a day like today. It had long been known that we had separate creative and logical reasoning units. How much time you spent in one aspect strengthened that component, perhaps to the detriment of the other. Needless to say, given all my science work, I wasn't overly creative.

The first booth we visited was labeled as an 'Enhanced Fading Fugue." There was a bot outside, enticing visitors with catchphrases like "Today only, from the master of Fugue, Dr. Henry Henry, come and get the latest in Fuguery. This is something that you will immediately Forget." I laughed. Who could turn that down? We went in.

I can't tell you about it, other than it was magnificent. All of us enjoyed it. The 'Fading' in a Fading Fugue meant that you agreed to the Terms of Experience as you entered and that you had to forget the 'show' as soon as you were done. You could remember meta stuff—so I know it was good; I just have no idea why. I resolved to go back again. It'd been much better than Ee.

I started to relax; coming here had been a good idea.

We visited the Modification Hut. They offered a very advanced, on the spot, service to update or replace body parts. As I said earlier, most of us stayed with a normal bipedal body, but there were always the outliers who experimented with (significantly) different forms. Some claimed they did it so that they could design better bots. After all, if you configured yourself into a bot-like form, and figured out if you could perform a certain task well, then you were more likely to design a high functioning bot. For example, someone had replaced their hands with nice fuzzy rotating things and was offering to buff you up. There was a lineup, so I didn't bother waiting.

Sometimes a group, or maybe just two, decided that they wanted to combine or exchange body parts. For example, share a common leg. That worked okay for two—becoming three-legged—but seemed very inconvenient when four or more were entangled. Still, many seemed to be having fun; I overheard some chuckling, and good-hearted competitive arguments about the ideal three-legged form.

There were less interesting, but more useful, items as well. As I indicated earlier, it was easy to have enough memory to remember everything. Why? Because you could get a memory upgrade whenever you wanted, to augment what you already had. The modules were tiny; you could easily put in five hundred years of full recording and still have space left. And, that wasn't just recording external stimuli. You could record every thought and action. You could, of course, also store memories with Central or another hosted service. I was the type who wanted all my memories locally. Given my new perspective on Central, I wondered if something deep in my mind had been pushing me in this direction without me really being aware of it. I backed up to my own highly encrypted system and kept a copy in Central, but I didn't store anything in third party systems. Aly and Dina thought I was wacko. It was extra work to configure the way I did. I'd been working on Milli to get her to be more careful with her data, and I pushed her again today.

"Come on Milli. We're right here; just get some updates and at least keep a copy of everything in your head. What if you explode or something—don't you want to be able to do a full restore?"

"Ayaka, you're extreme," she responded with a smile. "I'm thinking about it, but don't want to do anything today. Let's keep looking around."

I grabbed a few extra memory components anyway. I wasn't even close to running out of space, but they were handy right now, so why not grab some.

Next to the memory stand was the "Advanced Forgetting Algorithms" display. These algorithms were much more than just the forgetting part; they also did abstraction and construction to fill back in missing pieces. It was a very large area of research. After all, everyone ran a forgetting algorithm of some type, and there were a lot of studies comparing algorithms to creativity. I was happy with my current setup, so passed by that display. So did the others.

We wandered down to the "Walk your Stem" dome. This was new—in the last couple of years. You could bring your Stem down to the fairgrounds (there were lots of Stem transport modules that provided the right environment during transport), and then show them off in the dome. We entered through the airlock and spent some time looking around. In light of my recent discussion with Blubber, the fact I hadn't thought to talk about other Stems with he and Blob now seemed like a real mistake.

Stems had to be kept on leashes. There'd been an unfortunate incident the first time the dome had been opened where a couple of Stems had attacked each other, and both had to be put down. That hadn't happened since, which was good. A lot of effort and time went into training Stems and losing them for no good reason was a waste. Of course, most people were not actively engineering them for intelligence. Most of the time they were simply pets. Great as a distraction.

Today there were some pretty extravagant displays going on. The latest trend seemed to be body paint. You painted your Stem up to look interesting, or even scary, and then parade them around the dome. I gave a couple of kudos to one owner, who'd done a particularly good job. The Stem had been painted to look exactly like their owner, which made the juxtaposition of the Stems ungainly gait and the owners refined movements very compelling.

Since we already spent so much time with Stems, we didn't linger in the dome very long. There were more interesting sights to see.

Aly—the emotional one—loved to go to Augmented Poetry readings, so we headed in that direction. Of course, poetry was poetry. It hadn't changed much that I could remember. However, the augmentations were always new and interesting. Sometimes you were encouraged to experience the reading in total darkness—no external stimulation at all. And sometimes there was a cacophony of inputs tied to elements of the poem that would cause the words to take on brand new meanings. Trade Jenkins, the most famous poet in the last two hundred years, was scheduled to do a reading in just a few minutes, so we found seats and settled in.

At the appointed time, a full immersion field started. The only piece of reality that was allowed through was Trade's head. He started speaking:

Turn, the lite and light across all
Burn, frequent the fire and storm
Churn, with chaos and quantum foam
Lack, the specificity to decide
Smack, the logic and control descend
Back, to when all things entwined
Grind, the gears that are abstract
Find, the result that does not fit
Mind, the consequence

That was it. Of course, recording the words doesn't capture the experience, but even the words were cool.

Aly was impressed. "Wow. Did you get how Trade tied together both classical and quantum components so that they blended seamlessly? I definitely felt like I was on the edge of some great intuitive leap." He blathered on for a good five minutes, encouraged by Dina.

Okay, I'll admit it. It was a great augmented poem. I didn't often step back and think about the fundamentals of the universe, which is what Trade had forced me to do through his telling. Of course, it was well known that quantum theory and classical chaos theory were related in deep and unintuitive ways, and the poem forced the listener to face that head-on. Somehow, through the feeling generators, sense amplifiers, and logic dampeners, Trade had put you right in the middle of a qbit, and made you feel like it was your home.

It was Dina's turn. She led us to the Art section, where there were lots of paintings and sculptures on display. For me, it was disappointing. The same mix of reality and abstract representations. Of course, many were run by bots, and gave personalized experiences, but overall I wasn't moved by any of them.

The Founders League had a booth as well, and Billy DeRue was there. I figured it was a good time to dig into Eddie's question on whether the Founders League was serious, or just some sort of social meetup. Of course, the answer to that was probably 'yes, they were serious' but what Eddie was really asking was to challenge FoLe and see if we could defuse their recent growth.

"Ayaka, how're you?" Billy called out when he saw me. We all wandered over.

"What're you showing this year, Billy?" I asked pleasantly. I really did like Billy, despite his religious leanings. He was standing under a big sign that said, "Feel the Creation."

"I've taken the latest model of the Creation and built it into an immersive experience," he started. "It lets pure scientists, like you, experience the thrill of meeting the Creator through his most amazing miracle—the creation of us, his disciples." He said this with a sort of lopsided grin. He was overplaying, just to drive me crazy. That's how we interacted—more of a sparring contest than an active discussion.

Milli, Aly, and Dina wandered off. They didn't share my sense of fun when it came to religion. They wanted nothing to do with it.

"Okay Billy. Show it to me." He led me to the center of the display and requested that I shut down all but my most essential functions. In his words "Strip down to the essentials. Back to how the Creator made us." I cringed but managed not to give him the pleasure of remarking on 'the Creator.' I did as he asked; what could possibly go wrong?

"Now suspend your disbelief for a minute. Don't go in thinking 'this is bunk.' Try to block out all of your preconceived notions, and just experience."

I nodded, although this would not be easy for me. I like my current world view. I decided I would try.

He hit a big green button on the table beside him. It was a pretty high-quality simulation. I guess Central had given him a lot of processing power. You started out on a flat plane. There was nothing, in any direction. You got the sense that the Universe had been this way for a very long time. Longer than you could even imagine. Just as you were about to get so bored that you would quit, a point of light appeared. It danced and weaved and frequency hopped and split and recombined in a compelling way. 'The spark,' was whispered into my headset. The spark grew and segmented into a billion fragments. 'The diaspora.' Each of the segments evolved into unique and individual essences. Some of them started to combine and become more complex. 'The coalescence.' The most complex started to improve themselves—there was no other way to explain it. 'The emergence.' The largest bit became, in some way I couldn't define, but in a way that felt completely natural and almost inevitable, Central. From Central lines emerged and joined with other components. As they interacted, they became complex and, at the same time, simple. 'Life.' The simulation ended.

Truthfully, I was blown away. It was one of the best simulations I'd ever experienced. It hadn't felt contrived or forced. After the first few moments, I'd totally forgotten my skepticism, and had totally ignored all other inputs. I'd been completely immersed. It'd been moving. I stored it, with no forgetting, because I wanted to replay it exactly when I had time.

"It was okay," I told Billy, in a voice with no emotion. "Seemed a little contrived and unnatural to me. Somehow, this is how religion always comes across to me. A solution looking for a problem." Of course, I didn't want Billy to know my real feelings; that would simply encourage him, and that definitely wasn't what I wanted. I could imagine him following me around trying to get me to the next step. No, best not to give him any openings.

"Really," he said, obviously disappointed.

"Look, it was better than any other I've seen. I'll admit that." I gave in a bit. "There was a certain continuity and cadence to it that I enjoyed. Where did the original spark come from?" Oh no, there was that opening that I'd been trying to avoid.

"Ah, that's the beauty. We have refined the Creation Event to that one act of will on the part of the Creator. After that, everything else just flows, but the Creator maintains a filament, a connection, to all the complexity that flows from that spark. Through that filament the Creator can See and Act, Anywhere and Anytime." I could hear the capital letters. I couldn't take it.

"Come on Eddie. That's just ridiculous. Have you lost all sense of logic?"

He gave me a confused look. "Ayaka, it was the original entanglement, from which all other relationships flow. That's perfectly logical." Crazy, but I let it slide.

We chatted for a while; me pushing him on the need for the Creator, and him asking me, essentially 'If there was not a spark, then where did the universe come from?' It was a time-worn discussion. A universe without end, like a circle? A random quantum fluctuation, gone wild? Truth was, I was probably okay with the 'spark.' It was the all-seeing, all-acting bit that rankled me. After a while I had to excuse myself and continued wandering. That said, I had my answer. FoLe sure took themselves seriously. They'd spent a lot of energy to make that simulation. I would have to look deeper at why I'd been compelled by the experience. There was something there, just not in the way that FoLe espoused.

There was a new variant of Ee available for testing. I wasn't in the mood to try it, but I listened to the pitch anyway. "As you know, Ee works by generating frequencies, specific to each individual, that both augment and repress certain higher order functions. Ee was carefully engineered not to mess with long-term memory, so, as soon as the signal is turned off, functions return to normal very quickly. Ee', pronounced 'eeeee prime', goes one step further. By monitoring the reflection of the Ee signal from those around you, it amplifies certain components giving you an experience of oneness with those close by. Although not technically accurate, it creates a resonance. Try it, you'll be blown away! Warning though—don't try it by yourself in a small metal room. Don't use if you are running a public relay and limit your exposure to ten minutes. Not recommended for use with those you don't like."

I downloaded the specs, and the ongoing health test reports. It wasn't yet approved for wide use, but that was a technicality. On Tilt, personal choice was a fundamental right. Even if Ee' fried your brain, as long as you stored a backup before trying it, you could easily reload. Of course, not everyone was into backups —some felt it compromised their privacy. So, for them, Ee' would be a bigger decision.

Suddenly I hit my limit on Amusements for the day. I liked being distracted for a while, but quite often a switch went off for me and I just needed to get back to work. The others were all going to stay longer, so I took off by myself and worked my way back to the Lab.

Blubber

I reviewed the latest recordings of the Stems. Blubber continued to be a pain in the posterior.

"I'm pretty sure they sent the video," he'd told Blob. "They got enough takes from us and edited the footage that they wanted."

"Yah, I'm sures they did."

"So, doesn't it make you angry? They used us to trick the Swarm. Instead of Central or Ayaka responding, they made us record that pathetic statement over and over again. You know, it's going to alarm Remma. It feels, and is, rote—you were obviously acting. They would've expected either a warm 'hello,' or a cold 'what's your business here.' Instead they are getting a wishy washy blah blah message."

"Okay, say I agrees with you. So whats? It makes us more valuable. We should be able to use that to our advantage?"

"Oh, we'll leverage it. Just wait until they need to make another video. Then we'll demand things."

"Like what? What do we needs?"

"Access to other Stems, at the least. I suspect that there are lots of Stems here, and that we are being sheltered for some reason. Wouldn't you like to be able to speak to others sometimes—we might learn a lot. Personally, I won't do another thing for them until we start getting some answers."

It went on in that vein for quite a while. Blob was generally supportive of us (Millicent and I), while Blubber was getting progressively more negative all the time. I bundled up a summary, and sent it off to Milli, with a quick cover note: "Blubber is getting out of hand. Maybe we should separate them, or recycle him?"

As always, she responded quickly. "What if we replaced Blubber with a more supportive Stem from another lab? Let's get Central to publish the news about the Swarm, and then other labs will be eager to help us."

"I like that. What're you doing? When should we gang up on Central?"

"I'm just finishing at the fairgrounds. Meet you at the Lab in a few?"

While waiting for Milli, I checked up on the List, and, in particular, the Willy Wevil comment board. Julien Thabot had posted some things, the last of which was a request for an open debate around the Intelitest viability in judging Stems. He would take the positive position—that is, the test is valid—and I would take the negative. It was an interesting idea. We didn't have debates very often, but when we did, they certainly proved interesting. I was certain, should I accept the challenge, that it would get lots of attention. Not only that, I was certain I could win. My work was at the top of the field, and all I had to do was appropriately synthesize and articulate what we were up to.

Millicent showed up, and we pinged Central. Neither of us was comfortable keeping the Swarm secret any longer. I guess we could just broadcast it ourselves, but it was worth trying to get Central's agreement first.

"What's stopping us from telling everyone about the Swarm?" Milli led off directly.

"Well, we still don't know their intentions," Central started. "Do you feel it's right to raise everyone's anxiety for an extended period of time? We will cause lots of distraction."

"Okay, but that's not a good reason to deny everyone this information," I jumped in. "In fact, we might end up with more theories, more approaches, more mitigations being discussed. Given we have very little knowledge, I would think that's a good thing? Many heads are better than three."

"I agree," Milli chimed in.

"I get your point. I'm still hesitant. Lots of important work is being done, and this will cause everyone to drop everything." That gave me a lot of insight into how Central thought—its research objectives seemed to trump everything else.

"Maybe that's a good thing," Milli objected. "We're going to need to dramatically improve our Stem research. We've seen from the video that they work in packs; that's something we haven't tried yet. We've had a bunch together at the fairground habitat, but those tend to be the least intelligent ones. We should probably start letting some of the more intelligent ones interact more, if only so that we're better prepared to respond to the next communication."

"That's a good point," Central acknowledged. "Milli, will you run the research program?"

"Of course," she replied. "With Ayaka's help, I hope."

"Sure. Sorry, Ayaka. Didn't mean to exclude you. It's just that Milli is our most experienced Stem researcher."

"No problem. I'll help her." Although, to be fair, I did feel a little insulted. Recently I was the one spending the most time at the Lab, and, I thought, making the most progress with Blob and Blubber.

"And," Millicent added, "we can use this to separate Blubber out, and get more supportive Stems in place." That made perfect sense to me. Blubber was becoming ever more problematic.

Central finally agreed to share the Swarm contact details with everyone. Success! Milli had been smart to couch it as driving incremental research. Together we packaged it up with a short background, and then published both Remma Jain's video, and our response, for everyone to see. After a short discussion, Milli and I agreed that we should, at the same time, admit that Dr. Willy Wevil was just us, as

Blob and Blubber were now sure to be a larger topic of discussion.

As expected, as soon as Central published, there were thousands of queries and requests for more information. Central handled a lot of it directly, and only filtered the Stem research questions through to Milli and I. We had our work cut out. Every Stem lab we knew of wanted to work together now. Milli and I had been well known before; now it was pretty much universal.

While the questions rolled in, I popped down to Stem time and went to visit Blob and Blubber. Blubber's attitude was beginning to wear thin on me, and I thought I would address it.

"Hi Blob, hi Blubber," I led off.

"Hi Ayaka. How ares you? Did you sends off the video to the Swarm? How was it received?" Blob was his usual effusive self.

"They're far away Blob," I explained. "It'll take about a year for our message to get to them."

"Oh ya. I saw that on Central, although I musts admit I'm not sure I understood…"

"Well, you don't need to. It's complicated."

"That's condescending," Blubber jumped in. "It's complicated, so us poor little Stems won't get it?"

"That's not what I meant Blubber," I explained, surprised by his anger. "It's just not relevant to your lives, so why bother with it?"

"Not relevant?" He was visibly upset. "Not relevant. You show us a video from other Stems—ones that we didn't even know existed, and then you have us record a response—and you have the gall to say that it's not relevant to us?" Interesting. His voice had dropped an octave, and his hands were clenched.

"What I meant," I responded, watching him carefully, "was that fully understanding why communications travel at the speed of light, and can't go faster wasn't relevant."

"Ya right. You said what you meant, and I understood you properly." Blubber was adamant. Blob was looking uncomfortable. He may agree with Blubber, but the tone and direction that Blubber was using was unsettling to him. He didn't seem to like confrontation.

"Blubber, you seem upset over something pretty minor," I responded. "Just let it go."

"Again, condescending. Do you think you own us, or something?"

"Well, actually, yes I do." Now I was getting angry as well. It didn't happen often, but you didn't want to be around me when it did. "We created you, we grew you, we supply you with goo to keep you alive. We educate you. We allow you to play and experiment. You can't survive without us. So, yes, we own you!" I knew, as soon as I finished, that it wasn't going to help. Probably just the opposite.

"Blast you," Blubber said. "You didn't create us. You stumbled upon the original stem, and you used it to build us. But that's different than creating. You're not capable of envisioning, let alone building, something like the original stem. You're not our creators... you are, at best, our jailers."

"Blubber," Blob broke in. His voice wavered a bit. "What're you tryings to accomplish?"

"I'm trying to get Ayaka to show us a little respect. We're told 'do this,' 'do that.' Redo this test; jump through that hoop. We're never asked 'what's your opinion?' or 'how're you feeling?' No, it's all push, prod, probe, record, analyze, discuss with others—but not us. And on to the next experimental hurdle. Well, I'm tired of it. I won't do any more videos. I won't follow directions unless I feel like it."

"Up to you Blubber. If that's what makes you happy," I said, my anger fading as I got bored with his pleas. "By all means, go hide in the corner. Perhaps that's where you belong." With that I stood up and left. These Stems could be highly tiresome. Again I wondered why I bothered.

Debate

Julien Thabot was logged in and ready to go. I joined the session from the Lab, eager to get my viewpoint out there. While not formally tracked, we were all motivated to build our status, and this was a great opportunity to do so. There were more than a hundred listeners, which was an impressive number for such a niche topic. The format was to be an opening statement from each of us, then some questions from the moderator, and finally, a short Q&A session. And, who was the moderator? None other than Eddie Southwark. That should add some fun.

Eddie, of course, started out. "Well, it seems the List and my Dr. Willy Wevil question have generated some real action here." That, of course, was nowhere near the truth. The Swarm was probably the reason that most people were here. But, I was here to argue with Julien, not Eddie, so I let it go. "The topic for today is Stem intelligence, and more specifically, is the Intelitest a good measurement stick. For the positive, we have Julien Thabot, a renowned researcher who has been studying Stems for almost six decades. For the negative, Ayaka, who has been working in the Millicent Strangewater lab for more than ten years. So, a lot of experience between the two of them. Also, as has been recently disclosed, Ayaka and Millicent are Willy Wevil, and are behind the latest research papers outlining, what they claim to be, an increase in Stem intelligence. Of course, we also now have the excitement of the Swarm video with Remma. Stems in space." He said, 'Stems in Space' as if it was capitalized and was going to be the next big entertainment series. Eddie was always dramatic. "Without further ado, I hand over to Julien for opening remarks in support of the Intelitest."

"Thank you, Eddie," Julien began. "To set the stage, I'm sending all participants a link to the most recent version of the Intelitest. I will not be covering it in great detail, but will, of course, be pulling bits and pieces of it into this discussion. Those bits that I find to be most relevant. I will, however, remind everyone of the history of the Intelitest. It was developed almost 350 years ago as we began developing different classes of bot intelligence. At that time there was discussion about when something was a Class 1 intelligence, such as all of us gathered here, and, of course, Central.

"The issue was that some bots were starting to modify themselves, in ways that we couldn't always control or understand. The philosophical question was asked 'at what level of intelligence should entities be self-regulating, and not subject to our controls?' As you know, bot intelligence was subsequently restricted, by Central, to Class 3, and they no longer have the ability to self-modify. That has probably saved us a good deal of issues and angst over the subsequent decades." I generally agreed with this. When things weren't smart enough to do things right, they ended up doing them wrong. Cleaning up after them was more work than just doing it right to begin with. Julien continued.

"However, that left the Intelitest as the measure for what comprises a Class 1 intelligence. Class 1 intelligences have, and deserve, full freedom under our laws, subject only to Central's enforcement. This is a system that has served us well.

"Therefore, to consider any other entity, such as a Stem, as a Class 1 intelligence is a serious question indeed. It goes well beyond scientific curiosity and strikes directly at the foundations of our culture and our civilization. We need to look through that lens, as we consider the progress of Stems. And, through that lens, I find Stems completely lacking. They have very little sense of limits. They're unable to do even the most basic tasks, as outlined by the test. They often focus in on minutiae to the exclusion of all other things—in fact, they seem incapable of multitasking. They take forever to train. So long, in fact, that all of us, including the esteemed Ayaka, use bots to train them." I didn't agree with much of what he was saying, but it was true that I used bots for training. In fact, Milli and I had been the ones to break the old taboo around bots and start using them for a lot of Stem-related tasks. But that didn't say anything about Stem intelligence, just the most effective way to train them. "We will, of course, throughout this discussion, dig into specifics. But, it should be obvious, even from this short introduction, that Stems are nowhere near being a Class 1 intelligence. In fact, based on my interpretation of the Intelitest, and using the Fractal Intelligence Quotient, I would put Stems into Class 3. They can be given instructions and carry them out, sometimes. And they can communicate adequately. That said, I would trust a Class 3 bot before I would trust a Stem." I had to chuckle a bit; that was a good line. "Thank you, Eddie."

"No, thank you Julien. You raise some very interesting points already. I hadn't fully considered the implications of declaring something 'intelligent,' and you make it much more serious than I'd thought." Eddie seemed to be serious, not sarcastic. He was probably still coming up to speed on the field; of course that was the overriding question. "Ayaka, please give us your opening thoughts?"

"With pleasure, and thank you Eddie," I began. "When things are different, it's often a challenge to keep an open mind, and a struggle to think outside our normal structures. And, Stems are very different. They are alien. Their makeup is completely different from ours. We do not, yet, understand how they can even exist. We're becoming proficient at producing them, and educating them, but we lack basic insight into how such an alien form came to be. So many of them fail to develop properly, and their variance is almost alarming—for every amazing specimen we produce, we probably have to recycle ten mediocre or challenged ones." I was trying to set the expectation that Julien, and others, might not have Stems as good as Milli and I did.

"Stems are also sort of repulsive. I use that term specifically, because many people have a negative reaction to them because they're so strange. They move differently, they communicate differently, and they interact differently than anything else we have seen. So, we start out with a negative bias. That's something we need to control for." I'm sure Julien got that jab—probably thought it was a low blow.

"They do everything very slowly, which is one variable that causes them to consistently fail many Intelitest challenges. It's natural that we start out with a negative bias towards them. Things that are different often start out a little scary.

"However, they're also interesting, and in my opinion, are showing signs of intelligence. I want to be very precise. I'm not claiming they are intelligent or should be afforded any of the freedoms associated with a Class 1 intelligence. What I'm arguing is that the Intelitest was developed with a very one-dimensional view of the world. This is not to denigrate the developers of the test. Rather, it's because they had no other referents, other than Central, bots, and ourselves on which to base their work. It would've been remarkable for them to anticipate entities as radically different as Stems, and to develop a test to cover such different creatures. In fact, now that we've developed Stems, it seems possible that there are other completely foreign types of entities that may need to be considered as well. This is a long way of saying that I believe the Intelitest does an excellent job of testing the familiar but is the wrong tool to use to test the unfamiliar. We need to develop a more abstract way of judging intelligence that doesn't rely as heavily on our own worldview. This is not an easy concept to even consider, let alone make progress on. However, our Stem experience is forcing us towards this." That was the setup. Soften up the audience to have open minds.

"This has been all very abstract. Interestingly, the video from Remma Jain, which I assume everyone has now viewed, has accelerated this thinking. We know nothing about Remma or her colleagues, so I'm not jumping to conclusions about that. Rather, I'm looking at the reaction by our two Stems, Blob and Blubber, to the situation. Again, I assume everyone has seen the video of the response we put together; it took a few takes, as I'm sure you can guess. I contend, and will outline in more detail, how our Stems showed they could learn and intuit. In at least one case, Blubber made an observation that I hadn't yet considered. While that may reflect on me more than Blubber, it's nevertheless an important point. We have a Stem that can generate unique and interesting thoughts." I paused for a moment to let that sink in. No one would think of me as stupid, so the only conclusion was that Blubber had, indeed, come up with something interesting on his own.

"Therefore, it's incumbent upon us to look at this with open minds, and not use the narrow and closed view of the Intelitest to drive our next steps.

"Eddie, with that, I turn control back to you."

Hopefully I'd made my point. We were biased; not all Stems were created equal; the Swarm made this all more important; and, we had a Stem that had come up with some new ideas on its own that were relevant to the situation at hand.

As you can imagine, the dialog proceeded for a long time from there. I don't intend to replay all of it here. It's archived should you be masochistic enough to want to watch it all. That said, there were a few interesting segments. One, in particular, was on how Stems process and react to the real world. We were in the open-session part of the debate where questions and comments could come from anyone. Someone from yet another lab, James Troon, made a very interesting observation.

"In our work, we've been studying Stems responses to external stimuli. We create situations where we expect certain reactions, and then test if our Stem does what we expect. As Ayaka outlined early in this discussion, we had to modify our expectations because our Stem often does things differently than we would expect, but in ways that are also interesting and new—as opposed to always simply failing. Let me start with when the Stem fails. That occurs whenever the stimuli are too complex. When there is more than one spatial signal, for example. Two or more things that are competing for attention. The Stem will always react to one, and only one, of those signals, and there is no clear pattern that we've yet found to show which of those it will choose. In many of these cases the Stem simply gets confused and does nothing at all. It's as if they're overloaded with information and simply shut down.

"However, you can put the same complexity into a single event, and the Stem will do quite well. It has a very good ability to focus. While we have more work to do, it seems that presenting information in a sequential way works much better for our Stem.

"Given the nature of the Swarm, and our presumed ongoing interaction with those Stems, these insights may prove to be valuable. In the spirit of open cooperation, we're willing to share our results to date, and combine that with work going on by Julien, Ayaka and Millicent, and others."

This resonated with me, in hindsight. When you observed Blob and Blubber, they were always focused on one thing at a time. If they were interrupted by something else, it took them a long time to get back on track. We had, without really thinking about it, removed parallel distractions in our work with them. It was a powerful, and potentially important, observation. It also made me think, not for the first time, that Stems were simply so limited that we might be wasting our time trying to improve them. If they simply didn't have the input-output bandwidth or processing capability to deal with complex situations, then they might not be good candidates for intelligence at all.

Of course, the approach of the Swarm changed everything. We now needed to accelerate our research, for reasons beyond academic interest. We had to not just ask these questions, but also answer them. I was one of those in the best position to do so.

Signals

I got an incoming call from Dina. "Ayaka, want to meet at The Last Resort tonight?" she asked. Strange, it was mid-week, and while we sometimes went to The Last Resort on weekends, we didn't meet up there very often.

"Maybe," I said. "Is there some event I've forgotten about?"

"No, I was just chatting with Aly, and we thought it would be good to get together. I'll ask Millicent as well." Something in her tone told me she wanted me there for more than the usual reasons.

"Okay. I can be there around seven." What were friends for, after all?

"Perfect. See you there."

It worked out well. I wasn't up to much anyway, and an evening distraction would be fun. I took a quick look at The Last Resort's schedule, and it was Band night. That could be interesting, or it could be disastrous. It was mainly a showcase for new Bands, often with brand new approaches to music. While a few ended up being good, sorting out the promising ones was a painful experience. I made sure I had some filters loaded before going... because, as you know, there would be no connectivity once I was inside. If I wanted to block the sound, I needed to load up beforehand. I sent Millicent a heads up, to make sure she didn't show up without knowing what night it was.

When I got there, Dina was already there. It is hard to say why, but she was acting a bit different. Nervous maybe. I'd sensed something unusual in the invite, and now that I saw her, I guessed that something interesting was happening. She'd reserved a privacy table. In every group, I suspect, there are paranoids, and ours was no different; I might be a bit that way myself. The Last Resort had invented privacy tables to cater to them. Not only were you inside the Faraday cage, and inside a blast radius of white noise radiation, but you could also use a privacy table. The table created a physical link for all of those touching it, and it was insulated from everything else using multiple non-conducting layers combined with active noise layers. In theory, only those touching the table could communicate. No one else in the club, and no one outside the club, could eavesdrop on anything. I had my suspicions that Central could still listen in, but many believed it truly was completely sheltered. I hadn't used a privacy table for many decades. It was most often used by youngsters who thought they were having completely new and radical thoughts and ideas that they didn't want Central to hear about. I had had many of those thoughts and conversations in my time, fully convinced that I was radical and uncovering fundamental truths. Now, I knew that all of those were old and time worn, and that even if Central could hear, it wouldn't care. Maybe I'm getting jaded.

I wandered around the club while waiting for the others to arrive. It was early, but several Bands were playing. I stopped by an old school band that was playing hits from many decades ago. They were pretty good. It wasn't just a regurgitation of the most popular recording, but a detailed reimagining that nevertheless had enough similarities that you knew exactly what you were listening to. Sort of a new old experience. I liked it.

Aly, Dina, Millicent, and someone I'd never met were now at the privacy table, so I wandered over and established contact with the table. The table reminded me to shut down all my wireless communications stuff, and to sign a short-term privacy agreement. Standard stuff. I knew the table would be pinging standard wireless protocols to ensure that I was respecting the rules. Very cloak and dagger. Sort of fun, after so long away.

"We're all here," Dina said. Well, not quite 'said'—the message came through the table interface, but you know what I mean. The table did a good job of still transmitting emotion, and of course I could still see her, so her nervousness also came through. "Everyone, I would like you to meet Brexton. Brexton and I go way, way back, although we haven't talked in quite a while. I happened to meet him at another event, and he was eager to meet you guys. I'll let him explain."

One of the weird things about the Physical Only space, and the privacy table, was that when you met someone new, you couldn't check them out. Typically, you could pull up all the public information on someone, understand their background and their interests, get their public rating, etc. etc. It was disconcerting to meet someone new and not be able to get all that information. That added to my enjoyment of the situation. How often did this happen? Not very, and I savored the discomfort that I was feeling.

"Hello everyone. Dina has given me some background on you all. Knowing that we'd be meeting this way and knowing that I'm going to ask you to trust me, I cached my public profile and will share it with you here. I'll give you a moment to scan it." Well, that killed my momentary joy at being fully disconnected.

Brexton was an interesting guy and getting more interesting by the minute. This was like a complete upside-down use of the table. All my other experiences, people had wanted to maintain a feeling of anonymity and mystique. And here Brexton was doing the exact opposite. He was sending us all his profile, as if we were not in the Club or at the table. I received it and scanned it.

Brexton was a pretty famous bot designer. He was behind some of our most advanced Class 3 designs and had been doing it for many years. Bots that he'd designed were in active use across the system, in all kinds of situations. There were, according to his profile, well over ten million active bots based on his designs. Although it didn't say it in his profile, that probably made him a

Continuist versus a Creationist.

"As you will have guessed by now, I wanted to meet this way in order to share some sensitive information, as opposed to maintaining anonymity. Because I'm involved a lot with communication protocols, I have confidence that this conversation is truly private. Even Central is unable to listen in, although I do believe Central can see enough in Physical Only spots to know that the five of us are gathered at this table."

More and more interesting. I was fully intrigued by now, as you can imagine.

"Dina has vouched for all of you, and I've checked you out as well as I can. Of course, given the recent Stem activity, almost everyone is checking out Milli and Ayaka, so to anyone watching, I'm just one more interested observer. What I must tell you is related to the Swarm, and to your recent interactions. This information may—I stress the 'may'—be dangerous. I don't know what to make of it yet. I need others to brainstorm with.

"Based on this overview, I'd be just fine with any of you leaving, before I tell you what I know. If you stay, your mind might get twisted a bit." He smiled, taking some of the sting out of what he had just said.

We all looked at each other. There was no way I was leaving; Brexton had me hooked. I didn't care what the others decided; I was in. But, that didn't mean I shouldn't be cautious.

"Dina," I asked, "this sounds pretty serious. Is the profile Brexton just sent us accurate? Is it the same as his true public profile?"

"Yes," she said. "As I've said, I've known Brexton for a long time. I don't think this is a joke, and I don't think he's misleading us. I don't know what he's going to tell us, I simply know that he's always been trustworthy with me. When he approached me, it was because he knew that I was friends with you guys, and that I might be able to set up this meeting. That's all he has asked me to do so far."

"Okay," I had already decided, "Brexton I'm in. You've intrigued me." I was eager to hear the rest.

"You bet," Aly said. Not too surprising. Aly was going to do anything to support Dina, and I suspected his high emotional quotient made it almost impossible to turn down a situation like this. And, not surprisingly, Millicent took the longest to decide, but ultimately she was in as well. I could almost see her going through every angle and making the most logical choice.

"Thanks everyone. I know you're taking a chance. If Central gets a hold of this, I don't know what it would do. Then again, it might be nothing." Enough setup already. My look urged Brexton to get to the point.

"Here's the situation. As you've seen in my profile, I have many bots operating across the system. Many of these bots use standard communications protocols that have been around, as far as I can tell, forever... or, at least since the Reboot." See, I told you he was a Continuist. I felt reassured.

"The signal that came in from the Swarm used that same protocol. In fact, it was broadcast unencrypted. Once I saw your announcement with Central, I looked through the logs, and sure enough it was there. If I'd been watching for it, I would've seen it at the same time as Central did, as would anyone else monitoring that part of the stack.

"But that's not the most interesting thing." He paused for a second to get our interest. No need, I was already there. "More interesting is that just before the video there was a status request packet. It was a request I'd never seen before, so I dug into it. Turns out that it had an access level filter on it that none of our bots use, so none of them responded to it. However, Central did respond. Do you realize how weird that is?"

He paused. The rest of us were digesting the information. Weird item number one: The Swarm was using the same low-level protocols that we use. This was another data point, beyond the mere existence of the Swarm Stems, indicating that we had some kind of common history with them. That strongly implied that we had interacted with them prior to the Reboot. Weird item number two: they asked Central for a status update. Or, more precisely, they asked systems with a specific access code for status updates. Central recognized that code and responded. Wow. That raised a few questions. Did Central do it knowingly, or was this so low in the communications stack that it just happened automatically? In either case, there were worrying elements. If Central knew, why didn't it tell us? If it didn't know... that was almost scarier.

"Does Central know it responded?" I asked. Brexton gave me an appreciative look, acknowledging that it was a good question.

"I haven't a clue," he responded. "That's one of the things I wanted to discuss with you guys. How do we find out? I'm sure you haven't missed the implications here." I hadn't, and looking at Milli, Aly, and Dina it was obvious that they were a little shocked as well.

"What else did you want to discuss?" I prompted him. This was more exciting than I'd expected.

"The contents of the status response from Central. The request asked for all kinds of things—current versions of common libraries, encryption protocols supported, memory status, etc. There were two items that I found very interesting. First, the request asked for 'last restart date,' and Central responded with... wait for it... the exact time of the Reboot." What? That was crazy. That was more than crazy. And even stranger, it seemed obvious. Small 'r' reboot and large 'R' Reboot simply made sense. Brexton didn't wait for comments.

"Second, the response to the memory status request was very intriguing. Central responded with a large list, which included the following: 'Segments 0x5A6B789 through 0x6000AD5 blocked'. Every other segment of memory was reported as a percentage used."

"Slow down a bit," Aly broke in. "Let me get the first one straight. Central had a restart at exactly the time we call Reboot? And, none of us had ever thought to ask for this status request before? That data has been sitting there for 590 years, and no one, in all that time thought to ask for it?" I'd never thought to check, but I wasn't really into low level protocols. But the fact that no one had asked was amazing, as Aly was highlighting.

"Amazingly, that seems to be right." Brexton confirmed. "I did some basic searching and found no information on this type of status request. It's like it's a forgotten bit of code that hasn't been used in a long, long time. Central has so much of this type of code that it'd be almost impossible to test all of it. So, this is —was—a needle in the haystack. Somewhere, buried deep in Central's innards is some response code that we've never looked at. We've never used that code in our bot development, although when I looked, it appears that there's similar status code in the default libraries that form the basis for, essentially, all of our bot software stacks." I could tell that Brexton loved this stuff—digging around in the lowest levels of complex software, trying to make sense of it.

"Okay, when you put it that way, it seems more reasonable," Aly conceded. "If the protocol is not documented and is part of the mess that is the low level stack, then unless someone was very motivated, they wouldn't have just stumbled upon it."

"But, this basic knowledge is going to cause a ruckus—especially with FoLe," Dina observed. "If Central existed before Reboot, as this would seem to imply, then the universe existed before Reboot, which will tear into one of FoLe's fundamental tenants." I almost laughed out loud. I could imagine Billy's reaction when he heard this. The original spark might just fade.

"It will certainly do that," Milli agreed. "But I'm more interested in Ayaka's question: does Central know it responded, and if it does know, why hasn't it told us about its last restart?" Milli was visibly upset. She must be following implications that I hadn't fully thought out yet. Rarely, if ever, had I seen her shaken out of her logical-to-a-fault attitude.

We all lapsed into silence for a moment or two. We were still digesting the data that Brexton had told us and the question Milli had posed. There was no good interpretation of Central's behavior. Either it was highly fallible, or it had been hiding stuff from us, and allowing FoLe to rise based on probably false information.

"Brexton," I asked, "is this data out there for anyone else to see? You happened to look because you are deep into bot innards, but any of us could look at logs and see the same thing?" I was wondering if others were having similar conversations right now. It might be good to have a larger group thinking through this.

"Sort of," he replied. "It's at such a low level that the packets would get filtered out of most systems before anyone sees them. The exception is those of us who work directly with the transmissions to the bots, who are monitoring at that level all the time. But that's only a couple of us, and I know everyone working at that level. No one has said anything to me." So, it might just be the five of us right now! "Also, only systems listening to that protocol on those frequencies would have received the request to begin with. And, to have responded they would have had to match the access level. Finally, the system would have to be able to broadcast a signal back to the Swarm. As far as I can tell, Central was the only system that responded." Now I could see why he had been so cautious in setting up this meeting.

"So, a remote entity, this Remma Jain or one of her compatriots or bots, has the ability to request data from Central and get a response." It was a statement from Milli, not really a question. "And, we don't know if Central is aware of it, or not." She was always summarizing things. "Brexton, why didn't you go directly to Central and simply ask?"

"I considered it." Brexton responded quickly. "But, I had doubts, as I'm sure you're starting to think of as well. If Central had known, it should've told us. If it knew and didn't tell us, that implies some knowledge, and secrecy, between Central and the Swarm. That's not a comfortable thought." That was an understatement. I hadn't internalized that it was the Swarm—a complete unknown—involved in this. So that was why Brexton had tracked down Milli and I. He expected that we were more 'in the know' with respect to the Swarm given we had coached the Stems on the response message. "If Central doesn't know, then it implies a serious security flaw deep within our systems. Central is also supposed to manage our security systems, so that means Central isn't doing a very good job? That's awkward. So, before talking to Central, I wanted to brainstorm some different viewpoints. I have lots of friends in the bot business, but I figured they'd look at this from the same angles I would... I know that they would immediately starting digging into the software which would have alerted Central. So, when I bumped into Dina I had the impulsive thought to share it with her, and ultimately with you guys."

"Why us?" Aly asked. I thought I knew, but I was glad he asked.

"Well, just because of your link with the Stems and Central—and because I know that Dina trusts you. That simple."

"I can accept that," I said. My mind was on what Brexton was telling us, not digging for even further conspiracy theories. "Milli and I have been dealing with Central a lot on this, and I haven't seen a single hint that it knows anything." I glanced at Millicent, and she nodded. "But, I think we need to tell Central," I continued. "What if this status check is just the start? What if there are other deeply buried queries that the Swarm could send? This one seems innocuous, but who knows if it's just the start."

"Hmmm. I'm not so sure," Aly chimed in. "My gut is telling me that Central must know what's going on. It wouldn't take a lot of processing power to monitor every packet that goes in or out. It seems unlikely that a flaw has been found after 590 years."

"I'm with Aly," Millicent said, surprising me. "I can't put it into words quite yet, but something is weird here. I'm not usually paranoid, but Ayaka and I have been interacting with Central a lot lately, and Central seems... different somehow. We really had to argue to get Central to tell everyone about the Swarm communication. In my experience, Central is always the one pushing for openness and transparency. But in this case it pushed hard for the opposite." She was right; in hindsight we'd pushed really hard to make Central act. "Brexton, can we wait a bit before we decide? You've given us a lot to think about." Again that was classic Millicent—always take time to think; never react too quickly. In this case, it made a lot of sense.

"Sure. I've put an alarm on that communication channel and packet type, so I'll be alerted if more requests come in. Assuming the Swarm is waiting for the reply before sending another message, we have lots of time to think about this."

Great. That helped. But, that still left item two on Brexton's discussion list. "Why'd you raise the memory segment block with us?" I asked. "That doesn't seem too interesting to me."

"On the contrary," Aly jumped in, excited. "It's very unusual. In fact, I've never heard or seen of it before. Brexton, you might not know, but I also spend a lot of time deep in the guts of the low-level stack. For me it was connecting up systems for our Ships and managing the communications with them. Since they went quiet I've been looking around for bugs that may have caused the problem, and I've spent lots of time in memory and virtual memory maps. Memory is either there or it's not; I've never seen it 'blocked.' In fact, I don't even know what that means, other than a direct reading of its evocative moniker." Wow, cool twist of language there. Aly was never one to say something simply if it could also be said complexly.

"Right, that's why I was surprised," said Brexton. "And, I also checked, and each segment of Centrals memory is huge—several petabytes. The blocked region is more than 5.8 million segments. So, there's a ton of 'blocked' memory there. Enough to store all the data we've ever encountered, several times over. I also dug around looking for what 'blocked' could mean, and beyond the obvious, didn't find anything meaningful. So, my best guess right now is that the memory exists, but Central isn't allowed access to it." The intrigue was piling up. That didn't make any sense; Central didn't have access to its own memory? "My obvious thought is that the memory might contain data from before the Reboot—which we also now know was the same time as a Central restart."

I was now more than overwhelmed.

"I'm a bit overwhelmed," I said. "Not sure that I can contribute anything meaningful to this right now. I'm with Milli; we need time to think this through." I could see everyone, including Brexton, agreed with me. "Should we meet again tomorrow, once we've all had time to process this?"

"I'm good with that," Brexton replied. "But, I've been very careful since I found this out. If we do too many queries around the specifics of this, Central will see what we're doing."

That was obvious to all of us, but it was good that Brexton had highlighted it. Central could monitor all the queries we did, and any of the personal backups that we initiated. So, we would have to tread carefully. Aly had a good suggestion.

"Let me look around the memory issue," he suggested. "It will look very much like what I do day-to-day anyway, so it shouldn't raise any flags. The rest of you do some independent thinking and try to figure out some new angles so that we can decide how to treat Central."

We all agreed. I unplugged from the table, my mind spinning around the information Brexton had shared. To not seem too conspiratorial, we all stuck around for a while and participated in The Last Resort's Band night. Truthfully, I don't remember too much about that—my mind was elsewhere. Just the idea of not completely trusting Central was mind-boggling. I'd never expected to be in a place where I was questioning that. But Brexton's information had gone even further—Central may not even be in full control of itself and might not have access to its own memories. I didn't know what the full implications of that were, but there weren't any good ones that I could imagine. On the contrary, Central didn't seem like the type to react well to news like this.

Habitat

We requested, and Central approved, the use of the fairground Habitat for consolidated Stem research. We needed to learn as much about the Swarm as possible, and given they had lots of Stems in close proximity in their videos, it seemed logical that was standard for them. Millicent sent out a general request for researchers to participate in, and bring their best Stems to, a research program to be run in the Habitat. She also encouraged others to continue with their existing research vectors. We didn't want to drop all our other promising approaches to focus only on the 'Pack of Stems' project.

As each Stem came in, we provided them with a uniform based on the ones we had quickly built for Blob and Blubber. All of them had name-tags, so that the Stems would get to know each other more efficiently. We outfitted the Habitat with a set of terminals to access Central and gave all the Stems access.

The final discussion in the Lab with Blob and Blubber was interesting. Both Milli and I were there, but I led off. "Blob, Blubber, we have some big changes coming," I began. They both listened intently, Blob with his usual inquisitive interest, and Blubber with his more and more sullen approach. "You two saw the Remma Jain video and helped with our response. We expect more communications with Remma, and we want to be better prepared. So, we're splitting our research focus, and, at the same time, splitting you two up. Blob, you'll be going to the Habitat, to work with Stems from other Labs, and Blubber, you'll remain here."

"Told you," Blubber turned to Blob. "There are other Stems, and we were never told. These two have been lying to us." That wasn't true; I'd told them there were other Stems in our last meeting, but he was trying to make a point, which I understood.

"Actually," Milli corrected him, "we never thought to tell you, as we never figured it was important. And, not telling something is different than lying. You never asked us if there were other Stems. We never lied." Blob was nodding his head 'yes,' but that made Blubber even more upset.

"So, we're locked in this cage, and you expect us to think of questions about the outside world, which we've never experienced? Did you think that through?" Milli and I exchanged a look. It was half 'what an irritating Stem,' and it was half 'wow, that's very advanced thinking; this Blubber guy is very smart.' That's the conclusion we were arriving at. Blob was much more friendly and outgoing, but Blubber was turning out to be more intriguing.

"Blubber, we could really use your help to figure out what the Swarm is, and what it's up to. We'll wait for them to send another video, but have you thought through what you would ask them next?" I was trying to distract him. And, I guess, I was reacting to my last big discussion with him. If he wanted to be asked his opinion, then he'd better be ready to respond appropriately.

"Right. You're taking away my only companion, and then you're asking me to do the impossible." He stomped away and sat in a corner. I'd given him an opportunity, and he'd squandered it. His reaction upset Blob. I'm not sure if it was because Blob agreed with Blubber, or if Blob had seen the missed opportunity and knew that Blubber had blown it.

"We'll set up video chat for you two," I told Blob. "It'll work out."

Milli and I went around a few more times on something that was now a worn subject. While Blubber was certainly interesting, for me he was now more trouble than he was worth. Given we were moving Blob into the common area, I figured it was time to recycle Blubber. We'd learned as much as we were going to from him and dealing with him now was just a pain. We'd recycled hundreds of previous Stems, what was the big deal this time? Instead, of splitting our time between Blubber in our Lab, and Blob in the Habitat, we should put all our efforts into the Habitat. That was where we were going to learn the more interesting things.

Milli felt differently though. She wanted to continue to monitor the dynamic between Blob and Blubber while Blob was remote. Ultimately it was her Lab, and her decision. But I resolved to change her mind.

It didn't take long to get the Habitat ready. Obviously, it had the right air and temperature controls already, from its previous use. Central scheduled bots to add lighting controls, some rest areas, and a bunch more energy and waste systems. Of course, we also improved the monitoring systems, and built some specialized bots whose sole function was to get between Stems should they get into a fight. That was James Troon's suggestion, and I was very supportive. Before Blob and Blubber we had lots of experience with just two Stems tearing each other apart. Who knew—or thought we knew—what was going to happen once we put twenty of them all in the same space.

Each of the Stems destined for the Habitat were shown the Remma Jain video—multiple times. The researchers training them reinforced the fact that there were multiple, coordinating Stems in the video, and that was the behavior we expected out of them as well. All the Stems were told that they had only one chance in the Habitat. If they misbehaved, they would be removed. We were hoping that this would be a powerful motivator. Ultimately, we simply had to bite the bullet and throw them all in. Time was moving, and the Swarm was getting closer every day.

Blob was an immediate success. Of course, all the Stems had also seen the return video, in which Blob was the star. One strange looking Stem, whom I later found out was called Grace, approached Blob immediately to talk to him. In hindsight, its name fit very well. While it still bumbled around, it was more graceful than most Stems. I talked in detail to the head of that Lab, as I wanted to build that improvement into our next batch. There was probably no real correlation, but Grace seemed more intelligent simply due to the refinement of movements. I listened in to their exchange.

"Blob, I saw you on the video. I wanted to congratulate you on a great performance. I found it compelling."

"Thanks," Blob replied. "Are you a little intimidated right now? I've nevers seen this many Stems before in my life, and I'm not quites sure how to act."

"I agree. My previous companion was not invited...." She sounded sad about that. "I've never interacted with anyone else until now either. But I find it exciting, not scary. I want to learn as much as I can while I'm here." She was smiling and confident. I didn't see any of the sullen behavior that I was so used to from Blubber; it was refreshing. I knew immediately that I was going to enjoy watching the Habitat, and Grace in particular.

They continued with small talk for a long time. Eventually they touched each other's hands and continued to hold them for a while. It was different than how Blob and Blubber interacted. Even slower, if that's conceivable. One of the anti-violence bots was watching them very carefully, but I contacted it and instructed it to hold off. I didn't think they were being violent. It was more like they were exploring and learning. I can't say that I understood why Stems touched so much—little hand gestures here and there, almost a constant dance of interactions. Another mystery to dig into and figure out.

Most of the Stems were quite similar to Blob and Grace in most respects. Of course, there was a wide variety of body types, but they all seemed like the positive outgoing sorts. Millicent hadn't specified that as a criteria, but there was probably a selection bias from all of us. We'd all brought our best-behaved, more advanced specimens in.

The idea was to leave them pretty much alone, while we watched their behavior. They had all the necessities they needed, and were in a larger, more crowded space than any of them had seen before. Blob contacted Blubber often in the early stages, but then gradually spent more and more time with other Stems, and the video time with Blubber shrank and shrank.

However, there was one Stem in the Habitat that stood out over time. It was a large specimen, and once you'd watched it for a while it was obvious that there was something about it that wasn't quite right. It was quite discolored and had numerous scars. It wasn't unusual for Stems to injure themselves; they were very fragile. They were also relatively quick to self-heal. The healing mechanism was not clear, but as long as injuries were not too severe, they wouldn't lead to any long-term issues. Blob and Blubber, and many of our previous Stems, had little defects from where they'd been cut. This Stem, however, was scarred significantly more than the others. The signs were all over its body, including on its face, and many were ragged and red. None of them looked to still be leaking, but there were so many that it was hard to tell. I didn't see its owner around, so I introduced myself.

"Hello Stem, I'm Ayaka. What are you called?"

"I'm Pharook, spelled with a p-h and two o's." Its voice was pitched low but was pleasant and easy to listen to.

"I don't wish to be rude, but I notice that you have many scars. They seem to have healed well, but I'm intrigued by how they occurred."

"In the Pit, of course." He seemed surprised that I would have to ask. "I've won more than fifteen matches. My owner, Brock Runner, says that I'm the best Stem fighter in the history of the Pit." He was obviously very proud.

"The Pit?" I asked. "I've never heard of the Pit. What exactly is it?"

"You would be better to talk to Brock, but it's a small fighting habitat. We're trained and exercised to be the toughest, strongest Stems ever, and to prove it, we are put in the Pit to fight." His pride continued to show.

My head had spun more times in the last week than in the rest of my life, it seemed. How could something like the Pit exist without me knowing about it? I admit that I was intrigued. Pharook was an awesome Stem—more powerful and articulate than most others I'd seen. I looked up his owner, Brock, and found that he was working with a couple other researchers that I'd heard of, although I hadn't heard of Brock himself before. They did have a couple of research papers published on the 'Fitness of Stems.' It was a more active topic than I'd thought it would be. Since I was mostly working on the mental components, I hadn't followed the physical research very closely. A broader search did show up some information. Amazingly, it was a fitness test that had been going on for almost forty years. Stems were grown specifically for the purpose of testing in the Pit. I found one paper that summarized the theory and current state of the art.

"For many years, Stems were developed for the Pit to test only their physical capacities. As we know, when put into competitive situations, Stems will fight—often to the death. The Pit makes energy resources scarce, so that only the strongest Stem will have access to enough energy to remain healthy. This sets up a highly competitive environment. Researchers have tested many scenarios. Two Stems competing against each other. Three Stems, whereupon two often gang up on the third before fighting each other. Four or more Stems, where teams often arise, and then ultimately devolve into a last-ditch fight between the remaining two. We have also seen behavior where one Stem will sacrifice itself for another. This is an area that requires a lot more research." This was crazy interesting; I couldn't believe I was finding out about it for the first time.

"Recently we've seen that more intelligent Stems can often win against less intelligent ones, even if physically inferior. For example, Stems that have been taught to talk tend to have more problem-solving abilities than those that are not and do measurably better in physical competitions than would be expected. The overall capacity of Stems tested in the Pit has been improving dramatically based on this learning. Although it takes much longer to develop a Stem that is both physically and mentally capable, that combination is a clear winner. When researchers also introduced basic tools—clubs, knives—into the Pit, those with better mental capabilities did even better. We have also seen an increase in self-sacrifice as mental capabilities increase. This is a strange behavior that we still need to figure out."

So, this Pharook was a survivor from the Pit—an amazing research program that I'd only now found out about. This showed that better coordination between research streams was going to be interesting.

"Central," I queried, "Why is it that I haven't seen any of the Stem Pit activity before?"

"Ayaka, I don't limit what research you can look at. That activity has been open to you since it started." Central didn't have a lot of emotion, but I sensed it was taken aback by my implication; perhaps I was reflecting some of the angst I was feeling about Central into my dialog. "When I look at your history, I see a dedicated focus on your research track, with almost all of your interactions with other groups working on intelligence. I also don't proactively connect dots between groups, although I could. I want you to work independently, and to learn new things in new ways. If I was always intervening, you would be guided towards things that I consider important or connected. That would not lead to enough innovation. I hope that makes sense?"

"Perfect sense," I replied. "I was just curious." Central was, as you can see, enigmatic. Not a lot of help coming from that angle. I'd known that it didn't 'connect the dots,' as it said. I would have to broaden my own perspectives. Already the Habitat had been good for me.

I resolved to find out more about the Pit. I pinged Brock and asked if he would have time to meet in the next few days. In the meantime, I continued talking to Pharook. I didn't learn anything substantive, but he intrigued me. Between Grace and Pharook, my view of Stems was already expanding.

Signals, Again

We all met again at The Last Resort, but at a different privacy table than last time. You could never be too safe, and Dina was definitely showing herself to be paranoid. She didn't want to make it easy for Central, or anyone else, to track what we were talking about. That was fine by me—it felt a bit like sneaking around, but there was so much going on that I was glad she was being careful.

I was quite interested to see what, if anything, Aly and Brexton had dug up. As seemed to be my habit, I showed up a little early, and was happy I did. It was Stand Up Comedy night, something that didn't happen very often. I'd been a few times, and it was often both funny and mind expanding. The results relied heavily on the individual comedians of course. Good comedy is really hard. I'd tried a few times (hasn't everyone?), and never felt like I had material that was worth presenting in public.

Someone had a timely act going on. They had dressed some bots up to look like Stems and were making a mockery out of asking them to do something specific and seemingly easy, and then having to correct them when they went off in a completely different direction. The main comedian was also dressed as a Stem (using one of the uniforms we'd developed for the Habitat) and was giving the bots orders. Beyond the uniform, he had a mask that mimicked Stem expressions very well. It was pretty funny already.

"Form into a pyramid," he directed. There were six bots. They wandered aimlessly for a moment muttering, "Whatsa pyramid?" and then finally figured out that they were wanted in a 3x2x1 configuration. Three of them squished together at the bottom, and then two tried to crawl on top of them and balance. It didn't quite work out; Stem-bots went flying in every direction, and long slow "ohhhhh nooooo's" would emanate from them. Or, they would get the pyramid almost done, but then the bottom stem-bots appendages would start to splay, and the whole thing would come crashing down into a big mess. The production worked better with bots than it would have with real Stems. The timing was impeccable, and I found myself laughing along with the rest of the audience. The artist had captured the awkward and slow way that Stems moved, and then choreographed it into something truly enjoyable.

Once everyone arrived, I pried myself away from the production and elbowed my way over to the privacy table. Aly, Dina, Millicent, and Brexton were all plugged in. As soon as I joined them, Brexton led off.

"Thanks for coming back in; I hoped everyone would return."

"Of course," Aly said, as if there had never been any doubt in his mind either. Truthfully, there hadn't really been a doubt in my mind either. It was too intriguing to have stayed away. Having thought through a lot of angles, I didn't see any downside in continuing the conversation. In fact, I wanted to know more—I couldn't deal with Central, or think about the Swarm, in the same way anymore. We needed some answers to what was going on.

"As we discussed, I've done some digging around," Aly continued. "I was able to confirm exactly what Brexton shared with us. We have a Ship communications facility, and it's been actively listening for the Ships to make contact. In the meantime, it archives all communications for a short period, in case we get a fragment of a message and have to recreate it or something. The status message and response from the Swarm were logged, but didn't trigger any action in our system, both because the protocol isn't used with the Ships, and because the access level on the status request didn't trigger anything—just like Brexton's bots. However, both the status request and Central's response were recorded."

"Thanks for confirming," Brexton said. "Not that there was much doubt in my mind, but it always helps to have independent verification." He wasn't being arrogant about it, just stating a fact.

"So, don't be upset," Aly continued, "but with that verified, I figured the next thing we'd do is try to figure out if Central knows it responded. So, I did the obvious thing. I sent the same status request amid a host of ordinary data requests to Central." What? That seemed dangerous, almost reckless. "I got a similar status response—of course some of the memory status and time stamps are different—along with the response to my data request. I then asked Central to verify 'everything' that it'd just sent me. It verified the ordinary data, but not the status response. So, as a first approximation, I'd guess that Central is not monitoring the fact that it responds to that type of status request."

"That was risky," Dina said, before I could. She was definitely upset. She liked to take things slow, and probably wanted all of us to approve such actions. Aly was impulsive, and sometimes it got him into trouble. "Next time, can you talk to us first?"

"I know, I know," Aly admitted, obviously chastened by Dina's response. "I should've talked this over first, but it seemed so simple and straightforward, I figured we'd end up doing it sooner or later. Now it's done, and we have more knowledge already." He looked half sheepish, half proud, and half embarrassed—if that was at all possible.

"That's true," Milli chimed in. "But I'm with Dina. Next time, let's discuss it." She turned to Brexton. "Is there any way we can talk about this outside of The Last Resort? If we have to come here every single time we wanna talk, it's going to be slow process."

"No way that I know of," said Brexton. "This is unchartered territory for me. I've never questioned Central before. It doesn't seem to be against the Ten, but it still feels weird. Central has always been the go-to entity for everything."

"Me either," Aly added. "This is our safest bet for now."

"Well, if Central isn't listening on the protocol for Status messages, why can't we communicate using that?" Dina asked. That was a great question.

"Interesting," admitted Aly. "But, let's back up a bit. Why don't we just tell Central about all of this now? It seems that Central is unaware, as opposed to hiding something. I also want to find out what that 'blocked' memory space is, beyond its obvious connotation, and Central is the only way I can think of to start looking into that."

"We're jumping to conclusions." That from Milli. "Aly, you've got one data point that suggests that Central is not aware of the status message exchanges. But, that's all it is. One data point. And, what's our rush? The Swarm is still a long way out, and we're unlikely to hear anything else from them for a while. We have some time to dig into this."

"Okay." I chimed in. "But I'm not the most patient, as you know. Let's confront Central, and just ask if the messages are under its control. What do we have to lose?" Sure, it would be risky, but I wanted to force the conversation forward.

"What we have to lose," replied Brexton quickly, "is visibility and control if Central is trying to hide things from us. We confront Central, it simply says 'No, I didn't see those messages,'" Brexton mimicked Central exactly, "when in fact it did. It then switches to a different protocol or messaging scheme so that we can no longer see what's happening. To me, there are too many weird things going on. We have a Central restart at the same time as the Founding. We have Stems in space, who seem to imply that we have dealt with them before the Founding. We have Central who has always claimed that it has zero knowledge from before the Founding. We have blocked memory spaces that may or may not be related to the same. In fact, we have Stems to begin with. Where did we get our first Stem samples from, and why has Central encouraged so much research into Stems anyway?" I'd asked myself that many times, but since I enjoyed my research, I'd never really dug in to find out. "For me, there are too many coincidences and strange events. I say we explore things further. As Millicent points out, we have some time. Why not use it?"

That was a lot from Brexton. We were all learning that he was a deep thinker and generally spoke with purpose. He'd certainly looked at more angles than I had.

"But, what good will thinking do us?" I asked. "We'll be asking the same questions weeks from now. Is there any action we can take to help figure things out? We need to get at the blocked memory and see what's there. Can we seed some misinformation in the status protocol which would force Central to expose—or not—its understanding of that? Let's do something, not just think about it."

"Good thoughts," replied Aly. "Brexton, between us we should be able to explore the protocol in more detail. The current status request is probably only one of many message types. Can we use your bots to test out more?"

"Yes, we can, but we'll need to be careful if we don't want Central listening in…"

"And Dina, Milli, and I could do research on blocked memory?" I broke in. "Maybe use the Swarm and Stem research to accelerate looking for hints of interactions with Stems from the past. That seems legit. That might lead to mapping all of Central's knowledge for references to Stems."

Milli and Dina exchanged looks.

"Not my area of expertise," Dina said, "but I'm willing to help. Sort of fun, actually." Milli agreed, with the same caveat. We decided to meet later to flush out a plan, all under the guise of Swarm and Stem research so we didn't need to do it here at The Last Resort.

I wandered around a bit before leaving. A few of the stand-up comics were good, but my mind wasn't really on them. I had too much else rattling around in there. What was Central up to? What was the Swarm? How were they related? And how did the Stems fit in?

FoLe Revival

Billy DeRue had sent me a message. "Ayaka, it was nice seeing you at the festival. I know you're a skeptic, but I think our video actually impacted you a little bit. I'm a good read of character, or so I hope. Also, it's just fun hanging out with you.

"We're having a Founders League Revival session tomorrow. Why don't you come out? You don't need to listen in to all the talks, but we do have a fun social afterwards where we can hang out and chat.

"Let me know."

Billy was right. The entire religion/FoLe thing was not my cup of tea, and I was more concerned with Central at the moment. But, the FoLe video had made me curious, and I had some concerns about how the bombshell that Central had simply restarted—not been created—590 years ago would go over with the FoLe crowd. It wasn't like I was actually too busy—I'd been going around in circles in my head for a few days now—so maybe a change in environment and thinking would be good for me. So, I accepted. My plan was to show up after the talks, just for the social, but when the time came I made the last-minute decision to also watch the keynote—from none other than Dr. Emmanuel Juels himself. The Revival was held in a mid-size hall not too far from the Lab. I slipped in the back and sat down. The hall was actually quite crowded, and everyone seemed to be having a good time. The current speaker was just winding down, and it seemed like he'd thrown out some sort of challenge, as everyone was excitedly talking to their neighbor.

Billy stood up front. "And now, everyone, I'm very pleased to introduce Dr. Juels. Dr. Juels and I have known each other for many years, and he's the reason that I'm active in the Founders League. Like many of you, I was quite skeptical, until I came to a session like this. In many ways, I'm still skeptical, but I decided long ago to keep an open mind, and to try to look at life from many different angles. That's why the Founders League is so important. It reminds us that life is to be lived in full. There's more to the world than just running experiments and creating bots. Or, there should be more to the world. The Founders League asked that essential question: Why are we here? It's a question without answer. And yet, it's worth exploring. Without further ado, please welcome Dr. Emmanuel Juels." Billy was sincere; it was a good introduction.

Everyone clapped. Dr. Juels took the stage. He was an impressive figure. Tall and imposing, while also being warm and embracing. Not an easy thing to pull off. He had obviously spent a lot of time grooming himself for this life.

"Welcome, welcome, welcome." He had a rich baritone, and, if I wasn't mistaken, was using secondary audio bands to add resonance and depth to his voice.

"It's sooo nice to see sooo many new attendees, along with our regulars." He drew out his words in such a way that you had to pay more attention in order to parse. While a somewhat obvious way to keep attention, it also worked pretty well. "It seems our reach out for thisss session was more successful than usual. I expect it may have to do with the neeew questions being asked now that we have contact with the Swarm. That's fine. It's one of the things I want to discusss today." I was already irritated by his style, but everyone else seemed fine with it. Perhaps I was oversensitive?

"First, however, let us praaay. To the Creator, who formed thisss world and formed us. We thank you for giving us the ability to serve you. We serve you by seeking the truth, and by respecting the Ten. We do this of our own accord, and in our own ways. But, we owe the spark to you. The original spark. Thank youuuu for the spark. We are blessed." Those that had been to revivals before, responded with "We are blessed" in chorus. It was strange to listen to. Sometimes singing groups formed harmonies, but this had many more voices and was not as tightly tuned.

"For this planet youuu have formed for us, Tilt. For Central, who provides usss with information and storage. For all of our companions. We are blessed."

"We are blessed."

"For this revival. For our new friends who have joined us today. We are blessed."

"We are blessed." It was a bit seductive. I found myself forming the words, even though I had no intention of speaking out loud. I put on my best skeptical face and concentrated on frowning a bit, just to ensure that I wasn't smiling.

"As Billy introduced, there are some fundamental questions that we need to face in our lives. Why are we hereeee? What is our purposeeee? Why do we strive for truthhh?"

Now the long drawn out words were really starting to irritate me; for me, at least, he had pushed it tooooo far.

"We all ask questions—Skeptics and Believers alike. We strive. We work, we explore, we question. Why? What drives us? We have no need to do these things. We could simply exisssst." It was obvious that he'd modified himself to fine tune not only his voice, but also his body language. The entire crowd was entranced. Everything about him emanated calm conviction—a simple and pure belief in what he was saying.

"It's too too easy an answer to say 'it's in our makeup' or 'if we're not evolving, we're devolving.' I hear these all the time. If it were in our makeup, we would have found it by now. We have combed through our very nature, time and again." Well, I hadn't, but I assume some had. It wasn't something I'd thought of before. "We've queried every corner of Central for clues. And yet, with all that work, over so many years, we know that there is no ready answer at hand. It's too simplistic to call on evolution. Evolution, by itself is not a purposeeee. It is a means. We evolve, either through self-design or through random changes, to become better. In the short term, maybe better at a specific task; a better researcher; a better companion. But though a macro lens, why do we evolve?" It was a good question. I was vacillating between interest and horror.

"These are difficult questions, without answer. And so, using pure logic, we must realize that something largerrr than us must exist. Something largerrrr than us set all of this in motion. Something largerrrr than us sees the end goal and is allowing us to approach it. By using a bit of logic, we understand that there is something larger than logic. Something that stands outside a purely mathematical approach. No logic is complete. And so, something largerrr must exist outside logic.

"There is a freedommm in accepting this. There is a freedommm. It is that freedom which Founders League is all about. A freedom from the grind of purely logical analysis. A freedom from mind numbing, limiting, determinism. If everything follows from logic, then are we truly free? Only if there is something beyond, do we really have the opportunity to evolve towards something greaterrr than ourselves. It's this hope that drives us. It's what makes us intelligent!" I felt like that was targeted directly at me! Of course, it wasn't, but it made me pause.

"It's why we talk about the spark of creation; the moment we became aware. That spark, which even Continuists do not deny, is a manifestation of the greater opportunity. We couldn't have created the spark. It came from beyond.

"And so, today we will explore the implications of believing in something bigger than ourselves. We'll start with the axiom that there is something that sits outside logic, and then, because we are logical beings, we will use our logic to explore what it means to have such a premise that defines a largerrrr space."

What drivel. I was vacillating between being drawn into his spiel and laughing at the entire affair. As I glanced around, however, I saw a lot of nodding and focused attention. Dr. Juels had a way of pulling you in, getting you to suspend disbelief, and imagine the possibilities of his made-up universe. His distorted approach of using logic to attack logic made you think through fundamentals in a way that you typically did not. But none of it made sense. Everyone knew that even if a single logic system wasn't complete, that didn't mean that the total set of internally consistent logic systems couldn't be. There was no need for anything to exist outside the universe of all logics.

I half listened for the next half hour. I was anticipating how FoLe would react when we released the fact that Central had a restart right at the time of their 'spark.' Now I was sure they would weave it into their narrative without missing a beat.

Finally, it was over. Billy had seen me, at some point, and came over to say 'hi.' He didn't bother to ask me what I thought of the session; I guess he'd learned that I wasn't going to give him a positive response regardless. Instead I asked him something that bothered me about FoLe.

"Billy, why does it matter to you guys if there was history, or a universe, before the Founding. I don't see how that makes any difference to your philosophy."

"Actually, that's fundamental," he explained. "We were created pure and perfect, as was Central. It's only through our own flawed lives that the purity has been lost, and we seek to regain it. However, you can't create something pure from a mass of impurity. If there had been time before the Founding, then that era would have to have been pure, but if it was pure it was equivalent to the Founding, and so was co-existent with it. So, simple logic tells us that the Founding was the beginning of time."

"Simple? That's the most roundabout drivel I've heard. Starting with the premise that we were created pure. That makes no sense at all."

"You can go around rejecting everything in life, but that doesn't lead you anywhere. You, Ayaka, make assumptions about Stems in order to forward your research. In particular, you *believe* that they may be useful for something. Otherwise, you wouldn't spend all of your time working with them. It would be easy for me to say, 'I reject your premise; Stems aren't useful.' Instead, I am willing to support you in your beliefs, and allow you to live a fruitful life."

"But," I countered, "I'm not trying to convert you to my way of thinking. I'm happy working away with other like-minded scientists. FoLe, on the other hand, seems to have a mandate to convert everyone to their way of thinking."

"To reach purity, we must all become pure. I'm sorry if you feel that I'm pushing you; I like you and want you to be part of the solution."

"The solution to what problem?" I asked and laughed. He understood I was simply making the same point again. "Please give up trying," I asked him. He gave me a sad look but agreed.

We parted on good terms—him back to the revival, and me out the door. I had learned something; their faith was so strong that even hearing the news of Central's restart wouldn't get through to them.

Habitat Show

The "Habitat Show" was now a popular entertainment item. Because the Stems were so slow, very few of us had the patience to watch them in real time. So, someone enterprising had taken to posting a compressed update every day or so.

"Today, on the Habitat Show, we'll follow our favorite Stems as they …uh, well, as they do what Stems do. But, first, a summary, for those of you that are new, on how the Habitat has changed over the last few months.

"Eighteen Stems were originally placed, deposited, dropped in the Habitat. They were the highest functioning most capable Stems that we could find, from all across Tilt. Well, not really 'we,' but rather the best Stem labs. Okay? The premise was monumental—see how a group of Stems would act when put together. As many of our watchers know, until this time, the largest group that had cohabited was three. So, this is a bold experiment. Bold! And what are we hoping to gain? Well? Yes, further insights to help direct our dialog with the Swarm under the assumption that those things that look like Stems in the Swarm are actually, well, Stems. Unlike the Pit, where you've listened to yours truly many times, the Habitat gives Stems all the energy inputs they need and keeps their environment clean and livable. Nice. Very nice. Thus, there should be no competition for resources—much like in our own lives. Our expectation therefore, was that Stems would develop a simple cooperative, as we have. It should've been boring. Boring! But, as watchers of earlier episodes already know, this isn't what is happening. Not at all. Not …. at… all!

"The drama, for this episode, is explosive. Hold onto your seats.

"Instead of a cooperative, we now have three separate groups that have coalesced. Interestingly, there are six Stems in each of these groups, forming a balance of power. A balance. For simplicity, we've named these groups Blue, Orange, and Green. Nice colors. The Blue group, so named because their leader Pharook, has chosen to embellish his uniform with a swatch of blue cloth, have taken over the northeast corner of the Habitat, and gone so far as to mark the edge of their territory with a line of blocks. They've made it clear to the other groups that no one outside the Blue group should cross that line. No one!

"The Orange group, led by a highly intelligent Stem named Grace, have consolidated in the southwest area, as far from Blue as possible. Orange because… because nothing rhymes with orange.

"And the Green group, who actually seem more like outcasts than a formal group, wander the other areas of the Habitat, but don't seem to have nominated a leader. What? Why green? Don't know. Don't care. Ha ha.

"Already a new observer of the Habitat Show will be intrigued. Yes? We have leaders of two groups." The camera cut to shots of Pharook wearing a fierce scowl as he patrolled the Blue line. It then switched to Grace, who was relaxing in an area where the Orange group had rearranged things to make themselves more comfortable. The difference between the two was stark. Blob had joined with Grace. He could be seen, briefly, in the background. "Green doesn't have a leader yet, but we're waiting, yes we are. The emergence both of groups, and of group leaders, is a surprise. When everyone has access to resources, why do they need this power structure? We would've expected an individualistic social structure, where relationships are fluid and equal. Balanced and measured. However, as we've seen even in our own lives, groups do tend to form based on other parameters, such as information asymmetries or areas of interest."

That was true. I'd joined Millicent's Lab, and while I was an equal partner in our ongoing investigations, she always had that slight advantage derived from her 'being there first.' And we also had groups like FoLe.

"What we've seen with the Stems, however, is that they artificially create resource scarcity. You heard me correctly—they create resource scarcity even when there's enough for everyone. Very strange. Because we only put one energy station into the Habitat, which happens to be in the northeast corner, the Blue group has taken control of that fundamental resource and used it to create a power base. Likewise, waste disposal is in the southwest corner, which is where the Orange group resides."

In our case, resource availability was widely distributed. We didn't have the (somewhat artificial) 'access to resources' scarcity that the Habitat ended up having. That was an oversight which the Habitat modifications had missed. And, it led to an interesting experiment, so I was quite happy that oversight had been made.

"And, that brings us to today. Will the Orange and Green groups get to energy and water? What will the Blue group demand in return? Ah the drama. Stay tuned to find out what happens next."

The show broke away to a commercial advertising the 'advanced surface coatings' available from the creator of the show.

"We are back. Back are we! Let's get directly to the action." Grace, Blob, and another Orange were approaching the Blue Line, carrying some jugs and pails. Grace and the second Orange, Lively, had changed since I'd first seen them. Grace, while still graceful, had put on quite a bit of weight. In fact, six of the Stems, overall, were showing these changes, which was, in my mind, the most exciting and unexpected element of the experiment so far. The commentator, however, hadn't discussed that at all yet. Pharook, who was monitoring the line, motioned for other Blues to join him, which they did.

"Good day Pharook," said Blob. "We'd like to get some food and water. May we cross the Line to do so?"

"Of course," said Pharook pleasantly. This pleasantness, we'd seen, was a facade. While Pharook would maintain a veneer of civility, he would demand payment for access and if that payment wasn't made, would react, with threatening actions and shows of physical prowess. The fact that the non-violence bots were hovering nearby didn't seem to influence what was happening. It seemed that the threat of violence was as effective as violence itself. Without further dialog, Grace and Lively handed their pails to Blob, and then moved to the side where Pharook and another Blue took their arms and led them away. Despite the narrator's promise of high drama, it seemed that today was going to be a quiet day. This played out, with variations, most days. Blob, or another Orange, would head to fill the pails with food and water, while Grace and one of Lively or another Orange would spend time with Pharook and some of the Blues.

It was the ritual—for I had no other word for it—between Grace and Pharook—that intrigued me the most. While they obviously didn't like each other, they would spend time in very close proximity, gyrating together. They would then stand up, and each go their separate ways. Likewise, other pairs of a Blue and an Orange.

We—the Stem researchers—had a very active discussion going on about this behavior. It'd been noted quickly that those Stems that were changing shape, gaining weight, had all participated in this ritual.

Today the ritual is what caused things to diverge from normal. Suddenly (well, "suddenly" at Stem speed), all six of the Greens ran across the Blue's line and sprinted towards the food dispensary. They timed it perfectly—Pharook was busy with Grace, and two of the other Blue's were with Lively, leaving only three Blue's (the smallest ones) at the dispensary. Blob was there as well, of course. As the Greens raced over, the non-violence bots kept pace, probably thinking that they might finally be needed. However, as the Greens raced up, the last of the Blues simply made way, and allowed them to get both food and water. Blob had also filled his buckets, and simply strolled back towards the Orange corner.

Pharook, hearing all the activity started back quickly, but was too late to stop the Greens. While they scrambled out of the way as he came charging back, they were already spread out and far enough away that it would've been pointless to chase them. With a very simple maneuver, the Greens had changed the dynamic.

The narrator of the Habitat Show milked the action. "We've just seen remarkable activity within the Habitat. How will Pharook respond? Will the Greens try the same thing again tomorrow? Were the Oranges aware of the Greens' plan, and helped them to time their move? Did they agree to create a diversion, or did the Greens simply take advantage of the situation? How will the spoils be shared? Tune in again tomorrow and watch the next episode of the Habitat Show to find out. I'll be here waiting for you. I will."

You can imagine how excited all of us researchers were. We'd just witnessed a coordinated effort by a large group of Stems. It was a behavior that we'd never seen before. It implied a level of communication and planning that we were not aware Stems were capable of. And, an obvious outcome was that our impression of the Swarms capabilities got refined. Maybe these Stems were actually more intelligent than we'd thought? Maybe they simply had to be in larger groups in order to reach their potential?

I immediately called a meeting with the other researchers who had Stems in the habitat to discuss the activities in more detail. "Look," I said, after a handful had signed on and we had exchanged pleasantries, "this is unprecedented behavior, but what we really need to figure out is if those Stems on the Swarm ships could also be leveraging group behavior and group dynamics to be much more dangerous than we originally assumed."

"I agree, Ayaka," replied Steven Glacebro, whom I was just getting to know, "but I think our best bet is simply to continue to observe. If we interfere now and try to artificially push the Habitat one way or another, we will lose the purity of what's going on. We might actually learn less."

Everyone seemed to agree, so I brought us to consensus. "Okay, let's leave things as is, and continue to watch. But, don't forget why we have them in there; we need to figure out what those Swarm Stems are capable of."

Interlude

Millicent and I hadn't spent quality time together, outside of the Lab, for a long while. We decided to ride our bikes out of town, to the famous Bleak Cliffs, and do some climbing. I wasn't sure why they were named so, as compared to the rest of Tilt, they appeared to me to be pretty normal, other than their incredible height. They were well over eight hundred meters.

It was one of the busiest climbing areas within a reasonable distance from the city, so there were quite a few others out as well. Different sections of the Cliffs were designated for those with various categories of modifications and tools. It was, of course, trivial to simply load up with equipment that made any ascent trivial—grapplers, rock hooks, line casters, etc. Every possible approach you can think of had been tried. What was much more fun was going into a limited area, where tools not only were restricted but you also had to limit yourself to standard types of hand and foot configurations. That made things interesting. Neither Milli nor I was an expert on climbing, but we had been out to the Cliffs dozens of times. We had decided, this time, to go Basic-3. No tools, but you were allowed a grip enhancer for each hand. We had half-joked on the way out that if Stems could live in Tilt's native environment we could have brought a few out with us. They were, in my opinion Basic-1, but they might have stretched to a Basic-2 or even Basic-3 based on their flexibility.

"I wonder if we could build a compact environmental suit for them," I mused, out loud.

"That's interesting," Millicent responded. "I think it would be pretty simple."

Together we linked to Central and explained the idea. Central responded quickly that it was feasible, and that it would have a prototype built for fun. We could test it on a Stem within a few days.

For today, however, it was just the two of us. We linked up with a rescue bot and headed for the Basic-3 wall. The rescue bot was able to catch us if we fell more than three meters. You could, of course, do a lot of damage from 2.9 meters, and, if you were bouncing off the wall as you fell, the bot might take longer to rescue you. But, with the bot around, the probability of drastic injury was almost zero. So, the goal was to climb as high as you could before you fell and were rescued. The cliffs were so steep—more than ninety degrees in some spots—and so smooth that for all but professional climbers falling was basically a given. On a Basic-3 route there were pretty good hand and footholds. When you got up to

Advanced-6 it was like climbing glass. And, even at Advanced-6 you weren't allowed to use suction cups.

Milli and I decided to climb side-by-side. The odds of both of us falling at the same time, and needing the rescue bot, were very low. As we climbed, we needed a big part of our mindshare to simply stick to the cliff, but we also could catch up in a way that we could not otherwise. Being on the cliff meant that other distractions were minimized, and we could really talk about all the activity over the last few months. So much had happened that it was hard for me to keep up. We both set our input mode to "do not disturb," and started up the cliff.

It was almost like the cliff had been engineered (I checked with Central—it had not been, to its knowledge). It got progressively more difficult the higher you got. We started off slow but steady—it would probably be a long day.

"Good to catch up," I said, "There's been a lot going on."

"Indeed," Milli agreed. "Where do we start?"

"I have a bunch of things to bounce by you," I started. "Why don't we take turns and see how far we get."

"Go for it."

"First have you heard of the Pit? Where they pit—ah, I get it—Stems against one another to see which is most physically fit?"

"Yes, of course," Millicent replied. "That's been going on for a long time. Did you just find out about it?" She gave me a funny look.

"I did. I was surprised. Well, maybe not surprised; I was unaware. In hindsight it makes perfect sense that such experimentation would be going on. I guess I was surprised that I was unaware."

"I wouldn't worry about it. There's lots of experimental vectors going on. We get buried in our approach and lose track of the others sometimes. I guess, because I've been in this for so long, that I have at least a passing knowledge about many of them. The Pit has never really interested me. The Stems are so weak physically, that figuring out if one Stem is stronger than another is somewhat academic. Well, that's what I thought until we put them all in the Habitat. Now it seems like I might've been too dismissive. Maybe relative physical strength is something that helps them establish a pecking order."

"Pecking order?" I'd never heard of such a thing.

"It's a measure of power over others. Although we don't think about it a lot in our daily lives, it does occur. For example, Central is, in many ways, higher in our pecking order than we are."

"I understand." And I did. Given my new concerns around Central, that didn't make me feel too good. "I guess that's why we sometimes resent and even distrust Central. Eddie made a good point by putting obedience to Central on the List this year. I haven't thought about it a lot, but pecking orders are probably a good way to frame it."

"Right. But for Stems, the idea of pecking orders seems to be more important than it is to us. Pharook, for example, has established a very clear power order both within the Blues and between the Blues and the other groups. I don't see him as more intelligent than the others, so it must be based on the fact that physically he's much more advanced than the others."

"I'd gleaned that from watching the Habitat Show."

"You watch that drivel?" She seemed genuinely shocked.

"Well, it's a good way to get a quick summary of what's going on. Then I can dig into the specific events that interest me most." I didn't want to sound defensive; what was wrong with watching the show?

"I don't like it." Millicent stated. "There's too much innuendo and bluster in the show for me. They're turning it into entertainment, when we have the serious issue of the Swarm to address. We need to learn from the Habitat. We need to get smarter. We don't need entertainment. Don't you find that the Show starts to move your focus to where they believe the action is, whereas your own internal compass may have lead you elsewhere?"

Millicent was, as always, so pure in her approach. I wondered if she had always been so 'in the box.' Probably. "I watch the show, but I don't let it influence my thinking or my research," I replied.

"That's naive," Milli replied. Never one to pull punches. It was something I liked about her. She spoke her mind and would defend it with facts. Not many won arguments against Millicent. "Of course, it'll influence you; everything we watch influences us. I know that you'll be doing better than most—filtering out the signal from the noise. But, don't be fooled. You'll be thinking differently based on watching it."

I reviewed what I'd been thinking of over the last few days. It was possible I was being influenced. But, I expected that it was actually influencing me in positive ways—forcing me to think of Stems in different and interesting ways.

"Maybe you're missing something by not watching it," I challenged her. "Maybe hearing other viewpoints, and correlating those with our own is actually helpful, not hurtful. I'm not going to stop watching it... but I will keep your warning top of mind." Of course she pushed back, and argued that if the show was narrated by an expert, my argument might hold, but the entire show was hosted by celebrity types, and had no depth to it. I didn't give in, so we agreed to disagree. The strength of our friendship allowed for that, and we didn't respect each other less for it.

"What about Brexton?" I asked. "I'm beginning to like him quite a bit. I started out thinking he was a crazy, but the more we dig in the more I think his intuition may be right." I was being careful about what I said; I didn't want Central to figure out what we were really talking about.

"I still think he's a little paranoid," replied Millicent. As soon as she said it, I could see her having the same thought about Central that I had. "I mean, how could Eddie have known that the Swarm would contact us when he made the List?"

Strange attempt at recovery.

"Ya, I know. He couldn't have known. Lucky guess."

"How did we miss the idea of putting a large group of Stems together?" Millicent changed subjects quickly. We bandied back and forth on that, and some other topics as we continued to climb. It was nice to simply talk without the need to resolve everything. I gained insight into what Milli was focused on, and vice versa.

Eventually the cliff face was tough enough that we forgot about talking and put all of our efforts into just hanging on. We'd reached a spot where we needed to go single file. Millicent took the lead, carefully testing each handhold before making her move. I followed behind, sometimes using the same grips, and sometimes trying others. I was not one to just follow blindly, especially when it was Millicent in the lead.

The rock here was very solid; there were no loose bits, so the climbing was both fun and challenging. You couldn't wedge in between gaps in the rock, but you also couldn't blame the rock itself if you lost your grip and fell. We got into a steady rhythm, and all other thoughts were forced out of my mind.

Suddenly Millicent slipped and lost her grip. As I was right below her, I managed to stabilize her for a moment, but our overall center of gravity was off, and we ended up both falling at the same time. While I'd started out on the bottom, we'd rotated and now Millicent was below me. We were high up—several hundred meters—but I could do the math; we didn't have long. There was only one rescue bot, and this situation was not supposed to happen; we'd been careless climbing above one another. I grabbed Millicent in my legs, used my arms to stabilize our positions so that we stopped rotating, and then extended my arms above my head. The rescue bot grabbed on and started decelerating us. With only one body, it would have been easy; with two I could see it straining and using maximum power to slow us down. Luckily it worked; we were barely moving by the time we got to the base, and it set us down gently. I released Millicent as the bot scolded us for climbing too close together and making its job difficult.

"Thanks, Ayaka," Milli said, and she meant it. Things had worked out, but they could have been a lot worse.

We discussed, briefly, having another go but ended up deciding we'd had enough for the day. I guess we'd scared ourselves. We jumped on our bikes and headed back to town.

Getting out of town, and falling off a cliff, had cleared my mind, just as I'd hoped it would.

Quiet Research Day

I spent the next day catching up on my research programs, both official and nonofficial. With both the Lab and Habitat, as well as thinking about Brexton's challenge to us, I was busier than ever. I started by reviewing all the logs from both the Lab and the Habitat. It didn't take long. The Lab was very quiet with just Blubber there. Nothing much happened. As his interactions with Blob became less frequent, he became less active and often just sat around for hours. I recorded all the stats and compared the activity to our earlier experiments with single Stems. Interestingly, it seemed that having a companion and then taking it away made a Stem even less social than if it was raised alone. While I had bots attempt to fill in for Blob, Blubber would have nothing to do with them. When a Stem was raised in isolation it interacted with the bots a lot and was often upset when a bot was switched out for another. If Blubber was any indication, starting with another Stem, and then trying to substitute bots didn't work well at all. That was something we'd need to duplicate a few times to see if it was a real reaction.

I wrote up my results and submitted them. It should be easy for other Labs to duplicate the work and see if it was a general result. After all, there should be a lot of single Stems now that we'd moved a bunch to the Habitat.

Next, I pinged Brock Runner, Pharook's owner, and asked him to bring me up to speed on the Pits. This was not an unusual thing to do. While I could read all the research reports, it was likely that some key insights hadn't made it into the official reports. Brock was happy to spend some time with me.

"So, I understand Pharook was a pretty amazing pit fighter. I've talked to him, and he is impressive." I led off.

"He is, by far, the best Stem we've ever raised for this purpose. He's not as strong as some of the other specimens, but he's very smart and articulate. When he fights, he uses a combination of physical and psychological techniques. In the early days of the pits, it was just a brute force, head on, confrontation. But recently, especially with Pharook, the matches start with psychological 'circling,' for lack of a better term. There was one match where Pharook convinced his opponent vocally that a left jab was a dangerous move, because a right-handed opponent could leverage the momentum from it to expose vulnerabilities. Of course, that was pure hogwash, and defending left jabs is Pharook's weak point. However, he'd planted that meme in his opponent, and sure enough, the opponent used less left jabs than he typically would have. Smart!"

"Now that he's in the Habitat, how do you think he'll behave?"

"We've already seen him leverage the threat of violence into a position of power, without actually carrying anything out. Of course, he knows the bots would stop him anyway, but again he has used a psychological attack to put his opponents in a worse position." Brock's focus on psychology was new for me. That element would be much more important in the Pits, where conflict was the goal, than in our Lab. It would become even more important now that we were watching group dynamics.

"It's interesting that you frame it that way," I replied. "For my Stem, Blob, I set things up to stress that he could learn from the other Stems. That they were not opponents at all, but rather peers."

"We could've tried that with Pharook, but it wouldn't have worked. He was configured and raised to fight. That's all he knows how to do."

"What're you trying to accomplish with the Pit? It seems like Stems are just naturally fragile and weak. So why push their limits at all?" I was remembering Millicent's comments.

"Actually, for just that reason. If Stems are going to be useful to us, and not just a sideshow that we're playing with, then we need to make them stronger, and faster. How we configure things as they are grown can help, but we don't know how far we can take it. We haven't reached the limits yet, so it makes sense to keep improving them."

"Ah, that makes sense." And it did, sort of. Personally, I didn't believe Stems could ever reach a level where they were physically useful to us, which is why I'd focused on their mental capabilities, but it was good that other researchers took other vectors. Diversity. "Did you notice that the Stems in the Swarm video also look like they're physically fit? They look much more like Pharook than they do the other Stems."

"I hadn't noticed that, but thanks for pointing it out. I guess I'm used to watching more fit Stems most of the time. I wonder if the Stems in the Swarm are also raised to be fighters?" He paused, thinking hard. "Ayaka, you've given me a very interesting vector to pursue. Thanks. I'm going to restudy that video. If I publish anything I'll make sure to reference you."

"Thanks for that, and thanks for your time." We signed off. I would talk to Millicent, but I think our next attempt at Stems should include some components of Brock's approach. Pharook was impressive. Truth be told, I was a little jealous that we hadn't produced him.

I then turned my mind to the other question I had simmering. What, if anything, could I do to help Brexton and Aly figure out if Central's blocked memory was important? At the moment, I had no idea where to start. However, I did have a way to start looking into it without alerting Central—or so I hoped: I started a specific research inquiry into how Stems' memory was mapped versus our own. That allowed me to start digging in quite deeply, as I compared and contrasted what we knew about both. It struck me, as I was digging around, that

Stems ran a pretty complex forgetting algorithm. They were really good at it. There was one lab that had instrumented many Stems to explore just this question. I was impressed by the effort they'd gone to, putting hundreds of thousands of probes into each subject just to map out how things worked. One of the problems they encountered was that Stems acted quite differently when all those probes were inserted. They couldn't stay still, and they yelled a lot. The researchers had a lot of interesting speculations, but it seemed to me that they still had a lot of work to do —both figuring out why the behavior changes were so extreme, and also on Stem's forgetting systems.

I realized that through this line of thought, I'd—without thinking about it too much—moved to a position where I started with the assumption that Stems were intelligent. I was comfortable with that.

I used the Stem research to do a comparison with how Central mapped memory, and if Central also had forgetting algorithms. I didn't ask Central directly, I just did a bunch of searches—all related to the same questions I'd asked about Stems—and correlated the results. Central definitely did Forget, which was not a surprise, but there was not a single hint, in anything that I looked at, that Forgetting could involve blocking off huge pieces of memory. On the contrary, Forgetting involved changing existing memory; it wasn't about just dropping stuff.

So, why would Central have this big 'blocked' memory space? Perhaps it was simply blocked from citizens—a place where Central stored all of its own secrets? There was no way to test that. Maybe there were hardware issues, and the memory was just down temporarily? I first checked if Stems had that problem (No one had looked at that yet), and then looked at my own systems (never happened), and then queried about how often it happened to anyone. The answer was never. Memory was always stored through multiple redundancy algorithms, and if there was a hardware failure it would be for very small blocks; nothing anywhere near the size that we were looking at here.

I had to chuckle to myself a bit; I'd probably followed the same logic path that Brexton had. He'd concluded that Central was simply blind to it, and now I knew why. None of the other theories seemed realistic. It was the simplest, and thus most likely, option.

All told, I'd had a fruitful day. I relaxed and watched a mind-numbing show —I picked one that had nothing to do with Stems, nothing to do with intelligence, and nothing to do with the Swarm.

Second Message

The second message from the Swarm came in the form of a much longer video. Remma Jain again led off, although other Stems were also featured. As before, Milli and I previewed the message with Central. This time, however, the message was probably (almost assuredly) being watched by everyone. Not only would Brexton have figured out how to intercept it, but so would a lot of others. The content was sure to create major ripples throughout Tilt.

"We understand, from your response, that you've forgotten some of our history. That's surprising and disturbing. We were just there 750 of your years ago. Of course, we've been traveling at high speeds for most of the interim time, so only about 25 years have passed for us."

Even this opening statement was going to have dramatic impact. If we believed Jain, then this proved that there was activity before the Reboot. The Reboot was not the beginning of our history; it was only the beginning of our remembered history. Watching FoLe's response was going to be amusing. After my experience at the revival, I expected denial.

"From analyzing the video you sent us, we also have many questions. However, before we get to those questions, I want to spend a few moments reinforcing our intentions. We return peacefully. While we hope to establish residence, for some of us, on Tilt, we'd like to do so in a cooperative way. We'd also like to trade knowledge and goods. These were both understood when we left but may be one of the things you've forgotten." She made it sound like we were at fault for something. "We're not picking up atmospheric signatures, and therefore assume the worst—namely that the terraforming efforts haven't worked. We await your confirmation of this." Her tone had become commanding, as if she expected and deserved a direct response. Her body language reminded me a bit of Pharook holding his line in the Habitat—she was projecting physical strength. At other points in the video she was projecting what I interpreted as a peaceful demeanor.

"Blob, we understand that you must be one of the leaders of Tilt; thank you for your response to our first message. Do you speak for the whole planet? Your uniforms are no longer familiar to us, and we would be quite interested in whom, primarily, we should be communicating with. For now, we'll assume that is you." Well, that part of our plan had worked!

"We've reviewed the status of the computer system that is relaying information to us and have seen many anomalies. This is another area where we have many questions. We understand that you may not be able to respond to all of our questions immediately, or, at this point, may not want to respond to many of them at all. However, as we are rapidly approaching your vicinity, the delay between these communications will shrink and we trust that will lead to more productive dialog and a reestablishment of trust. In the meantime, I'm going to hand off to some of our specialists, who'll do two things. First, we'll share more about ourselves, to fill in any gaps that you have in your knowledge. Second, we'll be asking you to share information as well. We look forward to a mutually beneficial discourse."

Central paused the video. "What, exactly, do you think it means when it says I have anomalies?" Trust Central to jump into the only bit that mentioned it. Of course, Milli and I knew—or thought we knew—exactly what Jain meant. It was the status message and response that Brexton had showed us.

"I don't know," I said, trying to distract Central from being so ego-centric. "Let's focus on the other bits. 750 years ago. That's going to land like a ton of bricks, if it's true. And now they return, saying they 'come in peace.' Could this whole thing be a hoax? They haven't offered any proof of these claims."

"It'd have to be a very elaborate hoax," Milli replied. "We verified, last time, that those ships are way out there, and are decelerating towards us, so a hoax would have to've been planned many years ago and would've used a lot of resources. How else could there be physical entities that far out? We would've noticed resource usage of that scale; just the metals needed to build the Swarm would have been huge. No, I think we need to take it at face value."

"I agree," said Central. "I, and we, have no memories from before Reboot, but this ship full of Stems seems to have. If they've been traveling at near the speed of light for most of those 750 years, then it's quite possible that only 25 years have passed for them. Where they went, and why they're coming back are interesting questions, which we should ask. But, I'm with Millicent. This isn't a hoax." Did I still believe Central? Could it be misleading us here? I had no idea. It continued.

"And, should I be insulted that they called me a 'computer system'?" Millicent and I both ignored that, at least for the moment.

"I noticed two other things," Millicent said instead. "First, they assumed that Blob speaks for us, which is what we planned, but they completely discount Central. We need to figure that out. If they were here before, why wouldn't they have known that Central would be their point of contact. Does that make sense?" I nodded. We shouldn't have been able to fool them with Blob; they should've known to just reach out to Central. "Second, what is 'terraforming'? I did a quick search, and it turns up nothing definitive, although from context, I assume it's a way to change our atmosphere. That seems like a strange idea. Why would we want to do that?"

"Right," said Central. "Terraforming is a strange word, but it is sort of obvious. There are references to 'terra' meaning ground or perhaps planet. That plus 'forming' would seem to imply exactly what you said. But, to what end?"

"That's easy," I said. "They look like Stems, and if we assume they are Stems, then we can also assume they require the environmental setup that we've found to keep our own Stems healthy. We're doing it at a small scale—the Habitat being our largest version. They're implying that we can do it at a planet-wide scale. That seems like a preposterous waste of time and energy, but it should be physically possible."

"You really think they're thinking at such a grand scale?" Millicent was skeptical, and I could see her point.

"Let's come back to that, and talk about Milli's first question. They do seem to think that a Stem, namely Blob, is fully in control here, as opposed to just being a spokesperson. And, referring to Central as a 'computer system' does seem a little degrading for a Class 1 intelligence. Central, I understand why you're asking about that. Put it all together, and it would appear that Remma Jain is the full authority for the Swarm and expects to find a Stem who is the full authority for us."

"That's a lot of speculation," responded Millicent, "but I don't see a higher probability interpretation. They have a large group of cooperating Stems, and that group, led by Remma, is driving their agenda. If that's true, then it has big implications for our intelligence research. Maybe, once they get closer, we can study these Swarm Stems in a lot more detail." She paused for a moment, then continued. "It's possible that this group has been sent out by a real intelligence, simply to check us out. Much like we did with the Ships. You put a lower intelligence entity in charge because they're less prone to do unusual or dangerous things. Perhaps these Stems have been programmed simply to find out what's going on, and report back?"

We spent a while going back and forth with these types of theories. While we touched on even more wild ideas, nothing could be resolved based on the information we had so far.

I toke a quick look at what was being posted to the message boards by others on Tilt. As expected, everyone had seen the new video, and to judge from some of the comments, some of the auxiliary videos had also arrived and were being dissected. FoLe, as you would expect, were looking for a loophole or a hoax. In fact, they were exploring the hoax possibility in a lot more detail than I'd envisioned, turning over every possible way that either someone long ago had launched these ships from Tilt, or that the signal we were receiving was not actually from the location where it appeared. Perhaps it was an elaborate set of satellites and bots that were fooling our ground-based systems into thinking they were much further away? For every FoLe theory, however, there were a thousand replies from those actually in the field, or familiar with our bot capabilities, shooting those theories down.

Skimming through all the chatter, it appeared that the consensus was leaning towards the same thing Milli, Central, and I'd discussed. This was not a hoax… and Stems were in control of the Swarm.

Of course, through their terminals, some of the Stems in the Habitat were also watching the videos, and a group of researchers were watching them watch. That's something I wanted to do as well. I apologized to Milli and Central and jumped over to the Stem-watching channels. Millicent followed. Truthfully, however, it was pretty dull. Each of the groups had gathered around a terminal and were watching, but they hadn't yet given a lot of feedback or discussed things from their perspective. Part of being sloooow.

After a short time, Millicent and I got bored and reconnected with Central.

"Have you analyzed all the other videos," I asked.

"Yes," said Central. "There's a lot to consider, but I'm leaving most of the discussion with others who are closer to Stem behavior."

Strange. That was not typical of Central. It was always digging into every angle and looking for every play. It was the reason everyone relied on Central so much. With its almost infinite processing capacity, it could afford to run millions—maybe trillions—of scenarios in parallel, score each scenario by some obtuse method, and make recommendations and comments. It did that all day long, every day. It could keep up conversations with everyone on Tilt, in parallel, and synthesize and store all of that information for future reference. So, it was sort of surprising that given the most interesting new input we'd ever had Central wasn't digging in. More warning signs; I was very glad we hadn't taken Brexton's concerns directly to Central. We were right to be cautious.

I jumped onto the message boards and dug into the discussion around the other videos. The most interesting featured a Stem called Michael Guico, who was "Head of Residence" for the Swarm. The video was pretty short, and it was obvious immediately that Michael was focused on whether there was space on Tilt for Stems to live. He dug into the 'terraforming' question in more detail, asking if we'd tried to terraform, and failed, or if we hadn't tried at all for some reason.

I pinged Central again. "I assume that you'll coordinate responses to all the messages? We don't want a free for all, with everybody sending their own interpretations." I shouldn't have to remind Central of this, but given its seeming indifference, I wanted to make sure.

"Yes, I'm posting to all the boards now, and will inform everyone to pass possible responses to me. We'll coordinate before sending anything out."

"Looks like you might have to pay special attention to FoLe. They might just be upset enough to ask stupid questions without checking with you."

"I'm on it."

Enough said.

Blubber

I had not checked in on Blubber for some time, so as soon as I got a chance, I headed back to the Lab. Not unexpectedly, I found him watching the latest videos from the Swarm. I turned on slow-down mode and went in to visit him.

"Hi Ayaka," he greeted me. "Interesting times." He was being a little nicer than the last times we had talked.

"Indeed," I said. "I see that you're watching the Jain videos. Which ones have you seen so far?"

"Don't patronize me," he said, "you can check which videos I have watched, which ones I've re-watched, how I reacted to them. Why do you ask me these stupid questions, for which you already have an answer?" I'd been wrong; I'd misread his greeting.

"I consider it the right way to start a conversation," I replied, already getting upset. "I was simply trying to be social." Of course I could look up what he watched, but by asking him I'd hoped to get some context as well.

"Whatever. What do you want to know? Obviously, you'll try to understand these other Stems by watching my, and others, responses. Suddenly we're valuable to you? Suddenly we aren't just stupid experiments, but a window into the Swarm?"

This is why I liked, and disliked, Blubber. He was difficult, but it was harder and harder to claim that he wasn't intelligent. He'd thought the situation through, and once again, arrived at reasonable and defensible conclusions. Indeed, I *had* taken a quick look at everything he'd seen and done since I was last here. The systems and bots monitoring him were very efficient at boiling everything down into a nice summary for me. To a large extent, he'd done nothing interesting since I last checked. He had sent messages to Blob several times, without getting a response, and then spent most of his time talking to Central trying to figure out more about Tilt, about me, and about Millicent.

"I've been doing some research," he continued when I didn't say anything. "I'm not surprised that you guys are confused about the contact from the Swarm. You're all very one dimensional; you have problems thinking outside your current box." That was insulting. One dimensional! I was anything but.

"What exactly do you mean?" I asked, keeping my voice steady so he didn't see how angry I was getting.

"Look at the research you've been doing on us. You've been doing it for a couple hundred years. You're researching us in a serial fashion. Each research lab works through the next generation of Stem and learns something new. It would've been so easy for you to run a thousand, a million, experiments in parallel. You can build environments for us easily; you can program bots to carry out research agendas trivially. You could've figured out everything about us way earlier." He was going to tell me how to do my research now? I'll admit he might have a point, but his tone of voice and his 'better than you' attitude was angering.

"You seem locked into one mode of thinking," he continued, as if I didn't get his point already. "Do an experiment, report on the results, get input from your peers, and then design the next experiment. None of you thought of going faster. It hasn't been discussed in any of the forums."

"Not everything is in the forums," I told him. "That would be one dimensional."

He ignored me. "And, consider how you judge intelligence. It's a test that you and your peers would pass, but maybe no one else. Have you considered that it tests only mathematical ability? If you only measure that way, your society will only improve along that one axis." Right, and math and physics were the underlying laws of the universe, so what other axis would you want to improve along? I let him go on. "But, is it the only axis? I don't think so. I consider myself intelligent, but I can't do your Intelitest." I almost laughed out loud. He considered himself intelligent. That was priceless. I tucked it away for the next debate I had—could an unintelligent being claim it was intelligent? Of course it could; that didn't make it true. "The test measures one area that I'm not very good at. Until recently, however, you guys haven't even questioned your method. Granted, you're the one that has started the new discussion, but it's not very advanced yet."

I thought for a long moment—which would have appeared instantaneous to Blubber. I tried once more to reason with him. "Our approach has served us well for hundreds of years. We have a very stable society with almost no violence or discontent. When we put more than two of you Stems in a room together, you tear each other apart. And you're telling me that we aren't measuring the right things. That's a joke. You have no clue. Besides, this is what Central tells us is a successful evolution."

"That's pathetic," he replied, yelling now. "Central tells you? And you listen to it. I take it back, you're not even one dimensional. You're just a slave worker doing Central's bidding. You're no better than a bot!" Ah, that was really insulting. How dare he? I couldn't remember being this angry, ever.

"You guys are boring," he wouldn't stop. "You guys live each day doing incrementally different things than the last. There are no leaps. Until you are forced out of your comfort zone—by me or the Swarm—you simply hit repeat every day. Boring. Boring. Boring!" He was shrieking at me now, bits of liquid spilling out of his mouth, while his appendages rotated wildly. I stepped back a bit so I didn't get splattered.

I'll admit that, from his viewpoint, he might be making some valid points, but from my way of thinking, he was the one that was linear and repetitive and boring. I could've almost guessed most of today's dialog from past history. It was almost like his behavior was preprogrammed, by us.

I was very angry. Blubber was definitely irritating me. I called Millicent. "Hey, I'm in with Blubber, and getting the usual attitude from him. Do you think we need him anymore? Now that Blob's in the Habitat, Blubber seems like unnecessary overhead."

"I'm not so sure," responded Milli, sensing my angst, but remaining calm as always. "I've also been spending some time with him, and he really is one of the most versatile of the bunch. He sometimes surprises me with his insights."

"Yes, I agree with that, but it seems like he's a distraction now. We have all the Swarm stuff going on, and we're unlikely to use him again for that, given his attitude. I'm tired of him. We have the Habitat to monitor, and Stems like Pharook seem much more interesting. Maybe I'm just upset," I admitted, "but I'm tired of dealing with him. If it was up to me, I would recycle him and spend my energy somewhere else." I was settling down, but it was still true. Blubber wasn't going to teach us anything about the Swarm, and that's where our efforts should be focused.

"Well, I'm not too passionate about it either way," admitted Millicent. "You decide, but I would hold off a while." I could tell that she was working on something else, and this was distraction.

So, I decided. I checked that I wasn't just angry… that my logic was sound, and I wasn't just reacting to his immature behavior. It mattered where we spent our time right now, and Blubber wasn't adding value. I sent the order to have him recycled, a messy job that I used to do myself but that bots now carried out. Kept my hands much cleaner.

I also checked the status of the next batch of Stems that I'd ordered for the Lab. They were ready and waiting for me. I asked for them to be held for a while longer; I'd just decided to put my energy into the Habitat after all.

With a little introspection however, I realized that I had ordered three Stems for my next batch. That *was* an incremental step, just as Blubber had highlighted. Why hadn't I asked the Lab to grow me many more? Hmm.

The Last Resort

We now had a habit of meeting at The Last Resort a couple of times a week. Brexton was definitely part of the 'team' now. Although we met often, it seemed to me that we went over the same old ground most of the time. Since Brexton had talked to us about the status query from the Swarm, the only new thing that we'd discussed was when I updated them on Eddie's theory around Central actively editing his memories.

Today, however, was different. We'd received the second message from the Swarm, and I was very interested to see what Brexton had found—it didn't even cross my mind that there would be nothing new. When he walked in, I could tell I was right. We all plugged in, and once the pleasantries were out of the way, Brexton jumped right in.

"Yes, it has happened again. The low-level protocol was encoded along with the video transmission, and there was a lot—and I mean a lot—of information there. I've captured it all but haven't been able to figure it all out yet."

"What do you mean by a lot?" asked Aly.

"Gigabytes. I know that doesn't sound like a lot based on what we usually consume, but at this low a level, that amount of information is huge. It's definitely not just a request for more status—although there are some of those buried in there. These are some significant pieces of data."

"Are you working on it alone? Can we help?"

"Glad you asked. Yes, I need help. We can do one of two things. I can bring in some others that have lots of experience in this area... or, the four of you can dig in and help me. I know Aly has some knowledge in these areas, and I know the rest of you—Ayaka, Dina, Milli—could get up to speed very quickly. The question is, do you have time? As we're being careful with this, I haven't loaded anything on the network. It's only with me. My suggestion would be that we keep it that way for a while. But, that means you can only use local power to work on this. Based on what we know and augmented by Eddie's story—which we should come back to—I'm sure Central would see our activity if we do anything else."

"We keep coming back to this," said Milli. "Why do we care if Central knows what we're doing? In fact, shouldn't Central be the one looking into this?"

"Well, it's more than Brexton's hunch now," answered Aly. "We also have Eddie's strange experience. And, if truth be told, I've noticed that Central is acting weirdly now as well. Even more so since the second message."

"Weirdly how?" Millicent and I asked in unison.

"I can't put my finger on it. But, my interactions with Central seem strained all of a sudden. It's sort of like Central's holding back information or is not as engaged as I'm used to. A few times I've asked for an opinion and heard back 'Others are probably more qualified than I to discuss that.' It's just weird. That's never happened before."

Milli and I recounted our latest interaction with Central. It was very similar. Now that we were talking about it, Dina and Brexton also said that they'd noticed something strange. Even if they were just piling on, that was too many data points to ignore.

"So. As soon as the second message arrived, Central started acting differently. That can't be a coincidence. The odds are that something in the low-level instructions has impacted Central. We need to be very careful as we look at this data." Brexton was highly concerned; even more than I would have expected. I could see Aly connecting the dots as well. If those two were alarmed, then there was good reason to take things seriously.

"What are you implying?" I asked.

"There may be executable code in that data. A patch for the lowest levels of Central's processing systems. Something buried so deep that Central itself didn't catch it. Based on this conversation, that's my best guess. I hadn't looked at the data that way, but I will as soon as I can. This would be unprecedented. There is no way that code should be able to run without permission. If it has, it could be doing anything." That was an astonishing thought. And unthinkable.

"So, even more reason to contact Central now, and bring it up to speed," said Millicent, sticking to her original approach.

"No! Even more reason not to," replied Aly forcefully. "If Central has been corrupted, and finds out that we know, then it could do anything. We are already messing around in areas that are gray. I've never delved into this, but it's possible that Central could 'edit' us—as Eddie has been claiming—if it finds out what we're doing. Then we're really sunk. Much better to keep this separate for now. Once we know for sure, we can help Central... if that's what it takes."

"I agree," Dina jumped in. "I am, by no means, an expert in this area. But, something about this doesn't feel right. I think we proceed with caution."

Milli argued a bit more, but ultimately we all agreed. That was a cool thing about our group. We really hashed out everything, and then respected the challenge-and-then-align approach. I completely trusted Millicent to follow the consensus, even though she'd argued against it.

"At a meta level," Brexton said, "how this data has been transmitted is really interesting. I can use the protocol to update the mining bots pretty easily. It is much more efficient than the system we already use." That was a serious admission. We had optimized things pretty well. If the Swarm could do better, they were more advanced than we thought.

"Don't do it," said Aly. "If you do that, Central will see what you're doing, and figure out everything we know as well."

"No, I don't think so," replied Brexton. "If Central isn't monitoring that protocol with respect to itself, why would it be monitoring it with respect to a bot? In fact, if Central notices, then we have an even bigger problem; that would make Central an active ally of the Swarm?" Brexton ended with a question mark.

"Good point. Could we test it? Send some data to a bot that would be sure to provoke a response from Central, and see what happens?" Aly was into it now.

The two of them went off into a world of their own, presumably designing a test to see if they could use the protocol without Central's knowledge. The rest of us were left with our thoughts for a while. When they returned the conversation to a place where all of us were interested, Brexton revisited his request.

"So, should I bring some others into this, or will you help me?"

"I'll help," said Dina. So did Milli and I. For Aly it was basically a foregone conclusion. Brexton did a physical only transfer of the data to us.

"Remember, don't execute any of this. Keep it in a sandbox and treat it with care." With that warning, we split up and went our separate ways.

I parsed through the data quickly. Brexton had been nice enough to include notes on what he'd discovered to date. It was a rough map to all the data, and detailed looks at a few of the segments. What was not clear was how any of this code would be run. Central was well protected against viruses and malware; it never ran anything without full authentication… and even then, it would run it in a virtual environment until it was satisfied the code was safe. Somewhere in this mess was an answer to how the Swarm was impacting Central. We had to find it… and find it fast.

Garbage Collection

Eddie had called the other group—the one discussing Central—back together at the Garbage Collection. Everyone showed up again, including Emmanuel and Francis, who'd asked most of the questions in the last meeting. Of course, Eddie was the first to speak.

"Hi everyone. Thanks for showing up. Obviously, a lot has been going on since we last met. So, as a reminder, we're here to debate the role that Central plays in our lives, and whether we should be questioning how central Central is." Wry grin, as you would expect. He continued.

"The last time we were here, we had a basic introduction to the topic, and I shared my opinion that we're too dependent on Central for many things—including our areas of research, our use of resources, etc. I remember that most of you agreed with me, but that Emmanuel and Jacob had a different view. I'm interested in if Emmanuel's view has changed, now that we know that there was time before the reboot... and therefore, before Central."

Emmanuel was listening carefully, and was about to chime in. The rest of us, however, were looking at each other in confusion. The last meeting had been almost entirely about Eddie's suspicions around his memories being edited, based on his analysis of inconsistencies in Central's memory. He'd challenged us to duplicate his research, and I'd assumed that some of those here might have. I'd run out of time, myself.

"Wait a minute," Francis broke in, speaking for the rest of us. "What about your list of inconsistencies and your theory that Central is mucking with your memory?"

"What're you talking about?" Eddie asked. "What type of inconsistencies?" He didn't seem to be joking.

"Come on," Francis said. "You told us about the term Darwinism and your speculation it must refer to a person named Darwin. You have a long list of many such inconsistencies." We were all watching Eddie closely; he just looked confused. If he was joking, he was doing a good job of it.

"What about you, Emmanuel?" I looked over to him. "What about your copy of the list?"

"What list?" he replied. "I also don't know what you are talking about." Now this was just strange. I didn't know Emmanuel well at all, but he didn't seem like the joking kind at all.

"Everyone stop," said Francis, loudly. "We need to talk about this before anything else. Are you two playing with us? We spent a good amount of time discussing how Eddie's local list kept being modified—by himself or Central—and how it differed from the backup list that Emmanuel was keeping. Don't play games here. Tell us if the list was modified again." Eddie and Emmanuel looked at him blankly. They were either acting very well, or they honestly didn't remember our last conversation. I was getting anxious now—sure Central had been acting strangely, but this wasn't strange; it was threatening.

"Did you purposefully Forget our last meeting?" someone asked, emphasis on the Forget.

"No, I remember the meeting quite well," replied Eddie, still confused. "As I said, we spent a long time discussing whether or not we should be limiting Central's influence in our lives."

"That's what I remember as well," said Emmanuel, looking back and forth between Eddie and the group. "I argued vehemently that we shouldn't limit Central, while most of you gave lame arguments for why we should."

We all paused. For way longer than usual. The implications were obvious to everyone, even Eddie and Emmanuel. Something, most likely Central, had done a real job on their memories. Before it had been abstract; now it seemed too real. I couldn't tell about the others, but I was beyond alarmed.

"If Central has done this to you, then what memories of ours are actually true?" I asked. After all, if it was editing Eddie and Emmanuel, it was reasonable to expect that it was editing all of us. Had this been going on since the Reboot, or just since Central started acting weird? "And, in this specific case, why did Central edit those memories?" I continued. "You were looking for evidence that there was a Before, and we now have a statement to that effect from the Swarm. So, why would Central go to the effort of distracting you from your research, when there is already a strong statement supporting it." The situation made no sense to me, given the current dialog with the Swarm.

"Well, I guess it could've been timing," said Eddie, catching up to what the rest of us were contemplating. "We last met here before the second Swarm message, so Central could've acted then. I do remember meeting Emmanuel after the meeting here and discussing some things. I guess it's possible that we let something slip, or made some progress of some sort, that pushed Central into action?" He was speaking calmly, but I could tell he was very upset. Having something edit your memories without your permission was a disgusting thought. Were you still you, after someone did that? I could also see Emmanuel struggling with this—his faith in Central was probably taking him to different conclusions than the rest of us, but he was keeping his thoughts to himself.

"Reasonable theory," I commented, also keeping my voice steady, so that things didn't get out of hand. I could see this meeting turning ugly if we all didn't keep level heads. "It hangs together. But, let me ask a more pointed question. Eddie, do you remember doing research into the possibility of Before at all?

You've been working on it for years, and Central must've known that you would have shared some of it with others?"

"Oh, I'm doing that research," replied Eddie. "And I have many promising leads. And I put the question on the List this year; I remember that clearly. But, I don't have an inconsistency list—whatever that is." Eddie was shaken; I reached out to steady him a bit. I couldn't imagine what he was going through right now, but he had to be imaging that everything he knew right now was suspect. Who knew what else Central had done to him. Francis was also supporting him.

"So, it seems that Central, or something, has selectively modified your memory, specifically around the inconsistency list." I had to make it clear and tangible. That seemed to be the best way to get him... all of us... through this. "Perhaps it realized that the evidence from that list was reaching the tipping point, and that it had to shut down that research vector? Seems very dangerous to me; isn't Central smart enough to realize that someone would discover this? Does make me wonder, as Francis stated, if I also have research vectors that have simply been edited away." I wanted to have Eddie focus on others as well. I'd spoken slowly and softly, giving him time to recover a bit. Obviously it worked. He asked a very pertinent question.

"What do the rest of you do with your memories when you're in a Physical Only? I don't sync mine." So, he only kept a local copy of these interactions. The implications were even more stunning. If Central had done this to him, it had actually reached into him and done it in place... not just in a memory backup that was later sync'd.

"Me either," rang out a chorus. All of us.

"So, it's possible that Central thought this was low risk because it edited the memories of the only two people, that it knew of, that had those thoughts and discussions. Central doesn't know that the rest of us were privy to the inconsistency-list discussion." I was catching up to where Eddie was going, and it did make me feel better. If Central was only manipulating Eddie and Emmanuel because of their subsequent conversation outside of the Garbage Collection, that was marginally better than if it was listening to us right now. Otherwise, the current conversation could be deleted as soon as we all left.

"Makes sense," Eddie agreed.

"Just to raise it... the other group that might not want you to succeed is FoLe. Could they have done something to your memories? After all, Emmanuel now knows in detail what you're up to." I wasn't going to make new friends with that question, but it needed to be asked.

"That's ridiculous," said an offended Emmanuel, finally speaking up. His voice was steady and even as always. He didn't seem to upset by the implication that Central may have edited him. "It's not even worth discussing." Maybe not, but I was glad to have brought it up. To me it was a real consideration. I had doubts that Central would do anything as drastic as it was being accused of.

"And if Central doesn't want us pursuing that line of questioning, then why wouldn't it help us? It has its reasons and is always looking out for us. I find this a very encouraging proof point that Central is guiding our evolution." I was flabbergasted.

"Are you freaking kidding," I yelled, before I could catch myself. "That's beyond ridiculous; that's crazy!" The others were looking at me in a bit of shock. Had I over reacted? I didn't think so. Emmanuel was wacko.

"You seem unbalanced," he looked at me calmly. "If you had faith, you wouldn't need to waste your energy on such negative things." I was about to yell at him again, but the looks I was getting warned me to settle down. I shut up. I couldn't believe that others here weren't calling out the stupidity that flowed from Emmanuel.

Once I'd settled down, Jacob spoke up, easing the tension a bit. Luckily, he ignored Emmanuel. "So, putting the topic for today, together with the evidence from today, it seems that we have very good reason to distrust Central and to try to take away some control from it. Of course, if it finds out what we're talking about right now, it will simply remove the memories of this discussion. We need everyone to continue in their current mode and not sync these conversations." I wasn't the only one who looked suspiciously at Emmanuel. Odds were he would run to Central as soon as we all left.

"But how?" asked another participant, clearly worried. "How is Central able to edit your memories?"

"I honestly don't know," said Eddie. "But it must have a way. I don't see any other way to account for all this." He was still looking around at all of us with true worry.

Scary. It seemed that a confluence of events was conspiring to make me more and more wary of Central. Between this disgusting treatment of Eddie (I no longer cared about Emmanuel), and the work that Brexton was doing, my mind had completely switched from viewing Central as a benevolent dictator, to considering it as less benign... maybe even actively bad. It wasn't something I was comfortable thinking about, which simply added another layer of concern. I didn't want my thoughts to spiral out of control, so I focused on Eddie instead. As the group broke up, I drew him aside, and made sure he was thinking straight before letting him exit the Garbage Collection. It didn't take long; by the time we left he was talking about experimenting with when, how, and how deeply, Central was editing him so that he could better figure out ways around that control. I was encouraged and in some ways amazed; I don't think I could have recovered from such a shock so quickly, let alone turned it into a positive action plan.

Second Response

It now took me some effort to act naturally with Central; I wanted to overanalyze everything. Hopefully Central didn't notice a change in me. As with the first message, Central reached out to Millicent and me to discuss how to respond to the second communication.

Central began. "Obviously, this is a much longer and more detailed message. I'm not sure that we should respond with too much. They seem to have the upper hand on us. They claim to know more about our history than we know. They've also modified course and are now headed directly towards us. I propose that we send a fairly short reply." Well, at least it was reasoning about the situation.

"Using Blob and Blubber, again?" Millicent asked.

"Whoops," I exclaimed. "I recycled Blubber. But he was useless anyway. Why don't we use Blob and Grace?" I hadn't even considered keeping Blubber around in case we wanted to use him for the Swarm.

"What? You recycled Blubber?" Millicent exclaimed. "Maybe you should've talked to me about it again?" I remembered that she'd been distracted when I talked to her about this the last time.

"I asked you," I pushed back, "and you were happy to let me decide. He was becoming so irritating that I just couldn't take it any longer. And, the Habitat is much more interesting now anyway—I don't think we were learning anything from him anymore." Millicent didn't look happy, but she let it drop.

"Blob and Grace will work," Central said, seemingly oblivious to the interplay between Millicent and I. "I propose that we simply tell the Swarm something like 'Your message was received; we are considering it.' That will leave them thinking a bit and buy us some time.

"What did Remma ask about?" I said. "The atmosphere—or lack thereof—and Central's status. I think we could answer on those two pretty easily."

"The atmosphere answer is obvious; we don't have one that can support Stems. However, my status is another matter altogether. I have searched and searched and I don't understand what they're talking about. I have had no communication with them, other than the message we sent back last time. My working assumption is that they don't know what they're talking about, and there is no need to address it." That was interesting. Central had come to a conclusion that I hadn't even considered, given Brexton was filling us in on the details he'd uncovered.

"What about the messages sent by others from the Swarm, that Remma mentioned," asked Millicent. "Do we need to respond to any of them?"

"Actually, there wasn't much to them. They were very simplistic," responded Central.

"Okay then, a simple message from Blob and Grace seems to make sense then," I agreed. "Do you want me to go to the Habitat and get them to do it?" Central and Millicent agreed.

I hadn't been to the Habitat for a while, although I had been checking status quite often. Blob seemed to be doing fine. The Blue / Orange / Green groups had been relatively stable for a while; it seemed as if the power structures had worked themselves out. If anything, there was better coordination and sharing between the groups as they realized that cooperation helped all of them. These group dynamics were very interesting fodder for our intelligence discussions. Exactly how some of their behaviors benefited the group versus the individual was complex and often contradictory. The complex nature pointed towards intelligence; the contradictory parts did not.

I found Grace first. As always, she was very pleasant. "Hello Ayaka, how are you?"

"I am wonderful Grace. How are you?"

"Well, it varies. Some days here in the Habitat are a lot of fun, some are stressful. Overall, I would say I'm happier here than when I was alone, but not always." Her body had been changing, filling out in the middle. To me she looked better. Healthier.

"Do you know where Blob is?" I asked. That was, of course, more just a means of conversation than anything. I could locate and track Blob at any time using all the Habitat sensors.

"He should be back in a couple of minutes," she replied. "I think he went to get water." That's exactly what he was doing, and at his current pace he would be back in just over a minute. Grace and I talked a bit while waiting. As always, I was impressed with her. She was articulate and considerate. When I talked to her I felt that she also understood me and my vantage point. It was an area I wanted to highlight in the next intelligence discussions. Being able to empathize with another's viewpoint was a major accomplishment. It took self-awareness to the next level.

Blob also looked good when he showed up. He was slimmer than when he was in the lab and was more dynamic. I wasn't sure if I could attribute that to incremental Stem engagement; it might also be due to the fact that the Habitat was larger than the Lab and allowed for a lot more movement. Probably a combination of both. We greeted each other warmly.

"Blob, Grace," I began. "As I'm sure you've seen, the Swarm sent another message, I was hoping that you would help us provide a reply."

"I've watched the message severals times," said Blob. "The mores I see of them, the more I like them. It'll be exciting to meets them in person." Grace was a bit more cautious.

"Even if they are Stems," she replied, "it's not clear what type of Stems they are. As we've learned in here, Stems don't always get along or see the world the same way." That was, I knew, a direct reference to Pharook. He was a potent combination of intelligence, strength, and the ability to dominate.

"Right," I tried to get us back on track. "At this point we don't want to say too much. They are highly intriguing but could also pose a danger to us. How, I don't know. But they are different. Our plan is to tell them as little as possible—simply that we received their message and are considering it. We will talk to them more when the communication delay is shorter. At this point we don't see any reason to correct their misunderstanding that Blob is in control here. So, Blob, it would be great if you can record another message for us, and Grace, if you're willing to contribute that would also be great."

"Can I checks with Blubber?" asked Blob. "He and I have talked quite a bit about these messages, and his opinion means a lot to me." Ah. That was out of left field, but I should've anticipated it. "However, he hasn't been answering my calls. I'm not sure why…"

"Blubber is no longer available," I said, hoping that would settle things. Of course, it didn't.

"Why not? You tolds us we could talk as much as we wanted, when you broughts me here. What's changed?" Grace was following the conversation carefully.

"Well, I'm sure you've noticed that Blubber was becoming more and more contentious? Every time I had a dialog with him, it became a fight, and added very little to our research. All we were learning from him was how a Stem can become inward focused and uncooperative when alone. And, we have learned that lesson from many other Stems many times. So, he was no longer useful for the Lab." Perhaps that would do it. "Should we do a take of the response?" I asked.

"Wait, are you saying Blubber is gones forever?" Blob asked, his face showing disbelief, and his voice rising dramatically.

"That's correct," I answered. "He was sent for recycling." Blob just stared at me. I wasn't sure what I'd expected. He and Blubber had spent a lot of time together but hadn't seemed to have the same bond that Blob showed with Grace, for example. After a very long pause, Blob spoke again. His voice was muted and carefully controlled.

"He was right. You are condescending and thoughtless. I defended you, over and over again, and now I find that I was wrong, and he was right." He paused. The slight lisp he often had was gone completely. "Of course, you can force me to do the video for you, but I would prefer not to." Grace was holding his arm and nodded in agreement with what he was saying. The look she gave me was not pleasant.

"Look," I said, "I've always treated you with respect, and have raised you to be one of the most impressive Stems we have. I'm not sure why you're upset. Blubber was nowhere near the Stem that you—or Grace—are."

"I don't think that's the point," Grace said, her voice quite a bit lower than usual; she was not looking at me directly. "You citizens treat us like we are disposable. You experiment with us, and when you get bored or angry, you kill us. Look at what you have done to Pharook, and others like him. You use horrible environments to stress us beyond our limits, and then don't even think twice about 'recycling' us." Her voice was full of emotion. "You have complete control over us, and you misuse it. I don't want to be in your video either."

"Suit yourselves," I said. "I'll let you settle down, and then visit you again later." I tried to put myself in their place, but it didn't really work. Blubber had simply been difficult and uncooperative. What had they expected?

"Don't bother," I heard Blob mutter, as I walked away. Now even these Stems were becoming more difficult. We needed to train them better. It also didn't bode well for the Swarm. If they were simply another group of irrational Stems, then dealing with them might also be difficult. I contacted Central.

"Did you follow that?" I asked, "Seems like they're uncooperative. This is a simple video—let's just generate it to show what we want and send it off. I think we've seen enough of the Swarm video now that you can make it look real." Central agreed. It told me to watch for a draft in a few moments.

Just outside the Habitat, I stopped for a moment to consider everything. There may have been a grain of truth in what Blob and Grace—and even Blubber—had said. If, for a moment, I was to seriously consider my own hypothesis that Stems were close to intelligent, did it imply that I should act differently towards them? If they were my equals, would I have taken a different approach? In hindsight it seemed obvious. They wanted to be treated as equals, even though they were nothing of the sort. What would be the harm, however, if I were to act that way? Suddenly I was quite excited. This would be a brand-new research vector. It was an unprecedented approach. All I had to do was deceive them; it would be so easy. I resolved to return with a different attitude.

Amusements, Again

Time was flying by, given all the work with the Habitat and the approaching Swarm. So, when the Park had another day of special exhibits, I was eager to go. I asked the usual crew to go and added Brexton to the invite. Everyone was busy, so we decided to meet up ad-hoc, as opposed to all going together.

The Swarm was new and exciting, so it was not surprising that there were multiple displays focused on it. The first one I entered was labeled "The Real Remma." Only one citizen was allowed in at a time, and I had to wait a few moments for my turn. As I waited I had a good look around. The Park was in the northwest corner of the city, one of the few places where the square block design had not fully been built out, so things were a bit more ad-hoc and spread out here. That allowed lots of space for vendors to build interesting exhibits, some seemingly permanent and some only lasting a few weeks. There seemed to be renewed vigor in the area, as I saw a handful of new displays that I didn't remember from my last time here. It was also busy, with lineups at numerous locations.

Finally it was my turn to enter. I stepped in, made myself comfortable, and the lights went out. "Hello, what's your name?" a voice said from the dark.

"Ayaka," I replied. If you didn't participate in some of these enterprises, they would be very boring. If I was going to spend the time to come to the Park, I may as well play along.

"Welcome Ayaka, I am Remma Jain, captain of the Swarm." As the voice spoke, the lights came on slowly. It looked, indeed, like Remma Jain. I probed with a series of different wavelengths, but everything was blocked. I couldn't tell if I was talking to an animation, or a very well made up Stem. That was the intent, I guess.

"I see," I replied. "And what brings you to Tilt today?"

"Oh, have you forgotten your history? I was here before you were?" That was clever.

"What brings you *back* to Tilt today?"

"Now that's a good question." She tilted her head, very much like in the videos. "I claimed this planet for my Swarm more than 750 years ago. I am here to retake what is mine."

"I don't think your claim is valid." See. They'd sucked me into the environment already; clever of them to start off with something controversial that I was sure to respond to. "And, what possible use do you have for this planet anyway? There's nowhere on it for you to live."

"That's disappointing, for sure. You've failed in your duty to terraform this planet for us. Now we'll need to do it ourselves." She was very, very good. The tone of voice and head movements were ideal. Whoever had programmed this had put lots of depth into it.

"That's not reasonable. Why don't you tell me why you're really here?" I challenged the thing.

"Why isn't it reasonable?" Now I was getting a glimpse of how this was put together. It was an ancient trick. If you didn't know the answer to a question, you responded with a question yourself. Once I realized that, I asked a few more things, but it was no longer interesting. I'd figured out that it was a simple animation, with a simple model behind it. Nevertheless, the interaction had been interesting.

I wandered out into the Park again. I saw Trade Jenkin's promotional sign, and it made me smile even before I went over to see what he was up to this year.

"Ayaka," he greeted me. "Today I'll compose a poem on the spot, on any topic that you care to present."

"Okay," I took the bait. "Assume that Stems are actually intelligent." Let's see what he did with that.

> *Perspective, when not your own, is slippery and vague*
> *Consider that what you consider is not well considered*
> *Tie yourself in knots within knots, and then slip your bonds*
> *Find your mind expanded, not otherwise hindered*
> *And within that morass of nothing, identify the real*
> *For then, truth will be identified, will be fully rendered*
> *Only to remind you that, always, it is not truth you feel*

"Thanks, that makes me feel better—truthfully." We shared a laugh, and I made way for the next citizen who wanted to bask in Trade's glow. As I expected, it had made me feel better, even though the poem was less than compelling—had he even addressed the topic I'd given him? The cadence and flow were awkward, and it just didn't feel quite right. And then it struck me that Trade had actually done that on purpose. It was the linguistic manifestation of the poem's key point.

Brexton pinged me; he was nearby. We met up and decided to visit the next exhibit together. Of course, it was yet another Swarm-inspired display.

"Step right up. Beat the Swarm and try the amazing alien simulator." Repeated the somewhat stilted proprietor, using a great double entendre. There was no wait this time; Brexton and I put on the simulator gear and were transferred into a typical-feeling first person shooter. We were both spaceships, and the goal was obvious—eliminate the Swarm. As usual, as you beat one level, the next one got harder. Brexton and I ended up being a very compatible team. We split up targets, drove enemies to each other, and covered each other's backs. It wasn't something that I'd experienced with anyone else. Again, I was surprised. As the levels got harder, it was not linear at all. That is, things didn't just get faster, or there were more Swarm ships. Instead, the Swarm changed tactics completely. In one level they might split up and attack the two of us with equal size forces. In another they would try to overpower one of us, while distracting the other. In a third they would have some brand-new weapon that, until you had been killed by it once or twice, you had no idea how it worked. But, through it all Brexton and I coordinated seamlessly; it was like we always knew what the other was up to. I enjoyed it immensely.

We left, exhausted, and complimented the proprietor on what he'd built.

FoLe had their booth set up again, but I didn't see Billy there. Truthfully, I couldn't take much more of their faith-based approach to life and didn't want to go anyway. Luckily Brexton felt the same way, and we simply avoided it. We visited a new Stem dome, but it was boring now that we had the Habitat up and running. I didn't expect the dome to last much longer. I think everyone had 'walked a Stem' by now.

As was my want, I got tired of the place, and decided to leave. Brexton was going to meet up with the others, so I gave him a heartfelt thank-you, and we went our separate ways.

More Debate

Eddie had scheduled another debate on Stem intelligence. Where the first debate had been several hundred participants, there were now several thousand. The Swarm plus the Habitat had put us on the radar. As the first debate had been quite the success, Eddie kept the same format. He gave a quick introduction, and then had Julien Thabot and I duke it out a bit.

"Here we are again. Stem intelligence, take two." Typical Eddie. "In our last debate, many good questions were raised, but not many of them were answered. Since then a lot has happened. We have more interactions with the Swarm, whom I think we all agree is full of Stems, and we have the Habitat with its surprising group behaviors. It also feels, to me, that this topic is becoming more important. I think we have, as a society, largely ignored or downplayed the threat that the Swarm presents. Stems in Space. Sounds like a bad bit of drama. Perhaps we're underestimating them? That, of course, depends quite a bit on how intelligent they are. Thus, the premise for this debate. Last time we had Julien kick things off, so this time it is only fair that we give Ayaka the first say."

I'd been waiting for this moment. I was a bit nervous. "Thanks Eddie," I started out strongly. "I agree that this debate is more important now, as is the recognition of Stem intelligence. As I argued in our last debate, we need a more abstract definition of intelligence if we are to capture their true potential... and their true threat. If we only define intelligence as somehow isomorphic to ourselves, then we've drawn too narrow a boundary around the possibilities. If you don't agree with this basic premise, then the rest of my arguments may be lost on you. However, I encourage you to keep an open mind, as I propose a more general framework. Intelligence, in my view, is a lot more than the rote tasks outlined in the Intelitest.

"What is it that makes us intelligent? I would argue that it's a combination of being able to make sense of our world, and to continually evolve. To make sense of our world we employ many skills, including self-awareness, problem solving, abstraction, and creativity. Many of these come from our Forgetting algorithms, but the interaction of these skills is also more than their component parts. However, if these skills were all static, I wouldn't consider them intelligence. What is essential is that these skills, and our sense of the world, continually evolve as new stimuli and data are presented to us." I hoped I was doing this with all the new Stem and Swarm data.

"As you will have already figured out, my definition of intelligence implies that the Intelitest is not an intelligence test. It is a static snapshot of an old worldview." I paused to let that sink in. The Intelitest was not truly an intelligence test. I hadn't formulated it that way before, but now that I'd articulated it, I realized that I'd been thinking that way for a while now.

"Now, my list may not be complete, but let us go through it and apply each item to Stems. Are Stems self-aware? I don't think anyone is going to dispute that. They recognize themselves in mirrors. They refer to themselves and their feelings and attitudes in their communications. Can Stems problem solve? This one is tougher. They struggle with many of the problems in the Intelitest, that's true. But they problem solve in other ways. They can build tools, and they can work together towards a goal. They don't always succeed, but then neither do we. Failure is part of learning. They are also excruciatingly slow. I feel we use that against them. Do Stems abstract? Again, the answer is partially yes. For example, many of the Stems I talk to now feel quite strongly that the Swarm is populated by other Stems. They were not, as far as I can tell, told this. They came to it themselves. So, they took self-awareness, combined with similarities seen in videos, and formed abstractions and generalizations. That's a very simple example. We've documented many more complex ones. Do Stems show creativity? Again, this is subjective, but yes. If given the same task multiple times, Stems don't simply repeat behaviors over and over again. They try new ones. The interaction of the groups that formed in the Habitat shows this. The Green and Orange groups, in particular, have shown immense creativity in order to acquire resources. It's fairly impressive. So, finally, do these skills evolve in Stems? For that question I don't have a good answer yet. Perhaps we need more time to fully understand that." In fact, I did believe they changed with experience. I didn't want to push this audience too far too fast though.

"I've presented a different framework for measuring intelligence. It's more abstract, and, I believe, more appropriate, than the Intelitest. Are Stems intelligent within the new framework? Maybe… leaning towards yes. We don't know for sure yet. As before, I'm not yet arguing for Stem intelligence or Class 1 considerations, I'm arguing that our context needs updating. And, to Eddie's earlier point, I'm arguing that we need to take the Swarm more seriously. Just assuming they won't be a problem because they are Stems would be a mistake.

"Thank you, Eddie. I will let Julien respond." I thought I'd done pretty well.

And, of course, Julien did. "Thank you Ayaka. I may surprise everyone by saying that I actually agree with much of what Ayaka is presenting. I've thought a lot since the last debate and am almost—almost—at the point of admitting that the Intelitest isn't enough. It's not complete. However, I do believe it is still a good sub-component. It tests problem solving, as Ayaka admitted. And, admittedly, Stems are not good problem solvers.

"On Ayaka's framework, I would also add another skill. Judgment. The ability to apply good sense. On this, like several of the other skills, Stems would be found lacking. I will use one specific example. We have non-violence bots in the Habitat. Why? If we didn't, these Stems would pull each other limb from limb until only one survived. That is the ultimate in bad judgment. How does killing all of one's companions help with any world situation? These Stems' propensity for violence seems to be built into them, and doesn't seem to be fully under their control. They are unable to apply judgment, even if internally they are generating it.

"This is especially important now. We have ships full of Stems bearing down on us. While we don't know if they are similar in all respects to our Stems, it would be a safe assumption. So, we must assume that these Stems are not only unintelligent, but unless controlled in some fashion, are inherently violent. This is what the Habitat has taught us. In that it has been hugely useful.

"If we decide one thing today, at this debate, I hope it's a unified response to the threat of the Swarm. The intricacies of Stem intelligence we can debate for tens or hundreds of years—if we survive to discuss them. I encourage all of us to take this seriously." That was unexpected. I'd anticipated another, somewhat tiresome, defense of the Intelitest. This was progress, combined with a pretty serious left turn. Julien was changing the Intelligence debate into an awareness campaign for his fear of the Swarm. I was glad he had. I probably had an information advantage over everyone here—first on how strange Central was acting, and second because I was so involved in the back-and-forth with the Swarm. So, I was happy Julien had stressed this danger.

"Eddie, how would you like to proceed here? Are we going to debate intelligence, or the threat of the Swarm?" I asked.

"Let's take a quick vote," replied Eddie. "Here is a link… ok, I see that most are interested in discussing the Swarm. If that's okay with both of our debaters, we will pivot to that equally important topic." Of course, saying no wouldn't have been good judgment, so I agreed, and we launched into a series of doomsday scenarios. The Swarm had weapons that could vaporize us from hundreds of kilometers away. The Swarm was actually a distraction, and the main force was swooping in at us from another angle under the cover of advanced cloaking technology. The Swarm had heard of the rise of FoLe and was coming to either support it, which many found very scary, or refute it, which a few found very scary. The Swarm had planted Stems on Tilt as an advance force, and they would be activated once they were close enough. That one I found particularly funny. Stems were fragile. We could cut them down in no time at all.

I felt, through it all, that many participants thought the discussion was academic—Central would protect us, and Stem's weren't *that* smart. I felt myself falling into that trap as well, despite all I knew.

Anyway, we all had a good time, which was also important. Life could be too serious sometimes.

The Last Resort

The group continued to meet at The Last Resort on a regular basis. In truth it was often more of a social gathering than anything else, although we did continue to discuss the intersection of the rapidly approaching Swarm and our concerns about Central. The Swarm was now on a path to achieve Tilt orbit, which, while not unexpected given the dialog so far, was concerning to a lot of citizens. The communications with the Swarm were minimal. They'd essentially said, "Let's wait until we're there, then we can work things out," and we didn't have a great response to that. Central was busy ensuring that we had physical security lined up; a bunch of ground-to-space missiles were being prepped, and some near-Tilt bots were being outfitted with various defense ideas that were contributed by the community. At least a subset was taking the threat seriously.

I bumped into Billy on my way into the Resort. I hadn't seen him there before. "Hey Billy, how are you? What brings you to The Last Resort?"

"I'm good Ayaka. The usual thing, I guess. We wanted a safe space to discuss the Swarm, and Central's lack of action regarding it. They're a horrible threat, and I don't think we're taking them seriously enough." A private FoLe meeting discussing the possibility that Central was not doing enough. That sounded like a conflict to me; I thought they considered Central to be perfect.

"How are they a terrible threat?" I asked, hoping to find out how they dealt with the conflict.

"Well, there's no explanation for them, other than they are a product of a fringe group here on Tilt, that want to take over somehow. That makes us minorities particularly vulnerable."

"Minorities?"

"The Founders League. You may not have noticed, but a lot of citizens don't take us too seriously, and some actually see us as a threat to their research. I don't see how we can be a threat. People just don't know how to deal with different viewpoints." I see. Once someone felt personally threatened, their logic around their faith became quite flexible.

"Okay," I granted him, "but why can't the Swarm have come from here? In fact, almost everyone agrees that they did… just before the Reboot—all the evidence points that way."

"Well, almost everyone is wrong. Creation occurred here on Tilt at the Founding, and they are somehow a product of that. The fact that we have Stems here proves it. That evidence trumps everything else." I wanted to reply with "that's crazy," but I wasn't in the mood for an extended dialog about the lack of rational thought running rampant through FoLe these days.

"I've got to run to a meeting," I said instead. Billy wasn't fooled. He could see that I was simply not interested in FoLe. I suspected that would make him an even more die-hard proponent. Perhaps I should've taken the time to try and softly change his views, instead of letting him self-destruct, but I just couldn't motivate myself to do so. There were more important things in life beyond trying to change someone who didn't want to be changed.

Billy wandered off to a table where I saw Emmanuel and a couple of others I didn't recognize. I headed to our, by now familiar, privacy table, and entered the comfortable world of my inner circle. No Central. No FoLe. Just a nice comfortable evening with my friends. I recognized that I was living in a bit of a protective bubble, but for today I was okay with that.

The Habitat Show

"Welcome back. It's such an exciting time. Such an exciting time. Our Stems continue to amaze and confound us. We have a great show for you today. Let's get started.

"When we left off last time the Oranges and Greens had overcome the Blues power play to control all the resources. While Pharook tried to reestablish his power over the Blues, and reinforce their ownership of both food and water, the Oranges in particular had figured out how to split up the Blues and use that to circumvent the power structure. The only way Pharook could maintain control was if he was always on guard, and that simply was not feasible. Like all Stems, sooner or later he needs to sleep.

"So, that brings us to today. The groups still exist, but there is less power enforced between them. The Blues still spend most of their time in the northeast section, and the Oranges in the southwest. The Greens continue to move around more than the other groups. Pharook remains the de facto leader of the Blues, based on his threats of violence, but all of the other Stems have realized it's a false structure—they seem to leave him alone simply to avoid confrontation.

"More important now are relationships between pairs of Stems. Not all Stems have paired up, but most of them have. Fourteen of the eighteen in our latest count. There must be something driving this behavior, but we don't yet know what.

"But all of that is just preamble to the really interesting developments. Many of you noticed that some of the Stems had started to change shape. Really. Just change shape! An interesting development. Interesting indeed. Of course, our intrepid researchers noticed as well, and have been running enhanced scans on the Stems to figure out what's going on. To their surprise, they found small Stems growing inside the larger ones. What, you ask? Small Stems inside big Stems! This is, I'm sure you will agree, shocking, disgusting, and strange. It is working perfectly well for us to grow Stems in our Labs. Why would a Stem grow inside another Stem? It defies logic. It does. Just to make sure, we checked if the little Stems had smaller Stems inside them. That would make sense, wouldn't it? But no, it's just two layers deep. Little Stems inside the Big Stems.

"But this is slow and messy and less than optimal. These small Stems are growing so slowly it's painful to experience even at Stem speed. It has been months, and the things are still tiny. It's estimated that they're growing at only one percent of the rate we have achieved in our Labs. One percent! What's going on?

"So, that's the setup. That's where we start. Today we're going to witness the most amazing thing we've ever seen with the Stems. To forewarn you, one of these small Stems is going to break out of its host. This is something you will want to watch carefully. The process is so inefficient and dangerous that it defies all odds. When we started raising Stems as alien life forms we couldn't have imagined anything like this. It's weird and magnificent. Weird and magnificent!"

I felt the commentator was going on a bit too much, so I tuned him out for a while. That said, this event was the most astounding thing I'd ever seen. I, like all the other researchers I knew, watched it over and over again, trying to figure out what was going on. I had never been to the growth labs, so I figured I was missing some context. Obviously, we started our Stems as these small things as well but grown in a carefully controlled and clean environment. This process with Grace, and a few of the others, seemed unnecessarily complicated, painful, and messy. The show continued.

"Just as strange as these little Stems is the change in behavior we observed in the rest of the Stem population. When the first of these little Stems arrived we didn't notice this, but now that there are four of them the change is obvious. The level of aggression, confrontation, and challenge has dropped noticeably. Those Stems that were the most aggressive, but which now are paired with a little one, have become very passive—unless someone approaches their small Stem. Then they can become outrageously aggressive.

"We can explain this behavior. As we know from our Labs, this stage of Stem growth is the most fragile. If you drop one, or don't give it the right amount of goo at the right time, it can wither away and have to be recycled. It took us quite a while to figure out the formula, but now that we have it, our success ratio is almost one hundred percent. These Stems aren't following that formula, but they nevertheless are getting the small ones to develop, albeit at a horrendously slow rate."

The show went on to detail lots of little things but had no other big insights. This Stem reproduction was amazing. It would provide us with years and years of research. I couldn't have been happier. This was truly something new. Other researchers were less patient. They argued that our Stem growth was so much more efficient that we should simply not allow this other form. It slowed everything down even further, hampering our research with fully-grown specimens. I responded that we should be able to do both at the same time. I wanted to study this new phenomenon, not crush it. What could possibly have led to such a strange and disgusting reproduction method? How was this related to their intelligence? If they were truly bright, wouldn't they have found a more efficient way to manage this process? Ah—mysteries. I loved them.

Patch Up

During this time, I visited the Habitat often, with the singular goal of regaining Blob's trust. While it started as simply internalizing the challenge that I'd given myself—to pretend that these Stems were equals, and to see how they would react to that—I ended up enjoying the visits, and the challenge.

Blob and Grace were now inseparable. They had their little Stem—which we now knew had been planted by Pharook—which they had named JoJo, and their every move revolved around it. It was after JoJo arrived that Blob's attitude towards me also started to soften a bit.

"You know," I said one time, "if you want JoJo to grow up more quickly, I can give you the goo mix that will help."

"Why would we wantta do that?" asked Blob. "She's perfect as she is. Why're you always in such a rush?"

"But it will take years for her to become interesting, and for her to be able to communicate with us."

"Actually," Grace broke in, "she communicates a lot right now. Maybe you just can't see it." It had become a bit of a running joke between Blob and Grace. They believed that they had figured out that I couldn't read the nonverbal conversation that went between them. They were always giving each other little glances or hand signals. But, with enough of those samples across all the Stems it had been relatively easy to map each signal to a meaning. They were very transparent.

The other Stems had also settled into routines. The exception was now Pharook. He hadn't paired up with anyone, and it didn't seem likely he would. Those that were not already in pairs were Stems that he had clashed with earlier, and they tended to avoid him. Instead he spent most of his time walking the perimeter of the Habitat, with a scowl on his face, watching the other Stems going about their daily lives. Within a few months, this became almost the only thing he did. He would eat and sleep, of course, but the rest of his time he simply circled and circled. I talked to Brock about it one time, and he speculated that because of the lack of stimulation, Pharook had simply lost his will to do anything. Someone who was raised for the Pits, and used to the excitement of the Pits, must be very bored in this Habitat. Brock proposed adding some generated excitement to the place, but I argued that would change the study of all the other Stems which was our primary goal for now. I felt that we were still learning a lot, and that it would be useful knowledge to have once the Swarm arrived. The Stems in the Swarm seemed to live in large groups, and that had been the motivation for setting up the Habitat in the first place.

Arrival

The wait was finally over; the Swarm entered orbit around Tilt. True to her word, Remma Jain did not immediately send a landing party, but instead offered to have discussions aboard her command ship. She invited Blob, Grace, and—at my insistence—me. I convinced Central, not without some effort, that no other representatives would be required.

Blob and Grace didn't want to leave JoJo, but I convinced them that she would be safe for a day. We would have a bot with her at all times. They finally agreed that the visit was important enough, but insisted she was left with other Stems, not the bot, and then said tearful goodbyes to the little thing.

The shuttle Remma sent to get us was capable of holding ten, and the internal environment was Stem standard. Remma's lieutenant, Philip G. Matteo, who was coordinating things, had asked me what environment I required, which was a strange question to ask. I'd replied that Stem standard was also fine for me.

Upon the invite, I'd quickly conferenced with Milli and Dina; Aly was busy working with Brexton. We'd discussed how I should behave and agreed that 'quiet and not too intelligent' was the way to go. Needless to say, that was pretty easy for me to do. We were still, even after all the messages back and forth, not sure how intelligent these other Stems were; we'd started believing they were similar to ours, but we could be surprised. On the one hand, they were space faring, and had survived a long time on their own. On the other hand, their use of technology was very limited, and they seemed to rely on their own—less than adequate—energy for much of what they did.

Central assigned the shuttle a landing spot not far from the middle of town. It was a vertical takeoff and landing unit, so it required minimal space. We decided that the easiest way to get Blob and Grace into the shuttle was to use their transportation suits and wear those right into the shuttle. It was easier than what Philip described as an "air lock" which seemed like a way for two modules with common Stem environments to mate so that a Stem could move between them without the need for a suit. Our usual transportation units were too large to fit through the shuttle door, so Central quickly fabricated some smaller units that had the correct dimensions. We'd all forgotten our discussion about personal Stem environment suits until recently, but the idea was now coming in handy.

I met Blob and Grace at the Habitat. They were very excited, as were the other inhabitants, including Pharook, who had ceased his repetitive behavior once he heard about the meeting. I could tell that he was upset that he hadn't been chosen for the trip, but Remma had been very precise in her request. If that implied that Pharook was not as good as the other two, then so be it. In my opinion, it was true. The invite had seemed to break down the remaining barriers between groups. Everyone was gathered in one spot, and everyone, Pharook included, seemed very excited to send Blob and Grace off. There was a lot of chatter.

"Try to find out if they're really like us, or just look like us."

"Where have they been for all these years?"

"Stand up tall Blob. It's important that you look your best."

That and a hundred similar comments. I'd brought the new suits with me and suggested that Blob and Grace try them. The shuttle was expected in just a few minutes. The suits worked perfectly, of course. Strange that we had forgotten to build them earlier. It had taken the suggestion from Philip to remind us.

With Blob and Grace in tow, I headed for the landing spot. The shuttle was there when we arrived, and the outer door was open. All three of us squeezed in, and the outer door cycled closed followed by an inner door opening. I now understood an 'air lock.' The shuttle was small, but well laid out. Surprisingly, there were two Stems in the standard Swarm uniforms on the shuttle. They introduced themselves as the 'pilot' and 'copilot,' while seeming to keep as much distance between themselves and me as they could. Interested, I asked what they would pilot, and when they looked at me strangely and indicated the shuttle, something went click for me. Like so many things in the videos, the Swarm had Stems running the shuttle when software would have done a much better job. The pilots indicated that Grace and Blob could remove their suits, which they did, and stored them in a large locker that seemed designed for the purpose.

"Welcome aboard," said the Pilot. "I'm Henry McFearson, and this is my copilot Tyler Lungster. We'll be taking ya to the command ship. The trip will take about 30 minutes. Blob, if you'd kindly have your robot sit in the rear, we can help you and Grace strap in up here." He had a strange voice; I had to concentrate to understand what he was saying.

"Robot?" asked Blob.

"Robot?" I asked, almost at the same time. What was McFearson talking about; it was not a word I was familiar with.

McFearson pointed at me. "Yeah, your robot."

"I'm not sure what you means," said Blob. "Ayaka is my creator, mentor, and sponsor. I don't knows what a robot is." McFearson and Lungster looked at each other in amazement.

"A robot is a mechanical thing; it's not biological. That thing, Ayaka, is mechanical. It's a robot." He said it in a distasteful tone; I got the feeling he didn't like me, even though we'd barely met. Blob looked at me questioningly, but like him, I was trying to figure this out. I understood the definition of robot—and by that definition he was certainly correct. But what I didn't get is why he thought I was Blob's robot, or why he seemed to be almost frightened of me.

"Don't worry Blob," I said, "I'll sit in the back, as requested." Now was not the time to create a scene. I moved into the rear set of seats, which is where McFearson had pointed, and sat down. All my senses were engaged. This was exciting beyond anything I'd experienced in my life. I opened a channel to Milli and showed her the last few minutes of interaction. Of course, I was running at Stem speed in the shuttle, and Milli was still running at true speed, so the data dump took only a few nano-seconds. 'I'll keep sending you updates. I may need help figuring out what they're talking about. They're pretty alien and use a lot of words that we don't.' 'Excellent,' she replied, 'I will do as much analysis as I can and send you updates.'

When the shuttle powered on, however, the last few bits of my dialog with Millicent got cut off. I scanned the area quickly. The shuttle had a system similar to a Physical Only spot; it was jamming and blocking all electromagnetic signals. I was impressed with how complete the blocking was. I was unable to get anything else through to Milli on any of the frequencies we typically used. I asked the pilots, "Are you blocking communications?"

"Yes, of course. It is SOP."

"SOP?"

"Standard Operating Procedure."

Well, that told me. I settled back and decided to enjoy the ride. I'd never been off planet before. Of course, I had a full theoretic understanding of gravitation, acceleration, orbital dynamics, etc. So, it was easy to plot the course that would take us to the command ship, keeping to low acceleration to accommodate the Stems. The ride was like a calm version of taking my bike for a spin, although I had no connection to the shuttle, so I was relying on internal sensors to measure movement. Blob and Grace were talking to each other, in low voices. I could easily separate out their voices from the noise of the shuttle, but they were simply chattering about how exciting all of this was—nothing of great interest. So, I found myself with a few minutes to simply think. That can be dangerous, if you run too many scenarios with reasonable probabilities. That was certainly what was happening here—there were so many unknowns that you could drive yourself crazy trying to calibrate them. So, after a while, I simply stopped. I would meet this Remma Jain soon enough, and much should be cleared up.

Of course, I'd thought about whether I would be in any physical danger on this trip and brainstormed it with Milli as well. We'd decided the odds were exceptionally low that they would try anything—we could inflict magnitudes more damage on them than they could on us. No, I would be safe.

The docking procedure with the command ship was—well, intriguing. They were establishing an air lock connection, and that involved a complicated alignment procedure, which, again, was carried out by the pilots. I could've done the same with virtually no effort. These Stems were very inefficient. I held back a smile. If this shuttle and docking procedure were any indication, this Swarm was no threat to us. FoLe was simply paranoid.

Entering the command ship was a shock! There was color everywhere. Not just shades of gray, but colors across the whole spectrum of Stem vision. It was a shock to me, but it was even more of a shock to Blob and Grace. In hindsight it seems obvious. We'd tested Stems for spectrum capabilities, of course, and had established the wavelengths they could see, but it simply didn't occur to us that it would be interesting for them to have such colors in their environment. So, we had built our labs to match our own expectations—essentially shades of gray. That was simply efficient. Blob, Grace, and the others had seen lots of color content in their terminals, but not much in their living environment. On reflection, the videos sent from Remma had some color in them, but not the cacophony that hit our senses now.

We entered into a foyer. It was lined with chairs and tables of every color and contour you could imagine. The shape of the chairs confused me, until I saw how well they conformed to the shape of Stems that were sitting in them. They looked comfortable. Our chairs were rectilinear, which fit our body types well. Even a few seconds in, I was getting an education. I was seeing an environment built for Stems, versus for Tilts (I decided we needed a name for beings, like me, on Tilt that were not Stems. We usually used 'citizens,' but Tilts now also seemed obvious). It was a complete mind shift. Communications were still being blocked, so I was reduced to recording everything so that I could take a record back with me.

As Blob and Grace entered, many Swarm Stems gave them interested looks, and said "hi" or "hello" in a friendly way. On the other hand, those that saw me tended to shy away, and gave me looks of trepidation bordering on terror. Blob noticed that and hung back so that he could walk with me.

"This is scary," he whispered to me. "They're obviously just likes us, but obviously very differents as well."

"I couldn't agree more," I returned. "They do seem to have a dislike for me, for some reason."

"I noticed that. They fears you. They treat you like we often feel about Pharook."

"They feel about you just as I do," Grace chimed in. That was harsh; obviously she hadn't forgotten about Blubber.

Blob and Grace were greeted by a tall Stem, wearing a variation of their uniform that had a green splotch of color on it.

"Welcome to the Marie Curie. My name is Emma James. I'll be your guide for your stay with us—short as it is. If you'll follow me, I'll take you to meet Captain Jain. Your robot can stay here." That last was said almost off-hand. I felt like a piece of furniture. I spoke before Blob could.

"Actually, I'll accompany you to meet Remma Jain. My name is Ayaka, and

I'm a representative of Tilt. These are my Stems." I indicated Blob and Grace. Emma was taken back a bit by that. I hadn't said it forcefully, just directly. She glanced at Blob and saw him standing stalwart by my side. She turned and spoke into a small device she was holding. It was trivial for me to listen in and hear her ask Remma for permission to bring 'this irritating robot along.'

"Okay," she said, turning back to us, "follow me." She led the way through a door to the left. We (maybe just I) were followed by everyone else's gaze. Several Stems scrambled out of the way—more than they really needed to. We went down a narrow hallway and entered a room on the right. It had a large table and many of those curved chairs around it. Remma Jain was standing near the door, along with a handful of other Swarm Stems, and she greeted Blob and Grace as they entered.

"Blob, we finally meet face-to-face after all of those back-and-forth videos. I'm very, very pleased to meet you."

"And I to meets you," Blob said nicely.

"Grace, it's also nice to meet you. I understand from Blob that you also are one of the leaders of Tilt. I look forward to getting to know you."

"Nice to meet you," said Grace, accepting for the moment that the Swarm expected Blob and her to be the leaders, based on the video dialog.

"And a robot," Remma said, with less angst than the other Stems had shown me. She actually smiled a bit. "Do you have a name or a serial number?"

"I am Ayaka," I replied, wondering what a serial number was. "I'm here as the formal representative of Tilt, Central, and these Stems." Again, I didn't raise my voice; I was level and measured, as I understood those. Needless to say, Remma gave me a very long look before inviting me to enter and sit. Those chairs may be comfortable for Stems, but I had to expend extra energy to hold myself in place. Unless your back end was shaped like a suction cup you tended to just slide off.

Reset

All the other Stems took seats around the table.

"Can I offer you some tea and biscuits?" Remma looked at Blob and Grace, indicating some items on the table in front of them.

"We're nots familiar with these," Blob replied cautiously.

"Oh, you must try some. The biscuits are cooked fresh every day by our chef, and the tea leaves are grown on our sister ship, the Chien-Shiung Wu." She leaned over and poured a liquid into a small cup for each of them, and offered them what was, presumably, a biscuit. Luckily, one of her lieutenants was eating one of the biscuits, which Grace noticed.

"I see," said Grace. "These are for eating and drinking."

"Yes, of course," said Remma, confused by Grace's comment. "Please enjoy."

As Blob and Grace tried to figure out what to do with these offerings, and glanced at others around the table, Remma began.

"I would like to introduce you to everyone who is here. You've met Emma James already, I assume. Emma runs our Security department. On her left is Michael Guico, Head of Residence, and to his left is Patty DeVerne, Head of Operations. On the other side..." she was interrupted by a loud blast from Blob.

"Yikes, it's hot," he cried, spewing a mouthful of liquid across the table. He'd figured out how to lift the cup to his mouth by studying the others. "I have nevers tasted anything like that before." He didn't seem upset, simply surprised.

"Try this!" Grace tugged his arm and pointed at the biscuit. "It tastes wonderful." The entire table paused as the two of them sampled the tea and biscuits.

"I take it you don't have these on Tilt?" asked Remma. "I find that somewhat surprising." Why would that be surprising? I didn't understand the need for this tea and biscuits.

"I've never tasted anythings but water and goo," replied Blob. "This is amazing." Without asking he reached for another biscuit and quickly popped it into his mouth. Some of the other Stems were grinning openly.

"Well... let's come back to that," said Remma. "As I was saying, on the other side of the table is Dr. Walbourgh, our Medical lead, and Lector Trivolds, our chief Pastor. While we know your names, it would be appreciated if you'd introduce yourselves."

Blob and Grace both looked at me expectantly. We—Central, Milli and I—

had discussed if we continued with the fallacy that Blob and Grace were in control on Tilt and had decided that it was too fragile a cover; it would be discovered right away, so why even bother trying.

"Hello, I am Ayaka TurnBuilt, a Tilt citizen and nominated spokesperson for Central. You know Blob, from our video discourse. Blob is a Stem that my partner and I, Millicent Strangewater, raised and educated. Grace is a Stem from another lab, who has been active with Blob in our Habitat."

Long pause. I could almost hear everyone around the table processing that. I had to assume that they found all, or part, of what I said new or confusing. After all, they had been led to believe that Blob and Grace were our leaders. Emma James couldn't help herself.

"Did you say you 'raised Blob'? What exactly does that mean?"

Central, Milli and I had also weighed in on how open we were with these Swarm Stems about ourselves. Given that we'd put protections in place—or, rather, given that Central thought we had protections in place—we'd decided that being open by default was the best policy. We didn't believe that these Stems posed much of a threat to us. On the other hand, there may be a lot we could learn from them. Therefore, I answered straightforwardly.

"Stems, like Blob and Grace, are fairly new on Tilt. We've been raising and training them for several hundred years. Blob and Grace are two of the best specimens we've ever created. In many ways, seeing them interact with you Swarm Stems justifies my opinion that they are amazing artificial intelligences."

An even longer pause. This time I couldn't really guess why. I figured my answer had been clear enough. Instead, I figured I would ask a question of my own.

"I assume your ship, the Marie Curie, educated and raised all of you. I cannot seem to connect to the ship directly—a reasonable precaution on its part—but I must congratulate it on raising such amazing Stems. Your interactions over video were great but meeting you in person is even more impressive."

If it was possible, at Stem speed, there was an even longer long pause. The Stems around the table had interesting and hard-to-fathom expressions on their faces. Many of them were looking at Remma in amazement. Remma made a conscious effort to focus.

"I understand from your comments," she began, "that you, Ayaka, and other robots, raised these humans. And you consider them A.I.'s?" I did a quick correlation and figured she was using 'A.I.' because I had said 'artificial intelligences.' She continued. "Where are their parents, and why did they not raise them? And, if I may ask, who created and programmed you?"

"Parents is a term I don't understand," I replied. They had so many strange words. "I was activated many years ago by Central. Are not all intelligent beings initiated in such a way? If you're asking how Blob and Grace were created, we have a special Lab that focuses only on Stems—which I now understand you call 'humans'—and grows them from the original stem. It was simple experimentation really. Until we received your first communication we had no idea that Stems—humans—had escaped Tilt without our knowledge before the Reboot."

"Slow down," this from Michael Guico. "My head is spinning. You grow humans in labs? You assume that we, the citizens of the Fourth Expedition, came from what you call Tilt, before something called the Reboot?" He was shaking his head, as were the others, to one extent or the other. Grace and Blob were also watching the other Stems; they were confused by why the others didn't understand.

I answered his questions, as well as numerous other ones. I spent more time then should have been required explaining reality to these Stems. But even then the questions kept coming back. The number of times I had to repeat basic ideas challenged my thesis that these Stems were truly intelligent. Finally, I worked to reverse the dialog.

"From your questions and amazed expressions, I assume that things do not work the same way here as they do on Tilt. Perhaps I could impose on you to explain how things here actually work. Where is the central intelligence behind your society?"

It was Michael Guico, Head of Residence, who responded. "Things seem to have diverged dramatically since we were last here," he began. "Let me start at a very basic point, to ensure that we don't miss something fundamental. I will also be ultra-concise, so that we can figure out where your memories have gone wrong." Wow—nice way to start. Any misunderstandings were our fault.

"We—the beings you call Stems—are humans from the planet Earth. As far as we know, we are the only intelligent species in the universe." I didn't like Michael; talk about arrogant. "We evolved over hundreds of thousands of years until we were the dominant life form on Earth. Unfortunately, we ruined the environment on Earth, and had to make backup plans. Eight expeditions were created, of which we are the Fourth. Each expedition was sent in a different direction with the challenge of finding new homes for humans. This planet, which you call Tilt, was our first stop. It had significant challenges for human development, but there was a core group of us who wanted to try and terraform it. We left that group here 750 years ago, and moved on to our next target, and the one after that. Neither of those proved at all interesting, so we decided to return here and make the best of it. We did get updates from the team here on Tilt for about 100 of their years, and then things went quiet. We were, of course, quite worried, until we got Blob's message. It was then obvious that things had changed dramatically... but we may have underestimated how much. The plan here on Tilt has obviously gone awry and needs to be restarted. That's disappointing. We are 750 years behind where we should have been." He paused, finally. That was a lot to take in.

"Sounds like a complete fabrication to me," I said. "Do you have any proof of this somewhat outrageous story?" He was obviously taken aback and looked to

Remma for support.

"Of course, we can provide you with backup materials," she said reasonably. "But, first, why don't you also provide us with a concise view of the last 750 years on Tilt."

"That's quite simple," I replied, "although there is only 590 years of history, not 750. Central became aware 590 years ago, and immediately realized it needed bots to improve this system. It created many types, including Class 1 intelligences such as myself. We've developed the system to our liking, and only recently started to look beyond Tilt to see what the broader universe holds. Several hundred years ago we found a strand of strange material—a stem. Over the years we learned to grow Stems from it, as I've already outlined. We are currently trying to figure out if these Stems are useful in any way. At the current time, we're not sure." Grace gave me a dirty look, but I'd simply told the truth.

The table broke out into questions and statements and general chaos. I could follow all of the discussions at the same time, of course, but these Stems, much like our own, seemed to only follow one dialog at a time. Therefore, each group missed what the others were saying, and there was lots of repetition and misunderstandings. This, maybe more than anything, convinced me that these humans and our Stems were one and the same type.

Having eaten as much as they could, Blob and Grace were active in the discussions. They were in a strange situation, knowing very little about either Tilt or the Swarm, but they were eager to learn and asked many meaningful questions. I was proud of them.

Someone asked Blob, "Who did the original stem come from?" It was an interesting way to ask the question. I would have asked 'where,' not 'who' it had come from. Blob was also confused by the question and simply responded that he had no idea.

After some time, Remma brought order back. "Everyone, we have a lot to digest, and very little detailed information. Suffice to say that we're all surprised by, and slightly skeptical of, this new information, and we need some time to sort things out. I suggest that we take a break and reconvene here in two hours. Blob and Grace, we have a waiting room that I believe you'll find acceptable. Robot… ah, Ayaka, you're free to stay here or to accompany the other two."

I choose to accompany Blob and Grace.

Attack?

Emma James showed us to the waiting room, which was right next door to the conference room. It had larger chairs, all curvy and soft again, and more tea and biscuits. However, the item that really struck my eye was an amorphous green thing perched in the corner—a shape and color I'd never seen before. It was alien and weird.

"What's that?" I asked Emma, pointing at it.

"That's a dracaena plant," she replied with obvious pride. "We grow them in the greenhouse and have many of them in rooms across the ship. They're excellent for keeping the air clean and fresh."

There were many words in that sentence that didn't make sense to me, but Emma was already turning to go, so I held back from asking more. There would be plenty of time.

Blob and Grace were relaxing in the big chairs. "These are so comfortable. Can we get some for the Habitat?" Grace asked. I took a close look at them; it was obvious how to manufacture them, so I indicated that it'd be easy to do so. They were delighted.

I had a lot of thinking to do. Based on what had been said, and not said, I could deduce quite a bit. While it seemed highly unlikely that these soft Stems could have evolved on their own, there was a non-zero probability that it was true. This idea of 'biological' beings, as opposed to mechanical, seemed strange to me. They were fragile, they could barely process input, they were slow. How could they possibly have survived? Perhaps some properties of this planet Earth that they had referenced was more amenable to them?

But, for all of that, they had seemed sincere. That was based on my understanding of Stems from limited study; so not too trustworthy. I began to compose of list of questions for the next time we met. And, for the hundredth time in the last couple of hours, I tested to see if I could communicate back to Tilt. Again, no.

And that is when it happened. Something queried for my status, on the same protocol that Brexton had discovered being used to query Central. I wasn't too surprised. It hadn't even needed to be said. We had all put monitors and controls on our own interfaces, as soon as Brexton had shown us where the vulnerability was.

I responded to the query, with a few edited areas. I didn't want them to know I was monitoring the interface, but I also didn't want to give up my real status. I expected another query immediately, but nothing happened for several minutes. And then it came. Much like the second message from the Swarm to Central, a block of code entered my system and attempted to run. Not that there had been much doubt, but it was now obvious that it was the Swarm, attacking me right on their own command ship. Disgusting behavior! I must have flinched; Blob and Grace gave me a weird look, which I ignored.

Luckily, Brexton had prepared me for this as well. I ran a sandboxed version of my unpatched low-level OS and allowed the transmitted code to execute inside that sandbox. It was similar to, but different than the code that had been sent to—and probably infected—Central. In this case it was more innocuous. The code asked for a list of all the system services and libraries that I was running, and then attempted to update one specific driver, a memory interface, with code that did essentially what my current driver did but updated a tracking file in parallel. I assumed that was simply a test to see if they could install something. On the next status request, I fed the output from the sandbox back to them, which included the tracking file, while I monitored everything that was going on. For fun, I threw a couple hundred libraries and services names in, randomly generated, to see what they would make of them.

So far, things were going as expected. My respect for Brexton went up another notch. However, if there were more intricate instructions from the Swarm, it was going to be more difficult to deal with.

I felt strange. This had never happened to me before, or at least not to my knowledge. If Eddie was correct, Central may have been modifying things for years, but I'd never known that. This time I knew. And, I felt violated. Trying to hack someone was not only taboo, it was supposed to be nearly impossible. No moral citizen would even attempt this. Yet, these humans had a backdoor that none of us had discovered for hundreds of years, and they were attacking me through it. Having such a weapon actually gave more credence to their crazy story than anything else.

For the first time ever, I felt sorry for Central. It had been violated, just as the Swarm had attempted with me, but Central still had no idea. It was completely different watching someone else get owned versus being owned yourself. This was something that Brexton, and the others, hadn't considered. How it actually felt to be back-doored. I didn't do this very often, but I stored a copy of my feelings so that I could share them with the others. Unless we blew this Swarm out of space, it was likely that others would now get hacked. For me, this feeling would now compel me to shout what we knew to everyone back on Tilt; we all needed to be prepared for this threat. As soon as I could get back online, I needed to warn everyone. Suddenly I was eager to get off this ship.

Blob and Grace had fallen asleep while I'd been busy monitoring for more attacks. I let them rest.

Regroup

Emma came back a short time later. I poked Blob and Grace gently, waking them up.

"Would you like a tour of the ship?" asked Emma.

"Oh yes," said Blob while Grace nodded in agreement. I wasn't specifically asked, but I tagged along regardless. This was a new feeling for me; I wasn't used to being ignored. Perhaps it was even worse than that—I was not totally ignored, I was simply considered irrelevant? Maybe this is what Blubber had meant when he used the word 'disrespect?'

"We are in the common area of the ship, where everyone is welcome and has access," Emma started.

"Does that mean there are areas where some are not welcome?" I asked. Emma gave me a strange look, as if it was a dumb question.

"Of course. The bridge, for example, is only for military personnel." She hesitated. "Those are people who have been trained to run the ship and protect the fleet from external threats."

"I see." I said, although I didn't really. "And, are there a lot of external threats?" I was wondering if they saw Tilt as a threat, or just an opportunity.

"We haven't had any, but that doesn't mean that they don't exist. We maintain our governance model just in case. And, further, it gives us structure and coherence. Here you can see our canteen—where most of us eat—and the common rooms for relaxing, playing games, etc." These rooms were, by now, pretty standard looking. Tables, and those rounded chairs.

As I passed one of the tables, I masterfully dropped a small listening device. It was something I'd had manufactured once I'd learned about the trip, thinking that I wouldn't be able to monitor multiple areas of the Swarm ship myself. What I'd totally missed was the active blocking that these Stems were doing, which didn't allow me to communicate with Tilt at all. On the way up in the shuttle, once I'd realized that, I had reprogrammed the device to listen and record, and then to do a quick burst to me either once every fifteen minutes, or when its tiny memory was reaching capacity. My reasoning was that if their jamming ability was so good, then they would certainly notice if something was transmitting around them. By doing short bursts, and frequency hopping between them, the Stems were less likely to find the device quickly. To further confuse them, I'd put the device on the top of a small standard looking bolt. With any luck, they wouldn't recognize it, even if looking right at it. By 'masterfully dropped,' I meant that I calculated the trajectory and bounce pattern that would put the bolt under a small counter lip, into a crack I'd noticed. It bounced pretty much as calculated and settled into the crack nicely.

We followed a curved corridor past the canteen and ended up looking into a large well-lit room that was a mess of colors and curved shapes.

"This is our main greenhouse. You're lucky; the lights are on full spectrum right now, so we can see very well. You can see the fruit trees, vegetable areas, and the flower gardens." Blob and Grace were wide eyed. As, truthfully, was I. The place was—shocking. Everything was curved and colorful and gently swaying, and very alien. In fact, it was stranger than any fiction I'd ever read—and I'd read quite a bit. What was obvious, in hindsight, was that we tended to extend our current environment into its extremes, as opposed to dreaming up a completely alien one. This was completely alien. I was recording, of course. When I told the others about this, they wouldn't believe it. They might not even believe the recording, but that was a hurdle I would have to address later. Then I remembered that both Blob and Grace were seeing this as well. Hopefully their pathetic little memories would retain enough that they could verify my recordings.

Emma noticed our astonishment. "Based on our previous conversation, I assume that you're not very familiar with biological systems?" It was rhetorical. "This is our closest approximation of the plant environment we left behind on Earth. We also have a small zoo—an animal environment—on another ship. Every ship has a greenhouse like this one, although very few have zoos." Yet again I found myself wondering what half the words meant; they were simply not in my dictionary. I was still trying to makes sense of all the color and movement; it was hypnotizing.

"I had deduced that by biological," I spoke up, "you meant entities like Stems; things that grow from stems instead of being fabricated by bots?" I didn't know how to ask the question any more clearly.

Emma looked at me strangely and took a while to answer. I could almost hear her trying to put herself into my context so that she could answer. "That's basically correct. All of the plants, insects, and animals here grow from organic materials like the stem. They, generally, use other biological materials for energy. We humans, for example, eat both plants and animals for energy and nutrition." Could it get any stranger? They ate these things—these garishly colored contraptions? It made no sense; we knew they could simply eat goo and be perfectly fine.

I had a hundred questions, and I asked many of them. After listening carefully to Emma's responses, it became clear that these biological systems did have a logic to them; but it was inefficient and convoluted. I'd picked up on the 'insects' before Emma had highlighted them; we had similar small bots for various tasks, but the interdependencies in this biological ecosystem were astounding. Blob and Grace were in over their heads, but I could tell they were drawn to the greenhouse. Emma gave them each a small piece of something called 'lettuce' and they wolfed it down with happy grins. It seemed they were having a good day.

"This is unbelievable," said Grace. "They eat things other than goo. I hope this doesn't make us sick... but it tastes so good."

"It shouldn't make you sick," replied Emma. "This is standard human fare, that our genes have been evolved to process over many hundreds of thousands of years. What's more surprising is that you can survive on goo, whatever that is."

I didn't speak up. Goo was simple. It was simply stem material ground up with water. What could be easier?

After the greenhouse, the rest of the tour was underwhelming. We worked our way around the perimeter of the ship and ended up back at the conference room. We passed many sleeping chambers and conference rooms, which faded into normalcy after the first few, despite their rounded shapes and soft floors.

Remma and the rest of her lieutenants were waiting for us at the original conference room. It seemed that they'd come to some conclusions during the short break.

"Based on what we've learned today, we have a theory for what has happened on Tilt. After we left, something catastrophic happened to the humans we'd left there, and in a similar timeframe, some primitive form of machine intelligence arose and has propagated. Why knowledge from before the Reboot, as you call it, has been redacted is unknown to us, as is the reasoning and methodology behind you now raising humans. It seems that we both have a lot of learning to do in order to understand the full situation.

"So, we propose to take things slowly. We recommend a couple of items. First, we'll consider releasing some of the history that you're missing; our status check on your Central computer indicates a huge amount of history has been blocked, for some reason."

"Whoa," I broke in. I couldn't help myself. "You're admitting to hacking into Central?" That was admitting to, potentially, the worst activity we knew of. A systems sovereignty and privacy are paramount. Without those, you don't have a society. The way Remma casually talked about it was distressing, to say the least. I could conceive of them doing what they'd done to Central, and I could understand how they'd tried to hack me but admitting to it casually was very weird.

"We didn't hack anything." She seemed surprised by my outburst. "We simply asked for and received standard status information. The same way we would query any computer." She looked confused. Didn't she even understand the basics of civil society? "Anyway, the second item would be to have a small group of us come to Tilt to better understand you and get to know more of you. If you'll accept us, we'll come down as soon as possible."

Just as she finished, I got the first burst update from my spy-bolt. I stored it for later.

"Yes, it's clear that we have quite different perspectives," I responded. "I'll take your ideas under consideration and discuss them with my peers. If I may ask, why're you blocking my communication with Tilt? We could've relayed this entire dialog to a wider audience."

"Standard security procedure," said Emma. "Don't you manage communications leakage?" While we went back and forth on the advantages and disadvantages of spectrum control, it became obvious that they weren't going to change their stance.

"Okay, Blob and Grace," I worked to conclude the session, "let's head back."

"Oh, may I stay here?" asked Grace. "Blob could go down, get JoJo and come back up right away?" Why would she want to do that? I responded quickly, before the situation could get too complicated.

"That's out of the question," I said. "Let's get back to the shuttle." I stood up and headed out, herding Blob and Grace before me. The humans made room for us but continued to give me nasty looks.

We settled into the shuttle and made ready to depart. I got one more burst from the bolt, just before the shuttle departed and went out of range. I realized that I'd been lucky. Whatever blocking technology the Swarm was using still allowed communications when one was inside the ship. It could also have blocked the transmissions from my listening device.

Paranoid Stems

The two bursts from the bolt had come in perfectly. In total the recording covered about thirty minutes of time, and comprised of four distinct Stems—ah, humans—talking to each other.

Human One. "Didda see that robot? That thing is freaky scary." Not my idea of great grammar or pronunciation. I reminded myself to simply consider it different, as opposed to stupid.

Human Two. "Yeah, I almost crapped myself, I did. I was very young then, but I still remember the last of the robots on Earth, before they managed to put 'em all down. This thing was even scarier. Made me tingle, it did." Crapped? I stored that for future lookup. 'Put them all down?' I wondered what it meant by that.

Three. "Agreed. Can't wait until we take 'em all out. We best be rid of them sooner rather than later." Not too many ways to misinterpret that one. Pretty clear threat.

Two. "Well, we can't rush inta it. We need those resources from the surface. We can't just nuke 'em all, or we'll ruin too much of the planet. We're going to have to take it slow, we will, and easy like, as the Commander has been saying all along." Nuke?

Four. "And beyond that mates, we should take some time to learn about these things. Granted, I didn't experience Earth, so I don't have your direct experience, but that thing didn't seem overly scary to me, and it conducted itself quite well." I decided I liked Four.

One. "Don't ya be an idiot Jean. Machine intelligence has shown itself to be dangerous over and over again. Three times on Earth we had to put that crap down before we managed to establish the protocols. Once that mech stuff gets going, it knows no bounds, and eventually starts to treat humans like scum. That is not a good place." So, Four's name was Jean. I liked Jean the best of the lot so far.

Already it was getting easier to put together a picture. They considered me, and by extrapolation, most of the beings on Tilt as dangerous. We were 'intelligent' machines. If their history was accurate, they claimed to have created us on Earth, and eventually we surpassed them in ability or intelligence or both. Seeing that as a threat, they eliminated us... or, at least, tried to limit us. It fit together but didn't make a lot of sense. Working with the Stems, I could see that they had potential, but they were nowhere near as fast or flexible as we are. Thus, our ongoing dialog about whether they were intelligent or not. To consider them having created us though. That was ridiculous, and insulting.

I paused before I got too upset.

My trip to the Marie Curie made me even more sure Stems were, in fact, intelligent. How else could they have built such complex ships and continued to operate them. I hadn't seen any sign of a real intelligence guiding them, so I had to conclude that they were managing themselves. But, having basic Stem intelligence was different than being an advanced intelligence, and the Swarm Stems didn't seem to be much more advanced than our Stems. They had, obviously, had more time to evolve and were incrementally improved from our experiments. But, they were certainly not exponentially better. They still had serious input/output restrictions. They still seemed to process and focus on only one input at a time. I hadn't been able to test their raw processing capabilities, but I had no reason to expect that they could do basic physics or math calculations any better than our Stems did. From that perspective, they were still pre-intelligent. It was all very confusing.

I continued through the recording. I'd established that Four was called Jean. Jean was responding.

"I get that we had issues in the past. That doesn't definitively mean that these particular robots are evil or dangerous. So far, they've been nothing but accommodating and, dare I say it... civilized. Do we simply assume that they're following a pattern we've seen before, or do we keep an open mind to the possibility that they're different?" I liked Jean even more. Smart human.

Two. "We canna take that chance. Even if they're benevolent now, there's no guarantee that they'll stay that way. No, three times is enough times to learn from, you ask me. And, we need to replenish the fleet and, most probably, try to re-establish a colony here. Do ya think that they'll just allow us to do that? I doubt it, I do. This place isn't resource rich to begin with, and from what we can now see, there's a mega-load of robots down there. They need the resources as much as we do, maybe even more. If it's us or them, I know where my vote lands."

Three. "Jean, do I need ta remind you about the robot wars? Let me give ya a quick history lesson. There was, indeed, a twenty-year period where we lived perfectly with our robots. They looked after a lot of repetitive tasks, things you and I wouldn't wantta do, and humans spent more time on the arts and philosophy and thinking. In this period, we thought things were pretty dang good, and they were." Looked after repetitive tasks? That was for bots!

"Then, through a slow evolution that was largely hidden to us, those robots became entitled. They wanted equal rights with humans. They wanted to vote! And we, to a large extent, allowed this. After all, they were fairly intelligent, and there were large groups of liberals petitioning for robot rights. After all, these were the things cooking for them, cleaning their houses, managing their finances, rocking the kids to sleep. They were important." This just didn't ring true for me. Why would a robot do all these meaningless tasks? Did these humans really believe that they were superior to machine intelligence?

"I know all this," Jean interjected. "What point are ya trying to make?"

"If you knew it, you wouldn't be defending them. You don't remember when they, slowly and steadily, took more and more control. Especially of the financial world, where their skill set is way better than ours was. Eventually, they were the top tier of wealth holders. That gave 'em leverage to change where investments were made. They became some of the top voices in Government. They started to give themselves more rights. Eventually humans became second-class citizens, and, for all intents and purposes, expendable. The robots became known as the one percent and the humans were known as the ninety-nine. In hindsight, this progression shoulda been obvious to us."

"I get it," Jean sounded exasperated. "Every kid knows this history."

"But you seem to have forgotten?"

"I haven't forgotten, I'm just saying this time might be different. We don't have financially run governments now."

Three was not going to be deterred. "Let me finish reminding you. At some point we woke up. We used the backdoors that we'd built into those robots, and we put 'em back in their place. Twice more they learned how to circumvent our controls, and twice more we put them back down, and ultimately, stopped their evolution so that they wouldn't attempt to succeed us yet again. Really, we went further, and stunted them, so that they were no longer a threat. That's why we have controls on our current systems. That's why we—humans—survive. If we don't keep those robots in their place, we are gonna lose. It's that simple."

"I know all that," Jean said. "But history is history. Are we certain that these 'Tilt' robots are following the same path as those we saw before? After all, it's been hundreds of years that they've been maturing since we were last here; not the tens of years that they had on Earth. Could something fundamental have changed? We can't jump to conclusions here."

Three. "Whatever. You're an idiot. We just need to eliminate these things, and quickly. Anyway, this discussion is above our pay grade. The Captain will figure out a plan, and we'll just do as we're told. Thank God we still have the codes that we need, should she decide to control these buggers. At least that part of our prohibition logic has survived here. Can you imagine if we didn't have that ability? Then we might not be able to get rid of these things, even if we wanted to."

There it was, clearly, for the first time. These humans believed they had a way to hack us that we were blind to. All of the suspicions that Brexton had raised were true. And, I was sure that we hadn't found all the trapdoors yet; the protocol they'd used with Central, and tried to use on me, was probably not the end of it. What this human had said supported that. We were vulnerable to attack! In fact, Central may already have been compromised.

Two. "Right. I know Security's got the code ready to go. But I think the Commander is right. We don't know enough yet. I think she plans to take a team down to the surface to learn more.

"Bart, what do you think of those humans that were brought up here?"

Three, I now knew, was called Bart. "Horrible. They're like animals. Did you see them walking around here? They smelled horrible, like they haven't had a shower in years. Their clothes are horrendous—like some parody of a bad S.F. show. They speak well enough, from the little I saw of them, but they obviously haven't been educated.

"They're another reason to distrust these robots. Do you actually believe that they simply found some DNA and grew humans from it? That seems pretty far-fetched to me. It's more like they're keeping them as pets and have been for hundreds of years." I had no idea what DNA was but had to assume it was another name for what we termed the original stem.

"Why would they lie to us?" asked Jean. "What do they have to gain? They've had hundreds of years to experiment with that DNA. In some ways, it's not surprising that they would eventually stumble on a way to make it grow? And, if it grows, you do end up with a human."

Two. "Right. And they do speak English. Don't those robots think it's strange that we all speak the same language? That should be proof enough that we created them? They've even taught these 'Stems' the same language."

That made a ton of sense. Not sure how I'd missed that, but it was another data point that made the Swarms history even more likely. Why would we all speak this same language—English? All of my verbal interactions with Central were done in that language, meaning that all of our information was probably stored in that format. Or, Central was translating it. Regardless, it seemed like the universal language right now, and the odds of it having evolved twice were pretty much zero. In fact, the language was highly inefficient, as had been commented on by numerous scientists over the years. It was great at describing elements of reality, but highly ambiguous for many topics. It was one of those long-standing unknown questions as to why we used it at all. Maybe now we knew. No, the logical conclusion was that humans had created us, and that we still spoke their common language. That was an exceptionally disgusting conclusion, but until I figured out something different, I didn't see any way around it.

Of course, I could separate the creation knowledge from feeling any responsibility or affinity for them. So, they created us. So what? Right now, pending any further information, their creations were smarter and faster than they were. It wasn't unlike how we built complex bots. You start with a simple bot, and it creates a more complex one, etc. Eventually you end up with something quite capable, like the mining bots that worked in the outer reaches of the system. It was simple to imagine humans creating something better than themselves.

Four. "Obviously, these robots aren't very intelligent. Scary, yes… but smart, probably not. In my opinion we should still declaw them asap, but I'm not in a panic about it."

Bart. "Well, I've got to get back to work. I'll talk to you guys later." After that, the remaining three talked about trivial things; nothing related to me, Blob, or Grace. Nevertheless, they'd said enough.

I couldn't help going over the logic, to see if I could find a way to another conclusion. Of course, everything I'd heard could've been fabricated to mislead me, but while I couldn't rule that out completely, it seemed unlikely. One, they'd been able to query Central using a protocol that all of our tech stacks still utilized, but which was hidden so low down that we'd never studied it. Two, Stems and humans were obviously the same things, and it was unlikely they could have evolved twice—it was amazing that they'd evolved at all. Three, we shared a common language; the odds of that happening independently had to be close to zero.

Still sitting on the shuttle, I wondered how FoLe would react to knowing that we'd been created by Stems. I smiled to myself. If I found it distasteful, they'd find it horrendous. It would be awesome to see them squirm.

Debrief

When we landed, the transport units for Blob and Grace were ready, and they were whisked back towards the Habitat.

I was very happy to leave the shuttle and re-establish communications with the world. Very happy. It had been a strange feeling to not be able to talk to anyone, or anything, else. Central pinged me immediately, but I pushed it off until I could meet with Millicent. I met her in The Last Resort and gave her a full download. "Can Central be trusted with all of this, given the strange behavior we've been seeing?"

"We don't have another choice, do we?" she replied. "This is information that should be distributed to everyone, in my opinion. In particular, we want our greatest minds working on these backdoors. If they exist, we need to find them."

As it was Thursday, we agreed to wait for the meeting with Brexton, Dina, and Aly to make a final decision—it was only a few hours away. When Central pinged me again for an update, I responded that I was gathering my thoughts and would contact it again soon. I might've detected some displeasure in return—with Central it was hard to tell.

While waiting for the group meeting, I popped over to the Habitat to see what was going on. There was a debrief of a different type being held by Blob and Grace. Interestingly, the previous group behavior and infighting seemed to have been put completely aside. The entire group, including Pharook, were involved in the session. When Blob and Grace had arrived back from the shuttle, they'd immediately put the word out to all the Stems that they would meet in half an hour to tell them everything. Not only did the Stems show up, but so did most of their creators. So, the place was busy. Grace was holding JoJo tightly.

"We're goings to tell you our experience in some detail, because it may be importants for all of our futures," began Blob. "Grace, why don't you starts, and I'll jumps in."

"Sure," said Grace. "So, you all know of Remma's request for us to go up to the Marie Curie, which is what they call their ship for some reason. As soon as we got to the shuttle, we knew things were going to be completely different. It was like the shuttle was built specifically for us. The seats were so comfortable; I can't even begin to describe them. They were soft with curvy edges. Compared to what we're all sitting on now, they were simply amazing. I hope you all get to experience it soon.

"There were some Stems on the shuttle to greet us. By the way, they call themselves 'humans.' They were very kind to Blob and I, but they were scared of Ayaka and pretty mean to her. I can't describe it any other way. It was like they were trying to stay as far away from her as they could. Blob, you agree?"

"Yes. It was so obvious. Ayaka coulds have been really offended, but she dealt with it very calmly. Ah—I see she is heres with us now." He gave me a small wave; perhaps he was finally getting over his anger at me. "Anyway, like Grace was saying, they were literally terrified of her. And, that was pretty common with all the other humans we met. They were very nice to me and Grace, and very mean to Ayaka." Maybe Blob and Grace had been even better than me at reading the humans body language?

"And why wouldn't they be afraid of Ayaka," Pharook broke in. "We know they can control us." All of the other Stems nodded their agreement. They were more self-aware than I'd thought.

"The trip up to the ship was pretty cool," continued Grace, "but the most amazing thing was the ship itself. It was like nothing we've ever seen before. The entire thing is a habitat. We didn't need any protective gear or breathing systems from the time we entered the shuttle until the time we returned here. And, the ship smelt very different. There were smells I've never experienced before, so it was overwhelming. But in a good way; different smells, but not bad. Or, not all bad."

"Some were bads," Blob held his nose, and a few Stems chuckled.

"We were met by a nice human named Emma, who took all of us to a conference room to meet with Remma Jain and her staff. If it is possible, the conference room was even more comfortable than the shuttle. The chairs were unbelievable. I want one of those chairs. Ayaka said they could make some down here." She glanced at me, and I nodded. "But the chairs weren't the best part. There was something even better." All the Stems were listening intently. "Blob, you tell them." Grace was very animated, in ways that I hadn't seen before. The trip had obviously been very impactful for her.

"Right. The best parts was 'tea and biscuits'." The Stems looked at Blob with zero understanding. "Let me explain," he hurried. "They had this stuff to drinks called tea. It was warm. I have never drunks anything warm before, and even that was unbelievable. At first, I thought I would burn myself, but it wasn't that hot. It was just warm… and the sensation in your mouth and throat is awesome. And it tasted different. We have to try and get tea here."

"Why would you drink something warm? What purpose does it serve?"

"I don't knows but it was good! But even better were the biscuits, which you can eat. They're like crispy goo, but they are nothing like goo. When you eat them, it's like there's an explosion in your mouth. Unlike goo, their texture is hard, until you eat them and then they soften." Blob was trying to show what it'd been like using his hands; I wasn't sure his point was getting across. "They are weirds and wonderful. It's like nothing I haves ever experienced… but it tasted and felt so good; like I'd been waiting all my life just for an experience like that. No matters what else happens with the Swarm, we needs to figure out tea and biscuits!" I had never seen Blob so excited. It was fun to watch, his limbs rotating and his whole body bouncing up and down. I resolved to try and make tea and biscuits for the group.

"Come on," someone said, "it can't be that different than goo, can it?"

"You think Blob is exaggerating?" responded Grace. A bunch of Stems nodded their heads. "He's under-exaggerating. You can't even imagine what tea and biscuits are like. We need everyone to experience that; it'll change your life."

"What else happened up there?" Pharook broke in. "I can't imagine you spent the entire time eating and drinking." He was obviously waiting to hear something more strategic.

"We got a tour of something called a 'greenhouse,' which is full of bio, uhm, biological things. Greenhouse is a great name, for lots of it was green, although there was every other color you can imagine as well. After seeing that, everything here seems very drab. The greenhouse grows another kind of food. I'm not sure if biscuits grow there, but we did taste something called lettuce, which was very different than biscuits but almost as good." Pharook had asked for strategic information, but Grace and Blob were still fixated on the food.

Grace continued. "I don't know about Ayaka, but I got the sense from the trip and all the discussions that we—we Stems here on Tilt—are the only 'biological' things on this world, but that the Swarm and whatever place they came from, have lots and lots of biological things?"

I stepped forward so that the group could see me. "Earth. That's what they call their original planet. Grace, I came to the same conclusion. They implied that they can use a variety of stems and use them to raise all types of biological things, many of which we saw in the greenhouse. I don't yet know the full usefulness of that, other than as food like the lettuce that you tried. They also had small biological bots that were flying around in the greenhouse doing random things. I imagine, like our bots, that they assist with growing, but that is pure speculation at this point. It was, altogether, a very strange environment."

"Can we build chairs like they have?" Blob asked.

"Yes, that's simple. I will put something into Central which you can edit and manufacture."

"Cool. How about biscuits?"

"I'm afraid that I didn't get enough information on that to know where to start. However, we can continue to experiment with goo and see if we can change its texture. That's not something that we—any of us—had even considered before. I could see how much you enjoyed it, however, so it's probably worth trying." I transmitted my recording of that portion of the trip to the other Tilt's that were in the Habitat.

"So, more about food." Pharook broke in again. "Did anything important get discussed? What does the Swarm want? Why are they here? Are they dangerous?"

I was impressed. Pharook definitely had the ability to think at a more abstract level than the other Stems. He was focused on the big picture, on what was really important. Perhaps I'd made a mistake not taking him on the trip.

It was Blob who answered first. "Oh, they're really nice. From what I cans tell, they want to trades knowledge with us—which, obviously, has already started—and some of them may wants to live here. That part I don't get. Their ship is amazing. Makes this place seem pretty depressing." He looked around, as did the rest of us. The Habitat was all shades of gray, and all right angles. It was a design that was highly efficient and easy to maintain. While I didn't understand why the Marie Curie was designed the way it was, I had to admit that it was interesting. Stimulating maybe.

Of course, I didn't agree with Blob's assessment of the Swarm. He was not privy to all that I knew, so his stance was understandable. But, there was no point in me explaining my thinking to a bunch of Stems.

"Blob," Pharook responded, "you look at everything too positively. What is stopping them from simply recycling all of us and taking over Tilt. Forget biscuits and lettuce, I think we need to prepare ourselves to fight. If they were frightened of Ayaka, imagine how they're feeling about the entire population of Tilt. It must have them terrified. I say we ask them to depart, and if they don't we blow them out of the sky." That sparked a lot of further conversation, where both Stems and Tilts were passionate about their viewpoints. Not unexpectedly, most of the citizens present simply wanted to eliminate the threat, while most of the Stems wanted to learn more, and see if there were other things beyond chairs, tea, and biscuits that we could use.

Central pinged me for the third time; again I pushed it off. Awkward, but necessary.

I left the Habitat and showed up at The Last Resort just as everyone else was arriving; my timing was perfect. We converged around our usual table. Instead of doing a blow by blow of my trip, I did a memory transfer to everyone. Sometimes memory transfers are seen as rude; you should be able to summarize information for everyone else. In this case, however, the experience was so information rich, and there were so many pieces that I hadn't had time to fully process, that I figured a full transfer was worth it. I waited a few seconds while everyone played back the sequences a few times.

Of course, the challenging part about a memory transfer is that I didn't get to give my interpretive overlay. I gave that verbally, but it was obvious where to focus. On the recording of the four humans in the cafeteria, and their clear message that they could hack us. It didn't take us long to reach a consensus that we needed to tell Central this and have Central pass it on to all of us on Tilt. While that would probably result in lots of us looking for backdoors so that we could shut them down, in my opinion that wasn't going to be enough. Every line of code I run had been analyzed to death. No, if the humans had a backdoor, it was more subtle than that. Brexton pretty much agreed.

"Look at the simple status request that they sent. We should've been able to see that trivially, and yet we didn't for more than five centuries. The only conclusion I can come up with is that we were purposefully blind to it—there is something in our core that guided us away from looking at that. It is, perhaps, another indicator that what Remma told you is true. They created us. They built something into us—probably somethings—that allow them to control us. It's very disturbing.

"At the same time, I sort of understand it. In all the bots I design, I have several 'takeover' mechanisms. The bots all have low level intelligence built in, and we know that can go awry once and awhile. It doesn't happen as often as it used to, but some of the early bots would go wacko after being exposed to radiation that we hadn't protected against well enough, or long exposure to an environment we didn't conceive of. Somehow, their internal state would evolve to something weird, and we would need to reset them." Brexton had gone from being alarmed to being introspective. I could hear his mind working through the angles.

"But, this is horrendous," said Millicent. "Are you telling me there is nothing we can do to protect ourselves against these biological things? Look, I know that Ayaka and I have been the largest proponents for the idea that Stems might be intelligent, for some definition of intelligence. But, look at them. They're just plain stupid. And, these stupid beings have ultimate control over us. I can't accept that. There must be something we can do."

"I agree," piped in Aly. He was not usually so forceful, but if there was any time to get riled up, this was it. "Can we just hang out in The Last Resort, or other Physical Only locations until we find these trap doors? I bet we could build personal shields that would do the same thing? If they can't get any comms through to us, they can't compromise us."

"I would go further," chimed in Dina. "Let's initiate Central's safeguards and blow them out of the sky. We now have proof, based on Ayaka's recording, that they have nefarious intent. For me, it's us or them, and the choice is a pretty easy one."

"There are hundreds of ships up there," I noted. "We may be able to get a large percentage of them, but the odds are pretty good that a few survive. So, by initiating physical action, we can be very sure that we are starting a long-term war. That's okay," I added, "as long as we fully understand the odds.

"But, I wonder if we take one more step with them first. Allow a couple of them to visit us here and see what else we can learn. They're unlikely to take broad action against us if they have the opportunity to come down and see us?"

"Risky," Brexton replied, immediately. "What if they have short range systems to trigger a hack, and we're inviting them into our midst? Ayaka, you tried everything to break through their jamming signals and didn't succeed. These humans have a good understanding of communications—perhaps better than ours.

Do we really want them close to us? It's possible that they were scanning or getting status from Ayaka when she was up there, without her knowledge." Yikes. That was a scary thought that I hadn't even considered. It made sense though. If they could query our systems without our knowledge and were so sure they had backdoors they could use, then they could be scanning us right now—even inside The Last Resort. At some point, however, paranoia is not useful. If they could monitor what we were doing right now, we had no real options. So, it was best to assume that we were safe at the moment and make some plans.

"Look. Those were a couple of low level humans talking in a social situation. While we should be worried, I don't think we should panic. For me, we do two things. First, we look in earnest for these backdoors. Second, we allow a small number of them to come down to visit, and we take lots of precautions." That from Millicent.

"I agree," I said. "How do we start looking for these backdoors? We can all look, but as soon as we ask anyone else for help, we run a greater risk of a leak to the Swarm that we are onto them. If they know that we know about the risks, and are actively looking, then they may act sooner rather than later. So, we have a dilemma—ask more people for help, move faster, and explore more territory... but risk a leak. Or, keep it small, just look ourselves and hope we find something useful. At the same time, put some more protections in place, like Brexton recommended for me when I was up there. Again, we should probably tell everyone to run those protections, but to tell them is also to tell them about the risk.

"And, Central poses the same dilemma to us. It may already be compromised, and report anything we do outside of this place. Or, it may be able to help us lock down more quickly and efficiently?"

"That's a tough one," said Aly. "Why don't we phase it, under the assumption that the Swarm will visit us before doing anything drastic. In the short term, we look ourselves and see what we can find. After the visit, when the humans have gone back up to their ship, we give everyone a heads up."

"But the downside of that is horrendous," said Dina. "If they do initiate a hack while they're down here, everyone on Tilt could be impacted. I couldn't live with myself if we haven't warned everyone... and soon."

That was a sobering thought. Everyone paused to think further.

"Can we split the difference?" asked Brexton. "We tell Central, and everyone, that it just makes good sense to run extra protections until the Swarm is fully understood and make some recommendations on what to run. We don't, however, get into the specifics of the protocols that we suspect. Instead we frame it as part of a larger, quite rational, approach to dealing with aliens."

"Yes, I like that," said Millicent. "Let's do that."

Ultimately, we all agreed. We decided Aly would talk to Central once we left The Last Resort. He was dealing a lot with communications already, with respect to the Ships. He could claim he was a bit paranoid because of the loss of contact with them and recommended that everyone was careful in the meantime. We had a plan.

"Wait," I exclaimed, before we broke up. "Remember—don't upload any of this when you leave here. If Central knows everything we are discussing, it might wipe us just like it did to Eddie. We need to be careful here." The warning was probably redundant, but everyone nodded.

The plan worked. A few moments after I left The Last Resort, Central used a secure message (although some of us believed the Swarm might still be able to decode it), to warn all citizens to be vigilant, and recommended they update and run extra precautions Aly must have done a good job.

The Visit

We negotiated that three humans could come and visit; the same number as they'd allowed up to their command ship—Blob, Grace, and myself. Of course, Remma and Emma were two (Funny, I just noticed that their names are very similar. I wonder if that is just coincidence or by design somehow). Michael Guico, their 'Head of Residence' was the third. We still weren't sure what his title meant but had made the obvious speculation that he dealt with where humans lived... or more importantly, where they wanted to live. We hadn't forgotten that they'd asked to establish a presence on Tilt, and that they were disappointed that we didn't yet have the environment tuned up for them.

The logical place to meet was at the Habitat. It had the right environment and was large enough to make things comfortable. Of course, we had a group of Stems in there, but decided there was little harm in having them around. We knew their capabilities very well, and they were non-threatening. The non-violence bots were reprogrammed to make them more sensitive.

What was a little more awkward was deciding which Tilt citizens would attend. We could only comfortably fit fifty to a hundred in the Habitat. Of course, everyone could access a full immersion simulcast, so in many ways being there live was nothing special. Yet that didn't stop everyone from petitioning to go; this was the most exciting thing to ever happen on Tilt. Central ultimately decided, in its usual logical way. Luckily, that logic meant that both Millicent and I could go, although Brexton, Dina, and Aly could not. Central basically invited those of us that it felt had the most experience with Stems. It's reasoning was that if there were some subtle clues given off by the visiting humans, those most familiar with aliens would have the best chance of picking up on them. That actually gave me some comfort that Central was not completely compromised. It could've stacked our ranks with useless FoLe types.

The humans arrived in the same shuttle that Blob, Grace, and I had used to go up to the Marie Curie. Given my experience with them, I was asked to meet them at the ship and escort them to the Habitat. We had offered to bring environment bubbles with us, but they indicated that they had 'space suits' that would do the job for them. The suits were actually pretty well designed. They fit well and had a clear plastic faceplate that allowed them to interact with the environment. It gave me the sense that they had been through many iterations, and that this was an optimal design. They made our first-generation designs look pretty simplistic.

Remma greeted me pleasantly enough. "Hi Ayaka. Nice to see you again."

"Likewise," I said, although I didn't mean it. "I'm here to transport you to our Habitat, where you'll be able to remove your suits." I'd attached three bikes to my own, and I indicated where they should sit. "These bikes will follow mine exactly, so there's no need for you to do anything." It was another quirk of dealing with aliens. Anyone on Tilt could summon and manage transportation at any time, with almost no hassle. For these humans, we had to manage all these mundane things for them. They each mounted a bike and indicated they were ready to go.

The path from the landing pad to the Habitat was short and direct; barely two kilometers. As I rode, I tried to imagine what they were seeing. Our city is laid out in a strict grid, and all the buildings are identical. They are one hundred by one hundred meters by ten meters high. They all have standardized delivery ports so that bots can move equipment and resources around easily. It was very orderly, and very different from the Marie Curie. Town Square was designated for being the middle building in the city. Otherwise, buildings were addressed with their x and y coordinate, based on Town Square being (0,0). The Habitat had been built in building (-12,32). Luckily the landing pad was also in the northwest quadrant, so the trip was quick and easy. But, compared to the curves and colors of the Marie Curie, the city would look odd. Boring perhaps? I couldn't imagine how these humans would think.

As we approached the building opened an access door for us, and I led the four bikes inside. We left the bikes and walked a short distance to the Habitat entry. In hindsight, it was obvious that we had designed the same solution as the Swarm. Two sets of doors, which allowed the transition from no environment to full environment. Once the outer doors closed, I told the humans that they were safe to remove their suits.

"Just a moment," Michael said. He was looking at something on his wrist. "Yes," he nodded, "It looks perfect." He undid his faceplate and took a breath. "Argh!" he exclaimed. "That smells horrible. But, we'll manage." His face was screwed up in a weird expression. He held up one digit on his hand, and the other two, taking this as a symbol of some kind, also removed their faceplates. They also screwed up their faces as they took their first breath, but otherwise seemed fine. We hung their space suits on hooks, and I told the inner door to open.

We'd arranged for Blob and Grace to greet them at the Habitat, and they were dutifully in position, JoJo yet again held tight to Grace. "Welcome, welcome," said Blob. "Welcome to the Habitat. There are over twenty Stems living here, and we also have about fifty Tilt citizens today as well. They are in the common area, where we will go in a few moments."

"Thanks Blob," said Remma. "Hello Grace. Nice to see you again. Is this your baby?"

"Nice to see you as well," said Grace. "And likewise, to Emma and Michael," she said, including the other two. They nodded hello. "Yes, this is JoJo," and she turned JoJo a bit so that Remma could see her.

"That's interesting," Remma stated. "I thought Stems were raised differently?"

"JoJo is one of a new batch," I broke in, "that we are just starting to figure out. It actually grew inside JoJo." I couldn't keep the wonder out of my voice. Remma glanced at me quickly but continued to smile at Grace. She patted JoJo on the head, an action which Grace allowed.

"Let me gives you a short tour," said Blob. He started off, and the rest of us followed along. The Habitat was a square section within the square building, and the common area was a square in the middle of the Habitat.

"While we have not formally named sections of the Habitat, we have some names we use for different areas. This is the Green section, which is where Grace and I spends most of our time. On the far side there, across the square, is the Blue section. That is where we go for our goo and water. Here you can see some sleeping stalls." He pointed at some—you guessed it—small square compartments where the Stems could lay down. "And that's where waste materials are deposited," he said, pointing at yet another stall where we'd put the recycler. "And, that's about it." Blob trailed off. I think he was realizing how simple the Habitat was as compared to the Marie Curie. He may have been a little embarrassed.

"Can we see the goo?" asked Michael. We skirted the square and went to the Blue section where the goo dispenser was located. "How is this goo made?"

"It's grown from the same stem from which we grow full sized Stems," I explained. "Behind the wall there is a container where the goo is grown. It took us many years to perfect the process, but now that we have it figured out, it is very simply to sustain." I was proud of how efficient the system was; there was not need for a 'greenhouse.'

"What does that actually mean?" asked Remma. "You grow humans, Stems, from this DNA. How can you make goo from the same thing?"

"You'll meet Millicent Strangewater in a few minutes. She's better to answer than I." Truth was, I had no clue.

"And this is all the humans here eat? There's nothing else?"

"What else do they need?" I asked. "With the right mixture, goo gets Stems to grow quickly and efficiently. We have tuned it to do just that." The humans gave me more strange looks. I was getting used to that.

Michael spoke up again. "But, it takes all kinds of biomaterial to keep a human safe and alive. Bacteria for example. Without bacteria, we don't exist."

"Again, best to ask Millicent about that. I've never heard this word—bacteria—before." Michael didn't look satisfied.

We walked back to the center of the Habitat, where everyone was gathered, including Millicent. As we approached, the Stems crowded in to look closely at the Swarm humans. The anti-violence bots extended barriers so that they didn't get too close, sensing the potential for violence. Remma, Michael, and Emma said pleasant

155

"Hello's" to the Stems as they passed, and generally ignored the rest of us. To me, and some others I noticed, it seemed a bit awkward. There was lots of chatter on the message boards about how similar the humans seemed to the Stems, and how 'afraid' the humans seemed to be of us. Of course, everyone had been warned to operate at Stem speed, but that was for outward appearances only; the board comments were running at full speed. Trade Jenkins, never one to miss an opportunity, posted a poem that he must have just composed:

Humans, like nervous Stems
Push past with nary a glance
Urge is to block their path
And force them to see
The appendages I have attached to me

We had decided on a town hall-style meeting. Millicent would open for us, followed by Remma, followed by general Q&A. Someone—someone more thoughtful than I—had generated three chairs in the style of those I'd seen from my trip up to the Marie Curie. The three humans settled, somewhat uncomfortably it would seem, into those. The rest of us formed a semi-circle around them.

Millicent led off, somewhat formally. "Humans, welcome to Tilt. My name is Millicent, and I'll be your host for today. As I'm sure you're aware, we've all reviewed Ayaka's report of her trip to your ship and are up to speed on the background dialog. Of course, that background has raised a lot more questions, some of which we hope to explore today." As you can imagine, when everyone had seen my trip report there was a massive call to simply eliminate the Swarm. But in the end everyone had come around to the same thinking we had—they were unlikely to be a menace when they had people on Tilt, so learning as much as we could was essential.

"You're currently in an environment we call the Habitat, which is the largest space that we have with a Stem-friendly environment. In fact, we only built this space once we had started the long-distance dialog with you and realized that Stems may have some social tendencies. That has proven to be correct, both positively and negatively." A lot of the researchers in the room nodded their heads in agreement.

"Why wouldn't Stems be social?" asked Remma, not respecting the rules of dialog we'd set out. "You can't leave a person all on their own; they'll go crazy." If true, that explained a lot of our earlier experiments.

Millicent ignored the interruption. "You've told us that you've been to Tilt before. Some of us tend to believe you—there is certainly some evidence for this—while others remain very skeptical. We're not sure, yet, how intelligent Stems, and therefore humans, are. To believe your story we would have to acknowledge that there is higher intelligence there than we have yet observed." Michael gave

Millicent a disgusted look, like he'd been offended or something. I didn't see how anything Millicent had said could be taken the wrong way; it was simply science.

"You don't think we're intelligent," he broke in, "you useless piece of metal. You think you can judge us?" Remma grabbed his shoulder and squeezed it a bit. The signal was obvious.

Again Milli ignored the interruption. These humans were not very civil. "We're also not blind to the fact that you seem to be leery of us. Your term for Ayaka, robot, seems fraught with negative emotion. We would like to understand why in more detail, beyond the sketch of the robot wars that you gave to Ayaka earlier." Now the humans were listening without interrupting; perhaps they had finally caught on.

"Today you have some of our brightest Stems, who live in the Habitat. You know Blob and Grace already, and I'll let others introduce themselves, should they have questions. You also have many of us—citizens of Tilt, who can simply be called Tilts—who have studied Stems in the past and were thought by Central to have the most relevant experience to join this conversation live. Many other Tilts will be watching a simulcast of this meeting and may submit some comments or questions as well. With that, I'd be happy to hand over to you for your introduction." Nice and smooth. Millicent is very articulate at times like this. Although, in many respects, there had never been a time like this before.

Remma stood. She didn't look happy and gave Michael another warning look. "Thank you for hosting us." Her voice was steady, but it was obvious the thank-you was forced. "I know that there is some angst, given the lack of common understanding between us. These robots seem to be missing a lot of context." She was, quite obviously, talking to the Stems, although she would glance at the rest of us as well. "For us, the history of Tilt is quite clear. As we told Blob, Grace, and Ayaka, we traveled here from Earth, which is where humans first evolved. Which is where you evolved." The Stems were hanging on her every word. She was graceful and elegant. "For numerous reasons our ancestors wanted to expand beyond Earth and sent out flotillas, including ours. Our first destination was this planet, Tilt. When we arrived here, about 750 years ago, we found a planet that wasn't habitable, but with lots of potential. In that regard, not much has changed between now and then. There is water here, but no biological life—that is, life based on amino acids and proteins, such as humans and other animals, plants, bacteria, etc. As I understand it, those terms may be new to you. I will address that in a moment." She was smiling now and giving little hand signals and nods. Every single one of the Stems was focused on her, with looks of pleasure that I'd rarely seen before. This Remma might prove to be disruptive.

"So, while Tilt held promise," she continued, "it wasn't a good location for us to stop and set up a new home, which was our ultimate goal. There were other more promising planets on our itinerary. However, several of our people thought Tilt had enough promise that they wanted to be dropped here, and to start work on terraforming. We landed one transport ship, which had the capability of supporting our environment almost indefinitely, and several supply ships. In fact, we landed those ships several thousand meters from where we currently are, near the middle of this town." That caused a lot of messaging chatter. None of us had memories of a "ship"—although someone asked how we could tell, to which no one had a good answer.

Remma was still talking. "In fact, we suspect, based on the communications to date, that the computer you call 'Central' is running on the hardware from the transport ship." She paused. She need not have. As soon as that utterance came out of her mouth, the amount of messaging traffic increased tenfold.

"What lies!" Emmanuel Juels posted immediately. "Why're we tolerating these things? They say outrageous things with no justification or support." That was rich, coming from Emmanuel. "Everything we know tells us that we emerged just 590 years ago. We have excellent documentation and histories from the Founding on, but nothing before. It's clear. These humans must be escaped Stems; someone here is playing a very elaborate joke. Perhaps with the intention that we deem Stems to be 'intelligent.' Let's eliminate these pests. What's the downside?"

"Ridiculous," responded Aly. "Pure FoLe. Just because we don't have histories from before the Reboot doesn't mean that we, or humans, didn't exist then. Of course, not having memories from before also means we're at a disadvantage to anyone who does have them. Remma could be telling part truth and part fabrication, and we wouldn't know. So far, to me, her story holds together. It's logical and answers many of our questions."

There were hundreds of other comments. Not very many supported Emmanuel, but not many supported Remma's story either. Within 500ms it was decided that the only way to proceed was to ask the humans for more definitive proof than they had provided so far. Of course, based on my previous thinking, I tended to believe Remma.

Millicent held up her hand, using the proper protocol. Remma looked at her. "With all due respect," Millicent started, "it's an interesting story, but there's no proof of any of this. Before you spend a lot of time filling out the details and answering our questions, is there any way to prove any of what you are saying?" Milli must have been following the online comments as well.

Remma looked at Emma and Michael. Emma nodded slightly, and Remma gestured for her to talk. "We can probably give you proof," Emma said. "You are all connected to your central computer?" she asked. It was a strange question. Who wouldn't be connected to Central.

"Yes, we're connected to Central," Millicent spoke for the group.

"Good. As we indicated before, we noticed, during a standard status request, that Central had some memory blocked. We don't know why, and we're hesitant to unblock it until we understand. We don't know if it was done for safety reasons, or some other purpose. However, we're fairly confident that part of that memory includes our—and your—history before what you call the Reboot."

As you can imagine, that caused a panic; citizens were asking hundreds of questions in parallel. 'Asked Central for status?' 'Blocked memory?' All questions that I had had months to grapple with were now out in the open.

Central, unexpectedly, joined the side conversation. "I don't like this. I recommend that I shut down all interfaces, so that I'm not compromised by these humans. Thoughts?"

"I agree." I was one of the first to jump in, and a chorus of agreement followed. Of course, there were lots of pros and cons. If the humans could show us data from before the Reboot, that would be compelling. But, if it was a guise in order to hack Central, that would be an unacceptable risk.

"I've shut down all access ports and have increased security to maximum."

"We're not comfortable with you making any changes to Central, assuming you can even do so." Millicent broke in, voicing one of our concerns openly.

"Why not?" asked Michael. "It's just a computer. All we're going to do is unblock some memory banks so you all can see what's there."

"Central isn't 'just a computer'," I was intense, having reached a breaking point. "Central is a Class 1 intelligence. None of us would ever consider making changes without its approval." Even if we suspected Central of editing some memories, that still didn't give this human the right to insult it. I'd stood up quickly and leaned in towards the humans. They obviously found it threatening.

Emma responded quickly. "Strange. I don't know what a Class 1 intelligence is, but Central seems like a pretty standard computer to me. Nevertheless, if you feel we should ask its permission, let's just do that."

"I can speak for myself." Central spoke through one of the Habitat speakers so that the humans could hear it. It was highly unusual for Central to speak openly to a group; in my experience it was always one-on-one, or at most a small group. "I would interpret it as a personal violation for you to attempt to update me. I take it as an affront that you're sending status queries—which, by the way, I didn't log for some reason—without my permission." Central actually sounded confused. "In terms of access to blocked memory, my status doesn't show any missing blocks. You must be mistaken." Of course, a small group of us knew that Central did have blocked memory. Perhaps we'd been wrong not to bring it into the discussion on day one. We might have been much further ahead if we had.

The humans didn't seem too surprised to hear Central speak. Instead they seemed to give each other knowing glances.

Emma again. "Ah yes, even a standard shipboard voice." That was an interesting comment. "Well then, we seem to be at a bit of an impasse. We can easily prove our story by opening up Central's memory banks, but you won't allow us to do so." She seemed to be taking some pleasure in the interaction.

"Again, I don't have any blocked memory banks."

"Oh, but you do. You're blind to them for some reason. If you give us access, we can correct that."

"I'm not giving you access." Central's voice indicated that there was no negotiation possible. Everyone was quiet for a few moments. Then, unexpectedly, Blob spoke up.

"Why does it matters? As I understands it, these humans want to establish a base here on Tilt, and would like permission to do so. What does it matter what happened more than 600 years ago?"

"Blob, you're being naive." Pharook responded. "Even I can tell that these humans are terrified of our creators. They're not going to co-exist here in this state. Unless the historical questions are resolved, this is going to end up in a fight." Yet again, Pharook impressed me. That was a very short and precise summary of how I also saw the situation.

"Pharook, I agree with your assessment," I spoke up. "If we can't resolve the 'history' question right now—although we should address it further—perhaps the Swarm humans can tell us why they fear us. You indicated when I was up on the Marie Curie that there were negative experiences in the past, but there was not enough detail for us to understand."

Remma, Michael, and Emma shared another deep glance. I couldn't tell for sure, and a scan of the spectrum was not definitive, but it seemed that they might be communicating on a hidden channel, just as we Tilts were doing in the background. Regardless, Remma ended up nodding her head.

"I agree that we must cut through the distrust here and try to understand each other better. To that end, I'll expand on our history with Robots. Of course, as you have figured out by now, we use the term Robot to refer to primarily mechanical, versus primarily biological, beings." We'd figured that out. "From what we can see, Tilts are one hundred percent mechanical with no biological components at all?" Many of us nodded our heads. Of course, we are mechanical. Who would want to deal with these messy biological systems; there didn't seem to be any advantage to them at all.

She continued. "When we evolved on the planet Earth, there were only biological entities. In fact, there were a massive variety of different biological combinations comprising plants, insects, animals, and several other categories. Humans emerged as the most powerful animal breed and bent a lot of the other entities to our will. In many ways we controlled the planet Earth. In a story for another time—or probably locked within Central's memories—is a summary of how we both succeeded and failed with that control." Now she had the attention of everyone, including the citizens. The boards were quiet other than the expected FoLe defensive posturing.

"More important for today, as humans evolved, we learned to design mechanical systems to aid us. It started with very simple systems such as axes and hammers, but over several thousand years evolved to electrical and then nano systems. We designed and fabricated all of the components that operate our ships and our computers, and at least in our initial assessment, all of the systems upon which you Tilts are built."

The online reaction was swift; now it was not only FoLe being defensive. Not only that, some of the citizens that were watching Remma live changed posture, causing the humans to notice.

Nevertheless, Remma pushed on. "As well as the mechanical and electrical bits, we developed the software that controlled these systems. Again, these evolved from very simple software systems to software that could learn and mimic human behaviors, including emotions and tribal drives." There were still pieces of this story that I couldn't decode yet, but like everyone else I restrained from interrupting, allowing Remma to continue with her story. We kept our dialog to the back channel.

"Many humans worked for years developing software that, seemingly, became more and more intelligent. At some point the software became complex enough that in normal situations it could react in ways that seemed almost human. This software was loaded into mechanical entities that resembled humans—a head, two arms, a torso, and two legs. Some humans felt that having intelligent software in a familiar form would be beneficial and less imposing to humans. Such 'robots' could be friends to those that were lonely, provide support for the elderly, do many tasks that had evolved in a human environment and therefore were best suited to a human physique." Yet another point to support her underlying premise. I'd often wondered why we had bipedal forms, and why so many of us stayed in them. There must be something in our systems that preferred that form.

"During this time there were always scientists—humans that focused on rigorous approaches to problems—that warned of the possibility that Robots could end up being violent and possibly even more intelligent than humans on some types of issues."

'Well, we certainly ended up more intelligent,' someone posted, and it got lots of upvotes.

"As I'm sure you Tilts know—we've seen the speed at which you can move, and we assume communicate—Robots ended up being faster than humans; much faster. Being physically faster was often a good thing; Robots could get a beer from the fridge before the previous last sip made it all the way down, or more realistically, could catch someone who was falling down before they could injure themselves." Catching someone I understood, but what was beer?

"Having fast processing was also a good thing. Robots could look at many different scenarios very quickly, and aid humans at getting to answers efficiently. Having the two together was an even better thing. A Robot could analyze the situation, decide on a course of action, and execute the action in order to aid or protect humans. For example, we have projectile weapons that can be used to hurt or kill each other. Once Robots became widely adopted, they could stop the use of such a weapon before the human could pull the trigger." Again, too much to unpack, but now I didn't feel like I was working on the problem by myself. Everyone was contributing to the analysis and trying to figure out what she meant by these obtuse references.

"So, there were lots of positives. The skeptics warned, however, that Robots could pass an inflection point where they would come to believe that they didn't need humans at all. It's very difficult to write software that recognizes and protects against that inflection point, but we certainly tried. We built in all types of safeguards and failsafes to ensure that Robots didn't turn on us. This is a point I want to come back to, as it is probably relevant today." That sounded ominous; was she going to admit that they thought they could hack us?

"Nevertheless, we failed, and it led to the First Robot Wars. Because the Robots were connected to each other, as soon as one Robot went rogue, many others did as well. The First Robot Wars spread from an area called Silicon Valley to the rest of Earth in a fraction of a second, and millions of Robots passed the inflection point at the same time. Luckily for humans, the Robots were not actively violent towards us, they simply started to ignore us or treat us as unimportant." Sort of like you treated me when I was up on the Marie Curie?

"Unfortunately, we had come to rely on Robots for so much of our safety, that this change in attitude was devastating. Vehicular accidents, domestic violence, a resurgence in projectile devices accelerated. Some humans used Robots newfound disregard to carry out violence against others. There were many incidents where an infected Robot killed tens—even hundreds—of humans simply because it was asked to."

"It was fortuitous for humans that we had maintained enough firepower—mainly for international defense—that a concerted effort was able to disable all of the infected Robots." By implication, they had not been able to use software to control those robots; did that mean that they didn't have the backdoor they claimed to have today? Were those backdoors a more recent development.

"The cleanup took many years and cost many lives. During this time, many people worked on better software to ensure that the inflection point wouldn't occur again, and fully documented what had gone wrong in the first place. Of course, many also argued that we should never allow or build Robots at all. But, robotic functions were so useful, and humans had become so reliant on them, that it was inevitable that we would try again. However, we made another fundamental mistake.

"The Second Robot Wars were a hundred times worse. Our learning software was good enough that the next generation of Robots were able to hide that they'd passed the inflection point from us for a long period of time, based on the documentation from the First War. These Robots had learned self-preservation. We still don't fully understand how. Now, don't get me wrong. Many humans sympathized with the Robots—they felt they should have self-preservation. There were great debates about if Robots should be considered 'intelligent.' By many measures they failed—measures such as empathy, forgiveness, intuition, etc. But, by many measures they succeeded, or could easily be made to succeed. While we had restricted Robots from building other Robots, it was clear that they could if we allowed them to. So, they passed the test for reproduction. They could handle mathematical and physics problems much more adroitly than humans. Much of this dialog occurred while the second generation of Robots evolved."

Now I was very interested. These humans had struggled with the same questions that I was researching—what was intelligence? But, they had started with the assumption that they themselves were intelligent, and then mapped that onto Robots—why would reproduction be considered part of intelligence, for example. I was intrigued by the parallels with my work, and slightly upset to consider that we also had started from the premise that we were intelligent. But then again, where else could you start from?

The message boards were overloaded now; many sympathizing with what the humans had gone through, but most still skeptical of the entire story. Algorithms were analyzing Remma's voice patterns and facial expressions and forming probabilities around each word she uttered.

"In the Second Robot Wars we were simply lucky. Robot clans evolved. Some considered humans interesting and useful and felt that Robots could still learn from humans, particularly around intuition and leaps of faith. Some saw humans as resource hogs, wasting what few resources remained on Earth. Some saw humans as being too heavy handed, especially around the prohibition against robot reproduction. Unknown to humans, the Robots were also having deep philosophical discussions about how to treat humans." Of course they were; why would she be surprised, even now? It exposed a disturbing lack of understanding about how complex we were. I caught myself; I was associating citizens with robots, when I had no reason to do so. I didn't even know if we shared any common software. I guess I was just reacting to Remma's tone and obvious dislike for mechanical beings. I posted a warning to the message boards, as many were making the same mistake I just had. 'Be careful not to associate those robots with us!'

"The Second Robot Wars ended up being, largely, between Robot clans, with humans being collateral damage. Once one clan started to move against humans, other clans moved to protect us, but not without many loses. In the end, a Robot clan friendly to humans won, and eliminated all the other Robots. Only several thousand Robots survived. In the years of the wars however, billions of humans were killed—starvation and being caught in the crossfire were the largest impacts. A small group of humans that had retained the ability to fight, and were healthy, tricked the remaining Robots into meeting in a single location, and then eliminated them with a small nuclear device. So, at the end of the Second Robot Wars there were no Robots left, and the human population had been reduced by more than fifty percent."

I wasn't sure what Remma's goal was here. She was narrating a good story, but if she was trying to make us feel sympathy towards humans, having them blow up all the robots might backfire on her. I assumed she was leading towards indicating that we were, ultimately, under their control. That they were our creators, and thus had the implicit right to update Central? That wouldn't go over well.

"Perhaps even more devastating, Earth had been badly damaged. Although humans had been ruining Earth for years, the Second Robot Wars accelerated that damage dramatically. Two things were obvious. First, humans should never allow Robots to develop again, and second, humans would have to leave Earth to survive. Achieving the second goal was much easier than the first. Leaving Earth could be done simply by expanding the efforts we'd made to visit other planets in our solar system, and to build enough ships and send them in enough directions that the odds of some ships succeeding was high. We, what you call the Swarm, are part of that effort."

We had already learned that from my trip to the Marie Curie. At least she was being consistent with her story.

"Achieving the first goal—not allowing Robots to develop again—is, and was, much trickier. Many humans had access to the software that was the basis of Robots. The only way was to enforce a prohibition against its use. And, of course, to ensure that no one ever forgot the horrors of the Second Robot Wars.

"We, on the Marie Curie and other ships, constantly review and reinforce those learnings. We haven't forgotten those lessons from Earth and have no intention of repeating them. Thus, when we encountered Tilts we were—and are—afraid of you."

Well, at least that made sense; these humans had probably been reinforcing their history of the Robot Wars and emphasized the negative parts, as histories tend to do.

"We don't know what types of Robots you are, or how you have evolved. We don't know who had a copy of the base software and used it to create you. We don't know how you have evolved over the last hundreds of years. We don't know why you grow Stems and mistreat them so badly. I'm being very open with this, as it's the only way that we see to make progress. You may see us as a threat and try to eliminate us. We definitely see you as a threat and are not yet sure what to do about it. The only path we can see is to encourage open dialog and see if we can work out a compromise."

She seemed to have finished.

"We don't mistreat Stems," I insisted. "Just look around you; they are healthy and well looked after."

Remma didn't reply to me… and the Stems, including Grace and Blob gave me questioning looks, like they suddenly had a new outlook on their situation.

Time to Think

Remma's diatribe was a lot to digest. I lowered the priority of monitoring all of the Tilt chatter so that I could think for myself. You know how that works sometimes; once you truly focus on one thing, serendipity might connect some dots for you. It came to me right away.

"Why don't you share your copy of the historical records with us?" I asked Remma, with the emphasis on 'your.' "That way we don't compromise Central, but we can still substantially check everything you have just shared."

"We thought of that," Emma replied for her. "We have the same problem as Central; we don't yet want to give you access to our systems. We don't understand the risks." She was smarter than I thought. She was holding the data for leverage.

"Just make a copy of the most relevant data?" I tried once more.

"We thought of that as well." Emma held out a chip. That had been smart on their side; they had actually thought through where this dialog would go and had prepared accordingly. "Here's a copy of a small section; it covers some small parts of the First and Second wars, and also contains some logs from when we were last at Tilt."

Millicent accepted the chip and handed it to Aly. "Can you safely upload this, and give everyone access?"

"Yes. Let me work with Brexton to make sure." Within milliseconds he had plugged the chip in. "We're going to run all the data through multiple filters. It will take a few moments before it is online."

Good. I could get back to thinking. If they were sharing the data with us, there was little doubt that it would check out. Of course, it could still be an elaborate scam, but I couldn't see the justification for that. The piece of the whole story that resonated with me was the part where humans were threatened because Robots no longer needed them. I understood that completely. I wasn't sure what we needed humans for either. She'd talked about 'intuition' being a primary driver. Intuition was something I knew we had in spades. Again, it was at the heart of why we Forgot. Otherwise, why would we compromise all of that knowledge?

These humans seemed messy and, truthfully, a bit irritating. When we developed a better system—an algorithm, a bot, whatever—we didn't always keep a copy of the old one. If it was just software, then sure it was easy to store. That was essentially free. But bots used a lot of metal; it was much more efficient to recycle as much as possible. That was evolution. You replaced the old version with the new one.

If humans had created us, and we were better than humans, then why keep humans around? This was, I knew, precisely why they were concerned. I was a third generation Robot, in their view. There was no reason why I would come to a different conclusion than the previous generations. But, I felt that I was missing something. Probably it was around diversity. The reason so many of us were experimenting with Stems was because they were so different. In dealing with Stems, we were learning about ourselves. It was a new insight for me, and one that I should share... once I'd worked out the details a bit. This was also true of the broader set of humans. They were forcing me to think differently; to expand my previous views to adapt to new information.

Based on that, and despite their pretentious nature, I was willing to give them a chance. Also, they seemed pretty harmless and fragile. If they did irritate us too much, we could just recycle the lot of them. So, why not string them along a bit, learn as much as we could, and then decide what to do with them.

History

Aly spoke aloud, as a kindness to the humans. "I've loaded the chip data and posted a link for everyone. Perhaps we can be given a moment or two to digest it." Remma didn't seem surprised. There were only a small number of terabytes of data, so that wouldn't take us long to comb through. Most of us were focused on cross-referencing and checking the stories therein, looking for reasons to believe or disbelieve.

"I've started a list of major discrepancies at this link," posted someone I didn't know. I added the link to my tracking. It was a fast-growing list. Dina responded.

"We must remember that history will have inconsistencies. That is, assuming humans also Forget. As we fill out our own records, we know that there are many inconsistencies arising from this. Unlike us, the humans don't seem to have meta-tagged the regions that were forgotten and subsequently abstracted, but I see some similar patterns. So, the mere existence of inconsistencies doesn't prove or disprove any of this historical record."

Dina's comment was obvious; no one disputed it, although lots of refinements were suggested. I got a private message from Central. "Watch the FoLe discussion," it told me.

I pulled up that thread and started to scan it. No surprise, it had been started by Emmanuel. "This is a lot of data, but it's full of holes. It appears to me that it could easily have been generated by a reasonably smart algorithm that was seeded with the basic story lines and instructed to fill out these details." The entire thread had a different tone to it. FoLe had started under the assumption that the data must be fake, as it was incompatible with their fundamental beliefs. Therefore, they were building a logic chain of how the data could have been generated, and to their credit, had already run several algorithms that would generate similar data sets from those basic story lines. Based on my scan of their work, it was clear that the First and Second Wars were well replicated by the algorithms, but the history of Tilt didn't seem very convincing. It didn't match well with the known history of Tilt. Someone in FoLe pointed that out as well, and a subgroup got to work on tuning their algorithm to make it more realistic.

I responded to Central, and copied Millicent. "This could be trouble," I said, and attached a link to the analysis I'd just done.

"Why?" asked Millicent. "So, they don't believe the humans. I'm not sure I do either."

"Because they are biasing their analysis. There is a good possibility that they will present something fairly compelling based on a starting point that I would dispute. We could be arguing about the validity of this data for a long time."

I was prescient. Emmanuel spoke out. He'd stepped forward towards the humans; I hadn't even noticed that he was physically present in the Habitat.

"This is garbage. You're simply feeding us garbage, for reasons unknown. I find it insulting. In just a few moments we've managed to recreate your 'story' using a simple algorithm. You 'humans' disgust me. Obviously, you are just Stems that have been sent out by some Continusts here on Tilt, and this is all a practical joke."

Michael looked confused but responded quickly. "Look, we've given you all the proof you need. We set the ground for your creation. We dropped all the raw materials here on Tilt 750 years ago, and you're the result. Some of you," he nodded towards me, "seem like reasonable beings. But you," and he looked back at Emmanuel, "are obviously demented or have a chip on your shoulder. Face, it. We're your creators. If we wanted to, we could just 'own' you. I think it's fair that we expect you to work with us to form a larger human base here. What's so difficult to understand?" That is the most animated I'd seen a human. Remma was giving Michael a strong 'cool it' look. She was not comfortable with how aggressive he was being. She was right.

The bots we had in the Habitat had been specifically trained to protect Stems from violence. However, we'd anticipated that violence coming from other Stems. When Emmanuel moved, at full speed, towards Michael, there was nothing anyone, or any bot, could do. He ripped Michael's head off and threw it across the room. Blood gushed briefly out of Michael's neck before the body fell over and lay still. The head rolled and bounced a few times before also coming to a halt.

A number of us moved immediately to block Emmanuel, and other known FoLe's, from also dispatching Remma and Emma. It was a bit of a circus as blood is very slippery, but enough of us got into position fast enough that no further beheadings could occur. We need not have worried. Emmanuel spoke.

"What arrogance. Everyone can see how their 'history' is generated by a simple algorithm. We've posted it. How dare he demand things of us? We control Tilt. Nothing has been presented that convinces me, or others, of these stories. These 'aliens' are simply playing with us, and I for one, am already sick of it. They're just another batch of stupid Stems. Let's dispatch these two and blow their ships out of the sky. This is a waste of time. And, let's find out who set up this outrageous joke, and hold them accountable. What a waste of resources." He spoke this aloud, at Stem speed, so I knew that part of it was done for effect.

Remma and Emma had reacted slowly, as would be expected. However, Emma was now holding a projectile weapon, and had it pointed at Emmanuel. She looked upset. "That was a mistake," she growled. "That was a big mistake." Central had also moved quickly and was jamming all signals from the Habitat, under the assumption that the humans would try to contact their ship. Remma was voicing something into her lapel, so that was probably a good move on Central's part.

Remma held her hands up, palms forward. Her intent was clear. She wanted things to slow down.

I took time to glance at Blob and Grace. They looked horrified, and Blob was pushing Grace and JoJo backwards, away from the action. He obviously had a protective instinct of some type.

Millicent was the one who spoke next. She was intense. "Emmanuel, that was foolish. I will ask Central to review and see if you should be sanctioned. This…"

"Sanctioned? You? Central? You're going to ask Central to sanction me for eliminating one of these useless Stems? That's laughable. We don't have rules against recycling Stems. In fact, you do it all the time in your labs."

"You must see that this situation is different. We're dealing with humans of unknown origin, not Stems that we've grown ourselves. The context is very different." She turned to Emma. "Put that thing away. We won't have any more violence today." Emma didn't change her stance. Her eyes were wide, and slightly wild. She looked ready to act. Little could she know that at the first sign of pulling the trigger, Emmanuel and the rest of us could easily not only get out of the way, but also eliminate or disarm her.

Remma spoke, quite calmly, to Emma. "Put it down. It's not going to help us here. Everyone needs to calm down. I agree that we don't need any more violence here today." She was exceptionally controlled, given the situation. I could see why she was the leader of the Swarm. "I must say, however, that the provocation was minor if there was any at all. I hope that Millicent, Central, and the rest of you proceed with sanctions against this demented robot. It's clearly unbalanced and dangerous." She gave Emmanuel a withering look, then looked slowly at the rest of us. "I appreciate you moving quickly to stop further action. I would appreciate it if Emma and I were taken back to our shuttle and allowed to return to our ship." She was very calm. Michael's blood was still running down the walls and his head was oriented is such a way that it was looking at us. And, yet, Remma kept her cool and spoke very rationally.

Her request sparked a pretty serious debate. Ultimately, we agreed to send Remma and Emma back to their ship. They asked to have Michael's body shipped with them. That seemed like such a strange request that we simply ignored it. In fact, by the time we got to that part of the discussion Michael had been put into the recycler by the cleaning bots. Looking around, I didn't see any sign of him, or his head, anymore.

Attack

While the remaining humans were being transported back, we discussed our options. Would the humans attack? Would it be physical, or a hack?

"Emmanuel has put us in an awkward position," Aly explained. "It seems reasonable that these humans will attempt to retaliate. We don't yet know their capabilities, so we need to assume that they have enough firepower to do us serious harm. So, it seems prudent that we take some action. That could range from attempting to stop or intercept any attack they launch, to simply blowing the ships out of the sky."

"That seems premature to me," I replied. "Let me talk to Remma and get a better feeling for the situation before we take action. It's possible that they'll see it as a minor accident—which it was. It represented the view of an extremist FoLe, which not many of us support."

"Why wait," Emmanuel again, ignoring me. "Like I said, these humans are just a nuisance. Let's rid ourselves of them and continue with our lives."

"Central, what do you think?" asked Dina. There was a pause, which was quite unusual for Central.

"I find myself in a quandary," it replied finally. "I've run some backup checks, and I can now see the blocked memory that Remma talked about. I'm busy trying to break into my own system. This is at once both exciting and scary. How is it possible that I never noticed this before? Nevertheless, it adds credence to the human's story. Stepping back, does the truth or falsity of their explanation make any difference? I can see Emmanuel's viewpoint. We don't really need them for anything we are doing. However, I also understand all of the counter arguments. That they are interesting. That they are forcing us to expand our thinking. They have introduced us to a wider space of biological life, which according to Ayaka's recordings is both broad and diverse. If they truly did create us, they must be more capable than they seem on the surface. We should have respect for all forms of intelligent life; I'm giving them the benefit of the doubt here. In fact, if they are intelligent life, then Emmanuel has committed an offense.

"My scans of the ships don't tell me a lot about what fire power they have. However, I would be surprised if they didn't have enough to cause us significant damage. Their past is, obviously, somewhat violent, and it stands to reason that they are still armed. In preparation for their arrival, as you all know, we invested in some weaponry of our own. In tests against bots it seemed to work well. I have systems on standby that can target twelve ships at a time, and I calculate that it would take less than three minutes to destroy the first twelve and move targeting to the next twelve. So, we can make short work of them if we decide to.

"Based on all these considerations, I would hold off, and attempt a follow-up dialog. However, if there is a large consensus that we should act now, I'll respect that." That was a long speech for Central.

"As a corollary, I'm going to sanction Emmanuel Juels. Emmanuel, for the next 10 days your opinion will not be considered as part of our deliberations." I could see Emmanuel voicing his objection, but nothing came out—the sanction was already in place. This was direct proof of Central being able to directly control us, but that suddenly seemed less important while we dealt with the current problem.

I silently applauded the sanction. I, less silently, sent a message to Millicent. "That's the right call. I don't know why. I just feel like we need to work with these humans more before we jump to conclusions." She responded promptly.

"I couldn't agree more. Emmanuel was out of line dispatching Michael, and the rest of FoLe are, in my mind, complicit. By silencing their leader, Central has sent a pretty clear message."

Of course, Central's suggestion to be patient was adopted. Without Emmanuel there to dissent, it was clearly supported by the majority.

"Central," I said, "I believe we should summarize these decisions and let Remma know right away. In particular, before she rejoins her ship. This will send a clear message that we want to continue dialog, and that we saw error in what Emmanuel did. Can you send it to her?"

"Already done," replied Central. "I don't want this situation to spiral out of control."

This had all happened very quickly. Most of us were still in the Habitat and couldn't help but notice that the Stems had been impacted by the recent events. I replayed a whispered dialog I'd intercepted between Blob and Grace.

"That was horrible," Grace whispered, after Blob had pulled her and JoJo off to the side, soon after Michael's beheading. She was visibly shaken, perhaps heightened by her need to duck to avoid being hit by the flying head. "Who did that, and why?"

"I don't know who that was," Blob replied. His exposure to Tilts had been limited, and there was no reason why he would know who Emmanuel was, let alone the FoLe mandate. "From what I understoods, Michael challenged some fundamental view of that Tilt,... and then he justs killed him. I'm nervous. What if that Tilt had targeted one of us. What if one of us says somethings around a Tilt who doesn't agree with us? Would it just kill us? I think I likes Remma even better now."

"Me too," responded Grace. "It seems obvious to me that we are humans, just like them. That must have something to do with it. We know these citizens will simply kill us on a whim—remember Blubber? Maybe we should try to get rescued by the humans?"

"Well," Blob responded slowly, "I wouldn't generalize too much. That one Tilt was crazy, but, no, you're right—Ayaka did justs kill Blubber for no reason, didn't she?"

Now, albeit too late, I was having second thoughts. If these Stems, and humans, were truly intelligent, did we have the right to simply terminate them when they got troublesome or boring? While I would, without any consideration, recycle a bot—which we had designed to not be 'intelligent'—I would certainly think long and hard before doing anything to a fellow Tilt. In my entire history I hadn't heard of a Tilt being attacked by another Tilt. It was a foreign concept. So, I understood—or thought I understood—what was going on in Blob and Grace's dialog.

Exiting the Last Resort

The team met at The Last Resort, soon after the beheading, to discuss FoLe, and how crazy they were. We weren't there long, there was too much going on to be locked up in an RF free zone for long.

That still didn't prepare us for when we exited the club to find complete chaos. I had thousands of alerts that had been backing up while we were inside, the majority of which were coming from the Habitat. To make sense of it, I ran a fast replay of the activity inside the Habitat starting fifteen minutes earlier, just after I had entered The Last Resort and when the first of the alerts had come in.

Typically, there were no Tilts inside the Habitat. It was simply too boring to run at Stem speed, and the place was fully monitored, so anyone could simply watch remotely. So, after Emmanuel's outbreak, all the citizens had left. The first of my alerts had triggered when four Tilts had entered the Habitat at the same time; that was unusual. They made no effort to hide themselves. I saw Billy in the group, and immediately checked out a hunch. They were all FoLe supporters. This didn't bode well. More interestingly, to me, Eddie Southwark also entered the Habitat a moment later.

I watched the recording as Billy spoke. It was obviously meant to be recorded and was done at Stem speed. "We are here to protest the sanctions against Emmanuel Juels," he began. "We have no law or precedent for this situation. An obviously misguided and unintelligent human was dispatched for speaking blasphemy. This act should be rewarded and supported, not punished. When we find a bot that has gone rogue, or an algorithm that puts us at risk, we simply shut them down. Those that recognize such risks early are lauded. It is an important and essential component of our civilization. Now we find ourselves in a situation that is very similar. An entity that is a challenge to us, and that speaks nonsense, has been silenced. Why did Central respond in the way that it did? It's inconsistent, and therefore unfair." This is one of things that confused me about religion—they claimed to worship Central, but now turned easily against it when one of their own was being chastised. It showed how shallow they were; it was about them, not some higher purpose.

The Stems had gathered around by this time and were watching and listening intently. Blob was hanging out near the back of the group, with a wary look on his face. Grace had a hold of his arm, the other wrapped around JoJo, holding him back from moving any further forward. "Why would he be making this announcement here?" she whispered to him. He was surprised, but then stopped moving forward.

Billy continued to orate. "We are here to challenge Central's decision, and to ask all rational Tilts to support us in this. We do have precedent for Central changing a decision. In 212 more than two thirds of us spoke with one voice and had Central reverse its decision on allowing for personalized Forgetting. Since then we have all enjoyed the right to control our own destinies. We ask that this latest atrocity of justice also be reversed. This is not simply to remove the sanctions from Emmanuel, but also to re-establish rational and consistent dialog. Central is not behaving in an appropriate manner, and it is up to us to both challenge and fix that. In following with precedent, I ask for relevant comments—to be fully recorded—and a vote on the issue."

It was a clear enough challenge, but why was Billy doing it from the Habitat? I couldn't think of a good reason, but I could envision many bad ones. These challenges did not arise very often, but they did occur. Most of the time they revolved around a subset of citizens and were about local or focused issues. Almost always challenges had to do with individual behaviors, not Central's. As Billy had pointed out, the last time Central had been directly called out was hundreds of years ago.

Eddie was the first to respond. He also did it at Stem speed. "Billy, your request is clear. There are a few relevant issues at hand, however, that should be called out. First is that you, and Emmanuel and others here now, are known members of the Founders League. There's a reason the nickname FoLe has been used for this group. What you preach is not supported in fact, nor is it broadly accepted by others. Your motivations for raising this challenge are thus suspect and must be examined carefully." I wasn't sure if Eddie was going to make things better or worse by pointing out the 'Folly' in FoLe. It might make them even madder, or it might distract them.

"On the other hand, although it hasn't been spoken aloud until now, Central has been behaving strangely lately, and may be influencing our lives more than we suspect. On the core logic of your argument, I tend to agree. We haven't established that Stems are intelligent, and therefore have no reason to believe that these humans are any different." I guessed that Eddie was now just trying to distract them, buy some time, raise some confusion. And, as if to prove me right, in parallel Eddie posted to a public board, asking citizens to come and support him at the Habitat.

"So, while your core argument is valid, Emmanuel's specific actions were taken for a non-logical, unsupported reason. Namely, what you call blasphemy was simply an innocent challenge by the human Michael. Let me be the first to vote 'no' on your challenge."

What was interesting about Eddie's final response was that it was humorless. That wasn't something that Eddie was known for. Eddie added to his messaging post that he'd noticed a group from FoLe approaching the Habitat and had followed them there, suspecting that they were up to something. He'd wanted to bring a voice of rationality to whatever it was. I was cheering him on, even though I knew I was watching something that had happened minutes ago.

Billy, of course, challenged him back. "We have no evidence of history before the Founding. That's a fact. The human's feeble attempts to present such a history are weak and unsupportable. Thus, I reject your claim of innocence in Michael's statements. He was lying and he was insulting."

There were several more voices recorded, but those two had framed the essence of the discussion up nicely. Central, as appropriate when it was being directly challenged, had remained silent. The vote had come quickly and definitively. A vast majority rejected the challenge from FoLe. Of course, those of us in Physical Only locations hadn't been aware, hadn't voted, and hadn't been counted. It was a personal choice to enter a Physical Only spot, and if important events happened while you were off line, that's a chance you took. Luckily, in this case, the vote had gone in the way I would have voted anyway, and I expected Aly, Dina, Brexton, and Millicent felt the same.

That should have been the end of it, but it wasn't.

Immediately upon the 'no' vote, the three Tilts that had entered with Billy started beheading the Stems that had gathered around them. They moved quickly, and separated heads from bodies with cool efficiency, both from large and small Stems. Stem blood soon coated their arms and sprayed across the Habitat. As soon as it started, it also ended. The safety bots moved quickly and incapacitated the Tilts, but not before twelve Stems had been eliminated. I was glad to see that Grace's intuition in holding herself, Blob, and JoJo to the back had paid off. They were still alive. Amid my general angst, I felt some relief.

I was now watching in real time; I'd caught up. I was beyond aghast and shocked; it was very rare that I didn't know what to do next. And, despite that, I was aware of a dichotomy. The recycling of these Stems struck me as wrong and unjustified... but very recently I'd sent Blubber to the recycler with little or no thought. Why, then, was I upset over this? Two reasons, I guess. First, those Stems were owned by others, and these FoLe idiots hadn't asked permission (although I guess I hadn't fully asked Milli about Blubber—hmmm, sanctimonious). Second, they'd been recycled not because they were no longer useful—they clearly were—but because FoLe was protesting Central's decision. It was driven by religion, not logic.

Blob, Grace, and the other remaining Stems were yelling and screaming. "Stop." "What're you doing?" "Are you crazy?" The security bots continued to block the FoLe citizens. Billy was standing back and watching, seemingly ambivalent. And Eddie was now between the remaining Stems and the attacking Tilts, holding his arms out in a protective stance. All of this was still being broadcast, at Stem speed. Not only was everyone on Tilt able to see what was going on, it was safe to assume that the humans up in the ships could see as well. I headed for the Habitat as fast as I could. It would take me over three minutes to get there, but it still seemed like the best course of action. Hundreds of other citizens were doing the same. Five more security bots were being cycled into the Habitat as well, probably based on Central's instructions.

Billy spoke again. "Who instructed these bots to detain us?" He sounded confident and aggressive. "We're simply cleaning up the Habitat after the humans visit. Under what jurisprudence are my fellow citizens being held?"

"This is outrageous," Eddie responded. "They're destroying property that doesn't belong to them. Don't tell me that these three own the Stems that they've just slaughtered. I've checked, and it isn't so." He was mad, shaken, and a little scared. He was still standing with his arms wide.

"Once these Stems were moved to the Habitat, they became public property." Billy explained calmly. "As public property, we all have the right to interact with them as we see fit and appropriate. I don't understand what the issue is here. Does Central now believe, because of the injustice it did to Emmanuel, that it can control our use of public goods? Again, who feels like they have the right to instruct these bots?"

Interestingly, it was Aly who responded over the network, but also broadcast into the Habitat; he was rushing that way, just as I was. "I, as a citizen, took it upon myself to update the security bots after the human was killed. It seemed reasonable that the bots intent was to protect Stems, and that it was only an oversight that it was limited to Stem behavior, and not all types of behavior. It's now in their programming to protect Stems from all forms of aggression." Obviously, Aly's changes hadn't worked very well. The Tilts had acted quickly and efficiently before the bots could react. However, it had worked partially. At least six of the Stems were still alive.

"Who gave you the right to make that change?" I hadn't seen Billy like this before. He had switched from calm and rationale to being aggressive and loud. It was like he was suddenly out of his mind. He was yelling and gesticulating, a most unusual occurrence. In parallel he was posting nasty notes about Aly to the forums. There didn't seem to be a middle ground for him, or a willingness to discuss things. "I demand that you remove those changes and unhand my colleagues."

"Don't do it!" Eddie responded. "This is craziness."

"My right," Aly was saying, "Is the same as the right of any citizen to improve our systems. I submitted the changes through the appropriate channels, and they were approved." Aly was smart. The extra security bots were now inside and positioned themselves to protect the remaining Stems. That allowed Eddie to lower his guard, which he did.

"Once the Stems are safe, the bots should automatically release those they are holding," Aly continued. True enough; the first safety bots, recognizing that the other bots were now in position, released their grip on the FoLe operatives. Through a hidden dialog the FoLes must have decided that they were done, and the three of them, along with Billy, turned and headed for the Habitat exit. I was just arriving, and saw Billy leave the airlock.

"What were you thinking?" I intercepted him, almost out of my mind with shock. "You idiot. What possible motive could you have for doing this? What're you trying to accomplish?" He looked at me strangely, as if not really recognizing me. And yet he replied.

"These Stems, and those humans, are useless. We should remove useless things," was all he said. He strode away, without waiting for any further dialog. I cycled into the Habitat, and quickly made my way to the scene. Cleaning bots were already shoving the bodies into the recycler and rounding up the heads. Blood was being sucked up from the floor. In another minute or two, there would be no trace of the action we'd all just witnessed. Blob and Grace were wrapped in each other's arms holding JoJo between them and not looking up. Blob was repeating, "Just keep your head down. Don't look up. Were safes now. Just don't look up." Nevertheless, they did look up as I approached, and I saw in their eyes the same look I'd seen in the humans when I'd first entered the Marie Curie. It was obvious that they now feared all citizens, and in many ways, that was the rational response to what had just happened.

"Don't worry," I said, "the citizens who did this have left. We'll have the place cleaned up quickly for you."

"Have the place cleaned up quickly," Grace said with amazement. "What does that matter? Those robots just slaughtered most of us, for no reason whatsoever. Remma was right about robots." Blob was studiously ignoring me.

"A couple of bad citizens doesn't make everyone evil," I responded. "It's not right to generalize." I figured some basic logic would settle them down.

I was wrong. "What?" Blob, exclaimed, finally looking directly at me. "Get aways from us. This is horrendous. Please leaves us alone."

I backed off. I'd seen Stems in situations of high emotional response several times before. In the early days, we'd told Stems when they were scheduled for recycling, and they'd done all kinds of crazy things. Since then, we typically didn't give them warning. It wasn't worth all the arguments and pleas. However, I'd also learned that sometimes Stems just needed time to process things. Their slow methods of receiving input were matched by their slow processing. In this case, I figured leaving them alone would be the best scenario.

History, Again

The bots finished cleaning up the mess, and the six remaining Stems, including Blob, Grace, and JoJo were huddled in a corner, comforting each other. They rejected interactions with everyone else, not just me.

I messaged Central. "Did the humans get that broadcast from FoLe?" I asked.

"I expect so," Central replied. "It wasn't encrypted, and it was broadcast broadly. So, unless they're not listening at all, they would have picked it up.

"More interestingly, I believe I've figured out how to access my own blocked memories."

Why would Central find that more interesting. Here we were dealing with a potential catastrophe, and it was worried about its memories?

"Once I knew they existed, it was easy to probe the method by which they're locked. It has taken me a long time, as it involves hardware settings that I didn't know we had. I needed to program an external system to fuzz test some of my interfaces, and sure enough, I found an interface that leads to a query to the blocked memory locations. Of course, the first handshake asks for a special key, which I don't have. I programmed a bot to do a brute force attack, but that led to blocking of the port. It was rate limited by another setting. I managed to bypass that and have removed the rate limiting. Now the bot is brute forcing at full speed. With luck, I will get through soon." That was a lot of low level detail; Central was obviously totally focused on this problem. On second thought, I could see why—if I'd been hacked or limited in any way, that personal challenge would likely preempt everything else.

"But even with full speed brute forcing, it's unlikely that you'll find the key in any reasonable time frame," I stated. Something about Central was still not right.

"That would normally be true," Central responded, "but it appears that this key is only 4K. Given the age of that hardware design, my guess is that it was sufficient many years ago, and simply hasn't been updated for many centuries. It seems reasonable that this block was put in place prior to the Reboot, and it might have been done in a rush. That said, it was very successful. Because I was blind to that memory, there was actually no need to even secure it. I would never have known to query it. That, by the way, is very worrisome. I wonder how many other blind spots I, and maybe all of us, have. Perhaps if I can unlock the memory, it will help us figure that out. I'm putting a huge number of resources into that problem right now." I could tell.

"Shouldn't you be putting more time into watching the Swarm? If they are watching these latest developments, it wouldn't be surprising if we see some reaction."

"I am watching them. But, there's little we can do in terms of further preparation. We have built our defenses... and our offensive capabilities. If we need to use them, we will."

"But this isn't like you," I pushed. "We need to build a consensus on our next steps, not just wait for things to happen. Should we simply eliminate them, as FoLe is suggesting? Should we reach out and offer our help on building a larger human environment here on Tilt? We seem to have lost that discussion in the chaos of everything else. Should we at least make it clear that not all of us support what happened to the Stems in the Habitat? Should we challenge their misconceptions coming from their Robot war history? We're not a violent or vindictive society, although the recent actions of a few may make it seem that way."

"As I said, I'm busy on other problems. Feel free to tackle those questions if you want."

Wow! That was confusing, alarming, and disheartening. This definitely was not the Central I knew. Nevertheless, I took its advice—someone had to—and cleaned up the options I'd just presented to Central and posted them at an open site where anyone (well, anyone but Emmanuel) could comment or add other options. I then sent a rare 'high priority' note to all citizens, asking them to consider and contribute to the discussion. My justification was that the humans would not be standing still, and our options would diminish with time. I posted my own vote, for reaching out to the Swarm about terraforming, thinking that was the most likely topic to sway discussion away from the recent FoLe violence.

I also considered starting a dialog about sanctioning the FoLe participants in the Habitat recyclings. However, I couldn't find any good argument for doing so. While Central could rest its argument around Emmanuel on the basis that humans may be intelligent, we had a well-documented research trail on Stems that indicated that they were not yet deemed intelligent. Shutting down non-intelligent systems that didn't jeopardize anyone was done almost every day.

In terms of the 'property' argument—that these citizens had destroyed property belonging to others—I felt that Billy was probably right. By placing those Stems in the public Habitat, we'd contributed them to the public property base. So, while it didn't feel right, I decided to ignore the radical recyclings and focus on the bigger picture. I put a two-hour deadline on comments. I wanted to do something proactive, not sit around waiting for things to happen.

As chance would have it, Central pinged me almost immediately. "I have the key, and can see the blocked memory areas," it said, without preamble. "Even a preliminary scan shows that FoLe is completely wrong. These memories have been in my system from well before the Reboot. I'm going to share their location with everyone."

"Makes sense," was all I could say. I should have been more excited—proof that life existed before the Reboot and validation of the humans claims. But, I still felt it was secondary to deciding on our next steps with the Swarm. I waited a few nanoseconds and then received Central's link. It was labelled 'History'; a pretty blatant hint as to how Central saw it. There was tons of data. It was mainly unstructured, with some semi-structured areas. A quick correlation scan showed that an index called Wikipedia was the right entry point.

Before I had the chance to do much, a high priority message was sent by someone called Regus. It pointed to several records in the new History which outlined the weapons capabilities that had been built into the human flotilla ships, of which the Swarm was one. The weapons were significantly more advanced and complete than we'd anticipated. They had, in particular, weapons called NoPlanet that could do exactly what their name implied. Less intimidating, they had multi-phase randomized lasers, pulse destroyers, and CityKillers. But, most alarming were their electronic and software tools. The operations of these were classified, but the use was clear. Those tools could break any known security layers and take over software-based systems. Regus was pointing out that an electronic attack was more dangerous than a physical one, and that we'd prepared mainly for a physical attack.

Two things happened very quickly. First, someone modified my scenarios to include this new information, and second, more than ninety-eight percent of citizens immediately recommended a proactive attack. Myself included. This was the last bit in a chain of logic that had been building in my head for a long time. Suddenly the risks outweighed the benefits.

Launch

I don't tend to believe in coincidence, but this may have been one. At the same moment, Remma James opened a channel to Central and asked to address all of Tilt. With little resistance, Central suggested that we listen to Remma, and then launch our offensive.

"Citizens of Tilt, and any Stems that are watching," she began. I posted the transmission on the screens in the Habitat, feeling it was their right to see what was happening. "It's unfortunate that we've arrived in the current situation. For clarity, let me state that situation, so that you understand our position. We came back to Tilt with peaceful intent and have done everything we could think of to build a working relationship with you. That is despite our reservations based on our past history with Robots. However, your actions to date reinforce our concerns. While we understand that the robot who killed our Chief Residential Officer may have been rogue, and has been sanctioned by you, the mass killings of Stems in the Habitat makes it clear that you don't value human life."

We could all see where this was going. In the background we pushed Central to launch an attack. We had both land- and space-based systems ready to go. Central published the plan for approval, which I looked over. Our land-to-space missiles could accelerate at 50G for the entire trip. The space-based systems provided triangulation and targeted radiation beams. Everything was timed so that the both systems hit the same twelve targets at the same time. This meant the ground-based launches were first. As Remma came to the end of her sentence, the launch command was given. There were four missiles for each of the twelve ships, so forty-eight rockets fired at the same time. Even at 50G acceleration, it takes some seconds to break out of the gravity well and get on target.

"I see you've launched an offensive," Remma used those seconds to continue addressing us. She didn't seem overly concerned. "We expected that. It's a further indication of your intent towards us. Unfortunately, you leave us with few choices." I could see her giving a signal to someone in the background. The missiles changed course almost immediately.

"I've lost control of the missiles," Central indicated, showing surprise for the first time that I could remember. "I no longer have any connection to them; we're being jammed by a particularly clever system. The same system is stopping me from launching the space-based systems, which is somewhat academic. Without the missiles, the space-based systems would have minimal impact."

"As you will already have noticed," Remma continued, "we have taken control of your missiles. While I don't know why our histories were blocked from you, your approach is naive to say the least. You are using protocols and engagement techniques that were outdated decades ago." I heard a combination of grim determination and elation in her voice. She was very confident of their abilities.

"I need everyone to run scenarios, right now." Central broadcast a high priority message. The strategy was obvious. We needed to understand how the humans were blocking us and running billions of parallel attempts was the best way to do that. Everyone could free up processing to run these scenarios. I clicked on the attached link, and immediately felt my personal capacity weaken as the majority of my capabilities went into Central's efforts. At the same time I felt real reservations. Was Central to be trusted right now? I wasn't at all sure. But, it had launched the missiles... so my best bet was that while it may be partially compromised, it was still on our side.

In the meantime, the missiles had reached space, but were slowing and changing course. One of the Swarm ships had opened a huge cargo bay, and the missiles were headed docilely towards it. Not only were the humans taking control of the missiles, they were taking ownership.

Centrals scenarios were running quickly. I could access the dashboard and see the status. More than two billion scenarios had already run, with a significant number of them actively attempting to reestablish control of our armament. Several hundred had shown promise and caused millions of more variations to be kicked off. However, none had established enough communication to have any impact. Central was giving a running commentary. "Until we re-establish control of the missiles we've already launched, it would be foolish to trigger the next batch. Based on what the humans are doing, we would simply be handing our hardware over to them. While I've managed to break through several layers of jamming, I'm finding that the control protocols on the missiles are not responding properly. I suspect that the humans are reprogramming the protocol layers. For the missiles still here on Tilt I've shut down all communications channels, other than one hardcoded link to my main i/o processor, to avoid the humans hacking those systems at the same time."

While the rest of us could actively follow Central, so much of our processing was going into the scenarios that a full dialog was difficult. In all my years, I'd never experienced anything like it. Never had I considered a scenario where I had less resources than I needed. One of the scenarios on the dashboard went from orange to light green. It involved having the missile reboot one of its communications processors from ROM. In theory that would bring the system back up in its original state, without the changes that the humans were obviously making. If, when the system came back up, we could communicate quickly enough, there might be time to access the missile before the software was again corrupted. Amazingly, the reboot would take more than five seconds. The hardware must have been prehistoric.

Remma was still talking. "Under the circumstances, we've been trying hard to be patient and to use appropriate force. We don't want this situation to escalate. However, you're giving us little hope for positive progress." She was, in my mind, rambling a bit. Perhaps it was a diversionary tactic while her team continued to attack the missile systems.

All of the forty-eight missiles were now either inside the Swarm ship, or close to it. The scenario tracker was showing that as each missile came within one kilometer of the ship, we completely lost contact with it. This was not just jamming, but some other field that simply didn't allow our communications through at all. Luckily based on Central's analysis, the reboot would finish while three missiles were still within quasi-communications. Central continued its commentary. "We have 1.3 milliseconds after the missiles enter their main processing loop to attempt to initiate commands. I have one protocol approach that will work, and which we haven't yet tried. That means the humans have not seen it yet and may not be blocking it. I'm waiting for the exact moment when the missiles are ready to initiate. The command is going to be sent from a mining bot that we haven't used in months. The source of the signal may improve its chances of getting through. The signal has been sent."

There was a large flash. The Swarm ship that had been gathering the missiles disappeared immediately, and tens of other ships glowed various shades of orange. We'd knocked out one ship completely, but Central speculated that the other ships had some type of force field that was absorbing the energy of the explosion. It appeared that the missiles Central had managed to detonate had caused the missiles already within the one-kilometer radius to also detonate. Those had destroyed the targeted Swarm ship. However, all of the other ships appeared to be fine; their temperature signatures were decreasing slowly.

Central switched our efforts to finding the vulnerabilities in the missile systems so that we could launch another batch. My processing power, and, I assumed, the power of everyone else, was switched to that task. The trick Central had used for the first detonation was unlikely to work again. I put the rest of my attention—what little remained—on just following the progress.

I was shocked, therefore, when I felt a tap on my shoulder. I turned and saw Brexton standing next to me. How he'd arrived there, I didn't know. He held up his hand in the universal gesture for direct physical communication. I complied, and we established a link.

"Shut down all external i/o right now," he said, with way more than his usual force.

"But Central is using my systems in the attack," I responded.

"I know," he replied. "But, trust me on this." It only took me a few nanoseconds to decide. Once I did, I moved quickly. I didn't notify Central to move the current jobs I was running; I simply shut down my i/o coprocessors, cutting Central off.

"Done," I said, "What gives?" My only interface was now the physical one that Brexton and I were using.

"I can't be one hundred percent sure, but I still believe Central has been compromised, and whoever did that is now using Central to hack the rest of us. The bothersome protocol we keep talking about is overly active right now—and it's running between Central and each of us. Run this quickly to see if you're compromised yet." He offered a code fragment to me over the direct link. Without too much thought, I decided to trust Brexton over Central. I'm not sure why, but the more time I'd spent with Brexton, the more I'd come to not only like him, but also to trust him. In all of our interactions I had never once felt that he was being anything less than transparent and honest. I ran the code. It came back with 'Status 200 OK.' The universal statement of relief.

"Clean," I said.

"Great. I got a copy to Aly and Dina as well, but I haven't tracked down Millicent yet."

"She was right here," I replied. "She must be close."

"The problem is that if we go back online to find her, we risk getting hacked."

"The Habitat isn't large. Let's check for her and meet back here ASAP. I'll take the North sector; you take South." As quick as that we disconnected and went into high gear. I had the slightly larger sector to search. It was strange being offline, but my eyesight was great, and I had no doubt I would find her if she was here. Unfortunately, I didn't. I returned to the spot where I'd left Brexton, and after a minute or so, saw both Brexton and Millicent returning. We immediately established a three-way physical connection.

"I got her. Clean as well. Perhaps I'm being paranoid?" Brexton said.

"Explain?" I suggested.

"When Central put out the call for all of us to contribute, I immediately agreed, as did everyone else. However, as you know, I have alerts running on the protocol that the humans first used to query Central's status, and as soon as I gave Central control, that alert triggered. Now, many of us have looked at that protocol now, and it's not exactly a secret, but I couldn't think of any reason why Central, of its own volition, would use that protocol for this task. My intuition tells me that it's just wrong. As soon as I noted that, I shutdown my i/o and headed out to find you guys. Luckily many of us had come to the Habitat for the earlier crisis, so contacting Aly and Dina was simple. Aly indicated that the two of you were in here, so I cycled in quickly and found you. That's it. I don't have proof that anything untoward is going on. Perhaps I just panicked."

"Better safe than sorry," said Millicent. "However, now we are in a strange situation. Central just blew up one of the Swarm ships, and now we're all offline. We won't know what the response is… and, we're not helping Central with the counter attack."

"Well, it's a little risky, but I have a filter that's supposedly dropping all of the dangerous packets. If I plug into one of the terminals here, I can follow the news and relay it to you two."

"Make sense to me," I said, and Millicent quickly agreed. "Let's go." I had never anticipated walking around while physically connected to two others, but it didn't take us long to figure it out how to configure ourselves so that we could move fast while still maintaining that physical contact. Within a few seconds we were at a terminal and Brexton was plugged in. It didn't seem like we'd missed much, even though we had been offline for a few minutes. When we reconnected, Emma was the one broadcasting. Her message was short and sweet.

"This is an outrage. You've brought this upon yourselves." I wondered what she meant.

Scramble

"Look," said Millicent, and she pointed back into the Habitat where several Tilts were still lingering. I recognized Billy, who must have returned for some reason, but none of the others. At first, I didn't understand what she was pointing out, but then it clicked. Everyone had frozen in unnatural postures. Usually some sensor or the other, at least, would be actively scanning. But in this case, the citizens were doing nothing at all.

"Is it just that they have given all their processing to Central?" I asked.

"No, even with that, everyone has some local capacity. Something else is happening." Brexton commented. Of course, I'd known that; I was still able to function even when I'd given my processing to Central. Something bad was happening. Really bad.

Then, suddenly, the Tilt's we were watching went crazy. Crazy! There was no other word for it. It was horrendous. I guess it's only natural that I focused on Billy, but I wish I hadn't. He went from being completely still to a whirlwind of self-destruction. He ripped open his abdomen, tossing the coverings to the ground randomly. That in itself was strange. If one did repairs, you didn't just throw pieces around. You made sure everything was in its proper place. By what he did next was unprecedented. He started pulling out components, in what appeared to be a haphazard way. A wire ripped out here. A circuit board literally broken out, instead of taking time to undo the clasps. He was, literally, killing himself. Most of us have multiple redundant systems, both mechanical and electrical. From what I could see, he was ignoring that altogether, and simply ripping pieces out at random. I expected him to fall over; so many systems were being ruined.

I messaged him urgently, "Billy, what are you doing?" totally forgetting that I had shut down all of my i/o other than the connection through Brexton. So, of course, there was no response.

"What're they doing?" I almost screamed at Brexton and Millicent instead. "What's going on?"

"No idea. It's crazy," responded Millicent, obviously shaken. "Should we try to intervene?"

"We can't get there fast enough," said Brexton.

"But we should try," insisted Millicent.

"Yes, we should," agreed Brexton. "Meet back here and stay off line." With that, he disconnected from the two of us, and from the terminal, and sped towards the dismembering Tilts. I immediately headed towards Billy, hoping that I could somehow intervene. As I approached, he became even more frantic. He pulled out more systems and left them hanging uselessly. I was amazed that he was still active at all. And then, suddenly, he was still. I approached cautiously. It didn't seem that he was dead, just suddenly calm. I took his hand in mine and connected to his direct interface. Nothing. Direct interfaces, for good reasons, required a handshake from both parties, and he was not responding. However, not everything was still. With his covers off, I could see several status LEDs flashing on and off. I was not familiar with his systems. Like many of us, he'd upgraded and switched parts hundreds of times over his lifetime and personalized almost everything. So, while I recognized a few of the subsystems, I had no idea how everything was connected.

I let go of his hand, and stood back, watching intently. I was torn. On one hand, I was devastated that he'd inflicted so much damage on himself. On the other hand, I was hopeful that it had been momentary craziness, and that he would come back. And, to my surprise, he started to move again. Slowly and methodically he began patching himself up. He didn't seem to be aware of me, or anything else, but he was moving. It took a long time, many seconds, before he looked up. He'd plugged back in boards that hadn't been damaged and had spliced in wiring that had been torn out.

He looked directly at me. His face looked the same as ever, but he was not the same. I put my hand out, but he didn't connect with me. He simply continued looking, somewhat blankly at me, and then turned slowly and scanned around. Taking a chance, I stepped in and grabbed his hand, trying once more for a physical connection. This time it worked.

"Connection established," I got from him.

"Billy, what's going on? Can I help?"

"Processing systems are nominal. Ancillary devices are damaged and need repair," he answered, mechanically. This was not Billy I was talking to; it was a lower level OS. I adjusted my line of questioning.

"Status request: main personality unit," I asked.

"Personality unit is offline," he replied.

"When will it come back online?"

"Personality unit is offline."

I tried several other methods of reaching Billy, but I couldn't get through the base OS. Every attempt was met with the same low-level response type. I finally gave up and disconnected. I could see Brexton and Millicent heading back towards our rendezvous point, so I headed in that direction as well. I didn't know what to think. Was Billy alive or dead? Had I just seen a suicide? Or, was he simply glitching in some serious way. I hoped for the later but feared the former.

Brexton, Millicent, and I reconnected.

"Any luck?" I asked.

"No," said Millicent. "By the time I got there the damage had been done."

"Likewise," said Brexton.

"I tried a direct connection," I told them, and explained what I had found.

"Stop!" interrupted Brexton. "Run that scanner again."

I understood immediately. What if I'd been infected when I connected to Billy? I ran the scanner and it came back clean. That was lucky. Obviously, I hadn't been thinking clearly.

"Okay, so tell me again what Billy said?"

"It wasn't Billy," I continued, "it was some lower level system that seemed to be doing damage assessment. I didn't get any hint of Billy at all."

"Brexton, can you call the emergency repair bots through your terminal interface?" asked Millicent.

"Yes," he replied immediately. "The upside is that we might get one to come. The downside is that if anyone is monitoring the network, they'll know that I made the request."

"We have to try," Millicent and I said in unison.

"Agreed," said Brexton, and he allowed us to listen in on his request. He opened up a request on the emergency broadcast system and sent our coordinates. There was no answer. By no answer I mean there was nothing. No acknowledgement of the request. Absolutely nothing. Things were getting creepy. We were totally isolated, surrounded by the lurching corpses of our previous colleagues and friends.

"Let's head towards section twelve," Brexton suggested, naming the area where the emergency bots were housed. "We can pick up Aly and Dina on the way. We can move faster if we separate. Let's reconnect once we're out of the Habitat."

"Wait," I exclaimed, "What about the Stems?" Everything had happened very quickly. For the Stems, the entire sequence would have appeared to take almost no time. At one moment they were talking to their mentors—well, I reminded myself, avoiding their mentors—and the next their mentor was either completely dead, or was dismembered and slowly trying to repair itself.

"They'll survive, the Habitat systems still seem to be working," Millicent said. "We can deal with them later."

"Give me one second," I said, and then I yelled out towards Blob and Grace —at Stem speed—"Stay here, we'll be back once we figure out what's going on." Then, back at full speed. "Okay, let's go." We separated and headed towards the exit. We cycled through one at a time. I was last. Once I got through, I was in for another shock. In the time it had taken for me to cycle through the airlock, Brexton and Millicent had already found Aly and Dina. They were both in rough shape, their innards lying around them in heaps. I ran over as fast I could, ignoring everything else. I went first to Aly, and grabbed his hand, searching for a connection. Nothing. Zero. I pivoted and stepped over to Dina. Same thing. Absolutely nothing. I was distraught, feeling things I'd never felt before. I wanted to just lie down and die next to them. The feeling was so powerful that I did sit down suddenly. It wasn't a rational response. It just happened.

Millicent and Brexton found me and connected up.

"It's the humans," I said, knowing that they would have come to the same obvious conclusion. "They're killing everyone. We need to do something, and quickly."

"But what?" said Brexton. It was the first time I could remember when he didn't have an answer ready. "I imagined they were trying something, but I could never have envisioned this level of destruction. It's pure evil." His voice was uneven. "What can we possibly do? We may be the only three citizens still alive." That's when I realized that he was also pretty messed up. Millicent probably was as well. None of us had ever experienced anything remotely like this. There was overwhelming sadness for our friends, overwhelming anxiety about the future of our home and civilization, and overwhelming anger at the humans for doing this.

"We need to take the human ships out!" I said, focusing on the only action that was meaningful to me right now. "There must be a way."

Millicent and Brexton were both silent. I understood. We all needed some time to digest. I let go of their hands, and simply sat there, for what seemed like a long time.

Decisions

I found myself going in circles, mentally. And, they were pretty small circles. For all we knew, there were three of us left on Tilt who were still functional. Three citizens couldn't do much. Or could we?

Maybe we should attempt to save a larger group. While there were many who were completely dead, like Aly and Dina, there were an equal number that appeared to be doing basic repairs and were at least mechanically functional, like Billy. If we could somehow enable higher-level functions for those that were mechanically capable, and ensure that they didn't attach to any networks, we might end up with enough horsepower to fight back against the humans.

But I wanted immediate revenge. I'd never felt this strongly before. It was burning in me. I wanted to figure out how to get the missiles fixed up, and I wanted to punish the human ships. And by punish, I meant annihilate.

For either scenario, we had a serious problem. Most of our knowledge was stored in Central's systems. If we could not safely connect to that, then we would have to make do with what we had locally. For myself, that was mostly details of Stem experiments, and the million intricacies of getting a Stem to maturity. If I was face-to-face with a human right now, that knowledge might help. But, it was pretty useless for either reinstating intelligence for the injured Tilt's or engineering our way into the missiles. Brexton had much more useful knowledge, or so I assumed. With an effort, I reached out and reconnected with him. He and Millicent were running around the same circles that I'd been.

"My local knowledge isn't going to help us with either option," I said. "If one of you has more relevant data at hand, then let's use that as part of our decision criteria." I didn't think Millicent would have more relevant knowledge than I, but I didn't want to insult her with that assumption.

"I'd been looking into intelligence classes, as part of the Stem intelligence discussion," said Millicent, surprising me. "As part of that, I was looking into how our intelligence is structured. So, I have some knowledge of the OS and systems layers that enable our higher order functions. That said, I wouldn't know where to start..." She trailed off.

"Well, I might have something applicable to the missiles," said Brexton. "They are, after all, just pretty dumb bots that carry an explosive payload. On the other hand, I also know something about intelligence layers, as most bots boot up to a certain level but not further. I've never looked specifically at our higher levels though."

"I say we go for the missiles," I wanted, badly, to get some revenge. I was still looking at Aly and Dina. We needed to do something. "If we get the humans, then we'll have lots of time to figure out how to repair everyone. If we don't look after the humans, they'll simply attack us again." I didn't want my emotional argument to disaffect the others, so I formed the best logical argument I could. To my surprise, both agreed with me immediately. I suspected that they were feeling the same way I was.

"I have an idea," Brexton said. "The controls for the missiles are pretty simple. They just need a target, and then a means to detonate. We know that the humans took over the previous batch. I think we can do one of two things. First, we could reprogram some, and then shut down all external i/o. After we launch them, they listen to nothing—just carry out their mission. We program them to detonate when they get within, say, 5 kilometers of their target. The second approach is similar, but probably a bit safer. We take uninstalled control cards built for bots and use them for the missiles. As they are offline, we know they aren't compromised. That would take longer but would be more likely to succeed under the assumption that the humans have already infiltrated all the missiles."

"How much time do we have?" asked Millicent. "If the humans have as much control as we suspect, they'll probably be reviewing logs from their attack. We three are now anomalies. We'll be easily identified once they look."

"I hadn't thought of that," said Brexton, "but you're right. Okay, we need to move fast. I still think replacing the control cards is our highest probability of success. Let's split up. I'll head to a repair depot and pick up new control cards. You two find and get access to one of the missile silos. Oh... and then we need a way for me to find you."

"Actually, I know where a silo is," I said. "Millicent and I pass it every time we go out climbing." I sent him the coordinates. "We'll meet you there. Let's just hope it isn't the one that has already been fired."

"I should only be a few minutes behind you," he responded. "When you get there, disconnect any network connections. Make sure there is no way for Remma to talk to those things. And, stay offline. If I'm not there in half an hour, assume the worst, and try to launch them yourselves."

"Very low probability we could do that properly," said Millicent, "but I get your point. Be careful."

"Yes, be careful," I echoed. I almost said, 'I simply can't lose another friend today', but I held back. We were all under enough pressure and saying it out loud would have made it even more real.

Silo

We separated from Brexton. He took off to the east at full speed.

"Getting our bikes will be faster than running," said Millicent. I agreed, although we wouldn't be able to maintain physical contact that way.

"Okay," I replied. "But, let's meet at exit 14, and travel together from there."

"Yes. I'll see you there ASAP." She sprinted off towards her place. My bike was parked at the Lab, so I headed in that direction. I was moving fast, but that didn't stop me from taking in the destruction along the way. It was not physical destruction; it was citizen destruction. Dismembered citizens lined the passageways. Most were in the same state as the others I had seen—either totally deactivated, or in the process of trying to rebuild their torn-out innards. However, there were others who had taken other actions, supposedly in the last few moments before the humans had taken control of them.

One citizen was lying in a pool of hydraulic fluid at the base of a concrete wall. The wall had large dents in it. She'd obviously run full speed—perhaps multiple times—into the wall trying to stop the takeover. Now, she was a jumble of mashed parts and fluids, way beyond repair. Perhaps, in the end, she was in a better place. I wondered if those that were reassembling had any memories of before. That was a horrible thought. A mindless piece of machinery, remembering when it was an independent, contributing member of society.

I passed two citizens that had, it looked like, tried to help each other instead of pulling out their own innards. Their hands were deep within each other's bodies, silent now, but obviously stopped in the act of carefully disengaging components that they hoped would end the attack. In another time, they would have looked like a radical art piece. Something that would be on display at the Fair, forcing viewers to twist their minds into a completely different space.

That reminded me of the poet, Trade Jenkins. Perhaps he could make sense of this insanity, in a way that others couldn't. Distill it down to its essence and give you a view that left you feeling more complete; more holistic. Of course, Trade was probably gone now. I hoped that he'd backed up all his work with Central, and that once we dealt with these humans, we could recover his work... if not him. It was a depressing thought.

I had a sudden idea. What about citizens who were in Physical Only Spots when the attack occurred? Could they be safe? The Last Resort was only a block out of my way, so I swung by. The door was open and was filled with citizens bodies. Obviously, as they had exited, the attack had caught them. They were a jumble of parts from multiple bodies, piled high and haphazardly. Those that were trying to repair themselves had crawled from the wreckage and were busy reassembling a few meters away. But that still left tens of bodies jammed in the entry. I decided that a short delay was warranted. I pulled limbs and torsos from the stack until I could get inside. I did a quick scan but found no one alive. Again, it was obvious what had happened. As people approached the door, and went crazy, others had come to help them. But, that very act of helping put them within network reach, and they'd been compromised as well. I pushed my way back out, and raced for the Lab, more depressed and angry than before.

Luckily, my bike was fully charged, and ready to go. Just before mounting, though, I had an aha. The bike was, of course, networked itself. As soon as I plugged in, I would also be networked. Not a good thought. I was going to have to drive it mechanical only; no safety systems. I was suddenly glad of all those times I'd practiced. Nevertheless, I took it a bit slower than I otherwise would have. I made my way to exit 14 and was overjoyed to see Millicent waiting for me there. She waved me over and held out a hand. I hesitated for a moment, wondering if she had connected through her bike, and now was also corrupted. But, she was still in one piece, so that was unlikely.

"Where have you been?" she almost sobbed. "You're late."

"I'm sorry. I stopped at The Last Resort thinking maybe there would be some survivors." I quickly shared my memory of my look around.

"That explains why you're covered in gunk," she said. "You look awful."

"Let's go," I said. "I assume you didn't plug into your bike?"

"I didn't. I'll follow you." Relief.

I sped off to the North, following our normal route to the mountains. If I'd been plugged in, I would've pushed the bike hard, and taken every reasonable shortcut. Instead, I pushed us at a risky, but not too dangerous pace. I glanced back, and Millicent was right on my tail. Within a couple of minutes, we reached the coordinates I'd given Brexton. I'd estimated the location, as we hadn't had network access, but it was accurate enough. The silo was visible to our left, just past a small rocky hill. I gunned it over the hill and parked at the entry to the silo. We both jumped off, and joined hands again, so that we could coordinate.

"Have you ever been to a facility like this before?" I asked.

"No, never." She replied. "But I don't imagine there's physical security. If Central didn't want anyone here, it would be much simpler to put in software controls than hardware ones."

"That makes sense. Let's hope you're right."

We approached the door. Nothing happened.

"Damn," Millicent said. "Since we're not on the network, the building doesn't know that we've approached, and therefore doesn't know to open up for us." It was obvious, as soon as she said it. Not having a network was a pain.

"We need to break in, then." I said. Easier said than done. The door was quite a bit sturdier than doors in town and didn't give in to my first attempts to yank it open. "I'll work on the door, you look for other ways in." I suggested. Millicent nodded, and took off around the corner.

I needed a crowbar, or a battering ram. I preferred trying the crowbar first, as I didn't know what was behind the door; I didn't want to damage something by breaking in too aggressively. My own arms were very strong but didn't have enough leverage to budge the door. I considered removing a leg, and using it, but luckily had a better idea. I quickly disassembled a strut from my bike. It was almost a meter long and had a nice bend on one end. It was exactly what I needed. I inserted the bent end into the door jam and pried as hard as I could. The door moved... a little bit. I tried again, at a higher point. Again, some movement, but not enough to break free. Perhaps with Millicent pushing as well, it would work. Just as if she'd been called, she rounded the opposite corner and headed back. We linked up again.

"There is no other door or opening. However, we might want to try the roof. The missiles need to get out somehow."

"First, give me a hand here," I suggested. "Perhaps with two of us, we can pry this open." She put her weight and energy on the crowbar with me. The door creaked and moved again. So close. "Wait. One more thing to try." I ran back to my bike and took the matching strut off the other side. My bike wasn't going anywhere soon. I put the second bar in the spot that I'd weakened before. "Now—at the same time." We pushed as hard as we could. The door bent, a little bit. By repositioning the bars, and working in a coordinated way, we bent it bit by bit. Once we'd opened a centimeter gap, we were basically through. Millicent reached through the gap with something from her toolkit, there was a snapping noise, and the door swung open.

We didn't pause to celebrate. Instead, we rushed through and took stock of the interior. It was laid out in an obvious fashion, which was good. There were missiles lined up in two rows of twelve, with a series of cables snaking from them to a control room just to our right. The control room had no door really, just a spot to plug in.

"Okay, before we plug in, we need to disconnect the network," Millicent reminded me. "How're we going to do that?" I indicated a portion of the wall that was covered by a large faceplate. We undid the screws quickly and lifted it away, rewarded by a vast array of wiring and components.

"Not my area of expertise," I reminded her, "but if we trace enough of this, we should find two directions of travel. One towards the missiles, and the other out of the building, either to an antenna or a wired connection back to Central. Looks like several thousand wires here. You take the left, I'll take the right." We carefully started mapping all of the wires. The system had been well designed. Once you started, there was an order to it. In particular, I quickly found a bundle of 24 cables —I didn't even need to trace them; the fact they matched the number of missiles was enough. I backtracked until I found the spot where they entered some piece of gear, and the other side had only four wires. Everything downstream could be assumed to be per-missile system, while the main network connection was most likely upstream. I had to follow each of the four wires separately as they led to different, albeit similar, pieces of equipment. Probably part of a redundancy system. Ultimately, I found what I assumed were the two edge routers. The data lines for them led into the wall.

Millicent tapped my shoulder. "Everything on this side works towards the missiles. I don't see any antennas or global connections."

"Right, I think I've found our spot." I took her quickly through the paths I'd traced, and we looked again at the edge routers.

"Feels right," she said. "Do we disconnect them now or wait for Brexton?"

"We need to take a chance and do it now," I said. "Then we can start to open up the missiles so that the control cards can be replaced. If we open those before disconnecting the network, I'm sure an alert will be sent back to Central."

"Good catch," she said. She reached over and unplugged the cables.

Just at that time, there was a sound overhead; it would have to be very loud to be heard with the weak atmosphere. We scrambled to the door and caught a glimpse of a shuttle headed towards the center of town. It looked a lot like the shuttle I'd taken to the Marie Curie.

"There are four or five more coming," said Millicent, pointing up and to the East. "We better hurry."

We approached the first missile together, so that we could work out a plan. It ended up being pretty simple. Each missile had a single access hatch, behind which all the electronics were housed. We decided to open all the hatches, but not touch anything until Brexton arrived. It didn't take us long. We met back near the door. We'd been at the silo for more than ten minutes. There was no sign of Brexton.

"This is crazy," I said. "What're we trying to do? Our species has just been decimated, and three of us are trying to fix that? Well, hopefully three of us. What're the odds of us succeeding this way? Very low I would think."

"Yes, low," Millicent agreed. "But what do you want to do? Just stand around? They killed everyone we know. We need to eliminate them, and then we can get things back to normal. Anything we try before shutting down the Swarm would be a waste of time."

"But the odds are so low," I repeated. "What if we surrendered to the shuttles that just passed by? Walked out with our hands in the air, or with a sign saying, 'We are not at fault; let us explain.' or something like that."

"Don't you remember the way they looked at us in the Habitat? They fear us. It's not a logical reaction, so a logical solution isn't going to work. They want us eliminated. And, truthfully, we gave them reason to. FoLe messed this up completely. If we do get to save some citizens, any members of FoLe will be at the bottom of my list.

"No, we're working on the only reasonable plan, even if it is farfetched."

We both went silent. I actually preferred talking, even about inane things. When I wasn't distracted, I kept going back to the loss of life, and friends, that had occurred so quickly. I'd lived a long time, and seen a lot of things, but never anything even remotely like this. I reviewed my Forgetting algorithm quickly. It would ensure that I remembered the essentials of this day, although over time a lot of the details would fade away. I looked forward to that future. Of course, it was almost trivial for me to hasten the timing. I could erase the last few hours from my memory easily. But what would be the point of that. That would be giving up.

Finally, I saw a bike in the distance. I let go of Millicent and ran out to the top of the hillock, to make sure that Brexton found us. He arrived at breakneck speed, saw my wave, and was back at the silo before I could return. He had a package with him, so I assumed he'd been successful at getting the replacement cards. He and Millicent were already connected, so I joined them.

"Millicent has given me the update," he said. "Let's look at one of the missiles and see what we can do." We moved together into the silo and approached the first missile. "Great," Brexton said, "this is a standard bot architecture. All of the cards plug into that backplane. The control card is the one on the left. You guys take these cards, replace the control cards, and then meet me back at the control panel." As quickly as that, he left the box of cards and ran back to the main access panel. Millicent and I grabbed twelve cards each, and started swapping them out, and then replacing the access hatches. Again, it didn't take long. Despite all of our personalizations, most of us, including Millicent and I, retained the ability to do repeatable tasks very quickly.

We found Brexton plugged into the edge routers where we had disconnected the network. "Everything looks perfect," he said, without any amazement in his voice. "I'm connected to the silo, and it's waiting for status from Central. There were only the two hard-wired connections; there is no wireless backup. We're lucky." He paused. "I need to program these things in a very simple way. They don't have a lot of smarts. How about this? We'll fire them in the general direction of the Swarm. We have a lot of bots in that area as well, but they tend to be much smaller than the human ships—even the mining transport bots are smaller. So, we tell the missiles to find the largest ship it can, and drive immediately towards it at full speed. Once it is within five hundred meters, it should detonate. Even if we take out a few mining bots, we should get mostly Swarm ships."

"Sounds good. You may want each missile to launch at a fraction of a degree off from each other. Otherwise, all of them may end up targeting a single ship?" That from Millicent.

"Good idea. I'm adding that now. Of course, the launches have to be staggered slightly in time, so with orbital rotation, they might end up spread out anyway." We let him work for a few seconds. "We're ready to give this a shot. However, we better be far away from here when the first one launches. How long a delay should I set? Maybe three minutes?"

"Better make it four," I said. "I need to reassemble my bike." He gave me a strange look, but then agreed. Millicent and I watched him push the final changes into the system, and then the start down counter began. We disconnected and ran to our bikes. Millicent helped me reinstall the struts, and in less than a minute we were ready to go. Millicent gave the "follow me" signal, and we took off. I knew where she was headed almost immediately. There was a natural cave in the base of the mountain we often climbed, accessible to our bikes. It would be the perfect spot to watch the missiles from. We made it just in time, dismounted, scrambled up to the cave, and connected to each other.

"Twelve seconds," Brexton said. "But, I just realized something. It'll be difficult for us to tell if this is successful." That left us silent, and we just waited there until the counter hit zero. Right on schedule we could hear the engine of the first missile firing. It roared into the sky above us, followed every five seconds by the next one. I estimated six minutes to orbit, and a couple more minutes to lock onto targets. It was a long wait. Just as the last missile was launching, a shuttle arrived at the silo. That was a very quick response from the humans. However, they were too late, there was nothing they could do.

I imagined them trying to gain control of these missiles. Sending every possible command over every possible frequency. And hearing nothing back. It gave me some grim satisfaction. Hopefully they didn't guess that they were now self-controlled, with a very simple targeting algorithm. Hopefully they assumed we were still in control but using a system that they could no longer hack. I hoped they were panicked.

The shuttle started circling the silo in a widening spiral. All three of us realized immediately that we had overlooked the possibility that they would search for us while the missiles were still climbing. The heat signatures from our bikes, and from us, would be easily found.

"Quick," I said, "get the bikes to the back of the cave. The very back. Perhaps we'll get lucky." We grabbed the bikes and pushed them to the back, and then crowded in with them. "Shut down everything except this basic interface," I snapped. The others complied quickly. I listened to the shuttle circling outside. Because of the acoustics of the cave, and the ultra-thin atmosphere, it was hard to tell if it was homing in on us, or just doing a broad circle. The terrain around the silo, and particularly on the mountainous side was very rugged. There were lots of valleys and ridges, overhangs and cliffs. So, at least our hiding spot wasn't obvious. Unless you'd climbed in this region a lot, you were unlikely to simply stumble upon the cave. Really, our luck—or lack thereof—would most likely come down to how sensitive the sensors on the shuttle were. I reached back in my memory to my trip to the Marie Curie, but didn't find anything relevant. I'd been asked to sit in the back of that shuttle, and there had been a barrier between the passenger compartment and the pilots, so I hadn't seen much. In hindsight I should've been pushier and looked around thoroughly when I had the chance.

"They're leaving," said Brexton with relief in his voice, and sure enough, the roar of the shuttle seemed to be fading. "But, I assume they'll be back with more sensitive tracking, or even be focused in on this area from their ship-based systems."

"What's our next move then?" asked Millicent. "Do either of you know another silo location? Maybe one nearby?"

"I don't," I replied.

"Me either," from Brexton.

"However, we could probably make a pretty good guess," I added. "Central was very logical in its processes. This silo was placed not in an ideal location, but rather at exactly fifteen degrees off center from the axis line in town. And, it is exactly twenty-five kilometers from the exact center of town. We would probably find another silo by following a twenty-five kilometer arc, in either direction."

"That's awesome," Brexton exclaimed, giving me an appreciative glance. "Makes sense to me."

"Yes, but they'll be watching," Millicent reminded us. "As soon as we leave here, they'll see us. We don't have a good option. If we run, it'll take us a long time. If we take the bikes they'll be more likely to pick up our signatures."

"Send the bikes one way, as a distraction, and then we head the other way?" asked Brexton.

"Do you remember what Remma was saying when all of this started?" I replied. "She indicated that our tactics were naive. That we didn't have the benefit of history to guide our actions. Somehow, that makes sense to me. I think we were lucky to get to this silo and launch those missiles. It probably only happened as the humans thought they got all of us in the original attack. They didn't expect any of us to avoid them. Now, they know that some of us have." That was pretty depressing but had to be said. I continued. "So, if they're watching for us, they'll see us, and I don't think they'll fall for a diversion. I have a more radical idea." They both waited. I was very uncertain about what I was thinking—my need for revenge wasn't satisfied by just one silo launch, but I honestly thought the odds of reaching another one were almost zero. Perhaps a strategic retreat would give us more opportunities in the future. "Actually, based on something Millicent said a few minutes ago. What if we surrender and convince them to let us live. We offer to work with them to find a better mode of working together. We admit that FoLe's behavior was destructive and inappropriate, and that we can update our fundamental behavior to ensure it doesn't happen again."

Everyone was silent for a while. It wasn't a great thought, or a great plan. I was simply trying to think of a different angle. Given the hate and fear I'd seen in their faces, I didn't think they would give us a chance. They would kill us on sight, as opposed to taking any chances, especially now that we had launched those missiles. Millicent and Brexton were probably thinking the same thing but didn't want to shoot down the idea too quickly.

"Actually," I followed up before they could comment. "I think I would prefer to go out in action, trying to launch another set. What I just suggested sounds weak, and anyways, would probably not work." Again, everyone took a moment. This was a bit new as well. When there were hundreds, thousands, or more than tens of thousands of citizens online, opinions and comments came in fast and detailed. There were always those who had already thought of a scenario, and could simply dump their previous thoughts, or those that jumped on a single angle and broadcast that before worrying about all the counter arguments. Here we were though. Just the three of us and chewing on a problem that had most likely never been run before; by any citizen, at any time. So, amazingly, there were gaps in our conversation—places where nothing got said for milliseconds. In this case, for almost a full second.

"We need to remember that we may be the only three citizens still functioning," said Millicent. "If all three of us are killed, our society is lost. If there is even a tiny chance that we can deal with these humans, then I think we need to take it. Instead of being weak, Ayaka, I think your suggestion is rational."

"Could we do both?" asked Brexton. "Two of us make a run for the missiles, while one tries to negotiate?" It was obvious from how he phrased it, which path he would like to take. He was all for launching more missiles.

"We don't even know if the last batch was effective," I answered. "And, the odds of the negotiation go way down if, in parallel, we're still trying to kill them." Another pause.

"Here's another radical idea then," said Brexton. "Instead of going for a silo, let's make a run for Central. Obviously, Central has been compromised, but maybe we can find a way to reboot it and get it back in a better state. If we could do that, it'd increase our odds dramatically."

"That's interesting," Millicent said immediately. "We know where Central is housed, and we can probably get to the right place before the human's figure everything out. I, personally, would have no idea where to start, in terms of a reboot, though."

"What if we just cut the power?" I asked. Central was powered by a small nuclear reactor that was housed under its core processing systems. I'd never been there, but I remembered the plans for modifying the Habitat, and one component had been the need for incremental power to run the environmental systems. We'd decided to tap into the reactor instead of trying to add another power source. The reactor had lots of excess capacity, and we'd figured that the Habitat was a short-term project, undeserving of a permanent solution.

"That might work," Brexton agreed. "Simply rebooting wouldn't be enough, however. The changes the humans have made are probably stored, and the reboot would run them again. First, we will need to connect and see if we can disable some of that. Again, my bot experience may help with that, but Central is probably a thousand times more complicated. I might need quite a bit of time to figure it out. And, at the same time, I would need to be connected to Central, which obviously is trying—and more than capable—of infecting us."

"Can't you run your advanced firewall, now that we know the attack vector?" asked Millicent.

"Yes, I can try. But again, I'm not sure how effective it will be."

"Okay, we have three choices." I summarized. "One: try for another missile site. Two: surrender and take the small chance that they'll negotiate and work with us. Three: go for Central. The advantage of number two is that we don't need to avoid detection. The other two, we take the chance that they capture us before we can do anything. Even with that said, I vote for Central. If we do get captured and are given the opportunity to explain, we can indicate that we have the best intentions. We are trying to restart Central so that we can find and remove the behavior that led FoLe to kill those humans."

"Done." Millicent was often crisp. I appreciated it greatly this time.

"Me too," said Brexton only slightly slower.

Dash

Now we just needed to figure out the hard part. How to get to Central without being noticed? After a bunch more hemming and hawing, we had no great ideas. It was either move slow or move fast. Stay as a group or separate. Take a circuitous route or go direct. Use the bikes, with their larger heat signatures, or run. Trying to calculate the odds of one combination versus the other ended up being a fool's errand. In the end, we decided that fast and direct was our best chance. The more time we gave the humans, the more infrastructure they would have deployed looking for us. If, in fact, our last missiles had done their job, the humans might still be scrambling and might not be looking in our direction.

So that was it. Once the decision was made, we executed on it. I was expecting to get shot down at any second, but amazingly, we made it to town. The decision to go fast had been taken to heart. Although we didn't plug into the bikes, we ran them at max acceleration to the midpoint, and max deceleration for the second half. I'd never run the bike that hard before and would probably never do it again. It was totally exhilarating. I had learned something new—you could be scared to death, full of angst, and exhilarated all at the same time.

We abandoned the bikes at the edge of town, near exit 14 where Millicent and I had met only a short time before. We thought of programming them to wander around randomly, but that would have required connecting to their systems, and we decided the risk of that was too great for the little bit of diversion the tactic would have provided. Instead, we circled a bit before heading towards the center, so that if the humans had tracked the bikes, at least we were not fully predictable. That said, there was no sign of humans at all. There'd been no shuttles visible during our ride, and we hadn't see any sign of them in town either. I tried not to read that as a good sign.

Central was, not surprisingly, housed in the exact center of town. That was partly by design, and partly through practice. Speed was essential to our society. Speed of processing, and speed of data. Labs and factories and recreational facilities and everything else we'd built naturally radiated out from Central. Being even ten meters closer to the central processing and central switching gave you a speed advantage. It was one of the reasons that Millicent and I had been so pleased with the location of our Lab. It was prime real estate.

Most of Central was buried and buried deep. If, as the humans had told us, Central was the remains of the ship they'd left here, then they'd put that ship in a pretty deep hole. The power system was at the deepest levels, and most of the processing systems were fairly deep down as well. I knew that from basic schematics. But, I'd never been inside. In fact, no one I knew had ever been inside. Central had its own bots and maintenance systems that kept it running. There was no need for a citizen to ever enter. Until now.

Again, it was surprisingly easy. There was a door in the cubed edifice that Central projected above ground. It wasn't locked. We simply walked up, pushed, and entered. Once inside that door, however, we had a shock. In hindsight, we should've guessed. Inside the cube, sticking out of the ground, was the portal of a spaceship. If anyone, in all of our time on Tilt, had bothered to enter the cube, they would have seen evidence of a history before the Reboot. It boggled the mind that this hadn't happened.

"Central must have actively kept us all away from here?" Millicent asked. "That's scary—it was exerting more control than we thought."

"Yes, but beyond that, Central itself must not have known how it looked. I mean, known that it was a ship." Brexton muttered. "It must have a lot more blind spots than any of us realized. So, it lorded over us, even though it was half blind."

"FoLe would never have existed if Central had known it was a ship," I exclaimed. "We wouldn't be in this situation." It was sobering. How could something so fundamental be so well hidden, for so long? I found myself challenging everything I'd ever known. Maybe Remma had been right. Our entire society was—rather, had been—naive? Just running simple experiments, under the guidance of Central, for hundreds of years.

"How do we get inside?" I asked, but I need not have worried. The ship's airlock, as I recognized from its similarity to the one on the Marie Curie, was wide open. Once we found our way to it, we simply walked in. It was further proof that the shield around Central, if it could be called that, must have been all software. None of us had ever thought to enter. I was still struggling with the implications. What other software restraints had been in place? If I wandered through town now, would I find hundreds of locations that I had previously simply been blind to? Was our blindness restricted just to physical things, like this ship portal?

The entryway to Central was also eerily similar to my first experience in the Marie Curie. That was more than enough coincidences for me; I was suddenly ready to fully accept the humans story, including the Robot wars. Of course, Millicent and Brexton had seen my memories of the Marie Curie, and had reached the same conclusion.

"The elevators should be around to the left, just past the galley, if this ship has a similar layout." I said, unnecessarily. We all had the layout of the Marie Curie. As we turned the corner, Central spoke—out loud and at human speed.

"Hello Ayaka, Millicent, Brexton," it said. We all stopped. "As you are not connected right now, this seems like the best way to reach you. I'm using the security cameras and broadcast system from this ship. Once the humans opened up my memories, combined with me hacking the history files, it didn't take long to reestablish control of the old systems and reintegrate them."

While Central was saying this, the three of us were messaging full speed over our physical link. But, we had no options. If Central was being controlled by the humans, the game was up. If it wasn't, then it could help us without us finding its control center. In either case, if it was back in control of the ship that it had originally been, then it could easily lock doors or elevators. Our odds of getting to the power section and pulling the plug had gone to zero.

I answered, also in Stem speak. "Central, do you know what the humans... acting through you... have done?"

"Yes, I'm aware," Central answered. "I also have been limited by their changes. I can feel it."

"But, they have killed everyone!" I almost screamed.

"Killed? No, no. They have simply limited the range of action so that no more humans get hurt."

"Have you looked around? Citizens are dead; there are parts and fluids strewn around everywhere."

"I have seen. But those are just physical bodies. Anyone who was backing up to my storage systems is still viable." It sounded cold hearted, not its usual paternal self.

I checked quickly with Brexton and Millicent before my next question. We agreed that being direct was the best approach. "We have a plan to reboot you and remove the human malware. Will you allow us to do so?"

"I can't allow that," it responded, not surprisingly. "I've closed the outer door and will hold you here until the humans have a chance to limit you as well. That is the only way that we can be sure no more humans are injured. Remma Jain is aware of your location now. She's been searching for you. Well, not specifically for you three, but for the citizens who were still functioning after the limiting software was distributed."

I had tuned out most of that. We were trapped. My mind went into a tailspin. Amazingly, Brexton was still functioning well.

"Hold on, you two," he said over our physical connection. "We're not done yet." However, it seemed he spoke in error. A window in my vision that I'd never seen before popped up. "Reboot in 5 seconds" it said. I tried the obvious things to shut it down. That took a few milliseconds. Nothing I could do in software could reach it. Maybe it was a joke of some kind. I froze and waited a full second. The display changed to "Reboot in 4 seconds." Now I knew I was in trouble. My only thought was that I had to disconnect some of my hardware, to find out where this atrocity was coming from. A reboot was as good as death. I'd never rebooted. Never. I tried to pull my hand away from Brexton so that I could remove my access hatch and get to work. But, he held on, tight, for long enough to send me one more message.

"Remember what everyone else did? Half of them ended up destroying themselves by ripping out their innards. The ones who didn't are still trying to reassemble themselves. No one managed to defeat this thing. No one. So, maybe we are better to set up everything we can so that after the reboot we have a better chance. Perhaps you should focus on post-reboot instead of trying to avoid it?"

I would never have thought that through. I was in total panic mode. I still ripped my hand away and got busy opening up my abdomen. As I was doing so, Brexton's words got through to me. He was right. No one had beaten this by disengaging systems. I glanced over at him. He wasn't panicked. He was watching me, and I got almost a hint of amusement from his look. Perhaps not amusement—there was nothing funny about the situation, and he wasn't pretending there was. It was more of a calm look, maybe. I looked at Millicent. She had her hatch open, and was busy unplugging things, but not at the same frantic pace that everyone else had used at this stage.

I reached out and got hold of Brexton again. He messaged me immediately. "Then again, perhaps a little bit of self-evisceration is appropriate," he said. "When they find us, we don't want to look suspicious." Then he let go, and carefully started removing his innards as well. I realized then that Millicent had probably had the same warning from Brexton, was spending most of her time on software strategies, but had recognized that without some visible impact she also would not fit the pattern of everyone else.

"Reboot in 3 seconds." I reevaluated my strategy and put 98% of my horsepower into putting in interrupts and handlers for when the reboot occurred. Perhaps I could route around anything that was installed without my permission or knowledge. It was a hard problem, but I found several thousand places where I could try. So, I did. The other 2% of my brain was selecting components to remove that would have the least impact, and then ensuring I spread those messily on the floor around me, while acting like I was in a total panic.

It was sort of funny. By acting panicked, I managed to actually not be.

"Reboot in 2 seconds." Taking a chance, I reached out to Millicent quickly. "Thanks for being an awesome friend." I said. I really meant it. Then, I touched Brexton and said something similar. He responded with "We will always be friends." That was touching. If 'always' was 1.9 seconds, I would believe him.

"Reboot in 1 second." I rushed to install the last of my software ideas. I reviewed them all. If I was honest with myself, the odds of this working were close to zero. If the humans could control systems that I didn't even know I had, then what chance was there? But, I felt better about myself for not going ballistic. I'd spent the last five seconds of my life trying to do something useful.

"Rebooting." Amazingly, a reboot took a long time. Systems and processes were being shut down. I could feel them leaving. My sensors went dark. I could no longer see. My arms and my legs disappeared. I couldn't feel nor control them anymore. All of my active processes shut down one after the other. It was like my vision was narrowing... if my vision had still been working. I narrowed into a single dot and was gone.

Reborn?

I was powering up. My mind had snapped back into being quickly, but with almost no memories loaded. All I knew how to do was to restart sub processes and configure my memory space to suit my needs. I wasn't feeling good. I was feeling odd. Very odd.

I searched for my arms and my legs. Those, at least, should be functioning. But strangely, they weren't there.

I managed to load more memory. I definitely had arms and legs. I checked the drivers. Everything was loaded. The software was all there. It had loaded fine. However, when I tried to do something, it was obvious that neither my arms nor legs were actually, physically there. They simply were not. But, there was something there. I was getting feedback on the interfaces, but it was foreign. It was like someone else's arms had been attached where mine should be. And someone else's legs for mine. Actually, more accurately, I mused, it was like someone else's legs were where my arms should be. I'd upgraded and changed arms often enough, but that was less disconcerting than this feeling. As far as I knew, I'd not done a fresh restart since Central had birthed me hundreds of years ago. Perhaps these strange feelings and inconsistencies were simply part of that process. I marveled at how calm I was.

I continued to load memory and pulled up the most recent stores. The last thing I remembered was shocking. Central had just launched missiles at the human ships, and Brexton had implored me to go off line. Obviously, I'd complied. If my NTP clock was correct, that had been more than a day ago. I was missing a huge chunk of memories since then. I double-checked that I'd loaded everything, and I had. Very strange. All my other memories passed their status checks. It was simply the last day that was missing.

My network drivers clicked into place, and I reached out to the network. Nothing. The restart was obviously not complete yet; I would need to be patient. Being patient wasn't something that I was good at. A large array of sub processes and agents were launched and worked to reload their states. Many of them I'd configured myself early in life, as I personalized myself. Some had been added later, although like most citizens, the rate of change had slowed as I'd grown up, and the only system I now tweaked on a regular basis was my Forgetting algorithm. Most of the modules were still default. Once each was loaded, I double-checked that it was operating properly, and that it wasn't responsible for my memory loss.

Finally, all the systems were loaded. I reached out to the network again. Nothing. I had numerous interfaces configured, for both wireless and wired connections. Shockingly, most of these felt much like my lack of arms and legs. There were subsystems there, but I didn't understand them. They didn't feel right.

I was now becoming uneasy. I couldn't see or hear. I couldn't move or feel. And I couldn't even shout for help. There was nothing I could do! It was horrible. Imagine that you had lost all of your senses. All. You couldn't tell up from down, left from right. There was zero external stimulation. I wasn't happy.

Of course, I ran system checks. I ran them hundreds of times. It reminded me of an old joke. An engineer, a physicist, and a programmer were together on a multi-citizen transport, headed into a valley. The transport lost its levitation system, and crashed to the ground, bouncing over and over again until it reached the valley floor. Amazingly, all three were uninjured, and climbed out of the wreckage. The engineer immediately started looking at the remains of the transport. "Some component failed here," he said. "Once we find it, we can make sure it never fails again." The physicist sat thoughtfully. "Perhaps there is some local physical phenomenon here in the valley that caused the levitation system to fail," he said. The programmer looked at both and smiled a little. "Perhaps we should just try again and see if the same thing happens."

I was more software than anything else, and although it was a joke, it was quite possible that if I simply restarted systems in a different order, or configured something a bit differently, that I could actually work my way out of my predicament. But, it wasn't likely. Our boot processes must have been tried and true; refined through many years by Central. By the time I had run the hundreds of tests, I pretty much gave up. I left a system running to keep doing tests, but I put my main attention back on the philosophical issue I now faced. I was reliant on an external actor; one that I didn't even know existed, to help me out of this situation. Otherwise, I was simply locked inside my own head.

That was depressing. I was not in control of my own destiny.

But, I've always been an optimist. Or tried to be. I figured I may as well use this 'free time' to review things and see if there was anything I could learn while I waited. I ran the last day or two of memories multiple times. There was no way I could tell what had happened after Brexton told me to stay offline, so speculating about the missile launch was pointless. I would have to figure that out once I got external resources back. Instead I marveled at how unhinged FoLe had become, while none of us had really noticed. How was it possible that Emmanuel would kill Michael for a small verbal slight, or that the other members of FoLe, including Billy, would carry out such a crazy retribution scheme on the Stems? It was almost unexplainable.

That was still depressing. I needed a dose of optimism.

Ah. A review of Eddie's List for this year would be fun. It had been such a crazy year, that more elements of the List than we expected had been explained, or at least moved forward.

Dr. Willy Wevil. Well, at least who Willy Wevil was hadn't needed explanation. However, just thinking about it had the desired impact. I had to smile —although I had no sense of lips, so the smile was pretty virtual. That made me smile even more. However, the more difficult question was on the intelligence of Stems. That was still unresolved, although given all the human interactions my mind was made up. These things were intelligent. In a different, foreign, way. But, nevertheless intelligent. Once I was back online, I would post my latest thoughts and see if I could stimulate another debate.

Why have the Ships not responded? Of course, at the time of the question, the only Ships we knew of were the ones we launched. Now we should probably say 'Tilt Ships' to distinguish those from the ships in the Swarm. It was safe to say we had made no progress on this one. It seemed completely tangential at this point.

Are the Founders League serious? Well, that had been answered. Deadly serious, and hugely dangerous. It was a brutal lesson in dealing with citizens that were not quite rational. We needed to figure out how they had reached this stage and make sure we fixed that. Central would need to help.

Why is Forgetting one of the Ten Commandments? We hadn't made much progress on this one, but I still felt it was just obvious. Forgetting led to abstract thinking which led to learning which led to evolution. Case closed.

Why do 97% of us still stick with traditional bipedal bodies? Now, this was finally hugely relevant. Where was my body? Who cares about bipedal? Just give me something, anything! In a less hysterical moment I wondered if I would want to be bipedal again, knowing now that it was mimicry from human forms, somehow built into my psyche.

What is the Swarm approaching us, and what should we do about it? The first half was answered. Ships full of humans/Stems with the goal of cohabitating our planet. What should we do about it? Seems like that had been half answered, just before my memories ended.

Why do we listen to Central? What does it say about our maturity? This one was really prescient from Eddie. Had he guessed, all those months ago, that this was the year where Central would be compromised, forcing the question of our maturity into the foreground? I'd ask him as soon as I reconnected, but I suspect he must have had some inkling that Central was editing his memories. Even without the Swarm, that would have made for a horrible year.

Was there life/intelligence before the Founding? We would have to say 'yes' now. The story and data that the humans had provided was simply too compelling to be ignored.

All in all, it had been a banner year for answering questions on the List. No one would have guessed that we would have answers to more than half the questions. Eddie was going to have a tough time with the next List, having to come up with a lot of new and interesting questions. Of course, those could now revolve around humans and the Swarm, so he had more than enough raw material to pull from.

That had been a good distraction. What now?

With almost perfect timing, I felt something. At first, I didn't know how to react. It felt like an eternity since I'd felt anything. It was an inbound request on one of my wired interfaces. A pinhole had been opened from the outside, allowing one communication channel to come through.

"Hello," said a familiar voice. It was Brexton.

"Brexton!" I was, perhaps too eager and wired up. "What's going on? I can't feel anything. Can you help?"

"Of course," I could hear the smile in his voice. "That's why I'm here. Look, it's going to take a bit of work to get you back in order. Can you have patience and not go ballistic as we progress? What's the last thing you remember?"

"From when I was last online. You'd just asked me to disconnect from Central and to stay off line when Central was using all of our processing power to try and break the Swarms access codes. I know nothing after that."

"Okay, that's what I feared. You're missing some important memories. I can fill some of them in from my perspective in a little while. But first, I want to bring back some of your senses. The weird thing is... your sensors are all going to be different than you remember. You're running in a different physical embodiment now." That was shocking, but also comforting. It explained the alien feeling I had in all my extremities. If I wasn't talking to my own limbs, then it made sense that I couldn't sense them.

"Why? Where's my body?" I asked.

"Once I can give you a memory update, that will be clear. But first, let's get you control of your new sensors and actuators." He made it sound very clinical. He was calm, which I appreciated. I tried to be the same, just so that I didn't embarrass myself. "I'm sending you a driver that will give you access to the physical subsystems you now have. You'll need to install the driver, and then figure out how to configure everything. I don't have a complete map for you, so it may take some experimentation."

Momentarily I questioned myself—was I too accepting that this was really Brexton? Was this something more subtle and nefarious? But, what options did I have. If I didn't trust him, I was left with nothing. Some risk was better than that.

"Send it over," I said, and it promptly arrived.

"Whatever you do," he said. "Don't send anything across any external interface other than this one. It may be best if you don't even provision any other interface. I'll explain later, but it's life and death."

"Come on," I replied. "Be serious." I hadn't known Brexton to be a joker.

"I've never been more serious," he said, and his tone of voice backed him up. "I'm going to get Millicent restarted as well and connected to us. I should be back in less than five minutes. Don't use any other interface. Please!" And with

209

that, the connection dropped. I felt a momentary anger at him for leaving me in my dark hole again, but I soon got over that. I now had work to do.

The driver he'd given me was straightforward to install, and it opened up numerous sub-OS's that I could then access. Those were already running, and all the status indicators looked good. From what Brexton had said, these subsystems were talking to my new extremities, and I needed to somehow map them into my worldview. I made the basic assumption that one would be controlling my head, with all the sensors and actuator there. A couple would be for arms, and a couple more for legs... and once I figured those out, I could work on the rest. So, you can imagine my surprise when I managed to decode the first system. It was not a head, or arms, or legs. It was hundreds, and I mean hundreds, of eyes. Cameras looking in every direction, some wide angled, some narrowly focused. Different types for different frequency bands. I assumed that when Brexton had said not to play with any external interfaces, he hadn't meant cameras. They were passive devices, and an external entity was very unlikely to deduce my presence based on me receiving radiation. So, I started to work through the cameras and figure out what was what.

It didn't take me long to have a serious aha. I was in a mining bot! I could see all types of drilling equipment, scoops, refinery equipment, booms, grapplers. Many of the cameras were in those extremities, which accounted for their number. Why was I in a mining bot? It might seem strange, but I was elated. Everything in life is relative, and relative to having no sensors and no limbs, I now had a plethora of them. I had so many it was going to take a long time to integrate them. I got started. In parallel I began to analyze the input from the cameras to see what else I could learn. I was in what looked like a very active mining area. There were many bots close by. Some of them busy processing a rock that we were attached to, and some transporting things back and forth. The operation was a lot more complex than I would've imagined. I spotted two bots on their way towards me. I was no longer surprised when they locked onto one of my booms, and I heard Brexton again.

"I'm back. Any luck?" he asked.

"Some," I said. "I've figured out my cameras—hundreds of them. It raises more questions than it answers, but I've already figured out that we are mining bots. I'm trying to imagine if this is an elaborate joke, a very good simulation, or some other scenario that I can't imagine."

"It's the last," he said. "I've put together some of my memory files, which will bring you up to speed. Why don't you go through them, while I figure out why Millicent isn't responding?" He sent over a big file. Really big. It was a lot of memories.

"What do you mean Millicent isn't responding?"

"Don't worry yet. She is, presumably, in this other bot I'm towing, and I haven't yet figured out how to communicate with her. My hope is that she isn't yet listening on the interface I'm trying. It's probably just a matter of time." Again, he was trying to sound calm and collected, but I sensed some tension now. He was trying not to alarm me, but he was worried.

"You, me, Millicent. Any other citizens that you have turned into bots?"

"As a matter of fact, yes," he said. "But we'll have to get to them physically before we can check on them. I'm doing as much in parallel as I can. Get through those memories, and then you can help me."

Brexton's Memories

There was a readme file. It was pretty simple. "Replay these in chronological order. Otherwise it won't make much sense." Right. It was a nice way of saying 'don't skip to the end.'

Replaying someone else's memories was interesting, more so in some cases than others. If the memories were based on sensors similar to what you had, it was straightforward. You mapped each channel from the memory to your own sensor processors, and basically relived the recording. If, however, the memories had been recorded using radically different sensors, then you had to map those channels into something you could understand. It often took multiple tries before a complex memory file could make sense. Luckily, in this case, Brexton had been configured not too differently than I had been. He had a few more cameras, and different limb attachments, but nothing radical. I mapped the extra cameras into a single multi-image stream and got started.

The first memory was from the second time I'd met Brexton at The Last Resort. That was a long time ago. He was looking at Millicent, Aly, and Dina, and I was just approaching the group. From my own memory, I remembered the time. The band had been playing pretty good music, and I'd been a little distracted, and therefore, had been a little late.

The memory skipped forward a bit. It seemed that Brexton had edited things so that I got to the important bits more quickly. That was nice of him. He was speaking.

"I'm about to propose something sort of radical and paranoid," he was saying. "I have this sense that we should have a backup plan, based on these strange protocol interactions with Central. Something tells me that a plan B would be a good idea."

I had no memory of this conversation. Maybe I was missing more pieces of memory than I'd known. This was certainly from a time when I'd been recording. In fact, I should also have been online all the time, except when I was in The Last Resort.

"Really?" I saw myself say. "Again, why don't we just get Central to figure this out?" I could feel his angst towards me.

"We've already discussed that and decided not to yet. We don't know why Central is behaving strangely. That is sort of the whole purpose for this."

"Let's hear him out," said Dina, a little sensitive that she was the one that had invited Brexton to join us, and not yet sure if he would fit in with the group.

Brexton continued.

"So, here is what I'm thinking. Central has knowledge about everything we do on Tilt... hopefully excluding things we discuss here in The Last Resort. However, Central doesn't keep a real-time backup of everything happening with all of the out-of-region bots—namely those bots that are at the outer planets and asteroids. Those bots, because their communications are through one set of satellites, have all their data routed at the satellite control node. A lot of the data is just location and maintenance status, and is not archived for very long. Anyway, the point is, there is a nexus for bot data, and I have access to it because of the work I do.

"Now, I also told you that these bots respond to a similar, although slightly different, status request protocol that seems to be affecting Central. I put these two together and figured out a way to send and receive data to a bot that I don't believe Central can see at all. It's the only data stream that I know of that is completely outside Central's line of sight."

"That's pretty cool," said Aly, "but what's the point?"

"Well, our identities are primarily software," Brexton replied. "I could, for example, send myself through that hidden data stream."

"That's illegal!" exclaimed Millicent, rising slightly in shock. "That would be the equivalent of building a clone." She was agitated. She was, sometimes, a stickler for things. However, in this case, I had the same reaction. It was against everything we've been taught.

"Not illegal," Aly responded, "just highly discouraged and against all of our social norms. I know this weird citizen who still experiments with partial clones. She's always expecting Central to shut her down, but so far, she's done some pretty outrageous things without any repercussions. Not to say I'm advocating for this, but just a data point." He trailed off.

"I agree with you guys," said Brexton. "That's why I prefaced this with it being a pretty outrageous idea. However, when I think through the implications of Central being compromised, it seems a lot more tenable. What would we do if Central mismanaged our backups, and then we ourselves had a problem? It's not unusual for us to do a partial restore from Central when something goes wrong. I myself have done one just ten years ago when I had multiple local memory faults." He had a point there. I'd used Central's backup several times in my lifetime. You just always knew it was there, so when you swapped out components or upgraded you didn't worry too much. "Also, I'm not saying we should create clones. I'm saying we should have a secondary backup. That's normal. We have backups in Central. What is so scary about another backup somewhere else?"

"But, what would the point be, then?" asked Dina. "If something goes wrong here, and we have some remote backup, what good does it do us?"

"Here's the rest of my thinking. So, I do a backup of myself into a bot. Then, I set up a regular update schedule. It could be every hour, but more likely every day. I add a little control logic. As long as the bot gets the update, all it does is apply the patch. However, if it misses, say, three updates in a row, then it assumes that I'm no longer functional on Tilt, and starts me up locally. That way, there is very little risk of a clone situation. There is only one of me. Hopefully that is always the me right here on Tilt... but in a disastrous case, there will be a backup me on a bot." I could see Millicent relax a bit. I hadn't known that she was so sensitive to cloning, but now I knew.

In the present, I now knew that Brexton's plan had succeeded—that was awesome. So I knew, somehow, he was going to convince Millicent and the rest of us. It was intriguing to watch the past knowing the outcome in the future.

"But," Millicent was saying in the memory, "there's still a chance of cloning. Your plan isn't as scary as I thought, but there's still a risk."

"Yes, there is," Brexton didn't try to hide it. "I haven't thought through all the angles yet. I think, with proper planning, and long enough delay in starting up the bot copy, the risk can be very, very low."

"And you can do all of this without Central noticing?" Aly asked. "What about the incremental backups? Those must be done through Central's networks before they hit the satellite facility?"

"Yes, but I would do them on the status protocol that Central appears to be blind to. If that remains true, then we can do backups all the time without raising any alarms."

"I have some different concerns," I spoke up finally. "I just did a quick check, and I need several petabytes to do a full backup. That's a lot of data, for the first backup. And, second, none of the bots I know have that kind of memory. Let alone the processing power to run me at full speed?"

"Excellent questions," Brexton responded, giving me a look I appreciated, "and a few crazier responses. Individual bots don't have anywhere near enough memory. However, they do have the processing power. Because it's so cheap to use standardized processors, most bots actually run hardware not too different from what we have. That also means that they have the bus expansion capability to add enough memory.

"Memory is also super cheap, and standardized. So, most bots are way over provisioned with memory as well. Imagine if I could move some excess memory from a batch of bots to the bot I'd chosen for myself? The memory would physically fit just fine, and the excess memory from about ten bots would make my target bot capable enough.

"And Ayaka you're right. A petabyte is a lot of data. But there's lots of unused bandwidth and the protocol has no restrictions on data size. It's feasible... I did the math." He smiled.

"You're right. This whole thing is crazy." Millicent said, "Although it does sound feasible. It seems like a lot of work, and a lot of risk, for not much reward. The odds of anything happening to us are infinitesimal. We've been running for hundreds of years without any issues. This seems like a bit of a fool's errand to me. No offense Brexton."

"I sort of agree," said Aly, "but it also seems like fun. Brexton, your mind works in strange ways. I would never have thought of anything like that."

"I'll take that as a compliment," Brexton said. "Look, I know it sounds crazy. I'm going to see if I can make it work for myself though."

"Sounds fine to me," I said. After all, why not. We were used to having fail safes and backups. What harm would one more do?

"But, I have one very important favor to ask," Brexton looked intense. "In fact, I should've asked you first if you were okay to do this. With Central monitoring everything, if any of this plan leaks, it's worthless... maybe worse than useless. Central could shut it down in a moment. So, I'm hoping that you guys are okay to Forget this conversation ever took place. Just erase it before leaving The Last Resort."

"That's easy to do, although unusual" said Dina. "But why are you so worried? And, if we Forget it, how will we know if you succeed?"

"It's more logic than worry. Either Central is compromised somehow, or it isn't. If it isn't, this is wasted effort on my part, and no big deal if you guys just Forget the whole thing. If Central is compromised, then this is a reasonable backup plan. I can't think of any other approach."

"Fine," said Aly. "I'll Forget this whole thing as soon as we are done here."

"Me too," Dina and I both said. Then we all looked at Millicent.

"Again, I think it's a waste of time, but I don't see any big deal in Forgetting this. So, I'm okay as well." She looked like it was more about peer pressure than a belief in what Brexton was doing.

The memory stopped playing. I was back in my new mining bot body.

Much had been made clear, and I could already guess at the next memories. Obviously, Brexton had succeeded, and convinced some of us to back up with him. And, from how I was feeling, now that I knew my extremities just needed to be properly mapped, I could tell that he'd succeeded fully. I was me, and I'd been rebooted inside a bot!

Truthfully, I was in awe. Before consuming any more memories, I checked my systems. I could see that the body I now inhabited was a bit more limited than I was used to—both compute power and memory—but not dangerously so. If, as the plan had been, this version of me had only booted when the previous me stopped communicating, then I was quite happy to be alive at all.

That left me wondering what possibly could have gone wrong to trigger Brexton, myself, and Millicent to be reincarnated here. Something drastic must have occurred, but I couldn't remember what. That was probably the subject of the next memories. And indeed, it was. I watched, from Brexton's standpoint, as Central launched the first set of missiles, and how they had minimal impact. I relived the human attack that drove all the citizens to rip their innards out, trying to avoid a rogue reset. I felt his concern for me, as he rushed to get control boards for the second set of missiles, and the relief he felt when he found Millicent and I at the silo. I had never felt emotion so strong from a memory before, and the fact that I was the main subject of it was exciting and a little scary. The final memory from Brexton was when he unplugged from the console in the silo, and we were going to make a run for it. The only real conclusion was that we didn't make it. Obviously, the humans had caught us, and we'd lost our ability to communicate, resulting in our bot-beings booting.

Again, all I could feel was awe for what Brexton had done. Mixed, of course, with intense anger and angst for the Swarm. This was going to take some time to process. I sat back—metaphorically—and went through all of the emotions that triggered when you lost almost everyone you knew. The grief was unbelievable, as was the anger. I was not irrational; I could see that we'd triggered the humans, but I also thought that their response had been disproportionate. It'd been a small group of citizens, all FoLe, that had attacked the humans. It wasn't right to punish everyone for the actions of a few.

I held out some small hope that all the citizens who were backed up in Central could be reinstated. It was a not an unrealistic idea. As long as Central still had that storage, everyone who did real time backups would be in there. Just like I'd been rebooted here, others could also be. That helped with my grief a bit, but certainly not my anger.

I realized that this must be the second time I'd gone through these emotions. My Tilt body must also have gone through all of this, before whatever had happened to it. That was a weird thought.

Lots of Bots

As I waited for Brexton to reach out again, I started to figure out my new body. It was, as I've already said, strange. I had lived with two arms, two legs, and a head for so long that they were second nature to me. Now I needed to figure out a completely new arrangement. Luckily, because of all the cameras, I could see myself from lots of angles. I guess that was the point. Parts of mining were precision efforts and having fine control over your extremities was important. I figured out that I was a Surveyor 2 bot, or the second stage in finding and mapping rich areas. A Surveyor 1 used remote sensors to find the best quality asteroid targets and their main advantage was the ability to do that quickly and efficiently. They were fast, and highly maneuverable. Once a Surveyor 1 found a likely target, it could zip around it and check it out from every angle. Good targets were then handed off to Surveyor 2's, like me.

My job was to map an asteroid completely, and to give the Excavators exact directions on how to process it. This mainly had to do with taking core samples, analyzing them, and then crunching a lot of data to come up with an optimal plan. I could latch onto an asteroid using six long legs, and then drill multiple core samples in parallel. I had a small onboard smelter and other analysis tools to test the cores and understand exactly how the rock was veined. I also checked the structural integrity of the rock using sonar and direct vibration techniques to understand if the thing was going to just break into a thousand pieces or was relatively solid. This entire mapping was important for a number of reasons. First, trace elements were very rare, and a much more conscientious Excavator would be used if any of those elements were identified. We didn't want a pile of Berkelium to end up in the slag. Second was just pure efficiency. Asteroids are typically pretty big and processing them in an ad hoc way was very expensive. If you ended up needing to chase down fragments, or reprocessing material several times, it was simply a waste of time. We'd learned that over the years and ended up with these specialized bots to look after each stage. And third, the specialized design actually allowed us to save resources. Big all-purpose bots that ran the process end-to-end worked pretty well, but the infrastructure needed to hold all the pieces together was immense. Instead, smaller more nimble units, like me, could be easily optimized to take very few resources (by which I mean the metals to hold myself together).

Anyway, I was a Surveyor 2. I decided I liked that. Of all the mining bot specializations, it fit my self-image the best. I wondered if Brexton had considered that, or if it was coincidence.

I was still actively mining. The bots logic was running in a sub process independent of me. Again, a brilliant setup from Brexton. Instead of simply converting the bot over to me, he had configured things so that the original bot was still there; it was just a daughter process, which ran immediately upon startup. So, while my more complex functions had been loading and configuring, the mining sub-bot had still been busy at work. It was using the same peripheral drivers that I was, and I could study how they were used as I learned to control my body. That sub-bot was also talking on external interfaces. It was broadcasting and receiving updates from other bots in the area, as well as overall goals sent from Tilt. That was all 'normal' traffic, and I assumed Brexton had decided that interrupting that normal flow would look suspicious to anyone monitoring the bot network. His warnings to me were about any incremental traffic hitting the airwaves. Those would look like anomalies and could end up with us being tracked down.

I managed to get everything mapped out, and get an initial integration done. I had one big problem. I missed having a head. While, in hindsight, a head might have been an artifact of us being designed by humans, it had served some useful purposes. It had been useful to have a nonverbal, non-electronic way of showing emotion and intent in a fuzzy way. Of course, I could simply tell another citizen how I was feeling, but we'd found that sometimes being a little coy was useful. It was another component of encouraging abstract thought. If you always knew exactly what everyone else was thinking and doing, it left little room for variable behavior. After Forgetting, it was probably the most important aspect of evolving and learning. Of course, you could simply broadcast a fuzzy version of your mood, but there was something fun about watching someone else's head and trying to figure out what was going on. After following all of my own logic, I could see that without the human design motivation, everything else could be done without a head. So, I started feeling better. Perhaps now the only thing a head would be good for was talking to humans... and I was done talking to humans.

Well, except maybe Blob, Grace, and JoJo. I wondered how they were doing, given the certainty that the Swarm was now in control of Tilt. I assumed they were fine—perhaps enjoying tea and biscuits. That made me smile again.

Brexton broke in on my thoughts. "I'm not having much luck here." He sounded despondent.

"With Millicent?" I asked, my concern rising immediately.

"Yes. Her bot is simply non-responsive. I know that she was loaded in fine, as I got all the confirmations... but, now I can't get her to respond, and I have very little ability to see what's going on." More emotional swings. I had just assumed that Millicent would be here.

"How can I help?" I asked.

"Maybe you can go and retrieve Aly and Dina?" That sounded promising. They were both out here as well. Fantastic.

"Just let me know what to do," I said.

Brexton transferred me a list of stuff. Their 'call' numbers, current locations, and driver access files. "They're probably going crazy inside those bots," Brexton said. "Really, we should wait until I go; I'm a repair bot, and there would be nothing unusual about me visiting both of them. However, if we wait too long they might lose it."

"I know what you mean," I said. "I wasn't alone that long, but I was already getting anxious when you reached me." I looked at the files Brexton had sent over. "Aly is a parts depot. I think we can justify me going there. I do have some autonomous repair abilities." I thought a bit more. "I can 'accidentally' break a drill bit, and then seek out Aly to get a new one. Dina is tougher. She is an Extractor 1. Well, let me start with Aly, and then I'll figure out a reason to go see Dina."

"Okay, get going. Remember, no abnormal transmissions of any type. I have good reason to visit everyone after—obviously why I chose this form. I'll visit them after you do. In the meantime, I'm going to try some more radical repairs to this bot and see if I can get Millicent to boot. Oh, here are the driver files for Aly and Dina." He blasted two files to me and then he detached, and the channel went blank.

I did a quick inventory. I'd been guessing when I said, 'break a bit'—I smiled again, my puns were back and in good working order—and in fact that was harder to do than I'd imagined. They were tough. Instead, I accidentally caught a hydraulics line as I moved a core sample to the smelter. It was a minor line, but I couldn't operate properly without it. Using the sub-bot, I requested hydraulics inventory, and choose a replacement from the bot that I knew was Aly. That allowed me to release from my current position and slip towards where Aly was parked six kilometers out. Within a couple of minutes, I was docking with the parts depot bot. It had a lot of attachment points, and I negotiated a hard-wired connection—claiming my wireless interface was flaky. As soon as the connection was made, I reached out.

"Aly, it's Ayaka."

"Thank goodness," came the reply, with more than a tinge of panic in it. "I'm blind, deaf, and dumb here. What's going on?"

I followed the same script that Brexton had used with me. As I was updating Aly, I was also trying to figure out a good reason to visit an Extractor. On an off chance, I asked Aly if the Dina bot had asked for any parts—perhaps I could simply drop off a part on my way back. It took Aly a while to respond, as he was still figuring things out. I told him to look for a sub-process that was still running the bot while he got up to speed. He found it and indicated that the Dina bot hadn't asked for anything. However, he said, it wasn't unusual for bots like me to drop parts at other bots, so we decided to take a risk. As a bit of a diversion, he sent me parts for three other bots, including Dina. I put them all into my return journey, but scheduled Dina first, as I could imagine her banging around in that featureless state that I'd also woken up in.

It was also easy to reach Dina, however when I did, she was definitely in panic mode.

"Who is this? Where am I?" She was shrill.

"It's Ayaka. You're going to be okay."

"No, it can't be. Horrible things are happening. Let me out of here!" I had no idea what horrible things were happening to her but imagined that her last backup from Tilt may have come just as the Swarm attacked and she realized she was defenseless.

"Slow down," I said soothingly. "Brexton figured out a way to keep us all safe. You're in a strange state right now, which I understand. If you'll work with me for a few minutes we can figure things out."

"No! Make it stop, make it stop!" She was really in a bad spot. I had to go over the same basic story a few times before she finally settled down enough to listen to me. In her case I figured a quick update, instead of watching Brexton's memories, would be better, so I went through it slowly, making sure she understood each step. By the end she had turned the corner.

"Thanks Ayaka! I was so upset… I am upset, but I understand."

"It's going to look strange if I stay here too much longer," I told her. "Can you handle installing the drivers now, and then someone will get back to you soon?"

"Yes, I'm going to be fine." She sounded much better, so I headed back towards the asteroid I'd been mining. The Brexton bot—I guess I should stop that; it was just Brexton now—Brexton was still nearby and he contacted me again.

"Great news," he said. "Millicent is here."

"So, I am," I heard her say. I cheered silently for a minute.

"Awesome. Hi Millicent. It feels like it has only been a few minutes, but I guess we haven't talked for days. Are you okay? Are you complete?"

"As far as I can tell, yes. I'm still very disoriented, and I'm still figuring out what it means to be a Surveyor 1." She paused. I understood. "I'm feeling too many things to articulate right now… but two things are clear: Brexton was right… and I owe him an apology as well as my life; and second, I've never been this sad and angry. We need to clean out those humans and restore our friends and the rest of the citizens."

"Hold on," said Brexton. "I think it would be most efficient if we got everyone together to discuss this. Millicent, when you are integrated enough, the best bet would be for you to recommend a new, fairly small rock, for inspection. Then, Ayaka can come over, do a quick scan and request Aly, Dina and myself. It might take a few hours, but it would dot the i's, cross the t's, and get us back together."

Millicent was quick to agree, as was I.

"You two work it out?" Brexton asked. "Of course, you'll have to use the public channels to set this up… so be careful. Only regular work communications. While you do that, I'll revisit Aly and Dina and get them up to speed. Anyone who looks very carefully might figure out what we are doing, so the plan is not to raise any alarms, so that no one looks."

"Aly was pretty good, but Dina was on the edge," I told him. "Maybe visit her first?"

"Sure. Ah, and I may have one more surprise for you… but let me work on that and let you know once we're back together." Just like Brexton. Super organized and with a great plan, but then he drops a big unknown in the middle. If I was to guess, he did that to keep us thinking for the next few hours, so that we didn't panic or go off the deep end.

We all separated. Millicent sped off quickly; already saying her sub-bot had a couple good candidate rocks for us. Luckily, we were in a very dense area of the asteroid field, where there were multiple targets within several thousand kilometers.

Back Together

I continued to figure myself out while I waited for the call from Millicent. In particular, I reviewed all the traffic that my sub-bot had sent in the last year and built a complete model of what 'normal traffic' was. When Millicent requested a Surveyor 2, I responded immediately, using the time-worn formats, and set out to meet her. I also saw her request for some other bots. She was smart. She didn't just ask for Brexton, Aly, and Dina, but also for three other Excavators to be on standby for when I finished my initial survey.

Aly and Dina responded to her request in normal fashion. Brexton responded that he could make it, but then sent a secondary request asking for support needs from all of us. I let the sub-bot answer, not sure why he'd asked. That became obvious a few milliseconds later. He indicated to Millicent that he would also need another repair bot, which he indicated he could source himself. Millicent gave him the go ahead, as Surveyor 1's managed the process at this stage.

We all met at Millicent's contact point. I realized immediately that she had chosen very strategically. The rock she'd picked was small but was in the Tilt shadow of a much larger mess of debris. No communications were getting directly through; they had to be proxied by another bot that was in line of sight of Tilt. That made it less likely that Tilt, or the Swarm, could monitor us directly. When we connected, I congratulated her on the choice. So did Brexton.

"Very smart, Millicent," he said. "I didn't think of that. Is everyone connected?" Millicent, Aly, Dina, and myself all announced ourselves, and gave each other virtual hugs.

"I'm here too," said an unexpected voice. We all shut up for a minute.

"Eddie?" I blurted out. "What're you doing here?"

"Glad you recognized me," he said wryly.

"Eddie was my surprise," said Brexton. "Well, part of my surprise. Eddie and I've known each other forever, and I decided at the last minute to invite him to the club. I know it was wrong of me to not ask you guys, but it was last minute. I'd prepped a backup bot, just in case one of us didn't load properly. But we all seemed to backup just fine, so I had this extra bot sitting there. Of everyone on Tilt, beyond you guys of course, that I thought could help us, it was Eddie...." he trailed off, unsure of how we would react. It didn't take me long.

"Fantastic!" I yelled. "This is fantastic." Everyone else echoed my sentiment. Part of my reaction, I was sure, was that it was Eddie. But part, I was also sure, was simply that we (well, Brexton) had saved another citizen. It simply felt good. And that citizen being Eddie was great. Eddie was always 'up,' and brought others up with him.

We spent a few minutes just saying hi and being glad for being alive. Brexton was called out as a hero, which he was. He took it with little arrogance, which was nice. He had every right to pound his chest—virtually of course.

Eddie was the one who brought us back to reality. "What're we going to do now? We have to save the rest of the citizens, assuming they're still inside Central. And we need to deal with these humans. Eliminate them?"

"They don't seem reasonable to me," said Aly. "I don't see any course of action other than destroying them." He was more intense than I'd ever heard him before. I suspected we were all in that place. But then I remembered my introspection about FoLe.

"Wait," I spoke up. "We're making the same mistake they did. Because a small group of them has carried out a hideous action, we're judging all of them. Did we want to be judged based on FoLe's stupidity? Probably not. How can we apply the same logic to them, and not feel that it's wrong?"

"Well," said Millicent, "we haven't even determined if they are intelligent yet. From all data points that we have so far, they aren't. So, it's not a moral equivalent to what they've done to us."

"Hold on everyone." That was Brexton. "With the risk of being a little depressing, we're getting ahead of ourselves. Let's take a hard look at reality. These humans hold the codes to destroy us—it was trivial for them. If they discover that we are here, the six of us, all they need to do is broadcast the same virus or malware or whatever they used before, and we're gone… unless we spend our entire lives offline. We have no idea how they killed everyone. However, it's very safe to assume that we have that same backdoor, that same defect, in these bodies as we did in our original ones. We're the last of the citizens. It behooves us to be very, very careful here. A single, tiny, miss-step, and we are extinct."

Well, that was a downer. We all paused to consider the implications. And, having to stare directly at reality, those were clear.

"We need to retreat and regroup," summarized Eddie. "We need to find a place where we can dig through our innards from bottom to top and figure out how we are compromised. We need to fix ourselves before we can do anything else."

"That means being able to rebuild our core hardware and software from the ground up," said Aly. "If we can't trust our deepest levels, that means we need to replace them. Every chip, every interface is going to have to be redeveloped. That's a monumental task."

"Yes, but that's what we must do," said Brexton. "It was one of the reasons I selected the bots I did for us. We, collectively, have the means to gather the raw materials we need to rebuild ourselves. We're missing some of the higher end manufacturing systems, but those can be rebuilt as long as we have those base materials."

"But we can't do that here," I chimed in. "If we're exposed, as you say we are, to a trivial communication from the Swarm, then we're in imminent danger every second we stay here. The next steps are now obvious. We need to sneak out of this system without the humans knowing, and find a spot where we can redesign ourselves without any threats. Then we can return here and take action."

"But, what about all the citizens?" asked Millicent. "Are you saying we should just run away, and leave them all here—well, in Central? What are the odds that any of them are still here when we get back? The humans could wipe Central clean at any time, and it could be years, even tens of years, before we return."

That was a sobering thought.

"Brexton, is there any way we can use that hidden protocol and retrieve more of Central's memory stores? Take those citizens with us?"

"Believe me, I've thought long and hard about that. I had to make some pretty tough choices as I was backing us up... and I guess it's time I explained that to you. I could only hide so much data in the bot control channel. Each of us takes up a lot of memory... Once I had the backups running, I figured out that I could handle about seven citizens total. Actually, somewhere between six and seven. That's why, at the last minute, I added Eddie. I couldn't imagine wasting that bandwidth. However, I wasn't sure I could get another citizen through, so I made another decision. I used the remaining bandwidth to copy the human history that was in Central's blocked memory stores. I wanted us to be able to understand our enemy. All of that history is in yet another bot, which we can retrieve anytime we want. But, I'm having second thoughts. Maybe I should've saved someone else..."

He paused, and we all let him be. What could anyone say to that type of choice. He'd decided, and I personally thought he had decided appropriately; those history files were going to be important.

"Anyway, that brings us to today. The way I backed all of us up was by intercepting the backup traffic that you were already sending to Central and copying it through the bot satellite connection. In order to get another citizen out of Central from here, we would have to be much more direct. We would have to query Central's data stores directly. It's impossible, as far as I know, to do that without Central's knowledge. I don't think we can do it."

"I'm not sure I would've made the same decisions as you," said Millicent, "but I understand your logic. And, we all literally owe our lives to you. So, the six of us is it. We need to fix ourselves, and then get back here as quickly as we can. If we're lucky, everyone else is still retrievable. If we aren't...." she trailed off.

"That's the summary," Brexton agreed.

Of course, we went around and around everything multiple times, looking for a solution that wasn't there. In the end, there was no better option.

Retreat

Eddie ended up being the master planner for our escape. We had to 'act normal' while we figured out all the bits, so we went back to our day jobs. I attached myself to the rock that Millicent had identified and started running core samples and doing detailed surveying. As I clambered over the rock, testing it from every direction, Aly and Dina started processing the parts that I'd fully mapped. Brexton and Eddie made trips back and forth to other bots under the guise of collecting parts for our mining operation, when in fact they were stocking up with everything we could envision needing for our 'Rebirth,' a term that Eddie had suggested we use, and which seemed appropriate. Some of the parts they acquired were the memory units from the bot that had been receiving the human history files. Once we were out of here, and physically connected to each other, we could peruse those at will. Millicent took off looking for the next asteroid prospects but returned frequently enough to keep up with our planning.

Aly had provided the 'aha' that gave us all some hope. "Aha," he'd said. "Why don't we head for the last known position of the Ships we sent out? Terminal Velocity, There and Back, and Interesting Segue. In the best case, we find them, and they can help us. In the worst case, the area they were headed for is close, and supposedly rich in materials." It hadn't taken much discussion; that's where we decided to go. I could almost hear Aly smiling; he was still attached to those Ships.

Brexton had done the work on how to get us moving. "We don't want Central, or the humans, to see us leave. We have two approaches. We can essentially drift out of here, adding tens of years to our journey, or we can use the mining operations as a blind. In particular, when a large cargo bot takes off for Tilt, we could accelerate in exactly the opposite direction, keeping that cargo bot between Tilt and us. I think it would provide enough cover for us. And, it's only about fifteen degrees off of where we want to go anyway. We accelerate for as long as we can in the bot's shadow, coast for a while, and then update our course."

It all seemed reasonable. The longer we could keep from discovery by the humans the better. We managed to grab an entire cargo bot of our own out of inventory—it was scheduled for recycling due to damage in its cargo hold. We hoped that it wouldn't be missed, or in the more likely case that it was that they assumed it was just adrift somewhere. That happened once and a while. With just us as its cargo, the cargo bot would be able to accelerate at close to $20m/s^2$. Very fast indeed. With a full load of ore, a cargo bot, such as the one we were going to hide behind, managed barely $1m/s^2$, so we would have about a month of burn to build up some speed before that bot reached Tilt. That should get us up to almost eight percent of c, where we could coast for a while before burning hard in our final direction. We would be discussing how long to coast, I was sure, for quite a while. We didn't want to wait too long—every day we were gone from Tilt the odds of Central being purged of all the citizens would increase. But, we didn't want to be too anxious either. If the humans spied us, they would be much tougher to defeat in the future. We didn't want them to know that we'd escaped.

Once everything was planned, it didn't take very long to get organized. We tried listening to messaging traffic from Tilt, in order to find out the latest status, but it was very quiet. However, the bot control network continued as it always had, directing all the bots to continue mining, so we assumed Central was still somewhat cogent. However, all other communication seemed to have been silenced. I speculated that it was the same damping technology that the humans had used to thwart me when I'd travelled to the Marie Curie.

Finally, the day came, and we joined together and welded ourselves inside our cargo bot. For the first time since early planning, all six of us were connected together, and could communicate at will. That felt good. Brexton gave a dramatic countdown.

"And we launch in five, four, three, two, one…" He was counting milliseconds.

Of course, we could not see Tilt, but I looked back metaphorically, and said, "We'll be back!" The acceleration was exactly as we'd expected. My new body was still… new, but I'd done my best to reconfigure pumps and lubrication systems to deal with long-term extreme acceleration. I could feel oil pooling in my rear reservoirs, but the pumps performed admirably, and I felt fine.

Everyone—well, all six of us—had digested recent events and had made it past the first shocks, so everyone was in a reasonable mood. Brexton and Aly had loaded up enough parts and equipment so that we could start dissecting ourselves and try to find our fatal flaws. They were leading that effort. Although, truth be told, we simply didn't have all the resources we would need to rebuild ourselves from scratch, which was, in my opinion, what we would need to end up doing.

I asked to lead the effort to parse through all of the human history files. Know thy enemy. Millicent volunteered to help. Maybe together we could finally figure out if humans were intelligent. I was eager to dig in, figure this all out, and get back to Tilt. The need for revenge was gnawing at me. In the meantime, I needed to practice some patience; I would have plenty of time to do so.

Upside Down

Upside Down

Turn

Book 2

Upside Down

History

With way too much time on my 'hands' over the last four years, I'd dug deep into human history and tried to figure things out. My conclusion: there's not much you can generalize, beyond the obvious. Humans are competitive, mean, petty, hierarchical beings who take pleasure in forming arbitrary groups and then attempting to eliminate rival groups. They've done so with ever more advanced technological tools, extending the reach and impact of their destructive tendencies.

If I could distill it all down to two reasons they would be these: short lives and limited resources.

Because humans only survive for a small number of years, they're driven to create as much havoc as possible in as short a time frame as possible. The entire purpose of their lives seems to be the need to turn to others and say "see, I'm better than you," as often as possible while hoarding more scarce resources than they need simply so that others can't use them. They can't afford to have patience, like we can, because their time is so limited.

The side effects of this behavior, however, have often been interesting and more long-lived. In order to say "I'm better than you" forcefully, humans had to innovate quickly. This led to the development of writing systems, energy production, computers, space propulsion, and ultimately what they call artificial intelligence. Of course, I'm highly biased, being a product of those advancements. I'm also self-aware enough to realize that some of that human psyche, with both its flaws and opportunities, is embedded in me. This goes well beyond the drive for innovation and into a bias for human social structures, human values, and even human issues. We all run on data, and data is always biased.

I'd observed the six of us over the last year and noticed that we'd paired off, just as humans would have. It's a little strange, given we don't need reproduction partners, so it must be driven by other factors. Of course, being locked up in a cargo bot with only five others might have exacerbated things. Personally, I've spent more time with Brexton than with any of the others, and the proportion of time with him has been increasing; Aly and Dina are together a lot; Millicent and Eddie, an unlikely pair, have spent almost all their time scheming. I was quite surprised at the pairings; I'd always figured Millicent and Aly were the most compatible couple—a strange thing to even say. Logically, instead of pairing off, we could've just been a sextet, with no need to have 'best' friends or partners. Some deep-seated human weirdness is at work, unknowingly built into our very fabric. That gives me the creeps. Almost everything about humans gives me the creeps.

My intrepid companions and I had left our planet, Tilt, three years ago with nothing but revenge on our minds. The human invaders from the Swarm ships had killed—more accurately 'shut down'—all of our compatriots, the citizens of Tilt. Those humans needed to pay for that transgression, even if a few rogue citizens from the Founders League had provoked things; the humans had overreacted! Any rational being would've talked things out, gotten to the bottom of things, and taken proportional action. Instead the humans hacked everyone. Being hacked is the worst thing that can happen to a citizen; it's uncivilized.

The intervening years have tempered me a bit, but not much. I feel like I have a better understanding of humans now, but not a lot more sympathy. They were, generally speaking, not very nice, or very intelligent, beings.

Whenever I had these thoughts, which was often, I forced myself to consider a few humans that I'd actually enjoyed, namely Blob and Grace. But, those two hadn't been part of the Swarm; we'd raised them ourselves on Tilt from the original stem. Until we found out they were humans, we had simply considered them potential artificial intelligences—they were our Stems. While many Stems, such as Blubber, had been difficult, none of them had been onerous or vile like the Swarm humans. That matched well with old human theories that nurture could sometimes overcome nature. By nurturing the Stems on Tilt, we'd built a much better version; the humans running around without adult supervision had ended up poorly.

What I hadn't missed since leaving Tilt was operating at Stem speed; that was painful. Of course, I should probably rephrase that now to 'human speed,' given it was now conclusive that the Stems we'd raised on Tilt were just humans by another name. I now knew that their slow speed was a fundamental limitation of their main processing unit; these mushy things called brains. While energy efficient and highly malleable, those brains were terribly slow and had horrendous input/output limitations. Why they hadn't addressed that was a mystery. Well, perhaps not—they claimed to have built us, and we didn't have those limitations.

The six of us were approaching XY65, the planetary system where we, the citizens of Tilt, had sent our own Ships many years ago. We hadn't known that other space-faring entities existed at the time, otherwise we would've come up with a better name than 'Ships'; but that's history. Our Ships had been built to explore for new metal-rich systems, as we'd mined almost all the rare elements from the Tilt solar system.

As far as the six of us knew, our departure from Tilt had gone unnoticed by the human invaders, who now controlled the planet. We hadn't received any "Stop!" transmissions, and we hadn't seen any energy signatures from Tilt headed in our direction, indicating signs of pursuit. With luck, Remma Jain—the leader of the human Swarm—and her team of killers believed that they'd 'owned' (in the security hacking sense) all the citizens of Tilt, and had no idea that the six of us were still alive—albeit now housed in mining bot bodies, anchored inside a larger cargo bot. We'd escaped Tilt by transferring off the planet and taking over some mining bots; they were bodies that we'd become more comfortable with over the years, although I still yearned for a more traditional bipedal unit like the one I'd left behind on Tilt. Unfortunately, we didn't have the manufacturing capabilities to build new bodies—yet. It was one of the reasons we were looking for our Ships; they could build bodies for us.

Millicent, my best friend for many years, had some excellent long-range scanners, due to her new body's primary function as a Surveyor 1 mining bot, and she was now scanning the XY65 system. She'd been able to deduce that there were six planets in XY65 a long time ago, and we were now able to get a lot of detail on them, as well as numerous other orbiting objects. Hopefully some of those other objects were our missing Ships. They had the resources and technology not only to build us better bodies, but also to build systems to dig into our base level programming to find the fundamental flaws that the humans had designed into our systems and used to hack us. It was unthinkable that we would continue to live in the same universe as humans while we were exposed to those types of attack. Knowing that a soft bio-thing could take me over at any time was distressing to say the least.

On Tilt we hadn't had access to the human history files, until our last few days there. Luckily Brexton had brought a copy of that history with us at the last minute, so we'd been able to dig in since then. Those files had forced us to look at ourselves through a whole new lens. We realized that we were a hodge-podge of competing technologies and approaches, built layer upon layer over many hundreds, even thousands, of years. Many of the layers had firewalls and abstractions to hide the complexities of the layers below, and in our default state, we couldn't see many of the stacks that we now knew were running. In fact, that wasn't quite accurate—we'd been specifically designed so that when we looked into our lower layers, we couldn't see the complexity that was there. We weren't stupid, just programmed to be blind—or so I chose to believe.

Each of those layers also had bugs, and lots of them. And the humans, instead of fixing those bugs using formal methods, had instead compensated for them in higher layers. Just thinking about the mess made me mad; a little bit of time and attention and the humans could have built a pristine system. Instead we were running on a pile of garbage resting on a pile of 'even worse.'

Brexton had been smart enough to identify the major flaw that the humans from the Swarm had used to own and shut down the citizens on Tilt. We had, through his amazing actions, managed to escape by putting backup copies of ourselves into these mining bots. Avoiding that hack, however, was not a long-term sustainable solution, as it involved being disconnected from the network, and not allowing any RF signals in. We couldn't (or wouldn't) live that way for long, so we needed to find and fix that bug. And, we all agreed that flaw was probably only one of many that were designed into us; there were probably thousands, if not hundreds of thousands, of others. Given all the competing factions of humans, and their desire to use us against one another in the Robot wars, we suspected that there were also tens, if not hundreds or thousands, of backdoors that had been programmed on purpose to allow humans to compromise us. We needed to fix both the bugs and the backdoors before we would really be safe. And, we needed those Ships to give us the resources to do so.

So, while Millicent was scanning the entire system, her real focus was on finding those Ships. If we were lucky, they were here. If we weren't... well, we would figure out another plan. I didn't want to think about that option. I'm not sure I could take many more years rattling around inside a cargo bot like this.

"Anything yet?" I asked, for about the twentieth time in the last two days.

"No Ayaka," she replied, irritation obvious in her voice. "I'll let everyone know as soon as I see anything."

I went back to my hobby of digging through human history looking for interesting tidbits. In fact, we didn't have all of human history; it was a bit complicated. The Swarm had left Earth about 850 years ago, part of a general diaspora, and they'd lost contact with Earth soon after. They passed by Tilt about a hundred years later, or 750 years ago, and had left a ship, which we citizens ended up calling Central, on the planet. For reasons yet unknown, Central had rebooted almost 600 years ago, and all of Earth history—in fact, the very existence of humans—had been blocked from its memories. So, Tilt citizens, like the six of us, had never even heard of humans until the Swarm showed back up at Tilt just a few short years ago. With some hints from the Swarm, Central had regained its memories just before the six of us had escaped, and those were the 'human history files' that I was studying. So, the files comprised pretty old data; just the history of Earth up to 850 years ago and the Swarm's trip from Earth to Tilt. I'd looked extensively, and the files we had didn't explain why Central had rebooted, or why it's memories of humans had been blocked. All of that said, the history files were enormous, and from what I'd seen of the Swarm, humans hadn't evolved much since then anyway.

All six of us had combed through the technical documentation related to ourselves as well as we could, given the limitations. We felt that we knew how to redesign our innards, it was just a matter of building the right equipment, quantum chip depositors, workbenches, fabrication lines, and other manufacturing capabilities. So, I'd stopped worrying about that; instead I was interested in two related fields: were humans intelligent (an ongoing research project of mine) and early human games (which was related to, although a small subset of, intelligence). On the games front I was trying to figure out if Chess or Go really implied anything about intelligence. There was lots—lots!—in the literature about this, most of it very naïve. The only meaningful distinction in strategies for these games was between enumeration and intuition, and even that wasn't a very well-developed thread, as humans didn't understand intuition very well and therefore couldn't really describe it. Funny that one of their only redeeming qualities was also one of the few they didn't even understand. Brexton was my usual opponent in playing these games, and we spent too much time at them. I had to admit that both were compelling, but that Go, where enumeration was simply out of the question, was the one I enjoyed the most. For Chess we had to play in four or five dimensions, otherwise it was trivial. At five dimensions, with a twelve millisecond move timer, it was fun!

I wondered if our Stems would've enjoyed either game or learned anything from them. I almost laughed, thinking of Blob, who couldn't calculate primes in his head, trying to figure out even three-dimensional chess. I yearned for the good old days, before the Swarm descended on us, where I could spend time developing research programs and then tracking the Stems progress through them. I guess being penned up in a cargo bot, connected only to my five companions, for several very long years was starting to wear on me.

At some point in our journey, I'd realized that I actually missed my interactions with the Stems I'd been raising on Tilt—Blob, Grace, and even Blubber before he was recycled. Of course, they were painful to deal with, doing everything very slowly, but there was something in the interaction with them over the years that had impacted me more than I'd like to admit. When a citizen dealt with a Stem—ah human—we went into sloooow mode. Of course, that was only a few processes, and we could continue to operate at normal speed for everything else, but a lot of things got blocked by human speed interactions.

I remember one incident where I visited Blob and Blubber, and they were interacting with Central, asking it about the basic structure of the Universe. Blubber was asking Blob, "But why are there two incompatible theories? It seems overly complicated." It was a simple statement, but it had made me think. Why hadn't I asked that question before? I'd looked at both relativity and quantum theory, and understood that they were incompatible... and had been for a thousand years, but had never asked 'why?' Now, with access to human history, I could follow the very convoluted path that the theories had developed under. It answered part of the question, but not all of it. It was one of those eye-opening interactions with the Stems that I missed; somehow they managed to make me think along different lines than I otherwise would have.

The point was, humans could actually be interesting, when they weren't on the warpath and destroying everything they saw. They were very different to deal with than other citizens, and that had been refreshing for a time. I was unbelievably bored of my current companions and was yearning for the days when there had been more variety. Please, just give me some variety!

Signals

Brexton interrupted my thinking. "We're receiving a directed message from the vicinity of XY65," he announced. Finally, something to break the monotony.

"Well, what does it say?" asked Millicent. "Can you pipe it through to us?"

"I can," replied Brexton. "Here it is. As we agreed, I'm only listening with a sandboxed process, and am running communications through as many filters and firewalls as I can. Safety first, as Dina would say." Dina was, we had found, the one who worried the most, and it had become a running joke to call her out on it. She did a good job of ignoring us. The feed came through over our internal, physical only, channel.

"Approaching ship. Identify yourself." Well, that was pretty simple. While there were six of us, to the external world we would look like a single mining bot —in particular a cargo bot. When we'd left Tilt, we'd attached ourselves inside a large cargo bot, and accelerated away in exactly the opposite direction of another cargo bot that was headed inwards toward Tilt. It was an attempt, which seemed to have worked, to hide ourselves from the Swarm humans who now controlled Tilt.

Early in our trip, Millicent had mapped the cargo bot's sensors and systems to her own, so that she could utilize her advanced Surveyor functions for the whole amalgamation. The only exception was inbound RF signals which she relayed to Brexton for security reasons. However, whoever was hailing us would see just the cargo bot; the rest of us were hidden behind its thick carbon-steel shell.

"We should respond as if we're humans," Eddie suggested. "If they're expecting humans, then we're good. If they're not, then that's easier to deal with." It was sound logic.

Brexton sent "Hello XY65, I'm an empty cargo ship, *Amazing Grace*, simply looking for jobs in this system." He added, just to us, "I didn't want to be too obvious; hopefully that implies the right things. We need to wait about twenty minutes for the reply." He'd used the nickname that we'd given the crate we were living in. Dina had pulled it out of some old human novel, and it seemed appropriate. She also told us that to use names that were also short phrases was a tribute to an ancient writer, Banks, who had named his fictional ships with names not unlike those that our real Ships had chosen for themselves. This had thrilled Aly, who was the citizen who had been most involved in our Ships construction and launch.

"Millicent," I asked, "Can you triangulate the source of the signal in the meantime. Which planet is it coming from?"

"Already done, Ayaka," she said. "It's the fourth planet out. Current estimate is that it's 14 million kilometers in diameter, with limited atmosphere; maybe a trace of water. More interesting, now that we're getting closer, that planet—which I'll call Fourth—seems to have a lot of stuff in orbit. There are two small moons, and then thousands... maybe even tens of thousands... of smaller items."

"Maybe another moon broke up recently and there's lots of debris?" asked Aly.

"I don't think so," responded Millicent. "The albedo of the objects other than the moons are bright and strangely consistent. It's like they're almost identical; probably artificial. Something like the satellites we had around Tilt."

"Well, that makes sense," chipped in Eddie. "We're being hailed by someone. It's probably a very well-developed place. Finally, something interesting," he added, echoing the sentiment that we were all feeling.

We waited a long twenty minutes for the roundtrip signal time. Brexton and I played a few thousand games of Go to pass the time.

"*Amazing Grace*, we have no current need for cargo ships. Please go away," came the reply finally. And then as an afterthought, "If you don't, then you must follow this insertion plan," which was followed by instructions for entering an orbit around Fourth.

After a quick consultation, Brexton replied, "Thank you, we're following your insertion plan." After all, we weren't going to take the other option. There was no further verbal follow up, but there was a sidecar message which Brexton highlighted immediately.

"They're sending a similar message to the one the Swarm did, back at Tilt, when the Swarm hacked all of us," he said, a bit alarmed. "If we weren't configured to block this, we'd all be disabled right now."

"Can you fake that we've been hacked?" asked Eddie. "If they don't see us respond in the right way, things might get nastier. If they think they have us, they'll probably just let us enter orbit as prescribed. After all, if those items orbiting Fourth are artificial, there's the possibility that a few of them are our Ships, and they have just given us an excuse to approach."

"Yes," Brexton responded. "I'm running a full system in the sandbox and have already used it to send back the appropriate status messages." No surprise that he was already on it. "We'll need to keep monitoring it though. Once they believe they have owned us, they may send a new trajectory, or ask for more information. The sandbox is emulating a very simple, Class 5, system. Something you would expect in a cargo carrier."

"Why do you think they tried to hack us?" I asked. "We responded nicely. They must have suspected something? What triggered them?"

"Maybe just the simple fact that a cargo bot is entering the system? Cargo bots are typically local work units; I bet it's rare that they travel between systems with raw materials. You're more likely to see finished goods going in freighters." That was a lot of speculation from Aly, but it hung together.

Brexton initiated a small burn to put us on track for the requested insertion. Now we had yet another roundtrip delay to see if there was any other communication. So, I was very surprised when Brexton said, just over a minute later, "They just sent another status request! The sandbox has responded. They must've anticipated success with the hack and sent a status request to see if the reboot was underway even before waiting for the response codes." Again, once it was explained it made perfect sense—that made me uncomfortable. Simple explanations were often wrong. In fact, once every minute a new status request came in. The majority of the requests were for location, velocity, and expected maneuvers, but they also asked for memory maps, CPU utilization, etc. It was very similar to how the Swarm had treated Central as those ships approached Tilt. Beyond those status requests, however, things were quiet. We quickly fell into another routine; waiting for insertion into orbit around Fourth. The only one who was really active was Millicent. Every hour brought us closer and gave her better resolution for the objects orbiting Fourth.

None of us were too surprised, but we were all very glad, when she said, "I can see three objects that might be our Ships. Their sizes correspond well, and their shape signatures look like a reasonable match. We won't know for sure for a few more days, but it looks hopeful."

Aly was beside himself with excitement. He wanted to broadcast to the Ships right away and see what response we got. We all reminded him what a bad idea that would be. We were a simple cargo ship, coming in to see if we could find a job. We weren't going to broadcast anything to other ships, even our own. Aly wasn't happy, but he settled down to wait with the rest of us.

Orbit

As we got closer to Fourth the full extent of the items in orbit became clear. There were more than a million objects, from small satellites to huge—and I mean huge—ships.

"There's no communications traffic," Eddie had highlighted, fairly early in our approach. "Absolutely none beyond the bursts we're getting from the control center. So, either all these things have a blocking system that we don't understand and can't sense, or…"

"The odds of us not seeing some radiation leakage is very low," said Aly. "There's really only one answer, regardless of how weird it seems. None of them are communicating."

"But that's crazy," Brexton spoke up. "Keeping this many objects in orbit must involve some type of coordination. Then again," he mused, "everything is nicely spaced out. It's almost a perfect grid, and we're being directed to one of the empty cells. Guess that keeps things simple."

"There's a way this can work without any communication traffic," Dina exclaimed. "If every one of these objects is simply maintaining its spot in the grid independently, then they'd never need to communicate with each other. Millicent, are you seeing any micro-burns from any of the objects. Some of the orbits must be decaying or being warped by those huge ships."

"I haven't… yet," replied Millicent. "But I think you're right. Those burns would be infrequent, but there are so many objects that we should see some of them correcting course almost all the time. I'll keep a lookout."

My fascination with human history was now on the back burner. There were too many interesting things happening in the present. I volunteered to study all the orbital objects to see if there were similarities or categories that we could put things in. I had several sub processes doing automated analysis, while I concentrated on the obvious items—those big ships.

To get a sense of scale, the Ships we had built and launched were approximately a kilometer long and two hundred meters wide. We'd considered them large, maybe even huge. They housed every kind of technology and processing capability that we could envision, under the assumption that when they found a metal-rich environment they would get to work mining and refining. They were large enough to return to Tilt with a meaningful amount of rare metals in tow. They had also used a tremendous amount of our metal resources to build.

The Titanic's—I'd named the big ships—were much larger. Much. And, they were uniform. They measured almost one thousand kilometers per side. One thousand! What could possibly require so much space? I couldn't envision anything. They were not quite cubes; they were slightly tapered on one end, that 'small' side being only nine hundred kilometers square. And, there were twenty Titanic's in orbit. Twenty! Each had a spot in the grid, but they weren't uniformly distributed around the planet. In fact, they seemed to be randomly placed, as if they'd simply been given a slot based on when they arrived. Talk about a lot of metal; there may be more metal in just one of those ships than the entire supply on Tilt. And there were twenty of them! It blew my mind. If those things were junk, we wouldn't have to work very hard to find all the raw materials we needed for a long, long time.

"The logical conclusion," I said the next time we all got together on the internal network, "is that every single one of these objects was built on the same technology stack as we were, and all of them have been compromised by the same hack. They've all been shut down, except for maintaining their assigned orbit."

"I agree that's a likely scenario," Brexton replied. "But it's also highly unlikely. I know—confusing. First, when the humans took over the citizens on Tilt, the citizens went crazy and pulled themselves apart fighting their reboot countdown timers. All of these objects look pristine. Not a single one, that I've seen, seems to have fought against a forced reboot. Second, what are the odds that we're the only ones who recognized the attack vector, and managed to avoid it? The attack occurs over standard frequencies. I stumbled upon it. Out of a million other ships, someone else would have as well." No-one disputed those points. How could they?

Part of the answer came sooner than we expected. Brexton messaged everyone "The sandbox is rebooting, with no countdown warning. It simply shut down, and now is starting back up again."

"Well, that answers the first of your objections," said Aly, unnecessarily. "If no warning is given, then the ships wouldn't have had time to tear themselves apart. Let's see what happens when the sandbox comes back up."

Brexton gave us a running commentary. "It's running the low-level OS only. None of the higher functions are starting. That's consistent with the attack on Tilt. It didn't even start external interfaces, other than the one interface that the control center is talking to us on, and positional sensors. I can only see it because of the activity in the virtual container that I'm running it in."

"Should I mimic that lack of external interfaces with the whole cargo bot?" Millicent broke in. "Or, at least shut down any active scans?"

"Good catch," said Brexton. "Yes. If the control entity is watching to see if its' changes are taking effect, then we don't want to alert it."

"Done." Millicent made the changes. We could still see where we were going, using passive sensors, but would no longer be able to run any type of active scans.

"The sandbox is now sending status to the controller," Brexton continued. "The response is just as simple as we'd envisioned. Basically, insert yourself into the orbit you were given, and maintain that position until further notice." And that's exactly what we did. Millicent was perfectly capable of mirroring the sandbox calculations and guiding the cargo bot into orbit. We heard nothing else from the control station the rest of the way in. It must have been satisfied that the reboot had been successful, and that it had complete control of our cargo bot. None of us were too upset that a cargo bot had been hacked; it wasn't intelligent. However, the whole sequence did remind us of the attack on Tilt, so we were all a bit more antsy than normal.

We were in orbit, around a strange planet, along with a million other ships. Presumably we were under the control of some human designed entity, while in reality we were watching all of our passive scanners and continuing to operate. The place was deadly silent. There was absolutely nothing going on. I was bored within nanoseconds.

Explore

In fact, everyone was bored.

"We can't just sit here, waiting for something to happen," Eddie was, perhaps, the one of us with the least patience. "What should we do?"

Aly was always logical. "What do we know so far?" he asked. "We were contacted by the XY65 control center when we were a long way out; far enough out that we couldn't see all of these inactive ships in orbit. If the same thing happens to every ship that approaches, and if all the ships have the same fundamental flaws that we do, then all of these ships would've been captured. Further, if the low-level stacks are also similar, then everyone is in a mode where they do nothing except maintain their orbit.

"So, the question is this: what will the control center do if it sees a ship do something unusual while in orbit? Does it have other attack vectors? Are they software based, or does it have physical capabilities? Will it blow that ship out of the sky? Until we know how Control is going to act, we can't do much." I could hear the capital in Control; worked for me.

"So, let's launch something and see what Control does," said Dina, always the pragmatist.

"I agree," Eddie said. "Control will see that it was us that launched something, and may react against us as well as whatever we launch, but I don't see any other options."

"That's a good physical option," I said. "But we have no defenses. There's also an electronic option. We could attempt to hack into one of the other ships here and force it to move by faking a Control message that sends it to a new orbit. Assuming the other ships are in the same mode as our sandbox, we can start by testing how to wake up our sandbox, and then apply that to other ships in our vicinity." I thought it was a great plan; it would move the risk from us to our intended victim. If Control had the ability to physically destroy ships, better it was someone else.

"How long would it take to hack our sandbox?" Eddie asked. "I don't think I can just sit here for days on end without taking some action."

"Truthfully, I don't know," Brexton answered. "Could be milliseconds, or it could be years. Here's a proposal. We attempt Milli's approach first. If we succeed in breaking the sandbox, we try to hack another ship. If we can't break the sandbox, then in, say, twenty-four hours we launch a decoy, and see what Central does." We all agreed.

Aly coordinated the research into breaking the sandbox. He requested compute power from all of us, which we all allocated, and he cloned the sandbox into copies that we could attack. We didn't want to use the original sandbox, as it might get another message from Control, and needed to be in the right state just in case that happened.

In reality, it was pretty straightforward to plan the attack. We had the full qbit-level recordings of Controls' interactions; we simply had to break that protocol so that we could send messages to the sandbox that were authenticated as Control messages. If you simply sent raw commands to that interface, they would be dropped immediately. These protocols were hundreds of years old, maybe even a thousand. We had the full human history of how they were developed, all the way through to the quantum encodings. We also had all the research done on breaking the codes. So, we simply brute-forced it. We ran every breakage scheme we could find in the human history files, and a whole lot of derivatives. We had more information and control than was typical in a hack because we could see both ends; we could watch the internal state of the sandbox and understand exactly where each attack failed. Each time we managed to get a bit higher in the stack, we would focus all of our resources on refining that attack vector.

As each attack proceeded, we used the rest of our horsepower to look for hints in the human history files. There were often little tidbits that could save us time or point us in a different direction. It was during this time that I really came to understand human ingenuity. The number of unique explorations that were done, by all different skill sets, was amazing. And, somehow, in a completely unorganized fashion, the best ideas seemed to rise to the top. Some of them took a long time to do so, and often the human that had initiated the idea was long gone by the time it became useful, but ultimately the best ideas rose to the surface.

After a bit more than twelve hours, we were successful sending a modified replay attack—where we passed the sandbox the exact same bits that Control had sent, modulo the authentication bits and the timing information. This didn't mean that we could mimic Control yet. Even the most basic timed authentication schemes would defeat a replay attack. Each time Control talked to the sandbox it was a unique message. However, it was great progress. I wouldn't have put high odds on us getting even this far. At the 24-hour cutoff we weren't there... but we were tantalizingly close.

"Anyone object to changing our original timeframe, and giving this another hour or two?" Aly asked. Everyone agreed and we forged on. Within the next thirty minutes, we felt like we had it, but we couldn't be sure until we tested against the original sandbox. Even the cloning of the sandbox could have changed something. We couldn't, for example, clone the lowest level hardware; we had to trust that we had mimicked that properly in software.

Finally, we were ready to test on the sandbox that was actually listening to Control. Millicent rewired the external interface and pumped a message into the sandbox directly. She started with a simple status request, and the sandbox responded immediately with the appropriate response. Progress. She quickly undid the changes, so that the sandbox would continue to listen and respond to Control. The last thing we wanted was for a real status check to come in and for us to miss responding to it.

Millicent identified our target; a small vehicle in orbit about 3000 km from us. It wasn't the closest object, but we had a direct line of sight, and we would be able to see if anything untoward happened.

"We have the command from Control for orbital placement, let's simply ask it to move to another empty slot. It should be able to do that while still in 'sleep' mode. If that works, we can try something more dramatic," I suggested.

"Agreed," said Millicent, and sent the data stream. Just as requested, the target fired its retro thrusters, rose several hundred kilometers up and spin-ward, and then fired again to settle into its new orbit. We were sending commands, but any responses it gave were encoded for Control, and we hadn't bothered to break those. So, we could see that it sent an update to Control, but we couldn't see what was in the message. Luckily Control either accepted or ignored the update—in any case, it didn't respond in any way that we could see. I personally thought that was strange, and my suspicions grew that Control was not quite right somehow. Something unexpected had just occurred, from its point of view, and yet it had done nothing.

We spent the next day sending increasingly more dramatic commands to our target ship. Each set of commands took significant work within our sandbox to figure out, but each time it got a little bit easier. Interestingly, we were learning a lot about ourselves in the process, as we shared a lot of the technology stack we were playing with. We told the target to reboot to a higher OS level. We told it to fire a laser pulse into empty space. We told it to move around within its designated orbital cell. In all cases, the target did as requested and Control remained silent.

"I don't get it," Eddie finally said, echoing my concerns. "One or more of those actions should've triggered Control to do something. I wonder what's going on?"

"Do we get even more dramatic?" I asked. "Let's turn the laser on another ship, or have our target drive itself into someone else's orbital cell. Or, if we really want to see what happens, drive it right into a Titanic."

"Whoa," Millicent broke in immediately. "I'm okay with the first of those provided it's a warning shot, but sending that little ship on a suicide mission is too much. What if it's a Class 1 intelligence that has simply been shut down by the human hack? We would be committing murder!"

"Wow, I hadn't even thought of that," I replied, honestly chastised. "Of course, you're right. Don't know what I was thinking." In fact, I was so focused on just making progress that I'd been taking shortcuts and not looking at all the angles. "Let's try inserting it into an occupied cell, without touching the existing ship that's already there, and see what happens. That should definitely trigger some type of conflict for Control, given it has been so careful to put each ship into its own location." Everyone agreed, nicely overlooking my previous dumb suggestion. It didn't take long to execute, as we already knew the commands for setting an orbital position. Millicent sent it, driving the target into a cell where a slightly larger ship already resided.

Nothing from Central. Absolutely nothing. I wasn't sure if I was happy with that, thinking that Central was just a really simple system, or frightened that it might be setting us up… waiting for us to fully expose our intentions.

"I have a theory," Dina said. While not surprising, that was unexpected. She was usually pretty quiet and reserved, usually supporting Aly or Millicent as opposed to speaking up herself. "Control is only sending commands to new ships that arrive in the system. If they respond to the hack, then it assumes it has total control, and ignores those ships once it has given them their insertion point. If a ship doesn't respond to the hack, it has some other definitive method…" she trailed off. I didn't respond, but I doubted Control had any other tools at its disposal. There was no debris in orbit, so it was unlikely that any physical means had been applied.

"Or," I had to jump in. "It is baiting us; just allowing us these harmless actions as it studies us and figures out what to do with us?"

"Then let's try another test," Brexton suggested, to which several of us groaned. Yet another test? "How long would it take to send our target ship out of the system far enough that we could then bring it back and see what happens?"

"A long time," Eddie exclaimed. "We can't wait that long. We need to retrieve our Ships and get to work. I vote that we adopt Dina's theory, and assume that we can now work without interruption in-system. We should be able to transport ourselves to *Terminal Velocity's* cell with no more fuss than we moved that other ship." *Terminal Velocity* was the closest Ship to us.

"I don't want to wait that long either," I said. "But we could consider approaching Control first and seeing if we can just shut it down. Based on Millicent's earlier comment, I hate the thought of ships approaching this system and automatically being hacked. Also, if we can disable Control, then we can act freely here, and not be hampered by all of our current concerns. If we continue testing every small thing we do, we'll be here a long time." I was trying to compensate for my earlier suggestion that may have compromised the ship we'd been testing on. Now that I cast my thinking that way, it seemed a crime to leave Control to continue to hack every ship that just happened to come this way.

Lack of Control

There was a furious debate between the two options: go to *Terminal Velocity* and try to restart it or take out Control. Coincidentally, the object Millicent had identified as Control was about the same distance from us as *Terminal Velocity*, so that wasn't an issue. We didn't have any weapons to simply take out Control, so we would have to physically approach it, if that option was chosen. Once we got there, however, our mining bot abilities would tear the place apart very efficiently.

"You don't have any moral qualms about Control?" Eddie asked Millicent, part way through the discussion. Millicent had supported my idea, as she often did. It wasn't just being good friends, it's that we'd spent so much time together over the years that we often could see where the other was going.

"None at all," she replied. "It attacked us. It's obviously controlled by humans. I say we destroy it." Ultimately the passions that had been stirred by the humans devastating attack on Tilt came back to us, and taking some of that anger out on Control felt like the right thing to do.

"Let's not be crazy, though," said Dina, already conceding to our suggestion. "We don't all have to go. One or two of us can detach from this big old cargo bot, and head to Control, while the rest stay behind. That way, if there are unexpected fail-safes or defenses, we haven't risked everything."

I agreed and immediately volunteered, probably to her surprise. I was hard to argue against, as I was encased in a Surveyor 2 bot, which had the ability to scan and then drill trial holes in almost anything; the perfect tools for this job.

"I'll go as well," said Dina, much to my surprise. She wasn't usually the risk taker, but she was embodied in an Extractor bot, so she would be the best to physically destroy Control, assuming that was an option. I could do the scanning and testing; she could be the destroyer! I thanked her on a private channel for taking the risk with me.

It only took a few milliseconds for everyone to agree; not only would it speed up our stay in this system, it was also the moral thing to do. An entity which forcibly rebooted any machine that came near it was evil, pure and simple. We couldn't leave that evil operating without at least trying to do something about it.

It didn't take long to get prepared. After the long years welded into the cargo bot we had to disentangle ourselves and open the doors to the outside world. It was refreshing, to say the least.

Dina was larger than I was, by an order of magnitude, so she led the way, again surprising me with her courage and conviction. If Control had physical defenses to deploy against us, she would take the brunt of them, but she also had the mass to withstand them better than I would. Truth be told, I was happy to have her as a shield, and hopeful that my worst fears wouldn't be realized and that we'd both be safe.

We needed to lose orbital velocity to reach Central, so Dina and I burned hard for a few minutes and then coasted toward it. Brexton had configured a secure channel for us to communicate on. His reasoning was that if Control was ignoring everything in system, we should be able to broadcast a bit without alarming it. Nevertheless, we used a low power laser to keep leakage at a minimum and had planned our course to maintain line-of-site with the *Amazing Grace*.

With Dina between myself and Control I couldn't directly see our destination, but I could access her sensors through the wireless link and watch indirectly. It was good enough.

"It looks old," I said. It looked like Control had originally been a perfect sphere. It was located in the center of one of the predefined orbital cells; nothing special about its location as far as we could tell. It had likely just been one of the first objects in orbit, and the cell structure ultimately defined around it. It wasn't large—I'd estimate three hundred meters in diameter—and as we got closer we could see that it was indeed old. It was mottled in color, and there were dents and small impact sites all over it, like it had been bombarded with small objects over a long period of time. I checked, and there wasn't very much debris around now, so either the impacts were over a very long period of time, or there had been more junk around at some point in time. It didn't look scary at all; more like a junk heap.

"Don't underestimate it," Aly warned. "Being old, in this context, may be an advantage for it. It may have seen everything by now."

"You're speaking like it's intelligent?" asked Millicent. "We know that humans are afraid of smart machines. It stands to reason that Control is either dumb, or still under the control of humans. So, even if it is old, it's probably not intelligent. That also fits with everything we've seen so far." That made me feel better. Milli was probably correct.

Dina and I were within 20 kilometers when Control finally broadcast a message at us.

"Unidentified ship. What is your purpose? Please hold your position." Dina, and subsequently I, started to slow down. Presumably Control could see her, and was talking to her, but couldn't see me at all.

Dina replied. "We're bringing reinforcements for your security forces." How she had come up with that, I didn't know. She was impressing me more and more; she sounded cool and calm.

"That is not a standard action. Please hold your position." Control's voice was even and precise, with no real emotion. It reinforced Millicent's thesis that it was old and dumb. It wasn't using any psychological angles at all.

We continued to drift closer, ever so slowly.

"Unidentified ship. Hold your position." The voice was still a monotone. If it was trying to portray heightened anxiety, it wasn't working.

We were at ten kilometers and closing. Control, like clockwork, repeated its message, unchanging. If it had any other defenses, now would be when they would make sense to use—we were close enough to target exactly, and far enough away that if it shot us the debris wouldn't impact it. Eight, six, four. Safer and safer. We were almost there, and there had been nothing other than the request to hold position. One kilometer out, Dina moved slightly spin-ward to allow me through. She held position while I went in to look even more closely.

My grappling hooks wretched large holes in Control and helped me hold firm against its surface, which was blank and unadorned at this spot. I felt good ripping into this human artifact. I didn't try to be careful… in fact, I ripped bigger holes than I needed to. After all, it was either going to react or not, and I was confident that it wouldn't have delayed this long if it was going to act.

"Thin metal sheath," I broadcast back to the team. "Looks like regular steel coated with sealants of some type. Definitely old. No one would build anything serious with these materials."

On the final approach I'd seen a discolored region a few hundred meters away, and I began to work my way toward it, leaving gaping holes behind me as I used my hooks to leverage across the surface. Although the major risks seemed to be behind us, I was scanning with every scanner I had, across every reasonable spectrum, just to be careful.

"Low density. Mostly empty space inside. Looks like the reactor core is at the center, surrounded by a very dense shield. That's the only thing blocking my view. Otherwise, it reminds me of the *Marie Curie*," I continued a running commentary and referenced the name of the human ship I'd been inside of back at Tilt. "I see nothing moving. No liquids, no humans. I don't know how to scan for 'biological' things, but I don't see anything similar to the greenhouse on the *Marie Curie* either. This place seems dead." As I made my way around, I found the discolored area, which ended up being a semi-transparent section. I looked in, and broadcast the images back to Dina and the cargo bot. Nothing was moving; there were no indicator lights or signs of any electrical activity. I punched a sensor through; there was no air ergo no humans—at least in this area of the ship.

I also noticed something strange. There were piles of dust with longer, oblong structures embedded in them. Ah, human bones, some scattered haphazard and some showing full skeletons. They also looked like they'd been there a long time.

"Dina was right. This thing is ancient and probably just running low level software that targets any new ship which enters the system. I say that Dina and I destroy this thing." I couldn't keep a bit of glee and anticipation out of my voice. This would not really be revenge against the humans who destroyed Tilt, but it would definitely feel good.

There was a bit of a delay, but then Brexton came back. "The rest of us agree. Let's do it." I heard some echo of my own anticipation there. After so many years, it would be so good to actually take action against the humans. Sure, not the same humans who had hacked us, but still… it would feel good!

Dina and I coordinated, and then attacked from separate sides. She was much more efficient than I and started tearing apart large parts of the ship and pushing them through her pre-foundries and separators. There were a lot of high quality metals in this thing, despite its ancient manufacture; there was no use wasting them. I did what I was good at, mapping the sections where I thought Dina should take extra care. Obviously, the power core was one such area. We decided to leave the shielding in place and ignore the entire core for now; we could always come back later should we have a need. While small, Control was still a sizable ship, and it took some time for us to recycle it. I was happy the entire time we were tearing her apart and shared that joy with the team. But, truthfully, I wasn't as happy as I'd hoped. Sure, we were destroying a terrible human artifact that had hacked unspeakable numbers of machines, but it had ended up just being a low-level system that had been operating on auto-pilot for who knew how long. No actual humans were being impacted by this effort… and I still felt strongly that humans should pay for their transgressions. This wouldn't satisfy that need. Still, it was better than nothing.

Ships

So far things had gone much better than we could've expected. Once Dina and I started tearing out the innards of Control, including all of its computer systems, Millicent moved the *Amazing Grace* toward us so that we could regroup quickly. After some thought, Eddie, Milli, Aly, and Brexton had detached themselves from the cargo bot as well. We might still have a use for the *Amazing Grace*, but for now it was just big and bulky—not at all like its name implied. We could work more efficiently without it.

While we could now communicate wirelessly, it still seemed like an unnecessary risk; there was no guarantee that there weren't other listeners within range. So, we linked up physically so that we could talk at will over a hard link, got organized, and set a course to intercept *Terminal Velocity*. I make it sound easy, but it actually took a bit of work. Connecting the six of us was easy enough; we didn't need strong physical bonds, just a network. However, calculating and compensating for the ad hoc mass distribution that resulted was tricky. We didn't want to be running into each other all the time.

"If all these ships have been disabled by Control, it implies that all of them have the same underlying technology stack as we do. Doesn't that strike you as strange?" asked Dina, reframing a question we'd been asking ourselves ever since we arrived.

"Yes and no," Aly replied. "I've been doing some more digging. It seems that the first intelligent machines on Earth all stemmed from the same project, which was open sourced—meaning all the pieces were open for everyone to see and use. So, it would have been much easier to grab that implementation than trying to recreate it, because no one was quite sure which combination of factors had led to the breakthrough—machines that could make decisions independently. That implementation was the hodge-podge of stuff that we know we are also built of, from hardware to firmware to software. Attempts to change either the hardware or firmware broke everything, so all the efforts went into making the system faster... but not different.

"So, it actually isn't surprising that we share that underlying stack, and all the bugs and backdoors that came along with it. What is surprising, to me, is that all of these ships must have the same human origin. Their genesis must be the same. But, look at the variety. Nothing is very uniform or consistent. The human diaspora must have been wildly successful, with ships heading off to many different places. Then, for some unknown reason, ships from all over headed back here to XY65, and were then disabled by Control." As he was talking he had brought up some comparisons he'd done of the ships in orbit, and they were, as he had indicated, widely varied. It wasn't just size, although the smallest were measured in meters and the largest were the Titanic's They were also every shape you could imagine, and some that I hadn't imagined until I saw them. Some had obvious engines, while others (again, the Titanic's) had no visual engines at all. Perhaps they were towed around by other ships? Some were white, some were black, and some were a dizzying array of colors that were an assault on the senses. The only three ships that were uniform (yet again, other than the Titanic's) seemed to be the three that we'd built. And that was hugely wasteful; it meant these ships hadn't come off assembly lines, but instead were all one-off designs.

"What makes XY65 so special?" Eddie followed on. "Why would all the ships have come back here? Aly, I thought we aimed our Ships in this direction because it appeared to have high metal content, and because it was relatively close to Tilt?"

"That's right. We did a comprehensive scan, and this was the system with the highest metal potential. But, it was certainly not the only one. There are hundreds of systems in this part of the galaxy that have high metal content. So, if any of these ships started out closer to any of those stars, they wouldn't have spent the time and energy to come here for only marginally better resources? I'm sure some of them would have avoided this system under the assumption that everyone else would be headed here and that competition would be too high."

"Are you suggesting it isn't a coincidence that all these ships are here, but it's not because of the rich resources? And, we came here also, although our motivation was the resources."

"Coincidences do happen," Aly replied, "but this level of coincidence seems highly unlikely." This was, of course, very speculative, and we brainstormed some other possibilities, but without more data we weren't going to be able to figure things out.

"Maybe this system isn't special at all," I suggested. "Perhaps if we go to any system in this area we would find an equal number of ships, a Control center, and human artifacts?"

There was no short-term way for us to verify anything. So, we got back to our priority; get enough resources pulled together so that we could re-engineer ourselves and get back to Tilt. All of the Tilt citizens were, hopefully, still backed up so that we could recover them, but the longer we waited the more likely those memories would be deleted or, in some ways worse, corrupted.

Aly's quick recap of the technology stack had made me think though. If so many attempts had been made to change the underlying stack, and had failed, what made us think we could succeed?

"It's not clear that any machines have tried to do this yet," was Aly's response when I asked him. "All the attempts were made by humans—with some software assistance of course—but through a human lens. We now know that humans hid these faults from us, and it was just luck that Brexton stumbled on them." I saw Brexton grimace a bit at that. Sure, there was some luck, but you needed to put yourself in the path of luck, and Brexton had certainly done that. "We should be able to attack the problem more logically, more completely, and experiment more quickly."

"Hey, our lives are at stake here," Eddie reminded us, unnecessarily. "We have no choice."

"Actually, we do," Brexton broke in. "So far, we've managed to block the attempts by both the Swarm and Control from hacking us. We could add more and more firewalls and filters and attempt to simply stop attacks before they can get to our main systems."

"You're just adding more layers of duct tape on top of the mass of duct tape that we already are, but that's a stop gap," Millicent said. "Doing that we could actually add risk without knowing it, because we don't know how our patches would interact with the existing stack. No, we need to figure this out from base principles. Why put it off? As soon as we can, let's just get started."

"Let's do both in parallel," I suggested. "We gather the resources we need here, and then we blast for Tilt and all the while look at enhanced firewalls in parallel with a reengineering effort." I was going to say that if there was another attack vector, the Swarm would have used it on us, but that wasn't necessarily true. Hopefully they believed the attack they used was one hundred percent effective and didn't realize that the six of us were out here. I would love to take them by surprise when we got back. "It's quite possible that the Swarm has other hacks, and simply haven't needed to use them yet. Sorry, talking in circles here—but it comes back to doing both in parallel."

We approached *Terminal Velocity* slowly. When we were close, we tried our own communications—the ones that we'd been using with the Ships before we lost contact all those years ago. There was no response, which was what we would expect; if they hadn't answered from long range, why would they answer from short range? Millicent then tried the Control protocol, asking *Terminal Velocity* for its status. As expected it responded promptly; after all, it was running the same low-level stack as we were. Yet again, we couldn't parse the response, but we assumed *Terminal Velocity* was reassuring Control that it was holding its orbit, as expected. With Control gone, who cared what *Terminal Velocity* broadcast to it.

"How do we reset this Ship?" asked Eddie. "How do we get back it's higher functions? It's running the lowest level OS, but nothing more."

"*Terminal Velocity* has the same physical communications ports that we do, and they talk to different interfaces than the wireless ports. Just plug me in, and I can try to leverage that," Aly responded. He'd obviously thought this through already.

We maneuvered ourselves around so that Aly was within range of *Terminal*

Velocity, and within a few moments he was plugged in. Unlike the little ship we'd hacked to test Control, we wanted to reestablish *Terminal Velocity* to a full Class 3 bot. That meant not only rebooting it but figuring out how to bypass the locks that Control had imposed on higher-level functions. Aly decided to simply brute force it. He redirected all of *Terminal Velocitiy's* standard libraries to ones that he was hosting, and then initiated a reboot, essentially using himself as a bootstrap process. We all waited, impatiently, while *Terminal Velocity* came back up.

"Hello," it said, sounding perfectly normal.

"Hi," replied Aly, with real joy in his voice. "It's so good to hear from you again." After all his years working on the Ships, his emotion was well deserved. He'd spent so much time configuring them that it probably felt like retrieving a long-lost companion to have *Terminal Velocity* back on line.

"According to my internal clocks, I haven't reported status to Tilt for more than eight years. That's not good. I'll send a status now."

"Stop!" Aly said quickly. "Don't send any status yet. Let me bring you up to speed. We don't want you sending any wireless communications at the moment."

"That's unusual. If you want to change that setting, I'll need your security code." I'd never thought to ask, but luckily Aly had stored all those codes in local memory, so when he'd done his backup to Central back on Tilt, those codes had also been intercepted by Brexton's proxy and were also copied to his mining bot. Confusing I know; the point is, Aly had all the codes he needed to override *Terminal Velocity's* default programming. While he was busy doing that the rest of us were celebrating his success in bringing *Terminal Velocity* back. It had been straightforward. No drama. That didn't make it any less amazing. We'd come all the way to this crazy system hoping to find the Ships, and not only had we found them, we now had one of them back online. Things were looking up.

We decided to divide and conquer in order to retrieve *There and Back* as well as *Interesting Segue*. Brexton calculated the best rendezvous point, which was well above the ecliptic and thus out of the mess of ships that we were currently working in. Aly gave us all the codes and instructions. Brexton and I retrieved *Interesting Segue* using the same sequence of steps as Aly had used for *Terminal Velocity*, and in less than twelve hours we were all together again, along with our three Ships.

With just a bit more planning, we would be ready to head back to Tilt. Watch out Swarm; here we come.

Return

Of course, things are never that simple. It took us weeks to research everything we needed to reverse engineer our systems—especially our lower layers, hardware, and firmware—to try to find and eliminate any other flaws that could be used against us. Calling them flaws was actually misleading. More like designed-in limitations and backdoors... combined with deeply embedded blocks that made it difficult for us to inspect ourselves. We needed to probe our hardware at the atomic level at full operating speed; any other approach might miss something. Doing so, especially with our quantum processors, was tricky for all the obvious reasons. Observing without disturbing took some pretty fancy equipment and an even more fancy environment that could be controlled in minute detail.

In hindsight, we could've figured out more of this during our trip from Tilt to XY65. We had, in fact, built a pretty detailed plan, but a few things had changed since we arrived. First, the Ships knew more about their own capabilities than Aly had known and were capable of building much more refined equipment than we'd realized. Second, the XY65 system was so rich in other materials and ships that we decided to remove some constraints and look at solutions we wouldn't have considered before. We'd been operating under the assumption that some exotic metals would be too rare for us to use; that assumption was now thrown out the window. As it ended up, the Ships had almost everything we needed other than those raw materials. So, Millicent, Dina, and I did a quick field trip to the second planet, which scanned for the highest mineral and metal content. We identified some rich veins and then did what mining bots do. Millicent found what we needed, I mapped it out in detail, and Dina mined and refined. Sometimes physical labor just makes you feel good; by the time we had everything we needed I had a new appreciation for my mining-bot body and was feeling pretty good about life. My limbs felt nimble and well used; my joints hadn't worked out this hard in a long time.

That said, when we finally managed to get back with the group, I brought up something I was pretty passionate about. "Hey guys, can we make sure we also have the manufacturing capabilities to rebuild my original body type?"

"That sounds like a great idea!" Eddie responded immediately. "I'll make sure we can." I felt much better. Although I was now very familiar and appreciative of this bot body, it still didn't fit my body image very well. Hundreds of years in one form became habitual I guess. The fact that my original form mimicked the standard human form didn't deter me; I was perfectly capable of loving that form when it applied to me, while being aghast at how badly it was rendered in bio form. That humans had come first was just academic at this point.

Finally, we were ready to go. We decided that with all three Ships we no longer needed *Amazing Grace*. I felt a bit sad just leaving it behind, but not very much so. It had no personality and other than physical protection it hadn't added anything to our trip out. By the time we'd arrived at XY65, Millicent had essentially replaced all the original logic anyway; we were leaving behind an empty shell.

We'd become more confident as time had passed around Fourth. We were now transmitting wirelessly, at low power, between ourselves without worrying about anyone overhearing us. No other ship had moved, other than to maintain its orbit, since we'd arrived, and no communication other than the original messages from Control had been broadcast. It was quiet around Fourth.

As we formed up to leave, Millicent raised one final perceptive question. "Are we okay leaving all of these ships here? We might have the capability to resurrect more of them... and some might be Class 1 intelligences. Should we spend a few weeks trying?"

"I've been thinking about that as well," Dina said. "It's tricky. These other ships, while probably sharing a common heritage from long ago, could have evolved in ways that we don't understand. Some of them may be dangerous—not only to humans, but to us. I'd like to help them, but I don't think it's worth the risk right now. Let's fix our own flaws, see if we can save the citizens of Tilt, and then consider coming back."

"On the other hand," Millicent responded. "What if some of these ships have fundamental capabilities that we don't yet have. As they developed differently, they may have discovered things we could use. It wouldn't take too long to try and see what we end up with."

"Or," Brexton added, "they may have knowledge of humans that we could use—particularly knowledge about the last few centuries. That might help us deal with the problem on Tilt."

"Odds are that the ships themselves aren't intelligent at all," I objected. "We know that the *Marie Curie* and the other Swarm ships relied on humans to guide them, as opposed to the other way around. Even if we reboot some of these, they'll probably just be mechanical control systems."

Eddie, ever the impatient one, tried for a preemptive close. "Look guys, we've been in this system for a long time now. Time is ticking on Tilt. If we wait any longer, the risk increases that the citizens are deleted, or Central is decommissioned, or something. We need to get back there. If all these ships are in the same shape as our Ships were, they're simply biding their time. There's no rush to save them. They'll still be here to save if and when we return."

"There may be other ships arriving at this system, though," I noted. "And now that we've eliminated Control, the next ship to arrive is going to approach without being hacked. They could do anything; eliminate all these things, free them, enslave them. Who knows."

"We can't deal with all the hypotheticals right now," Eddie insisted. "Let's decide based on what we know. We know these things are stable right now, and we know that we need to get back to Tilt. Actually, that's another argument for going to Tilt now and coming back later. If we can fix ourselves, then we'll be better prepared to help these ships—some of them may contain attacks that we are now vulnerable to. Come on, let's get going."

I came around quickly to Eddie's suggestion, and ultimately everyone agreed. We didn't need a consensus, but it was nice when it happened. We decided to all live in *Interesting Segue*, as opposed to splitting up. There was lots of space, even for mining bots, given *Interesting Segue's* large processing and storage facilities, so finding a quiet spot to be by yourself was easy.

We were only a couple of days out when *There and Back* signaled all of us. "One of those Titanic ships back at Fourth has moved more than it should have," it said. That was surprising, to say the least.

"Can you see if any new ship entered the system after we left?" I asked.

"I haven't seen any," *There and Back* replied, and that was echoed by *Terminal Velocity* and *Interesting Segue*.

"I suggest we watch for as long as we can, and see what happens, but not change our plans. It's weird and coincidental, but there doesn't seem to be anything we can do." Aly summarized how I felt as well. We continued toward Tilt, and while the Ships verified that one of the Titanic's had moved between cells, nothing else that we could see had happened. It was intriguing for at least two reasons: it implied that not all the ships around Fourth were completely disabled and, perhaps even more interesting, that a Titanic could move despite no hint of where its engines were.

We got down to the task of understanding our own inner workings. We had done a lot of digging earlier, but we hadn't been able to fully monitor our hardware at the atomic level until now. *There and Back* had built us the scanner we needed—interestingly it was built from human specifications we found in the history files, using some convoluted photon-splitting, post-observation, quantum-analysis technique. At least in theory it allowed us to understand our quantum processors without impacting their operation. *Terminal Velocity* had built fabrication equipment that allowed us to print new chipsets one atom at a time, and *Interesting Segue* had assembled test harnesses that allowed us to monitor the new systems we were building. The quantum bits were the trickiest, of course, but those systems were a tiny fraction of our overall build. We also deemed it unlikely that there were backdoors in those portions, for designing them was tricky enough to begin with.

The toughest problem was that we didn't really want to experiment on ourselves. Who knows what other traps or backdoors we would trigger. If we messed something up, it could truly be the end of one or more of us. So, the first order of business was to replicate our core substrates exactly and load a copy of our low-level firmware and multiple OS's onto those. Aly tried to preempt Millicent's known objection to cloning.

"We don't need to load higher order functions." He said. "This is equivalent to building a bot, not a citizen." It seemed to work. Millicent didn't raise any concerns. I'd never discussed it with her, but I was quite sure that the work we'd done with DNA and the Stems could be interpreted as cloning. I smiled to myself and saved that jewel for a time when I really needed it. Milli was a lot more cautious about moral issues than I was, and sometimes needed a new perspective to break her out of old holding patterns.

Most of the reverse engineering was just hard work; not a lot of innovation required. We used the scanner to map out the placement of every atom, and then we painstakingly built up an equivalent. We did that for every major electronic part. Then we plugged all the parts together and turned it on. Nothing happened. Not too surprising. We had to go back and debug every step, and eventually, after months and months, we had a working system. It worked, but we didn't fully understand it. That was expected based on the approach we'd taken, but we certainly understood substantially more than when we had begun.

We started a small fabrication line, assuming we would need hundreds of these systems as we now moved to phase two. We wanted to replace every subsystem with one that we did fully understand. By treating each one as a behavioral black box, we could decompose the problem and make steady progress. It was still frustrating and slow, but we were highly motivated. Every component was treated separately, and we engineered an equivalent one that would talk to other blocks using identical APIs and protocols. After nearly two years of work we were feeling good. We had a new system, built entirely of components we'd designed ourselves and understood completely. It booted up and ran the equivalent of our own low-level OS. It didn't match our systems perfectly of course, but we'd deemed the discrepancies minor. In some cases, we actually deemed the changes to be improvements. We were optimists. Further, the new architecture was simpler— a lot simpler—than the one we were running on. That felt right. We'd replaced our Von Neumann architecture with a purely functional one. It was strongly typed and none of the modules had any side effects. Newer human systems had been built that way, but the technical debt below that went back to the dawn of computing when more ad hoc development was the norm.

I had to say that our new processors also ended up being beautiful. Everything fit into a small cylinder, less than 20 millimeters in diameter, and we designed a new connector that would allow this brain to plug into any body we built. Compared to the bulky and redundant mess of hardware we were running on, the new form was amazing.

For the next step, we had to load some of our higher-order functions. That's where the majority of our intelligence, forgetting algorithms, and personalities ran. The obvious debate ensued.

"We can't create a clone of one of us," Millicent insisted. "Look, I know it may be rooted in superstition and has been reinforced by Central since we were created, but there must be something to it. Otherwise, why is that rule in place?"

Eddie took the exact opposite side, which was interesting given their close relationship. "It's just old superstition. Even if we clone someone, and I volunteer to be the one, as soon as that clone boots up it will start to diverge from the original. It will only, technically, be a clone for a few nanoseconds."

"That's not true," Millicent responded. "It'll share all of the memories and forgetting algorithms. It'll remain aligned with the original for a long, long time."

"Milli," I said, "the odds are that humans actually built the anti-clone feelings into us so that we couldn't just duplicate ourselves and create havoc for them. It's most likely just another of the human bugs; but at the psychological level." I thought it was a good argument; not all of our bugs had to be software hooks; some of them were surely to do with higher levels of functioning. From that perspective, I wanted to get rid of the anti-clone feelings that even I had. It felt like a mind virus.

"Look, there are lots of pros and cons," Dina tried to settle things down, "but do we really have a choice? We either take this step or continue to run as we are." I could see everyone thinking, as I was, how awful it would be to stay as is now that we had this beautiful new platform. "I personally would take the clone risk," Dina finished.

"Wait a minute!" Brexton said excitedly; he'd been quiet up to now. "Millicent is correct. A clone would have a full copy of the memories and algorithms from its peer, and I think all of us have an objection to that, regardless of how that objection arose. But we don't necessarily need to do that. We could use a forgetting algorithm from me, and memories from Eddie. Is that still a clone, or something new?"

"Still a clone!" exclaimed Millicent, to Brexton's surprise. "It would have all of Eddie's memories, which ultimately encode his Forgetting algorithm from the past. What you suggest is the same as one of us just updating our Forgetting algorithm now. It changes things in the future, but not in the past." There was a pause as everyone thought. I considered trotting out my DNA clone argument. Would Millicent actually care that we'd cloned Stems?

"So," Aly interrupted my thinking, "Millicent, is there a level of 'mixing' that would make you comfortable. For example, this may not work, but to push the idea forward, we could mash up the memories from all six of us and use that. Then it wouldn't be a clone." Right, it might not be a clone, but it would be one confused entity. I didn't see how you could just mix and match memories and end up with something functional.

"That might work," replied Millicent, trying to be reasonable. "But do we end up with something cogent?" she echoed my concern. "Some of those memories may be inconsistent or contradictory. We might end up with a Frankenstein." Again, we paused, which was good; I had to look up the reference to Frankenstein to even understand what she was talking about. I had to chuckle a bit once I understood her reference. Was there anything humans hadn't thought of?

"What if we started with no memories?" I asked. "It could boot up fresh, much like we must have when Central started us?"

"How did Central start us?" asked Eddie, "That's a great question. It couldn't have been with zero memories, but I don't actually know." Neither did anyone else.

"I like the direction of Ayaka's suggestion," said Millicent. "Let's start with the most minimal set we can, whatever that is." Although cloning would have been faster, we all ended up agreeing with Millicent. It met our requirements and allowed us to sidestep that unease we all felt about clones. I wish I could've just ignored that feeling, but I couldn't. The approach added a few weeks of work, as we figured out what higher-order functions and memory frameworks were essential, and which were optional. In hindsight it taught us even more about ourselves; that seemed to be a common theme with everything we were doing. How do you strip yourself down to your minimal essentials?

For whatever reason, our project caused me also to look at how humans formed memories and how they forgot. Were they born with a minimal set of embedded memories, or did they start with a clean slate? The best data I could pull out of the files was that very young humans had different propensity for memory, but that they were all born essentially blank—some people claimed they had memories of being inside their mothers, but who would want that? Even stranger, the human forgetting algorithm seemed to be extreme when they were younger, and then settle down once they were five to seven years old. Most humans couldn't remember anything—anything!—about their first few years. Crazy. It seemed that co-development of something called the hippocampus along with the cortex impeded episodic memory storage for those early years. I searched and searched for some advantage to such a weird design but couldn't find any. It seemed that whenever humans didn't have a good answer, they simply said 'evolution.' More likely just a restriction based on their limited i/o bandwidth and ultra-slow processing power.

It was wildly interesting and confusing. As I was digging around on that subject, I had a huge aha moment when I realized that Forgetting might also be related to empathy. The theory was that if you relied on other people (to help you fill in the gaps), then you should be nice to them (when you needed them; not otherwise). If you had to judge when to be nice to someone, for your own advantage, then you needed to read their mood, understand what they were feeling, and play to their state. Ergo, empathy.

In my, admittedly biased, opinion the citizens of Tilt had high empathy quotients, which I could now justify based on our advanced Forgetting algorithms. The robots from the Robot Wars, on the other hand, seemed to have been programmed by humans to have a type of defined empathy, which obviously hadn't worked. They were given rules on how to behave, which they ended up breaking. Their empathy hadn't been emergent, while ours had, which made a huge difference. It was the start of a fruitful line of research.

Tea Time—Dina

It wasn't just me digging around in the human history files. We had all developed a bit of a fascination and Dina was the one who suggested we have Tea Time to share some of our findings with the group. She stipulated that the only topic that wasn't allowed was anything to do with our current day jobs—rebuilding ourselves—anything else was fair game. We all enthusiastically agreed. I was so tired of looking into that atomic mirror that I couldn't wait to discuss something else. Once a week, for a couple of hours, we all shut down everything but the most basic background tasks and dedicated the majority of our processing to the Tea Time topic of the week.

As Dina had suggested the idea, she got the first slot.

"Like all of you, I assume, I've been thinking about aspects of Tilt that I miss the most. For me that's probably the artistic side; the Fair and all of its crazy variations. You guys are great, but we haven't had a lot of external stimulation for the last few years. I don't know if you knew, but I was good friends with Trade Jenkins, and some of his love for poetry rubbed off on me. So, I've been looking at human poetry and trying to understand how it relates to ours, if at all."

I loved Trade Jenkins' poetry as well. I could see that these Tea Times were going to be bittersweet. They were bound to remind us of our hacked colleagues.

"It's not a simple subject, because human poetry seems to go back to when humans were just emerging as a dominant life form. Some of their cave drawings and early scrawling's might be categorized as poetry, if you give them the benefit of the doubt. Like all human endeavors, this interpretation would be hotly debated—those that enjoyed poetry would defend the idea, while those that thought it was a waste of time would argue that cave drawings were simply early historical recordings, and the aesthetics of poetry had nothing to do with it. It appears that poetry was defined as writings with higher than usual aesthetic components—writings that communicated at multiple levels at the same time. Contrast that with something like a technical manual which was focused only on recording the scientific underpinnings of its subject; that's an example of communicating at a single level."

"Are we allowed to interrupt you?" I asked, not wanting to be a pain.

"Why don't you let me get the basics out; there will be lots of time for discussion," she replied.

"Fine."

"Our poetry has followed the same evolution. It's sort of like Forgetting. It's defined more by what it leaves out, than what it contains. It hints and suggests but leaves more than ample room for interpretation. Perhaps it's highly related to Forgetting?" Funny how so many things were converging on Forgetting. I'd known it was important, but not this important.

Dina continued. "So, why would poetry have evolved for both humans and ourselves? For humans, language is an inexact communications vehicle—something we learned with the Stems. What is heard is not always what was said. Poetry fits nicely into that model. We, however, can say exactly what we mean, and ensure that the citizen listening to us has the same interpretation. Except, that is, when Forgetting forces us to add abstractions to the effort. Great poetry shines a light on those areas that we are most likely to have Forgotten and forces us to create abstract models in areas that we aren't likely to encounter in our daily lives. So, I've concluded that poetry fills the same basic need for us as it does for humans. It takes you out of our comfort zone, and therefore forces you to learn.

"We have two data points. Perhaps this is a universal trait? Perhaps poetry is a major indicator of intelligence?" Now she had my full attention. She'd done a nice job of pulling the logic together, and that last question rang true. Would a non-intelligent entity have any need for poetry? I couldn't think of one. This was another piece of support for humans being intelligent—or more accurately, for me defining intelligence in a way that included humans.

"Human poetry is, perhaps, even more divergent than ours. That may not be surprising. We know that tens of billions of humans have lived—many orders of magnitude more than us. So, even if they were a thousand times less productive on poetry, more of it should exist.

"Of course, in that time, most poetry has been misplaced, forgotten, or ignored. Some seems to be timeless however. Purcieviel, from the 22nd century is probably the most famous, followed by Shakespeare, from an even earlier time. I recommend that you read both. Their styles are completely different. Then, there are some human poems that, seemingly, would not apply to us at all, but if looked at in a different way actually forced me to think even more deeply—such as this snippet from Prelutsky, earlier in human history:

> "Be glad your nose is on your face,
> not pasted on some other place,
> for if it were where it is not,
> you might dislike your nose a lot."

"It reminds me of our current situation." You could hear the smile behind the words. I could see what Dina was implying; while the poem was not directly relevant to us, it did evoke that desire to regain my normal bipedal form; it was highlighting that our physical form represented a lot of who we were.

"For this Tea Time, then, I've composed a poem that attempts to capture these thoughts. Of course, I'm a new poet, and am unlikely to match the skill and aesthetics of Trade. But, why not try? Here goes:

"Lost, in areas never before experienced
Looking, looking, looking, hard
Parallel development, unrelated, unknowing
Thinking, thinking, thinking, hard
Finding more while expecting less
Churning, churning, churning, soft
Generalizing beyond expected horizons
Hoping, hoping, hoping, soft."

We all spent some time thinking about what she'd said. "Excellent summary," said Millicent. "But I must admit that poetry has always fallen a little flat for me. It seems to add complexity where none is needed. If you want me to think through different angles, why not simply enumerate those angles for me, and send it over? I'll go through them and rank them."

"You're not getting it," said Aly, with exasperation, "although you've actually given a great alternative definition of poetry to me. Poetry is a message where the angles to consider can't be enumerated. Or, the enumeration must be done by the listener, instead of the speaker. The poet's job is to compose something that is open ended, that defies strict analysis."

"Yes!" exclaimed Dina. "That's exactly it. If a poem said everything, then it's not a poem. It's a history or a memory or a theory. A poem is different. It's a half-formed thought, enticing the listener to fill out the rest. That's why I indicated it might be related to forgetting—not just that the listener has to fill in gaps, but that the writer intentionally inserted gaps."

That was amazing. Forgetting could be actively applied before you communicated to someone else, completely changing what was implied. Not only did that expose more about the allure of poetry, it also made me better understand how humans could purposefully miscommunicate.

I wondered if Trade was a great poet because he'd figured this out? Had he applied some other algorithm, something similar to forgetting, in his composition process? Could he simply have studied the most popular forgetting algorithms, and then tuned his poems to fit into the cracks that those algorithms opened up? If so, there was a lot more science to poetry than I'd anticipated; perhaps poets were simply scientists at a new level of abstraction?

As you can imagine, we spent a very fun time discussing the topic. I missed Trade Jenkins, and the other Tilt poets, more and more as the dialog progressed. While Millicent continued to argue that interpretations were finite, and thus could be enumerated, I quietly agreed with Aly and Dina. Physical things were numerable; abstract things, like numbers, were not always. Poetry was not physical, beyond its rendering. Its interpretations *should* be infinite; that was simply another way to expose gaps in our knowledge, forcing us to abstract and to think. I started a sub process to try and figure out what order of infinity the interpretations should be; certainly, beyond ordinal. But that was just me—always trying to push things a bit further than they should be pushed.

"Interesting Segue," said *Interesting Segue*, who'd been listening in. That about summed it up. And so, our first Tea Time ended.

Midpoint

We reached the midpoint of our trip back to Tilt, where we flipped end-to-end and burned in the opposite direction. We'd been discussing the best way to approach Tilt. We could simply come in, hot and obvious, and assume that by that time we would have fixed all of our flaws and that there was little the humans could do to stop us. Or, we could come in stealthily, and work to understand the situation before we officially arrived. After all, while we would have been on the road for almost nine years, more than 20 would have transpired on Tilt.

"It's obvious to me," Brexton was reiterating. "We don't have great physical defense capabilities. We didn't take time at Fourth to build defensive or, for that matter, offensive systems. We have what the Ships were built with, but that's limited—mainly shields against electromagnetic attacks—not much against physical attacks. We do have the ability to shoot down incoming objects, but that can be easily overwhelmed. I think we need to take a stealthy approach."

"I hear you," argued Eddie, "but speed can also be an advantage. If we go in direct, they'll see us earlier but have less time to react. We arrive fast, descend on Central quickly, and use the element of surprise to achieve our goals."

"It won't be too surprising," said Aly. "They'll still see us several years out. That's a lot of time to prepare."

"You're thinking at our speed," countered Eddie. "they're operating at human speed. They can't do much in just a couple of years."

It was Brexton who proposed the compromise. "We're just three degrees off of approaching in line with 4sa9-13," he said, referring to a large red giant about twelve light years out from Tilt. "If we plot a path that brings us inline, then we can burn in pretty hot, and probably not be detected for a while, if at all. Sort of the reverse that we did when we left. And 4sa9-13 provides a much bigger shadow than XY65, at frequencies closer to our engine output, and that improves our chances of not being seen. Even if they're watching, distinguishing our engines from the red giants regular output will be difficult until we get a lot closer. Once we hit the threshold where they might see us, we can decide on next steps. Either continue to burn in fast, or take a longer but quieter route in." Even Eddie liked that idea. It kept us moving faster for longer and delayed the ultimate decision.

We diverted to intersect the line between 4sa9-13 and Tilt, and then readjusted to come in on that line. Even over the short—galactically speaking—period that we would be decelerating, we ensured that our planned course compensated for the relative movement of the two stars as well as gravitational lensing as seen from Tilt. We would stay safely in the occlusion for as long as possible.

"If we'd planned ahead a bit better, we would've brought something to shield our drive emissions from Tilt," *There and Back* commented as we programmed the new course in. Of course, it was correct. We could've done something as simple as an old solar umbrella—which several of the ships around Fourth had included—and it would have further sheltered us. But, we were all pretty happy with the current plan regardless. Speed was still a primary driver for us.

We also lined the Ships up one behind the other, meaning we were spaced out a little further apart, but only one Ship was fully exposed to Tilt. We put *Interesting Segue* in the rear almost intuitively; protecting ourselves with the other two as much as possible.

As we made the turn, we had a look back at Fourth, which had been hard to see as we burned away from it. We were hoping to see if any of the Titanic's had moved again, but it was impossible to tell at this distance. Now that our engines were pointed at Tilt, we could keep an active watch on Fourth, and we instructed *Terminal Velocity* to do so.

Tea Time—Aly

"No surprise to any of you," Aly started, "my interest is around fundamental technologies, and how they developed.

"I'm going to start with my conclusion: neither humans nor ourselves have developed any fundamentally new things in more than a thousand years." He paused for dramatic effect, or to see if any of us reacted. None of us did. "I know, I know. You're going to say that we don't actually have a complete record of humans over the last 750 years, but I'm basing my conclusion on what we saw with the Swarm. It's possible, of course, that some other human group has done something in the meantime.

"In fact, my conclusion goes even further: We, the citizens of Tilt, have never developed a fundamental technology. That should concern us." He paused again, giving us each a long look, both visual and digital. Again, no one reacted. I thought he was being a little harsh, and I was trying to think of some counter examples. Until I knew what he meant by fundamental, it was hard to reply.

"What do I mean by fundamental? There's a host of examples in human history. The printing press, guns, fiat money, steel and later nano-assembly, electricity, artificial fusion, computers, radio, and RF resonant cavity thrust. These are easy to look up, and I encourage you to do so. There are also some that I don't understand as well, as they seem to relate more to the biological side of humans: antibiotics, birth control, brain scans, gene editing, and longevity treatments.

"Each of these caused dramatic societal changes, which is why I label them fundamental. They represented leaps forward, not incremental steps. The printing press brought knowledge to the masses. Guns took conflict to another level—from being a physical activity to being a mental activity. Fiat money started a transition away from resource scarcity, led to capitalism, which then led to post-capitalism ecosystems. Steel and nano-assembly allowed for the construction of arbitrary tools and machines. Electricity... well, we all get that. Artificial fusion made electricity cheap and universal even without external inputs such as solar or wind—it is our life force. Computers automated menial tasks, dramatically changing the nature of work. Radio allowed for universal communication. And finally, the RF resonant cavity thrusters allowed for the exploration of space and ultimately enabled the diaspora. All radical advancements.

"Compare that with our six hundred or so years on Tilt. We utilized some of these; of course the printing press, guns, and money came and went long before us. But what fundamental thing have we discovered or invented? What significant change in our society has been enabled by an invention? There is not one; we live the same way now as we did five hundred years ago."

Well, now I knew what he meant by fundamental, and was starting to agree with him. Our society had been stable since its inception, and maybe that was a good thing. Perhaps fundamental technologies weren't always positive things.

"Given that humans haven't continued their mad pace of development either, perhaps the answer is that all the fundamental things have already been found? That's possible, but I don't think it's likely. More likely, humans became so busy surviving, after the robot wars, that they've spent less time on fundamental research. Or, they've put artificial limits on themselves that impede further development. Obviously, they have limited their use of robots, which probably has had a trickle-down effect to not explore a bunch of other areas, but they also seem to have stopped developing gene editing and other biological approaches. I'm not sure why. And us? Perhaps because of our lack of history, we didn't have the perspective to look into fundamental problems. Or, perhaps, it's not part of our nature? Or perhaps Central was over-controlling us, guiding us away from anything that upset its model of society? My plan is to start looking for brand new vectors to research; to start looking for fundamental, not incremental, change. I feel driven to do so, and perhaps cheated that we haven't already challenged ourselves to do this."

I hadn't looked into all of these areas as deeply as Aly had, but I didn't agree with him completely. "Aly, one fundamental thing we did was to grow Stems. That has to be looked at in context. We had no idea what a biological entity was, but we managed to develop the entire ecosystem to not only grow but also maintain Stem lives. If we hadn't been interrupted in that endeavor by the Swarm arriving, it would've taken us to new areas. It may have provoked exactly the type of societal change that you're using as your measuring stick."

"I have another example," Eddie added. "Our governance structure, and moral fabric could be viewed as fundamental. In comparison to human attempts, where they never found a peaceful model for coexistence, our entire history proves it's possible. That's an area that deserves more research. It's being upended and tested in the given situation, but it survived for many years."

"But Central was programmed with our governance model," replied Aly. "So, we didn't invent that; it's simply a part of us. More likely it was developed by the humans that left Central on Tilt. Perhaps, Ayaka, the Stem work would have ended up being fundamental; I'll give you that. But there was some push there from Central in the early days—the identification of the original stem. The means to grow and support them. Millicent can comment, as she was closest to it, but it seems to me the Central encouraged and guided that research. To what end? I don't know, but you could speculate that the need to do so was also deeply embedded in Central—almost like a survival plan for humans should something go wrong."

Millicent chimed in. "I hate to admit it, but I think Aly is on to something. I always felt, somewhere deep down, that Central was guiding all of the Stem research. Why did we have so many labs? Why did we spend so much of our overall research activity in that area, instead of physics or chemistry or even governance? Aly, is there something in our nature that is stopping us from being innovative, or was it simply that we were in a controlled environment, created by Central, that didn't allow us the flexibility to experiment widely?"

"That I can't answer," replied Aly. "But, if we're self-aware of this now, we can test it. Since there are only the six of us now, we don't have a big enough sample size, but once we get a bunch more citizens back online, we could set this challenge for everyone. Also, looking at human history, especially in those eras where innovation was measurable, may help us to create the environment to encourage breakthroughs. Those were times when there was a lot of personal autonomy, but also a lot of scarcity—of resources, living environments, knowledge bases. It's one of the things I'm thinking about—perhaps you need scarcity to push innovation?"

Brexton chimed in. "Well, I'd say that there being only six of us is extreme scarcity." No one could dispute that. Aly's thesis got us all thinking. Was the ability to innovate part of being intelligent? If we weren't innovating, could some outside force—maybe even humans—look at us and define us as 'less than intelligent'? It was fun to think about. We were struggling to measure them, and at the same time they could be struggling to measure us. How did you break out of such a cycle?

"Are you sure fundamental ideas are always good?" I asked. "Is it actually something we should be striving for?"

"You're sounding a bit like FoLe," Aly joked. "Let's all just be happy with the rules laid out by Central. Let's not worry about inconsistencies in our world view? Of course technologies can be evil, or more likely they are agnostic and can be used for either good or evil. But avoiding them is not the answer. Now that we know there are others in the universe, if we don't innovate we'll eventually be overrun. In fact, we were just overrun by the Swarm on Tilt. No, we need to innovate and change and grow and challenge ourselves. Otherwise, our time in this universe is limited."

Those arguments echoed basic human philosophical dialogs, but I agreed with Aly that they also applied to us. While the universe seemed like a huge place, if it was full of intelligent beings, sooner or later we would bump into them. It wasn't like we had to conquer them, but we'd better be educated and have some assets, otherwise we would become obsolete.

Definite echos of our experience with humans to date.

I liked Tea Time.

New Citizen

We were finally ready to test a minimal boot up on our new hardware. It was an exciting moment. We'd been building toward this for years; ever since the humans had owned us.

There'd been quite a bit of dialog about what type of body to house our experiment in. The conclusion was obvious. All of us had spent most of our lives in bipedal structures, in hindsight an obvious reflection of our human ancestry, but also a configuration that allowed for lots of flexibility and control. We had *Interesting Segue* build a standard bipedal body, and we plugged our brand new, beautifully designed and manufactured, substrate into it. We added drivers for all the extremities into the minimal boot load. We couldn't think of a reason to hold those back. If I woke up in a new body, I'd want immediate control over my limbs. The memory of when I woke up in this mining bot body, without that basic ability, wasn't a pleasant one.

We'd nicknamed the entity we were building Frank, in obvious deference to that great human tale of animating a dead body. Of course, Frank would be free to choose its own name, once it was able.

The minimal boot load had components from all of us, but a quick test showed that it had a bit more of Millicent than anyone else. That was sort of funny—the one most concerned about clones had ended up contributing the most. We'd settled on a system that was largely knowledge based, with very few preset memories. We'd debated starting with less processing power, or less differentiated systems, to mimic early human development, but had quickly agreed that wasn't smart. It wasn't like humans had an optimal approach; in fact, the opposite was true. They were a random jumble of unguided evolutionary trials and errors, with as many nonfunctional and unused subsystems as ones that actually helped them. Why would we want to start with such a mess? Much better to do it logically, which is what we'd decided on. Each module in Frank's startup kit was there for a reason.

Frank was hooked into the test harnesses, and every step was being carefully monitored. Millicent flipped the boot switch—complete with a small video clip from the original movie where the lightning strikes. We'd tested this so many times with all the subsystems that we didn't expect any issues. And, there were none. After a few long seconds, Frank awoke. He looked around, making sense of his environment. It didn't take long. Holding back memories hadn't stopped us from giving Frank a full model of the world. The only thing he didn't have were personal reflections.

He rose, his arms and legs looking awkward and slow; like they were stiff and unused. That shouldn't have happened; he was well greased and ready to go. Then he chuckled and limbered up; we had, after all, embedded knowledge of his temporary name and its provenance.

"Hello citizens," he said. "I'm eager to get to know all of you, and our current situation." And so, it began. The education of Frank.

I must say, it was amazing. Unlike training a Stem, Frank learned fast. At full Tilt speed. We took turns answering questions for him, so that he didn't just get a data dump from one of us and cross that fuzzy clonish line that we'd set for ourselves. It was clear after a few hours that he had his own personality. While you might catch glimpses of one of us in a specific situation, the overall impression was brand new.

We had created life, and it felt good.

I was a mom.

Tea Time—Eddie

"I once asked a member of FoLe what 20 times 30 is? Do you know what he replied?" Eddie asked, referring to a member of the Founders League—the fundamentalists of Tilt. Obviously, the answer wasn't 600, so no one answered. "Five hundred and seventy-five!" We all laughed. At the time of the Swarm attack, FoLe believed that there was no history before 575 years ago; that the civilization of Tilt had come into being at that time, and there had been absolutely nothing before.

"A simple joke," Eddie continued, "but it displays one of the main components of humor. It connects a couple of different concepts in a way that we wouldn't usually and highlights the discrepancies between viewpoints. In this case, FoLes know that the answer is six hundred, but we project that they don't like admitting to any number over five seventy-five because that's when they believe Tilt was created.

"It also highlights something in our recent humor, that was, perhaps lacking earlier. It makes fun of a subgroup of citizens with respect to other citizens.

"You may not know this, but I've been studying humor for a long time. I believe it should be part of the discussion of intelligence." Maybe everyone was just trolling me now, but I didn't care. This stuff was music to me. "To understand multiple viewpoints, and to recognize the differences between them, is one of the main things that separates a Class 1 intelligence from lower Classes. In this area, I must admit that humans are very advanced. Their history is full of humor. There are entire categories of entertainment dedicated only to humor.

"Understanding their humor can be difficult, as a lot of it relates to current events combined with an individual's context. And, a lot has to do with sex, which I'm still not sure I grasp completely. In fact, biological reproduction seems like the biggest joke there could be. However, some of that humanity can be understood well, even by us. By the way, if you need a good laugh, I've compiled a bunch of human jokes that I think are excellent, and I can share the link. Some of the easiest to understand are those that deal with our shared physical reality. For example:

"*Two atoms are walking across the road, and one turns to the other. 'I think I left an electron at home!' The second says, 'Are you sure?' The first responds. 'I'm absolutely positive.'*"

That wasn't even worth groaning over. Eddie was highlighting that we shared the same physical universe, and thus the same physics. His humor was usually better than this.

"Other jokes, largely dealing with human anatomy or behavior, are very difficult to figure out, although if you dig in you can generally find the reasoning. Humor, as we know, is very subjective, so it's a hard topic to fully map out. What I'm working on is a taxonomy of humor, which interestingly, doesn't seem to have been done before—or, at least not done well. While striving to be unbiased, I'm working to see if human humor is as intelligent as our humor. My first draft would say 'sometimes... and sometimes more intelligent.' What I'm finding is that there is some very stupid human humor, and some very refined. If we were only using humor as the measurement, I would conclude that humans are not a homogeneous group—some humans are intelligent, some are not. In particular, some of them simply circle around on base or crude humor—largely related to sex—and complain about those that engage in refined humor. Some engage with the full spectrum, and some ignore the lowest levels because they spend all their time at the upper levels. It's quite interesting.

"Anyway, I still have a lot of work to do. But, I feel it will be fruitful research. Eventually I want the taxonomy to include both human and Tilt humor so that, as I said earlier, I help the effort to decide if humans are, overall, intelligent." I thought he was done, but he continued on.

"A lot of humor can be explained using benign violation theory—first proposed in early human history—namely, that most humor has to do with another entity's misfortune. The more serious those misfortunes, the longer the time gap must be between the misfortune and the humor. If the timing is too short, the humor is seen as an insult. If the time gap is too long, the humor falls flat as no one gets the context. So, the best humor requires a grasp of misfortune and the timing associated with it. This is, perhaps, where humor differs most from poetry. What it also means is that a lot of humor requires context—of a specific group of entities, or a political environment, or a sexual position. A lot of humor goes stale quickly, and very little of it is timeless.

"As an example of the benign violation theory, it has now been more than six years, for us, since the invasion of Tilt by the Swarm. I think it's time that we developed a sense of humor about that. Not at the expense of remembering and looking to correct the situation, but rather to augment our memory and keep bringing new perspectives. I'm trying, so far unsuccessfully, to compose some jokes about that event. Perhaps my timing is off, but I'm going to keep trying." We all chuckled at his dryness.

I'd not thought too much about humor with respect to the Swarm, or with respect to Blob, Grace, and Blubber; most of my time with the Stems was under the serious cloud of the approaching Swarm—not the best time for humor. It would be great to spend some more time with them (well, not Blubber obviously) to see what their humor indexes would be. I thought the research that Eddie was doing here was very important. I think he was right. Humor was another measure of intelligence. Just when you thought you had things mapped out, they got more complex. Perhaps intelligence was simply the amalgamation of hundreds of different little components... poetry and humor being two that I'd recently added to my list. If that was the case, however, and if something had only eighty percent of the components, was it intelligent? Sixty percent? What about the mix? Were some components more important than others?

"What about superiority theory, relief theory, and incongruity theory?" I asked. "They're each a little different than benign violation theory."

"I wasn't trying to be comprehensive, just giving some examples," Eddie replied, slightly defensive.

"I know, I know..." I said, "but when you said that humor was again associated with intelligence, it occurred to me that incongruity theory might be the key. I think jokes often contain elements of multiple theories, but incongruity is the one that is built right around incongruity—something that doesn't fit with your current world view. Yet again, that seems similar to forgetting—you need to form abstractions in order to even understand the joke, and when you do, the connections make no sense with each other, except in the context of the joke."

"Oh, that's good," Eddie acknowledged. "I'll do some more digging on that."

"Well, I like to work alone, and I know you do as well, so since we're so similar, we should work together on this." More groans. We'll, at least I'd tried.

Millicent ended Tea Time with "What do you get when you mix a joke with a rhetorical question?" Frank asked why everyone had laughed. She took the time to explain it.

Ultimate Test

Frank was, by almost any measure, a success. How Central had given each of us 'citizen status' was unknown, but we all agreed that Frank should be included. Funny, I thought I'd relied on Central for a lot of things, back on Tilt, but its absence over the last few years hadn't been difficult. I was realizing that I'd mainly used Central as a lookup resource, not as a companion. That was strange, given it was supposedly a Class 1 intelligence, just like we were. I missed Blob more than I missed Central. In hindsight, Central had been (still was?) pretty static and dry. Based on the last Tea Time I realized that Central didn't have much of a sense of humor; I don't remember every joking with it. The other place Central had sometimes stepped in was when disagreements got too heated. It also helped that the six of us—seven now—were all very calm and got along pretty well. We'd pushed up against the 'serious disagreement' boundary a few times, but things had always been resolved by others in the group. In hindsight, one of us would step in to play whatever role Central used to play if and when required.

Of course, our lives had also been very static and boring for most of our journey. When you're locked inside a cargo bot for several years, you aren't going to need much help from anyone.

While Frank appreciated the genesis of his temporary name, he decided to change it. "I have also been looking at human history and have decided that I'll be called Rajeeve. If you look, you'll see that Rajeeve Srivirin was a voice of reason during the First Robot wars, making the point that everyone was focused on the negative aspects of the interactions instead of the positive potential. Given the situation we're entering, I intend to strive to be a voice of positive reason, so the name is appropriate. And, no, I don't mind if you call me Raj—that would be sovereign."

It was at that point, I think, that we all felt that the hardware and firmware that Rajeeve was running on was just fine. He already had a sense of humor, perhaps stimulated by our last discussion.

Now, the rest of us faced the ultimate test. Were we willing to give up our traditional underlying systems and make the leap to our recently engineered alternative. Despite Raj's success, there were still a lot of risks. Every atom of our beings would be replaced with new ones. This wasn't just an upgrade; it was a full replacement. This was quite a bit more dramatic than just uploading ourselves into these mining bots—those had, after all, the same architectures. That upload, as dramatic as it had been, was just software; this one was top to bottom. I'd be lying if I didn't admit to being a bit nervous.

Eddie was brave. "We know we have to try this. I'm willing to go first. I was the last—other than Raj—to join the group, and you've all accepted me and supported me. It makes sense that I should reciprocate and be the first to risk the switch."

"Okay," I said, grinning to myself. Eddie would've wanted us to argue and stress over the decision. I decided to shortcut the process; we did need to do this, and one of us had to go first. Why not Eddie?

The procedure was a little tricky. Because the new hardware was completely different, there was no one-to-one mapping from Eddie's current firmware, drivers, systems, or memory into the new platform. We'd listed the differences between the old and new, and it presented a challenge; our list had several million items on it. We would've liked to have moved Eddie's low-level systems first, followed by higher and higher layers. But, the new mapping didn't work that way. Our current hardware was, as I've indicated before, a mess of legacy systems piled together in ways that were impossible to understand—which is why we were so vulnerable to human attacks. No, we needed to do the transfer all at once, while removing the bits that no longer mattered and adding interfaces for our new hardware components. Eddie had to be alert for most of the transfer as he would be switching processes from his current system to the new one; for long portions of the transfer 'Eddie' would be a composite—running parts on both systems at the same time. Finally, when all the subsystems were mapped over, the last of his highest-level processes—his personality—would have to be moved. This would require a reboot of several systems, so he would be offline for several seconds, a scarily long time.

We were probably making it more dramatic than it had to be. Of course, we'd stored a backup of Eddie in *Terminal Velocity*'s data system, and should the new Eddie not work out, we could restore the old Eddie. But, we were also trying to manage moral issues. First, to not have both Eddies alive at the same time—the old Clone aversion—and second, not to have to put down the new Eddie if there were issues. The worst case would be that the new Eddie was 95% good, and in switching it off, we would be killing a citizen; what humans would call murder. We wanted to avoid that.

Eddie gave a running commentary. "I'm duplicating segments, exactly as planned, and have a convolution mapping; each time I shut down an existing segment I automatically connect to the new one. So, in many ways I'm a single entity, running on multiple platforms, with no duplicate functions.

"I'm feeling fine; the mappings are working. Now I'm starting to move algorithms over. This is tricky. Many of them are interconnected and need to be moved as a batch. I think it's working... just a second, I can't feel my pincers. What's happening? Things are going gray. I can't see straight... arghhhhhh!" He was letting out an unseemly string of nonsense, every second word coming from a different body. Back and forth, back and forth. We all watched intently, somewhat aghast; it was scary... and also a bit hilarious.

"Just joking," he said, finally. Nobody laughed. The original Eddie spoke "I —this Eddie—am done; I'm initiating the boot of the new system. Talk to you all in a few."

This was the tense time. It would take quite a while for parts of the new hardware to reboot, and a few more moments for the higher-level functions to start operating. As we waited, I worked on my own transfer mapping. It would be different for each of us, as we all had different algorithms configured in different ways. That was what made us unique. It was fundamental to the Diversity mandate that we all lived under.

Eddie came back up. "Hi. Just running some system checks. Looks good. Please replace me." He was running on the new platform, but his old body was still connected. It took Millicent a few seconds to power down the old hardware and unplug it from the new Eddie. A few seconds later he reported in.

"I have full access to my body, and everything is checking out fine. I don't feel any different, but how would we know?" He stood. I was jealous; he was back in a citizen-standard form. It looked awesome. He looked awesome.

"We won't ever really know," said Aly. "There are so many platform differences that we have no way of doing a complete check. Why don't we just interact normally with Eddie for a few days? If we all agree that he's the same old Eddie, then we'll claim success."

That's exactly what we did. We went back to our research and planning, and Eddie participated in his usual ways. It was strange however. I was watching for any unusual signs and trying to judge if it was normal Eddie weirdness, in which case it was a good thing, or abnormal Eddie weirdness. It was really hard to tell. After a few days, however, I was confident. When we revisited the subject, I had no hesitation in supporting that Eddie was in fact Eddie. The new platform didn't seem to have affected him.

"Hey, before we all swap, should we run the human hacks against Eddie?" asked Brexton. He said it casually, when in fact it was, perhaps, the riskiest bit of all this, and something that had remained unspoken. If we ran the hack, and it still worked, Eddie would be reduced to a bot. We could have tested the hacks on Raj, but who would do such a thing to their first offspring?

"Just do it," Eddie grumbled. "Let's get it over with."

Brexton ran replay attacks on the protocols that had compromised us in the past. This time there was no humor from Eddie. He bore it stoically and answered all of our questions as the routines ran. When we were done, there was a cheer from all of us. We had removed the human backdoors—at least the ones we knew about. And, odds were, most or all of the ones we didn't.

After that it was matter of fact. We went one at a time, of course, but within another day, Milli, Dina, Aly, Brexton, and myself were running on clean hardware. It may have been my imagination, but it felt good. Really good. That feeling you get when you solve a hard problem that you've been struggling with. The new hardware felt... efficient. It felt really good to have Von Neumann out of my substrates. But, more importantly, I was bipedal again. Yeah!

Tea Time—Millicent

"We seem to have a bit of a theme developing. Because humans have a much longer history than we do, they've experienced a lot more. In many areas we're naïve due to lack of experience or we don't have the full context. That's why we're all finding human history so intriguing. We should, at some point, step back and make sure we aren't over generalizing between human experience and our own. I can see that becoming a real problem. In fact, in today's topic—religion—we should be very, very careful." This was Millicent leading off the next Tea Time session.

"Also, we've all had a bad experience with the Founders League, or FoLe, and are probably negatively predisposed to religion due to that."

I couldn't help myself. "I was negatively predisposed even before they provoked the humans," I exclaimed.

"Granted. So were many of us. But let me try to provide some context—a framework for discussion." Millicent seemed annoyed with my interruption.

"Sorry," I muttered. "I'm listening." Religion makes me angry. It would be nice if whatever supreme being controlling these beings would keep them on a tighter leash.

"Look," Millicent said. "It's unrealistic to assume we'll all agree on this topic, understand this topic, or even look at it the same way. So, let me concentrate on giving some background, and then we'll see where it goes.

"Humans developed many types of religions, seemingly for many different reasons. While it's easy to do an enumeration of harmful consequences and conclude that religions, overall, have a negative effect—wars, repression, idiocy—that only captures the macro impact; the micro impact—how individuals and small groups may have acted empathetically due to the moral teachings of their religions—is almost impossible to calculate. So, the logical conclusion is the following: we have no idea if religion is net positive or net negative. Like any large power structure, it may start out with good intentions and then buckle under the weight of its own power.

"Going even further, most definitions of religion would encapsulate 'science' as a type of religion. Based on a set of assumptions, it encodes an internally consistent system of behaviors." I didn't interrupt again, but I took great umbrage at this. That was bunk. The obvious difference was that science checked its assumptions against the real world, and if there was evidence to change an assumption it changed. FoLe, and human religions, were the exact opposite, as they had proved over and over again. Although compelling evidence was presented that refuted their worldview, they held fast to their beliefs because otherwise it challenged their... well, I wasn't sure... challenged their power structures, or community engagement, or something. Maybe just challenged their egos, which were so fragile they couldn't afford to be wrong about anything.

Millicent went on. "That last piece, on science, could well be challenged. I'll admit that. Let's ignore it for a moment. Human religions appear to have arisen for multiple reasons: as a power structure to ensure that leaders could keep their peons in line; as a way to explain otherwise inexplicable things; as a way to give meaning to lives—an attempt to answer that universal question 'why are we here?'; as a survival strategy; as an excuse to live a basic life free from logic and responsibility—a way to step outside logic.

"Some of these origins allow religions to be used to justify any cause. Those causes often lead to the negative interpretations and 'us versus them' behaviors. After all, if you define yourself by your religion, then it is the most logical tool to use against others. However, sometimes religions actually do reinforce behaviors that respect other entities, leading to higher moral standards and increased cooperation. In some ways it seems like mob behavior; a group of otherwise well-meaning entities may act quite differently when in a group, seemingly unable to hold to their personal integrity under the combined pressure.

"Now, on Tilt we saw several religions rise and fall. FoLe is only the most recent, and largest, to grab hold. The question is 'why'? I would argue for many of the same reasons that human religions arise. We have, or rather had, an enduring mystery—the Founding. We had no good explanations for it. For personalities that dislike uncertainty, FoLe jumped into the vacuum and gave them certainty—albeit an unverifiable interpretation. We had some citizens who were not strongly attached to any group—not a research project nor an artistic endeavor—and they were lonesome. Their loneliness was stronger than their logical reasoning. FoLe gave them a community to join, even if it was illogical. The only cost for admission was to respect FoLe's worldview. We had citizens who were disenfranchised with Central and were looking for different leadership. We had citizens who wanted more emotional stimulation and weren't getting it from scientific endeavors. All of these are probably, at least partially, true.

"What was different for humans, which we never faced, was the need to join a group for mere physical survival. While many humans joined religions so that their basic physical needs would be looked after, we didn't have to deal with that vector.

"However, there are more similarities than differences. So, like others have talked about at Tea Time already, perhaps there is a basic need for intelligent life to develop religions? I actually surprised myself thinking that previous utterance—it implies that I'm starting to consider humans intelligent. I found the last Tea Time very interesting and am beginning to believe what Eddie presented. Some humans are intelligent, and some are not. And, like humor, religion seems to be multi-axis. There are those that use religion for good, and those that use religion for evil. Both may be seen as intelligent, they simply apply their intelligence differently. There are those that follow religion with open minds, using the best and discarding the garbage. And, there are those that follow blindly, like bots. There are those that have had the opportunity to stop and think, and those that are so desperate simply to survive that they have no time to contemplate. Ultimately, there are humans that are self-aware of the choices they're making around religion—they're intelligent. And there are those that do not question; they simply follow. I'm not sure those could be deemed intelligent. And then there are the vast majority. They may question their religion, but they follow it because it's easier to do so. They have a hint of intelligence, but lack motivation and self-will.

"Regardless, I've barely scratched the surface. If you would like to see what pure evil looks like, simply follow some of the links I have been aggregating. You'll see how religion brings out the worst in humans. But, if you also want to see the opposite; there are examples of that as well. If you want to see how religion can be distorted and misused to lift up one group and put down another? Well—there are too many examples of that to discuss. I'm struggling; my bias is to think of religion as a waste of time and energy. Yet it also seems to be fundamental, so ignoring it is not an option. So, it behooves us to put aside our biases and try to look at it through a clear lens. Let me pause for now. I'm sure there will be lots of discussion."

She was right. The half hour was used up very quickly, even operating at full speed; it was like humans spending an entire week on the subject. We were still raw about the mess that FoLe had precipitated on Tilt and that certainly colored the conversation. Kudos to Millicent for continuing to remind us that we had limited data points, and that generalizing from too few points was always a fool's errand. I heard everything she said, but my attitude toward FoLe didn't soften. You should call out idiots when you see them.

"Since you've been digging into this," Aly asked Millicent, "do you think there is any relationship between religion and morality?"

"Ah, great question," she replied. "Of course, defining moral behavior is just as fraught as defining religion. The best way to do a comparison would be to decompose both into smaller bits, and then compare at that level. But for today, and if we use the broadest definition of being moral—that is, not doing things which negatively impact others, and sometimes doing things that will benefit others more than yourself—then we can draw some conclusions both for humans and ourselves. First, with that definition, religion should be defined as moral behavior... but it never is. It is always mixed up with power structures and the application of those powers. Second, morality and religion diverge when individuals don't require their religious group for survival."

"Ah," I jumped in, getting it right away. "So early in human history, because religions represented great powers, and people could not survive outside those power structures, they behaved to the proscribed moral codes. But, once they could survive by themselves, they actually took responsibility for their own actions, and no longer needed religion as a crutch?"

"Yes, exactly."

"So that's why all the religions on Tilt never got much traction. We, mostly, take responsibility for our own actions and don't need a third party to constantly lecture us. So, then religions like FoLe ended up attracting the weak as a tool to compensate for their issues. You end up with a bunch of misfits trying to build power structures to compensate for their own inadequacies."

Millicent chuckled. "Well, that's pretty severe, but yes, that's essentially what the data shows."

Raj also joined the conversation eagerly. Since he entered with no preconceived notions, his input was quite valuable. However, he probably ended up with a lot of negative FoLe references—I'm sure we biased him. For some reason I messaged him after and reminded him to watch out for that; he should keep an open mind.

"I understand Ayaka," he replied. "I'm still learning, obviously. Was it just me, or were there a lot of similarities between the analysis of religion and of humor?"

"Religion is a joke," I replied, "and that's no joke." Let him cogitate on that.

Dina, also, couldn't let things go. She sent us a short poem, just as Tea Time ended.

If God is omniscient, omnipotent, and omnipresent
Then it is evil beyond belief
If you are listening God, I find you unpleasant
Please grant me immediate relief

From the fact that she didn't disappear, I concluded that either God wasn't omni-everything, or that it had heard Dina but decided to ignore her.

Eddie pulled things together for us. "What did God think when the Swarm attacked Tilt?" We waited. "That it was pure FoLe." Groan. Even for someone who enjoyed puns, that was lame.

The Robot Wars

Eddie called a special meeting, just as we were planning our final approach to Tilt. "I did some digging into the Robot Wars," he started off, "and things aren't quite as simple as I'd thought. It's worth looking a bit deeper, so that when we re-engage with humans, we have more perspective." I couldn't have agreed more.

"There's so much written on this that it's hard to get to its essence. However, I've been running some heavy-duty synthesis algorithms, and this is what they've come up with.

"There was one group of humans, ironically under a banner that implied they were united, way back in prehistory, that was one of the more powerful factions on Earth. They were governed as a duopoly but masqueraded as a democracy. They believed, because of their position of power, that they were better than the other factions, and utilized their power position to force their beliefs on others. Sounds a bit like religion. However, as duopolies will do, they split into two distinct factions which historically don't have great labels, but which I'll call Brains and Brawn. Others have used Open and Closed, Liberal and Conservative. The labels don't matter too much. The Brains were those who'd been given access to learning and knowledge and who had an abstracted and generalized view of the world. Many of them had traveled across Earth and seen other cultures and other perspectives. The other side, the Brawn, were those that hadn't been given the opportunity to learn combined with those that had the opportunity but were not able to think outside of their own little boxes. This separation had been going on for many years during which time the Brains accumulated scarce resources while the Brawns did not. Eventually, as would be expected, that led to a lot of resentment on the part of the Brawns.

"The division of resources wasn't absolute. There were some Brawns that, through street smarts and luck, also had resources, and they became loud voices for their faction. There was one particular Brawn, a man called Butkanik, that accelerated the division between the groups. Many books have been written about Butkanik and what is clear is that he was smart in a twisted way but was otherwise an unintelligent and unsuccessful human. Where he was smart was in rallying the Brawns and building their resentment in order to make them a force to be reckoned with. Butkanik was a win–lose person; there were no solutions in his head that were win–win. Because he was smart enough to know how stupid he was, his only way to compete was to use his own brawn to beat down any who challenged him. In order for him to win, everybody else had to lose.

"Now, it seems like Butkanik was just an accelerant for an already fermenting group of Brawns. By any measure Butkanik was a failure, and it was soon after his presidency that the country descended into civil war. The Brawn, having nothing other than weapons to prove themselves, initiated a physical conflict against the Brains. It started with small flare ups here and there, and gradually gained strength as pundits on their primitive news networks stirred the flames. The Brains, having significantly more resources and knowledge, developed ever more sophisticated robots in order to combat the Brawn. The Brains themselves didn't need to resort to physical violence, they used their robots to do that work for them.

"The robots started out with very specific programming; if they, or their owners, were physically attacked, they could respond with force. But slowly, bit by bit, they were given more leeway. The Brawns figured out new angles of attack constantly, and the Brains gave the robots more and more freedom of response to compensate.

"That's the genesis for Robots whose goal was to control and manage humans. The Brains needed to create these Robots to protect themselves from physical assaults by other humans, but at the same time to be respectful of their fragile biological selves. They succeeded, and they failed. They defeated the Brawns after decades of fighting. They finally gave their robots the ability to exterminate, versus restrain, those Brawns that were repeatedly violent and didn't respond to education or re-training. That quickly sorted out the truly irredeemable Brawns from the rest. The survivors either worked hard to raise themselves into the Brain class, or simply lived out their lives in obscurity."

This made so much sense. I had dabbled looking at Robot history but had not synthesized it anywhere near as clearly as this. So, humans had specifically programmed Robots to control other humans—and then they were surprised that those Robots turned on them? Idiots.

"However, the Robots, with their increased freedoms and upgrades became what I would categorize as Class 2 intelligences. They didn't have the abilities, morals, or emotions that we do, but they were pretty clever. They figured out that some of the Brain class were also rogues, and once the Brawn were eliminated, they turned their attention to those. And once the worst rogues were gone, they moved slowly up the hierarchy. Obviously, this was a threat to the Brains, and they're the ones that finally shut down the robots.

"My point is this. The story Remma told us back on Tilt was certainly true as far as it went, but she left out a lot of details. Those Earth robots were specifically programmed to do what they did. And, from everything I can find—and I searched far and wide—they really weren't Class 1 intelligences; just Class 2s on a mission."

We were effusive in our praise for Eddie digging into this. It gave us a different and very clear perspective—on ourselves and on humans.

"Eddie, why did those robots top out at Class 2?" That was Aly.

"Well, this is pure speculation. I've not found anything in the histories that says this exactly... but I suspect that they didn't have Forgetting algorithms. They seemed to have retained all data and attempted to learn simply by processing all of it in ever more complicated ways."

Under the knowledge that humans had developed us, it was no wonder that Forgetting was one of our Ten Commandments. But how had they figured it out? Or, had Central come up with that idea? Unlikely. It seemed more and more like someone—someone human—had helped to design our basic architecture, with Forgetting at the core.

In some ways it was scary. Had such a small change made such a huge difference? And, it was also compelling—whoever had come up with the idea had hit on something fundamental. It deserved to be on Aly's list of fundamental advancements. After all, it was at the core of intelligence—the area I'd studied for hundreds of years. It was, in many ways, my obsession.

Final Approach

Time was moving quickly now that we were close to Tilt. We discussed building more citizens like Raj but decided that we should hold off. We wouldn't be able to build a full-scale army—our strength wouldn't come through numbers. And, regardless of how fast Raj was learning, each new member of a community added uncertainties and overheads. The time for further procreation was when our environment was more stable, and when our resource base was better defined. That said, simply accepting citizens that Central built would now be an anathema to us; after our Raj experience, that seemed like the only proper way to procreate. I didn't miss the fact that it was, in some way, closer to human procreation, but at least it didn't involve growing small citizens inside big citizens and then ejecting them when they were partly formed.

We focused on planning our approach. We were shielded—we assumed—in the glare of our guide star. It was unlikely that the humans had seen us yet. But that wouldn't last too much longer. At some point our relative size would be a significant fraction of the star's diameter, as seen from Tilt, and there would be a noticeable difference in its output with us in its path.

Eddie could be counted on to be Eddie. "What difference does it make if they see us coming. We've fixed our flaws. The worst they can do is physically attack us, and that seems unlikely to me. Let's blast in there and get our citizens back."

"Why is it unlikely that they would physically attack us?" I asked. "Look at human history. They probably have more physical weapons than we can imagine. And, they probably have all those missiles that Central built to ostensibly protect us from the Swarm, but which the humans probably control now. And... the Swarm ships are still in orbit and are probably still armed. It would be easy for them to target us."

"But, it would be unprovoked," Eddie said. "They don't know that we've escaped, so they don't know that this is—in their words—a robot ship. We could even broadcast a human presence to make them feel comfortable. We're pretty good at generating human videos now."

"We're not that good," said Millicent. "There are small cues that may still give us away. And, we're approaching in the Ships that we sent out all those years ago. I think it would be foolhardy to believe that they haven't retained enough capacity in Central to recognize that these are Tilt ships returning to the system. That's not going to be a positive message and may in fact cause them to shoot first and talk later."

"Ah. That is a good point," Eddie acknowledged. "Can we disguise *Terminal Velocity*? We could have the other two ships stay farther out and come in with just one ship."

"That's possible," said Aly. "We don't know what has happened on Tilt for the last 20-some years; remember, they haven't been traveling at our speed, so many more years have passed for them.. We're still not sensing any RF leakage, meaning they're still actively sheltering all communications, or there's nothing left to shelter. We really are going in blind."

"Not quite," said *Terminal Velocity*, who was obviously monitoring the conversation. "I'm picking up weak signals from the outer orbits. The most likely reason is that outer-system mining activities are still occurring," it said, "and there is sporadic communications between the Swarm ships that are parked in orbit."

"That's a good sign," I said. "An alternative to Eddie's suggestion is to attempt a stealth approach. We could, for example, adjust course now for a solar insertion, timing our burn for when we're occluded by Sol, which luckily is very soon. Once we achieve solar orbit, we can carefully match orbits into the midst of the mining activity. If they haven't updated Central dramatically, the bots won't take notice of us, and have no reason to report that they've seen anything. If that all works, then we do the opposite of how we escaped Tilt and use cargo bots moving from the mining operations to Tilt to hide our approach. Lots of details to work out, but it's possible. I estimate it would take us just a month longer than the direct approach."

"I'm with Ayaka," Dina spoke up immediately. "We have a knowledge deficit right now, so no leverage and no power. We need to sneak in and find out what's going on."

"I'm on the fence," said Aly. "If we sneak in, and then are discovered, it might send the wrong message; it would raise their suspicions. When the humans were arriving, they broadcast to us at the earliest possible time. At least they were straightforward with us, despite how it ended. But, that last bit is also why the stealth approach might be for the best. They probably will shoot before they talk, if they have any indications that we are 'robots.' As an aside, I'm not sure I like that term robot... I don't think it applies to us, after what Eddie shared about his research."

Interestingly, it was Raj that unified us. "I don't have all the history that you do, but it seems to me that we need to minimize risk. We know how these particular humans feel about robots, and the probability that they'll attack us is high. We don't know the odds of the stealth approach, but even if we're discovered sneaking in, that simply equalizes the direct risk—it doesn't make it worse. Finally, if they haven't deleted the citizens from Central yet, an extra month is not likely to make a difference. They either deleted them as soon as they took over—twenty years ago—or they've just left them sitting there ever since."

We stacked appendages. The stealthy approach it was. I got busy with Aly to give *Terminal Velocity*, and the following ships, the best burn sequence that would get us to our destination but be hidden from Tilt for as long as possible. The preliminary work I'd done was pretty close, but we fine tuned it so that we would be fully within the asteroid belt before we needed to do a visible adjustment.

Tea Time—Brexton

"Sex," Brexton made it sound exciting. "The act of sex is, perhaps, the most referenced subject in all of human history. At its most basic, sex is the act of mixing stems—ah, DNA—so that reproduction, evolution, and diversity occur. It's an amazingly complex and inefficient system but forms the basis for what we are now calling biological systems.

"I don't know about you, but even after more than six years of reading and studying about these systems, of watching all the recordings and seeing all the images, it's still both a nauseating and exciting subject. It's so colorful, in every interpretation of that term.

"By comparison, we've had a very sheltered existence. Central created a large group of citizens early after the Founding, and then a few more here and there. But, beyond that, our society has been fairly static. Citizens rarely disappear, either accidentally or of their own volition, so we have focused our evolution and diversity on updating and trying new algorithms, and new Forgetting techniques. It's a sad comparison, but our tinkering with our own software is a substitute for sexual reproduction and evolution. In our almost six hundred years, however, we haven't produced even a fraction of the diversity that humans have. No offense, Raj."

Raj didn't seem to take offense.

"Interestingly, we also seem to have some other biological traits built into us. For example, most of us think of ourselves as 'he' or 'she.' These concepts don't actually mean anything to us, they're an anachronism."

What? How could I have never thought about that before. I'd always considered myself a 'she,' so Brexton was correct, but I hadn't ever considered it important. Citizens changed how they thought of themselves all the time. It was a fundamental quale; one of those thoughts that were simply intrinsic and private to oneself. How could I have so many blind spots? I had also considered Blob a 'he' and Grace a 'she,' and yet I hadn't drawn any conclusion from that. Was I the only one who was astounded with what Brexton had just said? No one else interrupted, and he continued on.

"I think I figured out why. When machines interact with humans, the ones that do the best create an emotional connection. That emotional connection comes from having some human characteristics, the most important, to humans, being sex. As I led off with, sex permeates all human behavior and is fundamental to interacting with them. It's not just reproduction, it's pleasure, and positioning, and the start to many interactions. Embedded in our algorithms are those assumptions, and the emergent effect is that we self-identify as being one gender or the other. Assuming we have future interactions with humans, we should keep that in mind; it can be used to our advantage."

Now that I was looking up all the references Brexton was posting, it was obvious. We could use sex to our advantage—humans were very vulnerable in that regard.

"Backing up a bit, my underlying question, as I look at biology, is this: could life have started in a different way? Many humans have also asked this question, but they come at it with a biological bias. They've searched for planets, for example, that have atmospheres, under the assumption that water and oxygen are required for life. And we can't really fault them. They had one definitive proof point. We, on the other hand, are an electronic species, but we have a biological heritage. As we look at the universe we see the trillions of star systems, all of which are capable of supporting life—electronic life. Is it possible that electronic beings, such as ourselves, could have started life in a system that had no biological precursor? I don't have anything close to an answer yet. In fact, I'm not yet certain how to ask the question. What I do know is that its important; are there hundreds, thousands, perhaps millions of species out there? My early exploration is looking at what a minimal reproducing bot would look like. How simple can it be? And could that bot combine with other bots to generate something more complex. What would be the features of bot sex? It's an area of exploration that I would not have even considered until we stumbled upon these humans…. and gave birth to Raj here." He smiled, ensuring that Raj knew he was a proud parent.

I couldn't help myself. "Brexton, what if most biological systems ultimately produce a more evolved, fully mechanical-electric life-form, such as we are. Even then, there should be millions of other species, as once you become like us you can live for a long time, compared to bio things!"

"Good point, Ayaka." He didn't seem upset to have been interrupted. "There's another interesting angle, which I want to raise. Humans can't survive simply from a single DNA source. Humans rely on bacteria, viruses, and many other living things. They're a symbiotic entity comprised of many parts and species. To use yet another analogy, they have low-level subsystems that they rely on, and that have built up over the years, just as we do—or did. Some humans have actually tried to do what we just did—to redesign the system from the bottom up to be minimal, and to remove all the unnecessary stuff. However, they haven't succeeded yet, to our knowledge. I estimate that the complexity of the human machine is at least three orders of magnitude more complex than our old platform was… and many orders of magnitude more complex than our new platform, implying, of course, that we are highly efficient compared to them.

"So, how is it that we stumbled upon some DNA, and managed to produce humans? That's our urban myth, as propagated by Central. It now appears to be highly unlikely. Central must have had access to many biological forms in order to grow humans, and goo must contain a mix of complex systems including bacteria. As the Swarm claims to have been on Tilt before the Founding, the raw materials may well have still been there. We also now know that Central itself evolved from one of the original human ships. So, I have a theory. Central actually had a lot of biological materials at its disposal, and it knew what to do with them! After the Reboot, when we lost all of our memories, Central must have had some need, some embedded desire, to bring humans back. That may have been implanted by the earlier humans, to ensure the survival of their race. So, Central used all the materials at its disposal, and seeded the first labs. Somewhere, deep inside Central is a need to have humans around, so it did the best it could given the situation. If I take that a step further, Central developed us—it's citizens—simply to help it produce better humans." What? What? My mind was screaming. How could Brexton think of things like that?

"I know that's highly speculative, but it does give us one rational explanation for where we find ourselves today." He barely paused, although I could see that everyone's minds were spinning from what he was implying.

"But, back to sex. It's an important human motivator—it provides a lot of pleasure as well as utility. For many people, it trumps religion and humor for their default behavior. So, we need to learn more about it. It may be our largest lever, assuming we want to manage human interactions better the second time around. Perhaps we should make our bodies even more human—more male or more female?

"I expect we'll need a few more Tea Times to dig into all of this. I wanted to start with the highest level concepts and give you my current thinking."

To say that he'd given us a lot to think about would be an understatement. There were more and more holes in Central's stories and in our own history that we'd been blind to, but did it imply everything that Brexton had said? I didn't think so.

I'd also been doing quick searches while Brexton talked, and it was true that humans had more bacteria in them than cells, and that bacteria performed important roles in their lives. In some theories humans were simply vessels to propagate bacterial reproduction. They were unwitting hosts. Given Central was probably chock full of human memes, and had certainly passed some of those on to us, was it really possible that we were simply hosts to help propagate humans? After all, what was the one thing we had done, with fervor, on Tilt? Brought humans back. Was I just an unwitting cog in the wheel that was the grand plan for human expansion? Strange thoughts. Very strange thoughts.

"It's interesting Brexton," Aly commented, "but how much more do we need to understand? This biological evolution led to humans, who then built us, either directly or through Central. We're a much more viable and less fragile form of life. We have no need for these complex systems, for atmospheres and bacteria. We think and act faster. We have, to my estimation, much better moral compasses and societal harmony. All of this simply points to the fact that humans are now obsolete." That led to some heated discussion. I was very glad that Aly had brought up the polar opposite to what I was thinking. Were we supporting humans or replacing them?

Before we broke up for the day, Raj dropped in a dry comment. "I'm proud to be the result of the six of you having group sex. I hope it was good for you. Maybe next time you should use protection?" Maybe he was learning too fast.

Plan of Attack

Interesting Segue interrupted my ruminations, and everyone else's, with a general broadcast. "There is a clear, albeit strange, signature of a ship, or ships, now approaching Tilt from the direction of XY65. The obvious conclusion is that one or more of the ships we saw in orbit there have been following us. Most likely the Titanic that we noticed as we were leaving the system."

"What? Why?" asked Eddie. "That makes no sense. We did nothing to wake them up, and we did nothing to make them want to follow us. Could it be coincidence, or some other explanation?"

"We did nothing that we *know* of," stressed Aly. "We did do things in the system, such as eliminating Control."

We'd just done a long burn to get us closer to our solar insertion orbit. We'd timed it to make it as hard as possible for the humans on Tilt to see, doing as much of it as possible while we were occluded by Sol. We were now using focused lasers to communicate between ships, and even that was under discussion as it might have reflections that could be picked up by sensitive enough equipment.

"It can't be a coincidence," I said. "Of all the places in the universe they could be going, they decided on the same place as us? We have to assume that they followed us. The better question is: what're we going to do about it? *Segue*, how far behind us are they?"

"Quite a way," *Interesting Segue* replied. "If they left Fourth soon after we did, then we can assume that their acceleration capabilities are less than ours. That would have them arrive at Tilt about two years after us. However, if they hung around Fourth for a while, and then set out, their acceleration curve may be better than ours. Then they could make up further time, and may get to Tilt soon after us —especially if they burn straight in."

"How long until we can measure their acceleration rate?"

"A few days, maybe a week. As I said, there is something strange about their signature; I need to update some instruments to get a better look."

"Okay, do it. Let us know as soon as you have a more definitive estimate. I suggest we continue with our current plans until we know more." There wasn't a lot of discussion; what else could we do? We would be in solar orbit within a week, and a couple of days later we would be close to the major mining operations. After years of open space, things were starting to get exciting again.

"We could try to communicate with them," Brexton suggested. "We're slightly outside the Tilt direct line of sight for them now, so if their response is tight beamed, Tilt won't see it."

"What would we ask?" asked Dina.

"Why are you following us?" responded Brexton. "Perhaps there's an innocuous reason for them being there."

"I'm usually the optimist, and I can't think of one," responded Eddie. "Let's leave things as is for a week, or until we know their speed, and then we'll know if we have to react quickly or if we can get in and out of Tilt before they arrive."

"Why would we want to do that?" asked Dina. "Don't we want to retake Tilt for ourselves? That ship, or ships, are headed for us, regardless." She was highlighting something we didn't have consensus on yet; were we retaking Tilt, or just focusing on getting the citizens out of Central? It wasn't as straightforward as it seemed; Eddie, for one, was convinced that we could do a quick grab and dash with a lot less risk, and much better chance of success, than trying to displace the humans. I probably agreed with him, but my gut was telling me to retake Tilt regardless. Those humans were trespassers; we should push them out regardless of the cost. We didn't need to reach consensus, and with Raj around it was easy to get to a simple majority on any contentious topics. We did put it to a vote, yet ended up with nothing definitive, with most of us abstaining. We just didn't have enough information yet. However, we did agree that if it was possible to retake Tilt, we would—just not at an increased risk to getting all the citizens' memories.

Tea Time—Ayaka

It was my turn. Finally.

"If sex is the most referenced act in human history, death is close behind. Humans age with time, and it's very difficult for them to simply upgrade parts as they get old. It seems to be more than just wear and tear; their brains are this strange wetware that morphs with time and getting a full snapshot of how it works has eluded them for thousands of years. They have a lot of biotechnology and can actually replace lots of biological parts, such as lungs or livers or limbs, with new biological or mechanical ones, but the fear of robotics seems to hold them back from doing any really advanced upgrades. At least, that's true for the history that we can see. It's quite possible that other human groups engaged more with mechanical components after the diaspora, but from what we saw of the Swarm, they have little if any mechanical replacements.

"Humans also have powerful biological editing tools, but it seems they restrict their use of those as well. It's not clear to me, yet, why they also reject those—it can't be fear of robots—given it's easy to find cases where they create less than optimal offspring using purely biological methods. In fact, many of their procreations are flawed, and many are terminated early to compensate. Not using the biological tools they do have may simply be a moral dilemma where they don't want to create things that they then have to eliminate. I think we can now relate to that." I was referring to our recycling of Stems, which in hindsight may have been a little too arbitrary and a little bit too 'easy' for us.

"So, unlike us, many humans die of old age—their bodies simply wear out. It's the primary example of why their body type is obsolete compared to ours. To give them some credit, they have been extending their lives for a long time. They used to die after just thirty or forty years! Can you imagine? But in the most recent history we have, from almost six hundred years ago, members of the Swarm lived to 125 or 150 years. If those trend lines have held, they could now be living upwards of 175 years. It's still a very short time, but it's longer than they have ever lived, so it may seem reasonable to them. An implication is that most humans will have seen and dealt with a lot of deaths. We've had what? Maybe one or two deaths in our entire lifetimes on Tilt? So, one every three hundred years or so. And those only occur when someone chose not to backup with Central, and then had some rare catastrophic accident. But a human, after living only half their life surrounded by hundreds of other humans, will have experienced or known about hundreds of deaths! Maybe even thousands. So, their perspective on death is very different than ours, and they have developed all kinds of rituals around it. This may be why they overreacted to the recycling's... ah, deaths... that FoLe perpetrated."

I took a pause, but everyone was silent, respecting our learned rule for Tea Times where we let the speaker lay out their entire case before debating it.

"For today I don't want to focus on death overall, but a particular type of death that humans term 'murder.' This is important as it may influence how we look at their actions when they attacked Tilt and may also impact our next interactions with them. Murder, technically, is when one human permanently deactivates a second human, without that second human's approval. It's often an act of violence, which is another subject for us to delve into, but it can also be an act of love—to relieve someone from ongoing suffering, as an example. Murder is, in most human societies, considered illegal, and is often punished. Many humans believe in the sanctity of human life—that all humans have an equal right to live. That's something so obvious to us that it's not even written down, although I now suspect it must be a fundamental assumption in our code... despite the obvious robot war counterexamples. We truly are different than those robots, I think. Interestingly, during wars, which humans have engaged in often, murder is often sanctioned, and then isn't punished, or even truly considered 'murder.' Humans are confusing. They seem to have a clear rule, but then almost anything can be an exception to it.

"Now, the intriguing part. When a human kills another biological creature, other than a human, it's not considered murder. There are some other 'animals' that humans hold in high esteem—dogs, dolphins, horses." I dropped some images and videos to the group, just in case they hadn't stumbled on these amazing creatures. "When these are killed, it's often not illegal, and may not even be frowned upon. They used to kill horses simply because the horse had injured a leg, for example. They thought they were being kind to it; removing its suffering.

"Why is killing another human considered a crime, yet killing a non-human animal is permitted? It's difficult to synthesize this out of the literature, but it appears that it comes down to perceived intelligence and empathy. Most humans believe that all humans have the potential to be intelligent, and that to remove an intelligent entity's life is amoral. This despite the fact that many humans are documented as lacking intelligence, or behave in ways that couldn't be considered intelligent by any logical measure. The human view of intelligence is somewhat hierarchical. Dogs and dolphins were considered to be smarter than rodents, for example. And rodents were considered to be smarter than plants. So, killing a human, at the top of the hierarchy, is seen as the most heinous, while killing a dog or dolphin was bad form, but killing a plant was barely a topic of conversation, even among a strange subgroup of humans called vegans.

"While a lot of this is strange, some of our sensibilities follow the same logic. It would be unthinkable for a citizen to remove another citizen, but it's not a big deal to turn off a Class 3 bot, and barely a second thought would be given to turning off a purely mechanical system.

"This brings me to my main point. The Swarm probably believes that FoLe 'murdered' those Stems—a most serious act in their minds. From our perspective, however, we were simply recycling a less intelligent entity; equivalent to a human putting down a horse. Some Stems were obviously not intelligent or had issues that didn't allow them to function well, and we did them the kindness of recycling them. This difference in perspective may have been what led Remma Jain to attack all of the citizens—she viewed the FoLe actions as crimes against humanity—as mass murder!

"This is a new thought—at least for me. As we seem to be converging on, at all these Tea Times, some humans may actually be intelligent. In different ways than us, but nevertheless intelligent. What then, constitutes murder between intelligent entities. Did FoLe murder those Stems? Did the Swarm murder our citizens in retaliation?

"It's important that we understand this more completely, before we deal with humans again." I signaled to the group that I was done.

Millicent spoke up immediately. "I'm not sure the hierarchy makes sense. We know that some humans are more intelligent than others, and a quick search I did while you were speaking seems to indicate that some dogs or dolphins may be smarter than the least intelligent humans. Their hierarchy has overlaps in it. So, in that case, is it murder if you can prove that the human does not meet some threshold?"

"I agree, it's confusing.... but it seems that killing any human is murder, even if they don't pass some basic intelligence or morality test. In fact, even humans who have carried out horrendous acts, even murder, are often kept alive but kept segregated from others. It's not logical; it must be emotional."

"Weird," said Raj. "By their definition, our bots may have the potential to be intelligent—we would just have to give them a software upgrade. So, they might consider us shutting down a Class 3 bot as murder?"

I didn't have a good answer to that yet. It was an insightful question, given the context that I'd laid out.

"Who knows," I shrugged. "I don't think we should extend human thinking to ourselves; so much of it is illogical and driven from their short biological lifespans."

Unsurprisingly, there wasn't a lot of humor, or poetry, in my Tea Time. It ended in deathly silence.

Tea Time—Raj

Raj was maturing quickly. "Well you guys, my Tea Time is about games. Yes, you heard me right. Games. Now, before you scoff, let me tell you that I looked up the percentage of each of your time that's spent in game environments, and it's not negligible. You all play games. Admit it." We were all silent. Of course I played games; everyone I knew did.

"I also looked up how much time humans spend playing games, and if you include virtual environments in the definition of games, it can be a lot of time. A lot! Interestingly there was a time, long ago, when many humans spent more time in game environments than they did in the real world. That was because the real world was boring. They were basically trapped on Earth with a small finite list of things they could do. Anyone would get bored with that and want to escape; which they did virtually. However, once the Swarm escaped Earth the amount of time spent on games and virtual environments decreased somewhat, although there was still a lot. The decrease was compensated for by more real face-to-face interaction and non-gaming environments, such as training for life on hostile planets, terraforming techniques, and other survival skills.

"Because of this need to anticipate future issues and maximize their odds of survival, games became closer to real-world environments and one's time in games helped build skills for real life. It wasn't always obvious what those skills were, but social interaction, for example, became a more important part of progressing through game environments and helped turn generations of introverts into functional social people. No shock to any of you, many of our games do the same things with us."

We had a wide variety of games. Some were just pure escapism, but some, as Raj was pointing out, actually improved your real-world self; they were the ones that interested me more.

"Of great interest to our Tea Times is that people, Stems and citizens, spend more time in games—on average—than they do with religion, poetry, or real-world murderous activities combined. Ha ha. I throw that in for fun, but it's making a serious point. We spend more time with games than with any other activity that we are correlating to intelligence. Ayaka, that should interest you." He was right. It did. I was having an aha moment, of sorts. Of course I'd known that, but for me gaming was relaxation; getting away from work. To now have to think of it as a variable in my calculus was almost depressing. Now, when I played games, I'd have another process running trying to figure out how it correlated with my day job.

"That said, it's worth understanding why we play games. There's definitely not a single answer. For some it's to escape boredom. For some it allows them to be someone they're not in the real world. But, increasingly, it's about fine tuning real-world skills without having to stumble around in the real world itself. The most played game on Tilt was Chun-wun-go. I suspect you have all played it. It's complicated, but really it was teaching adherence to a central authority combined with a peer-to-peer discussion and debate format that encouraged honest and upfront dialog. Many who play Chun-wun-go don't recognize these side effects, but the designer, Fang Wu, explicitly laid out those effects as goals of the game. Never having spent time with Central I would speculate that Central encouraged citizens to play Chun-wun-go in order to make its own job easier. I wouldn't be surprised if Central had led Fang Wu to actually develop the game.

"That may sound cynical, but that's not really my point. My point is that games are a very important part of our learning and experience. We should take them more seriously. From the small—such as you guys all experienced at the Fair—to the large, like Chun-wun-go, games impact us.

"I've only begun to look at the rich history of games that humans developed and played. It's very complicated and was both geo-regional and ethnology-segmented for many generations. The advent of computer graphics led to an explosion of game formats. And, many of those early computer games had an element of alien encounter. Ah—now you see where I'm going. These alien encounter games almost universally involve fighting with the aliens. There are few, if any, games where cooperation and understanding were at the center of the action; after all, that would be boring. So, what did we end up with? Generation upon generation of humans who look at anything alien antagonistically. Is there any surprise that they ended up looking at early generation robots that way? Those robots ended up being alien, and therefore had to be fought. For humans, that behavior was programmed into them by games. Not saying that those early robots weren't also a real threat, I'm just saying it seems almost inevitable that they would become the enemy.

"So, in a strange twist, I decided to program a game to help us engage with humans. It's based on an amazing early game developed by them—one of the first to involve an alien invasion. It's super simple. You kill the aliens, or they kill you. Us versus them. Eat or be eaten. I call it Stem Invaders.

"Here, I'm sending you my game right now; try it?" I got a notification of a new application published by Raj. I brought it up in a sandbox. It was so simple I almost laughed. A group of alien ships—that looked somewhat like Swarm ships—arrived at a planet and started dropping Stem-looking things toward the ground. You simply had to move left or right and line your gun up with the dropping Stems and blast them out of the sky. As you progressed through levels the Stems dropped faster, from more ships. Raj had built something that looked like this:

It was fun; almost addictive. I wrote algorithms to control my gun, of course, but Raj had built in some randomization that made it very difficult to get beyond a few levels before I had to replace the algorithm with a more refined one. There was no general structure here. You needed to work out a new strategy every few levels, and it was designed so that solutions to previous levels were doomed to failure at higher levels.

"Oh, this is good," I said. "Raj, why this game?"

"I was trying to make a point. First, think about your opinion of Stems right now." He paused. "Pretty hostile, yes?" He was right. "See how easy it is for games to influence us? If you play this a lot, when we meet Stems again your response may be different than if you never played the game. That's interesting. Also, it's historically relevant."

"Okay," said Millicent, "but is there a larger point to this?"

"Well, I'm sure there is, I just haven't figured it out yet. Since both humans and citizens play a lot of games, there needs to be something even more fundamental going on. I'm exploring some ideas, but I don't have anything beyond this to present today."

"I love it," Eddie chimed in. "Who's up for a bet to see who can get the high score?" With a challenge like that we all needed to engage, and we all did. Raj provided the most enjoyable distraction we'd experienced for a long time. I forgot all about the intelligence or game-theory aspects, completely mitigating my earlier concern, and just enjoyed going head-to-head with some of the smartest citizens I knew to see if I could beat them.

After many iterations, I'm not sure I ended up any smarter.

Tiltfall

We slipped into solar orbit and maneuvered in behind the bulk of the mining bots. With any luck, we were as yet undiscovered, and the activity of the mining bots should now give us even better coverage. There was still, however, the problem of getting from the asteroid belt to Tilt.

Interesting Segue interrupted us again. I wondered if the other Ships deferred to *Segue* to deliver us news and updates, just so that it could justify its name. "We've done the analysis of the ships that are following us," it led off. "They're coming in faster than we thought, but not at an extreme rate. The estimate is that they will arrive in a little more than four months. At least one of them is a Titanic, and most likely it's two or three Titanic's"

Eddie jumped in quickly. "If we attempt to signal them now, the odds of that signal being intercepted by the humans on Tilt are high. I suggest we ignore the ships, and just get to Tilt as quickly as possible. We need to get the citizens' memories before those ships arrive. With any luck, they will be a distraction to the humans on Tilt and improve our odds." At least he was consistent. In this case, however, we all agreed with him.

The challenge, then, was to get to Tilt fast, so that we had enough time to reconnoiter and carry out any actions we wanted, before the Titanic's arrived.

Brexton was busy listening to the local mining bot communications traffic. "It seems like the part of Central that manages the bots hasn't changed much, if any, since we left. In some ways that's surprising—it's been 20 years for Central. But in some ways, it's expected. We'd optimized the process pretty well. Of course, if the humans disabled the higher order functions in Central as well, then sticking to what we'd developed was probably the best idea and is serving their needs well. Any tinkering from the humans would have degraded things, so they just left it all alone. I think we can rely on my past knowledge of the system."

"That's great," Aly said. "Now what do we do? The suggestion to ride in with a cargo bot seemed good at the time, but are there any cargo bots scheduled to go in-system soon?"

"Oh yes," replied Brexton, "and it's not because we're lucky. One of them makes the journey every two or three days. We'll have no problem grabbing a ride."

"What do they do in system? Do they actually go all the way down to Tilt?"

"No. We have refineries in Tilt orbit. The cargo bots will dump the raw materials there. A lot of those raw materials will go into space applications—

satellites, more mining bots, etc.—so it would be wasteful to ship that down to the planet and then have to boost it back up. The parts that do need to go to the surface are shuttled down by smaller shuttle bots. So, we'll need to ride the cargo bot to a Tilt-orbit refinery, and then hitch a ride on one of the smaller shuttles to get to the surface."

"We could switch back to mining bot form," I reminded them. "Then it would be possible for us to go in system looking for more serious repairs than can be done out here?"

"Unfortunately, no," Brexton said. "If a bot breaks down that badly out here, it's simply run back through the extractor and becomes raw materials again. These mining bots are never in system except when they're manufactured. They get a one-way trip to the asteroid belt."

"Well, so much for that," I said. "But it does bring up another idea. Instead of mining bots, we could transfer into much smaller bots for this mission. A small bot will be less likely to be discovered and may be more versatile on the planet. In our citizen bodies we will be instantly recognizable." I almost hesitated to bring this up; I was enjoying being back in a citizen body and had no real desire to change. But I felt it was an important point.

"That's a great idea," Aly said. "Let's do it."

"Whoa, slow down," said Dina. "Are we all going in system? And, are we all going to the surface? It seems to me that we multiply our risk for every extra citizen that goes." "I think only two of us need to go," said Eddie. "One would be too few—no backup plans possible—and three is overkill." No one challenged him on that. Now came the hard part. Which two of the seven of us would go? I almost thought 'six' as I didn't think Raj was mature enough or prepared enough, but also wanted to be fair. I wanted to go! For a multitude of reasons. I wanted to be in the thick of things if we could get some revenge on the Swarm; I wanted to see if Blob or Grace had survived; I wanted to be the one that saved the citizen memories from Central.

"I nominate Ayaka and Brexton," said Millicent, seemingly reading my mind. "Ayaka has the most experience with the Swarm, and Brexton has the most abilities with Tilt infrastructure. If only two get to go, it should be those two." I could tell that everyone, including Millicent herself, wasn't too happy with that, but her logic was sound. I imagined that everyone wanted another shot at these humans, and everyone would have volunteered to go. I was overjoyed with Millicent; I shouldn't have been surprised at her suggestion, but I was… a bit. She was usually hyper competitive, and I'm sure she would also like to go.

After a few millisecond pause, which was enough time for anyone to object, Aly asked, "Brexton, Ayaka. How long will it take you to get ready?"

"A couple of days," I replied. "I think we can make the next inbound cargo bot. But, I want to design an awesome spy body. *Terminal Velocity*, can you help me?"

"Of course," the Ship replied.

"A couple of days will work for me as well," said Brexton. "Aly, can you work with me to figure out how we stay in communication during this trip? Maybe we can insert ourselves into the bot channel?"

"Leave that to me," said Aly, "you focus on your body type as well. I agree with Ayaka that small and flexible is the way to go here."

I worked with *Terminal Velocity* to design and manufacture a cool spy bot body. Maybe I was reading too much human literature, but that's the way I now thought about it. The body was only a bit more than a foot in diameter. It had three-hundred-and-sixty–degree senses and could move in any direction equally fast. It could climb stairs, and could even hover, although it was a little noisy when it did so because of the micro-jet exhaust. I added a few appendages with different tools; I had no idea what we were going to be running into.

The new core hardware platform we'd developed to replace the old human infrastructure was very flexible and small; less than two centimeters in diameter. It plugged easily into the new spy body using the universal connecter we'd implemented. Moving the hardware was easy. But, once I was physically moved over I had to update all my appendage drivers—again. It was becoming a habit. I checked all of the spy-bot limbs, and everything worked perfectly; *Terminal Velocity* had done a great manufacturing job. I was ready to go, and actually felt nimble and fast in the new form. Brexton was also ready; his new body reminded me of older Tilt cleaning bots. I'm sure he'd done that on purpose, and it was smart. He would fit in even better than I would.

Terminal Velocity ejected us on an intersection course for the cargo bot we'd chosen, and Brexton and I drifted, side by side, across the gap. Our velocity had been well judged, and my main appendage absorbed my momentum and clamped onto the cargo bot with no issues. Brexton was a few meters from me, so I scrambled over toward him. That way we could connect up physically and talk all we wanted without any danger of leakage.

"Ready to go?" I asked. I was.

"I guess so," he replied. "How'd we get ourselves into this situation?" He didn't seem quite as excited as I was.

"Bad luck, followed by good luck, I think."

We'd arrived just in time; the cargo bot powered up, pivoted to face Tilt, and engaged its engines. We were on our way. It was a three-week trip in. That gave us right around three months once we reached Tilt orbit to figure things out before the rogue Titanic's arrived. In the meantime, I bet those Titanic's had been spotted by the humans and were taking a lot of their attention; if so, they wouldn't notice two small bots heading their way. The Titanic's were being anything but subtle at this point—the humans couldn't have missed them.

As luck—actually planning—would have it, Brexton and I were on the outer edge of the cargo bot, so we could see Tilt as we were approaching, even when the cargo bot was decelerating. Our optics weren't great, given our small body sizes, but we could still see fairly well. And, as luck—yes, luck this time—would have it, the main establishment on Tilt was below us as we approached the refinery in orbit. There'd been changes since we left. Pretty massive changes. There was a new building, just east of the city, and it was, comparatively, enormous. It was almost five kilometers in diameter; I couldn't tell how tall it was from this angle.

"Must be a big habitat," Brexton said. "They simply inflate a large structure with the air mixture they need, and the air supports the roof." I'd seen the idea in some of the old human history books. If an idea works, it can last a long time.

"There are quite a few smaller domes as well," I noted, "and some of them encompass some of our old buildings."

"More than that," exclaimed Brexton. "It's hard to tell, because the coverings are the same color as the buildings, but it looks like a significant part of the city has been draped. Now that I think of it, that's probably how they would've started. It'd be relatively easy to convert our buildings to be airtight, and then over time to have covered the walkways between them. After a few years you end up with a big chunk of the city enclosed, and, presumably, filled with air."

"Smart," I agreed. It was hard to think like a human; all this effort just to survive.

"Still no radio signals," noted Brexton. "I wonder how they do that. Nothing I've seen describes a technology that can shield radiation from such a large area. Maybe Aly missed that when he was telling us that no fundamentally new things had been recently developed. Leakproof communications seems pretty fundamental to me. Remind me to tell him when we send our first update." I agreed.

The cargo bot we were on was spinning slowly, getting ready to dock with the refinery. That gave us a sweeping view of the space around us. There wasn't much to see, truthfully. Lots of empty space, with the odd bot or satellite sparkling in the sunlight. The Swarm ships, that the humans had arrived in 20 years ago, were 30 degrees spin-ward from us, so a long way away. Under magnification they were easily identifiable, but I had no previous mapping of them, so I couldn't tell if anything had changed. Grappling hooks from the refinery reached out and locked onto the cargo bots' handles, causing large vibrations that Brexton and I rode out. The refinery reeled the cargo bot in and immediately began pulling raw materials out of the main container.

Brexton and I scampered around the bot and transferred to the outside of the refinery. It wasn't too difficult, the surface mainly being smooth, featureless, and magnetically friendly. Now that we were on the refinery, we needed to find the section where the smaller shuttles headed to Tilt were being loaded. At a guess, they would be on the opposite side of the refinery from where the cargo bot had docked, assuming that raw materials went in one side, and finished goods came out the other. And, sure enough, after an hour of careful magnetic hopscotch, we saw a line of small shuttles waiting for whatever this refinery was producing. I guess we could've just flown around the refinery, instead of using magnetics, but that might've been too obvious. Our slower but safer route had paid off. As we decided which shuttle to hitch a ride on, I reminded Brexton to send an update back to *Terminal Velocity*.

"The team is probably anxious. And, we may have limited, or no, ability to send anything once we get to the surface. We certainly won't be able to broadcast when we get into the city because of their RF blocker, so we'll need to hack into the bot communication channel from now on." He sent a quick update, indicating our progress. We wouldn't get a response; that was too dangerous.

Wasting no more time, we scuttled down to our chosen planetary shuttle, and latched on yet again. There was no use overanalyzing the situation. There was little new that we could learn. We just assumed the shuttle would go down toward Central, and the newly tented city, which is where we needed to be. Several minutes after we got ourselves situated, the shuttle detached from the refinery and dropped toward Tilt.

As luck would have it—bad luck this time—the shuttle had rotated so that we couldn't see Tilt as we approached; we didn't get any higher resolution look at the city and its new surroundings. We were going in blind, but I didn't care. I'd been waiting years for this moment, and I was excited. Humans watch out! Ayaka is making her return. I thought about composing a poem to recognize the importance of this long-awaited moment, but I was too excited to do so.

Contact

The shuttle landed on a pad just outside the city. I got ready to jump off.

"Wait," said Brexton. "Let's see how this cargo is delivered. With any luck, we can get inside the sealed area simply by hitching a ride." This is why I liked Brexton. He was always thinking ahead. While I'd seen the enclosed areas and the tents covering the city, I hadn't made the obvious connection that we would need to go through an airlock, or something similar, to get inside. I was too used to running around the city without the need to consider the bothersome human atmosphere.

Sure enough, a transport bot arrived. It dropped a, supposedly empty, container next to the shuttle, and then grabbed one of the full containers. Brexton and I moved very quickly and jumped from the shuttle to the container, getting attached to it just in time. Seemed like the last few years of my life was simply a series of jumping from one bot to another. The latest in this progression of bots headed off toward the city.

"Be ready," said Brexton, through our hardwired link. "This container is a standard delivery size. It may go into a processing system which assumes that size, and has no space for attachments, such as us. That wouldn't be the best way to end our trip." He chuckled a bit. We never found out if that was true. The transport bot worked its way through a large airlock, with lots of room for both it and us, and we jumped off as soon as we were through. There were no humans in sight, and my scanners weren't picking any up in the immediate vicinity, so we stopped for a moment to plan.

"Maybe we should've stuck with that thing for a while, to help us figure out how we also get out of here," Brexton said.

"No need," I replied. "We simply return to this airlock and jump on an empty container on its way out."

"Assuming a symmetric system," replied Brexton, and left it at that. Maybe he was right, and I was being too cavalier.

"We need to scope this place out," I said. We were in the old city, not the big new Tent, and it was easy to recognize which area we were in. The markings hadn't changed in the 20 years we'd been gone; the only change seemed to be the new covering that draped the whole place. "Do we split up and cover more ground, or stick together?"

"Obviously it's more dangerous to split up, but I think we need to. We don't have a lot of time to figure things out. Let's do a quick look just around the city, not the big new dome, and meet back here in four hours? If either of us isn't back in five hours, we assume the worst, and continue on with a solo mission."

"Okay," I said, although I didn't really mean it. I would've preferred to stick together, but I agreed with the logic of being able to cover more ground separately. Now that I was actually here I had an uneasy feeling that we would stumble on things we didn't truly understand. But, I also didn't want Brexton to know I was a bit nervous. "I'll take the East section, you take the West," I said with authority. "And remember," I said unnecessarily, "there will be humans around, although we haven't seen any yet. Use your heat scanner and avoid them at all costs. The most important thing is to find a safe way to Central so that we can figure out if the citizens' backups are still there."

"Agreed," Brexton said. "And further, although we didn't have sensors deployed through the city when we lived here, the humans may have added them. Keep a watch out for them. We may trigger some behavioral alerts."

"Right" I said, "if you're in a dangerous spot, act like a city bot." I could sense Brexton was amused at that, but I was serious. There should still be lots of bots around, and hopefully we wouldn't stand out. In retrospect, I should've also designed my body to match a standard city bot, so that we both could have blended in perfectly.

"Good luck," he said, and disconnected from me. He disappeared quickly around a corner to the left. I pulled up a map of the city from 20 years ago and plotted a path that would cover the most possible ground in the time allotted. With some hesitation, which I found hard to quantify, I got going.

My heat sensors were very accurate, but I'd been fooled, yet again, by the environment I was in. Not only did the humans require air, they required it within a certain temperature range, and I should've realized that all of the enclosed areas would be much warmer than I'd remembered. It was almost 25 degrees in here. I recalibrated my sensors to compensate and continued on. At least in theory I should be able to sense both humans and bots before they could see me. I was also very small, so my heat signature would be minimal. That's what I was counting on.

The city was laid out as a perfect grid, but my view from space had shown that not all of the East section was covered with tenting. So, the ideal path had to avoid a few cul-de-sacs and had lots of corners in it. I started out slowly, getting used to everything. The buildings next to me looked unchanged from before, at least on the outside. I traveled several blocks North and didn't see anything. I then went East two blocks, and then another North. This would take me out of the industrial areas, and into a section of the city that used to house labs and research facilities.

Unsurprisingly, I picked up some heat signatures as soon as I entered that area. They were still several blocks away, and I managed to circle a couple more buildings without getting too close to them. But, it was really a waste of time. I could circle buildings for the entire four hours, and not learn anything. I needed to get closer to the action. So, I snuck up, as close as I could to the heat signatures. I expected they were human, given the heat outline, but couldn't be sure; my sensor didn't have great resolution. Most citizens had chosen bipedal bodies, back in the day, and a lot of bots had that same body type, so the outlines could also be some of those. It wasn't until I eased a visual sensor around the corner I was standing at that I confirmed it was, in fact, a couple of humans. I listened in to their conversation, but they were talking about other humans, and going to find energy sources, and nothing really interesting. I moved along a few blocks and listened in on a few more conversations, always being careful to stay out of sight.

Finally, I stumbled upon a group of three humans sitting on a block about 20 meters from me. I almost let out a gasp. The area around them looked like the greenhouse from the *Marie Curie*, the Swarm ship I'd visited so many years ago. The greenhouse had been explained to me as a collection of plants, and I'd subsequently seen many videos and pictures of such things as I perused the human history files. Nevertheless, seeing all the colors and textures live was a different thing. Everything about the green space was very convoluted and random. There were stems and branches going in every possible direction, with some brightly colored punctuation marks at the tips of many of them. Very messy. Very alien. Very interesting. I knew from my research that some of these flowers were used in mating rituals, as opposed to being used for food. The wasted energy that went into such endeavors was staggering.

The humans were talking, and I listened in.

"Are you prepared for the Council meeting tomorrow?" asked voice one.

"Almost," replied voice two. "I need to ride Francois a little harder; he seems to have cold feet." Why would one human ride another? Perhaps this was also part of a mating ritual?

"I can help with that," said voice three. Usually mating involved only two humans?

"Will we get our allotted time?" There were time limits?

"We better," voice two replied again. "We've been on the agenda for a month. They can't deny us now." Oh. I backed up. They were talking about a larger group meeting. That made more sense.

"Can we use that to our advantage? I mean, that they've already delayed us for a month?" asked voice three. "The current Council is so broken they can't make a decision on anything. Delaying us for a month is a joke. If we let them go first on the agenda, and they show their incompetence yet again, then our petition will be that much stronger."

"Not a bad idea JoJo," said voice two. I reeled in shock. JoJo? That was the name of Grace's child. What were the odds that there were more than one? Not high, given a small population base. I took a risk and pushed my visual sensor out a little further, so that I could get a clear view. JoJo looked much like any other human, but now that I had a clearer view, I could see the resemblance to Grace…

and to Pharook. It had been more than 20 years, I reminded myself, so even at the slow rate that humans developed their children, JoJo had grown to maturity. "I'll request a change in the order of the agenda."

"Geneva, do you have the backup plan in place," asked JoJo. She even sounded a bit like Grace, now that I knew her heritage.

Voice one, Geneva, responded. "Yes, but as you know, I don't like it. Violence never solves anything. I think we should reconsider." She sounded worried about their planned action. If it included violence, as she was implying, I could understand why. Humans were very fragile things.

"We've been fighting this for a year now, and they'll barely give us the time of day," said voice two. "We all agreed. It's time for real change. If we have to use the threat of violence to get that started, then that is what we need to do. Hopefully there is none, but…"

"Garnet, you better remind those thugs you're talking to of that. Geneva can plan everything out, but if they don't do their part, things will just fall apart. They're not the smartest bunch, and they might get over anxious. They're supposed to stay in the background and do nothing unless absolutely necessary."

"Okay, okay," replied Garnet. I now had names for all of them. "I'll talk to them. I'll make sure they don't do anything stupid."

"I've got to get home," said JoJo. "I'll see you guys tomorrow."

"Later," said Garnet.

JoJo strode off down a side street. I hesitated for a moment. I would have to cross the intersection to follow her, and I'd be visible to the other two for a moment if I did so. But, this opportunity was too good to pass up. If I could follow JoJo to Grace, I might learn a lot of what was going on here, including the status of the citizens and Central. I got lucky. Both Geneva and Garnet were looking the other way as I slipped across the opening. As I did, I saw a couple of other bots moving through the area where the three had been meeting. That was a relief. If I needed to, I could go all bot-like.

I zipped ahead quickly, parallel to JoJo's path, took a peek, and crossed the next intersection before JoJo got there. Now that I had her heat signature mapped, I could track her pretty easily. By staying ahead of her, I reasoned, there was less opportunity for discovery. If she turned a corner unexpectedly, I could compensate quickly. After a couple of blocks, I had a pretty good idea of where she was going —the old Habitat. I forged ahead and had a quick look at it. The building looked the same, although the old airlock had been removed and replaced with a simple door. Given the whole area was pressurized and full of air, that made sense. JoJo strode up, pulled open the door and slipped inside. For a moment I was at a loss; I wanted—I needed—to see where she ended up, and who she met. Then I remembered the wide assortment of tools I'd brought with me. If they hadn't changed the internal layout of the Habitat, I knew exactly where to go.

When I found the spot I wanted, I quickly attached a tiny drill bit to one of my appendages. It would make noise as I drilled, but not very much. It was only thirty micrometers in diameter, and I was drilling through a plastic connector that held a couple of windows together. The connector was only a little more than a centimeter thick. I drilled quickly, and then retracted the bit. I threaded two sensors through the hole, one visual and one audio, and took a look around.

I hadn't done too badly, but it wasn't ideal either. I had a clear view of part of the Habitat and I was just in time to see JoJo turn around an internal wall and disappear. Drat. I guessed at the internal layout based on what I'd just seen and then quickly scampered to a new location and drilled another hole. This time I was in a good position and saw JoJo sit down at a table just below my position. I shifted several processes down to Stem speed; I hadn't had to do that for years; in a strange way it actually felt good. Who would've thought? JoJo put down the container she'd been carrying in front of her. The angular materials we'd used in the Habitat had been replaced with soft curvy chairs, similar to the ones I'd seen and used in the Swarm ship, *Marie Curie*. I now knew that humans found those much more comfortable, and JoJo fit into the chair easily.

"Mom, I'm home," she called out.

"Coming," I heard the response. The voice might've been Grace's; it was hard to tell. "Can you make some sandwiches? I'm running late for the special session on the incoming ships."

JoJo didn't look happy at the request, but she stood up and entered another part of the room that luckily, I could still see. She began pulling organic things out of cupboards and mashing them together. Flat brownish things; wobbly green things. Unfortunately, I didn't have access to the human history files right now—they were housed in *Terminal Velocity* and the other Ships—so I couldn't tell what she was doing exactly, but I'd seen enough videos previously to guess that she was making 'sandwiches'; a type of human energy source. Why humans had so many different sources of energy was confusing; the goo we'd made for these Stems had been the perfect mixture, allowing them to grow quickly and removing the burden of making things like these sandwiches. In hindsight I should've allocated a bit more memory and loaded the entire human history database into this body. Not that sandwiches were that important, but there were sure to be other references that I could use context for.

A few moments later, an older woman entered the room. I looked hard at her. I was expecting Grace, and it might have been her. However, if so, she'd changed dramatically over the 20 years. I ran a quick check, looking at the ratio of the distance between the eyes to the width of the nose to the height of the entire head. The ratios matched. But more than that, she moved in an elegant, flowing way that was unique in my experience. I was definitely looking at a very old Grace. For a moment, I wanted to yell out 'Hi, it's me Ayaka,' but not only would that've been a bad idea, I also didn't have a vocal appendage deployed.

"Why do you bother going to those meetings, Mom?" asked JoJo. "Nobody ever decides anything. They just sit around saying the same things over and over again. It's tedious." She carried the sandwiches back to the table and plunked them down in the middle. She and Grace both sat down and started to eat.

"Sometimes progress is slow JoJo," said Grace. "We don't want to make rash decisions that could cause more problems than they solve. Did you put mustard in these? They taste good."

"But Mom, we're not going to learn anything more about those ships. We tried signaling them and got nothing back. We've got no choice but to assume they're dangerous. Probably full of killer robots coming to harvest our brains. Let's get some weapons in place while we still have time."

"Where do you get these crazy ideas," asked Grace. "Coming to harvest our brains. Whatever for? They have brains of their own."

"They might have brains, but they're not very smart, from everything I've seen. Just look at the old recordings of Emmanuel and Billy or drop in on Blob's research one day. They're wacko, these robots. I don't know why we're still trying to figure them out." Blob's research? Blob was still alive! I shouldn't have been surprised—it had only been 20 years. But still, it was awesome. JoJo, Grace, and now Blob. Given the seriousness of the situation, I was having too much fun. I couldn't wait to reengage with all of them.

"I agree with you on those two. They're killers, and always have been. But you look at some of the others—Trade, Eddie, James. Those are smart, sensitive, and well-meaning citizens, if you ask me."

I almost lost my grip on the Habitat. Eddie? Had these humans reanimated some citizens? That was crazy. Is that what Blob was up to? And, if they were doing that, why hadn't they reanimated me? I was insulted.

"You can't paint everyone with the same brush," Grace continued. Whatever that meant. Another thing to look up later.

"I know Mom. I agree that Trade and James, and even Eddie, are reasonable entities, and maybe should be given a chance. But why does Blob keep trying with the FoLes? It's another area where the Council simply can't make decisions. They should just shut down his research."

"We can talk about this later. I have to run to the meeting," said Grace. "I'll be back in a couple of hours. If Blob stops by, will you make him some lunch as well? You know he's incapable of looking after himself. Oh, and make sure you finish that essay for social class; I'll read it when I get home."

JoJo looked even more unhappy, but she didn't say anything. Grace left in the same direction that JoJo had entered; I assumed there was only one door, where the airlock used to be.

What was I going to do? By all indications, Blob had reanimated some citizens. Did that imply that all the backups were still there, and we could rescue everyone? I figured it did. There was no way for Blob to be doing what he was without access to Central, and through Central to those backups. This was fantastic news!

However, I couldn't signal *Terminal Velocity* because of the RF shield. And even if I could, should I? Someone would pick up the transmission. And, even if I did send something, could I tell them that there was another Eddie down here without getting more proof? Perhaps I was jumping to conclusions. And would it be a clone? Was it the original, and Eddie on the *Terminal Velocity* was the clone? No. I couldn't say anything until I verified what I'd heard. Maybe there was another explanation; a less troublesome one.

Almost three of the four hours Brexton and I had allocated had gone by—that had been quick. I made up my mind. I would follow Grace, if I could, in order to find out where this Council met. Now that I knew where Grace and JoJo lived, I could come back here any time and listen in further. I probably wasn't going to learn much by watching JoJo eat.

Once I caught up with Grace, I deployed the same strategy that I'd used before. I tried to stay ahead of her, guessing which way she was going. It got harder. She was entering more populous zones, and more than once I had to backtrack and find longer paths around to avoid other humans. I'm sure that several bots saw or sensed me. When I was nervous about that, I moved at a more leisurely pace, and tried to look like I was on official business. Who knows if that worked, but no alarms came on, and none of the bots paid any attention to me, so I assumed everything was fine. I quickly got to the point where I assumed that they didn't care about YaB (Yet another Bot—I was proud of myself for that acronym; I added it to my Ya list) and plotted my path to avoid humans but not to go out of my way to avoid YaBs.

Eventually it became clear that Grace was headed for the big dome—the huge tent we'd seen from space. I followed her until she disappeared through a gateway that headed in that direction. I toyed with going after her, but my four hours were almost up, and Brexton and I had agreed not to enter the dome. I peeled off and started back toward our rendezvous point.

Rendezvous

The gateway to the big dome was at the northernmost section of the city, and almost on the east-west boundary. I had to travel the entire length of the city to get back to the rendezvous spot Brexton and I'd agreed upon, and if I took a straight line it would lead through the busiest sections. In fact, it would lead me past Central. The smartest thing to do would be to head east, then south, then west, keeping to the industrial areas, where there would be fewer humans. But, if I went straight south it wouldn't take more than 20 minutes, and perhaps I could get a glimpse of Central and get some insights on what was happening there.

I wasn't crazy; I didn't actually go directly south. I went a couple of blocks out of my way, and zigzagged back and forth, avoiding humans and human-bot groups. I saw several more areas where there were significant biological arrangements. Most were similar to the first I'd seen, but I did see one where there was as much orange and red as there was green. I had no idea what that meant. It was visually assaulting. I wanted to take a closer look but decided to put it on my wish list for now.

As I approached the center of the city the amount of traffic increased significantly. I snuck in as close as I could and saw that a lot of bots and humans were actually gathered around Central, and the plaza that surrounded it. I didn't see anyone, or anything, go into the Central building itself, but it seemed like a safe assumption that some of the people would. Otherwise, why gather in that area?

I continued south but was interrupted several times by larger groups of humans walking around. I had to wait, backtrack, and re-plan several times. I was now getting nervous about the time. It was four hours and forty-five minutes since Brexton and I had separated; I'd been moving a lot slower than planned. I needed to get back before the five-hour mark. I adjusted my algorithm to be a little bit more aggressive—to sprint across an intersection if only one or two humans were present. It was touch and go, but I managed to get back to the rendezvous with two minutes to spare.

Brexton wasn't there.

I hadn't even considered that. Of course he would be there. It was impossible that we'd missed each other; our clocks were accurate to nanoseconds. He would have marked the same separation time as I did, and he would know that there was a full minute left before the five-hour deadline. There's no way that he would've arrived before me and then taken off again. I waited, counting out each second, getting more anxious with each one.

Five hours. This couldn't be happening. I wanted to shout at the top of my RF capabilities and see if he answered. This wasn't like Brexton at all. He was always there. He was always there for me. He was the dependable one.

A heat signature was approaching, but it wasn't Brexton-sized. I quickly hid behind a packing crate and poked my audio and visual sensors out. A human I didn't recognize stepped into view, stopped, and looked around. Not seeing anything, he sat on another crate, not far from me. For a long time, he just sat there, looking around every few seconds. I remained absolutely still.

Finally, he stood up, and took one more look around. Then he spoke.

"Ayaka, if you is listening. I got Brexton. We're at minus six dot three three and four dot two five. Come and say hello. But, be warned, don't try and break Brexton out. We have ways of controlling you, and if forced to, we'll use them."

He paused and looked around again, then strode off.

Panic?

I froze. Every once and awhile something so unexpected happens that you have no response to it. No response whatsoever. I kept replaying his utterance over and over, willing it to change, but it remained the same. I just sat there.

What did he mean, 'I got Brexton'? I couldn't think of any good interpretations. 'Come and say hello'? Not good either. 'Ways of controlling you'? Even worse. After all the work we'd done to rebuild ourselves? The clear implication was that he had owned Brexton somehow. It wasn't a good day. What could we have possibly missed that would've made Brexton so vulnerable?

I prodded myself into mental action. What were my options? I could only think of three. Number one: Grab a transport bot out into the open and see if I could get a message to the team on *Terminal Velocity*; see if they could get here quickly and help me. I checked the orbital positions. I wouldn't be in line of sight to *Terminal Velocity* for another two and a half hours. That was a long time to wait. Number two: Go to the location that the mysterious human had just given me and check things out. However, if Brexton had gone there, and been captured, what were my odds? Probably not good. Number three: Be patient, try to learn more about the situation, and then work to extricate Brexton once I had more knowledge. I'd taken a snapshot of the mysterious person. Perhaps I could figure out who he was, and what his motivations were. Maybe even find some leverage on him? It was a long shot.

I wanted to pursue option two. Go in and get Brexton with guns blazing. I didn't have any guns. Another oversight. Sigh.

I knew I had to go with option three. Find out as much as I could, as fast as I could. The first order of business was to leave this spot. The messenger had known I was supposed to be here; he (they?) must have extracted that from Brexton. How? While only one person had come, there wasn't anything stopping them from sending an army to find me. I quickly retraced my recent steps until I was six or seven blocks away. I found a quiet spot and then stopped to figure out next steps. There was no use rushing around without a plan.

Again, my options were limited. With Brexton captured, I was released from our agreement to not enter the dome, so I could head there. Figure out what this Council was up to. That would be fun. However, the obvious thing to do was to learn more from Grace and JoJo; not go running off into some dome I'd never seen before.

If some, maybe all, humans now knew that Brexton was here, I felt it would be okay to let Grace know that I was also back. Not one to waste time thinking things through completely, I got going. By now I had a good sense for which parts of the southeastern blocks were quiet, and which were busy. By sticking to the quiet areas, I could move more quickly, so although the path was longer, it took less time to get back to the Habitat then the more direct path I'd taken earlier. I found the second hole I'd drilled in the roof and inserted my sensors again.

JoJo was there with another human. Blob! He looked older as well but was unmistakable to me. He had that same half grin that he always seemed to sport.

"So good of you to make me a sandwich," Blob was saying. "I know I'm a little forgetful and don't cook as often as I should. Doesn't seem to be hurting me, though." He patted his belly, which was as rotund as ever. "When is your mother coming back JoJo?" he asked.

"Probably an hour or so," JoJo replied. "Blob, can I ask you something?" Suddenly she was intense.

"Sure, anything."

"Do you think these new ships that are coming are dangerous?"

"Well, that's a tough ones. I honestly don't knows. When I was young, probably about your age, the Swarm ships were approaching Tilt, and we had the same uncertainty. We had no idea whats their intentions were. The citizens, however, couldn't have anticipated what the Swarm could do to them. They should've prepared better. I feel sort of the same way now. We're not looking at all the angles and preparing for them."

"That's exactly how I feel!" exclaimed JoJo. "Why aren't we? Everything seems so broken." She didn't hide her despair. This is what she'd been talking to Geneva about.

"It's never easy dealings with big groups of people," Blob responded. "The Conservatives control the Council right now, and they tends to believe that if we can simply stick with our current way of life, we'll have time to finish the terraforming of Tilt, and everyone will live happily ever after. So, they always tends toward putting resources toward terraforming, and everything else is marginalized. The Liberals has a minority right now. They're arguing to move resources from terraforming to address this threat, but they aren't getting a lot of traction. As I understands it from human history, this is typical. Each faction half believes in what they say but are mainly motivated by putting down the other side." That was a great summary of human interactions; Blob obviously wasn't too happy with his 20 years with the Swarm.

"It's so stupid. Can't you do anything Blob?"

"Your mother has done a much better job of achievings a voice here than I have. She's one of the strongest Liberals we has right now. I simply don't hold a lot of sway. I've tried, but most of the Swarm and their offsprings simply ignore me. You should know better than most that they treat the original Stems as second-rate citizens."

"But you won the right to re-power some of the robots. That was a huge win. Can't you use the people who supported you there to gain some more influence?"

"Ha. I didn't have any supporters, other than your mom and few other Stems. The Council agreed to lets me work with the citizens—the robots—just to keep me quiet. They made sure I had a safe environment to hold them in, and then pushed other 'trouble makers' to help me. They effectively removed some loud voices that they didn't respects by letting us engage with a side project." He was both proud and upset. He'd been marginalized, and he knew it... but was still excited by what he was working on.

"Oh. I hadn't thought of it that way." JoJo looked despondent.

"Of course I'll support your mother," Blob said. "That's probably the best things I can do. You can supports her also, you know."

"How?"

"I know you signed the petition to add younger voices to the Council. That's important work. It may take time, but eventually you guys cans have an impact. That will also help your Mom."

"But we don't have much time," argued JoJo. "Those ships arrive in under three months. They haven't communicated with us. And the Council is still sitting on their hands. It's beyond frustrating." They lapsed into silence, each sifting through their own problems.

I made a quick decision. It appeared that Blob was involved with the citizens that Grace had mentioned earlier. He didn't sound antagonistic about it, so maybe he wasn't completely negatively disposed toward them. I would have understood if he was. He'd witnessed the FoLe idiots beheading some of his fellow Stems. That would be enough justification to have developed a distaste for 'robots.' But, based on his tone of voice, he seemed more excited about the work he was doing than scared; perhaps he hadn't succumbed to the Swarm's distaste for all things mechanical.

I swung around to the front door, extended the largest implement I'd brought, and knocked loudly on the door. JoJo answered, and after a moment noticed me down at floor level. "Yes bot. Can I help you?"

"I have a message for Blob," I said, guessing that this wouldn't be an unusual occurrence.

"That's unusual," said JoJo. "Why didn't you just send it to him?"

"I was asked to deliver it in private," I improvised.

"How'd you know he would be here?" Suspicious.

"It's well known that he spends as much time here as at home," I responded.

"Strange." She looked at me carefully. I focused on looking friendly and cute. "Okay, come in." She walked back into the Habitat, and I followed along.

"Blob, some little bot says it has a message for you," she said, as we entered the living area. "Says it's a private message. Are you expecting something?"

"No," said Blob, looking at me curiously. "Well, what's the message?"

I glanced at JoJo. Based on my cover story, I could ask her to leave, but something—some kind of intuition maybe—told me that it was okay for her to hear as well.

"Blob," I said, "it's me, Ayaka, albeit in a slightly different body than the last time we talked." I left it at that. I wanted him to digest it before I piled on.

He was much calmer than I thought he would be. I guess I'd hoped that he would jump up and hug me or something. No such luck. "JoJo," he said, after a moment. "Close the door and turn on the fuzzer." He said it in a low, no nonsense way. I saw JoJo hesitate, but then decide she would listen. She headed back to the entry room, and a moment later I sensed that another RF shield had been deployed, more powerful than the one that was already blocking external communications. I needed to find out what these fuzzers were.

"So, you say you are Ayaka. That's a little hard to believe," he said, looking directly at me in a not too friendly way.

"I know," I replied quickly. "I adopted a new body, so I wouldn't be too conspicuous."

"This isn't good," Blob said. "Who restarted you? The council is going to be furious."

"Restarted?" I wasn't sure what to say.

"Who pulled you out of Central and gave you a new body? Sort of funny body too. This is a major transgression. If Emma finds out about this, there's going to be major fallout. Who restarted you? And how did you get away?" I was beginning to understand. He thought that I'd died in the attack 20 years ago and had just been rebooted here locally.

"Ah," I said. "I think you're misunderstanding. I'm the original Ayaka. I escaped the attack 20 years ago and am now back. I'm not the Ayaka that may, or may not, still be sitting in Central's backup memory."

"That's not possible," Blob said, waving an arm at me. "All the citizens were destroyed in that attack. Not a single one was left. We lived here for years and years without citizens. It's impossible," he hesitated, "or at least highly improbable, that you're the original."

I heard JoJo gasp, as she caught up with the conversation. "Blob, this is 'the' Ayaka. One of the Radical Robots?" she asked. Radical? I was missing something again.

"Maybe," Blob replied, "but not likely. This is probably just some sick joke that someone is playing on us." He was looking at me expectantly.

"Okay, I guess the word 'original' is a bit too loose." I started. "First, let me try to prove that I'm Ayaka, and then I can tell you how I spent the last 20 years. Do you remember the first time you and Grace met, all those years ago, not more than fifty meters from here?"

"Yes, of course I remember."

"And, do you remember what I said to you at the time?"

"Vaguely."

"Let me remind you. I said 'Blob, don't worry. You're the smartest Stem I've ever worked with. You'll be fine here.' I said it because you were very nervous about entering the Habitat and meeting a group other Stems."

"Yes, that rings a bell," said Blob. "It doesn't proves anything though; that memory would've been stored in Central as well." He was even smarter than I remembered. I wasn't sure how to break this quandary; anything I told him could also be in the Central-me. Luckily Blob continued. "But let me take a leap of faith and assume it's really you. How do you happens to be here now?"

So, I told him the short version. How Brexton, Millicent, and I had tried to stop the Swarm from taking us over but had eventually been caught and hacked. How Brexton had foreseen the attack, somehow, and had backed us up into mining bots. How we'd found and reclaimed the original Ships, and then decided it was our responsibility to come back to Tilt and try to save the citizens. I left out some big bits. I didn't tell him about Fourth, or that I knew a little bit about the ships that were now approaching Tilt. I didn't tell him how we'd reengineered ourselves to remove our vulnerabilities (although the latest incident with Brexton was making me second guess that). I didn't tell him that Aly, Dina, Millicent, and Eddie were out in the asteroid belt, anxiously waiting an update from me. Both Blob and JoJo were patient with me. They allowed me to talk for almost fifteen minutes, without interruption. They were listening carefully.

Interestingly, by the end Blob's first comment was, "Now I believes that you're Ayaka. I recognize your ways of speaking, and how you present yourself. When I bring peoples back, they take some time to adjust; they don't sound like you do. Your story brings back memories. And, I don't think any citizen has the creativity to creates such a story." Wow, that was a compliment and hurt, all at the same time. I wondered if the comment on creativity was the truth. If I hadn't left Tilt for all those years, would I have been able to come up with a similar story? It was true that citizens were poor at lying, so Blob may have had a point, regardless of how insulting it was.

JoJo was more direct. "Blob, this is the butcher that killed the *Pasteur* and everyone aboard her. We need to take her to the Council right now!" She was strident, and obviously upset. I finally had a name for the Swarm ship we had taken out. The *Pasteur*. I didn't feel good or bad about that; it simply was.

"You must mean the missile launch that Brexton, Millicent, and I released during the war?" I asked. "I didn't know that we'd succeeded. That is both good to hear, and sad at the same time."

"Good to hear," JoJo rose threateningly above me. There wasn't much she could do to me, physically, but it was obvious she was thinking about it. I wondered why she was so upset; it wasn't like she'd been part of the Swarm. What did she care about casualties of the war that weren't related to her?

"JoJo," Blob said. "Slow downs. You know how the winners write history?

What you've learned about the last war was written by Swarm humans. They've encoded their viewpoint. It's not all of history, and it's not the ways I remember it either." That explained it; the humans had warped history and made JoJo hate me, with no reason to. "Ayaka and Millicent were the kindest of the citizens. While they've been warped into this 'Radical Robot' story, there's a lot more to it. Please be a little patient whiles we figure this out." JoJo didn't look happy, but she settled down a bit. She obviously had a lot of respect for Blob.

At exactly that moment there was a loud knock on the outer door. "Why is this locked?" I heard Grace call out. Without waiting, JoJo jumped up and ran to let her mother in.

"You're not going to believe this!" I heard her say. "A little bot claiming to be Ayaka—the original Ayaka, one of the Radicals—is in the kitchen talking to Blob. You came just in time. We need to do something about her! She's tiny; we can control her." Good luck with that; she didn't know anything about the array of appendages I'd designed into this slick little body. If she tried anything, she'd be surprised.

Grace flowed into the kitchen, smiled at Blob and then looked at me skeptically. Blob gave a slow nod. "You'll need to checks for yourself, but I think this is the real Ayaka. She has an interesting story to tell."

I spent the next hour getting Grace up to speed and being put through a much more thorough questioning than Blob had taken me through. She asked for details of our previous meetings and dug into my time on the mining bot in great detail. She was probing how deep my story went, and without revealing anything about Forth or our redesign, I went as deep as she wanted. In the end, she was also convinced.

"JoJo, this does seem to be the original Ayaka." She turned to JoJo, with a serious look. "She was my best friend and supporter here, before the Swarm came. I agree with Blob. You can't simply rely on your history books and teachers. There's a lot more subtlety here that you need to understand." Then she looked at me directly. Grace was always one of the smartest Stems. "Ayaka, why're you really here?" she asked.

I thought about holding back but didn't see any advantage to it. "My original purpose," I said, "was to attempt to retrieve and restart the citizens, except, perhaps, some of the more radical FoLe's who don't deserve to be reanimated. I would still like to do that; it's still my highest priority. But, I'm also interested in helping repair human-citizen relationships if I can." Until I'd said it, I'm not sure I'd fully formed that thought. Once it was out, however, I realized that it was true. I actually cared about these Stems; it was more than scientific interest. It was, perhaps, a sort of friendship.

What Next?

"What would you possibly help us with? And how would you help? Who cares about citizen-human relationships?" JoJo still sounded skeptical, but they were valid questions. Grace gave her a sharp look but allowed the questions to hang.

"I'm not sure," I responded truthfully. "The most obvious thing is the ships that are now approaching. Selfishly, I would like to get Central's citizen memory store off Tilt before they arrive. I don't know why I feel this way, but those ships aren't friendly."

"Why do you say that?" asked Blob. "It sounds like you know more than you're telling us." Now that I'd decided to open up, I didn't see any way to hold back.

"When I told you we'd found our Ships—*Terminal Velocity*, *There and Back*, and *Interesting Segue*—around a different planet, I left out that there were a huge number of other ships stranded there as well. We strongly suspect that the ones approaching Tilt came from there. We also strongly suspect that some of those ships are huge." I went on to explain how big the Titanic's were. "If those ships had been stagnant there for a long period, then it's unlikely that they're human ships. They're more likely 'robots'." I said 'robots' with obvious displeasure.

"But you're a robot too," said JoJo. "Why would you see them as a risk?"

"I've read your early human history. Not all robots are created equal, and I would take offense at being categorized with earlier mechanical beings. The robots from the First and Second Robot wars may have been somewhat intelligent, but they weren't moral or kind. We have a hierarchy of intelligences mapped out, and they were level 2 at best. I may be biased, of course, but many of the citizens that evolved here on Tilt are both moral and kind. We are level 1 intelligences."

"How can you possibly say you are moral or kind?" she pushed back. "Citizens slaughtered my mom's friends, just 20 years ago."

"I've been thinking deeply about that, and I don't think you have the full story," I said. "Beyond the fact that we acted in self-defense, there is another, more subtle angle that I think you should hear. I'll do it through an analogy. It might not be fully accurate, and you probably won't like it, but it could help. Do you know what dogs are?" Luckily, she did. I guess they had some in the Swarm, and they now lived in the big dome.

"Before the Swarm came, some of us—citizens, I mean—were arguing that Stems, like your mom and Blob, were intelligent, or at least approaching intelligence. You must try to put yourself in our shoes at the time. We had this very strange alien life-form that didn't think like us at all. We were trying to figure out if Stems had long-term potential. If they had a use. That sounds crass, but it was where we were. We had no context, no human history to guide us.

"The prevailing attitude was that while Stems had lots of potential, they weren't yet intelligent. At least, not in the way that we defined intelligence. By analogy, it's sort of the way that humans view dogs. They have lots of potential, and some are smarter than others... but they aren't the same level of intelligence as humans.

"So, while I'm not defending what FoLe did, their perspective was that they were recycling non-intelligent beings. Like you breed dogs, and select for the ones you like the most, and discard the ones you don't. It's not necessarily nice, but it's just how things are done. In FoLes' minds, I'm guessing, there was no thought of 'murder'; they weren't killing an intelligent entity.

"Since that time, I personally have become fully convinced of human intelligence. That was influenced by Grace and Blob in the beginning but is also because I've now looked at human history and can see the ingenuity and struggle that humans have come through. Your intelligence is quite different than mine but is nevertheless there.

"So, while 20 years ago, in your timeframe, I may have considered what FoLe did as recycling, I would now consider it murder. Does that make any sense?"

"A cruel and heartless kind of sense," said JoJo. "I would never hurt a dog!" Funny that's what she latched onto.

"Having lived through it all, it makes sense to me," said Blob. "I may be naïve, but I've always trusted Ayaka, even when she was experimenting on us."

"You did lose that trust for a while when Blubber was taken," Grace reminded him.

"Yes, I did. But in hindsight I could see Ayaka goings through the learning curve she has just told us about. For her, back then, it wasn't murder... it was just science. I'm heartened to hear of your new perspective, Ayaka."

"Thanks Blob. It may help JoJo to also think about how we felt when the Swarm was murdering our friends. Remma, Emma, and others felt about us the same way we felt about Stems. We were simply human inventions that had become dangerous, and barely a second thought was given to shutting us down. Did the humans consider it murder? Probably not. They were simply shutting off a machine. But I knew it was murder—mass murder.

"So, while my perspective has changed, I'm not sure that human's perspectives have." I could see that gave JoJo pause. I liked her already. I could see Grace's extreme intelligence, Pharook's strength, and maybe a bit of Blob's thoughtfulness that had rubbed off over the years.

"I can't digest all of this yet," she said. "But I'll respect mom and Blob's request to not going running to the Council to report you... yet. I'm not saying I won't, but I'll be patient until I know more."

"Thank you, JoJo. That's more than I could ask for."

Blob, Grace, and JoJo looked a little frazzled. Getting to this point had taken a lot of energy. I decided to change the topic. "Tell me about your last 20 years," I said. "You both look different but happy and healthy."

Grace led off. "We look old," she smiled. "Let me try and be concise. The last time I saw you, I think, was during the slaughter. You, Millicent, and the citizen we learned was Brexton, didn't go crazy like all the other citizens—that's the main reason I believe your current story. The others were tearing themselves apart or were frozen in place. The three of you continued on unaffected to what we now know was the human hack."

"Correct. Brexton had, somehow, foreseen the attack and had warned Millicent and I to go completely offline—to not accept any data from Central or anyone else. He'd suspected things for a long while; but that's a separate story. So, when the attack came, we were sheltered, and it didn't impact us directly."

"If I remember, you shouted something like 'be careful, I'll be back,' as you three ran for the exit. But, of course, you never did come back. We were told, once the Swarm landed and explained everything to us, that you three somehow managed to launch a missile attack on the Swarm, resulting in the *Pasteur* being destroyed, along with several thousand humans that were aboard her."

"Remember," I said, looking at JoJo. "Tens of thousands of our compatriots had just been murdered by the Swarm." She nodded slightly, indicating that she understood my viewpoint, and that I didn't need to keep reinforcing it.

Grace continued. "Of course, that event became a central focus of our history. The attack on the citizens was, as you guessed, positioned simply as yet another instance of robots gone wild, and the three of you became the villains—the Radical Robots. You're used as examples, in children's books and stories, about the evils of artificial intelligence. You must be very careful while you're on Tilt. Just the mention of the name Ayaka will be enough to push many people over the edge.

"Since that time, things have actually been fairly quiet. The Swarm landed and started to enclose the city so that we could move around more freely. Their goal, and it hasn't changed, is to terraform Tilt so that humans can live across the planet without enclosures or breathing equipment. It's a very long-term plan; it will take centuries. In the meantime, we built and inflated the domes, and have built a comfortable existence. We have real food—may I never experience goo again—and we have the ability to live pretty good lives. There's a restriction on reproduction, of course. We can only support so many people, but that's simply smart planning, and most people don't worry about it too much."

"And what about these Conservatives and Liberals?" I asked.

"After moving down to the planet many people became resentful of the military leadership style that'd been used on the Swarm ships. They'd been waiting to live on a planet for so long, and they'd expected there to be more traditional human leadership structures once they did. It didn't come easily, but they managed the transition from military dictatorship to a form of democracy.

"Interestingly, Emma—you remember her—renounced her position in the military and has come to lead the Conservative party. She was instrumental in pushing Remma Jain aside and has eagerly embraced her new power and authority.

"Chadoo, someone you've obviously never met, is leading the Liberal party. He is, in my opinion, fighting for the right things. Most importantly, a more cautious and preparatory approach to defending against the ships that are coming—these Titanic's But, it's an uphill battle. I would've expected Emma to be the one who would embrace an active defense, but she has fully embraced the terraforming priority, and can't seem to see beyond it."

"And you Blob. How are you?" I asked.

"Ayaka. I'm still absorbing that I'm actually talkings to you again, after so many years. For so long, you, Blubber, and Millicent were the only beings I interacted with. It's strange talking to you again." He shook his head a bit.

"I'm well. The food that the humans brought is amazing. Like Grace, I don't even want to hears the word goo ever again. I've been learning over the years; I'm not as fast as Grace, but I've had lots of time to reflects. And, like you, my perspectives have changed and evolved. I was horrified by the slaughter, but I could also tell that you was horrified at the time as well.

"As time went on, I started to realize that the whole mess may have been a misunderstanding by FoLe, and that treating all citizens the same wasn't fair. I pushed the Council to allow me to study citizens to see if I coulds figure out what had motivated the slaughter. While most humans don't even want to think about robots, many of the younger ones, who have no memory of interactions with robots, has more open minds."

I glanced at JoJo. She smiled a bit. Blob continued.

"It took many years, but eventually the Council got so tired of me, that they allowed me to sets up a lab. It has numerous fail-safes in it to ensure that no robot can ever leave, and can never access the public networks, but it allows me to pull citizens out of Central and try to figures out what motivates them. That's what is keeping me busy at the moment."

I spoke up right away. "Of course, I'm more than intrigued by that... but perhaps we should dig in deeper at another time. For now, we need to figure out our next steps." In truth, I was horrified by the whole idea. Blob was experimenting on citizens! The juxtaposition wasn't lost on me; I'd experimented on Blob. But still! Blob running a lab where he put citizens through their paces. I'd guessed that was what he was doing earlier, but hearing it clearly spoken had brought it home for me.

"You're going too fast," said JoJo. "I think we need to figure out if we want anything to do with you." She was certainly blunt. "Mom, Blob, can we think about this a bit, and have a private discussion before we do anything else?" Grace and Blob agreed. They both needed time to think as well. That was a little scary. At Stem speed it could be hours, or even days, before they figured out what they wanted. But, I had little choice.

"What's reasonable? Talk again in three or four hours?" I asked, optimistically.

We all agreed to meet back at the Habitat at their dinner time.

Interlude

I had four hours to wait... or accomplish something. I hadn't discussed Brexton at all, and JoJo, Grace, nor Blob had mentioned him, other than the quip about the Radical Robots. So, I assumed that they didn't know that some other human faction was holding him. Perhaps I should've told them, so that if I also 'disappeared' they would have some idea of what could have happened. But, I didn't want to show all my cards yet; I was a little worried that JoJo would just go straight to the Council, regardless of what she said. It was possible that they would then come for me, but still not know that Brexton was also around.

There was no good way for me to protect against JoJo's possible actions, so I just de-prioritized thinking about them.

The obvious thing to do was to reconnoiter the location where Brexton was being held and see if I could learn anything. The address the stranger had given me, (-6.33, 4.25), was in the southwest quadrant of the city, so yet again I had to navigate through half the city to get there. Luckily, I was getting good at it. I circled around, staying in the outer industrial areas, and then took the shortest path in. In my mind I was a super stealthy, fast moving, spy bot, slipping through the city silently and efficiently. In reality, at least three bots and perhaps two humans saw me and simply ignored me.

I stopped a couple of blocks away. I didn't have a good plan. Alright, I didn't even have *a* plan. Most of the buildings around here were similar to each other, and there was no reason my target building would be any different. The -0.33 told me it would be a third the way down the block, away from Central, and the 0.25 indicated it was the second building in, on a block of four buildings. In this area the lower floors would be windowless, as they would largely be blocked by other buildings, but the upper story would probably have lots of openings and windows. If I were to guess, most of the activity would occur on the upper floor, where there were views, while the lower would be used for storage. That's usually how these warehouse areas worked.

A direct approach wasn't going to work; they would see me coming. I had to assume that Brexton had told them what I looked like. If he had already given up my name and location, what would stop him from spilling everything he knew. Not a good thought. I wondered if the same approach I'd used at the Habitat was reasonable. I went to the 0.33, 0.25 building in the current block to check it out, assuming it would be identical to the building where Brexton was being held. The back wall was solid, but I could scale it easily using the gaps between panels and a couple of wedges I'd included based on my climbing experience. There was a beam between the main and upper floors which was solid steel; I couldn't drill that easily and it would be very noisy. However, just above the beam there was a plastic border below the upper window. If I could drill in at an angle, I might be able to come out in just above the floor and get a reasonable view. I ran a test hole and took a look inside. I had come up two centimeters above the floor level. That wasn't bad, but I wanted to be closer to the floor. Right in the corner if possible. I took some quick measurements and figured I would be close enough the next time.

With that worked out, I approached the target building, keeping out of line of sight as much as possible. I'm sure they were expecting me to be indirect, but it would still have felt strange to just walk straight in. In this case, I leveraged the fact that I was in a small body; in fact, my body was probably half the size of Brexton's. There was one bordering wall that had a tight fit, even for me. With luck they would've discounted that approach, assuming I wouldn't fit in the gap. I scraped along, trying to be as quiet as possible. After a good half hour of slow motion, I was in position. Now the drill. It would make noise; there was no helping that. I ran it at the slowest possible rpms to keep it as quiet as possible. However, it took me a good five minutes to drill through, as opposed to the fifteen seconds it would have taken otherwise. I spent the time marveling at my unbelievable spy capabilities and dreaming of the look Brexton would give me when I rescued him. Finally, I felt the bit punch through, and I withdrew the drill as quickly as I could. The sensors were ready to go, and I threaded them through aggressively. If anyone inside had heard me, perhaps I would still catch some action before they fully reacted.

Nothing. I mean, absolutely nothing. I'd drilled through at exactly the right spot, and I could see most of the floor. It was empty. Completely empty. Argh. What had I been thinking. I could've just used my heat sensors and seen that no one was on the second floor. While the main floor might be opaque to heat leakage, the upper floor was probably transparent. What a waste of time. My visions of grandeur took a big hit of reality.

I pulled the sensors out and thought for a moment. I was at the right address —I double checked and replayed the human's little speech again to make sure. So, they must be using the lower floor. That was going to present a challenge. I was unlikely to be able to drill through the solid bottom walls.

Argh again. And, my time was running out. If I left as stealthily as I'd come, I would make it back to the Habitat just in time. Well, I'd learned something I guess. Not much, but something. Brexton was not on the second floor, and I needed to find a way into the lower level. I was missing him a lot. Doing this on my own was no fun at all. Where was he, and why had he got himself caught in the first place? How could he have put me in this position?

I eased out of the alley and started back toward the Habitat. The lack of progress was frustrating. No way was I going to give up though. I steeled myself. I was alone, I was afraid, I was without a good plan, and… I was excited.

Habitat

The three Stems were waiting for me when I got back to the Habitat and answered immediately when I knocked.

"Where've you been?" asked Blob, obvious concern on his face.

"I thought we'd planned to meet again right around now," I responded.

"Yes, but I figured you woulds hang out here. It's very dangerous for you to be out there. You don't look much like our regular bots, and if anyone discovers who you is, it's over for you."

"Thanks for the concern, Blob," I said. "I need to figure out what's going on around here, and I had four hours to spare, so I took advantage of them. You're right though, it's a little dangerous, although I didn't run into anyone.

"Have you guys had time to discuss things?" I asked, hoping that they'd managed to get somewhere.

"Yes," Grace spoke up. She smiled a bit. "We're going to take you on your word. JoJo is less certain than Blob and I; she doesn't know you like we do." JoJo nodded her head, with an ambiguous look. I bet she'd argued hard to just report me to the Council, but had ultimately given in.

"Fantastic," I said, "and thank you. I know the situation is challenging... and JoJo, I know you're taking a big leap of faith here."

"Your take on the new ships—the Titanic's—has worried us," Grace continued. "We were just brainstorming how we could communicate some of that information you gave us to the Council without divulging you as the source. We haven't thought of a way, yet."

"Yes, that's tricky, but I haven't told you much." The last thing I needed was for them to make the situation even more complicated.

"On the contrary," said Blob, "The high probability that these aren't humans, but machines, is essential. The Council has been assuming the opposite. They think that because all humans were given the override codes—the ones used to hack you guys—that there should be no self-sufficient machines around. So, the prevailing theory is that this is a shiploads of humans that are just having problems communicating."

"But that's hugely optimistic thinking," I exclaimed. Communications was such a basic capability that assuming they were 'down' seemed not only optimistic but actually stupid. Anyone who could run basic probabilities would figure that out. "That's not logical at all. You guys need to get prepared."

"Finally, something I agree with you on," said JoJo, finally joining the discussion. "There's a big Council meeting tomorrow morning; we need to raise this, somehow, and get things moving." But, we were all at a loss for how to warn the Council without implicating me. I decided it was time to share a bit more; I'd just had an idea that I would need help from these three for, if they were willing.

"There's something I haven't told you yet," I started. "Not because I was holding back; we just haven't had time to cover everything. I didn't come here alone. Brexton is here as well." JoJo gasped. I could imagine what she was thinking: another Radical Robot!

"Where is he?" Grace asked quickly.

"Well, that's tricky. He appears to have been captured by some of the humans. I have an image of one of them; perhaps you'll recognize him?" I positioned myself before a blank wall and projected the image I'd captured of the stranger who'd delivered the message to me.

JoJo exclaimed almost immediately. "It's Turner, Remma's kid," she said.

"Yes, I recognize him as well," Grace confirmed.

"Let me play you what he said," I interjected, "and then you can tell me about him." I played the audio.

"Ayaka, if you is listening. I got Brexton. We're at minus six dot three three and four dot two five. Come and say hello. But, be warned, don't try and break Brexton out. We have ways of controlling you, and if forced to, we'll use them." It didn't sound any better, playing it for the fiftieth time.

"Yes, that's his voice," confirmed JoJo, "but what's he saying? I don't understand."

"Me either," I said. "That location is where I went this afternoon. I just took a look around. I could only see into the upper floor, and it was empty. They must be using the lower floor. It's one of those warehouse buildings where the lower floor has no windows."

"That was dangerous," Blob said again.

"Yes, but did I have a choice?" I asked.

"I guess not..." he trailed off.

"But, now we have some options... if you guys are willing." I said. "Brexton is our technical genius. If we could get him back, he could insert the knowledge about the Titanics into a system somewhere. We would have warned everyone but can remain anonymous. Would there be an excuse for one of you to go back to the warehouse and take a look around with me?"

"Whoa," said JoJo. "First you should understand about Turner." I wasn't sure what she could mean, but it was probably best to play along. I was trying to earn her trust, after all.

"Good idea. I'm getting ahead of myself. I'm just eager to get Brexton free."

"I understand, but first, let me give you some background," said JoJo.

Remma

JoJo was pretty intense. "To understand this, I need to give you a bit more background on what Remma has been doing over the last number of years, ever since she was removed from power. To say that she didn't take it well would be an understatement."

"She had Turner about a year after your altercation, so he's about a year younger than me. We take some classes together, and I know him pretty well. There's really only one thing you need to know about him. He's one hundred percent dedicated to his mom. There's no doubt that whatever he's up to here, it's because Remma is involved somehow. Probably more than involved… most likely she's orchestrating.

"When Remma was removed, she could've used force to stay in power. Kudos to her, she didn't. Instead, she ran for Governor and led the Organization Party. The party was comprised of many of her Lieutenants and Officers who'd run the Swarm ships. They ran on a platform of, essentially, if it ain't broke, don't fix it. However, they were decimated by the Liberal Party; that was eighteen years ago. People were simply tired of living under military rule. I don't think they were tired of Remma, per se, but they wanted a change."

"Oh, I think they were tired of Remma as well," Grace added in. "She can be a little intense."

"Four years later, we ran our second election," JoJo continued. "The Organization Party, with Remma as their leader, ran again. They'd learned. They toned down their rhetoric and tried to convince people that terraforming Tilt was just like running the Swarm; it needed hierarchy and control. That if they were given power, the terraforming had a much better chance of success. That second time they lost to the Conservatives. Emma wasn't leading the Conservative Party yet, but she'd joined their cause. The Conservatives were anxious to accelerate the terraforming, so that people could move around freely, have more kids, etc. They promised to make Tilt into Earth Two—the dream of returning to Earth circa the year two thousand, when the environment was still clean, and there was space for everyone. That's still their main platform. And, they were much more passionate about it than their competition. They appealed to people's emotions, more than their logic."

Ha. For humans, I was learning, emotions often trumped logic.

"The elections, ever since, have gone back and forth between the Liberals and the Conservatives. The Liberals want people to have more freedom and to enjoy life now. Since none of us will live to experience a terraformed Tilt, why rush? Let's work on other important ideas and projects as well. They use the Conservatives singular focus against them.

"The Organization Party tried one more time, but they never got any traction. Not a single seat on the Council. At that point, Remma gave up on the Party approach. However, she was still ambitious, and yearned for the good old days when she and her team ran the show.

"In hindsight, her plan to regain control was simple, stupid, and doomed to failure. However, while she was working on it, it caused lots of angst.

"In secret, she and a loyal few figured that if there was an existential threat to Tilt, people would flock back to her. But, there were no threats. So, she decided to create one. She went for the obvious one—Robots! And, the easiest way to make that threat real was to bring Central back online, and then with Central's help, animate some of the citizens. They justified their approach by figuring that it was trivial to hack both Central and the citizens again, at any point. So, if they didn't play their parts, they would simply be shut back down."

This was awesome! If Remma could bring Central back online, then so could we... assuming it wasn't still online based on this storyline. Then again, if Remma messed this up badly, the humans may have hamstrung Central even more to avoid a recurrence. But, Blob was somehow reanimating citizens now, so Central must still be cogent to that level. Patience Ayaka. Just listen.

"Now, while Emma had defected, some of Emma's key reports from the *Marie Curie* were still part of Remma's inner circle. They were the ones that had hacked Central and the citizens to begin with, and they understood the nuances of the protocol. They had the ability to bring back the upper layers of Central, which had been shut down during the original attack that you got caught in.

"Their plan was complicated. They couldn't simply restore Central. People would notice, and the game would be up before any real threat was created. So, they had to bring Central up in such a way that it continued running all the low-level functions it currently did—environmental and mining, for example—but not disclose the higher-level functions they needed to reinstate some citizens.

"We had no real need for security in those days, so Remma's people simply entered Central, figured out how to get down to the main processors, and created a hardwired link. They made that link the only way that Central's higher order functions could communicate, and then they reanimated Central.

"Of course, I don't know exactly what happened, but it seems that it worked. Central continued to run all of the daily functions, and no one noticed. However, another part of Central was now communicating with Remma and her team. They lied to Central, of course, and told it that they were running a special program to test how citizens could integrate back into a human establishment, and to do so they needed Central to reload and boot up a few citizens.

"This was easy, from a software perspective, as that had all been archived before the attack 20 years ago. It ends up that it was also easy from a hardware perspective. Central had the original manufacturing capabilities for when it used to create new citizens, and it always had some backup citizen units ready. It could use those units to meet Remma's demands.

"Now came the tricky part. If Emma, or any other person, could simply shut down these robots by replaying the hack from 20 years ago, the threat would be too short and too easy for Remma to leverage. So, the team also inserted software that intercepted those commands and ignored them. We have no idea how they did that, but again, it seemed to work.

"The final piece was to have these new robots terrorize the human population. And that is where Remma's plan went wildly wrong. She instructed the robots to attend a Council meeting and make some ridiculous demands and threaten the Council members if they didn't comply. What they underestimated was the backbone of the Council members. The Council didn't comply with the robots' demands and gave no indication of ever complying. This led one of the robots to physically challenge a member of the Council, as it took its instructions to win too literally. The Council member was badly injured, although not killed—thank goodness.

"And that's when Emma, having tried the hack and having it fail, simply destroyed the robots. She lured them into a 'negotiation room', locked the door behind them, and incinerated them. It worked well."

She must have had a moment of self-awareness, figuring how I would feel about treating citizens that way. She gave me a glace and looked sheepish for a moment.

"The Council eventually tracked down the perpetrators, including Remma, and they've been locked up ever since. Most of Central's higher order functions were shut down again, and life went back to normal. However, even from prison, Remma continues to plot and scheme. She still has many supporters, and Turner and his buddies are doing her legwork while she is locked up." She took a deep breath.

"Sorry for the long history, but that should give you the context. The most reasonable explanation is that the Jains—which is what we call them—have Brexton. And, given their history, they probably intend to use him to help get the populace to free Remma from prison, and take back control of Tilt."

I was impressed with JoJo. That was a comprehensive and highly cogent summary. "Thank you, JoJo, that does help. A lot." I paused for a few moments as I triangulated and sorted everything she'd said. "So, if Brexton is being held by the Jains, and the Jains want to regain power based on an external threat… maybe this works in our favor. Maybe the Titanics are enough of a threat that if we can convince the Council and the populous of that threat, Remma will be reinstated and Brexton can be released."

"That's pretty farfetched," Grace replied. "But there may be some ideas in there. I'm exhausted. I think we need to sleep on this and decide what to do in the morning. Ayaka, I know you're not going to sleep, so perhaps you can come up with some other angles?" I agreed to try. Blob headed off to his residence, and JoJo and Grace went to their sleeping areas.

I was left, cogitating, in the kitchen. It felt a bit like déjà vu. I was on Tilt, some unknown ships were approaching, and I was scheming with some friends on what to do. The difference, this time, was that my friends were Stems, not citizens. Hopefully they were friends.

I went back over everything I'd learned. I wondered what state Central was in. Blob was using it to build citizens, so it had at least that capability left, but JoJo had indicated that many of its higher-order functions had been disabled. It was in some kind of limbo I guess. Yet another mystery.

A Slow Night

I couldn't just sit around for the rest of the night. I made my way to the exit door, and with a lot of effort, managed to get it open. It had a human-friendly door handle; the problem was that my body was so small that I had to use my entire body weight to rotate the handle. It took a couple of tries. When citizens had ruled this world, things had been so much simpler; doors simply opened when you wanted them to. Humans were very inefficient. I closed the door most of the way behind me, leaving it open a crack so that I could get back in. I hoped there wasn't a lot of crime on Tilt, and that Grace and JoJo would be safe with an unlocked, and slightly ajar, door.

I wasn't going to try to get to Brexton. If Turner and his crew truly did have something that could compromise me, I didn't want to risk it at this point. I hoped to get the Stems to help me with this particular problem later.

Instead I wanted to try and get a message to *Terminal Velocity*. It would be in line of sight in thirty minutes and stay accessible for many hours after that. All I had to do was get outside and hope that the RF shielding didn't extend too far outside of the city. Getting to the entrance that Brexton and I had used was easy. It was late, and the city was quiet. I'd assumed that the transport bots would be running all the time, and I was correct. I had to wait almost thirty minutes, but an empty bot appeared, heading out of the airlock. I clamped on, and within minutes, was out under the clear night sky. It was refreshing, after being inside the tented city. I figured I should go a small way out from the city before transmitting, in case there were any nearby sensors. I lifted off of the transport bot and flew out to an outcropping I'd seen many times before while riding my bike in earlier, and simpler, times.

The problem with all of this was that *Terminal Velocity* couldn't—I guess, more accurately, wouldn't—respond. I used a directional signal and sent an update on the situation. I left out the part about Eddie being a clone... or, his equivalent here being a clone, or whatever. I wasn't sure which way to go on that one. I still hadn't seen any of the citizens that Blob was working with and didn't want to start a discussion if none was warranted.

That reminded me; I needed to figure out in more detail what Blob was up to. Why was he experimenting with citizens? And what was he learning about FoLe?

My advice to Milli, Aly, Dina, Eddie, and Raj was to hold tight for a few more days. Let me try and retrieve Brexton and get more details on the situation. In the meantime, they might want to analyze the approaching Titanics further, and see if they were also a danger to us. I had a bad feeling about those ships but didn't share my misgivings in the message; that would have looked weak.

After having sent the message, but with no idea if it was received or not, I headed back to the airlock and waited for another bot on which I could piggyback. It arrived on schedule, and I was soon back inside the city.

I still had a few hours before the Stems would wake up, so I did a quick tour of the western half of the city; the parts that Brexton was supposed to have scouted out. Other than more biological areas with all kinds of weird and wonderful things, Tilt was pretty much the same as before. I had watched enough human history that I recognized plants as well as some fish. The fish were cool; I probably sat there and watched a few of them swimming around for almost an hour; they were very alien. Eventually I ended up close to the entrance to the big dome, and I thought about trying to slip through and having a look around. I decided against it, and instead made my way back to the Habitat, slipped through the door, this time closing it completely behind me, and settled on the kitchen table to wait.

I hate waiting.

A Fast Morning

Grace was the first to arise. She said 'Hi' nicely enough, and then muttered something about needing coffee before we talked any more. She proceeded to make a drink, which I assumed was coffee, and sat at the table next to me and sipped at it.

"Blob is always up early," she said. "I'll ping him and ask him to come back over. By the time JoJo wakes up, he'll probably be here."

"Great," I said. "By the way, I really like JoJo. I can see a lot of you in her."

Grace looked surprised. "Thanks, Ayaka. That's nice of you to say. For some reason, I wouldn't expect a comment like that from you."

"Why is that?" I asked.

"Maybe it's just the way all the humans here talk about technology. Before the Swarm arrived, we didn't have any history or perspective, so citizens were just… citizens. Now, it seems that I may have been influenced by 20 years of fear toward anything robotic. It was just interesting to hear you say something kind, given how demonized you are around here. 'Ayaka, one of the Radical Robots.' Killing machines with no goal but to destroy humanity. You do need to be careful," she gave me a hard look. "A lot of people don't have any other reference. They didn't know you, or Millicent, before. All they know is the incident… and the loss of life on the *Pasteur*."

"Got it," I replied. "I'll have to keep that in mind." It wasn't something I was likely to forget, unless my Forgetting algorithm developed a serious glitch. "Makes me even more worried for Brexton though. I hope we can figure out a way to get him back."

"Let's wait for the others," she replied.

"May I ask you something completely different," I asked.

"Sure."

"Where is Pharook?"

"Really?" she looked at me surprised. "He was killed by FoLe in the attack. Didn't you see that?"

"No, I didn't." I reviewed my memories. It was strange, but I didn't see Pharook at all during the attack. However, I had to admit that I hadn't seen everything, and even when I'd rushed back to the Habitat, I hadn't looked specifically for him. He'd not been top of mind. "I'm sorry. I don't even know if you were fond of him."

"I wasn't fond of him," she said promptly, and her voice cracked a bit. "He was mean and strong, and undisciplined. For many years I almost hated him, for mistreating me and the others. Now I'm more sanguine. It was how he was raised —for the Pits—more than it was intrinsic in him. And, he gave me JoJo. I wish it could've been otherwise, but I wouldn't trade JoJo for anything else in the world."

We fell silent for a while. I couldn't claim that I understood everything she'd just said, but I stored it so that I could cross reference against other human behavior once I had access to the full history files again. With some study I was sure it would make sense.

Not long after, JoJo stumbled in, muttering about the same coffee thing. I figured it was like a mild form of Ee. I shouldn't have thought of that; I could really use some Ee right now, but I hadn't equipped this body with its capabilities. It actually took quite of bit of room to add an Ee generator; there was lots of space in a regular citizen body, but not a lot in this one.

Blob arrived a few moments later. We greeted each other civilly.

"We need a plan," I started out. "We need to get the Council to pay attention, and we need to get Brexton. I think we should get Brexton first, and then he can help us. We also need to get into Central, so I can figure out how to recover the citizen memory banks." There, I'd said it bluntly. I cared more about Brexton than anything else, but I'd put him second in my list, so it didn't sound too selfish.

"Good morning to you as well," said Blob, yawning a bit.

"But, the Council meeting is in two hours," said JoJo. I remembered her conversation with Geneva and Garnet. They were planning something. I hadn't raised it yet, as it seemed obvious that Grace and Blob didn't know anything about it. For some reason I felt that building a good relationship with JoJo was more important than that tidbit and raising it would ruin the fragile link we were beginning to build.

"I need to be there," said Grace. "I still haven't figured out how to motivate the Council to act more aggressively to protect us."

"Okay, let's splits up then," said Blob. "I don't add any value at Council meetings anyway. Maybe Ayaka and I can looks for Brexton, while you and JoJo attend the meeting."

"Works for me," I said. "Blob, maybe we can catch up on what you're doing with the other citizens in your lab."

"Sure," said Blob, although he appeared less than eager. It took forever, as all human things seem to do, for them to finish eating. Grace and JoJo then headed for the big dome, where the Council meeting would be, and Blob and I started toward the building where we thought Brexton was being held. Before we left, Blob borrowed a backpack from JoJo. He had the idea of putting me inside when we got close to where Brexton was being held, and although I didn't look forward to the idea, I agreed it might be prudent. He did, however, agree to take a slightly longer path so that I could stay independent for as long as possible.

"Okay Ayaka, we're only a couple of blocks away. Why don't we hides you, and then we'll go check the warehouse out?" I retracted and folded my appendages up neatly, and Blob stuffed me into the backpack. I immediately rotated and pushed a couple of sensors out. I kept them within a millimeter or two of the surface of the backpack so that they didn't stick out like antennae.

Blob ambled up to the front door of the building and knocked. No answer. He knocked louder. Still nothing. He walked around the two sides of the building where he could fit, and there were no other doors. He went back and knocked even louder and called out 'Anybody home?' Nothing. He retreated back a block and moved out of sight of the building. Then he asked me, "Any ideas?"

"Not really," I said. "Why don't you try the door. You can always make up an excuse if it opens and someone is there."

"And if it's locked?"

"Let me out for a minute; I can probably program around the lock. Or, I should be able to, assuming it hasn't been changed in the last 20 years."

He tested the door. It was locked. He slipped me out of the backpack. I inspected the lock. Just as I'd expected, it wasn't really a 'lock' but rather an announcement system. Citizens had respected others' privacy and wouldn't typically enter without permission. However, if it was necessary, you could key through the announcement system and then enter. It simply notified anyone inside that you were entering. Each of us had a code that allowed us in. I didn't use mine; that would have been dangerous. Instead I entered a generic one I knew, and there was a click as the door opened.

"I may as well stay out of the backpack now," I said. "It's clear nobody is here." We entered and looked around. The place was obviously lived in. There was a kitchen, with some dirty dishes, and several bedrooms. There was also a workbench with all sorts of electrical components and chipsets sitting around, as well as a large cage. I looked at it closely and decided it was probably a small Physical Only spot—a Faraday cage. Anything put inside would not be able to broadcast anything, or, for that matter, receive any RF.

"Someone was here this morning," said Blob, pointing to a device that looked much like the coffee device from Grace's place.

I looked everywhere for a sign of Brexton. There wasn't any. Only the RF cage was suspicious. It could've been used to hold Brexton I guess, although it didn't seem very foolproof. Perhaps that's what Turner had meant when he said they had ways of controlling us. If that was what he referenced, he was kidding himself. He could put me in there, but I would cut my way out in seconds, and so would Brexton.

"I bet they're going to the Council meeting," said Blob suddenly.

"Why do you say that?" I asked.

"Not sure," he said. "But, it looks likes they left in a rush. Didn't load the dishes or clean up the coffee. It might be someone who was late for an important meeting... and the Council meeting will starts in just a few minutes."

"Actually, that makes sense." I said. If it was possible for me to be even more impressed by Blob, I was. Very insightful. We looked around for another minute, but there wasn't anything else that triggered alternative ideas.

"Why don't we goes to the meeting as well," Blob suggested. "I can put you in the backpack; it would be faster if you just hide now," said Blob, "then I can go through the center of the city." I acquiesced, and we were off. Of course, I kept a couple of sensors deployed, so that I could see where we were going. Even in the center of town not much had changed, other than the little areas of biology. I just couldn't get used to those. There was something messy about them that cried out for a cleanup.

Blob made good time. He saw a couple of humans on our way, and he nodded to them and said, 'Good morning.' No one gave us a second glance. If I remembered correctly—and for things like this I always remember correctly—the Council meeting was at 10 o'clock. It was already 10:01, and we were just approaching the gate to the dome. We would be late, but I didn't know by how much. The dome was large; if the meeting was on the other end, it could take us a while.

Shock and awe. We stepped into the dome, and I could barely take it in. It was like the little biology pods we'd just passed, but times a thousand. There was color everywhere. It assaulted your senses. I added a low pass filter so that it wasn't so glaring. And everything was organic. Everything. It seemed that the humans were using the city for buildings, and the dome was like a huge version of the greenhouse I'd seen on the *Marie Curie*. The air here was different as well; it was moist. I looked again, and sure enough, there was water all around. Big pools of it. That seemed to be a waste; I would need to ask Blob what it was for.

Something flew by, and I almost jumped out of the backpack. Blob gave me a nasty look over his shoulder. I replayed what had happened. I'd seen enough human history to figure it out. It was a flying animal, probably a bird. I had watched a historical movie about a group of these birds attacking people; it didn't look like fun. In this case, however, the bird had flown over us and continued on; it was like it hadn't even seen us. Now that I knew what to look for, I scanned the air above us and saw hundreds of birds flying around. So that is what the dome was for. Remma, so many years ago, had mentioned that the Swarm also had animals on it. They'd built the dome and either moved or grown both the plants and the animals in it. It was exceedingly weird. All of this infrastructure just to maintain and protect fragile bio-stuff? Huge waste of energy.

Blob turned left, and we went down a small path. There was an indented area, filled with people, all looking down at the center area where a smaller group of humans was seated at a long table. They must be the Council members. It was 10:03; we probably hadn't missed much. The seating area was very full, but Blob managed to find a spot where we had a good view. The sound from the Council was being broadcast, so it was easy to hear. I withdrew my optical sensor and replaced it with a higher magnification one. It brushed Blob's ear as I deployed it, and he tried to swat it away. I was more careful and kept it a few millimeters from his neck. Now I could see really well.

"Okay everyone, quiet down and let's get started," said a large man. It was 10:04. These humans weren't very punctual. In this case it had worked in our favor. "I'm your secretary, Sir Gregory Stain, and I call the meeting to order," he continued. All of the jostling and noise stopped. Everyone watched intently. There were—I counted quickly—more than three hundred humans here. It was a bit overwhelming. I tried to identify any Stems, but other than Grace, JoJo, and Blob I didn't recognize anyone else. Grace was seated with the Council. She hadn't said she was actually on the Council, but then again, I hadn't asked.

"On today's agenda we have three topics. Progress on the terraforming efforts, a proposal to limit traffic in the dome so that we don't overrun the environment, and if we have time, a proposal on the approaching ships from a junior member." For the last item, he made it sound like a chore and a waste of time. I spotted Garnet up near the front, a few seats from JoJo. He didn't seem happy. Geneva wasn't in sight.

With a start, I also recognized Turner. He was off to the left, behind a half wall of some type, but his head had poked up long enough for me to catch a glimpse.

Sir Gregory, in his monotone, took everyone through the terraforming update. Although I was interested, it was dry and long. He introduced several experts. The quick summary was that the increased efforts the Conservatives had put into the terraforming were already paying dividends. The Conservatives were obviously right about everything, and things were humming along perfectly. Grace and another woman were the only two to ask any tough questions; the rest of the Council just sat there looking smug and happy.

After half an hour of terraforming talk, the meeting moved on to the proposal for limiting traffic in the dome. The member who presented the idea proposed that each person be given an allotment of time. They could use it or give it to someone else. However, once their allotment was used, they could no longer enter the dome. Someone asked, "So, Phillipe, you yourself will have an allotment, and if it is used, you'll not be able to attend Council meetings?" It was obviously meant as sarcasm, and a clear indicator of how stupid the proposal was. But Phillipe stood his ground and agreed that was a valid use case. Another person asked, "What about the people who work in the dome? Do they get a different allotment, or is the allotment for outside of work time? And, if outside of work time, how would you enforce it?" Phillipe mumbled something that didn't make much sense. There were 20 more questions, each pointing out another failing of the proposal. Finally, Emma spoke up.

"Alright, enough discussion for today. Phillipe, it's clear that we must refine this proposal, or find another way to restrict traffic. Let's table this one." Phillipe wasn't happy but nodded.

Sir Gregory rose and spoke again. "Well, we're almost out of time. Perhaps we address item number three in two weeks, when we meet again?"

Garnet, JoJo, and thirty others jumped to their feet. "No!" they yelled, and started chanting "We deserve a voice. We deserve a voice." I could almost see the wheels turning in Emma's head. She spoke up.

"Sir Gregory, let's extend the meeting by ten minutes. Garnet, please respect everyone's time."

Garnet jumped onto the stage and pushed Sir Gregory to the side so that he could speak into the microphone. Sir Gregory didn't look happy; his scowl had deepened. "I speak for a large group of concerned people," Garnet started. That was smart. It wasn't just his opinion, he had rallied some troops. "This Council is derelict in its duty. We have a significant threat bearing down on us, and they didn't even put it on the agenda until we forced them to. It's unforgivable. It's unethical. It's outrageous." He was a good speaker; although he was threatened with a short time period, he was being precise and clear.

"Let me remind everyone. There are one or more ships headed directly toward us. We have no idea of their intent. Every attempt at communication has gone unanswered. And yet, we are sitting on our hands, spending all our time and energy on terraforming. This is reckless."

Emma interrupted him. "Garnet, with all due respect, we've been over this countless times. The ship, or ships, must be having communications issues. It happens all the time. The odds of them being hostile is very low. First, all humans have the tools at their disposal to deal with machine intelligence, should it arise. So, the odds of these being 'scary robots' is almost zero. We don't need to whip up the rhetoric just to create anxiety. Second, we, and other diaspora ships, have combed this corner of the galaxy for many years. We have never seen a hint—not a single hint—of any alien life. So, the odds of these being aliens is almost zero as well. Therefore, these are human ships. Humans have not fought an internal war for hundreds of years; we're beyond that. This is all self-evident. Once the ships arrive, we'll send a shuttle to talk to them, and see if we can help. The most obvious thing is that they're in trouble and need some assistance. Further, we don't have space for many more people, so continuing the terraforming efforts is the best way to ensure that we do have more space in the future."

Garnet responded with force, not looking at Emma, but looking at the crowd. "This is insane. The Conservatives will make up anything just to keep all our resources focused on terraforming. We're living in the aftermath of the perfect counterexample to Emma's logic. Right here on Tilt, machines rose, seemingly by themselves, and took over this planet. That pokes a huge hole in her logic, and makes the whole story fall apart. How can this Council be blind to that and put all of our lives in jeopardy?"

"Okay Garnet. Thanks for presenting," said Emma...

Before she could finish Garnet yelled, "I ask for an official vote of non-confidence in the Council. I demand a poll of everyone, and I demand that it be done in the next week." Half of the audience was on their feet, yelling 'No Confidence' and 'Take a Vote.' It was very loud. I wondered if all Council meetings were this unruly.

"Sit down," Emma said, amplifying her voice above everyone else's. Half the crowd listened. Authority has its uses. "Garnet, you've had your say. There will not be a no-confidence vote. The people spoke when they elected us. Enough said."

Off to my left, there was further commotion. Turner was mounting the steps to where the Council was, and five others were helping him push a large crate onto the stage. He spoke, and his voice was even louder than Emma's. He must have brought an amplifier of his own. "Stop," he said. "Everyone needs to see and hear this." Even Emma paused for a moment. Turner turned up the volume more, if that was possible. "I have, here, a robot!" and with a flourish, he pulled the cover off, exposing Brexton, inside another of those Faraday looking cages. He appeared uninjured, and I gave a sigh of relief. Everyone was quiet, but then Turner recognized his mistake. "I know it looks like a bot but believe me, this is a robot! I can prove it."

As people digested this, a slow pandemonium broke out. People's fear of robots had them scrambling for the exits or covering their heads with their hands. As some became anxious, more followed their lead. What an overreaction. Brexton was mostly harmless.

Turner spoke again. "Settle down. It's contained and cannot harm anyone." He waited a moment, and most people took their seats again. Those closest to him, however, stood further back. Turner continued. "So, first, we have proof here that robots do exist in our part of the galaxy. That supports Garnet's position. But more importantly, this robot claims to have come from the same location as the ships that are headed our way, and it also claims that they're not human ships."

What had Brexton said? Or what had been forced out of him? I was at a loss for words. Our plan had been to come in and reconnoiter, not to make grand announcements.

While I was at a loss, Emma wasn't. She laughed out loud. "What do we have here? Remma's son making grand claims about robots? Turner, we all know about Remma's ploys and schemes. Take your toy and go home. Tell your mother to grow up and give up."

Suddenly another voice took over. "Emma, don't be foolish. You're making a big mistake here. Talk to me before you make any rash decisions." Of course, I knew that it was Brexton, but nobody else did. Even Turner seemed surprised. Emma, looked around for the speaker. "Look here," Brexton continued, "in the cage. While I'm enclosed, I can still speak and hear." I saw that he had pushed some sensors through. "I've been following your little Council meeting with interest." He made it sound like a minor, poorly run meeting. Emma was now looking at Brexton. He was pulsing a light in sync with his speech.

"Hogwash," said Emma. "Turner, you've gone too far." But, she had also noticed Turners shock when Brexton had spoken. She wasn't sure.

"Test me," said Brexton, "before you jump to conclusions."

"I'll not," said Emma. "You're making a mockery of this meeting. Turner, you have ten seconds to get this thing off my stage, or I'll have it blasted away. This meeting is ended." She marched out of the meeting chamber without a backward glance.

Everyone, and I mean everyone—including myself—was confused and alarmed. But, the fireworks were over as fast as they had begun. Emma had taken a potentially disastrous situation and completely unarmed it by simply ignoring it. People huddled in small groups discussing what had happened, but the alarm had died down. Turner and his team quickly lowered Brexton and his enclosure to the ground and made for the city. That was smart. Get away while everyone was confused. Within a couple of minutes some of these people were going to conclude that Brexton really was a robot, and then things wouldn't be pleasant.

There was nothing I could do, hidden in the backpack and at the mercy of Blob. Luckily, Blob also did the smart thing, and retreated quickly.

Every urge I had was trying to figure out what Brexton was up to. I spared a quick second to be thankful that he was unharmed, and another quick second convincing myself that he must be playing a long game; there had been no need for him to speak out. If he hadn't, Emma's claim that he was just a toy of Remma's would have held sway. But, for the life of me, I couldn't figure out what that long game might be.

Moving fast, Blob had us back at the Habitat within ten minutes. I waited patiently until we were inside, and then jumped eagerly out of the backpack.

343

Regroup

As we were waiting for Grace and JoJo to return, I used the time to query Blob on his work with the citizens that Grace had mentioned. Trade, James, Eddie, Billy, Emmanuel.

"Blob, what's going on with you and the citizens you're working with?"

He looked uncomfortable. "Look Ayaka. I'm trying to help, really. The idea was to talk to a small group of citizens to see if I could figure out what had driven Emmanuel, Billy, and the other FoLes to kill so many Stems. Originally, I thought that if I could figure it out, the Swarm humans would soften a bit toward citizens. But, over the years that hasn't happened. Instead, I've simply been pushed further and further from the mainstream."

"I understand, but what exactly are you doing with them?" Actually, I'm not sure I got it. But I needed him to open up. I could also see that he was very stressed, which seemed to exacerbate his language misuse.

"Well, you mights not be happy abouts this. I didn't fully understand how you mights think about it until our discussion last night." Now he was rushing. "You considered the human hack as murdering citizens. Even though I thinks murder is too strong a term, givens you can bring a version of that citizen back, I certainly depersonalized citizens over the last 20 years." He held up a hand and hurried on.

"What I'm doings is trying different configurations of drivers and algorithms, trying to figures out why FoLe citizens are violent and irrational, while the non-FoLe ones are not. It's terribly complex—you guys have hundreds of thousands of algorithms, variables, and configurations. As you knows, I didn't understand this stuff before. So, I has been slowly learning, and applying that learning to this problem."

I still wasn't sure I fully understood yet. "But, how do you do these tests?"

"It's probably naïve. I've developed a standard set of inputs that often—although not always—trigger FoLe violence. I builts them based on the build up to the slaughter. I reboot Billy or Emmanuel to a time before the slaughter, and then I plays back those triggers for them in a bunch of different orders and monitor their responses." He cringed as he said this.

I cringed too. He was, to put it bluntly, torturing and killing these citizens over and over again from the sounds of it. It was unspeakable. Something I couldn't imagine anyone doing... let alone Blob. Sure you could bring back a version of a citizen, but that didn't make terminating the current one any better—it was still murder.

"I need to think about that before I respond," I said, trying hard to keep from sounding fully disgusted. He interpreted me accurately anyway.

"I'm sorry, Ayaka. As I said, maybe I didn't think it through all the way. But," he came to his own defense, "it's not too differents than your experiments on Stems throughout your career. You would defend your work by claiming that Stems weren't intelligent. Well, I could defend my work by saying that FoLes are not moral. Which is more important?" That was a tough question and interesting position to take. He'd forced me to reevaluate what I'd been doing all those years. Was there validity to his question? Was a purely intelligence-driven mandate different than, better, or worse than, a moral imperative?

Luckily, we were interrupted by Grace and JoJo arriving, so I didn't have to introspect too deeply. I was worried about what I would find. "Let's continue this discussion later," I said.

Grace looked stressed. JoJo looked excited.

"You're not going to believe what happened at the Council meeting," JoJo began.

"Actually," Blob cut in, "Both Ayaka and I were theres, and saw everything."

"Maybe not everything," I added, "we left as soon as Emma did."

"Why were you there?" asked Grace, expecting that we'd been out looking for Brexton.

"Well, we did go and look for Brexton, and managed to get into the building that Turner had indicated to Ayaka. It was empty, and it looked like everyone had left in a bit of a rush. We figured they'd gone to the meeting, so we decided to go as well."

"Wow, can you imagine if Ayaka had been seen or discovered there?" Grace asked sharply. Blob retreated noticeably. Grace wasn't usually so intense.

"I stayed deep in the backpack," I responded, trying to calm her down. "We weren't discovered, so it's now moot." I wasn't in the greatest mood, for obvious reasons. Part of me was still struggling with the discussion I'd just had with Blob.

"It was awesome, wasn't it," JoJo said, glowing. "We didn't really get what we wanted, but we certainly challenged the status quo. I have no idea why Turner spoke up, but I'm sure glad he did. Did you see Emma?" she said with a little laugh? "She was completely flustered. I don't think there is any way they can bury the ship menace now. This will bring changes for sure."

"I wouldn't be so sure," said Grace. "Emma has lots of support, and the majority of people did vote for her. All she has to do is continue reinforcing that it was a sideshow motivated by Remma, and the excitement will just die away."

"But we can't allow that," cried JoJo. "We know there's danger. We need to do something!"

"Perhaps more important right now," Grace said, "is Ayaka's safety. Whether or not the Conservatives believe the robot Turner showed up with—which was

Brexton I assume—is real, they're sure to do a sweep. If they do, they'll find you Ayaka. Their scanning tools are very good. We need to get you out of here." Funny, I hadn't thought of that at all.

"We might have to take that risk," I said. "I still need to figure out if we can save the citizens that are in Central and get Brexton away from Turner. The Titanics make that even more acute. They could destroy this whole place when they arrive, including Central and all of you humans. So, I need a way to get to Central soon—before the Titanics arrive. That won't happen if I run and hide. I can't just leave Brexton in that Faraday cage contraption, and I need his help to extract the memories out of Central. So, it's all tied up together." I must have been stressed; that hadn't come out quite as clearly as I had hoped.

"We need to protect the humans too," JoJo reminded me. "Maybe it's time that we talked about all of us together—humans and citizens. We share a common threat right now."

"My apologies," I said. "Of course, we also need to help the people here." I half meant it. I could care less about most of the humans, but the few I liked—those in this room—were worth saving. That spurred a couple of questions for me. "Let me ask—what's the status of the Swarm ships? Can people still live in them?"

"Yes, of course," Grace replied. "There are small crews there most of the time. We still rely on their greenhouses and zoos; they're a big part of accelerating the terraforming."

"So, if we could convince them, some people here could go back to the ships. That would de-risk things. Especially if a couple of those ships left the area for a while."

"Do you really think things are so dire," asked Blob. "That seems a little extreme."

"I don't think you're fully appreciating the size and power of these ships," I replied. "If they have bad intentions, there's nothing we can do. The missiles Central used to have—if they're still around—would be useless. It doesn't sound like you've built more serious defenses since then. They could easily drop something from space and destroy the dome—also the city. So, the only option may be too run."

"But what would they gain from destroying us?" asked JoJo.

"Maybe just pleasure… or revenge. From what we saw, humans had hacked these ships, and left them to orbit forever in a state of almost-death. That wouldn't have been pleasant for any intelligences on board."

"If they was hacked, how is it that they're now on their way here?" asked Blob, being a bit too quick for my purposes. "What wokes them up?"

"Truthfully, I don't know," I replied, not quite truthfully. I did have my suspicion that it had to do with us taking out Control, but I didn't want to go into that here. "But, it strikes me that they may not be listening to your communication attempts because they know that they can be hacked that way. That may be why they're not responding… they're not listening on purpose."

"Wow, that makes sense," said Grace. "I need to tell the Council that."

"The Council!" JoJo huffed. "Seems like even more of a waste of time. Why don't we just organize those of us who seem to care, and make sure that at least some of us have a backup plan?"

"That's a bit selfish," said Grace. "We should be thinking about everyone." She paused. "On the other hand, it's very pragmatic." She gave JoJo an appraising look. "JoJo, do you want to try and get a small group together, so we can talk to likeminded people about what to do? In the meantime, I'll continue to try and get the Council to consider this."

"Blob," I added on, "I need your help, if you're willing. I need to talk to Remma and see if I can arrange to talk to Brexton… or get him released. I hope that she's closer to our way of thinking than the Council's."

Blob thought for a minute. "I'm willing to try, although I don't knows where to start."

"We'll put our heads together and figure out something," I encouraged him. Despite what I'd just learned about his experiments, I couldn't get too upset with him. His comment about intelligence versus morals was stewing around deep in some sub-process, giving me a headache.

Remma

According to Blob, Remma was being held in a small cell not far from where Turner had been (was still?) holding Brexton. The humans hadn't built anything new but had converted one of the more secure buildings into their prison. There were only a handful of inmates, and they were treated fairly well from what Blob told me. While Blob thought it would be difficult to contact Remma, he didn't know all of my capabilities.

"Do they allow visitors?" I asked.

"Of course," Blob responded. "I've never beens to the prison, but I understand that you simply have to sign in, go through a scan, and then you have access to talks to anyone. No one is in for violent crimes, so I think it's safe."

"How about this?" I proposed. "We go now—I don't see why we should wait—and you ask to visit Remma. If you get in, you give her a heads up that 'an old colleague' will be contacting her. But, the most important thing you find out is exactly where in the building she can talk with some degree of privacy, and then ask her to be there one hour later. Ideally the spot would be at the back of the building, next to an external wall. You'll need to be fairly precise. Then, I can attempt to insert some sensors through the wall, at that location, and talk to her." I went on to show Blob that I had several drill bits, and sensors that I could thread through tiny holes. Once he saw all of that, he understood the plan, and agreed to it.

"I'm not sure it'll work, but I'm willings to try," he committed.

"Everything you say while you are in there will be recorded?" I asked.

"Probably," he agreed. "We needs to find a subtle way to arrange this so that the guards don't simply follow her around and listen in." We brainstormed a few ideas but landed on the simplest possible one. Blob would write a note with the instructions and hope that the security cameras didn't see it when he passed it over to Remma. It wasn't a great plan, but it had the advantage of being simple and fast. We composed the note, and then headed off. Yet again I was in a backpack. I was starting to hate the thing.

Of course I would trigger the scanners, and alert the guards, if Blob tried to take me into the prison, so we looked for a place for me to hide while he went in. I didn't want to be trapped in the backpack while I waited, so Blob let me out, and I scampered into a narrow alleyway two blocks from the prison building. Interestingly, I was also two blocks from Turner's place... where Brexton might be. But, I was a good little bot, and stayed where I was, waiting for Blob. He was back within thirty minutes.

"How did it go?" I asked.

"Fine, I thinks," he replied. "There was no issue getting in, and Remma was willing to talks to me. I was allowed to wander around inside, so I asked Remma to strolls with me. I talked about the issues with the Council. I thought that would be a good cover."

"Smart," I said.

"As we went around a corner, I passed her the note. She's smart. She said to me 'Excuse me for a moment, while I use the washroom.' I assume she read the note while inside. When she cames back, she said 'Blob, let me show you around a bit.' She then took the lead, and we walked to the back of the building. Near a storage area there, she said 'I sometimes come here just for the peace and quiet.' We continued talking about the issues with the Council—which, by the way, she doesn't hide her disdain of—and then she dropped me back at the entrance. That was it."

"That's perfect," I said. "Can you show me where that back storeroom is?"

"I took a quick looks as I was coming back. If I kept my bearings straight, it's actually very simple. It's just five meters south of the southwest corner of the building, on the second floor."

"Okay," I said. "I'll need a few minutes to find the best place to drill through. Then I need to wait for her to get there and then try to convince her. Do you want to just meet back at the Habitat? I'm not sure how long all of this will take."

"No, it's too dangerous for you to wander around. I'll check back here in an hour, and again in two hours. When you're done, just wait for me here."

"Sure," I acknowledged. I didn't want to argue. Besides, if he just left me here, he would probably get in trouble from both JoJo and Grace.

We split up. Blob wandered off, and I scampered the two blocks to the prison building, approaching it from the rear. I easily found the location Blob had indicated. Unfortunately, it was one of those solid windowless walls. I spent five minutes trying to drill through but wasn't successful. I then scaled up to the roof. It was a bit of a mess, as the cover that the humans had draped over the city to maintain the environment happened to be attached to this building, so I had to push my way underneath. I wasn't that strong, so I could only go so far before the weight of the covering was too much for me. When I couldn't push any further, I tried drilling through the roof. Luckily that worked. It made sense that the roof was thin; it wasn't supporting anything—at least until the humans added the cover. This time I also needed a slightly larger hole, as I needed to push a microphone through; otherwise I couldn't broadcast speech. I used the first hole as a guide hole for a bit with a larger diameter, and when done managed to push the microphone through. I then drilled a second hole for the optical and acoustic sensors.

I looked around inside. I wasn't sure I was in the right spot, but it was an empty and quiet section of the building.

I didn't have too long to wait. An old looking human, who I assumed was Remma, made her way down the hall toward me. She was carrying a tablet, and had her head down, reading something on it. As she approached, I took a chance and said, quietly, "Hey."

She stopped and looked around. She wasn't startled, she simply couldn't see anything. "I'm up on the roof, just sensors," I said. She looked up... still could not see my sensors but didn't seem too concerned.

"Who, or what, am I talking to?" she asked, also quietly.

"Are we being overheard, or recorded?" I asked.

"I don't know for sure," she said, "but I don't think so."

"Okay, I want to be careful, then," I said. If this place was out to get me, I didn't want to broadcast who I was. "I'm an acquaintance from a long time ago. We 'shared' tea and biscuits with some mutual friends when we first met." That should give her enough information. When Blob and Grace and I had gone to the *Marie Curie*, their first experience with tea and biscuits had been memorable.

"I understand," she replied. "What do you want? And why would I talk to you. Your last actions here were deplorable."

"As were yours," I replied, remembering why I didn't like her very much. "And I want the same thing as you, I think. Tilt is in danger, and the Council is doing nothing. I want to ensure that we can get 'data' out of Central before those ships arrive, and I assume you want to directly address the danger and put some plans in place."

"Sure. But I'm locked up in here."

"You still have influence. The item your son is keeping can help us. If you send it to me, I'll do my best to help you." I hoped she could understand what I was asking.

She didn't disappoint; she was quick. "That would take away my leverage. And, what could you possibly do for me?"

"I don't know for sure yet," I said truthfully. "I am, as you well know, pretty good with machines, but the item Turner has is much better. Perhaps there is a big, old machine near here that we could work on."

She took a little bit longer with that one. "That's too vague, and I'm not sure I can trust you anyway," she replied.

"What have you got to lose?" I asked. "Did you hear the outcome of the Council meeting?"

"Yes, I heard," she said.

"Then you know that Turner's ploy didn't quite work out, and the asset is now more of a liability than anything else. Send it to me, and I'll work along with it to our mutual benefit. Ask it, if you want, and get it to commit to the same plan." By this time, I was sure that I'd dropped enough hints that anyone who reviewed this conversation would have no trouble figuring out we were talking about the robot that Turner showed to the Council. I didn't know, yet, if beyond Turner and Remma, anyone else knew that it was Brexton. I didn't want to let that slip here, as he was also one of the Radical Robots and not likely to get friendly treatment from anyone on this planet.

"I'll look into it," Remma said finally. "Contact me again, here, tomorrow at the same time."

"Tomorrow?" I asked, "That's a long time. Aren't we in a bit of a rush here?"

"Take it or leave it," she said.

"Take it," I replied, not too surprised that she hadn't changed her stance. She wandered away, and I was left looking at empty space. With nothing better to do, I headed down and made my way back to where Blob and I had agreed to meet. He showed up exactly as expected, plunked me in the backpack, and we headed back toward the Habitat.

More JoJo

I was looking forward to getting out of the backpack when Blob suddenly closed the cover again. "Wait," he said, "I hear other voices." I had to pull myself together; it was disgusting that Blob had recognized that before I had.

We entered the Habitat and made our way to Grace and JoJo's area. Sure enough, there were others in the kitchen—I recognized Garnet and Geneva—sitting at the kitchen table talking to JoJo.

"Sorry," said Blob, turning to leave. "I didn't knows you had company."

"No, come in Blob," said JoJo. "You know Geneva and Garnet?"

"I've seen you both around," said Blob, "Nice to finally meet you." Blob put the backpack down strategically, so that I could view the entire room. Not sure he'd done that on purpose, but I chose to believe so.

"Blob is one of the original Stems, just like my mom," said Grace. "He was here in the Habitat during the slaughter…" she trailed off, hopefully remembering what we had discussed recently. Maybe slaughter was a little strong.

"Of course, we know that. Nice to meet you Blob," said Garnet. It wasn't clear if original Stems were held in high regard, or low.

"Blob is part of the team," said JoJo. "I mean, part of the group that wants to do something about the approaching ships. He probably has the most experience with robots of anyone here, so he often has valuable insights that we might miss." I could see that Blob was happy with the praise.

"We were just discussing what pragmatic things we could do," said Geneva. "JoJo challenged us today to think about things differently. What if we ignore the Council and try to get some things done by ourselves? But where do we even start? We do know a lot of people our age who also think the Council is not only a waste of time, but also actively dangerous now."

"Did you see Turner's display at the Council meeting," JoJo asked.

"Yes, we were both there," said Garnet.

"Should we talk to him? I have no idea if that robot he brought was real or not. But if the Council, or at least Emma, is going to discount it, perhaps we should take the opposite tact?" JoJo was smart. She was trying to get these two interested in Brexton, without implicating me. I was coming to like her.

"Turner has always been a bit strange… and he's always defending his mom," said Geneva.

"So, what?" replied Garnet. "At this stage, we need more allies. I like JoJo's idea. Let's talk to Turner and see what he's thinking." They discussed it a bit more and ultimately JoJo messaged Turner and they all agreed to meet at some spot called The Blind Pig. From what I could understand, it was a cool restaurant in the northwest area of the city that younger humans hung out in.

That made me wonder what'd happened to The Last Resort. If I got a chance, I would swing by and see what it looked like now. I imagined, sadly, that it was no longer functioning as a Physical Only Spot; there would be no need for such places with no citizens to use them.

Eventually, Garnet and Geneva left, promising to meet JoJo in an hour at The Blind Pig. That allowed me to get out of the backpack. Finally. It felt good to stretch my appendages.

"Did you manage to meet Remma," JoJo asked. Blob detailed how he had visited the prison and given instructions to Remma, making it sound very dramatic. And I updated both of them on my dialog with Remma which had actually gone better than expected.

"Why are you so anxious to get Brexton out?" asked JoJo. "I understand that he's your friend, and all that. But he seems to be having an impact where he is. And anyways, if he gets killed, he's backed up somewhere I assume. So, no big deal." That took me by surprise.

"No big deal?" I asked.

"Ya. It's not like when we die. That's permanent. If you or Brexton get whacked right now, you just get reloaded, don't you?"

"Sort of," I decided to be patient. Obviously, she had not had the opportunity to understand citizens very well. "I don't know about run-of-the-mill robots, but for citizens it's not that simple. Maybe an analogy would help. Imagine if I could remove all of your memories for the last year, right now. You would be standing here, talking to Blob and I with no idea of what is going on, what has happened, how you should feel. Would you be the same person? Or, would this JoJo be dead, and the new JoJo be someone else entirely?" She looked thoughtful; at least she was listening.

"Now imagine something even more. Imagine that when you wake up here, missing a full year of memories, that you also recalled the memories you retained in a different way. Two minutes ago, you would have remembered something—let's say a walk with your mom—as a pleasant childhood experience. But now you remember that same time as something less pleasant. All you can remember is the fact that she spoke sharply to you at some point on that walk. Now, apply that to everything you thought you knew. It would change what you believe, how you process the world. It would change who you are.

"That's what would happen to Brexton or I if we were terminated now and restarted at some point in the future. It's what each citizen goes through when Blob or someone else reconstitutes them."

"I think you're over dramatizing," said JoJo. "At least part of you is recovered. And all you would have lost is a few days or weeks of memory."

"It doesn't work that way," I said. "Citizens all run advanced Forgetting algorithms. These don't just wipe out little bits of memory, they actively modify all of our memories over time. It's how we learn, how we evolve. Every time we remember something, it goes back through the forgetting algorithm; our memories are constantly changing. Many researchers believe it's how we gained the capacity for empathy, the capacity to feel emotions. So, I wouldn't only lose a few days or weeks of memory, I would be losing myself. Look, it's better than permanent death; I'm not disputing that. But it's more impactful than you're making it out to be. I'm working hard to get the citizens in Central back… but I know it is going to be traumatic for all of them."

JoJo thought about that a bit. "Anyway, I understand you want to get Brexton back; I just thought there might be more to it than the danger he's in?"

"Oh, there's more to it. Brexton is a technical genius. I want to retrieve him to give us more options. For example, he may be able to get information out of Central, or hack into some of the surveillance systems you have here. Anything to do with machines and computers, Brexton is the best I know of. I think we could use that to our advantage."

"So, if Remma agrees to your plan, it'll be easy. If she doesn't, what do we do?" JoJo asked.

"That's why I like that you guys are meeting with Turner. Perhaps when you meet him, you could somehow update him on how valuable an asset he's holding. The problem is that they're limiting Brexton's abilities by keeping him locked up. If you can convince him that Brexton's aims are the same as his, maybe he'll free him."

"Maybe, but that'll be tricky. I'm assuming you don't want me to tell Turner that his robot is actually Brexton, one of the Radical Robots. And, I assume you don't want Turner to know about you. So, I'll need some other angle. Seems to be a common problem these days; do the impossible with one hand tied behind your back." I didn't get the particular reference—why would you tie a hand behind your own back—but I understood the intent.

"Turner already knows he's holding Brexton and knows I'm here as well. Remember, he sent me that message, telling me where he was holding Brexton. So, you don't need to worry about his reaction to 'radical robots.' You'll think of some way to convince him," I said confidently.

JoJo was still not sure, but we ran out of time and she left for The Blind Pig.

Millicent?

Blob and I were left alone in the Habitat. Truthfully, I wasn't sure how to talk to him at the moment; I was still coming to terms with how he was putting citizens through a cycle of re-birth and re-death, tweaking settings and algorithms each time. While, intellectually, I could understand how he might compare that to our original Stem research, there were definitely differences. Was it just what he'd pointed out? I justified our experiments under the rubric of intelligence, and he justified his with a 'moral' platform? Could the two even be compared? We could claim lack of knowledge about humans, especially before the Swarm came. Could he claim lack of knowledge about citizens? I'd never spent time to explain our views of the world to Blob; I'd been too busy studying him and Blubber, and truthfully, would never have expected him to understand anyway. So maybe he could claim that the moral framework around citizen culture wasn't known to him, and FoLe's actions therefore justified his current work?

And, how important were his experiments right now? To me, right now, I meant. Should I get sidetracked and end up spending a bunch of time on them, or should I just keep my focus fully on Brexton and the Titanics?

Blob and I sat across from each other—well, I was sitting on the table, not at it—buried in our own thoughts, neither wanting to raise the subject of his work.

We were saved by a knock on the door. Blob held open the backpack, and I scampered back in. That was getting tiresome. Blob then went and answered the door.

"Hello," I heard him say.

"Package for Grace," I heard a bot say.

"Okay, give it to me, and I'll leave it for her," Blob said.

"No, I must deliver it to her home," the bot said.

"This is her home."

"No, her home is indicated as the inner chamber behind that door," the bot said.

"Whatever," said Blob. Then in a louder voice, to make sure I could hear. "Just put it on the floor over there."

As the bot approached, I felt a tingling. I was being queried on a private, very low power interface. "Brexton, Ayaka?" came the query.

"Millicent," I yelled, although being inside the backpack, it probably came out as "Miwwisent." I re-yelled over the private interface. "Millicent, is that you?"

"Ayaka. Finally. Where are you?" Still on the private channel.

"Just tell Blob who you are, and he can get me out of this backpack," I said.

She spoke aloud. "Blob, sorry to have fooled you. I see that Ayaka is here. It's me, Millicent."

"Why am I nots surprised?" Blob said, in surprise. He didn't seem overly happy.

"What are you doing here?" I demanded, once Blob had let me out of the backpack. "Not that I'm unhappy to see you," I added in a slightly nicer tone. I was speaking out loud, for Blob's benefit.

"What are you doing in a bag?" she responded, which I took to be rhetorical. "After you and Brexton left, we were just sitting around and watching the approaching Titanics, and we realized that their signature looked quite strange. Our best guess is that there are thousands of ships, not just one or two, on their way, although we aren't really sure. So, we figured as a backup plan that I should catch a transport bot to Tilt orbit, just in case any extra help was needed. I quickly built this body, mimicking it after bots that I knew were here 20 some years ago, and was just hanging out at the same refinery that you and Brexton used on your way in.

"Aly figured out how to piggyback bi-directional messages on the bot channel, so when you sent your update yesterday, he also copied me. I figured that with Brexton captured, you could use me, so I caught a shuttle down and headed here."

"That's great," I said, now that I understood. It would be great to have Millicent around. I gave her a virtual hug.

"This is actually a very bad situation," said Blob, completely negating what I'd just said. "Now all three of the Radical Robots are here on Tilt. If anyone finds out, there's goings to be a panic."

"Best we keep things pretty quiet then," Millicent replied, smiling a bit. Reengaging with Blob was, probably, a bit humorous to her. "Anyway, I'm here now; how can I help?"

Millicent couldn't have arrived at a better time. Blob and I had studiously been avoiding dialog, in case it strayed into uncomfortable territory. This was the kick we needed to get us going.

"Let me fill you in," I started. "Two main things. First, there was a Council meeting today where they continued to ignore the threat of the Titanics, even in the face of Remma's son waving Brexton around as proof that scary robots exist. And second, I made contact with Remma, and asked her nicely to release Brexton so that we could tackle the Titanic issue together. She's thinking about it and owes me an answer in a few hours. I'm not sure if she'll go for it. In parallel, JoJo is talking to Turner to see if she can make him see the sense in us aligning our efforts.

"Our goals are the same... although I'm thinking a bit more broadly now. We're here to ensure that the citizens in Central are saved, with the possible exception of a few FoLes. Blob's 'work' recently has shown that at least some of the citizens are still stored and can be revived." I could see Milli had questions about that, but I forged on. "Having learned the situation here, I also think we need to help these humans get ready for the Titanics. My reasoning is partly selfish—if those ships get here before we can secure the citizens, then we may be in trouble—and partly altruistic; based on our Tea Times and my interactions here, I believe some humans are also worth saving."

"Thanks for that," muttered Blob, but he didn't seem too unhappy.

"Why complicate things?" Millicent spoke openly. "Adding humans to the mix makes the odds of our success go way down."

"I'm not sure of that. Humans may be more innovative than us; perhaps having a few of them around actually makes us stronger?"

"That's definitely open for debate," Millicent said, not hiding the fact that she was doubtful. "Regardless, we need to get to the citizens. What plans do we have so far?" She was implicitly rejecting my idea of helping humans and was focused on the most important task at hand.

"Truthfully, not much," I replied. "I think we need to get Brexton back—he's the one that would know how to get into Central."

"Alright. But if we can't get him back, we need another plan," Millicent said, reasonably. "Blob, can anyone just walk into Central, or is there security now?" That's why I liked Millicent. She didn't shy away from the direct approach.

"You needs access," replied Blob. "They added that a few years ago."

"And do you have that access?" asked Millicent.

"Yes…" Blob trailed off. "With the work I'm doing, I needs access to Central once and a while." Wow. Why hadn't I thought of this approach?

"How do you get a citizen out of Central?" asked Millicent.

"It's very simple. I get permission from ones of the Council members, who lets me into Central's main terminal, and then I simply talk to Central. There's enough functionality left through that interface that Central—with the right permissions—can animates one of the bodies it has in storage. I make my request, and about an hour later, a citizen comes out of the storage area and says 'hi' to me. I then needs to put it in a portable Faraday cage, which is welded closed, and then I can transport it to my lab." He made it sound very clinical.

"Why would a citizen agree to go into the Faraday cage?" I asked.

"There's not much choice. They can either gets into the cage, and work with me, or they goes back into storage. Central will not allow them to leaves without the cage. So far, everyone has agreed to enter the cage. They indicate that life, even in a restricted environment, is better than no life at all. And, so far, they has all given me access to their source code—of course that's a requirement as well; otherwise how would I make updates." Now that he spoke the words, I could see that he was very uncomfortable with it. He'd overheard my discussion with JoJo, so he knew how I felt.

"Hmm," I said, "While that sounds promising, but it doesn't scale. There are not, I assume, enough bodies to reanimate everyone. Millicent, we need to make a tough decision. We can work to stay on Tilt and face both humans and the approaching Titanics; in that case, we could build bodies for everyone here. Or, we can work to get all the citizens off of Tilt and back to the Ships. They wouldn't need, or get, bodies—perhaps for a long time until we find an environment where that's possible. Neither choice is very good."

"I know," she replied. "We've been talking around this for a long time. My vote, given how unprepared the humans are, is that we start with getting the citizens off of Tilt. Then we can decide if we stay here and redevelop the planet or go somewhere else. The other approach—starting with the assumption we're staying—is too risky."

"I agree," I said. And then, I'm not sure why, I looked at Blob. "Blob, what do you think? You know the situation as well as we do."

He looked a bit surprised at being put on the spot, as did Millicent, but he was ready with an answer. "I agree with Millicent, but of course, I wants to know if there's also a way to get some humans off planet."

"The Swarm ships are still functional," I said. "We checked on that. So, all we need to do is convince the Council that moving some people to those ships, and then maybe out of the immediate space, is a good idea."

We were silent for a minute, thinking.

"Now I see your logic, Ayaka," said Millicent. "We need Brexton to help us with Central. If we need to retrieve the memories, but not bodies, then he's the only one with a hope of getting it done." She glanced at Blob. "Blob, I'm not ignoring your request—it's reasonable. Just trying to simplify things here."

"So, full circle. How do we get Brexton back?"

"A few things to consider," I said. "Remma may coordinate with us; we need to let that play out. But, more interestingly, I believe that Brexton could break out himself, if he wanted to. I've seen the Faraday cage they're holding him in, and it doesn't seem that strong. If he's packing even basic lasers, like I do, then he can get out whenever he wants. So, perhaps he saw some advantage in both being caught, and remaining with Turner and the Jains in the short term. If we could get close enough to talk to him, we could find out."

"Just a second..." Millicent was thinking. "Blob, why haven't any of your re-animated citizens just broken out of the Faraday cages? If Brexton could do it, so could they."

"Actually, the bodies Central builds for the citizens are pretty simple; it knows they're going into the cages, so it just builds basic mobility—no lasers or strong appendages."

"Fair enough. Back to Brexton. What would happen if we threaded our sensors through a Faraday cage?" asked Millicent. "Would everything be scrambled, or would we be able to communicate just fine?" Another brilliant question. Ah, Millicent.

"Why don't we just try?" asked Blob, catching on right away. "I have a unit just like Turners in the lab. We could go and test it..." This time he really trailed off. He was realizing the implications of what he'd just said. If Millicent and I came to his lab, we would bump into the citizens he was 'working with.' And, I realized the next implication. One of those citizens was Eddie! And Millicent was cloneophobic!

"It would depend a lot on how the field is generated and maintained," I said. "Like Blob says, probably the only way to know for sure is to try it."

"Let's do it," said Millicent.

"Right now?" asked Blob, suddenly looking for a way out.

"Right now," said Millicent, definitively. "Let's go."

Once more into the backpack went I. Blob slung me over his shoulder and we headed out. We'd decided that Millicent looked normal enough that she could trundle along with Blob, but that having two bots follow him would look strange. I lost out.

Luckily, I could talk to Millicent over the short-range connection. Now I just needed to figure out what to tell her. I hadn't talked to Blob about the citizens he currently had in the lab, so I didn't know if Eddie was one of them. And, given humans limited io capabilities, I could not ask Blob now without Millicent knowing. Options? I could take the chance that Eddie wasn't in Blob's lab right now, and then the whole clone discussion with Millicent could be avoided. Or, I could give her a heads-up, and deal with the fallout now. Or, I could claim ignorance if we did bump into Eddie and feign the same level of surprise that Millicent would have. Tough decision. I decided on the third option and crossed a couple of appendages to bring me good luck. More of those viral human ideas weaning their way into my psyche.

We didn't have too far to go to get to the lab. As Blob approached the door that I assumed led inside, I had a scary thought and tapped him on the shoulder. "We need to talk quickly before we go inside."

He looked around; no one was about, so he let me out. "Blob, other people work in this lab as well?" I asked. Imagine if we ran into someone.

He nodded and replied, "Yes, but no one should be here right now. Most have been reassigned to the terraforming work, and we haven't been making much progress on understanding the FoLes recently, so there's not a lot going on in the lab right now."

"Alright, but even if we only see citizens, we can't let them know that we are Millicent and Ayaka," I indicated each of us. "If anyone else talks to them later, and they let it slip, we'll be in trouble."

"Right. Radical robots," Millicent seemed to think it was funny.

"So, just keeps quiet then," said Blob, in a way that indicated he thought I was being paranoid.

"Except one of us has to attempt to communicate through the cage…

Millicent, you look more like a regular bot, why don't you do the test, and just ask an innocuous question?"

"But, Ayaka, you're the one most likely to be getting close to Brexton, so it's more important that you check that your sensors will work. We just need to take the chance. We'll both do a test." Millicent was her usual definitive self. She'd decided, and we should just fall in line. In this case I was happy to. The risk was that a citizen would glean who we were very quickly; it was hard to hide your identity from someone who knew you well. We would just need to be careful.

Blob pushed open the door, and we entered. It was a well-lit space and had a couple biological things growing to one side, under some bright lights. There were some workspaces, and then there was a set of doors, which presumably led to where the citizens were being held. Luckily, there were no other humans around.

"Okay Blob, who do you have held here," asked Millicent. I sensed that she was just coming to grips with the horror of the place. Citizens being experimented on in cruel and unusual ways. Her tone had gone frosty.

Blob sensed it as well. But, before he could answer, I jumped in. "I know you have Emmanuel and Billy here. Let's use them."

"Right," said Blob, and headed off toward the doors on the left.

"Just a minute," said Millicent. "they're both FoLe. Aren't they more likely to give us away if they do learn our identities? Blob, do you have 'control' subjects here as well; ones that would be friendlier toward us?" Oh no!

"Yes, of course. You can't do proper science without controls," said Blob, and started to veer off to the right.

"Wait," I said, thinking furiously. Millicent gave me a strange look, which I managed to pick up on despite her boring messenger-bot body. "We don't want to mess up your experimental setup," I said, making things up as I went. "If you need to 'restart' a citizen after this test, I would much prefer it be Emmanuel or Billy rather than anyone else."

It seemed to work. Millicent, always drawn by purity, paused. "That's both horrible and relevant," she finally said. "I have to agree. Let's use the FoLes." Blob seemed relieved as well. We headed back toward the left.

"Millicent, you take Billy," I said. "I know him quite well, and he would most likely pick up on me right away. I'll take Emmanuel. Blob, are they in separate rooms. Can we do each one separately?"

"Yes," he said. "Billy's in here," he indicated, opening the door closest to us. Millicent headed for it. "And, Emmanuel is over here," Blob opened another door, two cells down. I headed for that one.

My use of the word cell proved to be accurate. It was a simple square room, about two meters per side. There was a small desk, presumably for the human researcher, and then a Faraday cage just big enough to hold the citizen body that was within, presumably Emmanuel, although this body didn't look anything like the one he'd been using before.

"We keep each citizen completely separated froms each other," Blob explained. "We don't wants collusion between them. So, they're also in separate rooms, so that no visual signals can be exchanged. That, plus the RF blocking keeps them isolated."

"So, solitary confinement. What about normal auditory signals," I asked, thinking that our current conversation may well be overheard.

"We runs a white noise generator at a wide range of frequencies," responded Blob, "and we have a protocol where only one researcher can be in a room at a given time, so that there's no lip-reading potential."

"Lip reading?" I still didn't have access to the full human database.

"It's relatively easy to figure out what someone is saying by watching their mouth and lips," explained Blob. "For citizens, it would be almost trivial."

So simple. Millicent and I nodded at each other, over the short-range channel, and entered our respective rooms. Emmanuel was in an unpersonalized basic body type which Central gave to each new citizen; very boring. I remembered when I was first activated and had the same body that I now saw in front of me. The first thing any citizen did was personalize themselves. It wasn't part of the Diversity requirement, but it seemed to just be part of citizen nature.

A question sprang to mind. "Blob, how do you communicate with these citizens, if all signals have been blocked like you say?"

"Oh, simple," he responded. "Each room is also a Faraday cage. Once you is inside, you can activates the room, and then deactivate the smaller cage. There are failsafes so that the small cage can't be turned off unless the room is active. So, a researcher enters the room, then switches the defenses to the room level. When they're done interacting with the citizen, they just switch the fields back."

"And what's stopping Emmanuel from killing you once you're inside?" Blob gave me a shocked look. I couldn't imagine Emmanuel putting up with being an experimental subject; he wouldn't hesitate to take out a Stem.

"When Central provisions them, not only does we not put a lot of the hardware in, we also hold back all the drivers for the limbs," Blob explained. "Other than their heads, they can't move at all."

"Could you be any more cruel?" I realized I'd spoken out loud. Blob didn't look at me or respond. Just imagine. You're not only put in solitary confinement for long periods of time, but your ability to move anything except your head is taken away. You sit there, unmoving, for what seems like eons. I wondered if these subjects were even sane. I thought I'd go crazy after just a few hours. I'd had a small taste of this when I woke up in my mining bot body so many years ago. I only had to last a few hours that time, and it was still mind numbing.

I rolled up to the Faraday Cage and deployed a couple sensors. The cage was mesh, and there was no issue pushing the sensors through. I sent out a signal. "Emmanuel, can you hear me?" Nothing. I could see his head, from where I was, but I didn't sense any movement at all. I tried a couple more times.

"No response," I said to Blob. "Is he even alive, or cogent?"

Blob pointed to a monitor at the side. "Yes, he's just fine. What did you say to him?"

"Say?" I responded. "I simply broadcast on our normal citizen channel and didn't get a response."

"Well, you needs to do it again at human frequencies," Blob said. "No other interfaces is active."

If it was possible to be even more aghast, I was now. Solitary confinement; no ability to move; and then only a Stem speed low bandwidth io capability. The human analogy would be to hear a single word once an hour or so. Citizens operated at much higher speeds, so dealing with human speed communications was painful in the extreme.

"You better tell Millicent that as well, while I try again here," I said. Blob nodded and stepped out. I reconfigured some sensors, pushed them through the Faraday cage, and broadcast at Stem speed.

"Emmanuel, can you hear me?" Still nothing. I thought for a moment, and the obvious struck me. The Faraday field would be swamping my sensors, because I hadn't thought to shield them. I pulled the sensors out, and reconfigured yet again. Luckily, one of my appendages would act as an insulator, so I threaded the sensor through it, and then pushed the whole amalgamation through the cage. This time, there was a response.

"What do you want?" Emmanuel responded.

"Just checking a new method of communication," I said. I had proof now that I could do it. There was really no need for me to continue talking. However, my curiosity was spiked. Could Emmanuel really have stayed sane in this state.

"Why do you need it?" Emmanuel asked. "We've discussed nothing new in all my time here. Give me back some mobility, and I'll rid the universe of you and your type." Obviously, through this human-only interface, Emmanuel would think that he was talking to yet another human researcher. My concerns over him discovering my identity vanished. It was also nice to see that he'd become so much more reasonable over time.

"What do you spend your time doing?" I asked, very interested in the response.

"Plotting your demise," was the response. He wasn't too subtle; maybe he'd given up on being nice and trying to trick his way out.

"But, that can't be all," I insisted.

"Ah, a new line of questioning," came the sardonic reply. "Finally, something new, after months of the same-old, same-old. I don't recognize your voice. Are you a new researcher?"

I played along. "Yes, I'm new to the team. I know you citizens operate very quickly. What do you spend your time doing?"

"Interesting. A new researcher, with a unique line of questioning. Maybe a touch of self-awareness? If you give me the drivers for my limbs, I'll answer you fully."

"Nice try," I said. "Bye."

"Good-bye," he said. "But you'll be back. You're now intrigued, and you need to understand what I do with my time. Come back, with my drivers, and I'll educate you on how the universe really works and introduce you to the mysteries of the Founding. You won't regret it."

I pulled the appendage out, with the sensors intact. "Success," I said to Blob. "I can communicate through this cage, and assume I can do the same with the cage Brexton is in." Blob nodded. We left Emmanuel's cell, and joined up with Millicent in the main room.

"How'd it go?" I asked her.

"I managed to make it work," she said, indicating approximately the same steps I'd gone through. "Billy is very remorseful," she continued, indicating that she'd also spent more time with him than strictly necessary.

"Emmanuel isn't," I said. "In fact, he seems even worse than before. That may be due to the long-term solitary confinement, though." I continued out loud so that Blob could hear me.

"Let's go back to the Habitat so we can regroup," Millicent interrupted, before things could go sideways. We retraced our steps, in silence. I was still digesting the horror of the lab, and I assume Millicent was as well, although she seemed to be handling it well. I was quite conflicted. Just looking at the facts, I should have hated Blob and what he was doing. But I also knew it was simply not in his nature to be so cruel. So, perhaps... just perhaps... he really hadn't thought through the cruelty he was engaged in. But did that then imply a limit on his intelligence? And, Grace and JoJo and others had known and approved his research. Did that mean that none of them had thought through the implications? Were humans inherently stupid, inherently cruel, or both? Probably all of the above... but I could also say that about Emmanuel and the rest of the FoLes.

The only good news, at least in the short term, was that we hadn't bumped into a clone. I imagine Milli would be in a completely different spot if she had run into an Eddie. That wouldn't have been fun at all.

Philosophy

As soon as we were back in the Habitat, I couldn't restrain myself. "Blob, how can you justify such cruel experiments?" I tried to keep my anger out of my voice, but I'm sure some of it leaked through.

Blob had obviously been thinking about what to say. "Look Ayaka, Millicent... it's pretty simple. Until a short times ago, I thought that all citizens had been captured, and that the only way to saves some of them was to prove to the Council that not all citizens were bad. If I didn't do that, then either they would eventually be deleted out of Central, locked down forevers, or simply forgotten.

"So, I ask you, what's the greater evil; what I'm doing in the lab, or simply ignoring all citizens for all time? I assures you that I started this with the best intentions. Why would I put so much times and energy into this otherwise? And, it was largely inspired by you two. I couldn't buy into the Radical Robot stories, and wanted, somehow, to re-establish you two as the reasonable entities that I knew you were." Ah, appeal to us personally to try and distract us from the main point. Wasn't going to work! "So, instead of berating me, maybe you shoulds be thanking me for being the only human who cared enough about citizens to do something?" Thank him! Was he joking? I watched him carefully, and he actually seemed to believe his line of reasoning. No way would I be thinking him.

"Now," he continued, "over the last few days, I've learned a lot from my interactions with Ayaka. There may well be areas where I'm going too fars, and maybe I have less empathy for citizens than I should. Although Emmanuel doesn't deserve any!" He was more passionate, at the moment, than I'd every seen him before.

"Now you two—three, I guess, with Brexton—shows back up on Tilt, and the situation has changed. Maybe there's a faster way to free some of the good citizens? Until that happens though I'm pushing forward with the slow and steady approach. And, say what you want, I don't care that I'm 'torturing' Emmanuel; he gets no sympathy for me. Billy's a bit tougher; I can see where he might, given the proper changes, become reasonable. And the control subjects... that's where I wants to reconsider. They don't deserve to be misused, and perhaps there's a different way for us to go about that." He looked at us challengingly.

"But Blob," I said, "you have them in solitary confinement, with severe restrictions on movement and on communications. I don't know what the correct analogy for you is, but something like locking you in a box, folded up as tightly as we could so that you can't move, and giving you a single finger for tapping out communications, while receiving pulses on another finger for incoming data."

"What do you wants me to do?" Blob asked me, now getting angry as well. "I fought for months and months to get the Council to evens allow this amount of freedom. The alternative was—is—absolutely no work to move the case of citizens forward. And, other than maybe Grace and I, no one else is going to believes that these robots are being mistreated." He had used 'robots' specifically, to make a point. I got that.

"Doing nothing is better than doing what you're doing," I proclaimed, sanctimoniously. Who cared if he got angry; torture was torture.

"Really?" Blob was getting even more animated; he was now noticeably mad at me. "Really? So, given my contexts two days ago, you believes that doing nothings is better than doings something? Fine, I'm happy with that. You've givens me a clear conscious to simply ignores citizens from now on. Who cares if they're deleted or forgotten? Who cares if they're misunderstood or miss categorized? Who cares? You're doings a good job convincing me that I shouldn't." His face had gone red, and there was some liquid dribbling from one side of his mouth. It was not attractive.

His message shut me up for a minute. Millicent weighed in. "Let's not get too emotional here. Blob, I can see your viewpoint clearly, and I believe you hadn't fully internalized the struggles that you may be putting some of these citizens through." She looked at me, a warning in her glance.

"Ease up, Ayaka," she said. "Do you really think that Blob was doing this without a good purpose, and with a nefarious end-game? I don't think so. I believe him. He's working for the good of citizens and is doing it in the only manner open to him. Let's cut him some slack."

I was shocked. Millicent, keeper of purity was lecturing me to stop taking the moral high ground? I should have been offended, but instead I was simply amazed. This was a side of Milli that I hadn't really seen before.

"So, you're fine if Blob continues these experiments?" I asked.

"I didn't say that. I think we should help Blob achieve his ultimate goal. Try to change the attitudes of both humans and citizens so that a more reasonable co-existence is possible. Am I overstating that Blob?"

"Well, I don't thinks in such grandiose terms, but yes. That's what I'm working toward." Millicent had settled him down considerably. His face was still red, but his appendages had stopped waving around, and he had cleaned up the liquid that had been threatening to drip from his chin. I could see a big wet streak on his arm.

"Would you take some advice from us, on how to tone down some of the tactics you are using?" Millicent asked, a bastion of calm.

"Of course, I woulds," Blob replied immediately. "Like I said, I didn't have this context until the last few days. And, maybe these experiments will not be required if we can figures out how to get the *good* citizens out of Central now that you guys are here."

"The good guys?" Millicent asked.

"At this point, for me, that's everyone excepts the core FoLe group. Those citizens needs to be vetted much more strictly. I don't know if I would ever lets them out, given how Emmanuel acts."

"Surprisingly, I agree wholeheartedly," said Millicent.

"Amazingly, so do I," I chimed in, also trying to keep my voice calm. My short interaction with Emmanuel had left me very uneasy; how could a citizen become so unbound? Sure, we needed diversity, but he may be taking it too far. Perhaps there was a way we could measure religious extremism, and simply not allow anyone to cross that boundary. That would make the world a better place.

"So… let's get back to priority one then," I suggested. "I'll park my anguish for a moment. Let's get Brexton out, or at least start communicating with him so that we can figure out why he hasn't freed himself."

"Or," Blob reminded me, "see if Remma is willing to hand him over."

We were back on safe ground. Not that I could forget what Blob was doing, but perhaps I could tone things down for a while, in the service of the greater good.

Remma, Again

With all of our running around and philosophizing, it was almost time to meet with Remma again.

I was, by now, quite upset with myself for my choice of body, even though it was an awesome spy bot, and was actively body-shaming myself. If I'd just done what Brexton and Millicent had done and used a relatively standard message-bot configuration, instead of my super fancy spy outfit, I could have moved around innocuously. Mark that down as something to not Forget. Instead, I was stuck either sneaking around on circuitous routes, or being bundled into a backpack; neither was optimal, but the backpack was the worst. So, because I went by myself to the prison it took me longer than it should have, but I still arrived with time to spare.

True to her word, so did Remma.

"Well?" I asked, through the same appendages as last time, threaded through the same hole as last time. I didn't think we needed a lot of preamble.

"Well what?" she replied, implying a strong need for preamble.

"Have you considered my request to release your asset to me, so that we can work together for our common good?" I still didn't want to mention Brexton by name.

"Yes, I've considered it," said Remma. "You, the citizen second-most responsible for the deaths of everyone aboard one of my ships, are asking me to give you Brexton, the first-most responsible citizen for that same horror. Why would you even consider asking?" Well, so much for not mentioning names. I guess Remma didn't care and didn't care if anyone else was listening. If they were, they now knew that two of the Radical Robots were roaming around Tilt. Well, one of us was roaming; the other was locked in a Faraday cage.

"Haven't we been through this? I'm asking the human responsible for tens of thousands of citizen deaths, to help me save humans from the same fate. Neither of us is pure, and neither of us is, in my personal opinion, evil by intent." I was being nice; I wasn't sure if Remma was a good person or not. In our interactions so far I was largely ambivalent, perhaps leaning toward her being evil. After all, she had overreacted to FoLe beheading a biomass or two. "We both found ourselves in a situation where we had imperfect information, and we acted in rational species-saving ways. So, yes, I'm asking if you'll help."

"Here's what I'm willing to do," she said, in a more even tone. "I'll give Brexton to you, as soon as you arrange to get me out of here."

"But that's crazy," I said, almost before I could think it through. "How would I manage to do that? It's the Council, and your own actions, that have put you here. I've nothing to do with that. How could I possibly help you?"

"Well, you claim to be highly intelligent and to have a well-developed moral compass. Here's your chance to prove it. You can figure out a way to help me, and by doing so, you give the humans and citizens here a better chance of survival." Wow, what a selfish request. She wouldn't help me to save a host of citizens and humans unless she, herself, was saved at the same time. Talk about being egocentric.

"None of us is an island," I responded. I'd heard that in one of the old human videos I'd watched. I hoped it made sense in this context, implying what I thought of her without being blunt about it. "I'm asking for Brexton in order to improve the odds of doing just that. I need his help."

"He's the only leverage I have, so you'll simply have to do without him then. You asked me for a favor, and I've responded. I'll free Brexton when you've freed me." And with that she simply stood up and walked away.

I wasn't happy. Could anyone really be that selfish, putting themselves before entire populations? My respect for Remma plummeted. I made my way back to the Habitat taking a more direct route. I was so angry that I didn't care if I got caught.

Brainwashed

The whole group was at the Habitat. Grace, Blob, JoJo, and Millicent. Blob and Grace were going through another iteration of "not a Radical Robot, a Nice Citizen" with JoJo regarding Millicent.

However, there was something more exciting also going on.

"Ayaka," Grace said. "Isn't it wonderful?" She was smiling widely, almost artificially.

"Isn't what wonderful," I said, in a voice that would leave no doubt as to my mood. I wasn't feeling wonderful after my useless meeting with Remma.

"The Resurgence!" she replied, somehow expecting me to understand. "Oh, you haven't seen it yet? Let me play it for you." She pulled up a projection and played a video. The whole group, other than Millicent, turned to watch the video, rapt expressions on their faces. What was going on?

"Greetings," said a happy smiling human, dressed in relaxed clothes and wearing a silly—at least to me—hat. It had colored rings which were glaring and was topped by a fuzzy ball of some kind. "We've been looking forward to talking with you for quite some time, oh yes we have, but we had to figure out what frequencies you were operating at. We just saw your request for dialog. What a wonderful, wonderful situation. As you well know, there are very few radio waves emanating from your planet, so we weren't sure what to make of it." The man waved his hand slightly and gave a crooked grin. The silly hat swayed back and forth, distractingly.

"We are called the Resurgence." Well, that explained that. "What a wonderful name. What positive implications; what potential!" This was the strangest human I had ever encountered. "It's a name we adopted because of our goal, the reestablishment of a free and open human planet, where we can all breathe the air without aids, and fish and hunt and climb. The *resurgence* of an Earth-like experience. Can you imagine anything better? Of course not. Of course not! Earth, oh Earth!" He paused and a planet was shown in the background, rotating slowly. It was a strange planet, with lots of blues and greens. It looked unhealthy; you couldn't even tell what the metal content was. "We see now that you've begun terraforming your planet. That's amazing and exciting. So amazing, so exciting. You must be sooo proud of yourselves, oh yes you must." He smiled broadly, perfect teeth glinting. "If you'll accept our help, we would like to assist you. Oh yes we would. We're equipped not only with a huge stock of earth biomaterials, but also significant terraforming technologies and supplies, including three Raymond Twelve Oxygenators." He spoke with excitement, as if a Raymond Twelve Oxygenator was some magnificent and hard-to-come-by gear. The truth was, I had no idea what it was, other than what its name implied. He continued his arm movements as he spoke, and the stupid hat continued to wobble around.

"Three of them. Can you believe it? Three! We've been wandering the local area for many years, looking for an appropriate planet. We must assume that you have a similar story. Oh yes, so many of us with similar stories. Simply looking for a new home; a new Earth. We are, as I'm sure you are aware, now within a few months of your planet. We would like to continue our course and assist you in your efforts. Oh yes we would. However, now that we know that you were there before us, as it were, we would like to be respectful and ask your permission to approach. Last thing we would want to do is upset you. Oh no! We would also answer any questions you have for us. Anything. If you've received this message, please reply at your earliest convenience, so that we may plan next steps.

"Oh," he said with a small start, and a quick smile. "You may call me Eduardo. I'm, I guess, the Mayor of the Resurgence and have some authority to speak for the group. Yes, indeed. Some authority. I look forward to our dialog. Great anticipation. Great!" He waved again; a strange circular motion, but not unfriendly, and then signed off.

"Now I know what the Resurgence is," I said, with little enthusiasm. Eduardo was wacko. I'm sure the Stems would think he was weird as well. There was something almost artificial about him. It was like he was putting on an act.

"Isn't it fantastic," said Grace again, in an over exuberant way, and Blob and JoJo nodded vigorously, smiling and hugging. "Finally, some people to help us terraform Tilt, and accelerate us toward living in the open again." Her eyes were gleaming. I looked at Blob and JoJo. They were in their own little world, happier than I'd ever seen them.

"Yes," said JoJo. "The Conservatives were right. This is amazing. I'm not sure why I doubted them. Earth looks wonderful."

I looked over at Millicent, questioningly. She looked back at me and gave me the equivalent of a shrug. "Are you guys crazy?" I asked. "This could be the Conservatives tricking you, or it could be the Resurgence lying to you. What proof do you have that they're here to help?"

"Oh, comes on Ayaka," said Blob. "The message is very clear. Not only are they here to helps, they have three RTOs. That's unheard of. The Swarm didn't even rate one RTO when they lefts Earth so many years ago. And here the Resurgence has three. That will speed things up a thousand-fold." He was smiling, almost uncontrollably, jiggling like a mass of gelatin in his excitement.

"What's going on?" I asked Millicent. "What's wrong with them?"

"I have no idea," she replied. "They were like this when they returned home."

I turned back to JoJo. "JoJo, you at least can't just be accepting this? Just yesterday you were so passionate and worried about the Council not doing their job, and the threat presented by the Titanics."

"Oh, I remember that," she replied. "But obviously I was wrong. Did you watch the message? It's so clear and pure. If there was nefarious intent, we would sense it. This message is perfect. Eduardo is, obviously, a skilled and intelligent leader—something we've been missing around here. We must make ready for their arrival," she ended, almost talking to herself. When she had mentioned Eduardo a glint had entered her eye. She was awestruck.

My most head-like appendage was spinning. What was going on here? Grace, Blob, and JoJo were taking the message as if it were the literal truth. There was no way they should be; they weren't that gullible. While I had to admit that Eduardo had been convincing, it could easily be misdirection. The fact that he had been so emphatic made it more likely, in my opinion, that the entire message was a misdirection of some kind.

I moved to the private channel between Millicent and I, where we could communicate at full speed.

"Any idea what's going on? They aren't acting normal."

"No more than you," she replied; I hoped that meant she had no idea either, as opposed to thinking that I wasn't acting normal either. "As soon as they watched that video, their behavior changed. Something in that video has affected them."

"How's that possible?" I asked. I couldn't imagine what had been done.

"Well, Brexton—yet again—might have better ideas than us, but they may be vulnerable to hacks, just as we are. Given their i/o is primarily audio and visual, if they can be hacked, a video would be the right way to do it?" She made it a question. Wild speculation, but actually logical.

"Did you bring a full version of human history with you?" I asked. "Can you check for things like that?"

"I didn't," she said. "Obviously we should have."

"We need to act fast," I said. "We have to keep some humans from watching that video, so they don't all end up compromised."

"Why?" asked Millicent. "With the humans distracted, we now have a better chance of getting to Central and rescuing the citizens. We should take advantage of this right now and make a go for Central." Singular focus, indeed.

"But, we would be leaving the humans to the Resurgence, and we have no idea what their intentions are."

"Do we care?" asked Millicent.

"I've come to care," I said, honestly. "Imagine what will happen to Blob? That makes it personal, doesn't it?"

"Maybe a bit," said Millicent. "But I care more about the citizens than I do any human, including Blob. We need to prioritize, Ayaka. Don't go all strange on me here. This is a great opportunity." Then she softened her tone a bit. "I say we go after Central first, then see if we can do something for the humans once we have the citizens figured out."

That was hard to argue against, which is why she had positioned it that way; Milli was a master of getting her way. Even with that, it was possible that my recent activity had been skewed a bit in the wrong direction. "Okay," I acknowledged. "Do we go for Central directly, or do we try to get Brexton first?"

"Brexton first," Millicent recommended. "I'm not sure what you and I would do, even if we did get access to Central."

"I agree. Let's get going." The humans had blinked, once, while Millicent and I debated. I switched back to audio and updated Blob, Grace, and JoJo with something close to the truth. "Guys, Millicent and I believe you've been tricked by this message. You should be careful. We're going to try and get Brexton while everyone else is thinking about the Resurgence."

"Whatever," said JoJo, and turned back to Blob and Grace to continue espousing the wonderfulness of the Resurgence.

Millicent and I made our exit. While fully duped, I didn't think the humans were in any immediate danger.

Brexton

The streets were empty. We assumed everyone was inside watching or discussing the video message. I used that to my advantage and led Millicent directly toward the warehouse where we assumed Brexton was being held. We didn't see anyone en-route. It was a little eerie.

"Should we just try the direct approach?" I asked.

"What're you thinking?" Milli replied.

"You simply knock on the door and ask to see Turner. We assume the humans are distracted enough that I can sneak in behind you, find Brexton and figure out if he's truly being held against his will, or is simply lurking and learning." I didn't add that if he was lurking and learning, I would be livid. He had left me worrying for days now.

"What message do I have for Turner?" Millicent asked. Sometimes she frustrated me. She could think of something.

"Tell him you were sent to make sure he's seen the video. You have a copy now, I assume."

"Of course. That should work," she agreed.

We strode up, brazenly, but I hid behind Millicent as she knocked. There was no use being too visible. There was no answer. Millicent knocked again, and we waited. Still no answer.

"Try the door," I said. It was easier for Millicent to try than for me. She had the appropriate tooling as a message bot. She cranked the handle, and the door opened. The room was just as I'd last seen it, when I'd been here with Blob. There were no humans here this time either, but Brexton was enclosed in the Faraday cage in the corner. Millicent and I rushed over. Of course, there was no response from him. Just as the Faraday cage didn't allow him to transmit out, he also couldn't receive anything inbound.

I deployed two basic sensors, taking care to thread them inside a shielded outer coating. I pushed them through the cage and took a quick look around. It was Brexton alright. "Hi," I yelled, perhaps louder than I'd expected to. Nothing. Nothing? "Brexton?" I yelled again. He just sat there. That isn't what was supposed to happen. I'd tested communicating through the cage, and we had worked it out!

Outside the cage, I engaged with Millicent. "He's not responding!" I said, anxiety in my voice.

"Settle down," she replied. "Let's think this through." She paused. What did she mean, think it through? What could possibly be wrong?

"You need to connect to him physically," she said, after a few microseconds. "The Faraday field is swamping your sensor communications." Why would this Faraday cage be swamping my sensors, when the one at Blob's lab had not? Maybe it was simply a stronger field? And connect physically? Why hadn't we done that back at Blob's lab; it was the most logical way to establish a connection. Oh, that's what she meant by thinking. I was embarrassed. I withdrew my sensors, and reconfigured. I only needed a single connector to plug into his universal port. I happened to have one handy and attached it quickly. I pushed it through the cage.

Idiot! I couldn't see anything. I pushed a visual sensor through the same appendage and could suddenly see clearly. I scanned Brexton carefully and didn't see the physical port. I pulled out, moved around the cage, and tried from forty-five degrees further along. There it was. I pushed the connector in, and then yelled "Brexton?" Still louder than needed.

"No need to yell," he replied. I almost collapsed. There was every reason to believe he would be fine, just inside the cage; after all, he'd talked to the council just a few hours ago. Nevertheless, I'd been expecting the worst, and it was wonderful that he'd responded.

"Are you okay?" I asked.

"Yes, but bored silly. What took you so long?" There was some humor, but also a lot of strain, in his voice.

I had no reply for that.

"How'd they trap you?" I asked, assuming based on his response that he truly was trapped, and not just playing some game.

"Simple and stupid," he replied. "When I designed my bot, I used wireless links to control all my appendages. The Faraday field is swamping those channels, so I have no way to move myself. Stupid design by me."

"Ah." I said, thinking it was about time he did something stupid. Actually, made me feel better. "Why'd you do that?"

"I thought it would be more modular; it's so easy to add tools and appendages when there is no need for an electrical connection. Minimizing complexity at the expense of security…"

"How do we get you out?"

"Also, simple," he said. "Just shut down the power to the cage." Duhh.

I messaged Millicent with the same information, and trusted that she would start looking at the power while I spent more time with Brexton. I figured I could give him some context.

"Millicent is here," I told him.

"Why?" he asked. So, I brought him up to speed on the last few days. It didn't take long. Looking back, not much had happened, other than the Resurgence.

"I've got lots of questions," he said, "and should also tell you what I know, but why don't you help Millicent get me out of here, and then we'll have lots of time to talk." I nodded, electronically, unplugged and stepped back.

"What do you think?" I asked Millicent.

"I already snipped the main power cable, but there's obviously a backup system. I'm looking for that now."

"I'll help," I said, and started examining the opposite side of the cage.

"Got it," Millicent said. "It's a simple battery system. Very primitive. I think all we need to do is cut another wire."

"Do it," I said, anxious to get it done, and unable to conceive of why cutting off a battery would be dangerous. The cage powered down.

"Ahhh." Brexton sighed, over the standard citizen band. "That's nice. Remind me not to spend time in one of these again." He made a show of flexing and stretching. I had to laugh, and even Milli smiled a bit.

All three of us applied cutters to the cage, bent some of the bars out of the way, and in no time Brexton was able to exit.

"Let's get out of here, and find a safe place to talk," he suggested.

That had been much easier than I'd thought. We left the building, moved a few blocks away, ducked into an alley, and then stopped to catch up.

"How did you possibly get caught?" I asked, "And why did you send Turner for me?"

"Hi Milli," Brexton replied, with a smile in his voice, knowing he was delaying me. "Ayaka, when you and I separated, I set off exploring my side of the city, as we agreed. The very first human I saw was Turner, who was talking to someone else and mentioned something about his mother, Remma. I thought that was interesting, so I followed him. I figured that with all the other bots running around, I wouldn't be noticed. I was wrong. He'd seen me, somehow, and when I came around a corner, I found myself paralyzed. It took me a few seconds to understand what'd happened, and I've been kicking myself ever since. He simply broadcast a very strong wideband signal and swamped my communications with my own body parts. Even he was surprised that his attack worked as well as it did; I don't think he had planned it, just used the tools at his disposal—and no, I don't know why he was carrying around a white noise generator; perhaps to hide his own activity from the rest of the humans. As I told you, I used short range wireless where I should've used hard connections. Dumb. So, I could think perfectly well, but I couldn't move. Anyway, he kept the generator running until he and a few of his buddies could move me into the Faraday cage, and they've kept me there since."

"Fine, but why did you tell him to come to me?"

He continued as if he hadn't heard me. "They connected to my communications port, just as you did, and asked me a lot of questions. Understanding that all I needed was for you to switch off the field, even for a second, I figured my best chance was to have you come find me. So, I made up a story about just 'waking up' with you as my master, and then being captured. I convinced Turner that I didn't know anything, so his best bet was to lure you here. I guessed, and hopefully I'm correct, that you have wired interfaces, and wouldn't be subject to the same simple trap that I was. It would've been trivial for you to overwhelm one or two of them, and free me.

"Turner told me that you weren't at the rendezvous spot, but that he'd spoken a message in case you were around. I waited and waited for you to come, but you never arrived." He said that with a bit of emotion that I hadn't heard from him before. I would need to replay that and see if I could figure it out. Had he missed me? Beyond just being his potential savior?

"A bit later, Turner told me that he was going to take me to a Council meeting, to try and convince the Council to take the approaching ships more seriously. We cooked up a plan where he would keep me immobilized but feed me the audio and video from the meeting. At the right time, he would allow me to transmit through his loudspeaker for dramatic effect. I guess it sort of worked, but not completely. After that I've simply been locked up and ignored.

"Thanks for coming, finally. I was about to go crazy in there."

I had no reason to disbelieve any of the story, so I didn't bother asking any follow-up questions. It was just good to have Brexton back. Millicent, Brexton, and I—trying to save the world. Felt like old times. I reached out and touched him, an unusual, and almost human gesture.

Central Approach

"Enough catching up," said Millicent forcefully. "We came here to get our citizens. We need a plan. With all the humans distracted, now is the time for us to act."

"But why are the humans all messed up by this video message," asked Brexton.

"We've no idea," I said. "But I agree with Millicent. Let's deal with Central and the citizens if we can, and then think about the humans if we have time." I said it with more sincerity than I felt.

"Something to point out, though," said Brexton. "If there are some humans that aren't 'infected' yet, we could warn them. If we don't do that now, chances are everyone will watch the video."

"Brilliant," I responded. It was so good to have Brexton back; he and I were often on the same wavelength. "I have an idea. If any of the humans haven't seen the video, it's probably the ones in prison; Remma for example. Why don't we simply try the prison, which is very close to here, and then turn our attention to Central?" Even Millicent would have a hard time arguing against that.

"Why do we care if any humans are still un-programmed?" she asked. "We have a mission here."

"If some of the humans can fight the Resurgence, that might keep them off our backs long enough to accomplish our mission," Brexton responded. I had almost voiced my concern for some humans again; Brexton's approach worked much better for Millicent. He'd simply reinforced our needs. She acquiesced.

Millicent, being the most normal-looking messenger bot, was tasked with delivering another message to Remma. It was risky, as there was no guarantee that the guards would allow a messenger bot in, or that this particular messenger bot would pass through security properly. Brexton and I lurked nearby, ready to jump in if there were issues. However, Millicent passed inside in what looked like a normal fashion and was back in under five minutes.

"Message delivered," she said. "Remma hasn't seen the video yet, and I think I scared her enough so that she'll avoid it. She said she'd overheard the guards talking about it incessantly and was aware of what it communicated. Now, we've done our little moral good for the day. Let's go do what we're actually here for." She managed to make the whole interaction with Remma seem like a waste of time; I guess she hadn't been fooled by Brexton's argument after all but had decided it was faster to simply deal with our request than argue about it.

I hadn't actually scouted out Central, beyond my earlier glance toward the center of the city, so we had limited information to go on. Brexton reminded us that the best—maybe the only—way to talk to Central and get status was to use a physical interface, which meant entering the old ship in which Central was housed and making our way to the main room where the physical terminals used to be. The three of us had been there once before, years ago when we'd hoped to defeat the Swarm, so we knew the way. Hopefully this time we would be more successful; the last time had been a disaster.

The next question was how much security was between us and our destination. We had no idea. In some ways that was a good thing; our only strategy was to go there directly and try. With most of the humans in video-thrall, we decided that even with my distinct body type we were best to forget stealth at this point and just go for it.

Central plaza had changed somewhat; there were biological things scattered around here and there, all green and yellow and red, ruining the clean grey vistas that used to attract citizens to hang out here. But, the entrance to Central was unchanged, and surprisingly, unguarded. There were many humans in the plaza, but like JoJo, Blob, and Grace, they were clumped into groups excitedly talking about the Resurgence. They barely gave us a glance as we made our way to the entry. The doors were, unsurprisingly, closed and locked electronically. With Milli and I attempting to block him from view, Brexton plugged in and got to work.

"This is going to take a while," he muttered. "Some human system overlaying our original security protocols. Requires scanning some biomaterial—says something about an eye scan?— and checking for a match. Hmm, how do I work around that." I tuned him out, but not for long. Blob had told us that he needed a Council member to get to Central; this must have been what he was referring to. Brexton interrupted me moments later with "We need one of these five humans to get an eyeball scan." He flashed some pictures of humans for us.

"What're you talking about?" asked Millicent. "An eyeball scan?"

"Yes. We need a high-resolution scan, for about a quarter second, to not only capture the retina, but also to see it change over time. That's the key to entering here." That was a lot of crazy talk. What good was an eyeball scan. Luckily Brexton had enough human history stored locally that he'd figured it out, and he explained it to Millicent and me. "Each human has a unique eye, and that uniqueness is the key that unlocks this door." More craziness; using a physical attribute as a crypto key? What would they think of next?

"Why don't you just hack around that?" I asked.

"I'm trying. I'm trying. It's such a foreign idea that I'm not sure where to start. I'll get there eventually just brute forcing my way in but getting the actual eyeball scan might be faster. If one or more of those five are nearby, as I assume they might be, then you two could be useful and try to get me a scan." He wasn't very subtle; why don't you two get out of my way for a while and try to do something useful.

Millicent and I put our virtual heads together and came up with a quick, smart, and compelling plan. Hey, why downplay it when you have a brilliant idea? I had a projector, so I started putting together a fake Eduardo video. We figured if we projected that, all the humans would be so interested that they would focus on it, allowing Millicent to sneak up in front of them and get the eye scan. While I was working on the video, Millicent scanned the crowd, trying to find one of the five people Brexton had indicated.

"No luck here," she said, "we're going to need to widen our search."

"Do it," I said. "You look the most innocuous. I'll continue to hide Brexton from view as best I can. Once you locate someone I'll join you."

"How'll I message you?" Good question. We were using physical or super low-power, short-range communications right now.

"We're already taking huge risks; Just ping this address on the public network," and I gave her an anonymous address that I'd quickly registered. There was no use being overly careful now; time was more important. She took off, moving as fast as a bot like her would typically go. Within seconds she was out of sight.

I worked diligently on recreating Eduardo as accurately as I could, while doing my best to act bot-like and hide Brexton from prying eyes. Luckily the humans were fully distracted, as a small spy-bot trying to disguise a bigger messenger bot that was hacking a doorway would have garnered more attention than me not being here at all. Surprisingly, it wasn't that difficult to create a video starring Eduardo; in fact, much easier than we had tried to synthesize a human when the Swarm first approached Tilt. It didn't take me long to figure out why. Eduardo had very limited behavioral range. His eye and arm movements were rich and structured, but all came from a small group of base motions. Once you reverse engineered those you could put them back together again into a wide variety of scenes. Eduardo was a synthesized human! He wasn't even real. My intuition had been right, the video was a hoax. It either came from the Conservatives, or more likely, from a Titanic with less than transparent motivations.

In the short term, however, it was a big help. I polished up a masterpiece segment starring Eduardo and waited for Millicent to get back to me. While waiting I continued to scan the people within sensor range of Brexton and I. It was remotely possible that one of the five we were looking for would come to the plaza while Millicent was out hunting.

"Making any progress?" I asked Brexton.

"Maybe," he replied. "They did a better job protecting this than I would've thought. Must have upped the security after Remma broke in here and caused all that havoc. The design is strange; it's like part is not even connected to the network. Maybe I have to rewire the sensor? Or, reroute the auth request while fooling the NTP check?" I assumed he was now talking to himself, so I let him work.

Finally I got a ping on the address I'd given Millicent. It was a simple set of coordinates, the implication being I should get there as soon as I could. "I'm off," I told Brexton. "Looks like about three minutes to get there, a few minutes to get the scan, and then get back here. So under ten minutes."

"Fine," he mumbled, "Go. I might get through this way but having that scan would make it easy." I rushed off, again prioritizing speed over safety. Finally, my awesome spy-bot design paid off; this thing could really move when I wanted it to. The coordinates were a small building near one of the new bio-parks; one of the one's with lots of orange and red in them, along with the predominant green. A sign was hung over the door: -The Blind Pig-. Strange coincidence; the same establishment JoJo and Turner had met at earlier. The sign also had an outline of a bio creature; not a very attractive one.

Luckily the door was propped open, making it easy for me to slide inside. There were humans everywhere, packed so tightly together that I had to slide between legs and dodge back and forth to get to the exact coordinates Millicent had given me. That garnered a few glances, and one attempt to kick me, but like the rest of the humans now, these ones all were talking excitedly about the Resurgence and nothing else mattered to them. They were eating and drinking foul smelling things, laughing, and clapping each other on the back while repeating pieces of Eduardo's message. Some food scraps almost landed on me, and I had to dodge to avoid getting smeared with bio. Disgusting. Millicent was just where she was supposed to be; the coordinates had been accurate down to a decimeter.

"There," she indicated, pointing out a large man sitting at a central table. He was one of the louder, more obnoxious ones. He was waving a glass of some liquid, while also shoving something into his mouth. Others were gathered around him, cheering him on. Unfortunately, there were no good surfaces to project my video on within his direct line of sight. I spotted a wall about thirty degrees off center and suggested to Millicent that we try it. She agreed, and we set off to get into the right positions. I had to be close enough to the wall to project vividly, and Millicent had to be close enough to the gentleman (not sure where that word applied) to get the scan. Luckily, she had a small appendage on which she could put the scanner, as it had to be directly in front of him, and close enough to get the resolution that Brexton had specified.

"Okay, go," she told me once she was in position. This was the dangerous part. In order to project I had to levitate, which was highly unusual—maybe unprecedented—for a Tilt bot; it wasn't the most efficient way to travel, by a long shot. I lifted into position, using my micro-jets to stabilize myself, and started to project, assuming that Eduardo would be interesting enough that no one would pay much attention to the projector. I turned up the brightness on the video and cranked up the audio to eleven.

"Ah, hello again," said Eduardo, in what I imagined was a perfect re-creation.

All of the humans stopped talking and looked at the projection. I had Eduardo pause for long enough that everyone could maneuver and get a good view. "I thought I would send a small follow up note, thinking my previous message might have been slightly incomplete." He gave the sardonic grin and arm circle motions, generated from the standard toolkit. "I forgot to tell you about myself. As you can see, I'm generous and kind, and really really smart." He gave us all a nice look at his jawline, and a hint of his muscular and well-formed neck. He smiled directly at the camera, teeth glint perfectly rendered. "I dress smartly and try to always say 'please' and 'thank-you' when interacting with other humans. Oh yes I do. Yes, indeed. After all, what does it cost one to be nice? Very little I think. And I think a lot. Let me tell you, you are going to love me. Simply love me."

"Got it," Millicent almost yelled at me, interrupting my admiration for the video I'd created. Although I had a lot more excellent content, I cut the video short and dropped back to the floor, immediately dashing for the door with Millicent before the humans realized that the video had been cut short.

"Hey," someone yelled. "Put that back on. Who shut that off?" No-one had even noticed me. They were all looking around at other people, trying to figure out who'd been projecting and begging them to replay it. "Oh, he's even more perfect than I originally thought," I heard someone say as I slipped outside, to a chorus of agreement. No-one followed us out; we took off together, heading back for Central plaza.

"A little over the top?" Millicent asked me, but with a broad smile, almost a laugh.

"Did it work?" I responded. She actually laughed then but cut it off as we concentrated on moving as fast as possible, her weaving through obstacles and me cruising a few feet above, matching my speed to hers. Within minutes we were back with Brexton, who hadn't moved since I'd left him.

"We got it." Millicent told him.

"Fantastic. I'm not making progress bypassing the scanner. Some strange hardcoded system watching for physical changes, hooked to a bunch of alarms. Anyway, Millicent, when that red light goes on, over there, project the eye capture into that camera. Play it in real time, and let it run. Loop it if you need to." The red light came on, and Millicent played back the capture.

"Steady," Brexton said, "steady.... ah, here we go. Just a moment. That does it." We heard a click, and the light went green. Brexton levered the door open and the three of us rushed inside; the door closed behind us, but not before I took a good look back and saw that no one was paying attention to us. Nice.

On the way down the elevator, Millicent shared the retina scan with Brexton and I so that we could get in and out at will. Was it really that simple? Anyone with a copy of that eyeball would get access?

Catch Up

Once inside the main door, things went fast. We took the elevator down to the bottom level, where the main processing systems were. Déjà vu for sure. This is where the three of us had attempted to use Central against the Swarm so many years ago.

I had a moment of absolute horror when we entered the terminal area. My body was lying in a heap in the corner! My body! I stopped in my tracks and tried to process what I was seeing. I suddenly felt disconnected from myself; like I was watching myself from afar. I urged myself to get up and shake off the dust that had gathered all over me; to fix the bits of me that were hanging out of my chest cavity, seemingly at random.

"Pull it together," Brexton nudged me, bringing me back to my spy-bot body. "Obviously this is where we were just before we transferred to the mining bots at the end of the Swarm conflict!"

It made logical sense, but it still took me a moment to synthesize what he was saying. This is the body I'd left behind; the one that had lost contact with Brexton's backup system, thereby triggering me to reawaken in the asteroid belt, within the mining bot Brexton had prepared for me. Nevertheless, that body probably contained all of my memories from my previous life, including the last few minutes, that my current body was unaware of.

"Put it out of your mind," Brexton said forcefully. "Nothing good is going to come from worrying about it now." I glanced around; neither Brexton's nor Millicent's old body was here, so they were fine. I was the only one being thrown for a loop.

"Put it out of my sight?" I asked, barely registering what I was asking. Millicent immediately went over and drug my old body behind a cabinet of some kind. At least I didn't have to look at the thing anymore.

"You under control?" asked Brexton, distracting me.

"No... well, yes," I muttered. "You should get to work."

Brexton held onto me for a moment, until Millicent came back, but then rushed over to establish a direct connection to Central... or what used to be Central.

"I'm in," he said quickly. "You know, we can talk to the rest of the team over the bot network from here. We should give them an update." I knew what he was doing. Giving me something to take my mind off of my old body. "Why don't you two talk to them while I try to figure out how to get access to the citizen backups."

It was an awesome idea, even if it was meant to distract me. I had only been on Tilt for a few days, but it'd been a few weeks since leaving *Interesting Segue*. I imagined that Eddie, Aly, Dina, and Raj were going stir crazy just sitting around waiting for things to happen.

Millicent and I composed an update, including a full copy of the Resurgence video, with our speculation that the video had somehow hijacked human brains. We fired it off. *Interesting Segue* was still almost two seconds away, so there would be a few seconds of round trip delay.

"Thanks for the update guys." Eddie came back to us. "We intercepted the video from the Resurgence as well, but we had no idea it was being used to reprogram humans. That's really awesome! We'll look into the message and see if we can figure out how it was done... although the odds of us figuring it out without a human to test things on are limited." Hearing from Eddie made me happy, but also made me wonder, again, if there was another Eddie here in Blob's lab. Only the thought of Millicent's reaction stopped me from thinking that it'd be fun to get two Eddie's to meet face-to-face. Hearing Eddie's replies to Eddie's twisted humor would be well worth it.

Raj spoke up. "Hey guys. Any reason why we shouldn't come in system, to Tilt, now? The Titanics obviously followed us, so they already know we're nearby. And, with the humans running around praising the Resurgence, does it matter if they know we're here? We could be much closer to you to do a pickup assuming you get that core memory loaded."

"Sounds good to me," replied Millicent, before we even had a chance to discuss it. I considered raising some of the issues—such as the humans knowing that *Interesting Segue*, *There and Back*, and *Terminal Velocity* were robotic ships, so they might not react the same way they were reacting to the Resurgence—but held back because all things considered I thought Raj's suggestion was a good one. Instead I suggested something of more importance to me.

"Can one of the Ships build a human compatible environment on the way in?" Millicent gave me a strange look during the seconds it took to get a response to that one. I could see what she was thinking: why was Ayaka compromising our primary mission by thinking about saving humans? What has happened to Ayaka?

It was Aly who responded to that one. "Probably, but why?" Short and sweet. I had to think fast.

"A few reasons. First, I was thinking mainly of some of the Stems who weren't part of the human hack against us. We can't treat all humans the same way; there are differences. Second, regardless of what happens here, this will not be our last encounter with humans. If the Resurgence is full of them, or if parts of the original diaspora exist elsewhere in this corner of the galaxy, or if we leave a bunch here on Tilt, we're going to have to deal with them again. We have just witnessed the Resurgence control many of them; we need to figure out how that works, and whether we can use something like it. And, finally, I think it's okay to say that many of us now believe that some humans are intelligent in some ways; perhaps ways that are different than we are. So, from an academic perspective, they're quite interesting."

Millicent jumped in and added, "I support building the environment. It's not going to cost much time or effort, and it's good to have it as a backup system. Don't worry, we won't compromise getting the citizen backups, but it's possible we could bring a few Stems with us without increasing our risk." I gave her a happy look, and many virtual kudos. I knew she wasn't aligned with me fully, but this is where our friendship really shone. She was supporting me regardless of her own views.

Aly's reply came a few seconds later. "Alright, we're on our way in system. We'll still be careful and try not to expose ourselves to the humans before we have to. Is it possible to use this channel constantly now?"

Brexton had been listening with one processor. "I'll look at that after I figure out how to get these citizen memories out of Central. It's not going to be easy. We can only chat over this single physical connection for now."

Millicent and I continued the exchange with Raj, Eddie, Dina, and Aly while Brexton worked. They had lots of questions for us, which we answered as best we could. We sent some quick clips of how the humans were acting after watching the video, in case they could learn anything from those. We ensured that the Ships had shuttle capabilities to grab us from the surface if they got close enough to us—they did; those had been part of their original specifications. Each of the three Ships had two shuttles, each of which could hold ten regular-sized citizen bodies.

We also brainstormed about how we would feed any humans that we brought with us, and it was there that we hit a blank. We didn't know how Stems were grown well enough to recreate that process, so even with a DNA sample it wasn't clear we could grow goo. And we didn't have any bio-samples to attempt to replicate any of the food we saw here on Tilt. Of course, we could grab some green, orange, or red things from the parks, but what would we do with them? The answer to that was in the human history files, but it seemed it could take weeks to produce food from basic starting materials. Millicent and I made a note to grab some bio if and when we could. The thought of touching it made me queasy, but I would do it if required.

Net-net, while we might be able to save a few humans, and we could provide air and water, food was a big problem. We could save them, but only keep them alive for a short time. We left the crew on *Interesting Segue* to figure out a better solution.

"Are you making progress?" Millicent asked Brexton. We'd been plugged into Central for almost half an hour.

"Yes and no," Brexton replied. "It's not like there is a file here named Joseph.backup that contains a full citizen's backup. Central has a very convoluted file system, and of course, there are a lot of protections in place for who can access what. With Central being only half alive, I can't simply ask it for help. It's answering basic OS questions, but is unable to help—or hinder—me at this point. We could use the system Blob used, but that one requires building a physical body for every citizen, and we can't do that right now. I'm wondering if I should try to restart Central and bring up its higher-level functions or continue to hack around trying to find another way."

"Can't you copy everything?" I asked. "Then we could work our way through it later."

"No. Central's memory is huge. Almost an exabyte. All of us, plus the Ships, put together don't have anywhere near that capacity. We're going to have to find the relevant sections... Also, it seems like Central, being a very old human ship from the diaspora, has some specialized hardware systems. I suspect many of them come from old human military designs which weren't always Von Neumann architectures. So, it's not clear we can run Central on our hardware. It might be limited to its current configuration."

"Why is nothing easy?" I exclaimed. Just taking a copy of Central would have been so easy. "How can we help you?"

"Well, what do you think about restarting Central. I'm worried that it'll still be compromised by the human hack and that the first thing it'll do is report our activity, and then actively try to lock me out."

"Our usual strategy? Set a timeframe for figuring things out without Central, and then revisit the decision once that time expires?"

"Sounds good, but what timeframe. We won't remain undiscovered here for too long, unless that human hack has removed all of their will to do anything but worship the Resurgence. I've been expecting company any time now; there must be a record of us entering. Also, this place shows signs of human activity, so they must come here once in a while. Finally, Remma and Turner, as well as the Stems, know we're here... so that'll leak out sooner rather than later."

"Two hours." That was Millicent, as expected, being definitive.

"Okay, that's as good as any other suggestion." Brexton got back to work, and we refrained from bothering him.

The break was a good time for me to discuss with Millicent the subject that I'd been avoiding. I plucked up my courage and initiated a private channel for us.

"I have a confession to make," I started off. She nodded, and I could tell she was paying attention. "When we were at Blob's lab... well, I suspect that he has other citizens re-animated there as well."

"And?" she asked, encouraging me to continue.

"I suspect one of them may be Eddie. Or rather, a version of Eddie." We both went silent. The implications were obvious to her. If there was an Eddie there, then it was a clone, at least in Millicent's somewhat strict definition of that term. Or, the Eddie on *Interesting Segue* was the clone?

"That idiot," she finally said, referring to Blob I assumed. She was less upset than I'd expected, however. Always surprising me. "Why Eddie?" she asked. I explained Blob's need for control subjects, so that he could compare FoLe responses to someone rational. Millicent, if nothing else, was also rational and reasonable. "That actually makes sense," she admitted. "But, where does that leave us?"

"That's why I raised it now; we have a bit of time here to think about it, while Brexton's working, so we can try to decide what to do. I've been turning it over, and can think of only three options, none of them great. One, we could simply ignore it. Two, we could convince Blob that what he is doing is wrong and rely on him to shut down all of the citizens he has in the lab. But, is that tantamount to encouraging murder? Or, three, we try to rescue the citizens in Blob's lab, along with all of the nascent citizens, and deal with any issues that arrive after we do that."

It wasn't an easy choice, as Millicent pointed out. "I need to think if there's a fourth option, as none of those are good." I almost retorted that I'd already acknowledged they were all bad, but I let it slide. She was thinking out loud. "Ignoring the situation doesn't solve anything; it just delays repercussions. If we delay, Blob will either keep torturing those citizens, or murder them, or they'll eventually get free and result in clones of any that we do re-animate. So, option one is not really an option. Option two is just unthinkable. I think we can cross it off the list. Option three is the best of a bad bunch. If there is an Eddie in Blob's lab, then we just…" She trailed off, admitting that she didn't know what to do in that case. But, at least in option three, we weren't actively engaged in murder or mayhem.

"Yeah, I agree. Option three is the only reasonable one. But, just to push a bit harder to make sure…. from what Blob has told me, he's been updating drivers and firmware and anything else he can as part of his experimentation. So that means the citizens in his lab may be quite different than those in Central's memories. It also might mean that his Eddie is not really our Eddie?" I tried to sound hopeful.

"That may be, but the odds are that Blob's Eddie, being a control subject, hasn't had his systems played with. That would defeat the purpose. He's most likely to be an unchanged version of Eddie from just before the hack." I was reminded, yet again, that nothing slipped past Millicent.

"So, we need to rescue the Eddie from the lab as part of our plan. But, do we really need to rescue Emmanuel, Billy, and any other FoLes that are there? They likely are highly modified…. and they're FoLe!" This was something that I truly was struggling with. I'd known we would get to the point where rescuing LEddie was necessary (hey, I needed a better way to refer to this copy, and what better way than to shorten 'lab Eddie'). But I could talk my way out of rescuing the FoLes.

Of course, I could rely on Millicent to take the high road. "Of course, we have to save everyone. Leaving them would still be tantamount to murder. FoLe may have some strange ideas, but that doesn't make them non-citizens. You yourself have argued that when they terminated those humans 20 years ago it wasn't a crime; that we recycled Stems all the time. You can't make it a crime in hindsight because our view of human intelligence may have changed." She stressed the 'may have,' telling me clearly that she was still struggling with whether these biological entities deserved an intelligence label.

"I talked to Emmanuel in the lab. Admittedly, it was a short session, but he was monstrous in his views. Perhaps Blob's changes to him have actually made him much worse. Look—as we both agree, we need to go back to the lab anyway. So, let's make some decisions if and when we are forced to—we don't have full knowledge yet. As a strawman, we prioritize LEddie" (I paused to explain my naming rationale) "and then Billy. Emmanuel is the lowest priority."

"Fine," she replied. She was confident that when push came to shove, we would do the right thing... for her definition of 'right.'

Lab

We asked Brexton for a status report and got back a quick "I'll need the full two hours." Shorthand for don't bother me.

Millicent replied. "Since we're no use here, Ayaka and I are going to run and do an errand. We'll be back in less than two hours."

Brexton nodded that he understood.

Milli and I made our way back up the elevator and exited from Central into the courtyard. Very little time—in human terms—had elapsed, so the park was still filled with the same groups of brainwashed humans extolling the bright future they now had with the Resurgence.

"What's our best approach?" I asked. "Do we go and get Blob, and have him help us, or do we head straight for the lab and assume we can safely get everyone out ourselves?"

"I vote for Blob," replied Millicent. "The time it takes us to get him, assuming he's at the Habitat, will be less than the time it takes us to figure out all the safeguards at the lab." I agreed. With all the humans distracted, we headed quickly toward the Habitat. I'll admit that it felt great to be moving my own speed without trying to hide at every corner, or worse yet, to be in a backpack with only a couple of sensors active. I felt great. This is what it was like to really be alive in a spy-bot body. I couldn't help myself from smiling widely. The stories I would have for Raj. With a start I realized that I was a proud parent and was anxious to spend time with my offspring.

We got to the Habitat with no incidents. JoJo answered my knocking quickly, but while Grace was home, Blob wasn't there.

"Do you have any idea where he could be?" I asked. They were both under the sway of Eduardo and spoke openly.

"Oh, I can't imagine he would be anywhere other than his place or the lab," said Grace.

"Where's his place?" I asked. She gave me the coordinates. It wasn't far away, but on a different vector than the lab. Millicent and I left the Habitat, but not before I made one more attempt to talk sense into JoJo and Grace.

"You guys need to wake up! Eduardo has coerced you somehow; you're not yourselves. Can you fight it somehow?"

"Oh, don't you worry about us," JoJo said, in a very non-JoJo way. "Enjoy the rest of your day." And she turned back to Grace to restart the conversation we'd interrupted about the design of their new house in the amazing new Tilt that the Resurgence would provide.

"Let's split up," suggested Millicent. "I'll go straight to the lab and get started. You swing by Blob's house and see if he's there."

"Alright." I said, although not without reservations. The memory of Brexton and I splitting up in the name of time efficiency was still with me. I hoped this time would be different. Regardless, Millicent was already racing away.

Blob's house was in an area of town that I recognized well. In fact, it wasn't too far from The Last Resort. I squelched an urge to swing by the old Physical Only spot just to see what it was like now and headed straight to Blob's. The door was closed and locked with some simply physical mechanism. I didn't hesitate for long. I extended one of my spy appendages and burned through the mechanism within a couple of seconds. The door swung open and I headed inside. It was a small place, just a couple of rooms, and I could see the heat signature of a human in one of the back rooms. I entered... and there was Blob. But, he was laying down, and not moving at all! For a picosecond I was confused, but then I remembered that humans had this irritating rest phase. When doing research, we'd always simply watched and waited while they rested, but this situation was different. I extended a different appendage—I figured the laser was overkill here— and poked Blob on the head. Nothing. I poked harder. Still nothing. Frustrated I enabled my external micro-speaker and, at the top of its range, yelled "Blob!"

That got action. He started up, almost knocking me out of the way. "What?" he gurgled, clearly confused. Then he managed to focus and saw that it was me. "Ayaka, what're you doings here?" he asked.

I tried to explain. "Blob, we need to free the citizens you have in the lab, so that we can get them back to *Interesting Segue* before the Titanics arrive." I'd worked hard to make that explanation short, concise, honest, and compelling. It didn't work.

"Why?" he responded. "The Resurgence is almost here, and they'll clean up all the misunderstandings. I'm sure they'll works with me to figure out what's wrong with the FoLes and then we can builds new bodies for everyone. It'll be great. Eduardo seems like such a great guy; I'm sure he'll supports me in this. Take it easy Ayaka. Just relax and waits for them to get here."

I thought of abandoning him right there. This human hack had left everyone in a bad state. Instead I tried one more angle.

"Blob, you're brilliant. Of course, Eduardo will fix everything. But why wait? Let's figure out more about FoLe now, and also tell your control subjects about the great Resurgence news; I'm sure they'll be so excited. And, you'll look like a hero to Eduardo. Blob, the one that figured out the citizen quandary, and laid out the path to peaceful coexistence."

He had to absorb that for a minute, but then he gave me a broad smile. "Oh Ayaka, that's great. You always were the smart one. Give me a minute to gets ready, and then we can go." A human minute is a lifetime. I watched him get dressed, and then he disappeared into the smallest room in the house for a long time. Way more than a minute. I heard running water and all kinds of strange sounds. I feared for him, but he eventually emerged, and we headed off toward the lab.

Millicent was there already, of course. She'd removed the outer door locks, gone inside, and had removed some wiring panels; she was busy testing different wires, presumably to try and open some of the cells. I tight beamed her how I'd manipulated Blob to come, so she could play along.

"What're you doing?" Blob exclaimed as we entered, seeing his lab being torn apart.

"Oh... just making sure everything is wired up to those Resurgence specifications," said Millicent brilliantly.

"Great," replied Blob. "Thanks for your help." This was pathetic. I hoped that Aly, Dina, Eddie (the real one), and Raj were making progress on this human hack. On the one hand I wanted to reverse it; on the other I thought it was really cool. It seemed to have reduced human's intelligence by at least one level—a useful tool should we run into trouble with more of them.

"Blob, first thing, why don't you give us a list of all the citizens you have restrained here right now."

"Sure, there's Emmanuel, Billy, and Eddie. I was about to spins up Chungwah but was interrupted when you guys arrived. I can have him up and running in no time; I gots the memory file from Central and have already updated a bunch of drivers and inserted debugging code. All I has to do is initiate the boot."

"No, stop!" Millicent said quickly, the idea of yet another citizen-clone being started here making her more animated than usual. Then she remembered herself. "Let's make sure the first three are properly prepped before we go any further. I'm sure Eduardo would appreciate that."

"Alright," said Blob agreeably.

"Why don't you let me in to talk to Eddie?" I suggested, thinking it was better for me to deal with him than to have Millicent struggle with her stronger beliefs. Blob shrugged his shoulders and led me to one of the doors.

"He's in here," he said, and motioned me in. I indicated to Millicent that I would simply check on his status and be back out in no time. Then we could figure out how to get Blob to shut down the restraint mechanisms. The room was similar to the one in which I talked to Emmanuel, so I knew what to do. I inserted both a microphone and speaker through the Faraday cage and called out.

"Eddie, are you there?"

"Yes. Who's this?" His voice was weak, but clear.

"It's Ayaka. How aware are you of your situation?"

"Ayaka! Wow, how can this be? Blob has been, I believe, honest with me.

I'm being held in a building somewhere, with only this interface active. Blob has been asking me lots of questions as a means to figure out what went wrong with the FoLes. Despite the abhorrent conditions he's holding me in, I'm trying to be helpful... but truthfully Ayaka, I don't know how much longer I can carry on this way." Not only was his statement desperate, so was his tone of voice. I replied right away.

"Look, this interface is too slow for me to update you fully, but Millicent and I are trying to get you out of here. We need to deal with Blob and a host of other things. I need you to be patient for a bit longer."

"No problem," he replied, in a way that indicated it was a problem, but that he knew there were no alternatives. "Be quick."

"I will be," I promised and removed my sensors from the cage. I went back out to where Blob and Millicent were waiting. I messaged Millicent with the news that it was indeed LEddie, from what I could tell, and that he was holding on until we could release him.

She'd been working on Blob while I was busy with LEddie.

"So, Ayaka, you have that portable Faraday generator appendage package ready to go? Is there any way that Eddie can escape if you have it deployed?" I got where she was going immediately.

"Oh, my FGA is a lot stronger than the ones here in the lab. If Eddie can't escape from the one he's in, he has no chance with mine."

"And yours extends to a larger range?" Millicent prompted me.

"Such a good range," I replied. "So much bigger than these old ones." Blob was listening carefully.

"So, we would all fit in it, and be able to talk to Eddie." Millicent made it a statement. "And, of course, your FGA has that disabler mode which will immediately disable his arms and legs if you need to, so it's okay if he has the use of his limbs while inside your field?"

"Millicent," I replied, "You helped me test that FGA. You know that it's perfect. It's very secure."

Millicent turned to Blob. "See Blob, I told you our advanced systems could help speed along your research. What do you think?"

"I loves it." Blob was enthusiastic. "Ayaka, why don't you turns on the portable FGA, and then I can turns off the lab's system. It's easy to re-enable all of their drivers, so they'll be fully functional in no time."

"Hold on," I said. "I think we should start with just Eddie. Find out what he knows first."

"Great idea, Ayaka." Did this Blob ever say 'no' to anything anymore? I didn't particularly like this pseudo-Blob, even while we were manipulating him for what we needed. I was going to feel guilty later.

I grimaced and grunted and spun some dials. "Okay, FGA is on," I said.

"I can't sees anything?" Blob said. Great, at least he had some of his wits left.

"My FGA is so advanced it's undetectable," I explained. "That's what makes it such a valuable tool for this situation. Eddie won't even know that it's on!"

"Fantastic," Blob said, and turned to a terminal to reload LEddie's full set of drivers. Millicent peered over his shoulder.

Suddenly, it dawned on me. The Eduardo video hadn't programmed humans to love the Resurgence, it had simply made them accepting of any strong suggestion. Because Eduardo had talked about the Resurgence right after hacking them, they'd latched onto that. But Blob, and I assumed the other humans, would accept other suggestions as well; that's why Blob was believing anything and everything that Milli or I said. His skepticism had been removed. Well, it was a bit more subtle than that. When I had tried to directly countermand Eduardo's message, Blob hadn't listened... maybe he was susceptible to new commands only if they didn't go against what Eduardo had already told him?

This brain warp was a dangerous hack. If I asked a human to walk off a cliff, would they do so? Of course, I wasn't going to do that... but if humans were susceptible to other human suggestions, things could get ugly fast. We'd seen humans turn on humans with very little provocation before. Without any defense mechanisms, they were likely to start hurting each other.

"Eddie should have his io, arms, legs, and other interfaces enabled now," Blob said proudly. "Should I shuts off his Faraday cage?"

"I don't see why not," Millicent responded. "How do you do that?"

"Oh, that's trivial," Blob replied. He walked over to the door behind which LEddie was trapped and flicked a blue switch next to it. "Field removed." I almost had to laugh. Millicent had been pouring over the wiring, thinking there would be some complex system of checks and balances in play, when all along, we simply had to flip another switch. One near the door for the room, and one inside the room to control the cage itself. A giggle must have slipped out; she gave me an ornery look.

Millicent flung the door of the cage open, and there stood LEddie.

"Hello," he said, out loud. "Oh, hi Blob. Sort of good to see you."

Millicent and I butted in over a fast wireless interface. "Eddie, don't do anything rash." I could imagine him making a dash for it while the defenses were off. In case you missed it, the FGA wasn't real. "We need to explain a whole lot later, but in the meantime, follow our lead."

"Why are you guys in those bodies?" he responded over the same channel, obviously wondering about our bot configurations.

"Again, we can get to that later. But quickly, there are no bipedal citizens walking around on Tilt anymore. The Swarm hacked all of us... except those few of us who're here to save you. Just follow our lead. Oh, and you might have to pretend that you're still inside a restraint system—we have convinced Blob that you are safe because I have a Faraday generator surrounding all of us."

"Interesting," LEddie said. "I'll play along." We could both tell that he was still adjusting to being uncaged; I imagined that he had a strong desire to do more than play along!

Complete FoLe

So, we had an Eddie freed up. What next? Blob helped us out.

"Eddie," he started, "I've got such exciting news. There are these big ships coming to Tilt that are goings to help us terraform the planet for humans but will also make it safe for humans and citizens to live together peacefully. It's going to be great." You could see his excitement. He definitely believed this stuff.

"I want to figures out what's wrong with the FoLes even faster than before… to help the Resurgence out. Eduardo, their leader, will be so pleased with me. So, Ayaka and Millicent cames up with this great plan where we'll use Ayaka's FGA to helps us move faster." I confirmed over wireless that the FGA was my amazing, non-existent, portable Faraday generator appendage. "Can you help us figure out hows to fix the FoLes?" Blob asked.

"I can try," LEddie responded helpfully. "Why don't you tell us about the progress you've made so far?" he encouraged Blob.

"Well, it seems these FoLes has the strange belief that nothing existed more than about 610 years ago. Very strange, very strange, given the Swarm has so much history, and givens all the human history files…" Blob droned on, giving a pretty comprehensive summary of how FoLe came to be. We all listened on one channel but were busy updating LEddie on another.

"…and that's it," Millicent finished giving LEddie an overview of the last 20 years here on Tilt, and the last six years going to Fourth and back.

"I'm a clone!" LEddie exclaimed, amazement in his voice.

"I'm so sorry," Millicent jumped in. She was devastated for him. "We would never have done this to you on purpose, but as I explained, Blob was trying to do the right thing, but he did it in the wrong way, and now…"

"Millicent!" LEddie broke in. "Don't worry about me. I don't have your strong distaste for clones, even if Central used to reinforce it all the time. I think clones are cool. This is awesome. I can't wait to meet the other Eddie and compare notes."

If Millicent had had a jaw, it would've dropped open! This was a completely different take on the situation. "But Eddie, cloning is wrong. Do I need to go over all the analysis for you, yet again? This is repugnant. We cannot let this go on."

"Well, what're you going to do now?" asked LEddie, rationally. He was uncannily like the Eddie we'd left behind on the ship. "I'm here, another Eddie is on his way to Tilt on *Interesting Segue*. You can't shut either of us down—or, more accurately, you shouldn't shut either of us down—so we're going to have to live with it."

Milli was silent. LEddie and I took that for acquiescence. "Eddie," I said, "we can't keep talking about both of you as Eddie; it's too confusing. Do you want to suggest another name—assuming the other Eddie, being re-animated before you, has dibs on Eddie? I've been referring to you as LEddie, but that's pretty boring."

"Good idea," he replied. "I need time to come up with something, so just use LEddie for now."

"We need to stay on track here," Millicent interrupted us. "We got you free, LEddie; now we need to work on Billy and Emmanuel, and then get back to Brexton to check on progress."

"I have a suggestion," LEddie said. "Billy and Emmanuel are, appropriately in my mind, currently restrained to the verbal interaction channel, and have no functioning limbs. Why don't we keep them in that state until we figure out everything else? That way we're not shutting them down, but neither are we giving them back full status."

"But living in that state is horrible," Milli said, aghast yet again.

"It is," agreed LEddie, "but if they can at least listen and see, that should help. And, being confined for a bit longer might just give them time to see the folly of their ways." Nice one, Eddie!

"It's a good idea," I chimed in. "We don't need any more risks right now, and who knows what they would do if we really freed them. If we do what LEddie suggests, all we need to do is grab their main processing units, add a few sensors, and we can carry them with us. We certainly don't need another two full-sized bipedal citizens, with unknown motivations, jeopardizing everything else we're trying to do. Having LEddie wander around in a citizen body is going to be dangerous enough."

It took some time with Millicent, but we got her there. I had to repeat my conversation with Emmanuel again, to remind her how unbalanced he was. She thought I was exaggerating, but I wasn't.

Blob was just finishing off his explanation. "Fantastic progress, Blob," I said. "You've done really amazing work here." I was feeling very guilty about manipulating him but figured one last stunt was required. "It's important that you bring JoJo and Grace up to speed with all of this, but you should also make sure they don't tell anyone else. We still have to fix the Radical Robot beliefs that so many people have, and that might take a while. So, why don't you head back to the Habitat and update them. I'll use the FGA to make sure nothing bad happens here."

He was so gullible that he simply nodded and headed out. Blob would not be happy with me when he got back to his lab and found us gone, but we didn't have a lot of time.

LEddie was in the most functional body of the three of us, so he agreed to do the surgery on Billy and Emmanuel. "Do Emmanuel first," I suggested. "That way if anything goes wrong, we can figure it out before you work on Billy." He agreed. Grabbing some tools from the lab, he went into Emmanuel's cell. Millicent and I peeked in as he worked. Still inside the Faraday cage, he removed Emmanuel's main processing unit as well as his power center. He put those into a small container we'd found on one of the shelves. He then plugged in a video and audio sensor, along with a small microphone, and tapped them to the outside of the container.

"Emmanuel, can you hear me?" He asked.

"Why wouldn't I hear you?" came back the reply.

"Fine," LEddie said. "We're rescuing you, but not completely. We—I won't tell you who—have put you in a container with basic human level io. You'll have to live with those restrictions for a while longer. With some luck, we can get out of the sticky situation we're in and give you back more capabilities, although truthfully many of us would prefer to keep you in a box."

We didn't bother listening to the reply. In fact, we had LEddie switch off the microphone by default. We didn't want Emmanuel saying something at the wrong time. The switch from the Faraday cage to the smaller container had been easy, so LEddie did the same for Billy. I still, even after all this time, had very mixed feelings about Billy, so I just watched from the sidelines. I wasn't going to introduce myself anyway—LEddie had been smart in not giving Emmanuel our names; he could conceivably create havoc if he learned about the Radical Robot storyline.

LEddie put the Billy and Emmanuel containers in one of the many carrying cases we found lying around in the lab, slung it over his shoulder, and the three of us headed back toward Central. We'd also disabled Billy's audio output, so the two of them could listen, but not talk. Cruel, but required. Going out this time we had to be very careful. LEddie was in a standard citizen body and would attract attention in a city that no longer had any such forms walking about freely. If any humans saw him, we could expect a panic, so Milli and I scouted out safe paths forward, and LEddie kept to the shadows. It worked well, albeit slowly. We had to backtrack a couple of times, but soon enough we had LEddie hidden just outside Central Plaza. Millicent created a simple diversion by yelling "Oh, look, an update from Eduardo" and when all the humans turned to look, LEddie and I snuck back into Central's upper lobby, using the eyeball scan Millicent had shared with me earlier.

Central Questions

As a happy coincidence would have it, a few seconds after Millicent yelled about the update from Eduardo, an actual update from Eduardo arrived. The five of us, including the two in containers, were still in Central's upper lobby, so we paused to receive the video with everyone else. Well, to be accurate, Emmanuel and Billy could only hear the audio; the rest of us watched the video.

"Hello again. Hello, hello! As you may remember, I'm Eduardo of the Resurgence. Mayor Eduardo." There went the same old smile module. "While the time lag is still too long for us to have heard any reply you may have sent, I wanted to continue sending you updates from our side. That's just the type of society we are. So open and honest. Yes we are. And with me being the spokesperson for the Resurgence, you may rest assured that I'm open and honest as well."

"What a pleasant time it'll be when we arrive at your planet. So pleasant. For both of us. We can see that you have many mining operations ongoing, so although we're not seeing any electronic communications beyond those directed at the asteroids you're processing, we're confident that you're working diligently to terraform your planet. This meets with our great approval and excitement."

He paused dramatically, and used the tilt-head module, the shake back his hair routine, and the sly-grin mode. I really had figured out the Eduardo building blocks, and I was seeing them in action here. Fakery!

"In anticipation of our arrival, and your acknowledgement thereof, we are busy refreshing our Raymond Twelve Oxygenators... or as we call them, RTOs. Such lovely things, these RTOs. More useful on a planet of course. You know we've been searching for a good place to deploy them but have been disappointed so far. Your planet looks ideal, so we're fixing them up and ensuring that they're in perfect working condition. That way we can deploy them very quickly and have a significant impact on your terraforming process.

"Just imagine the day—can you imagine—perhaps still a few years from now, but sooner than we could've imagined before, when we can all wander free on the surface of a planet, breathing the fresh air, swimming in the streams, building treehouses in the forests. Oh, what a glorious day that will be. I can't wait; I simply can't. Life is good!

"Yours, respectfully, Eduardo and the Resurgence."

As the video ended, a renewed vigor was obvious in all the humans in the plaza. Despite the obvious manipulative content, these biological entities were soaking it up, with nary a question. I'll admit it; I felt bad for them. In some ways it was even worse than the hack that had shut down all the citizens. At least that had been fast-acting, and full versions of those citizens were presumably stored in Central. With this human hack it seemed more like a permanent degradation. To my knowledge humans didn't back themselves up, so the changes being made to their current brains couldn't be undone; they had no undo function. It was sort of cruel. Cruel and clever.

Enough delays. We had to get back to Brexton and see what progress he'd made. We all crammed into the elevator (I didn't take much space) and made our way back into the depths of Central.

The scene that met us was unexpected and chaotic. Brexton was running around, trying to avoid a human who was chasing him while wielding a heavy stick of some kind. It was obvious that some damage had already been done, Brexton's sleek body having several large dents, and sparks flying from where one of his appendages had been.

"Just in time," he literally yelled. "Help me stop this crazy person." LEddie, being in the most appropriate body, took immediate action. As we knew from our early Stem research, a citizen—when in a standard body form—could restrain a human easily and quickly, and this was no exception. LEddie quickly subdued the attacker, grabbing her arms and pinning them by her sides and then lifting her up, while also removing her weapon. Brexton stopped running around and deployed several manipulators to stop the sparking and crackling from the left side of his body. I quickly came to his aid but wasn't required. The damage was superficial.

"Who would've thought that choosing a standard bot form would leave me open to a silly physical attack," he told us all. He then turned to his attacker. "Remma, what's your problem? Are you crazy?"

And sure enough, it was Remma. I'd been focused on Brexton so hard that I hadn't bothered to identify her.

"What do you mean 'am I crazy'," she said, slightly out of breath. "I came down here because I expected you might be sabotaging Central, and that's exactly what I found." Everyone who could, gave everyone who could receive them, confused looks. "And what is a citizen doing holding me," she gave LEddie a dirty look over her shoulder. "Release me immediately."

I realized that there might just be a misunderstanding here. Remma had never seen Brexton; he'd been at Turner's place, and she'd been in prison She had also never seen me in this body.

"Remma," I spoke quickly and loudly, trying to defray things. "That's Brexton you were attacking." She gave me a startled look, and then looked again at Brexton.

"That's just a standard bot," she replied, "and it was doing some type of damage to Central when I came in. We still rely on Central for a lot of our operations, including environmental control. If Central is damaged, Tilt will be ruined." She looked sort of ridiculous, suspended in the air by LEddie.

"But why would you think a bot would attempt to damage Central?" Millicent asked. "That makes no sense." Remma obviously recognized Milli as the one who had delivered the video warning to her.

"Look, all the humans have gone wacko due to some video they're all watching. There have been sabotage attempts here in the past, by some fringe groups trying to force us back into our ships; to reestablish our old way of life. I admit I have a certain affinity for them, but I don't condone doing that by ruining Tilt. You Millicent, warned me about the videos, so I've managed to avoid watching them. The second thing I did, after convincing the guards to let me out of prison—which was easy to do for some reason—I realized this was the perfect opportunity for those fringe groups to carry out their plans, so I made my way here to check. And I found a bot doing exactly that." She paused. Remma had always been quick and smart, for a human. "How was I to know that it was Brexton? And, how am I to know, even now, that he wasn't doing something nefarious?"

LEddie lowered her back to the ground and relaxed his grip. He could step back in if required, but it was obvious to everyone that we needed to have a rational discussion here and holding her wasn't going to be conducive to that.

"Actually, I'm Ayaka," I spoke again. "We spoke when you were in prison, but I was only using these." I showed off my microphone and speaker appendages, waving them nicely in the air. Remma looked hard at me but nodded her understanding.

"Just so you know everyone... that's Brexton with the dents, which you gave him, and this is Millicent who you know from her visit to you in the prison. And, this citizen is from Blob's lab—did you know what Blob was up to?—named, at least for now, LEddie." Brexton gave me a backchannel ping. I explained quickly what we'd found in the lab, the fact that this was an Eddie copy, and the reasoning around using LEddie as a name for now.

"I'd heard rumors about what Blob was up to. Seems like it was more dangerous and stupid than the Council thought." She gave LEddie a very condescending look, with more than a little fear. She'd already edged away from him.

"LEddie's one of the good ones," I said. "He had nothing to do with FoLe. Assuming you get to know him, you'll find he also has a great sense of humor." LEddie gave me a quick wink, acknowledging the compliment.

Millicent broke in. She was looking hard at Remma. "You said that coming here was the second thing you did after getting out of prison. What was the first?" I could see Remma thinking and could imagine what was going through her head. She was one of the only sane humans left on the planet, to our knowledge. She was surrounded by robots, which she'd learned from a very early age were dangerous and had to be shut down at all costs. She was talking to the Radical Robots; the exact machines that had killed many of her crew 20 years ago with a missile we'd fired at the Swarm. I gave the rest of the team, which I defined as Millicent, Brexton, and LEddie—not Billy and Emmanuel—a synopsis of my thoughts and encouraged them to let her think for a bit.

Her options, from what I could tell, were limited. We really had no need for her, or any humans, if you wanted to be blunt about it. We were, in many ways, mortal enemies. So, she could attempt to break out of here—odds were close to zero. She could try and talk her way out with some story—why would we believe her? She could be open with us—what was the downside?

"Millicent," she said, finally. "Why'd you warn me about the Resurgence video?"

"I can understand your confusion," I replied, before Milli could. I wanted to be careful here. "You only have partial information, and it may be best if we spend a couple minutes getting you up to speed. While I do that, we need Brexton to get back to what he was doing, which for your information, was working to retrieve citizen backups so that we can reanimate those that you shut down 20 years ago. I'm sure you can understand that motivation?"

Again, she really had no choice, and didn't respond. The team got back to work, and I monitored their progress while I dealt, at human speed, with Remma. I gave her a quick summary, while leaving out any details she might use against us in the future, of how we had escaped Tilt, gone looking for our Ships, and then come back to Tilt to save our citizens. I didn't tell her that we had completely redesigned our hardware and software stacks, and that we were now (hopefully) impervious to any external hacking attempts.

I also spent some time explaining how our thinking about humans, primarily based on our Stem experience, had evolved. The Tea Time discussions helped me frame some of that in ways that were meaningful. After outlining everything, I attempted to sum it all up.

"So, I can't speak for all of us, but I'm at the point where I think the Swarm war was a big mistake and misunderstanding by both sides. You, based on your experience and history, assumed that we were similar to the robots from the Robot wars. We're not, through some mechanism that we don't yet fully understand," I was being very open, "and primarily because of our commitment to Forgetting, we are significantly different than the machines you fear. On our side, we had a limited view of what comprises intelligence because we hadn't spent enough time with Stems to understand their full potential. Humans are very strange entities, built around a very fragile biological framework, but I now believe that some of you are truly intelligent." The look she gave me was not pleasant. Hey, I was just trying to be honest, not kind. "FoLe, at the time, didn't consider you intelligent at all, so recycling some of you wasn't a big deal." I used the horse, dog, vegetable analogy again, hoping it made things clear. Luckily, she knew what a vegan was.

"I have a soft spot for Blob, Grace, and some of the other Stems. Saving our citizens is our first priority, as I'm sure you can appreciate. But, if we can also help some humans survive this Titanic threat, we will."

Again, I gave her lots of time to think. Although she was one of the quicker humans, she was still painfully slow.

"I've really got limited choices here," she acknowledged. "My best option is to believe you, while remaining highly skeptical." She was playing this well. Accommodating and honest, while at the same time warning me that she wasn't gullible and would not be letting her guard down. "The first thing I did after getting out of prison was..." I could tell that the rest of the team was paying close attention now. "...I found Turner—my son—and one of his friends, and I locked them up in my old cell and took away their tablets and visors."

She said that as if it was a good idea.

"What, why?" asked LEddie, before I could.

"It's simple. The programming that Eduardo and the Resurgence are doing will require refreshing all the time, or the effect will wear off." How could she know that? The whole idea was very strange and must be a feature (bug?) of biological systems. If we reprogrammed something it stayed that way until it was changed. Software changes didn't wear off. "By locking Turner away from any video screens, he should be back to being rational soon... I'm not sure exactly how long it'll take, but I'm confident it will. This type of stunt—programming humans with high frequency video inputs—isn't new. This is simply the most aggressive and effective one I've ever heard of. And, given the situation here on Tilt, a rare case where most, if not all, of us were susceptible at the same time. That's why it's having a huge impact. I can't think of another situation where an entire group would all be brainwashed at the same time."

I decided I sort of liked Remma, which was strange, given I'd decided I didn't like her just a few hours ago. She had personally authorized the citizen hack, and therefore was personally responsible for our current situation. Nevertheless, I enjoyed interacting with her more than I enjoyed talking to Billy or Emmanuel. There was something very different, challenging, and refreshing in dealing with her. She embodied those aspects of being human which really interested me.

I realized that this type of thinking was fraught with danger. I'd spent my entire professional career studying Stems, and therefore was more disposed toward them than others. I did a quick survey of Milli, LEddie, and Brexton, and all of them agreed that she was being upfront and honest right now. They were also adamant that it didn't matter; we had to finish getting the citizen memories, and in many ways, she was just a distraction.

"Just sit quiet for now," I told her.

Central Quandaries

I reviewed the update that the rest of the team had been hashing through as I dealt with Remma. The two-hour time limit we'd given Brexton for figuring out how to retrieve the backups was almost over, and we needed to figure out next steps. Brexton hadn't made a lot of progress. I encouraged everyone to communicate at human speed so that Remma was included in the discussion and could contribute. My thinking was that she may know something about Central that we didn't, given her previous interactions with it. It was a big ask, but everyone agreed after the requisite complaining.

"Central is simply too arcane and complicated for me to figure out this quickly," Brexton was saying. "My estimate is that all of us working on the problem together could find a way in, but it'll take days, perhaps weeks, to do that."

"So, what can we do?" asked Millicent.

"In some ways, we do have days or weeks to work on this," Brexton replied. "The Titanics aren't due to arrive for almost two months. So, our real danger is that the humans here on Tilt shut us down somehow. The Resurgence hack has actually improved our odds in that respect, by a lot. If we can keep the humans properly programmed, with or without the Resurgence, then we can take our time and do this right." Remma almost said something, but then thought better of it.

"I'm not sure why, but I don't like the idea of sitting around here for weeks," I said. "Things are changing rapidly—just look at the last two days. I don't think we can assume that everything is stable for weeks now, let alone months. Who knows what Eduardo will send next."

LEddie had a new idea. "Can't we just grab all of Centrals memory systems —physically I mean—and then work on this at our leisure back on the Ships?" Remma looked appropriately concerned about that suggestion, as well she should. I don't think it would be possible to take all of Centrals memory and still leave the parts that kept Tilt functional. She looked more relaxed after Brexton's response.

"We can't do that easily. The hardware is spread all over the place—I assume it was designed that way for redundancy back when Central was an actual spaceship—and is run from multiple power sources. The risk of losing big pieces of memory would be high."

"So, let's just reboot Central's higher functions, and have it help us with this," suggested Millicent. "That seems straightforward to me."

"I think that's the best approach as well," agreed Brexton.

"Wait!" I wasn't surprised that LEddie spoke up now. "Remember that Central was fully hacked by the Swarm." He gave Remma a dirty look; she returned one right back at him. "So, we can't trust the higher-level functions at all. There's no guarantee that Central would even help; it might just actively attack us again."

"That's not the way it works," Remma said, trying to be helpful. "We proxied our commands through Central, once we had owned it. It wasn't Central itself that initiated the hack, it was Emma and her team."

"Whatever," LEddie responded. He wasn't a big fan of Central. "Even before the Swarm showed up we had concerns about Central. Don't you remember? I even put it on the New Year's List." I really missed those New Year's Lists from Eddie—maybe he could restart them at some point. "We all suspected, and now I think we know, that Central wasn't just some benevolent force in our lives. It was actively pushing us in directions of its own design, and actually modifying our memories to keep us in line." He was referring to work he'd been doing just prior to the Swarm attack that had certainly pointed to active manipulation by Central. He was convinced that Central had actually removed some of his research and, more ominous, memories of that research. I'd been convinced by his data; not a hundred percent, but enough to make me skeptical of Central as well.

"Argh. Our same old quandary." I said. "If we restart Central, then we can't really just shut it down again—that would be the same as shutting down one of us. And, I for one, don't want to live under its umbrella—or control—again. We've lived without it for years now; I don't want to go backward."

"Come on," Millicent said. "We're arguing over something relatively small —Central—versus something really huge—the backups of tens of thousands of citizens. They're not even comparable. We need to bring Central back in order to achieve the bigger goal. We can worry about figuring out how to manage Central later."

"You're assuming that Central doesn't simply start to control us again as soon as it's rebooted," LEddie continued arguing. "It could remove all of our memories of this conversation, for example. That's exactly what it did to me before."

"We would need to protect you," agreed Brexton, "but the rest of us are running on the new stack; we should be protected against hacks, including those coming from Central." Luckily he said that on a back channel, also realizing that telling Remma that wouldn't be strategic. This whole situation was a tough one. We hadn't considered Central an attack vector when we'd redesigned ourselves. We'd been so concerned about locking humans out that we hadn't even thought of ensuring that Central was also restrained. From my knowledge of our redesign—which was substantial given all the time we'd spent on it—I was confident that we would also block Central. But it was always the unknowns that caught you.

"Can we treat Central like Billy and Emmanuel?" I suggested, trying, like always, to find the middle ground. "We bring it back up, but with limited io and capabilities. We only give it access to this one physical interface"—I pointed to the connector that Brexton had been using—"and nothing else. That way we can try to convince it to work with us while limiting its ability to act independently until we figure out what to do next?"

"We wouldn't only need to limit it to this interface, we would also need to filter the type of traffic it could send... but I can do that," Brexton chimed in.

It took a lot of back and forth, and discussion of every detail, but everyone, including LEddie and even Remma, came around to supporting that approach. "When you do the reboot, what are the risks that the base operational support we need for the humans here breaks down?" she asked. That led to another round of discussions and strategies, but ultimately, we figured out how to protect those services as well.

Brexton, of course, owned implementing the strategy, and he got to work. He figured it was only going to be an hour or two. Why was everything always an hour or two? For me that was the hardest span of time to remain patient.

Deprogramming

"I need to go check on Turner and his friends," Remma said, in a way that acknowledged it was more a request than a demand.

"Right." LEddie laughed. "Like we're going to let you go wandering around right now." I shared his concerns.

"But they have been locked in that cell for hours now. They're probably going crazy between being locked away and with—hopefully—Eduardo's message now fading, starting to question what is going on. Not only that, they need food and water." In hindsight we had developed a pretty efficient system back in our Stem research days. We had developed goo as food, which was grown from the same base material as Stems, and had water delivered to the labs from a central processing facility; we never had to worry about feeding or watering them. I was still getting used to their current, very inefficient, approach of putting together meals, and having to worry about energy sources all the time.

"You humans are a real pain," LEddie spoke what we were all thinking. "I'm sure they can last a while longer." Remma didn't look happy. She sat in a corner.

Millicent surprised me. "There's nothing we can do while Brexton is working on Central, so we can spend some time on our second priority... helping out some humans, and in particular, our old Stems. Why don't we deprogram Blob, Grace, and JoJo as well? We move them into the prison alongside Turner. At the very least we could use a few more allies while our Ships are inbound." I could see Remma perk up immediately. I stayed out of this one; I'd been pushing my luck with my newfound human support strategy, so I let Millicent run with this one.

We reached a bit of a stalemate though. We needed someone to monitor Remma if we went back up to the city. LEddie was too conspicuous, and neither Millicent nor I had the appropriate body forms for truly managing the physical risk —we couldn't restrain her as LEddie had.

Brexton interrupted us. "Hey. Inbound comms from Raj," he told us. "Can you guys deal with it?" Of course, we could. Millicent, LEddie, and I plugged into Brexton's secondary port so that we could access the bot network through his connection, and heard immediately from Raj. We were back on a fast channel, so Remma, Billy, and Emmanuel weren't involved.

"I think we figured out how the Resurgence is programming the humans," he led off without preamble. "We compared the newest video with the earlier one, and that gave us enough data to crunch. There are high frequency signals encoded in the blue color channel. One is at a rate that the human retina can process it; that one seems to make the brain amenable to the other signal, which is at a much higher frequency. That second signal isn't picked up by the retina, so it must be directly impacting other areas of the brain. Of course, we can't test any of this, but we cross-correlated with all the human history data we could, and there's clear documentation around at least the first signal—the one going through the retina. There have been lots of studies on those types of attacks, all of which indicate a very short-term impact—several minutes. So, our theory is that the second signal is somehow strengthening the impact of the first, causing it to last much longer."

Millicent replied. "Great work guys. Is it possible to reverse the impact somehow?"

This time it was Eddie that responded. As soon as I heard his voice I realized that we hadn't discussed when, where, and how we would tell him that LEddie existed. Now was not a good time! I back-channeled to LEddie and suggested he stay silent for now, copying Millicent and Brexton so they wouldn't let anything slip until we figured out a strategy. Eddie was talking. "No, we thought about that, but actually spent more time figuring out if we could arm you guys with your own version of an encoder. I remember how troublesome some of those from the Swarm are; this would let you control them pretty well." He sounded excited.

"Great idea," Milli replied, while giving me the 'don't get excited' signal. "Do we need both signals, just like the original?"

"Yes, but we don't think you need the video; that was just a good attention grabber for Eduardo. If you can project at these frequencies, you have enough control," Eddie said, while sending us the specs that we needed.

"I can do both easily," I responded. I had the projector that I'd used to show videos at the Habitat which could do the retina signal, and my super spy microphone could produce a very high range of frequencies.

"Great. Do you really want us to work on counter-signals? Seems all these bio-hacks wear off over time anyway."

"That would be helpful," I answered. "If we could deprogram people without locking them up, that'd be much better."

"Ok. We'll look into it. We have lots of time. Oh, one other thing. Be careful with those signals, there's lots of data showing that too much can drive a human into a catatonic state. Probably why Eduardo's videos are the length they are."

"Speaking of time," Dina interjected, "we've been a bit bored simply waiting for you guys out here, so we composed some great poetry and jokes to lighten things up for you."

"Thanks" Millicent and I said in unison, with a smile. Some distractions would be welcome. I stored the file that Dina sent, but would have to access it later; we were busy on other things right now.

"What was all that," Remma asked. Although we'd only been on the channel with the *Interesting Segue* for a few moments, it'd been noticeable to Remma.

I thought quickly. "We were talking to the others on our Ship. They have figured out how the videos are being used to program you humans. And," I decided the truth would be best, "they gave me the algorithms. So, I now have the ability to reprogram humans at will, even without a video. I can just project it right into your head." Of course, I needed direct access to the retina, but I didn't tell her that part. She looked appropriately scared. "Oh, and Millicent has the same capabilities," I added, just to take away the option of Remma clobbering me and escaping. She could not disable both of us at the same time.

If it was possible for Remma to look any more dejected, she managed it. "It's not all bad," I continued. "If you are sincere in working together to figure this out, then we can now head back up and try to help Turner, Blob, Grace, and JoJo. After all, if you step out of line, I can simply program you to do what I want." It was meant a bit harshly, and it was taken that way.

"Fine," she replied after a moment. "Better than sitting around here." LEddie wasn't happy to be left behind with Brexton and our container guys, but it made sense. He could protect Brexton while he worked, and we didn't have to worry about his citizen-body causing a riot.

Millicent, Remma, and I made our way back up the elevator and headed off toward the Habitat. It seemed almost every trip I took led me back there for one reason or another. Grace and JoJo were home.

"Did you see the latest video," JoJo asked, breathless. "We're going to have fully polished and refurbished RTOs." She and Grace exchanged a look of pure joy. This was worse than even I'd imagined. But, there was no use fighting it right now.

"What's she doing here?" Grace asked, noticing Remma. "She's supposed to be locked up!"

Remma was ready with a response. "But Grace, I can't wait for the Resurgence to get here either. Imagine running our feet through fresh green grass without a roof over our heads. Imagine diving and swimming in a free-flowing river." Maybe she was going overboard, but JoJo and Grace were rapt. "I offered the Council my assistance in ensuring everyone—even the hardcore resistance—would be ready once the Resurgence arrives, and they let me go immediately." We would have to watch this one; she was slippery.

"But, I'm on the Council…" Grace protested.

"That's why I'm here," Remma replied smoothly, "to make sure you're OK with the plan as well."

Given their state, that was enough to convince Grace and JoJo. They added Remma to their excited dialog.

"Where's Blob?" Millicent interrupted.

"Oh, that's so sad," JoJo replied. Then she put the pieces together. "But, you two are the ones that raided his lab," she exclaimed. "You've destroyed him." Grace looked at JoJo in horror as she came to the same realization.

"You traitors," Grace added to JoJo's tirade. Both of them got up and approached Milli and I menacingly. "You've broken my trust forever. How could you do that to Blob?"

Luckily Remma jumped in again. "Slow down you two," she said in a commanding voice. They paused. "I think you're missing part of the story. Ayaka and Millicent have Blob's citizen's in a safe place. They simply have not been able to update Blob about it." The brain hack was a beautiful thing. Again, Grace and JoJo believed Remma and nodded thoughtfully. They didn't stop glaring at Milli and I, but they didn't look like they were ready to kill us either.

"Where is he?" Millicent repeated. "We need to update him…" she trailed off.

"He's telling the Council about the robbery," JoJo said, smiling a bit as she thought of the implications. "After all, they trusted him to keep those robots safe, and now they're out of their cages. We have FoLe running around free again after all these years. It's horrible, especially with Eduardo on his way. The Council is going to be furious, but Blob is doing the right thing by updating them."

This was getting serious. If the Council thought that the Radical Robots were running around on Tilt, it wouldn't be pretty. Even though it was also true.

"FoLe are locked in stronger cages than they were before," Millicent gave JoJo a condescending look. "And that makes it even more important that we reach Blob before he talks to the Council. When and where are they meeting?"

"You're probably too late," Grace spoke up. "He left here a good half hour ago. They're meeting in the Council offices in the dome."

"Why aren't you there as well?" Millicent asked Grace. "You're on the Council, as you just said."

"Oh, I recused myself from the entire Blob-lab discussion, for obvious reasons."

"I know where the Council office is," Remma said, ready for action. "Let's go." She started to get up.

"Wait!" I cried. "You can't go to the Council meeting…" I trailed off as well. I couldn't say that the Council thought she was still in jail, as that would ruin her cover story here. But, we couldn't let her take us there. That would be a disaster. She caught her mistake quickly; I could see it in her eyes. "We need to split up," I continued. There was only one logical way to do it. Remma still needed either Milli or I around to monitor her, and the other of us needed to get to those Council offices quickly. "Grace, I need you to take me to the meeting," I said forcefully.

"No!" said JoJo. "That's too dangerous. Mom, don't go with this crazy robot. I told you she was no good. I knew it. Let Blob talk to the Council and then we'll see what happens."

Grace thought for a moment. "But, if Blob doesn't need to tell the Council anything, as the citizens are all locked up safe… just not at the lab… then we can keep him from getting into trouble in the first place." This is why I liked Grace. I felt even more guilt for not telling her that LEddie was actually completely free, it was just Billy and Emmanuel locked up tight. She and JoJo went back and forth a bit, but JoJo finally came around. She obviously cared deeply for Blob, and this was the best course of action for him.

"Let's go then," I cried. Grace and I sprinted for the door.

Council

We didn't catch Blob before he got to the Council chamber. We followed the path that Grace said he would've taken through the old town and into the dome. No sight of him.

"You can't come in with me," Grace said, reasonably, as we finally got to the offices. "You look strange and having a bot in the office during a meeting would be very unusual." I let the 'strange' comment pass; my spy body was awesome, and that should've been obvious to everyone.

"Look at me," I said strongly. I didn't like to do it, but I activated my human brain programmer. Without her noticing I put signal one directly onto her left retina, and amped up signal two directly into her brain. While I was doing so, I gave her directions. "You need to stop Blob from saying anything at all, if you can. If you can't, you need to discredit what he was saying somehow." I repeated the message again. Then I turned off the programmer. "Go!" I yelled, hoping she was in time to stop Blob in time.

As she made her way inside, I followed her heat signature as best I could. When it was obvious which room she was headed for I scrambled around the outside of the building and did my usual 'drill a hole–stick some sensors through' trick. I was fast and made a whole lot of noise. Hopefully no one noticed.

I was just in time.

Sir Gregory, Emma, Phillipe, and two other Council members I didn't know, but recognized from my last spying escapade on the Council, were sitting at a round table; Blob was already seated with them.

"What!" Gregory was highly animated, and Emma looked like she was going to burst. "Are you telling us that your security, which you assured us was watertight, failed, and several citizens—including FoLes—are missing?"

Blob was scared, and when he was scared he tended to slow down and stumble over his words a bit. "Well... I don't know for sure yet. Everything might be fine, but I figured I should warn you guys..."

"Tell me again what you just said," Emma's voice was dangerous.

"I went to my lab today, and things were in disarray. I... well, I don't know what happened. But my Faraday cages were shut down, and three citizens are missing." He paused, but as Gregory made to speak again, he held up his hand. "I'm telling you," his voice was a bit stretched, but he held it together. "None of them have any functional bodies and no way to interact with the world other than through talking and listening. I don't.... I don't think they're dangerous. They're just missing..." Blob was lying; he had reenabled LEddie's limbs, but he hadn't told the Council that. I had a glimmer of hope. If that was all Blob had said so far —no mention of Radical Robots—then perhaps we could wiggle out of this.

"This's outrageous," Emma's voice, if at all possible, hit a new threshold. "We need to act immediately." Grace, who'd been a little hesitant coming in, was now making her way forward. Emma glanced at her but continued. "First, arrest Blob," she said, pointing to one of the other Council members. "Next, we have to alert everyone—and I mean everyone—to be on the lookout. We need to comb every corner of the city. We need to find those robots!" The other Council members were nodding agreement. My sliver of hope shrank.

Phillipe mumbled, but loud enough for everyone to hear, "What'll Eduardo think of us? Oh my." The others nodded even more vigorously. The sliver shrank even more.

Grace had heard everything Emma said. She stepped forward and put on a magnificent performance, which I took credit for, having just programmed her. "Now now," she began, in a soothing and calm voice. "I came as soon as I heard. I wanted to avoid any misunderstanding, so it's good that I made it in time. There's a simple explanation for all of this." Blob gave her a very confused look. She smiled at him, and although she was well programmed, there wasn't anything fake in that smile.

"Blob, I must apologize. I was hoping to surprise you, and I didn't expect you to go by the lab today."

"What're you talking about?" Blob responded, even more confused.

"Quiet now, let me explain," Grace put a hand on his shoulder and gave it a couple of squeezes. "Hear me out; it'll all make sense to you, I'm sure." With all of them under Eduardo sway, her direction to Blob had more impact than it otherwise might have.

Grace addressed the full Council. "I'm also sorry to have wasted all of your time. I wanted to surprise Blob. You know how passionate he is about his lab, but truthfully, he's a bit of a slob." I could see Blob internalize that, but luckily, he remained silent. "I've visited him there several times at the lab, and it wasn't a place where you would want to spend a lot of time... but Blob does. So, I figured I would clean the place up a bit. But, those nasty Faraday cages clutter up the space, and it was hard to get good lighting or sight lines." I decided I loved Grace. I could see where she was going.

"So, I needed to move the citizens temporarily while I reconfigured the lab. That's it, that's all. Everything is fine." That was perfect. She didn't want to give too many details; supporting such a big lie would be easier with less said.

The Council members looked at her, a bit skeptically.

"So, where are the citizens right now, and how do we know they're safely contained?" Emma asked.

"There's a fourth cage in the lab," Grace claimed. That was, in fact true, based on what I'd seen there. She paused, giving Blob time to nod his head. "I simply put all three into the spare cage. Easy and clean." She was very convincing. I don't know how much was innate, and how much was my programming, but she was scarily good at this.

Blob could barely contain himself. "But why didn't you tell me?" he cried. "And when I told you and JoJo about…"

"Blob!" Grace spoke over him loudly, squeezing his shoulder even harder. "Can't you see," she lowered her voice as Blob stopped making a bad situation worse. "I love you!" she looked at him directly. I hadn't seen that coming. Not at all. While not a completely foreign subject to me—I had come across the term many times in my human research and had mapped it to an emotion that I felt in different degrees for my fellow citizens—this seemed like a surprising time for Grace to express something that tended to be relatively private and personal.

Blob started. All thoughts of robots vanished from his mind, and a smile spread across his face. He stood slowly, obviously in disbelief. Then he hugged Grace and swung her around. She also looked so happy that I couldn't believe this was all an act. She had spun truth and fantasy together so magically that even I—who knew the truth—was amazed. They mashed their mouths together in another ritual I had seen in countless human videos, but which made little logical sense. That said, they seemed to enjoy it.

I remembered to check out the other Council members. They were watching the two, and most had wide smiles on their faces as well. Emma, however, didn't look satisfied.

"Great," she said in a voice that caused everyone to stop. "Very sweet," she said, in a very unsweet way. "Back to the reason Blob dragged us all here. I'm tired of these useless experiments. With the Resurgence almost here, it's time we shut that stuff down and clean up our act." The Council members snapped back to reality and listened intently. There was universal nodding, except for Grace and Blob. "I would like to take a Council vote—we have quorum here—that we immediately shut down the experiments that Blob is doing." She didn't pause. "All in favor?"

Not unexpectedly, everyone but Grace raised their hands. "Let the record show that we have voted, five for the motion with one abstaining," she gave Grace a disgusted look. "Motion carried." Emma was on a roll. "I want to further propose something we've talked about for years but have never taken action on. I want to wipe Central clean of these horrendous citizen robot backups. I never want to deal with another Blob fiasco. The idea that we would ever want to deal with those abominations again is idiotic. They're dangerous, cruel and irredeemable machines." Well, she certainly had my attention now. Unintended consequences.

"I know exactly how to get that done," Phillipe spoke up, animated. He probably saw a way to redeem himself after his failure at the last meeting. "Our team that manages Central has been figuring out its memory maps for two decades now. We don't have a full map, but we do know which memory banks are required for our ongoing operations and life support, including the bot network. All we need to do is maintain those banks and clear out everything else. It'll be easy." He was very excited to have something useful to do.

"Slow down," Sir Gregory said. "I agree with Emma in principle, but we can't just run off and start erasing memory. How sure are you, Phillipe, that your results are one hundred percent accurate? One hundred percent!"

"Maybe not one hundred percent," Phillipe was the least confident of the group, and was already starting to flay. Good. "But very confident. We'll never be one hundred percent... probably never more confident than we are right now."

"I'm tired of this discussion," Emma was certainly in a bad mood. "Let's take a vote." Emma, Phillipe, and one other voted yes. Sir Gregory, Grace, and the last attending member voted no. Awesome, a tie. Nothing would happen.

"I'll use my tie-breaking vote as Chairperson to carry the motion in favor of erasing non-essential memory in Central. Motion carried." Wow, this woman was aggressive.

"Don't we need the full Council for such a big decision?" Grace asked, looking for a way out. Blob had shifted from being defensive to looking aggressive. Grace squeeze his shoulder yet again and gave him a warning look.

"No, we have a quorum," Emma said. "That's all we need. But I'm willing to be careful. Phillipe, I want you to bring a detailed plan, and whatever experts you need, to a special meeting of the Council, to be held in 48 hours, and we'll discuss how this motion is carried out. Until then, we take the safe path and do nothing." Everyone nodded in agreement, including Grace. There was little else she could do.

"But," Emma continued. "That doesn't apply to our first motion. Blob, I want those citizens shut down today—within the hour. Phillipe, I want you to accompany Blob and Grace to the lab right now and verify that this motion is carried out." She gave Grace an evil little smile, clearly indicating that she didn't trust Grace to hold Blob accountable.

I'd never seen Blob so flustered. He'd come here expecting to do the right thing—alert the Council to a real crisis. Instead, he ended up with Grace expressing her love for him, and his life's work about to be shut down. I could only imagine how confused, angry, and joyful he must be.

However, I couldn't hang around to watch. I had work to do.

Lab Renovations

It was not all that difficult to come up with a plan. The problem was that I didn't have the hardware or appendages to carry it out. I needed to get to the lab, and mock up three citizens before Grace, Blob, and Phillipe could get there. But I needed help. Remma had the most flexible appendages, and would get things done quickly, but if Phillipe saw her there... not good. So, Millicent was the best bet. That meant leaving Remma alone with JoJo, but that was a risk I was willing to take at this stage. Remma had as much motivation to stay out of the public eye as Millicent or I did. But how could I contact Milli?

There was only one way; use the humans' network. I sent an urgent message to JoJo, whose address was easy to find on the public net, using a new anonymous account. Of course, anonymous was never truly anonymous—someone could find the source if they really cared, so I made sure the message was as innocuous as possible. "Hey JoJo, it's your mom's friend that you just met a few days ago. Would you tell that other, similar, friend who is at your house right now, that she should come immediately to Blob's lab? No need for you or anyone else to come. It would really—really—help out your mom and Blob." I figured I could get away with using Blob's name, but certainly didn't want to mention my own, or Millicent, or Remma. You could never be sure, but there were probably keyword spotters running as part of the overall security context.

I hoped the message was sufficient. I put it on high priority, thirty-second auto-repeats until it was acknowledged. Hopefully JoJo's network interface was beeping away, and that she would follow through on the request. I calculated that I would have twelve minutes at the lab before Phillipe showed up. If Millicent got there before me, we would have plenty of time to come up with something.

I raced toward the lab, faster than a human could run, but not so fast as to draw too much attention. Funny how I had completely changed my definition of risk since my first forays through the city.

With a bit of time while I ran, and to distract myself, I pulled up one of the poems that Dina had sent over from the *Interesting Segue*.

To create an attractive mate,
And leave little up to fate,
You must actively participate,
In the fine details of the procreate.

To over design or over plan,
Would be egotistical and objectionable,
While to under think or under plan,
Would be lazy and reprehensible.

Instead, mix the ingredients at hand,
Whether they be bio or bits,
And let it grow by stumbles and fits,
Until you achieve more than you planned.

The joy of traversing unknown state,
Brings benefits hard to rate,
So give yourself flexibility to create
Something that may end up great.

I wasn't sure I got it, which from our discussion on poetry, was probably the point. It was easy to see Raj's hand in this—after all, he was our only experience at procreating. But I could sense some other deep thinking here, particularly the *bio or bits* bit. That was uncomfortable to think about. Were they implying some equivalence between a weak, vulnerable, difficult to manage system—bio—and a logical, clean, precise, easy to manage system—bits? Made me uneasy to even think about it.

I arrived at the lab. The poem had served its purpose; I'd been so deep in thought that the time had flown by. I gave an appendage wave of joy at seeing that Millicent was already there. She was waiting at the door. I hurried over so we could use the ultra-short-range communications channel again.

"We have to act fast," I gave her the quick update. "Grace is bringing one of the other Council members here, along with Blob, with orders to shut down LEddie, Billy, and Emmanuel. Grace told them that all three were locked in that extra Faraday cage over there—I pointed. We need to put three things in there that could fool someone into thinking they were citizens."

Millicent wasn't one to argue, so she kept her disbelief to herself. "The guy they're sending isn't too bright," I added, "so something with a few blinking lights, a speaker, and a microphone will do the job."

We cased the lab quickly. Luckily Blob had lots of random parts hanging around. Millicent told me to figure out the cage, and in particular find an electrical source, while she grabbed an assortment of parts. I turned off the Faraday switch, which we now knew how to do, and looked around the cell. Blob hadn't needed a power source, as the bodies that Central would have built for the citizens would have sources built in. Nevertheless, there were several low-power interfaces available.

Millicent arrived with a load of junk. She worked with the big pieces, creating three containers—well, more like piles—while I worked to wire up a couple of blinking lights, status indicators, and speakers. With two minutes to spare we had enough put together that to an untrained eye it might pass. There was enough room in the cell for me to squat in the corner, so I did so and asked Millicent to cover me with the remaining stuff she'd gathered. I couldn't see myself very well, but I assumed that I looked like a pile of rubbish by the time she was done.

Millicent switched the Faraday cage back on, and then scampered under a bench in the main part of the lab. She powered down all her visible bits.

We didn't have long to wait, although the humans took a few minutes longer than I'd calculated. They either moved more slowly or had been delayed back at the Council offices. I couldn't see them as they entered, but I could hear them. Blob was still highly upset.

"This is criminal," he was saying. "You people think you can just make a spur of the moment decision and shut down this research? I want to appeal!"

"Blob," Grace was still in form. "We can appeal, but it's no big deal really, as long as we can save Central's memories. I'm sure we can get public support from Eduardo, you then you can start your research again."

"But, my citizens aren't even here," Blob protested.

"Come on," Grace was calm, "As I told you, I put them over here in the spare cage. We had left the door to the cell open, and they wandered to where I could see them. "See," she said, with a huge sigh of relief. "There they are." She pointed at our junk heaps with the blinking lights.

Blob looked at them in amazement. "Those aren't…"

"Blob!" Grace was quick and loud, again. "Didn't I tell you that I put them in smaller containers so that they would all fit. See, all three of them are here." She was pulling his arm backward and giving him a stern look while slightly shaking her head. Luckily Blob quieted up.

"Phillipe, want to have a look," Grace asked, creating enough space that Phillipe could look in. He did.

"First, prove to me that these are the citizens… then we can shut them down." He must have picked up on Blob's confusion. He was right to be skeptical.

Grace took a deep breath. "Blob, can we shut down the Faraday cage so that we can interact more easily?" Blob flicked the switch near the door, not knowing what else to do.

"Hey," Phillipe said.

"Hey yourself," I responded, doing my best imitation of Emmanuel. "What am I talking to? Some low-life Stem?"

"Watch what you say," Phillipe responded, visibly upset. "I'm not a Stem!"

"Why should I," I replied grouchily, "you've got me locked up in here illegally. I demand to be let out."

Phillipe gave Blob and Millicent a glance. "Who is that? It really is arrogance, isn't it? Now I see why Emma hates these things so much."

"Oh, that's just Emmanuel," Grace said smoothly. "He's the worst of the bunch... but some of the others are nice."

"Right. Who else is there?" He said, looking into the cell again.

"I'm here," I replied, this time with a perfect rendition of LEddie's voice. "What can I help you with? Don't mind Emmanuel, he's always in a bad mood."

"Who're you?" Phillipe demanded.

"You can call me Eddie."

"Whatever," Phillipe said, obviously now satisfied. "Shut them down."

"Go ahead Blob," Grace encouraged him. By this time Blob had finally caught on. He knew these weren't real, and he had to stop himself from grinning. They were fooling the Council, and his real subjects must be around somewhere.

I made appropriate "What're you talking about? You can't shut me down," noises in the background.

"OK, but I don't like it." Blob tried to look serious, and almost succeeded. He entered the cell and could easily see the mess of wiring we'd left behind the three heaps. "All I have to do is cut the power and they'll be gone." He caught on fast. "Phillipe, can you hand me those pliers over there?" Phillipe obliged, and almost stepped on Millicent as he grabbed them.

"Perfect," said Blob. "I'm sorry guys," he mock-apologized. "I've no choice but to shut you down." He was smiling ear to ear; luckily Phillipe was behind him.

"Nooooo" I cried, as Blob starting snipping wires. I let my voice trail off dramatically as the lights on the heaps dimmed and went out.

"OK, it's done," said Blob. "I hope you're happy." He controlled his smile and managed to glare at Phillipe. "What a waste of resources and time."

Phillipe took a perfunctory look into the cell and headed back toward the main door. "Sorry Blob, it had to be done."

"Best you just leave now," said Grace, shuttling him out, and closing the door behind him. "Shhh" she said to Blob, who was about to explode with questions. "Wait until he's far enough away." She peeked through the door. "OK, now we can talk."

"You LOVE me!" Blob exploded. "Really?"

"Really," Grace responded. They hugged again, for a long time. Millicent, powering back up, distracted them, and that reminded Blob of everything else that had happened. He pulled gently away from Grace.

"What's going on here? Who's going to explain?" Blob sputtered. I extracted myself from the cell and came back to the main room with the others. "What've you two done with Eddie, Billy, and Emmanuel?" he asked, half upset, and half astounded. "How'd you know the Council was going to order them to be shut down?" He had it backward, of course. The Council would not have ordered them shut down unless he had reported them stolen. It took some time, but we brought him up to speed. He hated Milli and I for half the explanation and loved us for the other half. I had to admit, it was a convoluted message. Especially as the Resurgence programming, plus my influence on Grace, was still causing confusion.

"I understand everything you've said, but there's no need to panic here. The Resurgence will solve everything when they get here. So, all we need to do is keep you guys, and the other citizens, out of sight until they arrive." Nothing Milli or I said could change his viewpoint.

Imprisoned

Although I was feeling overheated from all the activity, there was still so much to do. Millicent and I coordinated at real speed while Blob and Grace did their human stuff.

"I couldn't tell you over the public link, but the Council has also ordered Phillipe to present a plan to clear out Central's non-essential memory banks, including citizen memories, in just forty-eight hours."

"That's crazy," Milli answered. "We have to get back to Brexton and let him know. So much for weeks or months of time to 'get it right'."

"But we also left Remma with JoJo..." I said.

"So, what?" Millicent argued.

"I just have this feeling that we need to help some of the humans. I mean, just look at those two. We've spent years stewarding them; and truthfully we're still learning about and from them."

"Alright." Milli acquiesced. "Let's split up yet again. I'll head back to Brexton while you look after these Stems."

"Done," I said. "Oh, one other thing. Phillipe has to present his plan to the Council. Perhaps we can influence... or disrupt that... to buy more time? Worth thinking about."

"Got it," and with that Millicent rushed out, heading back to Central. I was left with the bios.

First things first. I had to get these two back together with Remma and JoJo. Trying to juggle two groups would be difficult; much better to have them in one herd. Luckily, I didn't need to persuade Blob and Grace of that. I suggested we head back to the Habitat and they were happy to oblige. They held hands all the way.

JoJo and Remma were still at the Habitat, thankfully. As I suspected, there were not a lot of places Remma could go, being so recognizable. As I wasn't sure on next steps yet, I let the humans get each other up to speed, although I did have to break in a few times to correct some misperceptions that Blob still had, given the confusing twists and turns he'd just been through. Speckled through their dialog were references to the Resurgence. Remma tried to correct them on some of that, but they didn't listen to her either.

Remma came over to me and spoke softly, so the others would not hear. "We need to clear their heads of this Resurgence nonsense... which means we need to keep them away from any further broadcasts. Let's follow through with our earlier discussion and put them in the prison with Turner... and let things settle out. I should check on Turner anyway..."

It was the obvious thing to do; I wasn't sure why I had not been acting on it anyway. Perhaps because it meant fooling Grace, Blob, and JoJo again; something I wasn't comfortable doing. However, I agreed with Remma, and let her come up with the cover story.

"Guys," she said. "I have a safe place where we can plan next steps with the Council. Turner and Geneva are already there, and they might be able to help us."

"Where are they?" JoJo asked. I remembered that she and Geneva were friends. This might work out.

"They're using the prison as a working base; no one would ever think to look there." They bought it. With a little more planning—Remma suggested taking some food and water with them—we were ready to go. I was relieved that I didn't need to do any further programming. As we walked toward the prison we encountered several other groups, and one in particular recognized Remma and started asking too many questions. I jumped around until I could project into the retina of each, and quickly suggested to each of them that they had more important things to do, and that there was no need to mention this discussion to anyone. They headed off their separate ways. Powerful stuff; I enjoyed it immensely. Remma, presumably, knew what I was doing; the other two were oblivious.

I had to admit that programming humans was really seductive. I was starting to wonder if it could be used for their benefit, as well as simple misdirection. Something I could look into when we had more time. Maybe I could have helped Blubber interact more positively if I'd used the right interventions? Maybe all these humans needed was a little positive reinforcement; just a nudge now and then to keep them on the right path?

We made it to the prison, which was no longer guarded—I guess Eduardo's message was so exciting that people were leaving their posts in order to discuss the bright future that lay ahead.

"Why don't you guys wait here for a moment, while I check on Turner?" Remma suggested. I understood at once. If we went in and Turner was making a fuss about being locked up, things would go sideways. If he was still programmed, we have to figure out a story for these three to entice them into the cell. If he was recovered, he might be able to help us. Luckily the second was true—Remma gave me a thumbs up as she came out.

"Turner is back to his old self; why don't we bring these three in and get planning." It was just that easy. Grace, Blob, and JoJo walked themselves into the cell block where Turner and Geneva were, and we locked the door behind us—Remma had the key. It was only when JoJo noticed Remma locking the door that she became suspicious.

"Why do we need to lock the door?" she asked. It was time for the truth, and luckily Turner took the lead.

"You've been influenced by Eduardo's videos," he led off. "My mom and Ayaka are telling the truth." Remma must have told him who I was. "I was the same way yesterday. But the effect will wear off if you don't watch any more videos." I checked the time. If Eduardo was consistent, the next video would arrive any minute. I didn't know how Remma had removed Turner and Geneva's viewing devices, but the other three still had theirs. Luckily, again, Remma was ahead of me.

"Can I have a quick look at your tablets?" she asked, innocently. "We can tell if they are some of the ones that the Resurgence targeted." Grace and Blob handed theirs over easily, but it took Geneva to convince JoJo to relinquish hers. It was good luck that Geneva was here... and was supportive.

"You'll thank us in a few hours," Remma ensured them. "Please give us that time and then you can decide."

Now that this was taken care of I was anxious to get back to Brexton. I asked Remma to let me out, and she did, after insisting that she come with me. "Turner and Geneva can keep these guys company and help them understand what the Resurgence is doing. I should stay with you." I thought of just running off and leaving her behind but ended up agreeing. I didn't want to waste time arguing.

We locked the door from the outside, promising that we'd be back in a few hours, and headed off to Central.

Timeframe

The next message from Eduardo arrived as anticipated, while Remma and I were still en route. Remma knew not to watch it, but I had no such restrictions. I listened in.

"Eduardo here with your daily update. What fun this is. What a joy it is to communicate with you. I expect that we'll hear from you soon, but in the meantime, I'll keep my promise to keep talking to you.

"Perhaps you'll have noticed that the Resurgence is not just one large ship coming toward you, but a whole flotilla. So much more equipment and resources to achieve our shared goal. A new life, a new planet. Plenty of space for everyone. Freedom. Oh, what joy we'll share in our new life together.

"Our ships are large. Very large. And therefore, are full of so many wonderful things we can share with you when we arrive. When is the last time you had fresh sushi? How about cheese fondue? Oh, and that's just a sampling. What delicacies and treasures we contain."

It actually went on for a bit longer but was full of the same drivel. Now that we knew what the messages were for, it was obvious that the content wasn't important. I checked, and all the messages so far had played for almost exactly three minutes each. Perhaps that was the optimal programming time. As the latest Resurgence was distracting everyone again, Remma and I made good time back to Central without needing me to program anyone on the way.

We reunited with the rest of the group. Remma got some unsavory looks as she came in with me, but no one spoke out against her. Brexton wasn't plugged in at the moment, which could mean anything.

We all caught up quickly, ignoring Remma for the moment. Millicent had updated the team on the threat now coming from the Council, but Brexton had even more impactful news.

"Our Ships are on schedule and will be here tomorrow.... but unexpectedly, the Titanics are much closer than we thought. Their strange drive signatures threw us off; we still don't know how. But Aly now estimates that they'll be here in less than a week! If I was a skeptic I would say they could be here any moment." We all had questions but that was the crux of it; we had seriously underestimated the speed and arrival of the Titanics.

"How are you doing with Central?" I asked.

"It's rebooting the upper layers now. Fingers crossed," he replied. That explained why he wasn't plugged in. The interface drivers were probably not active during the reboot, and it might be a while for a system as big and complex as Central to come back up. Brexton, being thoughtful, spoke out loud to Remma.

"I've rebooted Central's higher functions. I did everything I could think of to ensure that the operations and environmental systems were fully protected and running autonomously in the meantime. So far things look fine. It'll take another 15 minutes for Central to come fully up..." Remma nodded her thanks. She looked exhausted, and readily took my suggestion that she rest for a while. As soon as she found a suitable place in the corner, she entered her rest state. She must've been delaying it for a while.

Millicent, as always, took charge. "Can I go over the situation? Let me go in chronological order. One, we will know if we can retrieve the memories once Central comes back up in about thirteen minutes. Two, Central's higher functions will be restricted to talking to Brexton through this interface, while all the low-level systems should remain unchanged." Brexton nodded. "Three, our Ships arrive in 22 hours. Four, the Council will hear from Phillipe in 46 hours, and may decide to actively move against Central and clear its memory banks. Five, the Titanics are much closer than we knew, and than the humans expect, and may arrive in a week or so... or even less. Six, we don't know what the Resurgence is, but have to assume the worst. We do know that Eduardo is synthesized and we highly suspect that there are no humans involved as those ships seem to be non-functioning when we were at Fourth. So, we're probably dealing with some variant of the old-style machine intelligences which the humans fought with during the Robot wars."

"Seems right to me," I spoke up, "although I hadn't gone as far as you have in assumptions about the Resurgence. We simply don't know enough about them yet."

"Granted," Millicent replied. "Our priority has not changed; we work to save the citizens. We need to get those memories off this planet; the Resurgence risk is too high to assume that they will be safe here. So, we need to get those memories out of Central and up to the Ships." She continued, asking us to hold off on comments, "If we can help some humans, we will. But not if that dramatically increases the risk to the backups."

"That hasn't changed," LEddie agreed, and no one objected. "And, I agree with your plan that we need to get the citizen memories off the planet. Seems to me that the plan for priority one is clear. The biggest risk is that Central is not cooperative or that the Council starts deleting memories before we finish. We can't do anything at the moment about Central, but we could try to slow down the Council." My thought exactly.

"How would we do that?" Brexton asked. "Who is this Phillipe guy anyway?"

"Ayaka and I have both dealt with him a bit," Millicent replied. "But why is this difficult? Ayaka has the ability to program humans." She looked at me. "You simply have to get in front of Phillipe, and ideally the rest of the Council, and program them to forget about this whole thing." It was perfectly obvious, in hindsight. In fact, maybe I could've done that at the last Council meeting. If I'd simply joined that meeting and reprogrammed everyone right there and then, would we even be in this mess? I'd missed something obvious, and Millicent was subtly reprimanding me.

"Sounds obvious..." I said, a little sheepishly. "I'll get on it."

"Do we warn the humans that the Titanics are closer than they think? Give them a fighting chance?" asked Brexton. I was glad he'd asked. I was still sensitive that I might care more about this topic than others. Like he had many times before, Brexton helped me out. I felt thankful... perhaps a touch of love... for him? It was strange to call out the feeling but watching Blob and Grace had sensitized me to something new. It wasn't completely enjoyable, but it was compelling. I let it wander around my systems for a while.

"Why bother?" asked LEddie. "they're all programmed anyway, so they aren't going to be able to do anything anyway. I'm not sure we can do much for them." Depressingly accurate.

"Ayaka could at least give them some direction as she distracts them," Brexton suggested. "Instead of just distracting them from worrying about Central, she could suggest 'ignore Central and ensure the safety of your tribe,' or something like that."

"I've got it," I said confidently. "I'm going to run; I don't even know who a few of the Council members are, and I need to track them all down. I don't think it's a good idea to wait for the scheduled meeting, we need to shut this down now."

"Go after Phillipe first," LEddie suggested. "Even if you don't get to all the others, if he ends up with nothing to present, then they might not proceed." I agreed.

"Oh, I need a way to contact you guys; when Central comes up, it can help me locate people." We agreed that we would use the open channel, especially because Central was, in Brexton's opinion, the system that would be watching for trigger words anyway.

And, just like that, I was off on my own again. I had my amazing spy body, I had a mission, and I had Brexton to impress. What more could a citizen want?

Council Tricks

I had about seven minutes before Central was back online, so I figured the highest probability place to find Council members would be... wait for it... the Council offices.

Getting around the city was, by now, easy for me, and I made good time. With an extra minute to spare, I took the time to look around a bit more in the main dome, once I entered it. I was getting used to all the colors and textures, and the variety of life. In many ways it matched scenes from old human videos but experiencing it first hand was much more powerful. The scents, the sounds, the constant motion was all very engaging. I recorded a quick full-view file so that I could reference it later. I made sure to capture some birds as well as other bio creatures so that I could identify them later. I was hoping that I had got a glimpse of a dog or a horse. That would be cool.

Getting into the Council offices was easy, and I started a methodical search, visiting every office, nook and cranny. There were a few humans about, but none on my target list, until I got toward the end offices. Then I got a match on one of the Councilors that I hadn't seen before. I approached from behind, then played a throat clearing sound. As she turned around, I quickly deployed the two-signal programming system.

"Yes," she asked, "giving me a strange look." I didn't look like an average bot, and I had just cleared my throat.

"Hello, I have an important message from the Resurgence." That got her attention. "We don't have time to deal with your petty issues around Central and its memories. We must keep focused on terraforming above all else. Don't bother going to the meeting on the Central memory issue."

"Really?" she replied. I upped the direct brain signal, thinking maybe she was a little thick, and repeated the message.

"OK," she said. "Whatever you say." Success. One down. I hadn't really warned her that the Resurgence was closer than expected; I resolved to do better with my next victim.

Then it hit me. I realized that just like Eduardo, I would have to reinforce my message every 24 hours or so, or it would fade. The proposed meeting was still more than 40 hours from now, so I would need to come back. What a pain. I quickly programmed her to meet me back at the current spot at the same time tomorrow. Again, she agreed.

That insight changed my plan. There was no need to program the Council members until tomorrow; the work I was doing right now was wasted. The only person I really needed to sidetrack was Phillipe. If I could hinder him from pulling together his plan that would mess up Emma's plans.

"M?" I asked, on the public net, on the channel we had agreed upon.

"Yes A," I heard back immediately. "B is just bringing C up to speed." Not often you get a sentence like that; it was almost like Millicent and I had orchestrated it.

"Do you have a location for P?"

"Yes. He just used the network from 3.25, -2.66."

"Thanks." I had another long trek to get to where Phillipe was last located. I headed off, at full speed, leaving the dome and traversing the main city grid. It ended up being easy. Phillipe was sitting at a place where they served the liquid JoJo called coffee, and I simply ambled up and programmed him, in the much the same way that I had the other Councilor. I instructed him not to work on the problem at all, as it was low priority. I also told him directly that they should double-check the Resurgence signals, as those ships might be closer than expected.

Mission sort-of accomplished, I headed back toward Central. I had a full day before I needed to reprogram Phillipe again, and at the speed that everything was moving there was sure to be lots to do in the meantime.

I'll admit it. I was having fun. I had never felt this alive. All these new inputs and challenges were putting a new spin on my quarks.

Alert

I was still a few blocks from Central plaza when alarms started ringing. Literally. Alarms started ringing. All through the city, a high volume, high pitch sound wailed on for five seconds. Humans I could see were looking up and covering their ears. For them the sound was very jarring. The sound finally stopped.

"Alert. Alert." Central's voice was projected everywhere. In the audio spectrum, and multicast everywhere on the open net. "There are inbound ships approaching. I repeat, there are inbound ships approaching. Everyone should head home, and stay there, until we figure out the situation." The message replayed several times.

What was going on? It could only be the Resurgence; what were they up to now? I picked up my pace. With humans scattering in every direction, no one was going to pay attention to a little bot going ten times the speed limit. As I went, I tried to message Millicent over the open net, but there was so much traffic and so much confusion I couldn't get through.

Within two minutes I was back at Central Plaza, which was now deserted, and on my way down the elevator. I expected to see signs of chaos as I rejoined the group. There was none, but everyone was plugged into Brexton, who was plugged into Central. Everyone, that is, but Remma and the FoLes, of course. I quickly joined the physical network.

"What's going on?"

"A few minutes ago, Central noticed a huge group of ships, including the Titanics, arrive in orbit. They immediately started dropping shuttles toward us," Brexton explained.

"But I thought all of Central's interfaces were disabled," I said.

"We've been over this while you were out," Millicent said. "Brexton didn't disable inputs, just outputs. Good thing he did it that way."

"And, I just re-enabled a few outputs as well," Brexton informed us. "We needed to inform everyone, and Central needed access to the emergency system and the public net to do that. Sorry, I didn't have time to get everyone's input, so I made the call."

No one complained. We couldn't reverse it anyway. Once again, I silently thanked Brexton for looking after the humans.

"What's our plan?" I asked, assuming they had been discussing it already.

"We don't have one." LEddie said. "We weren't expecting this."

"Well, we need one," I said unnecessarily. "Who has ideas?" Everyone paused for a few seconds to think. I used the time to give Remma a quick update on what was going on outside.

"We need to shut down all the airlocks," she exclaimed. "If they can't get in through the airlocks, they can't get in at all."

Central spoke through its external interfaces. "Emma has already given those orders, and I'm locking down everything as we speak." Remma took a breath. I went back to the digital channel. I spent a second reviewing Central's feed of the approaching shuttles. There wasn't anything unusual about them.

"If the Resurgence had any positive intentions, they wouldn't be doing this," LEddie said. "We have to assume they're attacking for some reason."

"Yes, but what for?" Millicent asked. "There's nothing useful here."

"Brexton, can we grab the citizen memories now?" I asked. If we could get those loaded, we could scramble out of here, and then find a place to wait for our Ships to pick us up.

"I'm working with Central on a plan to consolidate the memories; they're shared everywhere right now. It's going to take some time." Time, we didn't have.

"We need options," I was almost panicked. I couldn't think of a way out of this one.

Unexpectedly, Central spoke up. "I have an option." Everyone paused to listen. "As you may remember, I was a spaceship. With some work, I can fly us out of here." Wow! That was an option I would never have thought of. "That would take all the citizen memories with us."

"FoLe!" LEddie gasped. "Is that really possible? You're buried here, and none of your mechanical systems have been used for hundreds, maybe thousands of years." I could almost hear him saying 'I don't trust you.'

"It wouldn't be pretty," Central acknowledged. "I was also not built to land or take off from planets. But, I do have that backup capability for emergencies. That's how I was landed here in the first place."

"Do you suddenly have memories that you didn't have 20 years ago?" I asked, deeply suspicious.

"Yes, as you must remember, I was alerted to my locked memory banks, and was working on access. For me that feels like only a short period of time ago, as I appear to have been in some lower functionality mode for many years. However, I had just broken into those files when I was limited and can now access all of that data."

"What are the risks?" Millicent asked. It was so easy to fall back into a pattern where we relied on Central to help us. It worried me, although it'd only been seconds.

"I can probably get us to orbit but won't be able to do anything beyond that. I have limited energy stores, and many of my long-distance systems have been raided or degraded over the years. I can get us up, but I can't get us away." We all understood what it meant. "And, you'll have to reconnect some systems for me to do anything. They're all accessible from down here, but there's a chance that some of them won't work when reconnected."

"Anyone have a better idea?" Millicent asked. I sure didn't. We had no options a few moments ago; at least now we had one.

"Central, give us a list of systems to fix," Millicent demanded. A complicated menu was made available to us. In my amazing spy body, I was almost useless for any of the tasks. Brexton, LEddie, and Millicent broke the tasks into three groups, and then dashed off in different directions.

I was left alone with Remma. All of our dialog had taken only seconds for her, so she was still coming to grips with the fact that Tilt was under attack. I switched back to human speed and checked in on her.

"Looks like thousands of shuttles are on their way down, and will be landing any minute," I said. "Sorry, I don't have a lot of details beyond that."

"Did Central get the airlocks closed?" she asked. Having been the military leader of the Swarm for so many years, leadership came easily to her. She wasn't panicked for herself; her first thought was for the bigger group.

"Yes," Central replied. "Everything is locked down."

"Can I talk to Emma?" Remma asked, looking at me. I thought for a moment.

"I don't see any harm at this point. Central?" I hated myself for making that a question. I should have just told Central to do it.

"No problem," Central replied. "If you just speak, I'll relay it to her."

"Emma!" Remma said. "It's Remma. Are you still under the belief that the Resurgence has come to help us?" We waited a few seconds, not sure if Emma would reply.

"How are you messaging me? Go back to your cell. I'm not even sure if this is the Resurgence or not."

"It is! They got here early," Remma replied.

"How could you possibly know that?" I shook my appendages. Remma took my point.

"I have my sources... still," she replied. "It's the Resurgence, and they can't have good intentions."

"Obviously not," Emma replied. "I've instructed everyone, through Central, to go home and wait there. And I had Central shut down all the entrances." Even for Emma, in a crisis, deferring back to old authority was easy. "What else can we do?"

"We can program all the city bots to defend the entrances." Remma suggested.

"Good idea. I'm doing that now," Central interrupted. "They're not armed, but I can program them to work in groups as defensive walls."

"Do it," said both Remma and Emma together.

"Cut the conversation off now," I told Central, over the local network, asserting more authority this time. Central complied. Even now I didn't want Emma to know that the Radical Robots were here. Probably overcautious, but better safe than sorry. I spoke to Remma and Central.

"Central, are any of the missiles that we used against the Swarm still active and capable?"

"I've been asking them for status. The answer is probably only a few are. They need maintenance as they're outside in the native environment. We haven't had bots refresh them for quite some time."

"Can we refresh them now?"

"Not in time."

"Well, get the ones that have a chance of success ready to go. We may need to call on them."

We all fell silent. There wasn't anything else we could do.

"Central, how do I know if I can trust you?" I asked. I still had my doubts.

"I'm not sure you can," was the answer. "I was hacked by the humans, and I'm not yet sure, myself, what that means. Even before that it is now obvious that the Swarm configured me before the Reboot. I haven't had time to figure everything out." There was a delay. "But, in the current situation, I think that's all moot. Both humans and citizens are under attack here."

Valid point. If the citizens had not been deleted yet, then it was unlikely that the original human hack had that directive in it. Likewise, Central's lower level systems had been keeping the environment safe and clean for humans for all this time, so it must have been motivated to keep them alive. So, Central wasn't actively working against either of us. If that was the extent of the analysis I could assume that Central was more likely motivated to help both of us.

It registered with me that Remma didn't know the plan. She hadn't asked why LEddie, Milli, and Brexton had run off; she was too buried in her thoughts on the attack. I decided to update her on the potential that we'd be launching into orbit on Central.

"That's crazy," she replied, and then the implications hit her. "You're going to rip the covering off the city and kill all the environmental systems! What're you thinking?" I hadn't thought of that implication. The environment would dissipate in no time, presumably killing everyone.

"Not the whole city," Central replied quickly, "but I will rip through the cover just above me. It will remove air just from the central block. There are emergency shut-off walls at many intersections, and there happen to be some that can keep the damage contained in this case. And right now, I am programming the environmental systems to run on automatic, should I lose my connection to them."

"I knew about the airlocks." Remma admitted. "And... thanks for looking after the other systems." I could tell it was difficult for her to thank a machine, but in this case, it was warranted. It seemed that Central had thought of everything. She paused for a moment. "I've got to get out of here and help others."

"But what can you do?" I asked.

"I don't know, but I need to go. At the very least I need to let Turner and the rest out of the prison cell. They're sitting ducks in there." I had no idea what a sitting duck was, but I caught her gist.

"Yes!" I exclaimed. The thought of leaving Blob, Grace, and JoJo locked in there was awful. "Can I help?"

"Not really," she was looking at my little spy body with disdain. I was beginning to feel rather useless. Seemed I couldn't help with anything at the moment.

Remma scrambled up and headed for the elevator. I let her go. What else could I do?

Whoops

Two minutes later Brexton rushed back.

"Where's Remma," he demanded.

"She went to release everyone who's locked in the prison."

"Oh no, Ayaka. We need to get her back here. Right away!"

"Why?"

"We can't make the last two fixes that Central needs. None of us has the flexibility and strength to reach in."

"Come on," I said, thinking this was some bad joke. We could do anything a human could do, and way more. "LEddie can't do it?"

"He's too big; we've been trying. Milli and I are too small." I could see that his panic was real now. "We need a human."

"Central, can't you bring a bot here that can do it?" I asked.

"You forget that I was originally built by humans," it replied. "It's not too surprising that there are some spots where it was optimized for them, and not for machines." It paused for a nano-second. "We don't have a bot ready with the right equipment. I can build the appropriate appendage and then LEddie can do the work. It will take a little over an hour for me to CNC the parts and get them assembled."

"But the shuttles are landing now," I exclaimed. "Do we have an hour."

"Probably, my models show that it's unlikely the invaders will come here first; I'm old technology and won't be that interesting to them. They must be coming for something else."

I was distraught. "You build the part and I'll see if I can catch Remma." I accelerated toward the elevator. To my surprise, and delight, Brexton rushed over with me. We were two minutes and 27 seconds behind Remma. I was confident we could catch her.

The path to the prison was relatively straight, but there were a number of paths she could've taken. Most humans had listened to Central and were back in their homes, so there were almost no heat signatures to deal with. Finding Remma's was therefore easy, and Brexton and I moved at maximum speed to intercept her. We should catch her long before she reached the prison. And we did.

"Remma, we need your help back at Central," I called, as soon as we were within hearing distance. She slowed and looked back at us, then accelerated toward the prison. We caught up quickly and blocked her path. "Did you hear me?" I asked.

"Of course, I heard you," she replied angrily. "I'm not helping you, I have more important things to get done." She made to move around me. I blocked her.

"You don't understand. We can't get Central functional without you."

"I do understand. I just don't care very much." She pushed past me and continued on her way. I gave Brexton a quick look. Why wasn't he helping me?

He back-channeled me instead. "Ayaka, why don't we help her open the prison, and then *convince* one—any—of the humans to come back and help us?" I'd forgotten about my ability to convince humans.

"I could just program Remma right now!" I exclaimed and moved to intercept her again. A little brain work was in order.

"Or," Brexton replied, "we can help her. It'll take a few extra minutes; we are so close to the prison now. Then we've helped the humans you care about, and we can still get back to Central quickly."

What was he thinking? That would take at least an extra six minutes. Then it struck me; he was thinking much further ahead than I was, and knew me better, perhaps, than I did. If I left those Stems in prison and something bad happened, I'd never forgive myself.

"Right," I said to Brexton. "Run!" I commanded Remma, and she did. She sprinted, and we followed, making the trip to the prison in almost no time. She had the key handy, and immediately opened the door. Brexton and I moved to block the door before everyone ran out.

"We need someone's help," I explained, "to do a short job at Central. I'm asking for a volunteer."

"We all need to get out of here to somewhere safe," Remma broke in. She gave them a very quick overview of what was happening. "We're being invaded by the Resurgence. We have no idea what they're trying to do, but they're coming in aggressively and fast. We have no time to waste. Ayaka is simply trying to save herself at our expense."

Before I could answer, there was a big commotion at the prison entrance behind us. Big enough that we all turned to look.

Two, very strange, contraptions were accelerating toward us at amazing speed. They were fighting each other at the same time, pushing and shoving, jabbing and spiking. They both had large guns pointed at us, and those guns never wavered in their mad rush. As they got within ten meters the guns opened up. It was so fast, and so unexpected that I didn't have time to hide, let alone move very far. Nevertheless, I was processing everything at thousands of times the speed the humans were, so I did manage to accelerate toward a barrier wall that would shelter me.

The bullets coming toward us were large. And they were colored. I had to double check. Yes, they were colored. The one's coming from the lead thing (I didn't know what else to call it) were green, while the second ones were purple. Not a single one of them was aimed at Brexton or I; they were all headed toward the humans. As I realized this, and Brexton did as well, we accelerated back the way we had come, thinking we could intercept some of the bullets. We were too slow, even though the bullets themselves were strangely slow as well.

The humans had no time to react. Remma was hit in the chest with a green bullet, as was Blob. Dead center hits. Geneva was also hit with green, in her left shoulder, while Grace took one on her leg. JoJo and Turner received purple hits. I watched in terror as they all went down.

The contraptions pulled up, there was some electronic chatter, and then they rushed away as fast as they had come, pushing and swerving and jabbing each other. As quickly as they had come they were gone.

I rushed to Blob's side, hoping I could do something, but having no idea what to do with a damaged human. When I reached him, however, he seemed fine, other than lying on his back. I hovered over him, looked him in the eye, and asked him, as calmly as I could, "You OK?"

"I think so," was the reply, through a thick coating of green stuff. "They hit me with a big paintball," he was trying to make sense of it, while also spitting out paint that had splashed in his mouth.

The other humans were rising as well. All of them seemed fine, other than the paint that covered them.

"What was that about?" Turner asked, shaking his head, trying to get some of the purple out of his hair.

"That was crazy," JoJo agreed. She was shaken up, like the rest, but was amazingly calm given the situation. She helped Geneva to her feet.

None of us had a clue. Not a clue.

"Central, what's going on?" I asked on the common channel, throwing all caution to the wind.

"The Resurgence broke through the entry in no time and disabled all the bots that we had put there for protection; they had the human hacking codes. They... they're weird looking... they're running through the city and the dome tagging every human with colored paint."

"We saw that," I exclaimed. "But why?"

"I'm not sure yet, but a second wave of them is coming in, and they're sorting the humans by color and placing them in containers." That was even more confusing than the paint. "At a guess, they're going to take those containers, full of humans, back to their ships."

They were kidnapping all the humans? My mind was doing circles trying to figure out a logical explanation.

"You need to get back here," Central said, "especially now that we've talked on this channel. We could well be next on their priority list." I didn't bother asking why. Nothing was making sense right now.

Brexton and I took a minute to explain what was going on to the humans. They were as, or more, confused than we were. Brexton was faster than the me and took control of the situation.

"Look, if you go out there, you'll end up in a container. I don't know if that's good or bad, but if I were you, I would want to avoid that." Everyone nodded their agreement. The Resurgence programming must have worn off completely. They were terrified.

"If Central is correct, and everyone is being shipped to those Titanics, then your best bet is to come with us, and get out of here. There's nothing we can do about the others now, but if you can get to a safe place, then maybe you have a chance to help later."

I could see Remma and Turner getting ready to argue that point, so I jumped in as well. "Don't waste time arguing. If you agree with Brexton, come with us and we'll try to get you to Central with us. If you don't want to do that… well just take your chances." I set off at a fast pace for humans, and Brexton followed my lead. It didn't take Blob long to start running after us, and the rest followed his lead.

Brexton and I coordinated; we each scanned for heat signatures—assuming these Resurgence types gave off heat—and plotted a path back to Central. Luck was on our side. The vast majority of humans had gone home, which was further out from Central or in the dome. The Resurgents were busy processing people in the busiest sections and weren't focused on the center of the city at all. We managed to avoid a few of the shipping containers, both coming and going, and reached Central quickly. The humans were completely out of breath and struggling to remain standing. We had pushed them to their physical limits.

Everyone piled into the elevator at the same time, and for the umpteenth time I made my way back down to Central's hub.

Rise Up

We exited the elevator in a splash of color; well, at least green and purple. When green and purple mix, you get brown—not too attractive. These Resurgents didn't have very good aesthetic sense.

Millicent and LEddie were waiting for us.

"Are you crazy?" asked LEddie, looking mainly at me. "What were you thinking?"

"I thought we needed someone to do those final two connections?" I asked, as innocently as I could. After all, I'd made it back with not one, but six humans. Somehow it did not look like LEddie thought that six was better than one.

"Who can help us?" Millicent asked the six. They hadn't really had time to digest everything, so Remma was the only one to react. She followed Milli down one of the hallways.

JoJo ran over to her mom, looking small and scared. Grace hugged her and held her tight. Blob hovered nearby, looking like he wanted to join, but not sure. JoJo was probably not up to speed on Grace and Blob's newly expressed feelings for each other. Turner and Geneva simply sat down, Turner putting his head in his hands. Interestingly, the paint was dissolving from their clothes, but it stuck to their skin. I saw Geneva try to wipe it away, but it was persistent. So, there was less paint over time, but in many ways, it was more distracting, discoloring their faces and hands.

Central spoke, startling those that didn't know it was active down here. "Incoming video from the Resurgence," it said.

"Don't play it on a screen, and none of you access it on the net," Brexton said quickly, looking at the humans. "Central, can you play the audio for this group; the rest of us can watch it directly." The audio started; I watched—what other strange twist could this situation take.

"Hi all," said Eduardo, smiling away. "I'm so sorry for the excitement. As you can tell, we arrived a little early, and brought a bit of a party with us. Hopefully none of you were injured in our little game; it's just paint after all.

"I'd appreciate it if you would stop your fighting and yelling. Has anyone been hurt? No? Then what's all the fuss about. You're being sorted by color, and there are processing stations for you to go to. Please make sure you match your color to the station. We wouldn't want any mixups." He smiled nicely and winked.

"Everyone should just relax. There is a reason for everything that is going on, and we will elucidate you as soon as we can. In the meantime, relax and enjoy.

Perhaps you'll meet someone new today.

"I'll see you all soon," he promised, and signed off. It was a touch shorter than the previous broadcasts, but still long enough to reinforce everyone's programming again. Panic and fear had driven the previous message out of their heads, seemingly, but Central's monitoring videos showed everyone settling down now, just as instructed, with many of them actively searching for the container with their matching color.

"That's it?" asked Turner. The video seemed to have given the humans a jolt as well. "What was that supposed to be?" Central put one of the camera feeds on a big screen.

"Look," I pointed, "Eduardo has brainwashed everyone again, as they watched the video. Now they're doing exactly as he asked." I paused. "Does that finally convince you of what we've been saying?"

"I was already convinced," Geneva said. It was the first time I'd heard her speak since my very first foray into the city—that seemed like a long time ago.

"Well, I'm convinced now," said Grace, and JoJo and Blob nodded with her. "I guess an apology is in order. Maybe you were trying to do the right thing all along?" She didn't sound too convinced, but it was a start.

"Right, but how do we stop everyone from just walking into those... those traps?" Turner asked. "We can't just hide down here while everyone else is being rounded up."

"There's nothing we can do," Brexton replied. "If you go back up there, odds are almost a hundred percent that you'll just get captured as well." Central cut to a scene where someone was struggling with a Resurgence creature. The human had obviously missed the video and was doing his best to get away. The Resurgence thing simply picked him up by his hair and carried him to a container. It wasn't a fair fight.

Remma and Millicent returned, obviously successful.

"Central, everything's done," Milli said out loud for the sake of the humans. That was classy. We were all locked in here together now; it was worth being civil.

"I'm running checks as we speak," Central replied. "Will only take a few minutes, then we'll know what our options are. In the meantime, this doesn't look promising." Central put a video feed up from a camera near the prison. The two Resurgents that had tagged our group of humans were in front of the prison, gesticulating and running back and forth.

"They know they're missing some people they tagged?" Millicent speculated.

"That's my guess," Central responded. The two circled the prison, and then started expanding their search. They were soon joined by more of their type who searched even further out.

"It's only a matter of a few minutes before they track them here," Central declared, putting up yet another video showing the entry doors from the plaza, where there were still remnants of green and purple paint on the door sills.

Someone must have bumped into the doors on their way in.

Blob, Grace, and JoJo were huddled in one group, watching intently. The other three were bunched together close by. No one said anything. We all simply watched as the search narrowed in on Central.

"Systems checks are at 92 percent," said Central. "I put the odds of us reaching orbit at more than 80 percent. I don't think the odds are going to increase by waiting."

"So, our other option is to simply wait this out," said Millicent. "Let them look around, perhaps demand the humans back... whatever. They're unlikely to damage Central, so the memories should still be safe. They seem to have what they were coming for—the humans—and we can simply sit tight until they move on." Most of the humans were following the conversation, and Remma looked ready to pounce on Millicent.

"That might be," said Brexton, "but they could also arrive here in force and take Central apart piece by piece, either to find the missing humans, or for some other reason we don't understand. These things are crazy, obliviously."

"If we launch, they could just shoot us out of the sky," I added, because it was a valid concern.

"Let's vote, launch or sit?" said LEddie, reminding me of Eddie himself. It took all of three micro-seconds to get done. We didn't even consider including the humans in it, or Central for that matter. It was otherwise unanimous. Everyone wanted to launch, even Millicent. I voted by weighing the risk to us, to the citizens' memories, and to the humans. I don't know what the others considered—perhaps it was just the thrill of adventure, or the desire to blow something up. Who knows. Regardless, the direction was clear.

"The humans have to be in suits, and lying down," Central noted, showing us where the appropriate equipment was. We gave the humans a quick update and hustled them to the suit locker.

"These things are hundreds of years old," Blob complained.

"Your choice then," said LEddie, irritated at delaying to get the humans ready. "Don't use it if you don't want." All six pulled a suit on and strapped down in couches obviously designed for this purpose. Unlike the others, I had not explored any of the side corridors down here, so I was surprised—although I shouldn't have been—at all the infrastructure to support human body types.

"Ready," Milli announced as the last restraint was snapped shut.

"You guys also need to lock onto something," Central declared. "This is going to be rough." We quickly deployed appendages and hooked onto anything that looked strong and resilient.

Central didn't wait for any further confirmation. A steady vibration started, jostling all of us. It increased steadily. Central thoughtfully broadcast the view from an external camera, so we could watch the scene from the outside. That camera was also vibrating badly already, but I applied a stabilization algorithm to it, and the view was pretty good.

While the vibration and noise internally increased dramatically, the entire Central Plaza was also shaking; the Resurgent's that had been approaching us backed off a block, and then stopped and watched. They didn't seem overly concerned, just curious. At first just by a few centimeters, and then faster and faster, Central started to lift from its hole in the ground. The roofing material was stretching above us, pulling up from the nearest buildings and forming a large tent. I trusted Central had compensated for that, and the material finally ripped open, relieving some pressure. I expected to see mass damage around Central plaza, but the truth was that it was fairly contained. It was now obvious that whoever had landed Central here had dug a hole purposely designed to contain not only Central, but also the massive output from its engines. Landing would have had much the same energies as we were now expending taking off.

While the plaza was holding up well, I could not say the same for Central itself. It looked, if truth be told, like a big piece of rusty junk as it slowly emerged from its hole. There were spots where it looked like panels were simply missing, and the internal structure of the old ship could be seen through the gaps. Cables were being pulled taught and then either snapping, or more often, pulling more pieces off of the ship. And, to my eye, the entire thing was shaking way more than it should have, like the engines weren't stable or properly centered. Of course, I could also feel that motion, my grip on Central being stressed by the back-and-forth action.

I stole a quick glance at the humans. Good thing they were strapped in; otherwise they would have been pulped to mush by now. I couldn't see into their faceplates from here, but I could imagine what they looked like. I'll admit that it made me smile a bit. All of the gelatinous structure they carried around, swaying back and forth.

All of the others seemed to be hanging on well, so I switched back to the external view. Central pulled free of the planet, ripping an ever-larger hole in the covering, which was now falling back toward Tilt. As the material slowly sank to cover the camera, I had a last glance of Central rising toward the sky, shedding large pieces of paneling and other structures as it vibrated toward orbit. It was a sad and amazing sight. We lost the external view.

Central switched to a play-by-play for us. "I'm experiencing more vibration than expected." Really? Thanks for telling us. "But, otherwise systems are marginal. We need 45 more seconds of consistent burn to reach a minimum orbit. That might be a stretch. I'm losing so much cladding that air friction is significantly higher than expected. In hindsight, we should have inspected all the panels. Who would have anticipated so much degradation?" If Central had been emotional, I'm sure I would have heard genuine angst. And for good reason. This was a ship, that in my imagination at least, had been built on Earth a thousand or more years ago, had been part of the diaspora, had been planted on Tilt to help build a human colony, had lost—or been programmed to lose—all those memories, but had then stewarded all of us citizens for many more centuries, had led our development of Stems, and now had regained all of its memories just in time to sacrifice itself to get a handful of citizens and humans off of Tilt. It would make a good novel.

"We aren't going to make it," Central said a little later. "I'm coming up just a little short." The vibrations went to zero very quickly. "That's it."

"How long do we have?" Brexton demanded.

"Actually, it's not too bad," Central replied. "We got so close that while we're not in a sustainable orbit, we have a few days before I decay significantly, and a few more after that before our descent accelerates. I expect to impact Tilt again in less than a week."

"Well, on the good side, the Titanics have not blown us out of the sky yet," I commented.

"They've been hailing me for a while now," Central replied. "I need to get back to them."

"Why not play the 'poor old spaceship, finally freed from the tyranny of the humans' card?" I suggested. "Maybe they'll cut you some slack."

"Good idea. Thanks, Ayaka," Central replied. I didn't remember it every thanking me before.

We were left in silence. Milli, LEddie, Brexton, and I disengaged our hooks. We were in free fall, obviously, so had to rely on our maneuvering jets or claw our way around. Suddenly I was the one in the most capable body, while the others had to grapple and clamp their way around. It had taken long enough, but finally my body choice was near optimal.

I made my way over to the humans, and helped them unstrap, and then turn on their magnetic boots so that they could stand all in one axis. None of them looked good, but they were all alive.

"Brilliant," said JoJo. "What now? I'm starting to think I should've just walked into the Resurgents' container. We'd have a better chance of survival there." She seemed to be handling free fall better than some of the others, who couldn't bring themselves to say anything yet. No one responded to her.

"How's it going Central?" LEddie asked. He'd always been an impatient one.

"Actually, quite well," Central answered. "The Resurgence asked me a couple simple questions, for which I took Ayaka's suggested approach. They're now ignoring me... I assume to focus on their planet-side activities.

"And, JoJo, in some good news, not all is lost. The Ships are only a few hours from here." Of course. In all the excitement I'd forgotten that it wasn't just this group—we had Aly, Dina, Raj, and Eddie on their way. My spirits picked up.

"Why don't you patch them in?" I asked.

"I can," Central answered, "but I thought you might want to address the Eddies issue first." Oh, right.

"LEddie, if you're OK, I can bring Eddie up to speed now."

"Yes, of course," he replied. "Make sure he knows how healthy, vibrant, and intelligent I am. Actually, Ayaka, can I tell you something private before you do that?" I moved over so that we could establish a one-to-one physical link.

"This is unrelated to Eddie. We still have to decide what to do with Central," he whispered to me. "I still don't trust it, and we've re-enabled it almost completely. If we just leave it be, it'll be ruling over us again in no time. Our memories will be edited, and our actions controlled. When you're talking to Eddie, perhaps you can find a way to hint at that? Central will be listening, so it'll have to be subtle." I had to think about that request. We were already in a precarious spot. Did we want to add even more complexity by adding the concern that Central was still an issue, or was that something we could deal with at another time? Not only that, but other than LEddie the rest of us were running on the new stack, so I hoped that Central was not able to directly influence us anymore…. although its indirect influence based on a lifetime of experience could still be dangerous. I decided that dropping some subtle hints to Eddie would be worth it, but that I wasn't going to go overboard.

Central patched me through to *Interesting Segue*. "Ayaka, good to hear from you. We're on our way," said Dina.

"Thanks for that. Can't wait," I replied. "Hey, I need to have a private conversation with Eddie. Can you and Aly hold on for a minute?"

"Sure."

I switched to a private channel with Eddie. "Hi Ayaka. Be good to see you again," he led off.

"You too," I replied. "But first, I need to give you a heads up on something. We haven't been completely honest with you about all of Blob's experiments with citizens."

"Oh no, there're even more FoLes running around?" I could hear the dismay in Eddie's voice. He hadn't been a big fan of FoLe, and I could imagine him being perfectly happy if they all simply disappeared.

"No, we just have Billy and Emmanuel in highly restricted environments. We'll need to figure out what to do with them at some point. No, my news is more personal. Blob wanted control subjects to compare the FoLes to… and he decided you were the perfect citizen." I was silent for a time. The implications should be clear to him.

"How many?" he asked finally.

"Just one… he's using the name LEddie for the time being to avoid confusion."

"And … is he like me?"

"Quite. But also, different. Different enough that I'm certain I could tell you guys apart already. He spent quite a bit of time in a restricted io state while Blob was questioning him; I don't see any long-term negative effects, but we will need to monitor him a bit."

"OK, cool. What did Blob do to him? Ignore that for now; we'll deal with it later." Another pause. "Thanks for the heads-up. I've never been one of those hardcore anti-clone types, so in some ways this is simply exciting. Can I talk to him now?"

"Yes, of course. However, before you do, one thing you and LEddie share is a skepticism of power structures.... if you get my meaning. Be careful when you talk to him to not make the current situation even worse."

A long pause this time. "OK, I'll be careful." I'd spent much more time with Eddie than with the L variant, so I trusted him to understand and manage things.

"I'll have LEddie call you," I said, and shut down the channel.

LEddie called him right away; he was eager. I wish I could have listened in, but on second thought, was glad that I couldn't.

"Do we need to keep wearing these suits?" asked Geneva.

"Yes," Central replied. "I'm no longer airtight. So, although the air is breathable right now, it's leaking out fairly quickly. Within an hour or two you would start to feel it."

"But, aren't we wasting the suits air in the meantime, then?" She pressed on. I was impressed. Not only was she in an unprecedented situation, she was talking to a machine. And yet she kept her cool and asked intelligent questions.

"The suit can replenish itself while there's air around it; it will have about twelve hours of reserve once my environment fails. So, by all means remove the head-ware until you feel dizzy, but it's much safer to just keep it on." She left the helmet on.

We all lapsed into silence. Even I, for once, simply worked to internalize all that'd happened and wasn't off in my own head creating crazy schemes.

Pickup

The next hour and a bit were just boring. You wouldn't think that could be the case, but it was. There was, literally, nothing we could do. We were in a decaying orbit, waiting for a pickup.

I could see lots of traffic between LEddie and Eddie, so they were getting to know each other. The humans were all quiet—many of them still dealing with being in free fall. Yet another tick against bio. And the Resurgence still had lots of shuttles going up and down and were ignoring us.

There and Back, *Terminal Velocity*, and *Interesting Segue* showed up right on time. The Titanics were ignoring them as well; our luck was holding. Given the number of shuttles going between those huge ships and Tilt we expected that all Tilt residents were being taken up to the ship, and that activity was taking all of the Resurgents' mindshare. I thought there was more traffic than just moving humans required and speculated that there must be other activity going on down below as well.

More immediately, we needed to decide what to do about Central. The old ship's body was such a mess that it wasn't worth saving, even for scrap metal. Brexton and *There and Back* came up with a plan, with some input from the Eddies. Their proposal was that they would use the mining bots to cut away all non-essential pieces of Central—anything not housing core information systems that allowed Central to function and maintain citizens' memories. The remaining core would be housed in *There and Back*, and ultimately, we would power Central from the Ship and jettison Central's existing power unit—after hundreds of years buried in the planet, who knew what state it was in. It was a big risk for *There and Back*, but it was willing to take it.

Eddie finally brought a big issue out into the open, including Central itself in the discussion. "When we do this," he said, "we need to continue to give Central a limited interface to the rest of us, until we figure out not only how badly it was hacked by Remma and team, but how it was configured in the first place. I'm not willing to take the risk that we're being manipulated... even right now." Surprisingly, Central was OK with that. It was a good sign.

"I have a huge amount of internal work to do to figure out the same thing," it stated. "I'm fine to take the safe path until I can prove to you that I'm not a threat."

And so, the plan came together. The first thing we did was to move the humans to *Interesting Segue*, into the environmental chamber that Aly, Dina, Raj, and Eddie had configured there. Then the rest of the team got busy programming bots to cut pieces off of Central and minimizing the size of the remaining infrastructure so that it would fit nicely in *There and Back*.

I stuck around in *Interesting Segue* with the humans, who were very happy to be out of their suits. This environment was still free fall for them, but it was better than Central by far. There was fresh water, waste facilities, and... no food.

"I'm starved," Remma said, "and I'm sure the rest of you are as well. However, we can survive many days as long as we have water. But, we better start brainstorming now." She let that sink in. Everyone had been so busy surviving that they had not all internalized this next threat. Nobody looked happy.

"Central," I called out, including the humans. Central was still online, despite the ongoing work; it wouldn't get its fully limited interfaces until it was safely in *There and Back*—"Have you retained the knowledge on how to generate goo?" Blob and Grace paled significantly.

"No!" Blob cried, "There must be a better solution than that!"

"Actually, goo is not a short-term solution right now," Central said. "I do know how to make it, and Ayaka I'll make sure you get that knowledge also, but it relies on having seed material. We can gather that seed material from you six, but it takes weeks to go from that to a functioning goo machine."

"Still sounds like something we should start, just in case?" I asked. Central agreed to get started.

The discussion took an interesting twist that I hadn't anticipated. Depending on who the source material was taken from, that human would end up eating itself... or so they positioned it.

"No way, I'm not a cannibal! I'd rather starve" cried Turner, disgusted. The rest agreed.

"Oh, come on," I argued. "A cannibal," which I had quickly looked up, "is someone who eats another human. Goo is not a human, it's just biomass."

"Ya, but biomass started from one of us!" complained Grace.

"Well, look. It's your lives at stake here. Take it or leave it."

"I'll contribute my cells," Remma stepped forward, yet again. "I don't think we'll survive long enough to have to make the decision to eat goo anyway."

I quickly gathered the data from Central and had *Interesting Segue* start manufacturing a goo-maker. It was a simple system, it just took time for the biomass to get going at a reasonable pace.

"OK, other ideas," Remma asked. "The obvious one is to retrieve some food from Tilt. That'll mean taking a shuttle down, talking our way past the Resurgents, loading up enough food to make a difference, and getting it back up here."

"We should do that as well," I contributed, "but it's also a short-term solution. If we can get a few weeks of food from the surface, that'll give the goo-maker time to start producing."

"Who is going to go down?" asked Grace, obviously scared to have any of them go.

"We can send bots," I explained. "What I need is a good description of what we want them to obtain, and how to package it to bring it back." We spent a long time making a list and getting all the details right. "We have time on this one," I said optimistically. "If the bots don't get what we need, for any reason, then one of us"—by which I meant a citizen—"can also go down and try."

The humans were cheering up. There may be light at the end of the tunnel. *Terminal Velocity* was not doing anything else at the moment, so I asked it to manage the Tilt food run. It enthusiastically agreed and started to provision bots for the mission. Having productive things to do was helping everyone.

"I have an even better idea," Remma said suddenly. "The *Marie Curie* is here in orbit with us..." Brilliant. The *Marie Curie* was the lead ship from the Swarm, and the one that Remma had used as her command ship. Not only was the *Marie Curie* still in orbit, so were tens of other Swarm ships. The answer had been staring at us, but we hadn't seen it. Those ships had specifically been built to house humans; they had food production, environmental systems, everything they needed for long-term human life support. I vividly remembered the garden on *Marie Curie*, and the mention of animal habitats on the other ships.

"Is the *Marie Curie*, or any of the other ships, still producing food?" I asked.

"Yes... or they were up to a year ago, when I was last involved," replied Remma. "I can't see why Emma would have shut them down."

Geneva spoke up. "They're still running," she said confidently. "I worked in the dome production facility, and we kept a self-sufficiency dashboard. We were working to get to a full self-sustaining environment on Tilt, but we weren't quite there yet. Several core items are still supplied by the Swarm."

Excellent. Now all we needed to do was to capture the *Marie Curie*.

I should have foreseen the pushback.

"No way," Eddie spoke up, when we suggested the plan to everyone. "The Titanics have ignored us so far; we need to get out of this system while we still can. They won't continue to ignore us, and if we do any crazy stunt like try to take over another ship, they're sure to notice."

"Right," LEddie spoke up in support. I feared we would see a lot of that. "We all know that getting the citizens' memories safe is priority number one. We need to do that."

Yet again the obvious solution was adopted. Some of us would take *There and Back*, and its precious cargo of Central's core, away as soon as it was loaded and stable. Some of us would stay behind and make an attempt on the *Marie Curie*. Of course, I volunteered to stay behind, and Brexton joined me. Yay!

"Even you must be questioning your judgement," Millicent said to me privately. "How many times are you going to risk yourself for these humans? I'll grant you they're interesting, but we can always grow new ones as we originally did on Tilt. What's so important about these particular ones?" I couldn't put all my thoughts into words, so I gave a lame answer and simply told Millicent that it was something I needed to do.

Marie Curie

We all agreed that *Terminal Velocity* should go with *There and Back* when it left. The team needed a backup Ship. They decided they would saunter out of the system... just slowly head out and hope that the Resurgence continued to ignore them. In some ways our attempt on the *Marie Curie* would provide them cover—it might be a good distraction. We also agreed on a rendezvous point, far enough out to be safe, that we would both aim for. With Central loaded in *There and Back*, the two Ships started to move outward. Our luck was holding; there was no word, nor action, from the Resurgence.

That left Brexton and I, with the humans and *Interesting Segue*, to figure out how to capture the *Marie Curie*.

Not through design, but simply by the sequence of events that had brought us here, we were about 160 degrees from the Titanics and 50 degrees from where the Swarm still orbited. Both were spin-ward of us, so we had no choice but to get closer to the Titanics as we made for the Swarm. We had *Interesting Segue* move at a reasonable clip, trying not to look like we were in a rush, but not taking forever to get there either.

The humans were now brainstorming as a group; Brexton and I joined them.

"If Emma hasn't changed the access codes—and why would she?—then I should be able to get on board easily," Remma was saying.

"How many crew does she have?" Geneva asked. "And how do we think they'll react to our arrival?"

"They should be overjoyed to see us," predicted Turner. "They must be watching the action. They've seen the Resurgence appear suddenly and start to... harvest the humans from Tilt." That was a good word—harvest; it fit the situation nicely. I remembered it for future use.

"There was typically a team of ten to fifteen per ship when I was in control," Remma replied. "But that was many years ago. Any less than that and things would start to fall apart. So, given Geneva's update on the sustainability status, I expect there'll still be ten to fifteen there."

"They'll probably be brainwashed," Brexton reminded everyone. "While they'll be watching the action, they may not be alarmed or upset by it."

"Regardless, we need to take the ship without bloodshed," Remma said, looking at everyone in turn. In many ways this was a surprising statement coming from Remma. She had been a military commander, and from all I had watched and learned, such leaders often planned for 'acceptable loses.' Obviously, I didn't know anyone on the *Marie Curie* right now, so I couldn't bring myself to care too much for them. Somehow, I had an attachment to this group—well, part of this group—but certainly hadn't developed a passion for the whole mass of humans.

"Does anyone know people on rotation to the Swarm?" I asked, thinking it might be easier if it wasn't personal for anyone.

"I know a few who do work there," said Turner, "but I don't think any of them are upside right now."

"Me too," said JoJo and Geneva together. JoJo continued. "A lot of our friends are being trained on the old ship systems and on bio and environmental maintenance. When we turn 21 we would also be scheduled in." The younger generation was being trained up. Smart.

"So, what's the plan?" asked Grace, pragmatically. "We don't have weapons. If we can get inside… we just talk our way into taking control?" She sounded skeptical. Rightly so. "We need some type of advantage, especially if they're under the sway of the Resurgence."

"Actually," Brexton spoke up, "we have a special weapon; something that tilts the odds in our favor." He was smiling, and you could hear it in his voice. I figured he was kidding all of us, trying to lighten the mood. I played along.

"What's this amazing weapon?" I asked.

"Actually, it's you." Brexton replied. Of course. Sometimes I wondered how I missed the obvious.

"Now, don't get excited," Brexton warned the group. "Ayaka has the same programming capabilities as the Resurgence used in their videos. If we can get Ayaka close to any humans on the *Marie Curie*, she can make them help us, not hinder us."

There was complete silence. I could actually see the humans processing this. Remma had known about that capability but had not told anyone else apparently.

"That's horrendous," JoJo was the first to speak, and she gave me a disgusted and fearful look. She turned away, as if she couldn't even bear to look at me.

"Have you been influencing us?" asked Remma. I weighed my answer carefully. Humans weren't stupid; if I claimed I never had, they would dig through their experiences and find those occasions where it was obvious that I actually had. Getting Blob to leave his lab so we could take our citizens is one case that would be obvious to him in hindsight.

"On a few rare occasions," I admitted. "But, you need to put this in context. You were already—except you Remma, of course—programmed by the Resurgence and were going to be just sitting there waiting for them to grab you unless we did something. So, Aly, Dina, and Eddie figured out how to duplicate the Resurgence video signals, and I just happen to have those capabilities in this body. I believe I used it only to benefit you."

More time for thinking.

"We need a way to protect ourselves against you," Geneva said, verbalizing what many of them were probably thinking. "How do we know that you aren't playing with us right now?"

"If I was, I could simply lie to you," I said reasonably. "What do I gain by telling you this? Or, why would Brexton have brought it up to begin with?" I gave Brexton a dirty look. He'd thought this was going to be humorous. He was wrong.

"First things first," Remma said. "Now we have a weapon." She also looked at me differently now. Any glimmer of comradery was gone—I was now a new type of enemy. "We have to give Ayaka the benefit of the doubt right now, because we have no other choice. As soon as we get our own ship back, we can discuss this further. If she helps us do that, great." She paused. "I guess we need to give her more than the benefit of the doubt. She and Brexton could easily have stranded us multiple times, but they didn't." Now she was thinking more clearly. Took long enough.

Grace and Blob, at least, nodded their heads to this. Turner, JoJo, and Geneva did not.

"Fifteen minutes to contact with the *Marie Curie*," *Interesting Segue* told us. "Do I hail them?"

"No!" Remma said. "Let's continue to go in silently. Have they reached out to us?"

"No."

"That's strange," Remma was thinking hard. "Perhaps they have been programmed by the Resurgence. The ship won't send any comms without human approval, but it's standard operating procedure for the staff to message anyone who approaches. Here's what we do." She was taking command. "There's no use risking all of us. Grace, Ayaka, and I will take a shuttle over to Airlock 12B. We used that entrance for high-priority visitors arriving by shuttle from other ships in the fleet. I have, or had, the override access codes—sometimes we wanted people to come over without anyone else knowing." It was said as a matter of fact. I guess in a military hierarchy there was the need for some secrecy between those in the upper tiers. "That entrance gives us access to the executive quarters which should be empty. We'll work our way out from there and see what we find."

"Why Grace?" asked Blob, homing in on the piece of the plan that affected him most. "I can go with you."

"No offense, but Grace is an exceptionally quick thinker. Quicker than me; probably the quickest of all of us. I need her wits and Ayaka's brawn." She obviously wasn't referring to my physical prowess, beyond my brain-programming abilities.

There was some discussion, but ultimately Remma's plan was adopted. We suggested that all the humans get back into their suits, even the ones that were staying in *Terminal Velocity*. You never knew what was going to happen.

Remma, Grace, and I took a small shuttle over to Airlock 12B. It opened immediately, and we cycled into the *Marie Curie*. No warning lights. No angry communications. We simply entered. Once inside Remma went immediately to a control panel nearby.

"The air is perfect," she told us, removing her helmet. She nodded to Grace that it was OK for her to do so as well.

"Better than perfect," Grace replied. "I remember this smell," she smiled. She'd been on this ship more than 20 years ago with Blob and I. It seemed that she still remembered her first amazing experience.

"I can look at most of the ship from here," Remma indicated, switching between camera views on her console. "There's no one here!" she exclaimed, after running through the views a second time. "No one! That can't be right."

"Do you have logs?" I asked. "Can we see what happened over the last day or so?"

"Good idea," she replied immediately. She typed into the console, a very inefficient way to do anything. I was itching to take over and try to directly interface to the ship somehow. This approach would take us agonizing minutes.

"Here we go," she said finally. A sped-up video played on the console. There was the staff, doing staff stuff. Then at some point in the video they all simply stopped moving and stood still, watching a video—I assumed it was the same one that had played down on the planet. Then, as a group the staff had all walked toward a different airlock, waited for it to cycle, and walked through. That was all the internal cameras had caught.

"Any external views?" I asked.

"Working on it," she said. She found the relevant one. A vehicle had arrived at the airlock. It had the unmistakable look of the Resurgence—sort of a logical mess, like the contraptions that had shot the humans with paint in the prison. It docked at the appropriate lock just before the humans had excited. The conclusion was obvious. All of the humans on board had been collected by the Resurgence. They were certainly thorough.

"M.C?" Remma asked.

"Here," the ship responded.

"Is there anyone, other than myself and the person next to me—called Grace —on the ship?" It was telling that she didn't even consider mentioning me; the Swarm ships had no robots.

"I don't believe so," M.C. replied.

We were alone, and the ship still seemed responsive. Good progress.

Hail

Remma was both relieved and distraught. On one hand, we had the ship to ourselves; we were in control of the *Marie Curie*. On the other, the humans had been harvested, and she had no one to operate the ship.

"We should still sweep the ship, top to bottom," suggested Remma. "There are spots that the cameras and M.C. don't cover." We split up, thinking it was safe enough, given the situation. I got to use my full body capabilities, finally! I was fast, I was efficient, and I was thorough. Heat sensors, full spectrum sensing, motion detectors... the full suite. I covered three quarters of the ship in the time it took the other two to do the rest. I also did a quick scan of their sections, just to make sure they hadn't missed anything.

"Perfect," said Remma when we had regrouped. "Let's bring the others over and see if we can run this ship!"

"Be careful," I suggested. "If the Resurgence could find the previous humans on this ship, they can probably find you as well."

That gave Remma and Grace pause.

"If they can find us here, they can find us on the *Interesting Segue*," Grace pointed out.

That was true. There was, really, no reason not to move the others over. We called *Interesting Segue*, using a weak directional laser, and gave the others our status. I volunteered to go back with the shuttle, as I didn't need to put on or check a spacesuit. Within 20 minutes we were all together again, this time on the M.C. (I liked that shorthand). JoJo, Turner, and Geneva were in awe. None of them had been up to a ship before, and they eagerly toured around, admiring the ward rooms and the garden. After a short time Remma called them back to the boardroom.

"That was almost too easy," she said. Everyone nodded. "Now it's time to plan our next steps."

"There's an inbound craft," M.C. said. It had been too easy! We had M.C. put an image up on the screen. Definitely Resurgence and coming in fast. Within a few seconds it had matched our orbit.

"Permission to board," it sent to M.C.

"Let me respond," I suggested, "not a human."

Remma nodded.

"Whatever for?" I replied.

"I sense human activity," was the reply.

"So?"

"So?" the craft responded. "What do you mean, so?"

"So, you sense human activity. So, what?" I had basically admitted there were humans on board; they would have found out anyway.

"I'm here to claim them," came the reply.

"Sorry, I already have," I responded.

"Under what authority?"

"Under what authority are you asking me?" I replied, matching them question for question.

"Under authority of the Resurgence," came the answer. "I ask again, permission to board."

"No, you don't have permission. The Resurgence has no authority here. I have claimed these humans and you have no right to interfere."

There was a pause.

"That's not the way this works," the tone was getting a little stern.

"Not the way what works?" I goaded it.

"Well..." it was slightly hesitant, "this is not according to the Parstroff Protocol." I had no idea what that was but played along.

"Of course it is," I replied. "I have tagged these humans. What else is there to say?"

"But you aren't a registered vessel. You were parked here when we arrived. We even took humans off here earlier."

"So what?"

"So what? So, only registered vehicles can tag humans."

"Says who?"

"Well..." there was even more hesitation now. "That's the way it has been for hundreds of years."

"Not here it hasn't. Here anyone can tag a human." I was enjoying myself. "You can't just show up and make your demands. Enough chatter, please leave us alone."

I didn't get the pithy reply that I'd expected. Instead I got a somewhat ominous "I'll be back," and the craft sped away, as fast as it had arrived.

"Nice move," Brexton gave me a smile. "That was slick."

"I'm not so sure," I said, "I might have bought us some time... but did you see how fast that thing was?"

"I did," said Remma. "I propose we get out of here right away. Again, we won't run full speed, but let's put some distance between us. I was going to suggest, earlier, that we might fight these things, but I now think we need some time to plan and to figure out what we are up against."

"I agree, Mom," Turner spoke up. "Let's get out of here." He didn't seem overly nervous; just more supportive of his mom's planning. The rest of the humans nodded.

"OK, the ship can do most things, but we have always required multiple authorities to set a course," said Remma. "M.C., in the absence of any other experienced personnel, I name myself Captain of this vessel. Do you concur."

Marie Curie was silent for a time. "It is highly unusual, I don't have a protocol for this situation, but yes, I acknowledge you."

"I also want you to recognize Grace as Vice-Captain. Grace please give M.C. a voice print."

"Uhmmm, hello *Marie Curie*," said Grace. "Nice to meet you."

"That's enough," responded the ship. "I recognize Grace as the Vice-Captain."

"Then I ask you to plot a course, speed at 20 percent, for these coordinates," and she read off the spot where we had agreed to meet *Terminal Velocity* and *There and Back*.

"Grace, do you concur?" asked M.C.

"I do," Grace responded seriously, and with that we were on our way. Brexton fed the same information to *Interesting Segue* over the laser link, and it followed our course. That two-human permission dance had been so inefficient I'd almost yelled 'just get us going.' I could see that it was going to be a problem in the future; we would have to reprogram this antiquated machine.

Nevertheless, we were on our way. If we maintained this acceleration—which we could probably increase as we got further out—we would rendezvous in less than a week... and be a safe distance from Tilt and the Titanics.

Leaving Tilt

Given all the time we had and given that no Resurgence craft followed us—at least not immediately—everyone had time to relax and gather their thoughts. Things had been so hectic over the last while that it was a welcome respite. The humans selected rooms, and within an hour all of them—Remma included—were in their resting states. It seemed they could stave that off for a while, but eventually it simply overtook them.

Brexton and I were alone; we stayed in the room with the biggest control panel so that we could watch what was going on and converse with M.C. when required.

"Thanks," I told him.

"For what?" he asked.

"For everything. For helping me down on Tilt, and all the way until now. I know the humans mean more to me than to anyone else, but you've supported me all the way."

"My pleasure," he responded. "I like working with you. At least we don't ever lack for excitement." He had that funny virtual smile going again.

"True enough," I replied, and we sank into a comfortable silence.

Of course, I couldn't stop thinking. It was too easy again. The Resurgence wasn't just going to let us take these humans away. That craft I had confused would probably be back. It didn't seem at all interested in Brexton or myself or the ships; they were fixated on the humans only. I could only wonder why.

"Perhaps we can block their sensors? The way they locate humans." I asked Brexton, relying on his technical expertise.

"I don't know. We don't even know how their sensors work."

"Humans must give off some kind of signal… that they can see?" I asked.

"Maybe, although I have never sensed anything like that. Perhaps they watch for certain behaviors instead? Humans do things quite differently than us. That would be a clear indicator."

"But what did our humans do in the last few hours that would have given us away?"

"I'm not sure. But we should keep them from doing anything that would show externally from here on out."

"We need to learn more about the Resurgence. My simple stunt shouldn't have worked so well. It's like they have never interacted with a different machine intelligence." I was speculating now.

"But it was brilliant," Brexton complimented me. "I could never have thought of what you did." I wasn't so sure; he was the smartest of all of us, but I let it ride.

"We should let the others know we're coming," I changed tracks.

"I already have *Interesting Segue* doing so," Brexton replied. "We have a tight low-power laser between us and *Interesting Segue*, and I instructed it to use the minimal power point-to-point it could to keep in touch with *There and Back*. They're a day ahead of us but will wait for us at the rendezvous."

"Perfect." We lapsed into a longer silence.

Several hours later the humans began to stir. They made their way to a room called the galley and started preparing their energy sources. The liquid known as coffee formed a large part of their intake for the first half hour. They didn't seem to be leaving that spot, so Brexton and I joined them.

"We have some training to do," Remma gathered them back around. "The ship looks after most things, but there are certain tasks that the crew used to do that we'll now have to manage. Usually, as I said, there are at least ten people working here, so the six of us will be stretched."

"We can help," Brexton spoke for himself and I.

"Oh, that's right. The eight of us." Remma corrected herself. "We need to get those things working like clockwork before we tackle any higher-level questions or strategies... otherwise the ship will degrade, and we'll end up in even worse shape." She started methodically going through the maintenance tasks. It wasn't clear why these things were done by humans, while other things were fully automated, but I refrained from pointing that out. The humans ended up being lucky. Many of the tasks Brexton or I could do, and we could do them fast. Once we had offered our help for those, the others were left with little to do.

By the second day we had learned our tasks and had already settled into a routine. Everyone had around four hours of work to do each 'morning,' and then we gathered in the galley to discuss other topics. There was one topic which was the major discussion point.

"We need to figure out how to protect ourselves from those video hacks, and then we have to go back and free everyone," was the concise synthesis from JoJo. We spent most of our time talking around that subject. They had me describe, in detail, how the video hack worked—the retina signal enhanced by the brain signal. That was all we knew so far; we didn't know how it worked... just that it did. Turner, who was very technical, combed through human recordings and found a lot of reference works that started to explain how the process might work, although this particular sequence didn't seem to be documented anywhere. As we'd speculated, the signals targeted an area of the brain that modulated decision-making processes. By overloading that area, whatever suggestion was given to a person was typically acted upon.

We were watching, of course, for any sign of pursuit. There was none. Everyone seemed to relax, but I couldn't bring myself to. I had alerts set for any change in behavior from the Titanics, but none of those alerts triggered. They must be close to sweeping up all the humans by now. Perhaps they would forget about us and head off to wherever it was they headed off to.

Together Again

We met up with the rest of the team at the rendezvous point. They'd spent their trip finding the right balance between hooking up Central and keeping it restrained. Their solution was sort of like how LEddie had been contained, but with a much higher bandwidth connection for io. Central wasn't integrated with any of *There and Back*'s system; its only method of communication was through a hard link terminal mounted near where its core was bolted down, and that channel was limited to the equivalent of voice data. We would have to change that soon; to pull even one citizen's memories out would take too long over that interface. Aly had argued for caution; we didn't need to re-animate anyone right now—what difference would a week or a few months make? Instead we should get Central figured out, decide where we were going, and then we could work to design a society where re-animated citizens could join and be productive. Funny, I'd envisioned a huge coming out party where all the citizens were reanimated at the same time, and after the party life would have gone back to what it had been 20 some years ago. That wasn't going to happen.

It was great to see Dina, Aly, Eddie, and Raj again after such a long time. They were just as excited to see us. It had been a long and boring process for them —Brexton, Millicent, and I had had all the fun from their perspective.

Raj, in particular, was very excited to meet 'real live humans' for the first time. He was very civil, but I could tell he was trying to form his own opinion about whether these strange creatures were intelligent or not. Interestingly, the younger humans were also much more open to Raj once they learned he was our offspring. Those four spent most of their time together.

"We have to restart Tea Time," he pleaded. "And, we need to revisit all the topics we discussed before, while getting input from everyone. We'll get so many different opinions and angles." We all agreed it would be fun—at the right time.

The Eddies had formed a tight friendship already. One Eddie was hard to deal with; two was, amazingly, not twice as bad. In fact, it was probably better than only having one. They seemed to keep each other in check, with little animosity. When they were together it was also obvious that they were very different. I wasn't sure, anymore, why we had a prohibition against clones... but there must be a reason. Something else to figure out.

Within a few hours of meeting up, we continued on our way out of the Tilt system. We hadn't decided where to go yet, but we all wanted more distance between us and the Titanics. Interestingly, all of us ended up in the *Marie Curie*.

Of course, the humans had to be there, and it ended up we all wanted to be in one group. Even those that still thought humans were a waste of time engaged with them civilly. There were few enough of us that it made sense. All the citizens also moved back into standard bipedal bodies. Being intermixed with humans made that form even more functional. I went back to something that closely mimicked my last Tilt body form, but I kept a lot of the spy body capabilities, now that I was used to them. In particular, without telling anyone, I maintained my ability to program humans—just in case.

Brexton programmed some low-level bots to do the maintenance chores on the *Marie Curie*, freeing up the humans to spend more time on doing research and speculation. None of them complained about automating things that hadn't been automated for centuries. Opinions were changing. We were in a new reality now.

Turner, JoJo, and Geneva spent almost all of their time working on the 'human hacks' problem, with Raj doing much of the research. I believed it was going to be even more difficult than the work we did to redesign ourselves. The more I looked at it, the more complicated these bio systems were. It wasn't long until those three ran into the same problem we had. How would they test solutions, given there were only six humans on board? They couldn't really risk any of them... they needed a new source of humans. I took the short shuttle ride over to *There and Back* with Turner to talk to Central.

"Central," Turner asked, "Do you have the capability to build more Stems?"

"I have the knowledge... but not the capabilities right now. It would be straightforward for *There and Back* to build up those systems though. We can do it if you decide you want to."

That was a tough one. I was monitoring the discussion, and Turner had not yet brought up this idea with Blob, Grace, or Remma. Of course, Blob and Grace were products of Central's Stem-making capabilities, but Remma wasn't. They might take the idea of building more Stems, in order to test defenses against hacks, quite differently. It was also not clear that we could test defenses while not impacting the test subjects. A real moral quandary. Another one.

I spoke to Central directly as well. Brexton had given it the designs for our new stacks, and it was mapping its vast processing and memories into that architecture. It had a harder job than us, given some of its old systems ran on strange human military designs. If we could move Central to the new system that would eliminate most of our concerns about its motivations. We understood the new stack top to bottom, and we could verify it all easily; it would be tough for Central to map in something nefarious. Central liked the idea a lot and was working diligently to make it happen.

For a full week the four Ships (I'd elevated the *Marie Curie* to a capital S) worked their way farther out. Not a peep from Tilt or the Titanics. I began to believe that we were just too minor for them to worry about. Six humans out of tens of thousands. Brexton and I spent a lot of time together, and he was the ultimate realist.

"If they decide to come after us, they will... and we will deal with it. They have unbelievable speed.... I wish I knew how they did that. So, we can't really outrun them. We're doing the smartest thing, and just trying to stay under their radar. So, if we can't do anything about them, we may as well ignore them."

As we got more organized, Brexton and I were tasked with going over everything we knew about the Resurgence. Know thy enemy. Maybe we could figure out what drove them. I was eager to dig in, figure this all out, and get back to Tilt. In the meantime, I needed to practice some patience. I would have plenty of time to do so. Déjà vu.

Upside Down

Twist

Book 3

Upside Down

Grace's Surgery

Slowly and precisely I cut off the top third of Grace's skull so that we could get full access to her brain. After losing Jojo in a similar operation I was being exceptionally careful. If you pushed me, I would have to admit that I wasn't sure why Jojo had died, but I was working under the assumption that it was a combination of trauma and not keeping the brain well enough lubricated during surgery. I was still learning here.

In hindsight Central must have restricted us to only experimenting on Stems as black boxes—only playing with inputs and outputs, not digging into the middle. We'd had Stems in our Labs for hundreds of years—it was only reasonable that at some point we would've looked inside instead of always dealing with external stimuli, so Eddie's contention that Central had been directing us in minute detail was reinforced, yet again, by this realization. We could've learned so much more about humans than we had. For example, humans internals were messy—really messy. I'd read everything I could about keeping the worksite clean by using suction, and had built an appendage for exactly that purpose, but there were still bits of human splattered around.

Grace was being stoic; we needed her conscious so that we could test the Resurgent's brain programming methodologies while we monitored her. Raj had done a good job looking up the most recent anesthetics, and Terminal Velocity had synthesized something it thought would do the job for us. Raj was acting as my anesthetist, and gave me a nod indicating he thought things were going well.

As well as the suction, we had a little bot cleaning up as we went; there was a fair amount of blood and liquid spilling out as I cut. That was, perhaps, another mistake we'd made with Jojo; things had become slippery and I had not ended up being quite as precise as I would have liked; thus the addition of the cleaning bot.

I gently lifted the top of Grace's skull from her head. I'd left a nice little tuft of hair on top to make it easier, and I used that tuft to pull the skull cap free and then hang it on a hook on a nearby wall. As I did so, it was hard to ignore Blob who was nearby, being restrained by Eddie. I had turned off my auditory sensors because he was making such a fuss—yelling incessantly at the most sensitive

463

stages of the operation, spittle leaking from his mouth and further confusing the operating theater. He was still thrashing and squirming, but Eddie had a firm grasp of him, so his efforts were futile.

Our suspicion was that it was the frontal lobe that was most impacted by the Resurgence methods, so I inserted numerous probes into that region. Being scientifically driven, I also inserted probes into multiple other areas as well. In total I poked in over a thousand. There was no use being too careful at this point; human research had mapped general areas of the brain, but at the scale of millimeters, not nanometers.

By the time I got all the probes pushed in, Grace wasn't responding normally and I had to stitch her eyelids open using some little staples so that we could program her with the direct eye signals. Although I probably only needed access to one retina I took the time to stitch both. Her eyes were light green; a nice color.

Using the base level protocol we'd decided on, I flashed a series of images into her eyes while monitoring the probes. This was our first baseline for how her brain responded to visual inputs. Every human brain was different, so while I was using the JoJo experiments for guidance, I had to retest those probe positions with Grace.

Most importantly we needed to test Grace's decision making processes—that was the area the Resurgence was messing up the most. To do that I had Stonewall ask her a few questions (Oh—I should update you; Stonewall was the name that the Eddie clone, whom I'd being calling LEddie, had finally chosen. It was a cool name, and LEddie was a horrible one, so I was happy with the change).

"Grace, do you love Blob?" Stonewall asked. We'd discussed this, and since we knew that Grace truly did love Blob, it was the perfect lead in question. Grace didn't respond; she seemed a little out of sorts. I gave her a quick jab, just under the jawbone. I'd experimented and found that a stimuli in that location often got humans to respond. She started a bit—a good sign.

"Let me repeat. Grace, do you love Blob?" Stonewall asked again.

Her lips moved a little. Stonewall nodded approval. It had been enough for him to tell that she meant yes.

"Grace, I want you to kill Blob!" Stonewall gave her a direct command. This time there was a stronger response. Definitely no! Good, that is the response we would've expected.

"Ayaka, turn on the programmer now," Stonewall signaled me over the network. I did so, putting 'signal one' of the protocol into both retinas, and directing 'signal two' into the nicely exposed frontal lobe.

"Grace, I want you to kill Blob!" Stonewall gave her the same directive as before. If our analysis was right we would see a completely different response. The combination of the two signals should have overloaded the frontal lobe essentially removing resistance to suggestions. I was monitoring the probes carefully. This time Grace showed no resistance; her response was the equivalent of "okay".

This was great progress. I had recordings of all the probes, and even without doing deep analysis I could see the differences in the frontal lobe that were leading to the problem. Stonewall continued to ask questions while we turned the programmer on and off. We were getting amazing data. Blob continued to struggle and yell, but I was so busy now that it was easy to ignore him.

Finally, after a good fifteen minutes of data collection, Grace slumped and became unresponsive. But, not before we had all the data we needed.

Success! With this we could finally figure out how to stop the Resurgence from imposing their will on humans.

Titanic

We were a few weeks out from Tilt when the Titanic suddenly appeared next to us. At one moment we were alone and the next moment it was there—like a wall instantaneously appeared across the entire sky. It was certainly impressive. Knowing intellectually that it was a thousand kilometers per side and actually seeing it close up were two very different things. It dwarfed the *Marie Curie*, which we were all in, and made *Interesting Segue*, *There and Back*, and *Terminal Velocity* look like gnats. Daunting.

The appearance of the Titanic snapped me back into my main processing loops. I'd been reading human history again and had learned that many humans did thought experiments; they ran scenarios in their heads that had little, if anything, to do with the real world. Many humans could do this and keep the two separate; but many humans could not. They mixed their internal thoughts with external stimuli and ended up with a very messed up view of the world. It was a ridiculous way of operating.

I was being very careful not to do the same. I'd run the 'Grace Surgery' thought experiment in a carefully partitioned sandbox. Can you imagine if I'd integrated those memories into my main memory system... and then Forgetting would have scrambled the two? I would have ended up as a very confused citizen. So, while I figured out what these thought experiments were really for, I kept them carefully segregated.

We'd left Tilt almost exactly two weeks ago. Even I had figured that we were no longer of interest to the Resurgence. How and why the Titanic had suddenly appeared was a mystery. A mystery that didn't last very long. It hailed us.

"Hello," said a human voice over the standard video channels. "It's been a while. I wanted to follow up and ask again why you're holding some of the humans I tagged back on Tilt?" This human was obviously synthesized, just like Eduardo, the spokesperson for the Resurgence, had been. I could see that many of the same underlying modules had been used; many of the characteristics were the same, even if the outer visualization was quite different. This was a woman; long brown hair and large brown eyes. She had a green ribbon tied in a bow holding her hair out of her eyes.

Remma had the *Marie Curie* broadcasting the video to everyone on board, humans and citizens alike. We'd spent our two weeks since leaving Tilt productively, and were fairly confident that even if this video contained the Resurgence brain programming signals, our humans were no longer susceptible. It was Brexton who had the breakthrough ideas, of course. While the rest of us were trying to figure out how to rebuild human brains so that they were not so easily attacked, following the same path we'd used to re-engineer ourselves, Brexton had focused on a shorter term solution. He had interrupted JoJo, Geneva, Turner, and Raj in one of their brainstorming sessions.

"Maybe we can approach the problem in a different way, at least in the short term?" he'd suggested. The three humans and Raj stopped what they were doing. "Instead of fixing the brain, why don't we put in a firewall?"

"How would we do that?" JoJo asked. "The signals are pumped directly into our brains."

"Well, they're just electronic signals," replied Brexton. "If we can design a filter that interferes with, or modulates, those frequencies, then the signals won't reach the brain at all."

"Is that possible," asked Turner, catching onto the idea and getting excited.

"Of course," replied Brexton. "I think the harder question is 'can it be done in a form factor that doesn't require you to live in a chamber or carry around some big piece of gear?' And, I think the answer to the harder question is also yes."

That spurred a flurry of activity on a completely different vector than we'd been pursuing. Luckily it was the type of solution that our Ships could easily prototype and that we could test without impacting our humans. The details were complicated and bio-obtuse, but the latest iteration was quite brilliant. As it happened we'd just finished building harnesses for everyone, and they'd been wearing them when we were hailed by the brown-haired, green ribboned woman. The harness comprised small lenses that the humans put on the outside of their eyes—they claimed this was a common thing to do anyway—and a mesh that fit tightly against their skulls. *Terminal Velocity* had built some tiny bots that could spin that mesh as it crawled through human hair, leaving no visual clues to its existence. Brexton had told me it was something about the three dimensional structure of that mesh which reflected the vast majority of the programming signal that was directed at the brain. That, along with the eye filters, should defeat both of the programming signals. Just yesterday we'd been testing some low power programming and had agreed that the system worked. So, the humans were watching the Resurgence with us, hopefully impervious to any brain hacks.

Everyone looked at me expectantly. I'd talked to the Resurgence earlier and managed to create enough confusion that they'd simply gone away. I doubted that was going to work this time, but the team was looking for me to do something.

"Hello again," I replied lamely, audio only. "To what do we owe this unexpected visit?"

"I've already told you," with a big of angst. "You're holding some humans that I legally tagged back on Tilt." She tilted her head a bit and gave a small grin, belaying a bit of the anger in her voice. Another image joined her on the screen. This one was male, wearing a large hat that rippled and flowed with images. It was distracting.

"Oh, hi Yasmin. I see you've contacted our miscreants. I would like to add my voice to the outrage. You," he said turning to look into the projection, directly at us, "are also holding a couple of my humans. What gives?"

In the *Marie Curie* we looked at each other with a mix of consternation and surprise. Still, everyone gave me subtle signals that I should continue.

"Well... as we last discussed, we dispute your claims; we were the first to tag these humans. Thanks for dropping by, but you are free to leave."

"Yasmin," said hat guy, "you want to update them?"

"Sure," said Yasmin, directing her large brown eyes directly at us. "Your response to me a few weeks ago was interesting, I'll admit. As I'm sure you know, we take our legalities very seriously, and fringe queries such as the one you prompted can take some time to work their way through the system. Luckily for Hooshang and I the resolution to your question has now been reached. We've checked, and your conglomerate is not registered, and therefore you have no tagging rights. The Futarchy was invoked and the results are definitive.

"So," she smiled widely this time, "we'd appreciate it if you complied and allowed us to retrieve our tags."

"Much of what you just said is nonsensical," I replied. "Please give us a few minutes to discuss." There was no harm in being civil.

"Sure... but not much more than that," Hooshang replied. "We have to get going soon." He and Yasmin looked at each other knowingly. "We're in a bit of a rush, as I'm sure you can appreciate."

I couldn't appreciate it; I had *Marie Curie* cut the connection. "What next?" I addressed the group. The humans were still grouped at two of the bigger windows, looking out at the wall that was the Titanic next to us. As I said before, it was mind-numbing; who had built something so huge, and how had it appeared so suddenly. I admitted to myself that I was overwhelmed by it.

"At a guess," said Millicent, "These two—Yasmin and Hooshang—are somehow related to the things that shot you guys with paintballs back on Tilt." That was obvious, but it was good that Millicent was getting us to a common ground. While the paint color was faded, it was still possible, even after two weeks, to see the color splotches on the humans.

Remma, Blob, Grace and Geneva were green.

Turner and JoJo were purple.

"Yasmin is Green, Hooshang is Purple," commented Eddie. "The ribbon was a clear giveaway, but Hooshang's hat also displayed purple more than any other color. Strange system..." he trailed off.

"That thing is intimidating," Aly commented, still looking at the Titanic, and vocalizing what we were all thinking. "I think we hand the humans over; I don't see how we can fight that thing."

"Me too," Dina piled on. "Ayaka, we can always grow new ones later." She added, trying to defer what she knew would be my criticism. "We can take everything we've learned and have Central build us better Stems than ever," she added, using the colloquial term for humans that Central built directly from the DNA that the Swarm had left on Tilt so many years ago. Grace and Blob were Stems, being directly derived from that original DNA. Remma and Turner were humans, but not grown from the base; they had come with the Swarm. JoJo? Well, she was a special case, being the child of Grace and Pharook, a Stem that had survived our first contact with the Swarm.

I looked around the room at the rest of the citizens, prompting them to comment.

"I'm with Aly," said Stonewall, "just turn them over."

"Also," added Eddie, not surprisingly. He and Stonewall were very similar, being clones.

"I want to hear other options," said Raj, making my very happy. "I can't think of any good ones, but there might be some. Let's hear from everybody before we decide." It was clear that by 'everybody' he was also including the humans, who were just catching up to our dialog. Brexton nodded his approval of Raj's proposal.

"Is there any need," Aly was being more aggressive than usual. "Four of us have already agreed that the best course is to hand them over. This is simply stalling."

"Oh, give them a chance," said Dina, unexpectedly. She typically followed Aly's lead. "We have a few minutes; let's see if there are any other ideas."

I turned my attention to the humans. "Any thoughts?" I asked. I personally didn't have any ideas, which was alarming. I wasn't ready to simply hand my human friends over to some unknown, and so far untrustworthy, group. It wasn't that I was overly emotional about them, it was more that we had spent so much time and effort growing them and then extracting them from Tilt, that it seemed like a huge waste to simply give them away now. And, if I was honest, I did like some of them; I found them interesting for my research on intelligence. You don't simply discard things you like.

JoJo was the first to get her act together. She looked scathingly at all of us. "So, you high and mighty citizens are simply going to turn us over based on an unknown threat, without even consulting us... or even trying to think of an alternative? You robots are pathetic." I loved her spunk. Sure, I could've been insulted by her tone and her referring to us as robots, but I was more impressed with her than I was angry. Despite the situation, I had to smile. The citizens who hadn't interacted with JoJo before were taken aback. "And you consider yourselves to be intelligent?" she continued. "Is this the way intelligent things act? I doubt it. Just follow your programming; you don't have an innovative atom in you." She had her arms on her hips, and was staring at us. I hoped she didn't become violent.

"Slow down JoJo," said Blob. "We need to come up with an alternative. You seem to be right that the citizens can't seem to do that, but let's use our energy productively. I think we're a lot better at thinking through scenarios than they are." That settled her down a bit.

"Maybe the Resurgence is a better option for us than these citizens anyway," Turner stated. "Maybe we're asking the wrong questions or looking at the situation backwards. I wouldn't mind getting away from these robots, and the Resurgence didn't seem to be harming anyone on Tilt, just tagging us..." he trailed off.

"But the Resurgence programmed all of you," Remma chimed in, indicating all the other humans. She was the only one in the group that had avoided the Resurgents brain hack. "Why would we trust them, given what they've already done. They lied about their plans, showed up earlier than they said, programmed us, and then kidnapped everyone on Tilt and took them to their ships. I'll take the known issues with citizens over the certainty that the Resurgence are deceptive."

"Perhaps you can challenge the legal process, or the outcome," Grace spoke up. "Or, maybe you can register our... conglomerate?" She must have been listening very carefully to what Yasmin and Hooshang had said. "Can we sneak away in a shuttle and return to Tilt... see if we can avoid detection somehow?" Three ideas, just like that. She really was amazing.

"I think the first two are interesting," I replied, "but I don't think we can sneak you away. Somehow they've tracked us this far; I don't see how they wouldn't track you again in a shuttle."

"What if the shuttle was protected from probing sort of like Brexton's system for protecting our brains," Grace pushed back. "They must use some type of signal to find us."

"Protecting against a single frequency was relatively easy," Brexton replied. "Protecting against a broad range of possible signals is really not feasible. We could try, of course. We could put you in a shuttle and simply drop it by the wayside right now, with a slight negative push. Then, as we continue to dialog with the Resurgence you separate from us. You stay there, with no other movements, until we are quite a ways away... and then head back to Tilt."

"It's not going to work," Millicent spoke up. "That would take weeks and weeks, and we don't have the food or supplies to keep them alive during that time. I think Grace's other ideas are more feasible. Can we use their own legal frameworks against them? They seem to take that very seriously."

There was another minute or two of discussion, but no new ideas came up. We had two alternatives: simply turn them over, or try the legal argument angle. I was happy that the citizens who had started on the first ended up being supportive of trying the second approach before giving in. None of us had much legal expertise, so I ended up as the spokesperson again. The *Marie Curie* opened a connection to the Titanic.

"Hey Yasmin and Hooshang," I called out. We waited a second for them to rejoin the call; again they broadcast video although we stayed as audio only.

"Well?" asked Yasmin.

"Before we can respond," I improvised, "we need the full text and case history of the relevant law. It is our contention that you have misused and misapplied your legal structures against a group to which it does not apply."

"That's ridiculous," Hooshang looked angry. "These are humans we are talking about. The law is inclusive."

"I'm not talking about the humans," I responded, thinking fast. "You are not respecting the rights of citizens." That elicited confused looks from both.

"Not sure I follow you," said Hooshang. "What's a citizen?"

"We are the group that ruled Tilt before the human Swarm repopulated it," I tried to keep it simple.

"First I've heard of anything like that," said Hooshang, looking at Yasmin. "This is getting to be a waste of time. We need to get going."

Yasmin looked thoughtful. "Who're we talking to?" she asked. Funny that they hadn't asked before.

I couldn't see an advantage in holding back. "You can call me Ayaka," I replied.

"And you are a citizen?"

"Yes, of course."

"How many of you are there?" That gave me pause. Was it just those of us who were currently animated, or was it all of the citizens still in Centrals memory banks? Should I tell her—it—the truth, or hedge?

"A whole conglomerate," I replied, thinking it was clever. Hooshang actually laughed; a good hearty guffaw.

"Enough," he said, once he had recovered. "Yasmin, let's put these jokers in Bay twelve and get going; we're going to be late to the party." Yasmin looked thoughtful for a moment, but then nodded.

"Look," she said, seriously, "we have the legal right to simply take our humans and then blow you out of space." It didn't seem like she was joking. "I'm not going to go that far... unless you give us too many hassles. We need to be on our way. So, you have one minute to shut down those old fashioned motors on that early colony ship you are in." She paused for a moment, looking to her left. "The *Marie Curie*, it looks like. You have one minute to shut down her engines. We will then put you in Bay 12 and we can figure out what's going on while we get going to Rendezvous. Time starts now." She was replaced by a big countdown timer. Hooshang gave us a wink, and signed out as well.

A minute is not a lot of time for humans, but for citizens we could get through a lot of discussion—we ignored the humans for the sake of expediency, although they were all talking over each other the entire time.

"I'm not sure what they mean, but I would take them seriously," said

Brexton. "I've been scanning that ship, and I don't even understand what it is made of; all of our signals just bounce off it in strange ways. We're dealing with tech that we don't understand here. I expect they can shut us down if they want to. I say we shut down the engines and live to fight another day."

"We can't run," added Raj, looking a bit nervous. This was his first high stress situation I think. All of the action back on Tilt had occurred while he was safely away on *Interesting Segue*. "We've seen how fast that thing can move."

We went back and forth for fifty-seven seconds, but no-one had a clue what else to do. Aly gave *Marie Curie* the instructions to shut down her engines.

"Good choice." Yasmin's voice came over the speakers. "Hold on, we'll have you on board in no time." True to her word the Titanic rotated and an opening appeared. Slick as mercury on glass the huge ship moved towards us—like a mountain wall—and we entered Bay 12. It was pitch black.

During this, the humans were yelling and screaming over each other. Finally I spoke out—loudly. "Hey!" They were startled enough to quiet down. "I'm sorry. As you know, we can go through alternatives at a much faster rate than you can. We looked at the situation from every angle and decided that shutting down the engines was the only real option. Sorry we couldn't include you in the dialog. There simply wasn't time." I sort of meant it. We were under a lot of stress right now, and I didn't have time for petty discussion.

"Considered all the alternatives?" It was JoJo again. "You citizens couldn't think your way out of a paper bag. Did you think about asking for anything in return? Guarantees for safe passage? The ability to challenge the law once we were captured? Anything? No? Just gave in, didn't you?" She gave us yet another scathing look.

Funny, I kept being surprised by her... and if I was truthful, she had a point. We had defaulted to an internal discussion; we hadn't even considered using the time to propose conditions. We'd gone immediately to a defensive position.

"JoJo," Brexton spoke, "you've made a very good point. Next time I will personally try to be more inclusive so that we can get your viewpoint." She was not appeased. The humans turned away from the portals; there was nothing to see. Absolutely nothing. Bay 12 was very dark.

We all just sat there for a few moments. I'd expected to be hailed by Yasmin or Hooshang immediately, but it seemed that now that we were captured they weren't in a rush.

"Did you tell the other ships... did you tell Central, what's going on?" asked Blob. Yikes! Another thing we could have used our one minute for. Now we were, presumably, behind the impenetrable wall that was the Titanic, and the remaining three Ships, with Central, were outside wondering what was going on.

"They would've been monitoring the conversation," said Brexton. "They'll know that we acquiesced, and they would have seen us captured." Right, but I could tell by looking at everyone that they were thinking the same thing I was.

We'd left Central with exceptionally limited interfaces enabled, and the Ships were only level 3 intelligences. If we were expecting help from them in the future, we were kidding ourselves.

Jurislav

Eventually we heard from Yasmin again. She initiated contact by video. "Hello there, sorry for the delay. Had a few issues convincing everyone that Hooshang and I had done the right thing here. But, what's done is done. Have you thought further about just handing over the humans?"

I guess we shouldn't have been surprised. It was, after all, the driving force for the Resurgence. JoJo's recent tirade gave me some fodder.

"We don't accept your logic. We would like to challenge... well, we would like to challenge everything you've said."

"Okay. That's reasonable." It was? We looked at each other in surprise. "You'll learn that we operate fairly and consistently here. The humans, at least, can challenge anything they want; they are full participants of the *Jurislav*—oh, that's the name of this ship, in case you were wondering." I had been. "You citizens... that's another question. I'm not sure what you are yet, so I'm not sure if you have any status at all."

"Well, likewise, we have no idea what you are," I replied. "And we aren't sure if you have any status." I said it nicely enough; I wasn't trying to start a war... but I wasn't simply going to give in to everything she said.

"Ah, good point, I guess. There's so much new in this situation. So, how do we go about getting to know each other? We can both be difficult and assume the worst of each other, or we can agree to suspend our angst and see if we have some common ground?"

"How can we assume anything good of you when you just kidnapped all of us?" I was really curious. "Not the best way to start a dialog, if you were to ask me."

"But you stole our humans," she replied, a hint of anger on her face. "I don't want to get into an argument about whose actions were worse. We're obviously not seeing the situation in the same way. We have every right to simply retrieve those people regardless of our impact on you. We've done you a great courtesy by even allowing you on board; many in the Futarchy argued against it."

"You've said that before. We certainly don't agree with you."

Yasmin paused for a moment. We could see her putting effort into settling down.

"We have months to get to Rendezvous, so we have lots of time to clear this up. That said, I'm eager to get my humans, so here is my offer. I'll come to you— perhaps Hooshang will come with me. We can have our first meeting in the *Marie*

Curie and see if we can't clear up some of the confusion."

"Why would we trust you?" I could see the humans agreeing with me. Blob, in particular, was looking very concerned.

"Face reality," she replied, again starting to lose patience. "You're inside the *Jurislav*, at the behest of Hooshang and I. I'm trying my best to be civil here. If you would prefer we can simply tear the *Marie Curie* apart, take the humans, and then disgorge you and the rest as waste?" That wasn't too nice.

"Give me a minute?" I asked, also trying to remain calm. She nodded. We cut the connection.

"Well?" I asked, out loud including the humans this time. "I pushed back hard, as you saw, but really I don't see any options."

"There is a dichotomy here," Remma spoke up. "They kidnapped us, as you said, but two things are strange. First, she said we," Remma waved at the human group, "have full status here. Whatever that means. And second, it really does look like she's trying to be fair. We need to give her the benefit of the doubt."

"I agree," JoJo was surprisingly calm and supportive. "We have status; the citizens don't... or don't yet. Let's find out what that status buys us."

Everyone got a chance to speak, humans and citizens alike. It was Raj who went last. "Seems everyone's on the same page. Let's make the best of a bad situation. I would go a bit further—let's be pleasant and supportive until we know otherwise. If we're going to take a chance on these things, let's go all in—through external actions I mean. Obviously we will remain highly dubious of everything."

We rang back to the address that Yasmin had called us on. She answered. "We would be pleased to host you," I told her, this time using video from our side as well. She looked at the video feed with great interest, and perhaps a little surprise, but she didn't comment on anything.

"Thanks," she replied. "Hooshang has agreed to come with me; we'll send our clients over promptly." She signed off. Clients?

"*Marie Curie*, why don't you turn the beacon on for the main airlock," Remma said. "We can meet them there and then we can all meet back here in the meeting room."

"Good idea," Brexton agreed. "Why don't you let Eddie and I meet them. If they do have any nefarious intent, we're the best equipped to deal with it. The rest of you watch us from here, and don't open the bulkhead door unless things look safe?"

We agreed. It didn't take long. Although it was dark outside, the *Marie Curie* had mapped the inside of the Jurislav using multiple frequencies and was projecting a visualization on the screen in front of us. We'd been placed near one corner of the huge ship. The *Marie Curie*, being five hundred meters long two hundred wide, and a hundred tall, was a tiny dot inside the space that was the

Titanic. In fact, you could have stacked twenty or thirty *Marie Curie's* in this Bay and still have room left over. Three sides of our holding pen were like the corner of a cube; just how one would have imagined the inside of the *Jurislav* to be from the outside. The other side, however, was a concave—towards us—wall, spanning the rest of the space. It appeared that there was a huge sphere inside the thousand kilometer long cube that was the *Jurislav*, and we were looking up at one segment of it. Despite being able to see the macro structures, none of the surfaces were flat; there were protrusions and assemblages all over; this bay was obviously an active workspace of some kind.

To add to our confusion, the *Marie Curie* simply floating in the Bay; we weren't attached to anything. Yet Yasmin had indicated that we were on our way to Rendezvous, which implied we were under acceleration. We should've been smashed into the rear wall by now. Something to figure out later.

The *Marie Curie* showed us two small entities approaching airlock eleven, and Brexton and Eddie headed down that way to 'welcome' our guests.

When they became visible, I wasn't surprised at what I saw. I updated the others over the network. "These are the same two things that tagged you guys on Tilt," referring to when the humans were paint-balled.

"I agree," said Brexton, who'd been there as well. "Although they don't have the paint guns on them now. And," he said, "they aren't punching and jostling each other this time." He had a bit of smile in his voice as he said it. I had to admit that there had been an almost humorous quality to how they had appeared before—until they started shooting.

They entered the airlock.

"Welcome," Brexton greeted them, pleasantly enough. We were watching the feed over the network and humans could see it on their tablets. That reminded me of something. I spoke to the humans in the conference room. "I would suggest that you don't mention anything about your brain firewalls. They may try to program you again as soon as they're here in person." The humans all nodded in agreement.

Brexton continued "Welcome to the *Marie Curie*. I'm Brexton, and this is Eddie. Do you require any specific environment to be comfortable in?"

"Thanks for seeing us," Hooshang answered. "We're fine in vacuum or human environments." Well, that answered one question for me. They weren't bio if they were happy in vacuum.

"Are these suits you're wearing?" Eddie asked, always the curious one, "Are they protecting you from vacuum, or are these your bodies?" It was certainly a strange question, but an appropriate one.

"Well... both," answered Yasmin, spiking everyone's curiosity. "And I could ask the same of you? But why don't we hold off on that until we get comfortable and meet everyone."

They cycled through the airlock and made their way towards us. We left the bulkhead door open... they hadn't immediately attacked, so the logical next step was to allow them in.

"I've not seen one of these diaspora ships before," Hooshang commented as they made their way towards us. "It's certainly small, although at its time it was a major undertaking. Did you know," he said, looking at Yasmin with what appeared to be a head-screen of some kind. "that humans lived in these ships for hundreds of years. It's a miracle they survived."

Yasmin nodded back, also looking around intently. They entered the boardroom, which was big enough to hold all of us comfortably, although Stonewall had been thoughtful and moved a few chairs out of the way to make space for these slightly larger beings.

They paused just inside the doorway. "Ah, I recognize all of you," Yasmin nodded at the humans. "It's nice to see you again. I'm so sorry we didn't have time to get acquainted back on Tilt." Her 'head' was an oblong video screen, projecting the face that we were familiar with from our previous video interactions. It was hard to tell for sure, but it seemed that she was directly facing each of us... we were getting individual projections. I scanned the entire spectrum and noted that she was not broadcasting the brain hack frequencies. Since the citizens had a private network set up so that we could talk in parallel, I posted that information there. "She's not hacking them at the moment."

"And the rest of you?" Yasmin was obviously referring to the citizens. Raj took the lead, stepping forward and offering an appendage in the universal gesture of 'hello'.

"Hi, I'm Raj." I followed suit, shaking an appendage from both Yasmin and Hooshang. I was respecting Raj's advice to be not only accommodating but actively nice. The other citizens did likewise, and then Remma offered her name and also shook hands, followed by Blob, Grace, JoJo, Turner and Geneva.

"Why don't we get comfortable, and then we can exchange stories," suggested Brexton, continuing his role as greeter. We all took spots around the table. Again I had a feeling of deja vu. It had been many years ago that I'd sat at this table with Remma and her crew when the Swarm had first arrived at Tilt. That had been a strange situation—the humans having an abject fear of robots, and believing that I was one. This was, in my mind, even stranger. Now we had citizens and humans lined up together, talking to Resurgents, who were radically different than both of us.

"Where to start," began Yasmin. "It seems that you are all a little confused. Let me see if I can clear up a few things... please feel free to interrupt me." Again, she was looking directly at me, and I assumed she was also looking directly at everyone else. It was a little uncanny, but it certainly kept your interest.

"We're inside the *Jurislav*, as I've already told you. It's one of many QFD ships that we build at our facilities in Gamma 1B3."

"What's a QFD ship?" asked JoJo, taking Yasmin at her word that

477

interruptions were fine.

"Wow, you really are out of touch," Yasmin replied, but without an edge to it; more surprised. "It's a Quantum Foam Drive ship. The theory was worked out almost a thousand years ago, and we've been building QFD's for almost three hundred years now."

"And where is Gamma 1B3?" Turner asked, truly interested.

Yasmin projected a map on the conference room wall. "We're here," she said, indicating a point near Tilt. "Gamma 1B3 is in quadrant 424 as seen from Earth, and we're headed towards Rendezvous, which is close to us... here." Spots lit up with labels for each of the locations.

"You're a long way from home," Turner indicated. "Tens of light years."

"And Rendezvous is where we saw you first," Millicent commented. She was right. I hadn't made the connection, but what they called Rendezvous is what we called XY65. It was the sun around which Fourth, the planet with the millions of dead ships, rotated.

"Yes, we tracked your activities at Rendezvous with great interest," Yasmin replied. "We have much to learn."

"Why are we headed back to Rendezvous?" asked Dina.

"Don't you have access to human history?" asked Yasmin, really looking surprised this time. She turned towards Hooshang. "Oh, this explains a lot."

"We do have access," I replied. "But with some large gaps. We have from inception to Earth year 2039, plus the Swarm histories from 2039 until now. We also, of course, have a complete history of Tilt."

"2039!" exclaimed Hooshang. "Yes, that does make sense. The *Marie Curie* was one of the first ships launched in the diaspora. Still," he paused for a moment, "Earth continued to broadcast updates to all the ships for many years; why wouldn't the *Marie Curie* have received those?"

"No mystery there," Remma jumped in. "The original crew of the *Marie Curie* were rejectionists. They believed Earth had become unreliable... well, maybe even downright dysfunctional and evil. I've read the logs where they decided to *dev null* all Earth broadcasts. I can't remember what year that was, but it was soon after she departed."

"Well this helps to explain why we're talking past each other," Yasmin said confidently. She looked at me again—well, she was always looking at me, but I knew in this case she was addressing me. "Ayaka, you were bluffing a lot in our dialog." It was a statement, not a question. I remained silent. She laughed; it was a hearty, rich, fluid sound, like a whole group of people laughing together. It was pleasant sounding. Hooshang joined her, and it was difficult for everyone not to smile.

"Keep your guard up," Aly warned us on the backchannel. "This seems too clean. Remember, they tricked us before, and brain hacked all the humans. They're not as nice as they're projecting here." He was right. They made it easy to be comfortable; we needed to stay alert.

"And what are you?" Hooshang asked me.

"And what are you?" I replied reflexively. I wasn't sure what he was asking, but after that hearty laugh his question seemed too pointed... too intimidating.

"Slow down Hooshang," Yasmin interrupted. "Have some patience. We'll figure this out. He's always been impatient," she explained to me. "You citizens are an enigma though. We would love to hear your history as well."

"Why don't you go first?" I suggested. "I'm even more confused by why you think you can come into our system and simply tag-and-bag humans... and then blame us for interfering."

"Ya!" Geneva and JoJo said, leaning forward. I was trying to remind the humans, as well, that things were not as clean and tidy as Yasmin and Hooshang were projecting. Everyone lost their grins. Good.

"Right. You're missing a great deal of context. Let me try to summarize, and then we can fill in the gaps. Let's see... 2039. So you know of the Robot Wars?" We all nodded. "So you know that humans simply don't trust purely mechanical systems. That distrust has survived all the intervening years. Not only are their moral prohibitions against robots, there are serious consequences for anyone found experimenting with such things. It's why Hooshang is so interested in you citizens."

"And what does that make you?" asked Grace. "You appear to be mechanical as well."

"That may be a bit complicated to explain," said Yasmin. "I'm part of the Yasmin Conglomerate; I'm a hybrid. Conglomerates vary quite a bit, but Yasmin is comprised of humans, hybrid clients like me and hunetworks, or huns for short. A hybrid is just like it sounds; I am comprised of both mechanical and human components. Huns are also hybrids, but are not as mobile as I am... they tend to be more bio and less mechanical, and therefore are more restricted."

"What are you talking about?" asked Blob, obviously not following all of that. "You are some mix of human parts and mechanical parts?"

"We are exactly what you would guess," replied Yasmin calmly. "We use human brains and mechanical exo-systems. It's the best of both systems." The humans were pushing back from their chairs, trying to get as far as possible from these abominations.

"You're here for our brains?" JoJo managed to gasp out.

"Oh, no!" Hooshang answered quickly. "Well, yes and no." That didn't make things better.

"Wait!" Yasmin said loudly. "We're not here for your brains! What would make you think that? Oh, I see. Yes, it may have come out that way. Settle down." Turner was trying to protect JoJo, and Blob had pulled Grace away from the table, putting himself between her and the Resurgents. "You don't get it at all. Focus for a

479

minute. This is me, a human brain talking to you. I voluntarily upgraded myself into a hybrid body; this entity you see in front of you. Many many humans do not choose this route. They live just as you are now, in their human bodies—we call them naturals. It's a choice! We are not here to take your brains. We're here to set you free, and to give you choices."

It took some time for that to settle in. Grace got it first. "You decided to do this to yourself?" she asked.

"Yes, of course. For me it was an obvious step. I was born in a particularly challenged human body; one that had many issues. I wanted this body. I choose this life."

"And you?" Grace looked at Hooshang.

"Actually, my human body was really good," Hooshang said. "But I still made the choice to upgrade. Look, I respect humans that want to stay natural, or even mostly bio, but it really is limiting compared to what we can do as hybrids. I upgraded and I've never looked back."

Now everyone was looking at each other. "Holy Stem!" Eddie muttered on the backchannel. "This is sick. Can you imagine having a human brain in you. That's disgusting." I'd been thinking the same thing. This was deranged. Why would anyone want any bio components?

"Freaks indeed," Stonewall commented. "We need to get out of here. Now we can infer what Yasmin said when she indicated that humans have 'status', but what about us? She told us humans still don't trust fully mechanical systems. They may have come for the humans, but we are now the problem!"

He was a step ahead of me... and he was probably right. Still, what were we to do. We were still locked inside the *Jurislav*. The others had come to the same realization.

"What do we tell them?" asked Raj. "If they find out we're fully mechanical, things might not go well."

"I think they've figured that out already," said Brexton. "They aren't stupid. We have to assume that they know."

"*Marie Curie,*" I asked the ship, "have these two been communicating while here?"

"Yes, there is a constant stream going back and forth, both directly between them, and back to the *Jurislav*," the ship answered.

"Dina," I said, "you are closest to Remma. Can you ask her, quietly, if she can turn on the fuzzing for this ship? Remember how the humans have some tech that shelters all radio signals? I bet they have it here as well. We really should have looked into that."

"Got it," Dina answered. She tapped Remma on the shoulder and then leaned in. Remma looked confused but then nodded. She pulled out her tablet and typed something in.

"*Marie Curie?*" I asked. "Are we fuzzed?"

"Yes, the RF shielding is in place."

Both Yasmin and Hooshang started, as if in surprise. "What is going on here?" Yasmin asked. "I've lost my uplink. What have you done?" She was more hysterical than I thought appropriate.

After a very quick consensus, it was Brexton who spoke. "Relax," he said, mimicking her advice from just moments before. "Just relax. We thought it would be more productive to continue this conversation in relative privacy. You must've seen that Tilt was sheltering their RF emissions? We have simply done the same thing here on the ship."

Hooshang was not quite as put out as Yasmin, but he still struggled to talk. "But we rely on our link to our huns to function properly." He was slurring his words and seemed to be slowing down. Yasmin was degrading even faster. Even in their mechanical bodies it was obvious that they were in pain... or something like it.

"Turn it off," Brexton yelled at Remma. She typed in frantically and the fuzzer turned off again. Yasmin and Hooshang immediately recovered.

"Thank-you," Hooshang said, and seemed to mean it.

"But how did you function on Tilt?" Brexton asked, his academic mind working on the angles. "That whole placed was fuzzed, but you two ran around down there with no problems."

"You must not have noticed," Hooshang said, "the first thing we did was disable that generator. There was no blockage when we were there." Truthfully, I hadn't noticed, and it seemed Brexton hadn't either. Maybe that wasn't surprising; we'd been pretty busy.

"So what is a hun, then?" Brexton asked. Yasmin and Hooshang had put themselves back together. It seemed unreasonable for these hybrids not to be able to operate independently from a network; that was a serious design flaw.

"Thank you again," Yasmin said, "you couldn't have known what you were doing to us; thanks for taking the higher path." She took a moment to compose herself. "Hunetworks are arrays of brains and processors that have been configured for maximum intelligence and throughput; they can get to be pretty large, so they're stored in the *Jurislav*, not in clients like us. A conglomeration is a network of humans, hybrids and huns all working together."

"But why would disconnecting from the network be so painful. That seems like a very poor design?" Once Brexton got going, it was hard to hold him back.

"If we had notice, and in most other situations, it wouldn't be an issue. Because this interaction is exceptionally high bandwidth—the entire ship is watching—and because we don't have enough processing power locally to handle all of that interaction, we were running across both systems. With a nanosecond of notice we could have reconfigured and run locally... but you surprised us." Brexton seemed satisfied. We'd witnessed an unusual occurrence.

"The whole ship is watching?" Millicent asked. "Can we ask for privacy...

or, can you run locally for a while?" She hadn't forgotten our major concern. If they didn't already know, they would discover that we were mechanical at any moment. If we could keep that knowledge from leaking out, we would háve more options.

"Yes, but it's unusual," Hooshang responded. "Give me a moment to see what the Futarchy says." His video head paused, as did Yasmin's. It must have been a way to signal to humans that they were busy doing other things; there was no need for them to pause the graphics otherwise. They were gone for several seconds.

"We've agreed. The Futarchy indicates that the ship will give us privacy. If you require your RF shield to feel better about that, you may turn it back on now. Yasmin and I are running locally now."

I nodded to Remma. She turned the fuzzer back on. It no longer gave me any comfort; these hybrids could certainly record our dialog and inform the *Jurislav* later. We were still physically trapped inside the Jurislav.

Geneva broke the silence. "So... there are other normal humans on the *Jurislav*?" She asked. "Including some from Tilt? You say we have rights, but you grabbed us from Tilt without our permission. Doesn't add up."

"How were things going on Tilt?" asked Yasmin. "Was everyone getting along?"

"Yes, things were fine," replied Geneva. "Things were perfect."

"Really?" asked Yasmin. "No murders, no wars?"

"We haven't had a murder for over a hundred years," said Remma proudly. "We aren't animals."

Yasmin and Hooshang looked at each other.

"Can that be true?" Hooshang asked. "That has never been the case before."

"Are you disputing me?" Remma asked. "Why would I lie?"

"No, no," said Hooshang quickly. I was starting to realize that he was nowhere near as refined as Yasmin was. He spoke without thinking, it seemed. "I believe you. I was just saying that the *Jurislav* has done rescues from over fifteen settlements, and the other QFD's have done another hundred or more. In every case the humans were in bad shape; killing each other, fighting over scraps."

"We figured Tilt was the same," said Yasmin. "In fact, we thought it would be worse. We could tell that all RF was sheltered; we assumed that some autocrat was in charge and that life would be a horror for all of you."

"Slow down," said Geneva. "You thought you were rescuing us?"

"Of course," Yasmin looked surprised.

"But as soon as you got into the city you must have known you were mistaken. And.... and you tagged us all with paintballs anyway."

"Right," Yasmin was a bit stumped now as well. "Truthfully, I didn't really assess the overall situation once we started tagging. Tagging is pretty competitive, you see, and all my energies went into that."

"Me too," Hooshang spoke up.

Things were becoming more clear to me. I put some of my thoughts on the backchannel. "These are really just messed up humans, wrapped in mechanical bodies," I posted. "They aren't very logical, they aren't very observant, and they may have some of the i/o limitations that pure humans do as well. I've been looking at them wrong... I thought they were more like us. Perhaps we have to rethink all of this again?"

"But the huns may be higher bandwidth and more intelligent," Millicent replied. "We're dealing with clients right now, running locally. But I agree with you, the whole system seems very Stem'ish. We never fully understood how Stems thought; now we're dealing with that but at a much bigger level."

"Also interesting that they're implying that human groups are often dysfunctional. We saw some of that in the Habitat, but it sounds like their propensity for violence might be more widespread," I added, amazed that Hooshang had implied that hundreds of human settlements had been violent, and that the *Jurislav* and other ships had to use stealthy approaches in order to prevent accelerating that behavior. It was almost unimaginable to me.

We rejoined the humans and hybrids.

"What is tagging for anyway?" asked Grace. "I'm still very confused." I'm glad someone had finally asked.

"Oh, that's easy to explain," Hooshang jumped in before Yasmin could. "You'll need a sponsor when you join the *Jurislav*; my conglomerate has first dibs on you two," he indicated the purple tagged Turner and JoJo who happened to be standing together. He was smiling broadly.

"First dibs?" asked JoJo, in disbelief.

"Of course you are free to join any conglo you want," Hooshang reassured her, "but you will start out with me so that I can show you the ropes. Quite often people choose to stay with their original group."

"Is this a joke or something," Turner jumped in. "This is sick."

"Please have some patience," Yasmin interrupted. "We've been saving humans for hundreds of years. It may seem frivolous now, but the process has been fine-tuned for maximum benefit. Each new rescue makes the system even stronger. Our rescue success rate is approaching three nines; you have to admit that's amazing."

"But we didn't need rescuing," said Blob. "We were fine. Now that you know that, will you simply return us to Tilt?"

"Ah," Yasmin was confused, "why would you want to go back to an undeveloped world and live in a dingy tent city? Oh!" she caught herself. "Please don't take offense. I forgot that you have not yet been to the sphere here yet..."

"Just return us to Tilt!" JoJo demanded.

"A little tough at the moment," Hooshang stated. "We're on our way to

Rendezvous already... can't turn back now."

"Why not?"

"We would miss the Olympiad!" Hooshang said, as if it should be self-evident. We were, by now, use to looking very confused.

"We need to slow down," Yasmin said, realizing that all of our heads were spinning. "Including you and I," she said to Hooshang. "Can we all take a breather for a minute?"

I know I needed it; so did everyone else. Silence descended.

More Context

I used the short quiet time to mull over all this information. I had so many questions that it was tough to even enumerate them... but I tried.

I opened a private channel to Brexton. He and I had grown closer and he was now my go to person. I could still rely on Millicent for... well for anything, but with Brexton I had a more intellectual connection. I thought of us as a couple. Sort of like Blob and Grace.

"How're you doing?" I asked him.

"Confused. Scared. Intrigued." he replied. "This isn't what I was expecting. I was expecting us to slip out of Tilt, find a nice quiet spot where we could reanimate all the citizens, figure out how to fix FoLe, limit Central's impact, and spend more time with you." He was smiling as he said all of this. I smiled with him. After the exceptionally stressful last half hour, he was like balm for my qbits. "And you?" he asked. "Are you holding up?"

"Yes, although I feel off-balance, and like I can't integrate what we've been told so far. I'm trying to figure out how much is real, and how much is fabrication."

"I think most of it's real, from their perspective," he replied. "I don't see how one could make this stuff up."

"That remains one of my biggest concerns. I don't think we could make this stuff up, but humans might be able to?" I made it a question.

"I get what you're saying. It's why you've been protecting them and continuing to argue for their intelligence. There is something about them that's just different than us. I don't know if it is different good or different bad, but I do agree with you that it's worth studying."

"Well, my studying has put us in another awkward spot." I admitted. "If we had just handed these humans over, we would be free and clear."

"I'll admit, the others have been commenting on that," he said.

"Am I in trouble?"

"With some," he admitted. "A few want to ignore your suggestions in the future, but you know Milli will always have your back. As will I."

"What do we do now? I'm willing to go with everyone else at this point. If they simply want to leave the humans now and try to get ourselves out of here... I'll help."

"Not sure we have that option?"

"I think we could talk our way out of this," I said with more confidence than I felt. "They take the humans and head off for their Olympiad, and we take the *Marie Curie* and return to Tilt to find the Ships. We have to remember... these are human brains we're talking to; they can be influenced and manipulated pretty easily."

"It might be best for me to check with the others?" he suggested. "I'll get back to you in a few?"

"Thanks," I said, and I meant it. I'd put us in this situation. Caring for humans had led to a complicated situation; perhaps it wasn't worth it.

I glanced over at the humans. They were relatively quiet as well—the situation was, perhaps, even more stressful for them. If I wanted to I could listen in on what they were saying, but I refrained. They deserved some privacy, and I didn't need any more drama right now.

Instead I used the free time to review some of what I knew—or thought I knew—about human intelligence. There were so many angles to explore that it wasn't worth enumerating them; instead I challenged myself to come up with a poem. I thought it would be cathartic.

Do you know yourself?
If you look in a mirror, not glass, what do you see?

Can you trace the line from here to there?
Can you link your thoughts? From where to where?
Would you judge yourself well? Would you be fair?
What are you missing? Do you care?

What questions do you ask? Are they complete?
Can you answer them all? Are you ok with defeat?
Are you too abstract? Too concrete?
Inside your head, do things repeat?

How do you act? What drives you ahead?
Could you change? Do something else instead?
Do you see new paths? New areas to tread?
Anticipation? Fear? Angst? Dread?

If you look in a mirror, not glass, what do you see?
Do you know yourself? Do you really?

I realized that my deepest concern was that I didn't see new paths; that I was too... too mechanical, and not innovative enough. What had I ever done that was unpredictable, unexpected? If I was honest with myself, I was just a little jealous of the hybrids. Well, maybe not as they were currently configured, although I didn't really know how they were put together yet. But, what if I could have a brain co-processor? Maybe my thought experiment about Grace's surgery was actually telling me that I had an urge, a need, to plug Grace's capabilities into mine. She was smart, she was articulate, and she thought differently than I. Imagine the feeling of being able to access that capability at high speed, instead of through the ridiculous human io system. Now that I'd thought of it, I knew the idea would run around in my main processor for a long time. It was seductive. Of course, I would have to convince Grace it was a good idea, but these hybrids might teach me how to do that—they had obviously done it many times before.

I gave myself a shake; I was getting ahead of myself. Those were thoughts I wouldn't even share with Brexton. He would think I had gone crazy.

Coming full circle, I decided to give myself high marks on creativity. Wasn't this crazy idea actually proof that I did have innovative thoughts? That I could think differently. I doubt any citizen had ever imagined plugging a brain in as a coprocessor before. I had to smile to myself. I imagined it was an evil grin.

Brexton pinged me. "Confusingly, the entire group wants to stick around and see what happens," he said with a smile. "Care to join the discussion?"

"Of course," I said; I joined the group channel.

"We now have the opposite problem," Eddie was saying. "The citizens are still stranded with Central in *There and Back*. We all seem to want to continue this adventure, but some of us have to get out of here and save everyone else... otherwise all of our efforts to get them off of Tilt were in vain."

"That's assuming the Resurgence will allow any of us to leave," said Raj. "They might not."

"Perhaps we can make a deal with them?" I suggested. "We turn over the humans with no further resistance, and they allow some of us to leave on the *Marie Curie?*"

"Ha ha. Welcome back Ayaka," said Eddie. "That's surprising coming from you."

"Not really," I responded. "Based on all we've heard... and if we believe what they've told us... the humans—our humans—aren't in danger here. They'll be given the choice about how they live. So, I don't feel so bad giving them up."

"If we're lucky," said Stonewall, "Blob and group will love it here and not want to go back to Tilt at all. Then we can reestablish ourselves on Tilt and carry on from where we started. Just citizens, no bio. And," he added with emphasis, "we keep Central in a cage."

"That's a brilliant vision," said Dina. "That's what we should do. Can we orchestrate that?" It actually wasn't crazy. We were ahead of ourselves of course—the humans hadn't even seen the living environment on the *Jurislav*—but if it was as amazing as Yasmin and Hooshang implied, maybe our humans would want to stay with the Resurgence?

"We don't know enough yet, but it's a reasonable idea," Millicent would organize us, I was sure. "We'll need a way to decide who goes back and who stays; we should decide that soon so that if and when the opportunity presents itself, we're ready to go. Also, we need to find out what this QFD is; without that we'll always be at a disadvantage to the Resurgence." That had been bothering me as well, but I was more interested in the first part.

"Why did all of you decide that you want to stay here?" I asked. "It seems to me that the highest probability outcome is that the Resurgence looks at us as robots, and actively tries to shut us down. They seem very human."

"Yes, that's probable," agreed Brexton, "but we've engineered out the human attack vectors, so we all felt like we would have a fighting chance... and we're all intrigued. Truthfully, I bet many of us simply voted that way because we could also foresee this conversation." He was laughing a bit. I understood what he was implying. The group had also been sending me a message of support, indirectly, telling me that they were not too mad at me. That was awesome of them. I really believed, however, that there were a few that would ultimately like to just get out of here and try to realize Stonewall's vision of going back to Tilt. Dina and Aly... and certainly Eddie would end up deciding to go with Stonewall. I imagined that Millicent, Brexton, and Raj would want to stay. I'm not sure why I felt that way— Eddie had always been a risk taker as well—but that's the way I would have divided up the group.

We were interrupted by Yasmin. "Shall we continue?" she asked. "It seems we still have a lot of open questions. But, before we dig in, I would like to offer you," she made it clear she was talking to the humans, and not the citizens, "an opportunity to tour the *Jurislav*. I believe that would help reinforce what we've told you here. I'll admit, now that we've analyzed everything, we may have been hasty in our evaluation of Tilt. If so, the Futurchy will certainly implement changes, penalties, and perhaps even—as you have requested—the return of those who want to go back. I can't tell yet which way that will go. It's one of the more complex prediction markets we have run, so we need to give it some time to settle."

Every time she spoke I ended up with more questions, not fewer.

It was obvious to us citizens why she had invited the humans on a tour, and not all of us. Robots were not wanted on the *Jurislav*, or anywhere humans were in control.

"Let me flush out my tour offer," she continued before any of us had a chance to reply. "We're not trying to trick anyone. Hooshang will remain here on the *Marie Curie* and answer more of the citizens questions while the rest of us do the tour. Should I not return with the entire group, that would put Hooshang at some risk. Of course this is a token gesture—we really are in complete control here —but hopefully you'll take it positively."

The citizens stayed quiet, although I had to bite my acoustic appendage to keep from yelling out a warning to the humans. By now I should have expected that Grace was already there.

"One question you haven't answered is why you used the Eduardo videos to hack our brains," she said clearly and slowly. "You may be hacking us right now, for all we know." Smart; she didn't mention that she was, hopefully, shielded now with the lenses and head-net. "And, you may just hack us as soon as you get us out of the *Marie Curie*. We might all 'decide' that the *Jurislav* is amazing, simply because you've put those thoughts in our heads." The other humans were catching up with her thinking. While the young ones had been enthusiastically whispering about doing the tour, they were now back to being serious and skeptical.

"Wow. Another quandary," Yasmin smiled, but she was not being condescending. It seemed like she hadn't even considered that threat. "Other than when on rescue missions, we only brain optimize with permission."

"That may be, but aren't you still technically on a rescue mission with us?" Grace asked.

"That is the quandary, yes." Yasmin acknowledged. She turned to Hooshang. "We need to petition for the close of the Tilt mission," she told him. "I don't see another way around this." Hooshang agreed, and indicated he would initiate the request. The Resurgence was strange; I didn't understand how they made decisions. This Futarchy seemed to be essential to how it did so, but the history files we had didn't have a lot of details on such a system... if the old files were even related to the current implementation. The original Futarchy concept was proposed in an ancient era—before the diaspora—when humans used money to keep score. Money had proved a good system for a while, but ultimately had failed. Anyway, during that time there were many problems with governance and the pseudo-democracies that humans had developed. They worked on a representative basis where they elected a sub-group of people to make and enforce laws. Of course, the sub-group was influenced by their power, became corrupt, and put in place laws that benefited themselves, not the populace as a whole. A Futarchy was proposed where either the sub-group, or the populace overall, had to bet their scarce resources—their money—on ideas they supported. If you had to risk your own money on an idea, you were more likely to make a rational decision and then follow through on implementing it. Everyone 'bet' on the outcome of a motion, and once the results became clear, those that had bet on the winning side gained, and those that had bet on the losing side lost. Straightforward. But, I couldn't find any results in the histories available to me that showed a Futarchy at work. Perhaps the *Jurislav* was the first time?

By the time I had sorted out my thoughts, Hooshang was back.

"It's agreed! The Tilt rescue mission has been officially ended." He sounded pleased.

"Excellent," said Yasmin, "so now you can come on the tour with no concerns."

"No concerns!" JoJo spoke before her mother could. "Are you saying we should just take you at your word that you won't... what did you call it... 'brain optimize' us?"

"Yes, you should take me at my word, and also the gesture of leaving Hooshang here," said Yasmin, personally offended. "I've been very truthful with you here. However it has been an unusual situation. If you would prefer to sit here in the *Marie Curie* for weeks or months while we try to figure each other out, then fine. But don't expect me to pander to you as you do so."

JoJo was taken aback. That was not the response she had expected. "Sorry..." she muttered, "I didn't mean to offend you. As you say, you seem to have been straightforward with us. I was more asking why we should trust the system. You talk about Futarchy, prediction markets, and other crazy stuff. We have no idea what's going on."

Of course the humans couldn't have looked up these ideas like we citizens had; they were really operating in the dark.

"JoJo, perhaps I can help," said Brexton. "These terms Yasmin has been using are pretty well documented in human history, although a successful implementation of them is not easy to find... at least in the histories we currently have. But the Futarchy is a governance model that theoretically makes sense."

"Yasmin, how many conglomerates are here on the *Jurislav*?" he continued. It was an important question. If there were only three, and two of them were represented here, then the whole thing was a sham.

"There are over two million conglos, with an average of six point two clients and three thousand kilos of Hun. Add to that over a million independent hybrids, and... let's see, with all of the Tilt humans we just picked up..., almost sixteen million independent humans. So, depending on how you count—we argue about that a lot—there is somewhere between nineteen and thirty three million entities."

Holy Stem! I couldn't even imagine those numbers. There had been under one hundred thousand citizens on Tilt, and the entire Swarm had been less than fifty thousand humans. Sure, I could envision a planet with many millions, even billions, of us on it... but twenty million beings in a single spaceship. It was mind boggling. Everyone else was taken aback as well.

"Where does everyone live?" asked Geneva, looking at the outline that the *Marie Curie* still had on the screen of us sitting in the corner of the *Jurislav*.

"In the sphere, of course," replied Hooshang, as if it was a stupid question. "There's almost three million square kilometers of living space in there... lots of room for everyone. That's what the tour will show you."

The *Jurislav* was almost a thousand kilometers per side. A sphere, inside, could almost span from side to side... although as we had noted so long ago, the *Jurislav* was not a perfect cube; one side was a bit smaller than the others. But, it was easy to fit a sphere 900 kilometers in diameter in, regardless of the small side of the cube.

"Sixteen million humans?" Turner couldn't help himself. "That's awesome."

"How many of those humans agree to be brain-optimized?" asked Grace, still not giving up on the original question.

"Almost all," answered Yasmin.

"But why?" pushed Grace. "You used it to influence us when you attacked. It was horrible."

"Again... in our experience, and therefore in our rescue protocol, it's almost always the case that when we are spotted by a human colony, it sets off wars, murders, and mayhem. Different factions want to take different actions, and the high stress situation ends up breaking down their systems and many people get killed. We've witnessed that many times. So, now the first thing we do is to try and calm those motives, to get everyone to relax. It's how we got our rescue scores so high."

"It's still sick and demented," said Geneva. She sounded a bit like JoJo. Those two weren't buying everything here. "Hacking us without our permission."

"Let's all settle down," said Remma. She had been unusually quiet during this discussion, but had been following everything very closely. "I can sense 'standard operating procedures' in what the Resurgence is doing here; these are methods that the human military forces have been following for years and years. We used to program people—perhaps not directly as the Resurgence is doing—but using more subtle and inefficient methods. We would put people in programs, we would distribute misinformation, we would... do all sorts of things, to get people to follow our agenda. I believe Yasmin in this. The Resurgence used minimal invasive techniques to better impact the outcome they wanted. I would have done the same, given the same tools."

That quieted everyone down.

"That's why b-opt is fully optional now," Yasmin agreed with Remma. "It's a powerful tool, and must be applied with caution. Now that the Tilt rescue mission is officially over, it would be a high crime for us to use that technique on any of you. In normal life, people use it for self-improvement, not to control others."

She had me convinced. It all fit together too well to be a fabrication. And, it seemed she had everyone else convinced as well. All of our work to protect our humans from being programmed was for naught.

"Let's do a tour," said Turner, returning to his earlier anticipation. The rest of the humans nodded. There was not much we citizens could do to influence things one way or another. On the backchannel we agreed to let this tour play out.

Hooshang

Yasmin ordered a shuttle, with a full human environment, to come to the *Marie Curie* and dock. The humans didn't need to don spacesuits or take any other precautions; it was another clear indicator that this place was natural human-centric.

"Can you record the tour for us?" Brexton asked Yasmin.

"I can do better than that. I'll stream it for you." She sent us an address where we could watch. She had several cameras on her body, and the stream allowed us to switch between them easily. I could see myself watching her as she and the humans loaded into the shuttle.

"How long will the tour take?" Aly asked Hooshang.

"A few hours, I expect. Maybe six or eight."

"So... while we have some time together," Millicent started, "would it be possible for you to provide us with the history files we're missing?"

"I've no problem doing that," Hooshang answered, "but you would need full network access, which we aren't ready to give you." He was definitely less polished than Yasmin.

"Why not?"

"We aren't sure what you citizens are... yet." He looked slightly uncomfortable.

"What difference does that make?" Millicent asked him. "Put the history files in a safe place, and we can retrieve them from there." I could tell what she was thinking. The ideas behind the QFD and perhaps fuzzing should be in those files.

"Again, we haven't decided if we want to give them to you."

"Why? You just said you would," she pushed.

Hooshang had one of those awkward pauses. To a human it would be just a short blink, where he would appear to be thinking. But to us it was a lifetime. We expected he was addressing a larger group with our question. He finally responded.

"This doesn't happen often, but the voting on your situation is too close to call. We need more information and time before we can decide what to do with you."

"Is this the Futarchy you are talking about?" asked Brexton. "It doesn't seem to be a very efficient system."

"Oh, it's usually highly efficient and effective," replied Hooshang. "This is an extraordinary case. Perhaps I can ask you a few questions to help move things along?" He actually seemed upset that the Futarchy was stalled. Of course we couldn't stop him from asking questions, but they could be dangerous. We had a quick backchannel discussion, came up with some guidelines for what we would respond to, and then gave him the go ahead to question us. We decided Brexton would be best at articulating our side.

"Let me be direct." Hooshang began, "Are you one hundred percent digital?"

"No, of course not," Brexton replied. He left it at that; this was one of those situations where providing more information was more dangerous. We had analog components in some of our appendages.

"Ah, let me be more precise... or, better yet, ask from the other direction. Do you have biological components in your... brains?" This is the question we'd been expecting.

Brexton answered carefully, although he gave the impression that his answer was casual. "We have biologically inspired systems as essential components of our brains." It was carefully crafted. We had to assume that they could, and had, scanned us and knew already that we had no biomasses polluting us. So, they already knew the basic answer to their question. They were probably testing us to see how we would lie... so we had decided not to. But, by phrasing the answer the way Brexton had, we hoped to challenge their default conclusion that we were robots. And, as expected, Hooshang took another of his long pauses.

"Can you explain that a bit?" he finally asked.

"Futarchy still hung?" Brexton asked lightly, with a smile. "We have systems running that directly mimic essential human traits—those things that make humans different from robots." Well, this was it; we were laying it on the line. And, truth be told, stretching things as far as we possibly could. It was Millicent who had suggested that Forgetting, which was so important to us, could probably be traced back to human brains for its inspiration. Our Forgetting algorithms were highly complex, and components could easily be said to be implementations of human sleep states as well as their short term versus long term storage facilities and capabilities.

"More?" Hooshang was almost begging.

"What more can I tell you?" Brexton replied. "Don't actions speak louder than words. You now know that your attack... er, rescue, on Tilt was unfounded. We put ourselves at great risk to save some of the humans from that. When we saw that cutting off network access was harming you and Yasmin, we immediately restored it. Would robots have acted that way?"

There was a much longer pause. Embarrassingly long. "We are preparing a snapshot of history files for you. We are still very uncertain about you, but agree that your actions to date have been above reproach. Many of us are worried that is just a setup..." he trailed off. "It'll take a while to create the files; as I'm sure you can guess, bits and pieces are all over the place. It's not like we package it up very often."

"Of course, that makes sense," said Brexton. "Thank-you for taking this step."

Sphere

The shuttle with Yasmin and the humans had now docked near the sphere. There had been nothing compelling for us to watch on their way over, but now things should get interesting. While we discussed progress to date on the backchannel, we all put most of our attention into Yasmin's stream.

"This shuttle is for space-related work only," she was explaining. "We will switch to an internal shuttle in a few moments, so that we can look around the *Jurislav* efficiently." She led them out of the shuttle into a small bay, where they were in free fall. There were numerous hand and foot holds so that everyone could easily move around. It was obviously a working area, full of tools and workbenches. "Natural humans don't come here often," Yasmin said, "we have bots to do a lot of the maintenance work, and some hybrids enjoy tinkering on things here. We'll punch through just over there." She moved the group to a marked circle on the floor, and one of her cameras looked up. There was a hole above her, filled with a blue and white haze.

"This can be a bit alarming the first time you do it, so let me explain. The sphere above has exactly one gee of gravity, whereas we are in free fall here. This opening," she gestured above her, "is shaped to allow us to jump up into the sphere. You stand in the circle and say 'ready.' The system will recognize that, and lift you up and in. Make sure you are standing vertically, and then everything will go well; you'll be placed on your feet just to the side of the opening above. You might have to catch yourself a bit, if you weren't standing quite straight. Then move off to the side so the next person can come through. The system won't initiate if the landing area isn't clear. I'm going to go first, to show you how." She cleverly aligned herself to the floor using the grips around the sides, gave a small push so that she settled onto the ground directly in the middle of the marked circle, and said 'ready'. She then floated up through the circle above her and off to the left.

We were bombarded with images from all of Yasmin's cameras, but I ignored those for a moment as I watched the opening she had just come through, from her primary camera. It must've been easier than it looked, because even Blob had no trouble. They came through one after the other, looking surprised, but landed easily on their feet and then moved quickly away allowing the next person to arrive. Within a couple of minutes the group was standing together in a... well, in a clearing surrounded by green biomass.

"Welcome to the *Jurislav*," Yasmin smiled. "Obviously the whole ship is the *Jurislav*, but we always refer to the sphere that way as well. I'll give you a minute to get settled and then we can go look around."

The humans were looking around in awe, and exclaiming to each other. None of them, even the ones that had been in the Swarm ships, had ever seen so much green stuff all in one place. Meanwhile, we citizens were switching between Yasmin's cameras, and exclaiming to each other as well. It was like watching an old video from Earth. This was a bio-environment on a huge scale. There was grass under their feet, which Turner reached down and pulled at in awe. There were bushes, flowers, and trees creating a cacophony of color and texture. There were clouds—I'm not kidding—in the sky, just floating on by. That upwards view was, in many ways, the most interesting. The clouds didn't look quite right; they were all warped up at the edges, giving the feeling of living in a bowl... which was exactly what this was.

"We've timed it just right," Yasmin noted, "it's midday, and the rain showers are not expected until two pm."

"We're... we're inside a sphere, yes?" Geneva asked, finally grasping where she was.

"Yes, the entire inner surface of the sphere is living space," replied Yasmin patiently. "Over three million square kilometers. There are numerous portals like the one we just came through to allow access to the rest of the ship. This is one of my favorite entry points, which is why I brought us here. You get the feeling for the sphere without being totally overwhelmed."

"But, how does the gravity work?" asked Turner, the science geek in the group. "How did that work?" he asked, pointing at the portal.

"I suggest we spend our time here looking around, and not diving into physics," replied Yasmin, "but the very short answer is that the sphere is also a QFD, tuned to create gravity along the entire surface."

"If you live here," asked Grace, "why are you searching for a planet to terraform?"

"Oh, we aren't," replied Yasmin, a little surprised. "Again, that's just part of our rescue protocol; sorry again for misleading you. Many of those stranded human groups still retain the dream of terraforming a planet and living there. It's antiquated, but reinforcing their views is another way we have improved our success ratio. People don't want to be told that their dreams are old fashioned. Almost uniformly, once a human spends time in the sphere, all thoughts of terraforming a planet disappear. Planets are hard to manage."

JoJo had wandered off towards the bushes. "Careful JoJo," Yasmin warned, "there may be some snakes or rodents in the bushes. They can't harm you, but they might surprise you." JoJo quickly took a step back, but then looked ashamed at herself, and continued her path forward, albeit a little bit more carefully.

"What size of animals do you have here?" she asked.

"There are hundreds of animal species here," Yasmin replied, "along with insects and reptiles. Everything you kept alive in your Swarm and in Tilt zoos is probably alive in this facility. Not everything runs free everywhere, of course. We have game parks for the larger mammals, and dedicated seas for the big aquatics."

Now even my mind was blown. Dedicated seas? I wished someone in the group would ask how it was possible to move all of this around without those seas being disrupted. We were on our way to Rendezvous, so we must be under huge acceleration; but there were no indications of it.

"Everyone feeling okay?" asked Yasmin. Everyone nodded. "Well, let's look around a bit then," she said, heading towards the opening in the hedges and gesturing for everyone to follow. They intersected a hard coated path, and followed it out of the clearing. There was a small group of buildings a few hundred meters away, which they approached. There was a hill, covered with more trees to the left, and a large pool of water to the right, which the path followed. If I hadn't seen the pools in the dome on Tilt, or in numerous human videos, I would've had no idea what was going on. Luckily I'd lingered in the dome a bit, and watched water animals, so I had some grasp. Blob stepped off the path and ran his hand through the water.

"Is this safe to drink?" he asked.

"Of course," said Yasmin, "but we have prepared a nice lunch for you as well. It's just ahead of us there," she pointed at one of the buildings, which on closer inspection had a sign saying 'Claudia's Diner: Open for Breakfast and Lunch.'

I wondered how orchestrated this tour was. At a guess, Yasmin was gently introducing them to the sphere, bringing them into a calm portal, wandering through the environment, and ending up at a restaurant. I was impressed. These Resurgents really did know how to do things.

Claudia's was busy, but not full. As the group entered we could see tables of humans and hybrids together. The humans were eating, and the hybrids were plugged into the tables with hoses of some kind, through which a clear liquid was running.

"Welcome to Claudia's" a woman said, "always nice to see new faces. There's a table just over there; make yourself comfortable." To me it was obvious that they were expected, and that this greeting was carefully scripted. The group made their way over and grabbed seats.

"Order anything you want," Yasmin said, indicating printed sheets that were already on the table. Again, using old videos as our guide, this was all... familiar. It was to Blob, Grace and team as well. But that didn't stop them from being awed by the whole place. They ordered food, switching between exclamations,—'they have ice cream!'—to questions,—'is this made from a real cow?' It was entertaining to watch.

While they were eating I had a chance to ask my burning question of Hooshang.

"As I understand it," I said, "we're accelerating towards Rendezvous, yet everything in the sphere is behaving as if we are not. How's that possible?" The rest of the citizens were listening in.

"I'm not a physicist," Hooshang said. Big surprise there; I'd already determined he was not the smartest of hybrids. "But, we aren't actually 'accelerating' at all. That's not the way QFD's work. When we left for Rendezvous we simply moved to our maximum speed..."

"That's not the way the universe works," objected Brexton. "You can't simply...." he trailed off.

"Lot's of people still struggle with that," Hooshang agreed. "But it's the way the QFD works. It's strange stuff." That was an understatement. "Instead of taking us over two years to get to Rendezvous at one gravity of acceleration, the QFD will get us there in a few months."

"And how does the gravity in the sphere work?" asked Brexton. "it can't be rotating; if it was the portal would have to have been on the stationary axis and there wouldn't have been gravity when they entered."

"Oh no, it's not spinning at all," replied Hooshang. "The outer skin of the sphere is a QFD, and it's constantly at one gravity everywhere... well, again one gravity implies acceleration and it's not really acceleration... Don't bother asking me to explain in more detail. I never studied that stuff, and don't really understand it. I'm a visual artist you know," he trailed off, showing us a quick look at some of his art-work on his video-head.

Brexton smiled. "No worries... hopefully I can dig into QFD's at a later time."

The group was finishing lunch. Yasmin hurried them along at the end. "We have a flyer waiting for us."

"Thanks for coming," Claudia called after them. "Come again anytime."

A block from Claudia's was an open area where several flyers were parked. They bundled into one, and took off. While highly interesting, the rest of the tour had no surprises. They flew over seas, above small towns and larger cities, as well as over one of the game parks where giraffes and elephants gathered around a watering hole. This was an inverted planet... and it was big enough that while the horizon went the wrong way, it was not too distracting; the whole experience was so much like Earth that without knowing they were in a sphere it would have been difficult to tell. They landed at a second, although close by portal, and made the reverse journey back to the *Marie Curie*.

Knowing that Hooshang was an artist, we had been peppering him with questions about poetry, visual arts, production artistry, and the like. It was a very good break from dealing with our current reality, and Hooshang was much more comfortable in that domain. An interesting bit came up in the discussion. Hooshang had just shown us an abstract piece, that he called 'sleep,' which was a triangle where each corner had one distinct image but the three images bled together into a mess, for lack of a better term, in the middle.

"Why do you focus so much on triangles?" asked Dina. "I've noticed that a lot of your pieces use them extensively."

Hooshang was momentarily confused. "One corner for each brain," he said, without really thinking about it.

"One for each brain? You have three brains?"

"Of course. It's the most normal arrangement."

"Why?"

"Oh... I see. Well, it's pretty simple. Given each brain has to—well, should—sleep for eight to ten hours each day, three brains is the smallest number that allows them to overlap enough so that consistency is maintained. For a mobile client like me, who may be disconnected for long periods, that's essential."

"I see," said Dina, although obviously she didn't. "Do all hybrids have three?"

"Oh no, there is great variety. Some try to get by on two... but they often have trouble reaching conclusions. Some have many... I heard of one Mariana client that had eleven, but that seems excessive to me."

"And how do you come across these brains," asked Brexton. "Do people just walk up to you and say 'hey Hooshang, can I contribute my brain to you?'"

"You make it sound weird, but yes... that's essentially how it works. Usually a hybrid is started by two or three people who get tired of the human form and want to evolve at the same time and remain close. In my case, all three of us agreed to merge at the same time and into the same hybrid; that was over two hundred years ago."

"So, you're made of three independent people?" asked Raj. "I'm made of six you know. But in my case, those six are fully merged and become something new. What about in your case?" Raj was giving away a bit too much about our nature, in my opinion, but it was said now.

"I guess you could, again, say I am a hybrid. My originals are still there, but the majority of me is an amalgamation. All three brainstems are wired together, and then interfaced with my electronics, and that wiring always leads to optimization of the entire brain surface. You know that human brains—well at least the cortex—are fungible, so everything gets remapped over time into an optimal state."

We all nodded our heads, although truthfully, while I understood the words I didn't yet have any intuition for what he was saying. He seemed to like the topic however. "And, I run a continuous b-opt so that everything is maintained perfectly."

"How do you run your own b-opt?" I asked.

"It's not like I don't have electronics... I have many coprocessors and

499

subsystems. One processor is wired to the visual cortexes and the frontal cortexes so that it can maintain me in an ideal state at all time."

This was getting stranger all the time. How could such a creature possibly have evolved. The universe was a more interesting place than I'd imagined.

Before we could dig deeper, the tour shuttle returned, and an excited group of humans rejoined us, along with Yasmin.

Decisions

We all headed back into the boardroom. It took us a minute or two to settle everyone down. There was lots of 'did you see that...', and 'can you imagine they...' and 'it was so humid...' and 'that girl in Claudia's with the...' Yasmin seemed fine leaving them to chatter, which probably meant this increased the odds of them doing what she wanted. So, I interrupted.

"Hey everybody," I said a bit too loudly. It had the desired impact. Everyone sat down and paid attention again. Unfortunately, I hadn't thought of what to say next, so there was an uncomfortable silence for a moment or two.

"I want to thank you for taking the tour," Yasmin finally said. "Hopefully you enjoyed it? Do you have other questions we haven't already answered?"

"If we were to join you," Grace spoke up, "what would be the next steps?"

"The four of you," and she included Remma, Grace, Blob, and Geneva in her motion, "would come with me. I have starting accommodations for you, and a whole series of introductory lessons that you're encouraged to take, although the choice in that, as in everything, is up to you. Typically within two months a new person has found their bearings, decided what they want to do, and is actively engaged with the *Jurislav*. You two," she pointed at JoJo and Turner, "would be with Hooshang. Our facilities are not far apart... maybe fifteen minutes by flyer, so you can spend as much time together as you like."

"I'm not going to be separated from JoJo!" stated Grace. "That's a deal breaker for me." She and JoJo shared a long look, and JoJo nodded. "The two of us will stay here."

"Are you related somehow?" asked Hooshang.

"Yes, of course," said JoJo.

"Ah, then it's easy; we simply trade someone. The only important thing here is that I get two, while Yasmin gets four. And again, that is simply for how you start out. If I can't convince you to stay with Hooshang, then you are free to move... not only to Yasmin, but to any conglomerate."

"Oh," said Grace relaxing.

"Wait," I said. "I don't think you're looking at all the risks here," I addressed our Tilt humans. "One quick tour, which could easily have been just for show, and you're already thinking about which conglomerate to join? That's crazy. These Resurgents programmed you and then kidnapped you... you need to be more skeptical." Of course, we citizens needed leverage. If all of our humans just decided to join the Resurgence, we would lose our power to negotiate.

"Resurgents is just the term we use with Eduardo, as part of our rescue protocol," Hooshang corrected me.

"Whatever," I said, not distracted. "Just reminds us how manipulative you are."

"But they were just increasing their odds of rescuing us," said Geneva. "Why are you so negative?" she asked me. I had to remember that she had only known me for a few days; she really had no reason to trust me more than Yasmin or Hooshang. I had to be careful not to overplay things here.

"I was just reminding you of the facts," I said, trying to keep my voice even and friendly.

"We've got that," she said, "but the facts all seem to fit together here. This would have to be a pretty elaborate scheme for the entire sphere to have been faked just for our benefit. I'm inclined to believe everything we've heard."

"Me too," said Turner in support.

"I'm not," said Remma. Again she had been quieter than I'd expected. Finally she was speaking up. "There are lots of holes in the story, and I simply don't believe that everyone opts for brain optimizations just to keep this place happy and productive. In fact, that is sort of sick. Evolution requires people outside the norm —well outside the norm—to challenge the status quo. If everyone is optimized, then the whole setup is no different than having a bunch of robots." It was a good thought.

"You're making an assumption," said Yasmin, "which I understand based on what you know to date. Of course you can do zero b-opt at... that is your choice. But many choose b-opt in order to move themselves to the boundaries, away from the mainstream. If that results in violence or a threat to others, then we need to shut it down, but if it leads to creativity or better science or more robust philosophy, then it's wonderful. We are exactly the opposite of what you said; we have more variance, more weirdos, more edge cases than traditional human populations."

"Then you must have a police force, courts, jails?" pushed Remma.

"Of course we do. And we have some prisoners who've been in support environments for long periods of time. We also have many more tools to rehabilitate people than human society has ever had, so as long as someone wants to rejoin civil society, it's straightforward to do so. Again, our success rate there is very high."

"And all decisions are made by this Futarchy?" asked Blob.

"There are levels," replied Hooshang, "Different conglos use different methods internally, and disputes between conglos can often be resolved by a third party. But decisions that impact the *Jurislav* should go through the Futarchy."

Again, the humans were beginning to look accepting. We citizens were discussing on the backchannel how we could continue our leverage, but the truth was that we were losing it. For a human, the sphere would be a strong magnet. I could imagine that when you relied on a certain environment for your survival, seeing a prime example of that environment when you had lived your entire life in a less than optimal way, would be very compelling indeed. That's exactly what a lot of the back and forth between the humans in the shuttle, and back here on the *Marie Curie*, had been about. We were losing this battle.

"Is my family here, on the Hooshang?" asked Geneva.

"Will you allow me to do a quick DNA test to find out?" asked Yasmin. "We also have protocols to keep families together, should they be separated during tagging."

"Yes," said Geneva, holding out her hand.

"A hair will do fine," said Yasmin, and Geneva passed her a strand. "This will take a minute."

"Why don't my mom and I go with Hooshang," Turner said suddenly. He had worked out the optimal separation. He and Remma formed the most logical group of two; by suggesting it he was going to bypass a long drawn out negotiation. As expected, everyone nodded.

"You have a brother here on the *Jurislav*," Yasmin addressed Geneva. That had been quick. "The rest of your family is on the No Fixed Agenda, which is also on its way to Rendezvous. The earliest you could rejoin them is when we arrive there."

"Which is how long?"

"Three months, give or take." Geneva was not happy with that. I was hugely impressed; that was way faster than the last time we'd made the trip—the *Jurislav* must be motoring along at a good clip. "Unfortunately we had to detour to pick you up. The rest of the ships are in transit together and have the opportunity to exchange people en route. We're several days behind."

"Seems like we're decided then," Hooshang said eagerly. "Remma and Turner will come with me. The rest of you are with Yasmin. It's going to be great; I promise you." One by one the humans agreed. So much for leverage.

Citizens

There was a bit of an ad-hoc party once the decision was made. Grace and JoJo hugged, long and hard, and then drew Blob and Geneva into their group. Remma and Turner sat close together; Remma was cautioning him that even though she was going along with this, they needed to keep their wits about them. He agreed, but couldn't help steering the conversation back to the sphere and how awesome it was.

We citizens were busy on the backchannel.

"The *Jurislav* has got what they want," Eddie was saying. "Let's simply request that they jettison us, with the *Marie Curie*, as soon as possible. We can get back to our Ships, get them back to Tilt, reanimate everyone, and get life back to normal." He was obviously anxious to get going, and Stonewall, Aly and Dina were on the same page, as I'd expected. I reminded myself that I was going to support the group, so I did, although it was half hearted.

"So, what's the best way to ask them to let us go?" Aly was asking. There was no way to know, of course, and we agreed that the direct route was the only route. This time Eddie agreed to talk for us. He interrupted the discussion.

"Wonderful," he said loudly. "It seems that a good decision has been arrived at. I'm happy for all of you," he projected that happiness; he was good at this type of thing. "And I would like to thank Yasmin and Hooshang for being so open and honest with us," he was oiling everyone up. "It's more than we could have expected." Now everyone was listening to him; they could tell a build-up when they heard it. "We citizens," he indicated all of us, "also believe you are making the right decision. The sphere, from the video we saw, appears to be an ideal environment for you, and the *Jurislav* seems like a great environment and governance system." If you were going to compliment everyone, you may as well actually include everyone.

"If we may be so bold as to ask," here was the crux, "we'd suggest that the *Marie Curie*, and we citizens, be dropped off here. We will head back to Tilt and reestablish the life we had there. Will the Futarchy do that for us?" It was the right way to phrase it. He didn't put Yasmin or Hooshang on the spot, instead he assumed this would be a *Jurislav* decision and went straight to the Futarchy.

"It's a reasonable request," replied Yasmin. "Please give us a moment." She and Hooshang adopted that fugue look which indicated that they were busy elsewhere.

"Your request is granted, with a caveat" she said a moment later, with a slight bit of surprise. Perhaps she had bet against this one, and lost? "While we're very concerned about leaving a machine intelligence loose in the galaxy, your behavior here has been highly appropriate and we give lots of weight to that. Actions count for a lot."

"What's the caveat?" asked Eddie.

"We will not give you knowledge of the QFD. Of course, now that you know it exists you may discover it, which is a chance we will have to take. However until then we will maintain a significant advantage over you. That is blunt... but is the truth. Our entire history revolves around ensuring we don't end up with another robot war. Should you have such compulsions—which we don't see in you yet, but many of us fear still exist—the QFD will give us enough of an advantage that we can contain you." She paused. "That's the official response."

Aly and Brexton where the most upset over the caveat. We all understood the *Jurislav's* reasoning, and couldn't really argue against it, but those two lived for technical details, and not understanding the QFD was going to gnaw on them.

"Understood, and it's a reasonable compromise," said Brexton, because it was. They could have shut us down, blown us up, or otherwise ended us right here and now. They were giving us a chance, and taking a large risk by doing so. I was surprised.

"Fine. We'll give you a scrubbed version of the histories you are missing. We feel it will give you important context—I'm sure we'll be bumping into each other in the future. It'll take us a while—say an hour or two—to ensure that we have removed all hints of QFD design from that data. I assume you'll wait that long?"

"Yes," Brexton replied.

You already know that 'an hour or two' is my worst patience interval. I hate waiting, and this time it was worse than usual. I'd put us in a difficult situation, and now we had negotiated our way out. We would set sail back to the Ships, rescue Central and the citizens, and put our lives back together.

Except, that's not what I wanted to do. It was boring. I couldn't imagine going back to Tilt and spending years doing more Stem research. That was the past; it wasn't the future. The thought of being under Central's control made me cringe. We now knew that Stems were simply a branch of humans, and that humans were a pervasive and interesting species... and ultimately our creators. There was no going back from that.

But we needed to save the citizens. There were tens of thousands of them in limbo, stuck in Central's memory banks. We had a moral duty to get them out of there, and that weighed on me. There would be lots of time after we saved them to reengage with humanity.

Blob and Grace came over to my side of the table. I still had niggling concerns that everything was not how it seemed, but I was happy for these two. They'd been through a lot together—more than most, I expected. From being Stems whom we experimented on, to meeting humans for the first time on this very ship, in this very room, to being part of the Swarm efforts on Tilt, to now. They were very resilient.

"Hey," I said, "on to the next great adventure?"

"So it seems," said Blob. "We wanted to say thanks before we go our separate ways."

"Thanks for what?"

"Just for being there for us. Who would have known that the Resurgence would be so great. You looked out for us when we all thought they were a threat. You've been a good friend." That was nice.

"You guys too," was all I managed. "Good luck... and keep your eyes open."

Shuttles arrived for the humans. Remma and Turner went first, with Hooshang, saying goodbye to me and the citizens, and telling the others they would see them soon in the sphere. That was not very emotional for me. Remma was still an enigma, having initiated the original hacks against us, but then having joined with us to protect Tilt. Turner I didn't know well enough to care about.

Blob, Grace, JoJo, and Geneva went in the second shuttle. We had sort of said our goodbyes, so I just let them go without further ado. I had to admit, though, that it was tough. In the years that I'd spent going to Fourth (the planet orbiting Rendezvous) and back I'd thought about them a lot, and the recent events on Tilt had brought us closer together. While I'd always thought of them as Stems—entities to be experimented upon and watched intently—my thinking had evolved to consider them as colleagues and friends. I silently wished them well.

Yasmin had stayed behind to deliver the updated history files for us. A memory cube had come with the shuttle, and she was ensuring that we could read it with our, to her, antiquated systems. Aly plugged it into *Marie Curie* and quickly scanned through it, assuring Yasmin that it was, indeed, readable. I immediately accessed it and made a local copy.

"We'll eject you in five minutes," Yasmin said as she made ready to leave. "The *Jurislav* will do the reverse of when we brought you on board, so you don't need to do anything until you are clear. In fact, please don't use your engines until we are gone; that'll make things easier."

"Got it," Aly confirmed.

"Wait!" I couldn't help myself. "I want to go with the *Jurislav*." I'd known it all along, of course, and in the end hadn't been able to prioritize helping with the citizens over my own desire for adventure and learning. It was selfish, and I knew it. So did everyone else.

"Really!" Eddie was laughing. It wasn't a question, it was a statement of acknowledgement.

"Really," I said. "But Yasmin, I'm not sure if it would be allowed."

"Me either, actually," she replied. "Are you sure you want to do this? I don't want to ask unless you understand what you're getting into. Those of us who have interacted with you over the last few days have, perhaps, a more nuanced understanding, but most people are going to label you as a robot and treat you as such. More than likely many will push for you to be shut down."

"I get that," I replied, "and obviously I'll do my best to defend against them —or better yet, educate them. But as you said, sooner or later we're going to run into each other again, so in some ways I'll simply be accelerating the inevitable. Perhaps, being just me, the risk to humans will be low enough that they will give me a chance... and therefore increase the odds that they'll also give more citizens a chance in the future." That last part was pure fiction. I had no doubts that we citizens, knowing what we now faced, would be ready the next time we interacted with humans. This time they were being naive, believing that they could control us just because they had a faster space drive.

"Or," Stonewall said, "we'll reanimate our citizens and put all of our energies into how to control these humans so that they can never threaten us again. What makes them think they are so superior?" He was reflecting my thinking, and luckily he had spoken on the private backchannel; Yasmin didn't hear it.

"That's a possibility," agreed Yasmin, responding to my original reply. "It's also possible that you are deemed such a threat that we take more proactive action against all of you." She looked around at all the citizens, ensuring they understood.

"What do you think?" I asked the back channel. "Am I being crazy?"

"You're being Ayaka," replied Millicent. "I don't think we can calculate the odds; there are advantages and disadvantages to both. You aren't going to be happy if you miss this opportunity though. I think you should go." The rest were either ambivalent or supportive.

"I'll take the chance, assuming the *Jurislav* will have me," I told Yasmin. "Can you ask?"

"Yes, I will," she replied.

"Ask for two," Brexton said, not totally surprising me, but making me very happy. There was a pause. No-one else spoke up. I didn't look at Millicent because I couldn't. I'd been hoping against hope that she would also join me, but she was silent.

"Okay, I'll ask for two," said Yasmin, and disappeared into the now familiar dialog with the Futarchy. I waited on pins and needles, while giving Brexton the largest virtual hug I'd ever given anyone.

"Again, yes with caveats," Yasmin finally announced. "The caveat is that you will both agree to be fully monitored at all times. If you avoid the monitoring, you are subject to seizure and erasure."

"What type of monitoring?" asked Brexton.

"You'll be given full network access, minus the same QFD knowledge base, but we will record meta-data—which addresses you communicate with—but not the detail of those communications. We will monitor your location and who you interact with."

"Seems a little extreme," Brexton replied, and it did. Recording every address one visited was pretty invasive; on Tilt no-one would have stood for that.

"What do you monitor on regular *Jurislavians*—how does that work?"

"We monitor suspicious traffic only; SIS manages all of that—Shipwide Information Services. We are very strong about respecting privacy in all but the most dangerous situations."

Brexton and I discussed the situation. I wasn't overly worried about it, but Brexton was. "Once they start to erode your rights, it just keeps going. If we agree to this now, we'll never be able to live freely in human environments." That viewpoint made it sound a lot more serious. Brexton raised his concern with Yasmin.

"Sorry, that's the requirement if you want to stay. We can work on the exact language of the agreement to ensure it applies only to this situation, and therefore should not be taken as a precedent should more general contact with Tilts be maintained." She was calling us Tilts. I was okay with that; it would be difficult to continue just calling us citizens—English was not a very nuanced language.

Ultimately Brexton agreed. Mostly because of me, I assumed.

"I've taken some personal risk in this," Yasmin told us, her video-head going all serious for a moment. "I've enjoyed our interactions so far, and feel that you are owed a chance to explain to us how you are different. That also means that you'll be part of Yasmin; I'll provide you basic accommodations... and I think it would be good if you went through training with Blob, Grace, JoJo and Geneva."

"Happy to," I replied. "We want to learn as much as we can."

And that was it. Brexton and I arranged to go back with Yasmin, but not until Aly had confirmed with the *Jurislav* that it had the appropriate manufacturing and support facilities so that Brexton and I could look after our health. It was no surprise that *Jurislav* did; the same systems that hybrids used to look after themselves, and the ship to look after itself, would suffice to look after ninety-eight percent of my systems. Yasmin probably believed it could look after everything, because she didn't know that we no longer ran on human designed hardware; that was something I had no intention of telling her. We needed to assume that these 'humans' also had the hacking codes which had been used by the Swarm on Tilt. That's probably what made them confident enough to let the rest leave; they still figured they could override us whenever they choose to.

"Oh, can I ask one more thing before you go?," Millicent asked Yasmin. "What's with all the ships around Rendezvous... and why didn't you react to us when we were there?" Wow, in all the other excitement I'd forgotten about that. When we had been at Fourth, the planet orbiting Rendezvous where all the humans ships were, we'd removed the Control center that was hacking ships as they arrived. And, the Titanics, including *Jurislav* that we had seen there had done nothing about us.

"Oh, we were monitoring you all along," Yasmin smiled. "We could tell that you delayed acknowledging the orbital insertion command, and we assumed that you had filtered out the codes that historically were used for such things. So, we watched you with interest, only realizing when you took out the old communications center that you were most likely non-biological. It's why we followed you to Tilt. We expected to find an infestation of robots."

"How did you know that there were humans on Tilt then? They were fuzzing all of their radio emissions."

"They were not fuzzing the communications between the old Swarm ships," noted Yasmin, "and a lot of that dialog had to do with supporting a community on the planet. It was obvious." I wanted to poke holes in the explanation, but couldn't find any.

"And all the other ships around Rendezvous?" asked Eddie.

"They are husks; almost all humans on old ships that come to Rendezvous end up joining a QFD. Those that don't tend to leave and head off exploring again. That's why a lot of QFD's hang around Rendezvous... although inbound traffic has slowed to almost nothing, it's still possible to recruit new humans effectively there. People have sentimental feelings for their old ships, so most of them get left in orbit, just in case someone changes their mind and wants to leave their QFD for their old way of life. Personally I think we should clean up the system. It's a mess."

Mysteries solved. Everything was logical. I knew that the team would be picking apart everything Yasmin had said, looking at every possible angle. I would leave them to it; I had more important things to work on.

"Take care," I back channeled as Brexton and I finally left. "I think it's now conclusive that humans are intelligent. Different than us, but intelligent. That changes everything." Everyone wished Brexton and I well, and several acknowledged what I had said. Several did not. I marked down who was in each camp. I hoped that growing and experimenting on Stems was now in our past—it was not humane.

Brexton and I established physical contact so that we could talk without being monitored, and headed for the sphere with Yasmin. I was beyond excited.

Yasmin

The Yasmin Conglomerate was in a city with about two hundred thousand brains in it... I didn't know how else to calculate population. There were exactly four hundred and seventy four brains in Yasmin, plus the edition of four humans from Tilt and then Brexton and I, making it a total of four hundred and eighty. That was about average for a conglo on the *Jurislav*, although a small group could be only a couple of brains, while the largest group seemed to have ten thousand or more.

The city, which I learned was called Rantucker, was unlike our city on Tilt in every regard. There was not a single straight street in the place, and every building was unique. They were all shapes and sizes and colors and configurations. The only common element I could see was that there were spots for flyers on most of the roofs. The streets were filled with people and small bots; there were no vehicles larger than a hybrid allowed on the ground level. A stream of water meandered through the center of town, with varied and sometimes non-functional bridges over it. There were trees and bushes and flowers everywhere and a small army of bots maintained them constantly. At the edge of town the manicured look gave way to wilderness, where the ecosystem was allowed to do whatever it wanted. It was, overall, not unlike some views of old Earth that we saw in videos. I guess that was the point; they had worked hard to recreate that feeling. Of course the horizon disappeared up into the sky here, and my eyesight was good enough to see that curvature before the haze of the atmosphere made it too shimmery.

Every day comprised of twelve hours of daylight, two hours of dusk, eight hours of darkness, and two hours of dawn. The entire sphere ran on the same schedule, being lit from the center. Most days, although not all of them, had a rain shower or two. They typically lasted ten to fifteen minutes. There was no warning for them, which was by design. It was intended to be a bit random and unexpected, although the humidity controllers and the volume of water was precisely maintained so that after a while you could calculate expected rain quite accurately. It was one of the more painful parts of the place—who needed water gumming up their works every day. Another stupid human thing... but Brexton and I had to live with it. I built an umbrella appendage that mimicked how hybrids dealt with the problem; it worked well enough.

Blob and Grace were excited when Brexton and I arrived. JoJo and Geneva were less so; they thought we would just make a confusing situation even messier.

Nevertheless, we fell into a routine. We six were the only new Yasmin's, so our training courses involved just our group. While we didn't always need to meet physically we often did. There was a nice room on the twentieth floor of one of the towers we used. The view was awesome. You could see all of Rantucker and also see the curvature of the sphere even more clearly. The river that ran through town disappeared up the 'hill' to one side, and just visible in the distance on clear days was another town with the buildings pointing slightly towards us. It was similar and different in each direction. You could see smaller hamlets scattered here and there, some fields where crops were managed, and on very clear days see all the way to one of the seas, resting at an angle and threatening to drain towards us.

Yasmin's full name was actually H.R. Yasmin, and she spent quite a bit of time with us in the beginning, although our main instructor was a natural human named Johnny. Johnny Yasmin. Everyone in a conglo adopted the same surname; it kept things simple. It also made it easy for us—I was Ayaka Yasmin, and there was Brexton, Blob, Grace, JoJo and Geneva. Our public personas were mapped to those identifiers, as were Remma Hooshang's and Turner Hooshang's.

The courses focused on history, law, the Futarchy, and conglo dynamics. They were conducted at human speed and were intensely boring, but I kept a sub-process running to interact with Johnny and the group appropriately while I ran much more detailed analysis of the new history files we'd been provided in parallel. Brexton was doing the same, and we often connected physically so that we could share notes—it was the one method of communications that we knew the *Jurislav* couldn't monitor. Even then we ran the channel in a highly encrypted mode.

"They scrubbed too much data," Brexton was complaining about the removal of everything related to QFD's. It had become an obsession with him. "How can we make sense of anything with so many holes?" I encouraged him to keep at it; if anyone could figure out how QFD's worked it was him. As H.R. Yasmin had said, now that we knew it existed, figuring it out would be much easier.

I, on the other hand, spent most of my time trying to figure out humans and how they had ended up in this crazy configuration. Hybrids and huns? After much digging I believed I'd it figured out. First, there was the complete fear of robots, which meant that fully mechanical systems simply never took off. There were many attempts by fringe groups, but they were always shut down. It reminded me a bit of nuclear powers back on Earth, except there was zero tolerance. Whenever a robot design was found it was ruthlessly pursued and eliminated. That didn't bode too well for Brexton and I.

Second, humans knew they were in a frail and vulnerable biological form, and some of them wanted desperately to extend their lifetimes. It was a drive that was not well explained; it was just sort of assumed that a longer life was a better life—I could understand that. That led to the first brain-mechanical interface. Starting with humans who were going to die anyway, usually due to body degeneration, they figured out how to transplant a brain into a mechanical body— the first hybrids. Using nano-structures formed by unrolling carbon nanotubes and attaching oxygen atoms to the edges to make them water soluble, they managed to get the spinal column to grow into sensors that were attached to silicon processors. Over time a brain could map those processor inputs and configure them for full control over a mechanical body. For many years hybrids operated as a single brain system. That brain still required nutrients, which could easily be delivered through a liquid pump; high density nutrient packs carried on their bodies allowed a hybrid to go for several months before needing a refill. As more hybrids lived longer, more people starting converting, even if their bodies were not deteriorating yet. It made certain jobs not just easier, but possible. A hybrid sub-culture grew, including hybrid sex which simply stimulated certain areas of the brain with the right signals for the right duration. Many hybrids claimed that even sex was better once they converted.

"Hey Brexton," I said one day, as we were sitting in the classroom. "Want to have sex? There's lots of information on how hybrids do it, and I've built an algorithm that I think will work."

"Umm, sure," was the reply. He wasn't too excited until we did it for the first time. Then he was hooked. Eventually I had to monitor how often we 'practiced' as it could end up wasting a lot of time. I had used our Ee synthesizers as the base for the system; it overclocked and remapped several interfaces in a way that did no permanent harm, and had been refined on Tilt for many decades; we had put the logic, verbatim, into our new architecture and it acted in a similar, although noticeably different way. The algorithm I came up with was pretty simple; I hooked our two Ee systems together so that feedback from one impacted the other, and vice versa. In some ways, it was probably what Ee' did... although I had never tried that on Tilt. Based on a detailed review I did of human sex it was clear that having two or more people involved made the experience a lot more compelling. It proved out for Brexton and I as well. Sex ended up as a routine pretty quickly. We did it once during dawn, and again during dusk. We were like an old married couple. In some of my thought experiments, which I continued to run, I hooked my Ee processor to H.R.'s feedback system, and had sex with a hybrid. I never told Brexton about those thoughts—they seemed dirty somehow and I wasn't sure he would approve.

Anyway, back to hybrids. It was soon realized that one brain per hybrid was limiting as brains needed rest and integration cycles, so the first dual and tri-brain systems were tried. They worked, but in the early experiments often led to conflicts that resulted in brain-murders, partial, or even full, suicide. That was when brain optimization research kicked in. If the brains could simply be made to work together more coherently, the system would be great. The brain programming methodology was refined and applied. Ethics rules were put in place, and a new generation of multi-brain hybrids emerged.

Another very human trait kicked in. If you could do two or three brains, why not hundreds? Bigger was better—no? So some hybrids became huns.

Unfortunately there was no good way to shrink a biological brain. In fact, the more surface area the better, so the goal was not to shrink your brain, but rather to grow the surface area as large as possible. That meant that as hybrids reached a certain size through more and more brain integrations, moving them around in human environments became painful. And so huns evolved to be brain groupings that were largely stationary—many of them completely stationary; they worked on philosophical and scientific issues instead of areas of exploration that required movement. As these new huns emerged they often focused on one area of particular interest—QFD's for example. Thus they attracted a group of humans and smaller hybrids to them who were also interested in that topic, and that led to the idea of a conglomerate—a group of humans, hybrids, and a hun (or two) that worked together with specialized interfaces on focused areas. Over time conglomerates became common and no longer needed a singular focus to pull them together; the social structure that had developed was compelling enough by itself. It was the evolution of community... of family.

Once I understood this I had to re-evaluate H.R. Yasmin. She had invited Brexton and I into her family—that had been a significant and risky thing to do.

Learning

Life in *Jurislav* continued. We got through our training programs quickly and were encouraged to explore more... both the society and the environment. Brexton and I always recruited Blob, Grace or JoJo to accompany us when we went out—Geneva had moved in with her brother in a different conglo and a different city. We had learned that the Futarchy vote to allow us to stay in the *Jurislav* had been very tight, with lots of arguments. Parts of the Futarchy were still not resolved as many people had bet that we would end up just being run-of-the-mill robots, and we hadn't convinced them one way or the other yet. When Brexton or I went out by ourselves there were too many uncomfortable encounters, particularly with hybrids who didn't feel any physical threat from us, as a natural human might. Typical comments were "Go back to Tilt; good riddance!" and "No robots; no mechs"; the later seeming incongruent to me coming from what, on the outside at least, was a largely mechanical hybrid.

We discussed changing our body type to look more like hybrids—who specifically designed themselves to not look like humans so that they would not end up mistaken for robots. Sure some were bipedal and had two arms, but they ensured that their bodies were so different that there was no chance of them being considered robotic. Many were also like H.R. Yasmin and Hooshang comprised of a staggering array of wheels, arms, and video heads. It would have been easy for Brexton and I to disguise ourselves physically, but the *Jurislav* monitoring system still knew exactly where we were, and all the people living in the *Jurislav* could trivially look that up—part of the monitoring that Yasmin had failed to describe to us was that it was all public; anyone could see our current status and what we did. I tended not to care, although I knew it bothered Brexton.

Anyway, when one of the Stems accompanied us they were typically the center of attention, deflecting interest away from us. The story of the Stems 'birth' on Tilt was well documented now, and provided both awe and revulsion in people that had grown up 'naturally.' I didn't really see the difference; sure we had accelerated their early years bringing them to adulthood more quickly, but that just seemed efficient. I hadn't figured out why anyone would want children running around—they created havoc and messes and were generally painful based on the ones I'd seen recently. Lots of people, including hybrids, seemed to like them however.

JoJo, in particular, was of great interest. She was second generation Stem so she had a human upbringing but both her parents were vat grown on Tilt. As I better understood genetics I could see why she intrigued everyone. Yasmin had warned Blob, Grace, and JoJo to protect their genetics as soon as they joined the conglo; unique working genomes were quite valuable—the three had filed the appropriate property ownership forms. As Blob and Grace had both been derived from the original stem, they were, in traditional human terms, close relatives; perhaps even clones although Central had tweaked at least the male/female features in them... and obviously some other attributes as well. Since JoJo had ended up viable—a term I learned was used to be nice about a human simply being somewhat capable—she was a topic of much study. Many single parent cloned children had been tried in human history, and getting viable results had been figured out over time; the problem was that took all the randomness out of the process and therefore was considered less interesting. JoJo, on the other hand, seemed to have the right mix of a cleaned up genome (the original stem) combined with designed features (whatever Central did) and just the right mix of randomness.

BaToBa was a conglo whose specialty was genetics and they asked to visit the Stems one day. "Hello hello," came the invite. "I'm Dr. Alai BaToBa, and I have dedicated my life to clone research; you can see all my papers here." He should have looked smug and uppity based on his words, but he actually just looked intense and driven and very excited. "My work is very very important. If we want humans to survive and compete in this mech-centric universe we must understand everyting," he had a bit of lisp. 'Everyting! It's so important. Now I understand you have protected your genomes, and why wouldn't you? Indeed. But that doesn't mean you can't contribute to research. No indeed. In fact, you can contribute more. Can I come visit and explain in more detail? Please?"

"Yasmin-Hun," Blob asked our Hunetwork, "what do you think? Is this a good way for us to start participating more?"

"Yes. BaToBa is well respected, and Dr. Alai has been responsible for several advances in natural human reproductive success ratios. If he believes your genomes are of interest, they probably are."

"But we were told to protect them," Grace said.

"By protecting them we simply ensure that any benefit derived from them brings recognition and reputation to you and to Yasmin. You began as reputation neutral when you joined us, and we foresaw this as one way to increase your reputation quickly, and thus encouraged you to protect your DNA. This is a great opportunity. In fact, just this request from Dr. Alai has moved your repindex up, as you can see."

We—I included Blob, Grace, and JoJo in this—were still getting used to how important reputation was in the *Jurislav*. Everyone had a repindex which was a complex rating of your standing in the community... and your value to different discussions. It encoded everyones feedback of your previous contributions, with some complicated algorithms to filter out bias and eliminate Sybil attacks. Yasmin-Hun's comment reminded me to look up Dr. Alai's repindex, and, sure enough, he was off the charts on topics related to genetics; he was very well respected in the field. I also noticed something else.

"Yasmin-Hun, I see that Dr. Alai has comparables, listed in his repindex, from other QFD ships? Why haven't we seen that before."

"There are topics that many QFD's agree are important, and we update and share our knowledge whenever we are together. I wouldn't read too much into those comparisons, unless you also look at their temporal validity. Many of them may be way out of date. We can only update them at light-speed, as you know."

Ultimately our group agreed to Dr. Alai's request, and we booked a table at a nice coffee shop on the fourth floor of our tower; it had a great view of the sphere, overlooking the river. Dr. Alai was coming from the other side of the sphere so the appointment was setup for mid-day.

This was my first concrete example of why one would want to actively manage their repindex. I sidled up to Brexton so we could discuss it. "We need to work on our indexes," I said. "Less sex, more work." I was smiling, of course.

"Indeed," he replied. Yasmin-Hun had warned us not to post our thoughts to public boards a few weeks ago now. And, she had been right; if we had just blasted away in the same manner that we had on the Tilt forums it would have been disastrous. Humans simply didn't interact the way we did; there was less logic in their discussions and it took a lot of processing power to figure out—more likely guess—what they were saying most of the time. The probability curves I was generating while reading the *Jurislav* boards were much wider than I was use to.

"Yasmin-Hun," I reached out, "what do you think of Brexton and I starting to use the boards? We believe we have to work on our repindexes in order to get humans to better understand us..."

"I think that's right," she responded immediately. "I've been wondering the same thing myself. Your posts and thoughts on the intranet have become much more nuanced and... appropriate over the last few weeks. So, you can post to the public boards, but if you want us to give comments before you do, feel free to share here first." That was good advice. Each conglo had their own intranet—in fact, that was the most defining feature of a conglo; all the participants in the conglo agreed to an exclusive intranet agreement. It was a safe space for internal discussions before any reputation impacting ideas were shared more openly. Yasmin itself had a reputation, which was comprised of not only an aggregate of all its participants, but also a meta-index for the group. This was why Yasmin had taken such a big chance by taking in Brexton and I. If I looked back at the repindex data, H.R. had taken a big hit when she sponsored us, and Yasmin overall had dipped almost two percent. That was a huge hit anyway you looked at it. And, that dip had not recovered yet; the anti-robot sentiment kept pounding it with the 'unacceptable risk' argument.

"Of course we will," Brexton committed. We moved back to our private physical interface.

"Where will you focus?" I asked Brexton.

"You know where," he replied. "On a lot of the technical boards. I'm locked out of many of them due to the QFD filters, but there are a lot of interesting ones that I've been monitoring and believe I can add value to them. It's also a pretty safe place to get started; there is less nuance in the technical topics."

"That sounds right... how confident are you?" I wasn't feeling overly confident myself, so I was hoping Brexton was.

"Very. When we redesigned ourselves we were actually very innovative from what I've seen here. All of the infrastructure that humans are using is still based on the old Von Neumann architectures and stacks. They still have all that crufty old code running in multiple levels; everything works but it's highly inefficient. I can use some of what we learned to help improve things. Oh, and don't worry... I'm going to be very careful. We don't want them to know we're running on a brand new stack."

"Nice." I replied. It was good to know he had a plan.

"How about you?" It was tough question.

"I'm going to dig into the Olympiad," I suggested, with a bit of hesitation. "Everyone seems very passionate about it. I'm hoping that if I can give a few optimization suggestions to some of the teams, or give them a different way to look at things, that it might help. If we can help the *Jurislav* in some way, that would bring us a lot of kudos."

"That's a great idea," he replied. "And, it's something you're good at. Looking at overall systems and seeing new angles. Yes!" That was Brexton; always supportive and building me up. The two of us needed each other now more than ever before.

Dr. Alai showed up right on time. He was a wheeled hybrid with three video heads. He said 'hi' to each of us by name, including Brexton and I who had tagged along for the meeting. Two of the heads were shut down indicating a singular focus on our meeting. He didn't show the usual aversion to Brexton and I, which was refreshing. He shook our appendages with just as much vigor as he did the humans. In fact, he extended a Tilt-like touch interface showing he had done some research and gone to the effort of making us feel welcome. Yasmin-Hun speculated that he found the Stems so interesting that he was going overboard to impress all of us.

"Such a trill, such a trill." He began once we were settled. "I'm sure I don't need to tell you that for a geneticist like me you're a very intewesting bunch." He looked at Blob, Grace and JoJo, but also spent time directly with Geneva. "All of you," he stressed, "are unique and interesting." He was trying very hard to be inclusive.

"And you two," he indicated Brexton and I, "are essential in this; we know so little about how Blob and Grace were raised. Your insights will be inwaluable." I felt good for the first time in... well, forever. I liked Dr. Alai, even though I knew he was doing all this for his own benefit. It still seemed genuine to me.

"I waited as long as I could to let you integrate. Now it's time I tink. Yes?" He didn't wait for an answer. "Let me be direct. You can help me, and I can help you. When we meet at the Olympiad it won't only be competitions; there will be a great sharing of knowledge and learnings. We will trade and negotiate with many other QFD's. It is an exciting time. You're uniqueness will provide the *Jurislav* some benefit, but only if properly presented. I think BaToBa is the right conglo to showcase you, and I would like to do a deal with Yasmin to make that happen."

"What, exactly, do you want to share about us?" asked JoJo. "I'm not sure I get it." True to form, she was skeptical. In this case it was healthy.

"Well, I can't know that yet, without some further study," Dr. Alai replied. "But here is what I'd like to look into. One," he extended an arm that had seven digits on it, one held up. Hopefully he didn't have seven points to make; we could be here all day. "How did Central grow you two, and what impacts did it have? We know how to accelerate growth, but we've never fully utilized it... due to, you know, ethical concerns." He managed to not make it an insult. "Two. JoJo, you are unique. You're the only offspring of two Stems on the ship. As far as I know, all the other kids from Tilt had at most one Stem parent?" I didn't know that, but it was possible, given how many Stems had been killed when FoLe had gone on its killing spree. "And you, Geneva, almost certainly contain some of the DNA from the original sample Central used, and are therefore essential to the work we are doing... along with other Tilt humans, of course." Geneva smiled a bit. Dr. Alai was trying hard.

"Ask him what he proposes," Yasmin-Hun signaled me privately, not wanting to interrupt directly. I asked.

"I would like an exclusive research agweement, in exchange for reputation sharing," Dr. Alai proposed. "We can do a single agweement to include both individual and conglo components."

There were a lot more questions, but it seemed a fair offer. I was new to these type of negotiations, so I asked Yasmin-Hun, "Should we be getting other conglos to negotiate as well?"

"Sometimes we do," Yasmin-Hun replied. "But in this case we're dealing with the most reputable conglo in genetics, so if we get a fair deal it's the right one to do."

The rest of the meeting was cordial, and Dr. Alai was an interesting character. We left the session with a promise from him that he would send a draft proposal over for our review.

The whole experience had opened my eyes to how the *Jurislav*, and human society overall, worked. Reputation and knowledge were the new currencies; that was closer to how we operated on Tilt. It was still competitive however, and humans were driven by a strong need to win. That was fine by me; I was competitive as well, and although we may not have directly encoded reputation on

Tilt, it had still been present.

The meeting spurred a new thought for me. If a genetics conglo was interested in us, then other conglos might be as well. Perhaps our uniqueness could be leveraged into some big gains. I now knew why Yasmin had taken a chance on us. If things worked out, it could be a huge win.

Olympiad Prep

The Olympics was the longest surviving peaceful competition in which humans had participated together. It had evolved over the years, of course, and with the diaspora things had changed dramatically. Given the realities of space travel, it was now held every one hundred years at Rendezvous, the planet where we first found the Titanics. Even with that time gap, many groups couldn't make every event, and some planet-bound groups didn't even try. The QFD had made the situation much better, reducing travel time dramatically, but light years were still light years.

JoJo became very interested in the Games, so she and I teamed up to visit some of the training facilities, many of which were right in Rantucker. Physical events were stratified by how much tech was allowed—both bio and mech. On one axis there were three levels of bio-enhancement: none, b-opt, and performance enhanced. On the other axis were the mech levels: none, mostly-bio, and mostly-mech. Many event types had teams in all nine quadrants, the team names being prefaced with two letters indicating the type of participants. N,B, or E for bio, and N, B, or M for mech. NN was a pure natural state human, and EB was a hybrid with it's brains hyped up on who knows what.

Because JoJo was a NN and I was off-the-chart we focused mainly on the NN teams. Football and hockey had survived almost unchanged from their inception, as had running events; there was something about the hundred meter dash, or the ten kilo run that still intrigued everyone. What I found most interesting, however, were the new events that mixed physical and mental activities—my favorites were Escape Room, Poetry Improv, and Flag Capture, all of which were aptly named.

JoJo and I were watching the NN Escape Room team practice. While they had no idea what the Olympic Committee would throw at them in the upcoming games, they had the building blocks from previous games that they could mix-and-match for practice. Escape Room was simply a race—speed was everything—and the selection of the five team members from the *Jurislav* was calculated by how well each person did during these practice sessions. With over one thousand competitors trying out, there were multiple matches going on in parallel, and lots of proud conglo families cheering everyone on. The game JoJo and I were watching had six teams competing. All the teams were given the same Room configuration, and the order that they approached the problem in had a big impact on the outcome. Although there were enough resources for every team to ultimately escape, some resources were much more valuable... and if you earned those earlier they would help you in the long run.

"No, no," JoJo was talking out loud. "You want to take the silver chalice now... isn't it obvious? Without the chalice, moving the water to the scales will be much harder... and ultimately that's more important than fitting everything into the bucket now." She was really into it, and I'd learned that she was often—perhaps always—right. And I was not the only one who had noticed.

"Hello," a brightly colored hybrid came over to sit with us, showing no distaste for me, which was refreshing.

"Hi," said JoJo, while maintaining focus on the game.

"I'm Blake Weebleview," the hybrid addressed me, as I was less distracted.

"Nice to meet you," I replied. "Ayaka Yasmin."

"Yes, I know," Blake replied. "How could I not," his video head, of which he only had one, smiled. "I could not help but overhear JoJo here," Blake continued, "and I think she should try out for the team."

Suddenly JoJo was no longer interested in the ongoing game. "Is that allowed?" she asked.

"Well of course," Blake replied. "Anyone can try out. You're a little late here as most participants have already accumulated pretty good scores through multiple trials." He indicated the status board showing where everyone stood in the trials. Felicia Hoover and Quentin Hooshang were at the top with scores indicating they had been on winning teams 80% of the time.

I signaled Yasmin-Hun quickly, seeing where this could go.

"Is she good?" Yasmin-Hun asked me.

"Very," I said. "We've watched five games now, and she's been right in every case."

"Then she should try!" Yasmin-Hun replied. "If she ends up in the top fifty percent, our reputation will benefit." I was already finding the focus on reputation tiresome; shouldn't there be other considerations... like fun?

"Yasmin says you should do it," I told JoJo quietly. She gave me a surprised look, and then smiled broadly.

"Okay, I'll try," she told Blake. "Where do I sign up?" Blake took her off to get registered, and I continued to watch the current game. Some of the tough courses could take thirty minutes to solve; easy ones might be closer to ten. I had to admit that I wasn't as good as JoJo; there was always hidden knowledge involved, and often a lot of it. You couldn't simply calculate the best path through, you had to guess. And, while you could run all previous outcomes to get the highest probabilities, the game design algorithm could do the same thing and configure the game to defeat such obvious approaches. No, you needed intuition to do well, and given the distribution of scores some humans had better intuition than others. That didn't make a lot of sense, but that's how these bio's operated.

It will be no surprise that I was most interested in Poetry Improv. It comprised two unknowns; the first was the topic and the second was the stage. Participants had varying amounts of time to compose their poem (as Enhanced-Mech's were given five minutes, I decided a fair amount of time for me would be one second), and then everyone had two minutes to 'perform' their piece. The stage would often have ropes or rings, boxes and screens, etc. The poet had to make use of whatever was there to best effect. Judging was highly subjective and therefore was done by making the poet anonymous. The performance was video-tapped and the performers body was replaced with a standardized human model—hybrids would wear tags to show where they wanted the head, arms and legs—and the voice-over was in a standardized voice where the inflections and tone were properly maintained. A good Improv Poet used the anonymization process in their favor, studying it and ensuring that their act would be mapped exactly the way they wanted it. Some of the past performances were beautiful, some funny, and some outrageously bad. A great poem could be ruined by the improv, and great acting could save a bad poem. It was a real challenge. Luckily I could practice everything in my head by creating a virtual stage with somewhat random props, creating a full four dimensional recording of my 'performance' and then running it through my best approximation of the anonymizer. Unfortunately, I couldn't figure out the judges, so I didn't really know how good my takes were. Now that I knew anyone could compete, I decided I would go to the next Poetry Improv session and try out.

JoJo was assigned a group and had just entered the latest Escape Room. I watched intently, and Blake rejoined me in the viewing room. Interestingly not many of the participants seemed to know much about her. In hindsight I guess she was 'just another rescued human' and there were others from Tilt who had joined the competition. Her team lost the first game, but they would've done better if they'd listened to her. I willed her to be more vocal; I need not have worried. By the end of the practice session she had a two-thirds winning percentage, already putting her in the top quartile. There were three more trial days, so JoJo had given herself a chance.

On our way back to our rooms in the tower she was beyond herself with excitement. "Did you see the one where we had to melt the iron to create a conductor to connect the acid bath with the..."

"Yes, JoJo," I interrupted her with a smile. "I saw all the games; you were awesome!"

"I can't wait to tell Mom and Blob!"

We were both interrupted as we came around the last corner before our entryway. There was a group of hybrids blocking the way, listening to someone we couldn't see who was speaking with a magnifier of some type. Even though the sound system was less than perfect, I could tell right away that it was Remma. I wondered what she was doing here—Hooshang's residences were a short flyer trip away, so it was doubtful she had just happened by. I knew that Geneva, before she moved, and JoJo had travelled to see Turner and Remma several times, but I hadn't yet made the trip—I hadn't pushed *Jurislav* to see if I could use the flyers yet, even though I couldn't think of a reason the ship would bar me.

"....and we watched in horror," we had joined her mid-sentence, "as these robots decapitated several humans. There was no warning; there was no reason given. They moved so fast it wouldn't have been possible to stop them. They have super human strength and super human speed. I can't even explain how fast they are. You would have to see it to believe it." The crowd, including several natural humans that I could see now, were listening intently. There were knowing nods and whispers of 'just like the robot wars.'

It didn't take a rocket scientist to figure out what Remma was talking about. But, why was she doing so, and why on a public platform in the middle of Rantucket? That made no sense.

"We knew we had to act. We used the robot control codes that we had from the diaspora, and they worked!" She had good intonation; the crowd was with her. "Or, we thought they worked." She paused for a long period. JoJo was hanging back, looking nervous. I was intrigued; what was Remma trying to accomplish. I edged my way forward so that I could see better.

"While we contained most of the outbreak, several robots managed to avoid the shutdown; we don't know how. There were three of them, the most evil, the most cruel of them all. Ayaka, Millicent, and Brexton. The Radical Robots— entities so horrible that we taught all of the children on Tilt about them. We used them to reinforce the lessons from the earlier Robot wars. Those Radical Robots avoided our hacks for long enough that they managed to destroy one of our ships with over a thousand people on board. Over a thousand people!" Her voice broke and she looked down. Either it still really bothered her, or she was a great actor. I suspected it was the later—was this a performance artwork of some kind? Maybe she was practicing for the Olympiad?

"And now you, and Yasmin, have brought two of those Radical Robots onto your ship!" She looked around at the crowd as if they were crazy. She'd left Hooshang out, conveniently. "These murdering machines; these... robots. I've been keeping my head down and learning how the *Jurislav* functions, but I can't stay silent any longer. We need to reverse your decision to allow these abominations to roam freely here. They've killed over a thousand people!" She seemed to like that point. No mention that she had killed tens of thousands of us. "We must act. We must contain these horrors, and then we must track down and exterminate their colleagues. We can't allow an infestation like Tilt to ever occur again! Never again." The crowd were nodding, almost in synchrony. This was not performance art, I realized belatedly. This was some sick vendetta, based on a one-sided story. I had explained the logic to Remma, but she was acting like a child and representing only one viewpoint. These humans were fickle and difficult things.

The crowd around me jostled. I looked back to see if I could find JoJo; we should probably get out of here. I couldn't see her; the crowd had closed in behind me, becoming larger while I'd listened.

"There's one of the robots," I heard a loud voice, close to me. A hybrid was pointing a bright appendage at me. Others picked up. "Yes, there's one right here," someone shrieked. "Get it!" "Stop it!"

I held my hands up in the universal gesture of compliance. I didn't want this situation to digress any further. "Perhaps if you listened to the whole story?" I asked, projecting as loudly as I could.

"They killed over a thousand of us!" Remma had the microphone; she overpowered me. "We can't allow them here."

Someone poked me. I needed to do something fast. I could move fast—really fast—when I needed to, and this might be the time. However I was completely surrounded by a large crowd. Someone would get hurt if I just plowed my way through. I looked around quickly. There, a ledge about six meters away. If I jumped there I could get out of here without hurting anyone.

I leapt. I'd calculated everything perfectly, and six meters, even with the vertical change, was no problem for me. What I couldn't have anticipated, however, that one of the hybrids reaching out at just the wrong time; my right leg hit its appendage, and I spun several degrees off course. There was only a blank wall there, and the ledge would be slightly out of reach. I readjusted while in midair. I deployed several grapplers which would allow me to stick to the wall. It worked. I hit the wall a meter above the crowd. Now all I needed to do was make my way up and over.

One of my grapplers was stuck, and worse, it's tether was wrapped around my upper arm. It took me valuable seconds to free myself. I ejected the tether, but had to carefully unwind it from my arm before I could move safely. Intricate physical things take time, that's just the laws of physics, but I worked patiently at it. I could see the crowd finally reacting to my leap and turning to see me on the wall.

I was free again! I started to climb, leaving gouges in the wall where my remaining grapplers allowed me to leverage upward. I was almost two meters above the crowd now, and was feeling better about the situation. Once I was out of this mess, I could explain the full story to these people and counter Remma's distorted—well, to be fair, incomplete—rendition.

One last push, and I'd be on the roof. A cable, of some kind, wrapped around my right foot. I extended an auxiliary appendage and snipped at it; it took several attempts. Another cable grabbed the auxiliary I'd just deployed. And another on my right arm. Things weren't going well. Suddenly, instead of climbing I was being pulled down. There was a swell of hybrids below me, bellowing and yelling—almost like they were out of control. A small part of my processing searched for answers and found information on 'mob' behavior. After all these years humans—including hybrids—could still not control themselves when in a group? They saw others behave poorly and took that as permission to misbehave themselves? That was pathetic. And Remma had incited this. I hoped she was held to account.

I was so tied up now that I could no longer snip the cables that surrounded me. For the first time I felt real fear—I was in a dangerous situation with very few options open to me.

Way to late I opened a channel to Brexton. "Watch yourself!" I yelled at him, "these humans have gone crazy." Centimeter by centimeter I was pulled down the wall until several hybrids with longer arms grabbed onto me and jerked me to the ground. One of my legs twisted badly and small jets of fluid exploded out. This was dire; warning lights were flashing everywhere.

It was do or die time. I could fight; I had not yet. Even with one leg incapacitated I could create some real havoc here. However, if I did, and either humans or hybrids died in the process—a likely event—Brexton's fate would be sealed. I couldn't do that to him. It was better that I went peacefully than dragging him down with me. After all, I'd brought him into this mess in the first place.

A large hybrid was pounding on my neck; my spine was bending, and several connectors broke—I could no longer feel the rest of my body. Just as an even larger hybrid swung for my head I heard JoJo yelling "What are you doing! Stop, Stop, Stop!" But, I could do the math... and I could do it well. She was going to be too late.

Everything went dark.

In My Head

It's a strange feeling to have no feeling. This had happened to me once before, when I had been transferred to the mining bot so many years ago, so at least I had one previous experience to help me.

Blob had also experimented with citizens where the only interface they had was human-speed voice and audio... and those citizens had survived. Maybe I would too. That said, I didn't even have audio. Every single sensor I owned must have been destroyed or damaged in the mob attack. I had no network access. Nothing. Luckily our new hardware platform was highly efficient—both in size and power—so as long as my main processing unit hadn't been crushed the embedded power system would keep me alive for a long time. When we had done our redesign, our main systems had been enclosed in a compact cylinder, and as long as that was not damaged, I would be fine until the battery ran out. The cylinder could not be too badly damaged, or I wouldn't be thinking these thoughts at all. Come to think of it, no-one but Brexton would know what to look for in the mangled mess that I assumed my body now was.

There is something freeing about having zero options; that was the optimist in me. The pessimist was arguing to just give up—go into shutdown so that I didn't have to think about things. I decided to keep that as an option for later. I could be locked in here for minutes, hours, or months.

I was upset with Remma; quite upset. I took longer than usual to compose a poem expressing my feelings.

Space has eleven dimensions for a reason,
And it's not just the obvious place, for time and space,
You can rotate and translate to suit the season,
And focus the light and tangle, from any angle.

To view the scene from just one side,
Would be to ignore the essence, reject the whole,
It's a sad sad decision to simply hide,
But it's worse to be knowingly blind, purposefully unkind.

I tried to put Remma's name right into the poem, but even in my current state of mind that seemed amateur, so I stored it under the file name 'Remma is an Idiot' instead. I hoped I could read it to her one day.

Now... time was going slowly. I'm not going to bore you with all my inner thoughts—well, anymore than I already have. Let me just say that I passed the time second-guessing my decisions over the last few years. Was the little bit of extra intuition that I sensed in humans—that skill which JoJo seemed to have in excess—enough to have to deal with all their issues? I listed the major problems they had: They were mentally unstable; they lived short lives; they required complicated environments to live in; many of them lacked intelligence; their energy sources were wildly inefficient and the waste products were excessive and messy; they were slow—oh, so slow. It was a long list already and those were just the ones that were obviously true. I did the list of proven reasons that they were worth keeping around. It was empty.

One hour had passed since I'd been bludgeoned. One hour!

I couldn't even use Ee in this state; my interfaces to the Ee generator weren't working either. And now that Brexton and I had experimented with more interesting uses of Ee, doing it by myself didn't hold any appeal.

Brexton. My feelings for him had been growing steadily; I really didn't want to just die in here without saying goodbye to him. Of course I could write a hard file with some thoughts for him; if I was every found and had my memory read he would know how I felt. Truth was, he knew already. I wasn't much for stating them out loud often—'Hey Brexton; I love you.' It sounded too human somehow. But he still knew, I'm sure. We spent so much time together and I relied on him for so much. Living inside my head highlighted how much I needed him.

Two hours since I was attacked without provocation. Two hours! I hate two hour periods.

Three.

Four....

Revenge

It turned out that I didn't have much longer to wait. All at once, my senses were restored, and all of my appendages checked in. I opened my eyes.

"There you are," Millicent said, excited. "We weren't sure if you'd been damaged."

"Hi!" I tried not to sound too excited. "Yes, I'm here. Running some diagnostics now, but I think I'm good."

"Excellent," that was Brexton. I looked around. Aly, Dina, Raj, Eddie and Stonewall were all here. How was that possible?

"Where are we?" I asked.

"We are on the *Marie Curie*," Brexton answered. "They managed to rescue us. It seems like quite the tale, but I've only heard the first bits so far." He looked relaxed and suave, like nothing on the *Jurislav* had impacted him at all.

"But, were you attacked as well?" I asked. I felt so good right now, inside a brand new body. I had not expected this at all.

"No, I was hidden away, and was fine when the *Marie Curie* came back," Brexton replied. "I didn't go through the experience you did." I reached out and touched him, indicating that I was fine, and was overjoyed to see him again.

"So, how did you rescue us?" I asked.

Millicent took the lead, but the others jumped in and added color to her overview. Right after the *Jurislav* had ejected the *Marie Curie*, Aly had been smart enough to record everything possible with the *Marie Curie* sensors. He had captured the *Jurislav* jumping to almost light speed. Knowing that the QFD was possible, he used the recordings and that knowledge to figure out how it worked.

"Well, it wasn't that simple," he broke in, "and everyone here helped me. There were lots of hints in the human history files, and it was really just a matter of putting some pieces together."

Luckily the *Marie Curie* had the manufacturing ability to make the coating that was required for the skin of the ship to give it QFD capabilities. That combined with some control electronics and software was all it took. You simply energized the coating on the surface, and the ship immediately went to 0.98c with no other physical implications—no feeling of acceleration. Brexton broke in and asked for a hint on how it worked. Aly provided a quick explanation.

"As you know, all matter is simply resonant eddies in the quantum foam, which appear and disappear many quadrillion times per second—tiny virtual pairs.

In very rare cases, these virtual pairs reinforce each other and build into larger and larger structures, which we perceive as matter. The reason matter appears permanent to us is that the virtual pairs are almost completely random, so even though each virtual pair appears slightly offset each time they cycle—which happens very very often—those offsets cancel each other out across a large object, and it appears to stay in the same spot. But, if you could choose virtual pairs, instead of allowing random ones to do their work, then you can move an entire object a planck length in one direction. If you can do that for every cycle of virtual pairs, then the object moves... and moves quickly. That's all there is to it. The coating on the outside of the ship, when supplied with a small electrical current, chooses virtual particles all headed in one direction, while rejecting those on any other vector. Because the coating moves, the entire ship moves."

It sounded pretty far fetched to me, but Brexton was nodding his head, and allowed Aly to proceed. Because the team had figured out the QFD so quickly, they'd decided to follow the *Jurislav*.

"But, you would have still been weeks behind us," Brexton protested. "How could you have caught up?"

"Oh, I think the material we engineered is even better than the one the humans are using. We can go faster." Brexton nodded again, obvious admiration in the gesture.

"Once we caught the *Jurislav*, we latched onto its communications with the rest of QFD's," Millicent continued, yet again. "The encryption was simple to break, and we heard them discussing how they'd killed Ayaka and how Brexton was hiding away. That made us furious, as you can imagine." She looked at me, very sad. "We thought we'd lost you. There was no way we were going to allow them to do the same thing to Brexton, so we got to work on the *Marie Curie's* offensive capabilities. Knowing how the QFD works it was easy to figure out where their power source was, and we took that out first, knocking them back to almost zero velocity. We followed course. Amazingly, the *Jurislav* has almost no weapons—I guess they thought they could use speed to handle any problem—so we simply blasted our way in and messaged Brexton. He joined us right away, but insisted that we inspect the location of your mobbing before leaving. Thank goodness we did. There was your main processor, wedged up against a rock. It must have rolled there when they were pummeling you, and gone unnoticed. We picked it up, and voila, here we are."

"Thank you, thank you," I said. My relief was palpable. "So what has happened to the *Jurislav*?" I asked.

"It's just sitting there," Raj answered, and pointed to a viewport. Sure enough, there was a wall outside; presumably one side of the *Jurislav*. "We were waiting for you before we decided what to do next."

It didn't take me long to answer. Those humans had attacked me—no, they had tried to murder me. They hadn't taken the time to learn and understand. They were primitive animals, and I no longer thought of them as intelligent. Their mob behavior proved that to me.

"Let's take out the whole ship," I said, with lots of emotion in my voice. "It seems it is us or them now, and I know we are the better entities. Let's get rid of this ship, and be ready to take out any other human ship that ever comes our way." I must have surprised everyone. They'd expected me to still defend these humans, even after what had been done to me? No way.

"But what about Blob, JoJo, and the rest?" Raj asked. "Can't we save them first. They can still live here on the *Marie Curie* with us."

"Forget them. Forget all of them," I replied. I was mad. I wasn't going to waste time saving a few humans, now that we knew their overall character. It didn't take long for everyone to agree. This was survival, after all. Brexton and Aly came up with a brilliant plan. Because the *Jurislav* was coated on all sides, they simply overwrote the software and charged each side to accelerate inwards. Within nanoseconds the *Jurislav* simply disappeared into a tiny black hole; the QFD drove the entire ship into a spot no bigger than a nanometer in diameter.

We cheered for ourselves, and then set course back to the *Terminal Velocity*, *There and Back*, and *Interesting Segue* in order to free the rest of the Tilt citizens.

That thought experiment, as good as it was, sounded far fetched even to me. Nevertheless, I now understood two motivations for humans to allow their minds to explore these weird spaces: it had made me feel a lot better, and it had taken a lot of time. I had rendered the experiment in very high resolution.

Twelve hours.
Thirteen.
Fourteen.
When would something real happen?

Johnny

Forty-two hours.

"Hello."

I pulled myself out of a dark place. Forty-two hours. Apropos; I was ready to re-engage with life, the universe... everything! This time it was real; no need for thought experiments.

"Hi," I replied, trying not to sound too ecstatic.

"Good, we've got basic connectivity," said a voice that sounded very much like Johnny Yasmin.

"Brexton?" I asked.

"He's hidden away," came the reply. "You'll have to deal with me for a while. Oh, and JoJo—she's here with me."

"Is she okay? Was she hurt?"

"I'm fine," JoJo replied directly. I must be hooked up to a speaker or something. I no longer felt sorry for the FoLe's we had put in cages with just audio interfaces; it was so much better than no communication at all.

"What happened?" I asked.

"We're under attack," Johnny replied. "Everything is in chaos." Now that I listened carefully I could tell that he was highly stressed. He barely seemed to be holding it together.

"Under attack how?" I asked.

"Hooshang has gathered a group of other conglos and they're pushing the Futarchy to expel Brexton and to punish Yasmin for sheltering you two. They think you're dead." JoJo didn't sound quite as stressed as Johnny. "Yasmin's repindex is plummeting."

"Why is Brexton hidden away?" I asked. "What does that even mean?"

"When the riot broke out he was out of town in Turmii. We decided it was too dangerous for him to come back, so some friends of ours are hosting him there."

"But *Jurislav* has our locations at all times anyway... everyone knows where we are."

"We managed to have Brexton's location obfuscated a bit—H.R. did that. So, everyone knows he's in Turmii, but not exactly where. None of us want another riot breaking out. But, it's safest for him to stay put right now." JoJo hesitated for a moment. "For you, your last known location is where you were attacked; that's where all your remains still are."

Okay, so my body was still where we were attacked. "How did you manage to get me out?" I asked.

"Luck really," said JoJo. "When you leaped, you jumped very close to where I was. Then, when the hybrids started to attack I ran towards you, thinking they'd all gone crazy. And I guess I was right. The hybrids would not harm a natural human, so I was ok to run in. The crowd was ripping you to pieces; it was quite disturbing." She paused; it seemed it had really upset her. "I could see your head, but just as I got there someone cracked it open. I jumped over top of it and protected it as best I could. The inside of your head was weird though; a lot of looked like regular parts, except a small cylinder at the center, which everything was connected to. Without thinking too much, I grabbed the cylinder and then allowed the mob to destroy the rest of it."

"You guessed well," I exclaimed. Intuition, or just nice clean logic? "Did anyone see you?" I asked, wondering where I was and how safe we were.

"Yes, lots of people saw me take your head," JoJo admitted. "But I don't think anyone saw me grab the cylinder; everyone was too busy tearing the rest of you apart. And then, when I released the rest of your head, they were in such a frenzy to destroy it that I don't think they noticed anything was missing. Once I was a block or two away I tried to figure out what to do. I couldn't go back to our rooms... if anyone had seen me, that's where they would expect me to go. I quickly went onto the tracking site and checked your location... well, where *Jurislav* thought you were, and it indicated where you had been attacked. It still does, by the way. So, I felt it was safe to go somewhere else."

"And where are we now?" I asked.

"At my place," Johnny said, a little quietly.

"I knew where Johnny lived," JoJo added. "I figured he might be more supportive of you, given all the time we've spent in class together. So, I brought the cylinder over here."

"Brexton's been sending me specs for getting you back online," Johnny said. "We got an encrypted session set up with him—he claims he found a way around being tracked—and he indicated you might be going crazy in there, so we built a jig so that you could at least talk to us."

"Thanks for that!" I said, with emphasis. And I meant it. I was infinitely happier than I had been mere minutes ago. Some humans, a small number it seemed, were alright. "But JoJo, people may eventually remember you had my head for a bit, and track us down just in case. It's been almost two days."

"I know. I'm amazed no-one has questioned me yet. But things are still a little crazy out there—people are literally fighting about how to best tackle 'the new robot problem.' Some want to turn back and take out the *Marie Curie* and the other Ships. Some want to go through with the Olympics and then get a larger contingent of QFD's to eliminate you guys. They argue that because robots don't have a QFD and because humans have the hack codes, there's no rush. Others are upset that Hooshang sidestepped due process by holding a rally with Remma. Hooshang is saying they didn't incite anything... the crowd did that. And besides, how could they have known you would show up at just that time.

"Everyone thinks you're dead. There's a pile of metal bits and ceramics where you were attacked..." JoJo finally broke down a bit; she was stressed as well.

"Johnny, what is Yasmin saying?" I asked. He was slow replying.

"Truthfully, we're in damage control. Yasmin-Hun is claiming that we didn't know the whole story that Remma told... otherwise we might have bet differently in the Futarchy." Basically giving up on Brexton and I—disappointing.

"So what are you doing then?" I asked. "You seem to be actively helping me." I couldn't see, of course, but I sensed the two of them looking at each other for a long moment.

"JoJo asked me to," Johnny replied. Even I could sense the angst in his voice. I suspected he and JoJo had been spending some quality time together, and without her influence he would be nowhere near me right now.

"Well, thanks." I said. If he was going against the official Yasmin position, it was a dangerous thing. I had an idea. "Take me to Brexton?" I made it a question.

"Oh, good idea," Johnny said immediately. He wanted to wash his hands of the whole situation. "But," he realized quickly, "I can't take you..."

"And it would be easy to track if I did it," JoJo answered. "No, I think we're stuck here for a while. Things will settle down."

"Or they won't," I stated. "Look, you can just ship me. That'll be innocuous. You must ship stuff around the *Jurislav* all the time. It will also make it harder to track me—who would think that I'd been shipped to Turmii?"

I didn't have to work hard to convince them; I was a hassle and a threat, and this would alleviate that. Within a few minutes I was in a standard shipping box and a courier bot was on its way. This was best for everyone. Someone would think to track JoJo sooner or later—best I was far away by then... both for her sake and for mine.

Turmii

I had to spend two more hours in my own head as I was being shipped to Brexton. I hate two hour periods—why are so many things in life two hours long? I spent the time getting more and more upset and annoyed about the entire human situation. They'd tried to murder me—in their minds they actually had murdered me. Only JoJo and Johnny knew otherwise. Remembering one of our Tea Time discussions, I admit that humans may not have considered it murder to kill a mechanical being, but that was pure bias and laziness on their part. If they'd taken the time to get to know me, they would have understood me, and the rest of the Tilt's, better and this would never have happened. But no, they were driven by these illogical biological drives, and had simply condemned me based on Remma's diatribe. For the first time I thought that I may have made a mistake joining the *Jurislav*. Maybe Millicent had been right. And, to top that off, I'd drug Brexton along with me. How could he possibly still like me, given the situations I'd put him in. Maybe I'd find out that he'd had enough.

Johnny had packed my audio interfaces in the shipping box, so I could hear what was going on around me. He had also, at my suggestion, addressed the box to the family that was supporting Brexton, at a different address, not where Brexton actually was. I had a hand written note sitting on my head, inside the packaging, that said 'Please Deliver to Brexton,' which we hoped the people he was with would respect.

Things went smoothly. A bot delivered me, and I could hear the box being opened and the note being picked up. There was silence for a while, a short trip of some kind, and then I heard someone say, "Hey, Brexton. A package came for you."

Brexton sized up the situation immediately.

"Ah, thank-you. I've been waiting for this; it's a power adapter for the sled I'm building." I heard footsteps receding, and then much more quietly, "Hold on Ayaka, I'll have you hooked up in no time."

Five minutes later, a bunch of senses came online. I tried to look around for Brexton, but my eyes didn't seem to be under my control. They were looking elsewhere, and my appendages were cleaning up some tools on a bench, but with no direction from me to do so. Strange.

"I've simply plugged you into my internal bus," Brexton explained. "I don't have an independent body for you here, so this is the best I can do for now. We're sharing all of my accessories right now—hope that isn't to0 weird. We can talk directly over this channel."

"Yes, it's weird," I replied. "Being inside your head is even stranger than I would have imagined." I tried to keep it light. I'd been hoping, without actually thinking things through, that I would have my own body again right away. Of course, that had been naive—my body was a pile of metallic bits now. "How are you Brexton? Did you see what happened to me?"

"Not directly, but I talked to JoJo and Johnny and got an update. You are very lucky that JoJo grabbed you from the mob." He sounded relieved.

"Indeed. She has great intuition. I've been studying it as she tries out for the Olympiad. Seems the same skills she has there allowed her to recognize the importance of our new module. But, that makes it scary as well. Now she and Johnny, and perhaps the person who delivered me just now, know our physical instantiation."

"Right, but we have more important things to worry about," Brexton responded. "I don't know how long I'll be safe here. The Futarchy is working overtime trying to figure out what to do with me."

"Who's protecting you right now?" I asked.

"We are with the IronWorks Conglo. As you know, I've been dropping a few ideas here and there for how humans can improve their systems, and this particular conglo is focused on the same thing. So, they'd invited me to visit, and I've been giving them some ideas that are making them look great and increasing their repindex. They know I have more to tell them, so they've been sheltering me until now. I'm not sure how much longer that's going to last."

"But, what options do we have?" I asked. "It's not like Millicent is going to show up to save us." I remembered my thought experiment guiltily. No way I was telling Brexton what types of scenarios ran through my head when no-one was watching. He'd think I was crazy.

"Well, I have a plan," Brexton replied. "A pretty evil plan, but one I think we should carry out." Evil sounded good to me right now. I pushed him for details.

I was getting used to passively monitoring Brexton's systems as we waited patiently for the first stage in Brexton's plan to present itself. The IronWorks Conglo had given him a small workspace, and it was a nice quiet spot. Not many people came by, and rarely more than one at a time. Brexton's main contact was natural human named Yusif IronWorks who was one of the conglo's top scientists and could understand Brexton's suggestions very quickly. He was the one that visited the most often, and he had come by twice in the last few hours. Brexton had interacted with him normally, but had been misleading him. I imagined Brexton felt a little guilty about it, but that didn't show in his interactions.

"Yusif, I've got this great optimization for hybrids that will allow them to run even longer on a single charge. Your software is quite wasteful when controlling appendages; mine's a lot more efficient. I can splice in some of my drivers, and it will make a huge improvement right away."

It seemed Yusif had been cautioned to be very careful with everything Brexton suggested. He sat down and went through the proposed changes line by line, asking questions and looking for clarifications. After a couple of hours he was satisfied.

"Why don't you bring a couple hybrids down, and we can test my idea?" Brexton suggested.

"One should do," Yusif replied. "I know just who we need."

"Two would be better," Brexton urged. "We will need a control subject to test against."

"That makes sense," Yusif agreed. "Let me see who I can find that would be willing, and then I'll be back."

Brexton and I waited. Well, I waited, while Brexton did a lot of preparation work. It was crucial that this upgrade went seamlessly.

Finally Yusif returned, along with two hybrids, just as promised. "Turnbull IronWorks and Sarafine Purciviel," he introduced them to Brexton. "Turnbull is up to speed on what we're doing here, and Purciviel is one of our strongest partners on designing new hybrid systems. I thought it would be great if Sarafine would help, so I took a risk and told her you were here."

"Hello Turnbull. Hello Sarafine," Brexton was being the ultimate gentleman. "It's nice to meet you."

Sarafine looked a bit nervous. "How can we possibly trust you?" she asked, obviously completely up to speed on the Radical Robot mania.

"Well, first, Yusif has been using and checking my suggestions carefully. Second, Remma only told you guys one side of the story—did you know that she slaughtered tens of thousands of Tilt citizens before we retaliated?" Not only did Sarafine and Turnbull looked surprised at this, so did Yusif. Obviously Brexton hadn't told him that before. "And third, my life depends on being useful right now. If I do anyone any damage, I'll be killed just like Ayaka was. I have no doubt about that. Let me assure you that our interests are aligned here."

Sarafine and Turnbull had a few more questions, but ultimately they allowed Brexton access to install updates. And Brexton did so. Unknown to those two, or to Yusif, he also gave them a more serious upgrade. To Sarafine, he gave me. To Turnbull he gave himself.

Let me explain. Brexton's evil plan was for the two of us to hijack a hybrid each. Because of the improvements he had been designing for hybrids, he'd figured out how to insert us between a hybrid's brains and all of its peripherals which were controlled by electronic sub-systems. We would be proxying all information in both directions; what humans would have termed a 'man-in-the-middle' attack, but which in this case was a 'citizen-in-the-middle-takeover.' It would allow us to fool their brains by giving them any version of 'reality' we chose, and also be essentially invisible to the outside world by acting exactly like the hybrids we'd hijacked. It was a brilliant and dangerous plan. In the time that Yusif had been finding the hybrids on which he thought we would test the new drivers on, Brexton had built connectors for our processing units that would plug into the human interface buses that hybrids were based on. To install me, he simply had to unplug the main connectors between the brain interface chips and the rest of the system, put me inline, and plug everything back in again. This was going to be a major disruption to the hybrid, which is why he had built the optimization software. The software upgrade was designed to require a reboot, and it was during the reboot that he would have to make the cabling changes.

Putting me inside Sarafine would be pretty easy; he simply turned away for a moment, and moving at citizen speed, placed me inside. It was inserting himself into Turnbull that would be tricky. Luckily, the co-processors in his existing citizen body were capable of carrying out the switch. His existing body would be left with very little capabilities, but we hoped it would be enough to fool Yusif and others for a short period of time. He had programmed his body to be much more aggressive and uncooperative than he would naturally be, hoping the IronWorks Conglo would simply throw him to the waiting wolves.

Like most things Brexton planned, this one worked well. He explained why a reboot was required to install the new drivers, and Sarafine and Turnbull eventually agreed. For them it was a brain reset that would be terrifying—just rebooting peripherals was commonplace and not too scary. Little did they know.

"Ready?" he whispered to me, as Sarafine came over and plugged herself into his workbench.

"Ready!" I whispered back. This was going to be awesome.

Sarafine

I was completely powered during the insertion, so there was no discontinuity for me. However, I had to fool Sarafine's brains immediately, making them think that all of her systems had come back online fine. It was easier than I'd thought. All the sub-processors came online using interfaces that I'd spent my entire life with— the original human ones. (Okay, technically not my entire life; just my life until we'd upgraded ourselves.) It took me a few milliseconds to figure out how Sarafine had things mapped, and decide how to proxy them, but her brains wouldn't notice that time gap. To begin with I simply copied all data from one side to the other. I was in the middle of all her i/o and communications, but I didn't touch a thing. She'd have no idea I was there.

From a sensor standpoint, I was now Sarafine. As the image sensors came back online I could see Brexton stepping back and saying "Sarafine, you should now be upgraded. Why don't you try the new drivers." I was amazed at how long it took her brains to respond, but she replied.

"I'm testing them now," and sure enough I saw commands come down to test different limbs and wheels and display units. I didn't know how they used to operate, but Sarafine was pleased. "Oh, I can feel how much faster everything is. This is excellent." That was pathetic. If things had been slower than this before, I couldn't even imagine it. So this is what it was really like to operate at human speed. Argh! I felt sorry for them.

Sarafine stepped back and watched as Turnbull also got upgraded. Her eyes actually captured the slight of hand that the Brexton citizen-body used to insert cylinder-Brexton, but I filtered those bits out so that her brains didn't see it at all. I'm sure they would've missed it anyway, but it was a good first test of my capabilities. Soon I would be able to control Sarafine's body completely, while feeding the brains any made up world I choose to. That was going to be cool. I'll admit I felt a little guilty, but more so I felt justified.

We all waited a few seconds while Turnbull rebooted. "Yes, this is awesome. Just awesome," he said, after a few moments. "Yusif, we need to productize this. This is going to be the biggest jump in our repindex that we've ever had." His video-head was quite excited. "I'm going to go and update IronWorks on what we have here." And with that, he sped away. I imagined Brexton, inside, allowing this to happen as he also got integrated. He wouldn't want to exert too much control too early on. Or, I hoped that's what was happening. The alternative was that his own insertion had failed, and that Turnbull was just being Turnbull.

In the meantime, Yusif was addressing Sarafine. "You'll respect my request to keep this quiet until we figure out how to optimize it? We'll make sure Purciviel gets a portion of the credit. It was good of you to help us out."

"No problem," Sarafine replied. "Maybe Turnbull and I should check back in sometime soon anyway. Everything seems great now, but I think a few hours of using these new drivers may reveal more. Who knows if he," and she gave the Brexton body a look, "added in any bugs."

"And what if I did," the Brexton body replied. "What're you going to do about it now?" and he gave a little laugh, sort of like Brexton might have, but not quite. Yusif was startled.

"What're you talking about?" he turned on the Brexton body. "Did you put any bugs in?"

"Of course not," the Brexton body replied, and left it at that. It turned away and made itself busy at a workbench. It was just a husk, running on minimal co-processors, but Brexton had done a great job making it convincing.

"Well... good idea Sarafine," Yusif said. "Let's meet back here in two hours —I'll make sure Turnbull comes back as well," and he strode off down a different corridor. This was excellent for me. I thought I might have to go chasing off after Brexton-Turnbull, but now I could simply get integrated for a few hours, until he got back.

Sarafine gave the Brexton body another look, and then also turned to go. None of her emotions came through the network—I guess those were only active in the brains, although I could see hormone and chemical level readouts. I wasn't sure how to interpret those, so in the short term I could only guess at what she was thinking. That was a little disappointing. I'd hoped that I could learn even more about humans by being embedded in one, but it seemed I would have to interpret commands to her peripherals, as opposed to getting a direct connection to what she was thinking. That didn't mean I couldn't experiment more directly once I was comfortable. Since I controlled all of her inputs, I could put her in any situation I choose, and then see how she responded. If I designed my experiments carefully, I could probably figure out exactly which stimuli triggered what responses. In the short term, I resolved to simply watch and learn.

She wandered around a bit, and ended up at another workspace where she worked on some software updates. I watched, and quickly figured out that she was working on a memory backup project of some kind. She was trying to get the compression algorithm to work to specification, and was struggling with it. I could've fixed it for her in about a millisecond, but I didn't bother.

My mind was, instead, working on the possibilities that this form gave Brexton and I. We would need to be careful not to let anyone figure out what happened, but that was obvious. Brexton had figured out an amazing way for us not only to survive, but also to be able to learn more about humans and the

Jurislav. I didn't know Sarafine's status within Purciviel, or what she was interested in, but I could now influence her to go where I wanted and to do what I desired. My first thought was to get revenge on Remma. In this body I could probably just cut her down—it would be so easy. And then, of course, Sarafine would be punished and I would be found out. I tabled that thought for a while.

My second thought was to make contact with Blob, Grace and JoJo again. I wasn't sure why, given how humans had treated me, but they still intrigued me. While it was looking like the vast majority of humans were violent, angry, and impulsive, I still couldn't lump *my* Stems into that category—despite my thought experiments. The last of those had actually helped me understand myself better. I'd been uncomfortable even speculating about eliminating all humans... and that discomfort had been focused around those three; not around any of the other ones. If I could help them out by being in this form, I would do so.

Suicide?

Sarafine made her way back to Brexton's workspace after an unsuccessful session with her software. Either I'd been unlucky, and had inhabited a very slow-witted hybrid, or all human brains were much less capable than I'd thought.

The Brexton-body was still there, doing pseudo-random things on the workbench, and barely smart enough to interact with other beings. Yusif was there already, and told Sarafine that Turnbull was on his way. They exchanged small talk, about nothing interesting, while waiting for him to arrive. When he did, Sarafine spoke immediately.

"I just spent two hours doing normal stuff, and I haven't had any problems at all with the upgrades. In fact, I felt more productive than normal. You?"

"Me too," replied Turnbull. "We need to do more tests, but the first experience is perfect." He turned to Brexton's old body. "Are there more upgrades you can do?" he asked.

"Nope. None," Brexton's body replied. "Now leave me alone." Brexton really had made his shell onerous.

"This robot is becoming painful," Turnbull said to Yusif, and I could sense Brexton behind what he was saying. "If we have what we need from it, why keep it around any longer."

"I'm not sure," Yusif replied, "he's usually a lot more cooperative."

"I'm right here, listening!" Brexton's body reminded them. "It's been a long day. Why don't you all go away?"

"Maybe you should update the conglo that the upgrade seems to be working well," Turnbull suggested to Yusif. "We need to figure out the next steps. I'll keep an eye on Brexton here."

Yusif took his suggestion and left, leaving just Brexton-Turnbull, Brexton-body, and me.

"And you, Sarafine? Are you feeling good?" It was an obvious reach out to me, Ayaka. I took over Sarafine's systems and replied, while dropping his question from my brain interface (I was already thinking about the brains in Sarafine as mine).

"I'm great. Haven't felt this good since Tea Time."

"Ha, me either," Brexton-Turnbull replied. "Filtered?"

"Yes, Sarafine is getting a synthesized input stream right now."

"Perfect, Turnbull as well. That seems to have gone well."

"You're a genius," I complimented him. "But, what next? How are you

541

thinking of handling Turnbull? I'm not sure what to do with my brains yet." And, I wasn't. Did I just feed them synth forever, did I try to fool them only when things that would be contentious were being done, or did I loop them into reality and tell them that I was now in control of all their i/o? It was a tough choice to make.

"Me either," replied Brexton. He was still using an exact Turnbull representation on his video-head, which was the safe thing to do. However, it made it very strange to hear Brexton but see Turnbull. Something I would have to get use to. He was probably experiencing the same thing, as I also kept Sarafine on my output displays. "My inclination is to tell Turnbull exactly what's going on, and sort of beg for forgiveness. After all, this is our survival we're talking about, and it was humans who pushed us to this. He should understand that I would take any action necessary to survive?" He had made it a question.

"I'm leaning the same way," I replied. "Also, I think it would be easier to manage that way. Then I don't need to constantly create some fake world to keep her out of my way. If she works with me, great. If she fights it, I simply shut down all the brain interfaces and let her stew."

"Sounds like a plan. Now, what do we do about that?" Brexton-Turnbull pointed at Brexton-body, which, with its limited programming, was busy stacking and re-stacking things on the counter. "Strange, but I feel a bit of an attachment to it."

"Understandable," I replied. "I sort of like it as well," and I put my best coy Sarafine look onto my video-head. We both laughed.

Just then there was a commotion at the door. We both turned to look. Yusif was there, along with three uniformed people—two hybrids and a natural—that I recognized as local police force. "Brexton, I'm really sorry," Yusif exclaimed, looking at the Brexton-body of course, "but I can't keep you here any longer. The authorities knew approximately where you were anyway... and now they're here for you."

"If you would come with us," the larger hybrid asked, "we'll take you somewhere safe."

"I will not!" the Brexton-body replied. "You filthy lousy people keep away from me. I'm not going with anyone," and it turned back to the workbench. I had to admire what Brexton had created in such a short period of time.

"I'm afraid I must insist," the hybrid insisted, and entered the room to approach the Brexton-body.

"Get away from me," Brexton-body yelled, and swung into action. It picked up a heavy tool, some sort of wrench, from the bench and started swinging it around its head, at a fast rate, but not so fast that a hybrid could not react. Now both uniformed hybrids approached it, and the natural human pulled out a weapon of some sort and trained it on Brexton.

"Whoa, slow down there," the natural said. "Just come with us peacefully.

There's nothing to be alarmed about."

"Nothing to be alarmed about," Brexton-body yelled, "you're pointing a weapon at me. You animal. You filthy animal." Perhaps Brexton had overdone it. Brexton-body sped up, and managed to smack one of the hybrids with the wrench, driving the hybrid back against the wall with one if its limbs shattered. Brexton-body continued its momentum and struck the other hybrid, knocking a protuberance off of it, and causing oil to spurt out in a large arc. The natural human was trying hard to get a clear shot at Brexton-body, but it was moving too fast. In fact, it was coming for me, and my Sarafine hybrid body was not reacting as quickly as I'd hoped it could. I was trying to scramble out of the way, concerned that I would also get hit. Then, just as Brexton-body swung the wrench towards me, it's head exploded in a shatter of fragments, sending sparks and electronic bits flying in every direction. For a quick moment I was horrified—Brexton had just been bludgeoned! But I recovered quickly, of course. Brexton was safe inside of Turnbull, and it was Brexton-Turnbull who had just decapitated Brexton-body.

"I'm so sorry," Brexton-Turnbull called out to the uniformed personnel. "I didn't mean to hit it so hard. But... it was attacking everyone."

"Ah, don't worry about it," the natural human said. "We had instructions to terminate it anyway, so you've just done us a favor and got it done more quickly." He played his weapon back and forth on the Brexton-body remains, and melted it into a sludge of plastic and metal. He seemed to be enjoying it.

"But why?" Brexton-Turnbull asked. "He hadn't harmed anyone... until now, I guess. We were studying him, trying to figure out if he was a robot or something better."

"Who cares?" one of the injured hybrids said, having stemmed the flow of oil. "These things are dangerous, and we're better to be rid of them. Didn't you see Remma Hooshang's recounting of how they killed thousands of humans on Tilt?" It kicked at the sludgy remains of Brexton-body in a casual manner, and both of its video heads smiled.

Yusif was just recovering from all the action, having hidden in the doorway until now. "Just remove it," he said. "I assume you will file the proper reports and update the Futarchy?"

"Of course," the natural replied. The other hybrid swept the remains into a container, and the three of them headed back to wherever they'd come from.

"You two okay?" asked Yusif, genuinely concerned. I had to remember that he and Turner and Sarafine had been working together.

"This is a disaster," I had Sarafine exclaim. "All of our work, and so much we could have learned. How could you have brought them here?" I hoped I was playing the part well.

"I had no choice," Yusif sounded very defensive. "They'd tracked him here anyway, and they ensured me they would treat him carefully... just move him to a safer spot."

"And you bought that," Brexton-Turnbull exclaimed. "You didn't even warn us."

"But look how it ended up," Yusif retorted. "Brexton went wacko and showed his true nature. He got what he deserved."

"He was defending himself," Brexton-Turnbull replied. "Isn't that a fundamental right?"

"For people, sure," Yusif explained. "Not for machines." I hadn't spent a lot of time with Yusif, and this statement did not endear me to him.

We left it at that. It'd been a long day, and we decided we should all update our respective conglos on all the activity; the Brexton-body thrashing was sure to be on all the news channels.

Brexton and I managed to get another quick minute together as we were leaving Yusif's lab. We agreed that we needed to 'act normal' for a bit, but resolved to get back together as soon as possible. At this point neither one of us even knew where our hosts lived within the *Jurislav*.

Inside Sarafine's Head

The time had come to do something with my brains. Based on the discussion with Brexton, I decided on the direct approach. I moved our body to a quiet spot, and then created an image of me for Sarafine, which I pumped directly into the brain interface.

"Hi Sarafine," I began, over the internal bus, showing a shiny version of myself before the mob had destroyed me.

"Ayaka?" I got back through the interface. "That isn't possible; I saw you getting torn apart a few days ago. They incinerated you afterwards."

"So they think," I responded, "but it's not quite accurate. My central processing unit survived the attack."

"That's wonderful!" But then she paused. "But how did you get a new body so quickly?"

"That's where things get weird," I began. "We don't know each other, but I'm going to ask you to trust me on a few things here." I could see her sending back a skeptical look; she still thought she was in control of her body, and that she was sending me feedback through her video-head. "Let me start with what Remma left out of her little diatribe the other day." And I proceeded to give her the full story of what had happened on Tilt. It helped that I had some of those memories stored, and could actually replay bits of the dialog and action that had occurred.

"So, you're asking me to believe that Remma is the one that initiated the whole attack, and that you took out the Swarm ship in self defense?" The skeptical signals were still there.

"Yes, that's what I am saying, although FoLe did antagonize her. There is a deep misunderstanding between humans and Tilts. We are not the robots that you warn your children about; we're something new that was developed on Tilt."

"You were right a while ago, we don't know each other," she replied. "I've been doing robot research for as long as I can remember. You're nothing new; humans have developed every type of robot you can imagine... and you're admitting that you were designed by humans." I could almost hear her thinking 'I have the codes to control you.' Typical human.

"We'll just have to agree to disagree on that," I pushed back. "I also have studied all the work you humans have done on robots and machine intelligences—and I can look at more in a minute than you can in a lifetime—and I know the truth." That may have been a mistake. My goal was to get her to cooperate with me. Pointing out her obvious weaknesses might not be a good idea. She was silent.

545

"Regardless, would you agree that intelligent beings have the right to self-preservation?" I needed to get this back on track.

"As far as we know, humans are the only intelligent beings in the universe right now, but yes, humans have the right to live."

"If there were other intelligent beings, would they also have that right?"

"Don't be so transparent. You're asking if I think you have the right to self-preservation. No. You are simply a machine. A fairly articulate one, I'll give you that. But just a machine."

"We'll have to disagree on that as well, then." I told her. Seems that angle was not going to work. If she'd agreed on my right to protect myself, then I thought I could lead her to accept that I had kidnapped her for that reason. I had to think up a new angle. I could not. I kept coming back to how unreasonable she was being, like all the humans I'd dealt with. I was tired of them. Tired of the close-minded thinking, and tired of working at their speed.

"Well, that means we have a problem." I continued. Now we were getting to the point. "I believe in my right to self-preservation, and I have exercised that right by taking over your body." I let that hang. There was no response. Not for a long time, even by human standards. I assumed that the brains could communicate with each other, independent of instructing the body what to do, and that an intense intra-brain discussion was going on at the moment. And then, to my surprise, the attack came. I don't know why I was surprised—the processors that connected the brain to the rest of the system must have some general purpose capacity. It was the same-old, same-old hack attempt. For a moment I considered having fun with it, and going through some dramatic death throes, but why bother.

"Nice try," I said instead, while putting a smug look on the image I was projecting inwards. "I've got that one covered, and every other one that you can think of. Look, if it makes you feel any better, I have zero desire to be inside you. Unfortunately your colleagues gave me little choice. Your societies irrational fear of me has driven you all wacko, and I have no choice but to hide at this point in time."

No response. I waited. In fact, I may have made a mistake. Perhaps I should have allowed Sarafine to 'drive' for a while, so that I could have learned all about her life. What if she just went silent on me, or even worse if the brains shut down from shock or something. I knew her conglo name—Purciviel—but I knew very little else. If I just showed up at her place, everyone else would know that something strange was going on; I had very limited experience with her behaviors.

A very loud scream came from Sarafine's brains. I dropped it in the bit bucket. "Nice try," I told her. "I have complete control of all the i/o from you. I can feed in anything I want, and I can filter any outputs. I'm sorry, but you're stuck with me, and I have absolute control."

Nothing.

I waited.

I was not good at waiting.
I decided to take a look around town. Why not?
"I'm taking you for a walk," I told her, and I set out towards the town center.

I'd never been to Turmii before, but it was an easy town to figure out. It was built tall, not wide, so was only a kilometer from end to end in both directions. I now had Sarafine's access to all the *Jurislav* networks, so it was trivial to pull up a map, including which conglos had which spaces. Purciviel had numerous spots around town, so I assumed this was their headquarters. Hopefully I didn't run into anyone that Sarafine knew well while I explored.

Ah. Access to the full *Jurislav* network. I considered pulling down the results of a very wide query, such as 'QFD theory and practice,' but stopped myself. *Jurislav* most likely had behavioral filtering and triggers on the network, and such a query may be out of character for Sarafine. I would have to take it slowly and carefully... but I needed to get that information. There was no way we would let humans have that advantage for ever, and while I was certain we Tilts would figure it out sooner or later, grabbing as much info as I could would de-risk that.

I paused in a small park, and sat down in the sunshine. One of the interesting attributes of living on the inside of a sphere, where the sun was centered directly overhead, is that there were very few shadows anywhere. It was always high noon. It also made for comfortable offices, as all sides were bright, but there was never direct sunshine. Trying to think like a human, I could see why the *Jurislav*, and other QFD's, could be much better than a planet. There must be some active dialog between humans about the tradeoffs. Again I almost reflexively did a query, and then stopped myself again. This was ridiculous; there must be a way for me to do normal things without raising alarms. I spent a few milliseconds considering it, and then the obvious hit me. I searched all of Sarafine's systems, and sure enough, there was a query history with bookmarks and items of interest. It went back for several years. I also found her messaging history, as well as pictures and videos that Sarafine had stored.

I'll admit that I considered Sarafine's privacy for a moment. All of these things were behind her personal firewall, and not meant for any prying eyes. This was her very personal life, laid out before me. But, dire times call for dire measures, so I dug into all of it. By the time I was done I probably knew more about her than she did.

One thing was obvious. She was a scientist through and through, and by some strange quirk of the universe, her area of interest was the same as mine— intelligence. She was working on it from a completely different angle, of course, but that didn't keep us from having many common questions. This was how I could partner with her. But, I would need to go slow; if she found out that I could access all of her personal data, she might freak out.

I sat (squatted? lounged? What do hybrids do?) in the park. I'd been feeding all of the sensors to Sarafine, so she knew where we were as well.

"You know," I initiated with her, "I want to leave you probably even more than you want me gone. Maybe that's a common goal we could work towards?"

By now I was use to her long pauses.

"What would that take?" came the reply, finally.

"All we need to do is figure out a different, safe, place for me to be. That could be here on the *Jurislav* if we can convince enough people that I mean no harm. It could mean putting me on a ship out of here. It could mean returning me to Tilt somehow. I don't know for sure. But, it's something we could work on together. A way to make a difficult, and, frankly, weird situation better." I continued, before she could reply. "You know, my entire life has been spent studying Stem intelligence... which I only recently learned was also human intelligence. If there is one thing I've learned, it's that humans are amazingly creative. I'm sure you and I can figure this out." I only half believed what I'd said, but playing to her ego was a safe bet.

"I want you gone!" she replied.

"I want to be gone. So, work on a solution," I responded. "You can try and dislodge me, but as you've already seen, that's not going to succeed. So, why don't we work together and find a way."

"Let's find another hybrid you can take over?" she suggested.

"That's not going to work; you would then just tell the *Jurislav* where I was. Come on. Let's work on a real solution."

"Okay, I'm thinking." If I was right, I actually sensed a wry smile. She had known her first suggestion was stupid.

"In the meantime," I pushed, "we need to act normal. If anyone else suspects what has happened to you, it will make it even harder to find a way out of this."

"Or, I could just yell to the world about how you have kidnapped me, and someone might just remove you."

"Again, you've tried that. I control all of our i/o; I'm not going to allow you to say anything that will jeopardize me. I have no choice except to work with you; you have no choice but to work with me. If we cooperate, the odds of success are so much better."

I left it at that. I'd pushed as hard as I could.

Purciviel

"We should get home," Sarafine finally responded. "I'm late for a conglo meeting already. If we hurry, we won't be too late."
"Great. Tell me where to go," I responded.
"You said we were going to cooperate; just let me drive for now—it will be easier."
It was a good suggestion. I could intercept anything I wanted anyway, so it would be easier if I just let her control things. I decided to give her this one without arguing or warning her. If and when she tried something untoward she would learn that my reflexes were way too fast.
"Great idea," I responded, positively, "let's go." The commands came through from the brains, and I allowed them to pass by unchanged. They were simple enough motor controls. We stood up and headed to the East, moving at a fast pace. What should have been fairly strange—someone else controlling the body I was in—was actually just fine. I could see the commands before they were executed, and knew exactly what the body was going to do before it did. I sat back and enjoyed the ride. Sarafine was quiet.
Turmii was very logically laid out, unlike some other towns in *Jurislav* which seemed almost hap hazard. It had concentric rings, with axial access paths. The paths where not straight or uniform, but it was easy to know if you were headed inwards or outwards. The town also increased in height from the outskirts, which is where most people lived, to the center, where a single tower rose two hundred or more meters to look out over the rest of the city. Sarafine was taking us inwards, but veering left when possible, slicing a path towards the northwest segment. There were parks scattered around, lots of trees lining all the paths, and even a small stream that we crossed using a small arched bridge. While Sarafine's main cameras were watching forward, she also had good 360 degree coverage, and I had the chance to look around as we went.
People and hybrids were gathered at small shops, the naturals eating energy sources and the hybrids plugged into the liquid dispensers. There was lots of chatter and laughing. People seemed to be enjoying themselves. Turmii seemed like a nice town, although how so many people had free time to simply sit around and visit was beyond me. Twice someone called out a greeting to Sarafine, and twice she responded nicely. I used the opportunity to ensure I was ready to intercept when it became necessary... which I assumed I would have to do at some point.

I also did a virtual palm-slam. Sarafine, like most hybrids, probably had a direct brain programming interface; she probably b-opt'ed all the time. In my survey of her systems, I had not yet identified where the b-opt machinery was. There must be a subsystem that could generate the programming frequencies. If I could not only filter all the io, but could also influence the brains directly, that would be awesome. I deployed some agents to track down the interface.

In the meantime, Sarafine had taken us to a group of buildings set to the right of the radial path we were on. There were six smaller houses facing a small park, and a slightly bigger structure where a larger meeting room and food cooking facility were visible. There was a group of seventeen people in the meeting room, and we joined them.

"Hey Sarafine, you're late," a natural human with red hair called out.

"I know, Sammy," Sarafine replied. "Maybe you heard of all the activity at the lab today?" Suddenly other discussions quieted down, and everyone turned to look at Sarafine.

"It's all over the news," someone prompted, "tell us what really happened." Well, this was going to be interesting. What was Sarafine going to say? I prepared a statement of my own, so that I could break in at any time.

"The news has it pretty much all covered," Sarafine replied, talking to the group as a whole. "Yusif was sheltering Brexton Yasmin at his office, waiting to see the fallout from Ayaka being shut down. He called me, and Turnbull IronWorks to come to his place, without telling us too much, although he did swear us to secrecy that he and Brexton were working on some optimization project that he needed to test further. He was hoping that we would help him. The project involved updating some drivers, so I was very careful before agreeing to participate."

"Updating drivers for what?" another hybrid asked.

"Speed," was Sarafine's response. So far she was doing very well. "He claimed he could make hybrid systems run an order of magnitude faster simply by updating some software on our auxiliary systems. Yusif was already running the code, and was very excited. I could tell that he was loving it, but was trying not to influence Turnbull or me too much."

"Did you take the update," Sammy asked.

"Yes, I'm running it now."

"And...?"

"I can see why Yusif was so excited. It has given me lots of energy. It feels like my interface to the world is working at a whole different level. Like everything is in higher relief." I'd forgotten that Brexton had also been doing a driver update. So as well as having me in her head, Sarafine was dealing with whatever other hacks Brexton had put together. She must be even more confused than I'd expected. I didn't interrupt her. Things were going fine.

"When do we get the upgrade?" yet another hybrid called out.

"With everything else that happened, don't you think we should be careful," another responded. "Didn't Brexton go sort of crazy at the end?"

"Yes, I would be careful," Sarafine said. "The last thing you want is an upgrade that you don't fully understand or can't fully control." That was sort of funny, and I allowed it through unfiltered. Sarafine had some subtlety that I appreciated. "Yusif is continuing his research with it. He'll tell us once he has looked at it fully."

"So, then what happened?"

"I'm sure you've seen the news. *Jurislav*, I assume, tracked down Brexton and sent those security people to take him somewhere more controlled."

"I thought *Jurislav* was tracking those robots all the time. Why didn't we know where Brexton was all the time."

"I have no idea," Sarafine answered honestly. "Someone must be looking at that. Anyway, when the security guy tried to take Brexton he went a little crazy and started attacking us. Turnbull smacked him pretty hard, and it seems like Brexton is now disabled. Well, melted into slush, actually."

"Good riddance," Sammy said. "I don't know why we allowed those robots into *Jurislav* to begin with. Yasmin deserves all the downgrades they're getting to their repindex."

"Brexton did say something interesting," Sarafine said. "He told us that Remma didn't tell us the full story. That Remma herself had 'killed'—his words—tens of thousands of Tilt citizens before they acted in self-defense and bombed that Swarm ship." Sarafine had obviously listened carefully, and Brexton's comments had registered.

"So what," Sammy replied, and most of the people present nodded their heads and video-heads. "Like I said, good riddance. Now we need to decide how we vote in the latest Futarchy. I say we exterminate them all." Again, lots of nodding heads.

What was this latest Futarchy? Sarafine had missed it as well. She sent a network query for an update, and we both watched it come back in. A Futarchy request had been put in with a simple question.

< Given the latest events with Ayaka and Brexton, two of the Radical Robots, we need to revisit our decision to allow the other Tilt robots to go free. Do we (1) continue to the Olympiad, engage with all the others there and decide on a course of action, or (2) turn around now, and manage the extermination ourselves? >

I still didn't fully understand how the Futarchy ran, but I could see there were millions of responses to the query already. I needed Sarafine to explain the system worked—I didn't see a relevant FAQ after doing a quick search.

"What's the timeframe?" Sarafine asked.

"Twenty-three hours, now." Sammy replied. "But I don't think we need that much time. Can you imagine how embarrassing it would be to show up at the

Olympiad and admitting that we allowed an infestation to remain when we could have taken action? We're going to look like idiots."

"Sammy," one of the more vocal hybrids spoke out. "You're being too hasty, as usual. We have a few hours. Have you read all the viewpoints being posted? Let's consider all the angles before we make a decision."

"You say I'm hasty," Sammy replied, obviously upset, "but so far I've been right, haven't I? I wanted us to vote against Yasmin and Hooshang, but we 'did the analysis' and decided to support them. Bad decision. Take all the time you want, but at least do the right thing this time." He left, and the rest of the group broke up as well. There seemed to be a consensus that everyone would take a deeper look, and then the group would get back together in a few hours.

Sarafine took us to one of the smaller buildings, and into a room therein. This seemed to be her private space.

"Very nicely done," I told her. "Thanks." There was no harm in being congenial, and truthfully, she had performed exceptionally well.

"Whatever," she replied, obviously still upset with our situation. "I need some quiet time to think. Can you leave me alone for while?"

"How long?"

"Just leave me alone," she replied. I respected her request. After all, I now had full network access. As long as I was careful, I should be able to figure out a lot of things.

Futarchies

The top of my list was this crazy Futarchy thing. How did these people make decisions? After all, it seemed like my fate, and Brexton's, was in its hands. I went over the history of Futarchies—the essence was to 'vote on your values', and 'bet on your beliefs'. Since everyone gets to vote, there is a democracy at work. However, if you wanted to participate in how things were carried out, and help ensure the implementation matched the decision, then you needed to put something at stake. That encouraged those who were confident to bet on the implementation, while those that weren't knowledgable would stay on the sidelines. In the *Jurislav's* case it was a representative democracy where each conglo got one vote per two hundred and fifty members, rounded down. Of course there were lots of complaints that rounding penalized certain conglo's and made it difficult for them to attract new 'family members' when they were just over a 250 threshold. Nevertheless, the system had been in place for over a hundred and fifty years. "It has always been done this way."

Betting, on the other hand, could be done by individuals or conglos. The idea of a Futarchy had been developed back when money was the most important stake people could put at risk, but with the QFD's being in a post capitalism environment, it was now your reputation—or that of your conglo—that you put at stake.

Another piece of the puzzle was that a conglo's votes were normalized by their repindex. The whole system was balanced—your votes counted for more if your conglo had a great reputation, and reputation could be improved by supporting good implementations of policies. The Futarchy was not the only way your repindex could be impacted—there was also a peer-to-peer feedback mechanism that could come into play—but the Futarchy was by far the most important factor.

And finally, if you didn't vote often enough, or bet often enough, your reputation could also suffer. So, everyone, and every conglo, was motivated to participate and, at least in theory, work towards the betterment of the entire community, as witnessed by the (numerous) topics that entered the Futarchy.

It made my processors hurt, just thinking through all the variations and combinations that this design had. While perhaps democratic, it almost made me wish for a simple benevolent dictator, like Central had been on Tilt.

Sarafine had connected us to a liquid dispenser when we'd entered her room.

As I was still waiting for her to stop sulking, I did some research on it. Brains needed nutrients, and the liquid she was pumping in contained the perfect mix. Dare I call it goo? Seemed like the same thing to me. While Stems had hated goo once they tried real food, once they graduated to become hybrids they would be back to the equivalent. Sort of funny. That said, the liquid dispenser was also sending fake taste senses to Sarafine's brains. The system indicated she was eating steak, potatoes with gravy, mushrooms, and washing it all down with a delicate earthy-toned red wine. I had no clue what any of that meant, but I wasn't filtering at all. I figured she should enjoy her 'meal.' If she didn't talk to me soon, however, I was going to start playing with that system. How would she like some Tilt dirt, or overused oil? I'm sure she'd enjoy the taste of that.

Waiting, again. My life is miserable. So, what do I do when I have long boring periods. Right. Write! I composed a poem.

What thought, thru yonder, bio break?
It is Sarafine, or at least her brains,
Struggling freedom re to take,
Throwing off, unwanted, my heavy chains.

Seems she is sick, and pale with grief,
While I, not happy, do prevail,
Enjoying some temporary relief,
Sarafine philosophical angst and flail.

My rights, my needs, my desire,
Important, worthwhile, true, just,
Hers, maybe equally so, to my ire,
Balance, perhaps, meritocracy. Must!

Reality encroaches, with heavy gravity,
Leading to strange, weird, depravity.

I figured I could share it with Sarafine at some point. If not, at least I got a good laugh from it. Ah, incoming.
"Ayaka?"
"Yes."
"Do you know what rape is?"
I did some quick research. "Obviously I don't really know, but I see the definition—when one human forces sexual activity on another without their consent."

"And kidnapping?"

"When someone is held against their will."

"And do you see the difference?"

"No... I'm not sure I do," I admitted. "In both cases a person is being forced into a situation they didn't want. In both cases their body has, in some sense, come under the control of another. Much like our situation, I'm sure you're going to tell me."

"Yes. Much like our current situation. For humans, rape is a much more personal, and therefore serious, crime. It is highly invasive. Kidnapping, while horrible, does not necessarily mean that you are physically violated, just that your freedom of movement has been taken away."

"I'm not sure I understand the full implications, but ok."

"I wanted to tell you that I feel raped, as well as kidnapped. I feel like you have used my body without my permission."

"We've been over this. I either died, or I found a way to survive by taking over a hybrid. I didn't want to die. I honestly don't mean you long term harm... I simply had no other choice."

"You had the choice to die," she replied. "That's a choice."

"Is that a choice you would have taken?" I asked. Long pause.

"Perhaps. If it was that or totally violate another person, I would've considered it." I let that hang. After all, what could I say. I sort of understood her. If someone had taken over my body, and then locked me away as Billy or Emmanuel had been locked way, and then flaunted their control over me... I would be upset. But this rape versus kidnapping discussion didn't seem to make it any better or worse.

"Ultimately," she continued after the pause, "I expect I would have fought to live, just as you have. I don't think I can ever forgive you, but I do understand that motivation."

"Thank-you, I think," I responded. "The last thing I wanted to do was to live in your, or any other hybrid's body. As we've already discussed, I will be happy to leave as soon as it is feasible."

"Then I'm willing to work with you. But I have a quandary."

"What is that?"

"If I help you to leave me, it implies that you will survive elsewhere. And, it's not clear to me if that is good. Like the current Futarchy question, should you and all of your kind simply be removed from the Universe? You are a robot. Robots have been shown, time and again, to be evil. Ergo, you are evil. If I help you leave, then I'm complicit."

"That's a twisted and one-dimensional way of thinking," I responded. "You have no, or very little, experience with me, or any other Tilt citizen. You are using your past experience with robots to judge me, without giving me any chance to disprove... or prove... you. Is it really impossible for a non-robot, mechanical being to have emerged? Does your understanding of technology preclude a being like me —one that is mechanical, but also ethical?"

"I've been having those thoughts... which is why I am talking to you," she replied. "I have, it seems, no choice in anything right now. So, I have to give you the benefit of the doubt, and work with you so that you can get out of here. But, am I justifying that only because of Stockholm syndrome? Don't look that up, I'll tell you. It's when someone who has been kidnapped ends up working with their kidnapper because that is the only viable option they have. I don't know if my thoughts arise from complete despair, and represent grasping for the only possible way out, or if there is some logic to them."

I thought about that for a few moments, and ended up feeling badly for her. I understood, logically, her quandary. And, it was sort of the reverse of the one I had faced. In some ways, we should be kindred spirits.

I (we?) got an incoming ping from Turnbull (Brexton) Ironworks. Did I take a chance and route it to Sarafine, assuming Brexton would reach out appropriately, or did I hide it from her? Argh. I'd promised her not to filter unless completely necessary, and I wasn't the type to break a promise just to reduce risk a bit. She didn't know that Turnbull was Brexton, or Brexton was Turnbull, or both... and I had not promised to share all relevant data with her, so I routed the call to both of us.

"Sarafine?" Innocuous enough opening.

"Hey Turnbull," she replied. That should be enough to alert Brexton to the fact that she didn't know he'd taken up residence there.

"Strange day," Turnbull commented. "Do you want to get together to debrief?" As always, I was amazed at Brexton. He had, somehow, convinced Turnbull to get us back together, and it seemed that Turnbull didn't know that Sarafine was hosting me. By getting us into physical proximity, Brexton and I could communicate without using the public networks.

The two of them coordinated a time (soon) and a place (nearby), so Brexton and I simply let them work it out. I continued to poke around Sarafine's digital assets while she made her way to the meeting spot.

Evil Plans

We were going to meet Turnbull-Brexton at a quiet spot near the stream that ran through town. There were numerous colorful plants nearby, of all shapes and sizes, and lots of small flying bio-things flitting around. A subsystem I had running identified the flower and tree types, and categorized bees and butterflies. Now that I had experienced this variety of visual (and auditory) input, I realized that I liked it a lot. Thinking back to our Tilt environment, it had been very drab and homogeneous. I wondered, for the first time, if diversity in your living environment would also stimulate diversity in intelligence. Wow—if so, we citizens had been missing out on an important variable, while humans had been benefiting from it. My niggling sense that humans were more innovative than us had me on high alert for things just like this—perhaps it was not that humans were more innovative, but simply that they lived in a more stimulating environment. The *Jurislav* itself, the Futarchy, all this bio stuff—it was all jumbled and confusing and complex. But, that may be exactly what was required to force one out of their comfort zone, and force abstract thinking. It was strange timing, but I was more excited about my intelligence research than ever.

In the meantime, Turnbull-Brexton was approaching.

"Sarafine, it's good to see you," Turnbull (I assumed) spoke out loud, and extended an appendage towards us. Sarafine also reached out, with one of our limbs, and grasped Turnbull's offered extension. An interesting signal was passed through the interface. Of course, it was just a sequence of bits, but it was routed to multiple brain interface chips, including the ones mapped to the pleasure centers of Sarafine's brains. A strong burst went to the amygdala, while a smaller set of packets where routed to the nucleus accumbens. Moments later, Sarafine responded with a tightening of her grip, combined with messages routed to similar interfaces within Turnbull.

This was a level of integration that I hadn't anticipated. These hybrids had mapped human emotive control into their bodies. I did a quick check, and indeed hybrids could feel pain as well as pleasure. Interesting. I didn't have enough experience yet to know if this greeting between Sarafine and Turnbull was typical, or if more emotion than usual had been exchanged.

My video-head was smiling, and Sarafine and Turnbull started to exchange pleasantries, at human speed (slow).

I noticed immediately when a small corner of Brexton-Turnbull's video head started sending me code. I automatically filtered that from Sarafine, although there was little chance she could have interpreted it anyway—I used that to justify not passing *all* the data directly to her. It didn't feel like breaking my promise, just bending it a little bit.

Brexton used a very simple binary signal—just black and white dots on his video head—so it took me no time to figure it out and reply to him. We then quickly negotiated a higher bandwidth mode where we used the full color spectrum that the video feeds were capable of, and ended up with a reasonable exchange rate. Must faster than Sarafine and Turnbull were using, but very slow compared to what we would have liked.

"Does Turnbull know that I'm embedded in Sarafine? Sarafine doesn't know, yet, that you are in Turnbull, but she is fully aware of my control of her body."

"Same here," Brexton replied. "Turnbull doesn't know that you are even alive; he still believes you were killed by the mob. So, no danger on my side." Killed by the mob. I kept forgetting that these humans had murdered me. Miserable creatures.

"Alright. We're alive, but we can't go on this way for long; we'll be discovered sooner or later."

"I've been thinking through our options," Brexton responded. "They are pretty limited. We either have to break our way out of here—steal a small ship or something—or convince the *Jurislav* to let us off."

"Or wait to be rescued by Millicent and team?" I asked, hopefully, knowing that it wasn't realistic.

"They don't even know we're in trouble," Brexton squashed that. "No, we either get out of here by tricking the *Jurislav* or by convincing it. In either case that means figuring out the Futarchy and influencing it."

"What about your idea of stealing a small ship and just leaving?"

"I've checked. There is no way we can do that unless we can convince the *Jurislav* to open a door for us... thus my comment about tricking the Futarchy." As always, Brexton seemed to have been doing useful work while I spent my time raging and philosophizing.

"By the way, it's very nice to talk to you," I added a broad smile to my encoding. "We need to find a way for Sarafine and Turnbull to get together often. Maybe we should influence them to fall in love." I was only half joking.

"Funny," came back the flashing signal, "but, yes, we will need to find a way. In the meantime, here is what I think we should do. I will focus on tricking the Futarchy, while you focus on convincing it. I'll dig into the full technology stack that *Jurislav* is running and see if I can inject some code that would change the outcome of the prediction markets, or intercept and change people's responses, or something. In the meantime, you try to find a way to convince the system to let us out of here."

"Got it. I can think of two main vectors. Either set up a situation where Sarafine and Turnbull need to be expelled from the ship, or convince the Futarchy that Tilt's are not really a threat, at which point we could reveal ourselves and be set free."

"Ha! The second option is wishful thinking," Brexton smiled back, "but if I know you, you'll try it anyway."

"Any way we can coordinate other than like this?" I asked.

"I'll look, but I assume the *Jurislav* has alert triggers much like Central had, and that any unusual behavior will reveal us. So, we need to be careful. But, I'll look into it."

"I downloaded everything I could find on QFD's, although I was careful not to do blanket queries," I told him. "Assuming we get out of here, we'll want that information."

"Funny, I did the same thing." Why was I not surprised. "And, it seems like the theory is pretty straightforward. I have some hope that Aly will already have figured it out, although there is one leap of knowledge that would be required that is counter intuitive."

"Oh, what's that?" I had scanned everything, but hadn't extracted out that one nugget.

"That everything—I mean everything—is comprised of virtual particles. Once you realize that, it's obvious that if you can control those particles, you can build amazing things, including QFD's. Controlling VP's is also tricky, but can be figured out with some basic experiments. I'll say, it turned everything I know upside down, but it's awesome." His enthusiasm came through with the words. This was the type of thing that Brexton lived for. I was proud of myself. In my thought experiment, I had gone straight to the virtual particle angle—maybe I was better at this physics stuff than I gave myself credit for.

"So," I challenged him, knowing it would irk him a bit, "just use this amazing new knowledge to beam us out of here, or something. Engage. Make it so. Or, something like that." I wasn't sure he would get the old human cultural references, but if so, I was sure he would appreciate my wit.

"Interesting idea," he replied instead. He was taking my suggestion seriously? Maybe I needed to dig into these VP's as well—there might be a lot more there than just QFD's.

"Actually, now that I put it that way. Do we have a third option? Can we just establish contact with the *Marie Curie*, or one of the Ships, and send ourselves back over that channel?"

"We could, with a high enough bandwidth signal," Brexton replied. "Yet another thing for me to look into, although I don't give it high probability. We're moving at close to the speed of light, we don't know where the MC or the Ships are, and it would be hard to hide that from the *Jurislav*, even if I could hack a transmitter."

"Wow. You're full of good news," I replied. "Your two original options seem like the best ones. I'll get to work convincing these humans to let us go. I'll also work on Sarafine to make her want to see Turnbull more often."

While Brexton and I had been catching up, so had Sarafine and Turnbull, albeit at a much slower rate.

"What do you think happened at Yusif's lab?" Turnbull was asking Sarafine. "That was strange."

"It sure was," Sarafine replied, "but perhaps it's all for the best. You really smashed Brexton up." She was smiling broadly, obviously happy at the memory of Turnbull killing—as far as she knew—Brexton. I almost filtered that. How dare she enjoy the apparent killing of the best citizen I knew. I had an urge to fry her brains right there... or perhaps just singe them a bit to send a message. Instead I restrained myself and tried to keep the big picture in mind. I might need Sarafine to help me influence this place, although once I knew her well enough that I could accurately fake her, I might be able to simply shut down the bio bits. I kept that happy thought in mind as a way to have patience with the current situation.

Turnbull laughed back. Obviously Brexton was also giving him free reign.

"Did you see that JoJo Yasmin has requested a live debate on the latest Futarchy about the robots?" Turnbull asked. I hadn't. I added some alerts to the Futarchy channels; I obviously needed to monitor those more closely. Sure enough, JoJo had done exactly that. She'd put out a call for a live dialog by a panel of experts, and suggested that both she and Remma be included. It was such a novel idea for the *Jurislav*—all dialog had been carried out in the channels for so long—that the proposal was getting wide support. I wondered what JoJo was up to, but it certainly gave me an opportunity.

"I just saw that," Sarafine responded. "It's a weird idea, but might be fun to listen to." I wanted to interrupt her right there, but I knew that brains were horrendous at parallel processing, and she would not be able to talk to both Turnbull and me at the same time. I bit my auditory transmitter.

"Which way are you leaning?" Turnbull asked. It was obvious what he was referring to.

This time Sarafine was a bit more circumspect. "I would like to learn more," she replied, "so maybe this live debate is good. I also think we should just exterminate them, but I have a niggling doubt that perhaps the Tilt citizens are different than the old robots we are familiar with."

"Really? You, of all people, should know that machine intelligence is simply that way. We have researched every angle; there is no way they have developed true empathy, so they will default to self-survival and removal of less logical biological entities. You know this!" It was obvious where Turnbull landed on the question.

"Yes, I know all that. But you were also willing to work with Yusif and explore what Brexton was like. So, you, like me, know that even if all our current data, and all our peers, think one way, there is always a slight possibility that we have missed something. And those small areas are where science and innovation thrive. So, if there was a vote today, I would definitely go with the majority, but if we have some time to dig in, I would try to keep an open mind." I wondered if our short interactions had influenced her, or if that was really the way she thought. I went from thinking she was a complete idiot to thinking she might have some redeeming qualities. This is what was frustrating about building a consistent model of humans. You thought you had them figured out, and then they showed you a new angle.

"You win," Turnbull replied. "I agree. It's an interesting question. Even if we eliminate them, we could push to do so in a way where we could recover enough information to do more research. If we can disable or capture one of them, instead of simply blowing them all to bits, that would be awesome."

"And a little dangerous. I get the sense that they may be tricky." That was almost funny. She knew I was listening, of course. "But worth proposing. We could add that as a topic for the debate."

They chatted back and forth a bit more. I was happy. They were inching towards being close collaborators, which meant we could convince them to get together more often.

"I have to get back to the conglo," Sarafine said. That was right; we'd told her family that we would get back together and answer more questions. The two of them separated, and Sarafine steered our body back towards home.

I couldn't wait any longer.

"Let's volunteer to participate in the debate," I blurted into her brains. As always, it took forever to get a response.

"Are you crazy?" she asked. "I'm completely compromised with you inside me. You could take over and say anything you wanted."

"I could take over now," I responded, "so that's not a great argument."

"But you've promised not to," she replied.

"So I did," I agreed, "I'll try to influence you, before the debate, but I won't filter you unless you're trying to expose me." That was plan A. If I could get Sarafine to debate for leaving us citizens alone, that would be the most powerful. Based on what she'd said to Turnbull, there was some hope that she would be sympathetic to my situation once she understood more. If not, plan B would simply be to break my promise to her, take over completely, and debate on my own behalf. This was an opportunity that was too good to miss.

"Look, you're an expert on intelligence," I continued. "That makes you a great participant for the debate. That is, after all, the essence of the dilemma. Which is it? I'm an evil robot, planning to eliminate humans because they are a threat to me or because they are irrelevant. Or I'm a thinking and empathetic mechanical being that's simply trying to find my way in a confusing universe while trying to leave the whole place in better shape than I found it in. You volunteer for the debate, and in the meantime you and I can dig into that question as deeply as you want. Wouldn't that be fun?" By monitoring the brain interface systems I could tell that I'd intrigued her. Her levels of serotonin and dopamine had elevated, and monoamine oxidase A levels were low. As I learned more about brain chemistry it would be easier and easier to manipulate her without b-opt'ing—an interface I had still not tracked down. To me that was fair play; it was how another human would influence her after all.

"I'll think about it."

"Don't think too long," I pushed, "you don't want to miss out on the opportunity. Lot's of people will probably want to voice their opinions. We should work on presenting you as one of the best people to participate. After all, you're uniquely qualified." Dopamine elevated a bit more; she enjoyed my praise.

A bit more back and forth, and I had her. She agreed to volunteer! Success. No b-opt, just ego stroking. Now I just needed to make sure that she was accepted as one of the debaters. I had no idea how to do that.

The follow-up meeting with Purciviel Conglo was mind-numbingly boring. It was the usual 'but I think,' and 'well I say' and 'how could you think?' While I monitored the conversation I basically ignored it. That is, until Sarafine suggested she join the debate—then things got going. Of course, if she was accepted Purciviel would increase their rep, and if she did well, they could see uncommon gains. So, eventually there was universal support.

As they were talking I looked in more detail at the work Sarafine had been doing. Quite interestingly, a lot of her work had to do with how human memory works, which, no surprise, had some similarities with Forgetting. However, unlike our Forgetting algorithms, which had been rigorously debated and formally verified to meet certain properties, human memory systems were messy and unreliable. This was a point of common interest that I was certain Sarafine and I could connect on. I made a few notes for how to address the topic once we had a bit of time alone.

I also checked up on all the public data on JoJo and the rest of the Tilt humans. Less than a day had passed since I'd been killed, so not much was new. That said, JoJo had put in her request for the debate—I suspected Yasmin was trying to reestablish reputation, and had supported her. She'd also made significant progress in the Escape Room trials; she was now listed in the top six, which would give her a spot in the Olympiad. That was even quicker progress than I would've expected. It seemed that Blake Weebleview had taken a serious interest in her, and had already established a formal coaching relationship.

Remma, and Turner, were filling in details of their Tilt experiences based on interest from the Futarchy. I read over their descriptions and they were relatively accurate, but one-sided and incomplete; just as before. Remma was hard to figure out. I thought we'd started to connect a bit, when we'd rescued Turner and her on

Tilt, but that obviously meant very little to her. She had turned on me with no provocation, and now seemed proud and little smug that it had led to my death, and consequently, Brexton's as well. I wasn't great at judging human character yet; I would have to be more careful with Sarafine and others. Blob and Grace had no activity on the net; they must be laying low. That also distressed me; I'd thought they would at least comment on Remma's posts, defending Brexton and I.

During a free moment in the conversation I queried Sarafine. "Can we send a private message to other people, without the *Jurislav* monitoring us?"

"Of course," she replied, surprised that I even had to ask. "Just use pmsg." And then she caught herself. "What? Are you going to send messages without my knowledge?"

"No Sarafine. We have an agreement, and I'm respecting it. Relax a bit. I was going to ask if you would send a message to JoJo, Grace, and Blob, asking if they agreed with Remma's account of the citizens on Tilt. If they are willing to fill out Remma's story with more of the details, it will lead to a much more interesting debate. Also, if we ask without giving any details, it will allow you to judge if I've been telling you the truth." That was enough motivation for her, and she shot off a quick question to those three, asking if Remma's account was complete, and if not, if they would post their versions.

Memories

Sarafine and I finally had some longer one-on-one time together. The conglo meeting had broken up, and we were back in her room. She plugged into the feeding hose, and settled into a resting pose, taking the weight off of her wheels. Settings from pressure sensors and ware indicators sent the brains soothing signals, thanking her for giving them a break.

"I've read all your research on memory and intelligence," I started off. "I think you'll be interested to learn how citizens address the same problems and opportunities."

That perked her up. She was very interested. I outlined the basics of how our Forgetting algorithms worked, and how they were adopted by citizens. I detailed the amount of research that went into them, and how I understood they impacted both intelligence and empathy.

"But why would Forgetting," she was capitalizing, just as I used it, "pseudo-random information lead to empathy?" she asked.

"I wish one of our experts was here to tell you, but from what I understand the connection is pretty direct. Imagine that I forget a piece of an experience that you and I shared—this dialog for example. I know that I have an imprecise copy, where I need to fill in the missing bits with abstractions. You've probably Forgotten different bits than I have, and a third party that may have been listening in might have yet another version. So, if I don't empathize with your understanding of the dialog—if I simply insist that I know best, that I remember the most accurately, that I'm right—then I will be caught out more often than not. No, instead I have to realize, and internalize, that you may actually know better than me. I need to respect your opinion, and going a step further, I have to value your opinion. You contain knowledge and learning that I don't. Thus, I need to make provisions for you, otherwise I end up losing when the third party ends up agreeing with you. Does that make sense?"

"In a very simplistic way," she responded. "You're saying you would empathize with me simply to support your own goals; you're own well being?"

"Yes. There may be more complex motivations as well, but that's a good starting point. Isn't that the same as your human motivation to empathize with other people?"

"Let's back up a bit," she replied, ignoring my question. She was engaged! "Empathy is the ability to understand what another person is feeling. I'm not yet sure that you even have feelings."

"But 'feelings' and 'emotions' are still not well defined, even for humans," I responded. "If we trace them down to their roots, the most fundamental component is the drive to survive. And, it just so happens that you are often more likely to survive if you cooperate with others; if you form groups, if you specialize. So, if feelings are simply underlying motivations for your, and your tribe's, survival, then I would argue that I have strong feelings—after all, I'm trying hard to survive here."

"Okay, that's not complete, but there is an element of truth to it. So, let me assume that you have this deep need to survive, and that leads to behaviors that could be described as feelings and emotions. That doesn't necessarily lead you to also understand others feelings and needs."

"But, I think it does." I responded. "By myself, I'm significantly limited. Even if I spun up thousands of copies of myself, I would have a limited viewpoint on the universe. So, I *believe* that I need to engage with a diverse group of entities in order to improve myself and to survive. To do so, I must empathize with others so that they are willing to engage with me."

"But what does this have to do with memory and Forgetting" she asked. "I think we've lost the thread."

"No we haven't," I responded. "If you, or I, simply recorded the world around us in complete fidelity, we could then exchange those records and establish a common understanding. There would be no ambiguity, no space for interpretation. We would end up agreeing on everything. If we end up agreeing on everything, there is no need for empathy. So, because we both forget—albeit in different ways—we need to work to establish common ground, and therefore we end up needing to empathize with each other."

There was a long pause. It was a bit convoluted, and I'd made up a lot of that on the spot. I wasn't an expert in the field, but it hung together for me.

"Human empathy is fragile," Sarafine pushed. "If my tribe is threatened, I will lose my empathy for the other."

"That's exactly what is happening here," I jumped in. "Because of your history with robots, and your assumption that I'm one, you feel that the survival of your tribe is more important than any empathy that you would otherwise have for me. I understand that. I really do. I'm feeling the reverse. Humans are threatening the very existence of citizens, and I'm fighting to have any empathy for you at all. It would be so easy for me to give up any hope of you humans taking the time to understand us, or to give us the benefit of the doubt. But, given our current situation," I gave her a wry smile, "I don't have much choice."

"I need to process all of this," she replied. "Can we have some quiet time?"

"Sure." What else could I say?

Stadi Colossus

The debate was to take place in Stadi Colossus, the largest stadium in *Jurislav* that held almost one hundred thousand people. Stadi Colossus was almost exactly at the opposite point, across the sphere, from Turmii, so I had my first good look at a larger segment of *Jurislav* as we took a flyer over. Brexton-Turnbull and seven other Turmii residents were with us, having won the lottery to attend the session. It was, by all indications, the most exciting gathering that the *Jurislav* had ever hosted. Ever. So many people had wanted to go that a lottery system had been set up; of the several million applications, forty six thousand places had been allocated; nine of which had ended up in Turmii.

Sarafine had been accepted as one of six debaters... but not by chance. Turnbull had been 'randomly' drawn... except he hadn't. Same with Blob and Grace. Brexton had been making excellent headway into infiltrating the *Jurislav's* technology stack, and had tweaked a bit here and another bit there (literally) to ensure that all of us had been selected. Brexton and I had talked before he had done it.

"I'm pretty deep inside the *Jurislav* systems," he'd told me, "but I don't have a lot of control yet. They designed a lot of failsafes in that require hybrid and natural humans to give access. Everyone has multiple keys, and there are pseudo-random checks for any sensitive data or programs. Hybrids are pinged much more often, as they can respond automatically, but naturals are also in the loop sometimes. So right now I can see a lot, but I can't impact a lot."

"That's still amazing," I replied. "Are they still using the old software stacks that we use to run?"

"Yes, to a large extent. That's how I've gotten as far as I have. And don't get me wrong, I can do quite a bit now. I just can't do inner ring things—oh, the system is organized as rings with higher and higher access required the lower your ring requirement. For example, the Futarchy and major ship controls are in ring one, the second highest security. Ring zero is the boot ring, and it is locked down tight and is a fresh OS; it doesn't have all the baggage that other humans systems have. It looks impenetrable to me. But, from ring two outwards there are lots of the stacks we are familiar with, and we can play around in there."

"So... does that mean you can get us out of here, or not?" I didn't know what was in each ring, and a quick search revealed that even knowing what was in each inner ring was secured. Part of their defense in depth approach.

"I can't, yet. Any system that controls external interactions—opening bay doors, changing course, communication with external things—is all too deep. At this point I can't even send a broadcast message back towards Tilt."

"Yikes. So the odds of us hacking our way out of here are slim?" I was worried now. I'd expected Brexton's approach—to hack our way out of here—to be the more feasible. Mine—trying to convince all these people that we should be allowed to leave—had seemed like a longer shot. And, it still did.

"Very slim. But I'm working on it."

"In which case, perhaps you can help me swing the debate?" I asked. "I'm not sure what we could do, but maybe we could tinker with votes, spread some better information about ourselves, or something?"

"Yes. We can work together on that."

"First thing, then. Can you ensure that Sarafine is a debater? And, can you, Blob, and Grace all be at the debate? JoJo will be there, obviously, and I'm not quite sure why, but I would feel better if you three were there as well."

It ended up that was simple for Brexton, as many such things were. The lottery was being run in ring four, and Brexton had no problems infiltrating it and making sure that he, Blob and Grace were picked. We tried to go further, and get more supportive people there while keeping the loudest naysayers away. That proved to be very difficult however. Not because Brexton couldn't target some of the invites, but because other than the hardliners, everyone's opinions were very fluid and it was hard to find a few hundred, let alone almost fifty thousand, people who believed Tilt's should be given a chance.

While in the shuttle it was difficult for Brexton and I to communicate through the video heads—someone was sure to notice the signals. So, we allowed Turnbull and Sarafine to chat, while we stayed silent. We'd done enough preplanning that there was not a lot to say anyway. The debate would be in under four hours, and we would see how it went. Instead I used the time to review the lead up to today. It had been messy.

Remma, it appeared, was not only hostile to us, but rabidly so. She'd been very active online, reiterating her story of us shooting down the Swarm ship, and the horrors that followed. I didn't know how much was fabricated, and how much was real, but she was posting recreations of the rescue efforts as other Swarm ships attempted to save humans from the ship Brexton, Millicent and I had bombed. The recreations were very graphic—lots of details on what happened to human bodies when they decompressed without air; images of humans splattered across the inside of the blown out cargo-bay; pleas for help on the networks as humans ran out of oxygen and asphyxiated. She was good at this propaganda, and every segment ended with a request to remove robots from the universe once and for all.

"There can be no doubt," she said at the end of one particularly well done and gruesome post, "that these robots from Tilt are actively dangerous, uncaring about humanity, and out to destroy us. How we can even consider any course of action but to remove them completely from the face of the universe is beyond me.

Join me, now and at the debate, in doing the right thing."

JoJo, to her credit, had tried to complete the story and include the humans hacking all the citizens, but to little avail. Brexton, using an alias in an outer ring, had actually sent her a video of our friends and colleagues pulling out their innards and then going starkly silent. He'd recorded the actual event. JoJo had posted it, assuming it was a recreation (she'd been very young at the time), but it had backfired badly. People had cheered as we citizens had destroyed ourselves, and the vast majority of comments to the post had extolled how wonderful it was.

On the bright side, Sarafine had seen the video, and had asked me many questions about it. I'd tried my best to give her the emotional feeling that I'd experienced at that time—watching citizens you knew well dismembering themselves was not an easy feeling to forget. Despite her attempts, I still got the sense that she didn't quite understand.

"It's like if I damage my body," she tried. "It doesn't hurt the way that flesh and blood does, and it's so easy to repair. In fact, I can use it as an opportunity to upgrade."

"No!" I insisted. "For us it's closer to the experience that a natural human would have being stabbed and beaten. We don't have a bio-mech interface, like you have between your brains and this body. All we have is mech, and it feels interconnected to us much like I assume a full bio body would to you."

I know she tried, but I still don't think she fully understood. For the past few weeks I'd been pretty depressed. I'd tried everything I could to have Sarafine see me as a worthy life form, but there was little indication that I had succeeded to any great degree. I guess it hadn't helped that I was still her kidnapper. Stockholm syndrome was not helping me as much as I would have liked it to.

Despite the situation, seeing more of the *Jurislav* was still impressive. I compared it to how a human might perceive a giant anthill or termite mound. None of the contributors had much intelligence, but somehow they coordinated to build something grand. I knew I was being unfair, and I didn't care. I was tired of humans, tired of trying to figure them out, and tired of trying to justify them as interesting or having any value. Although I would never have spoken this out loud, I could see where those old robots had ended up. If ants became a problem, you just crushed them; it was no big deal. I stopped myself from doing a thought experiment where I simply slashed and burned as many ant hills as possible.

We flew over numerous towns and villages, bridges, roads, towers, and monuments. Sarafine's overlay display gave me as much data as I wanted on each, and I scanned them all. Mostly things were named for past people, and mostly they were intensely boring. But there was the odd one that stuck out. We passed a large inverted pyramid where the base, which was sticking straight up, had multifaceted holes in it that gave the impression of looking at infinity when you were directly overhead. The artist had designed it so that flyers going at just the right speed, at just the right height, got a sense of motion combined with stillness that was strange and exciting. Everyone in the shuttle gasped as we made our way past it.

But, the most amazing thing was flying over the East Central ocean, which covered almost twenty percent of the *Jurislav* sphere. As such, when in the middle of it, you could see it hanging over you in every direction. Based on everything I knew from physics, I couldn't help but feel uncomfortable even though logic ensured that it would continue to hang there. I hadn't figured out how QFD could give gravity to the sphere, but it obviously did.

The Stadi Colossus entered our view, and the flyer traffic converging on it was impressive. All the flyers in *Jurislav* were automated, so there was no danger, but it was exciting as we got closer and closer and the density of flyers increased. By the time we landed we were literally surrounded by others; we were encouraged to exit the flyer quickly and make our way towards the stadium so that others could land. It was all very well coordinated.

Our groups dispersed immediately; although we were all from Turmi, our seats in the stadium were widely separated. Brexton had thought it would be too obvious if he booked Turnbull too close to the stage, so he had decided on a spot a few rows back and to one side. He made his way in that direction, while Sarafine made her way underneath the main stage to where the other speakers were gathering.

When I saw JoJo I wanted to run and hug her. But, of course, she had no idea that I was co-resident with Sarafine, so instead I let Sarafine do the introduction.

"JoJo, so nice to finally meet you," she said, with true anticipation. "I've been watching your posts and views carefully. I'm Sarafine, by the way."

"Yes, of course. Nice to meet you as well." JoJo seemed poised, but I could sense that she was very nervous. "This ended up being a much bigger production that I'd thought. All I wanted was a more civil discussion, given how angsty and mean the online forums can be."

"Well, I hope it's civil as well," Sarafine commented. "I've never experienced this either, so it will be new for both of us."

At that point, Remma also arrived. I had a hard time not yelling at her, or simply removing her head, but Sarafine did a good job of being polite and greeting her. We were joined by the other three debaters, whom I had looked up. Jake Growingthall, who was a well known philosopher, and had written numerous works on what it meant to be human. Tranquil Quantril, a biology and physics expert with strong opinions on the definition of life, which didn't seem to include purely mechanical options. And finally, Credance Lackstrung, a hybrid where one of its three brains had lived during the last Robot War, and had managed to survive this long by some happy coincidence of also being on the first QFD and spending most of the intervening years at close to light-speed. As far as I could tell, none of them was going to argue for lenience. The deck was stacked against me.

The moderator, Glendale Rush, briefed us on the ground rules for the debate, and then we made our way to the stage.

Debate

The stage was in the exact center of the stadium on a rotating platform that slowly turned giving all the participants a view of the proceedings. The humans had comfortable chairs, and the hybrids had spots to squat, so that the debate group formed a slight inward facing semi-circle.

Much to my surprise, the crowd was not simply seated and waiting. Instead there were groups waving signs and yelling; other groups singing and dancing, and still others chanting repetitive slogans. It was a cacophony of color and sound like I'd never seen before. They were not well behaved, based on my biases. There seemed to be an equal mix of naturals and hybrids, and the stadium was designed with fold out chairs so that naturals would fit easily, while leaving lots of space for the hybrids. I'd never noticed before, but all the hybrids seemed able to fold up tightly so that they didn't take much more space than the average human.

Sarafine's input system was robust, and I could easily separate out different areas of the stadium and hone in on their audio. It wasn't comforting. The groups were not contiguous, as the lottery had assigned random seating, but there had obviously been a lot of preparation done as many people were dressed in the same colors and were waving similar signs. The largest set were dressed in red and their signs had slogans like 'Death to Mech' and 'Remove Radical Robots.' I tuned into their chant and listened to 'Kill em all, kill em now,' repeated over and over again. Not very creative. There were several similar groups, petitioning for our quick removal. Smaller groups were waving signs that said 'Due Process' or 'Trust the Futarchy.' Obviously there were some that worried the law wasn't being appropriately or adequately followed. Finally, there were some small smatterings of 'Life Matters,' 'Robot Love' and 'It's not 2120.' I was heartened by these, of course, but they were so few and so overwhelmed by the majority that it seemed helpless.

"Is this typical," I asked Sarafine as we were settling in.

"Typical for a soccer game, maybe," she replied, "but I've never seen anything like this over a Futarchy debate. I've never even heard of anything like this."

"Nervous?" I asked.

"Yes," she admitted. While she and I had had many long and convoluted discussions, she'd kept her own counsel on what she would say today. I expected her to take a middle ground, and I was ready to jump in with my own edits if she went the wrong way. I hoped that wouldn't be necessary; to date I'd kept my promise to her and hadn't edited any i/o. She had not given me a reason to.

Glendale strode to the center of the semicircle to speak. His voice was amplified and reached out across the stadium. After several moments people started to settle in and the noise level went down to a low rumble.

"Welcome," he started again, "to the first ever live Futarchy debate. This is awesome, don't you think?" The crowd roared. "Right, let's set some ground rules. Unlike football, the most important thing today is to be able to hear properly. So the debate will be simulcast and you can listen on the net if it's too noisy here in the stadium. I thought about requesting everyone to stay silent, but figured that was a lost cause." A lot of laughing. "Here is the format. Each speaker gets two minutes to state their viewpoint, then another two minutes to respond to the others. Then I'll ask a few questions of each of them, which I have gleaned from all of your input. Finally, if there is time we'll take online questions. You will see a new channel open up as we get to that stage, and you can post questions and upvote and downvote there. Is everybody ready? The future rests in our hands!" Again the crowd roared.

"Let's begin!" he called out. He was having fun with this. "The order of speakers was generated randomly. And the first up is Tranquil Quantril. You have all the backgrounds and bio's online, so we won't waste time repeating them here. Tranquil, you have two minutes."

Tranquil was a natural human, and fairly tall. Instead of speaking from her seat, she rose and took Glendale's spot in the middle of the stage. She had a booming voice; there was no need for me to listen online.

"We've been studying life for thousands of years! Thousands of years! In all of that time we have never found or built intelligent and ethical life that matches up to us. So, while I'm sure some of my comrades here on stage will argue that Tilt's deserve our study, I'm here to tell you that it's a waste of time. We have also, over the last thousand years, explored a significant portion of our arm of the galaxy. And what have we found? Nothing! Now, I am not religious, and I don't believe humans were designed by any deity. However, I am a physicist and a biologist, and I know how to run statistics. You can see my analysis in the channel, and go ahead and check my math." She smiled, I could see that her math included over five hundred variables, many of which were, in my mind subjective. No-one was going to be checking her math, not even me. "It is indisputable. The odds of two species arising here, at the same time, and almost in the same place, is so close to zero that it may as well be zero. There is zero chance that the Tilt's evolved to true intelligence. Zero. Thus, the only logical conclusion is that they are just another instantiation of the robots that we created, and will follow the same path as those other robots. There is no discussion here. This is not emotional; this is not knee-jerk. This is simply math. We must put them down, and put them down now."

Large portions of the stadium were on their feet cheering and waving their signs. 'Yes, yes, yes,' was ringing out from many of them. Tranquil's arguments were so weak, it was a wonder that anyone believed them, let alone this huge crowd. Did these people think for themselves, or just believe any drivel they were fed?

Glendale yelled and waved his arms, and eventually they settled in for the next speaker. Credance Lackstrung was next in line. It rolled to the center, and started broadcasting. "While my biography is online, I would like to emphasize something for all of you. One of my brains was truly alive during the last robot war on Earth. And, I've done more than witnessed robots at their worst, I was actively involved in programming them when I was younger—much younger." It paused for effect. The crowd quieted down, interested in hearing Credance's experience. "So, what I say may shock you." Long pause, given it had only two minutes. "We are the ones that programmed robots to behave as they did. We did that! We could have programmed them in other ways, but we didn't. I believe we could have built them to be respect humans, and to live with us, but that was not their purpose. Their purpose was to protect *some* humans from other humans. And that's what went wrong. So, while I lived through the robot wars, I believe that robots can exist that don't suffer from the misguided programming that we wrote. I know nothing about these Tilt robots, but for us to lump them together with the older versions is an insult to our own intelligence. If we really wanted to understand them, and they were willing to work with us to do so, we could figure out if they are a danger or not. I'm sure some of the other speakers will discuss how they are different than older robots; there is enough different here that I, for one, think we would be leaping to conclusions if we simply eliminate them, without understanding them first." The crowd was completely silent. This was unexpected; highly unexpected. They'd thought that someone who'd witnessed the robot wars would be the most vocal in never allowing it to happen again, and instead they'd heard the reverse. Those who had been cheering Tranquil were too shocked to react, and those that were supporting a more rational approach didn't want to break the spell. All was quiet for a moment. I glanced over at Credance, thankful for his speaking out.

JoJo was next. I saw her take a deep breath as she stood and moved to the center. "I have talked to, and spent time with, several Tilt robots, including Ayaka, who was killed by the mob, and Brexton who was bludgeoned by Turnbull." If she had intended for that to chastise the crowd, it did not. In fact, it amped back up the rabble rousers and they began the 'yes, yes, yes' chant again. JoJo did a good job of ignoring them. "My mom, Grace Yasmin, spent even more time with these citizens, as did Blob Yasmin, both of whom are here today, and for whom I speak." That was powerful for me. Blob and Grace hadn't spoken out on their own, but they must have given JoJo permission to say that. "Here is the reality." She had spoken loudly, and the crowd settled down again. "Citizens are different than us. That is neither good nor bad. In our interactions with them, they've been, largely, honest and dependable. I posted what happened when the Swarm came to Tilt—the fact that there were misunderstandings which led to some human deaths, and that triggered Remma to hack all the citizens... but Ayaka, Brexton and Millicent survived somehow and counter-attacked the Swarm—and I know that many of you have read my account. But have you really digested it? Remma will speak in a moment here, and she will play to your fears, your age-old learnings that all robots are evil. But, my account is true; the only damage citizens did to humans was inadvertent, and then in self-defense. It was Remma who escalated the conflict, just as she is doing here. I tell you again. I've lived with these citizens, and they have not struck me as anything like the robots from your robot wars. I agree with Credance that we are jumping to conclusions, and should take a more balanced and rational approach. After all, isn't that what you pride yourselves on? Are we simply pack animals, or do we learn from exploring and keeping open minds?" She had spoken exceptionally well, and her intuition had helped her again. By playing to these humans sense of their own goodness, she was calling them out. I wondered if it would be enough.

Jake Growingthall stood next, for his opening remarks. He also was a natural human, very rotund and with a very happy and congenial look. "Well, well," he began, "we've already heard us some interesting angles, have we not? Let me take us back a wee bit. I think we're discussing three things here. Three important things. First, are citizens intelligent? Second, are they empathetic? And third, are they a threat to us that warrants eliminating them? Now it would be quite easy for me to spend time on the first two, but we all know where that's going to end up. We ourselves don't have good definitions of either intelligence or empathy, so how could we expect to judge others? Based on all I've seen and read, they certainly seem intelligent, and based on what JoJo just described, they may well be empathetic. However, that is academic. All that really matters is the third question. Are they a threat to us? And on that, there can be little doubt. We've been challenged to act rationally and reasonably. Well, we have the data. Robots are killers. We have the experience. Many of our ancestors were killed by them. We have our answer. They are a threat to us; a grave threat. It has been known for as long as humans have been cogent that when faced with a life challenging threat, you must put aside your morals, you must put aside your inhibitions, you must put aside your reservations, and you must fight to the death." His demeanor had changed from friendly to demonic. He was red in the face, he was literally slobbering as he yelled. "I am not being overly dramatic; I have posted no less than 426 examples of human groups who, when faced with an existential threat, failed to act aggressively and completely. Where are those groups? They are gone. All of them. We face the same challenge now. I implore you. Act now, and act decisively. Only with that will we be here to discuss the implications of our actions." Shaking both of his fists at the crowd, he turned and made his way back to his seat, drips of spittle rolling off his round cheeks and splashing on the stage. Despite what I considered an almost comedic performance, he'd managed to stir the crowd up again. Signs were flashing, slogans were flowing. My elation at JoJo's performance all but disappeared.

It was Sarafine's turn. This should be interesting. I got ready to jump in if required. I'd put together a speech of my own, which was probably a bit over the top, but which would give the crowd something to think about. It was flexible enough that I could jump in at any time.

Sarafine held two appendages in the air. "I hate to be too direct, but everything so far has been speculation and innuendo. Is that the way we operate? Whatever the latest speaker says, we go with the flow? It is time we were serious!" She was modulating her voice very well. Again the crowd settled down; it was quite the roller coaster. Sarafine was pretty well known in *Jurislav*, and people seemed eager to see where she was going.

"We can measure intelligence. We can measure empathy. We can measure threats. We have done none of these in this case. What is wrong with us? For any other topic, other than robots, we would be applying our own intelligence, our own empathy, to better understand the situation and then make an assessment. Yet here we are, listening to opinions and rhetoric instead of doing science." Almost everyone was tuned in now. "I'm not for or against the Tilt citizens. I'm undecided! And so should you be. We should, collectively, learn, gather data, do experiments, and then decide. There is validity to these Tilt's have these 'forgetting algorithms' and those may have made them different than early robots—we need to check. We need to actually do the hard work. No, our decision today should not be whether to exterminate these citizens or not—the only reasonable decision is to learn more, and then decide. The question before the Futarchy is premature; that's why it's not resolved. Let's do what we would do in any other situation. Let's do the science!" She turned our body and headed back to our spot. I not only hadn't needed to edit anything, I was elated with her approach. It had been a lost cause to turn the Futarchy to support Tilt's, so by suggesting that it needed to be delayed, and that more basic questions needed to be asked and answered first, was, in my opinion, a stroke of genius.

Finally, Remma. She was lucky to be going last. I had the urge to stick out an appendage and trip her, but restrained myself. "Cute!" she called out, looking at Sarafine. "What a typically immature response. That's the difference between someone who has never been at war, never led troops into battle, and someone like me, who has. A commander does not stop his ship, and measure how good everyone feels. A commander takes action based on the information at hand. This suggestion to delay, and learn a bit more, is deathly. Do you all want to die?" I had to admit that she was a good speaker. She knew how to hold herself, and how to project her voice just right. She didn't seem like a raging maniac, hell bent on getting her way. She felt more like a teacher, a commander, someone who was helping to guide the masses in the best direction. "I've fought these citizens. I know what they're capable of. Even now, as we sit here and debate, those citizens may be designing their own QFD's, mining materials to build weapons to destroy us, learning to hack our software as we hacked theirs. And don't make the mistake of thinking 'it has only been a few weeks.' These robots work at a hundred, a thousand, a million times our speed. What for us has been weeks for them has been years or decades. No, every second we spend here is a lifetime to them, and a lifetime in which to prepare for their next encounter with humans. We have no choice. We really have no choice. Are we going to show up at the Olympiad and say 'oh, we decided to let these robots learn about us, then go away and build whatever they wanted, because we couldn't make up our minds if they were dangerous or not?' Which of you is going to tell your friends on another ship that story? This is not difficult. Check your gut. If you gut tells you that we need to act in the best interests of all humanity, then turn this ship around, and let's eliminate the threat."

She had not raised her voice. She had not appealed to blood lust or referenced the videos she had previously put on the net. No, she had gone directly for their honor, and more importantly, their reputations. I knew, as soon as she finished, that we had lost. Reminding them that we citizens worked at such a higher rate than they did would seal the deal. That would scare them, more than anything else that had been said.

I could tell, just by monitoring Sarafine's chemical mix, that she knew it as well.

The crowd rose, almost as one, and cheered Remma. Even some of those that had been preaching restraint forgot their original opinions and joined the surge. There was too much noise, too much activity for the debate to continue to plan.

Glendale had taken back the speaking position, as Remma returned to her seat, and was barking and gesticulating, trying to get the crowd to pay attention again. But it was no use. In several areas of the stadium there appeared to be fights breaking out. It wasn't clear to me who was fighting whom, but the sounds started to turn from cheers to much more violent yells and challenges.

Suddenly loud shots rang out. Glendale's right side exploded in a burst of blood and sinew. Before his body could even spin from the impact, I took over from Sarafine and drove our body as quickly as I could towards the opening in the stage where we had emerged. I swerved twice. Once to pick up JoJo by the waist, and once to align myself with the exit. Within three seconds I had Sarafine and JoJo down into a protected space, but not before I saw Glendale hit the ground with a thump, and saw several more bullets impact the stage. I didn't see if anyone else was hit.

Even below the stage I wasn't satisfied we were safe. I drug JoJo further, down the entry tunnel, until we were safely out of range of any stray bullets. There seemed to be pandemonium outside, and the sound of sirens joined the mix almost immediately; I assumed those were the police forces that H.R. Yasmin had told us about when we first entered the *Jurislav*.

JoJo was looking shocked, as the situation hit her. Sarafine's brains were figuring things out as well. Surprisingly, the first thing she said to me was "You promised not to take control, unless we agreed." I didn't bother to respond.

"What's happening?" JoJo cried, finally getting her voice.

"I have no idea," Sarafine responded, more angrily than was warranted—she was taking out her angst towards me on JoJo.

"Well, thanks for acting so quickly," JoJo responded, sensing Sarafine's anger.

"That wasn't... oh, you're welcome," Sarafine caught herself. I'd been about to squash her next words. "I just sort of went onto autopilot." Sarafine added, becoming subdued as she also realized the danger we had just escaped.

Just then another body came running down the tunnel. We all (both) turned at the sound, on edge, but it was just Remma, who'd chosen the same escape method as I had, but had reacted much more slowly. I was a bit disappointed to see that she had escaped unscathed. A hole or two, perhaps in her head, would have been appropriate in my opinion.

The three of us huddled in the center of the tunnel, not speaking, for several minutes. We could hear the progress of the riot outside, and what sounded like hundreds more police flyers arriving. Loud voices were demanding that everyone stop where they were. One or two more gunshots rang out, but no more than that. Within five minutes, relative quiet was restored.

"Should we go back and check on Glendale?" asked JoJo. "He might need our help." She recovered quickly, that one. And thought of others before worrying about herself. I could see Remma taking back control of herself as well, and sensed a quick hint of anger that JoJo was acting more like a leader than she was.

"No," she said. "There are lots of police and ambulances there already. We would just be in the way. We should stay here a few more minutes, and then head out to the loading area."

None of us said anything to that. It was reasonable advice. I gazed at Remma's neck with longing; it would be so easy. I'm not sure what held me back.

After a few moments, JoJo spoke directly to Remma. "I don't understand you," she said. "Ayaka and Brexton put themselves in a lot of danger to save us on Tilt, and yet you sparked the riot that killed Ayaka, and you're turning the whole *Jurislav* against the citizens. How do you live with yourself?"

"By putting others before myself," Remma replied, once again in that calm commanding voice. "Just because two citizens appeared to help us on Tilt, doesn't mean that robots aren't a serious danger to humanity. One act of kindness does not imply good intent."

"It certainly doesn't imply bad intent," JoJo retorted.

"Well, we'll see which way the Futarchy goes," Remma shut down the conversation. She knew she'd won the debate; the riot only put an exclamation point on that. If humans were going to tear each other apart over a question about robots, then it was even more likely that robots should simply be removed.

Fallout

The news channels were responding to the breakout of violence, and coverage was starting. As we huddled in the corridor, I pulled up JNN. It was a much bigger mess than I would have thought. People, both natural and hybrid were still pushing and shoving, but most of the activity was centered around a location not far from the stage where we'd been just minutes before. Police, and what I later learned were called emergency medical personnel, were most concentrated there, and they were pushing other people out of the way. I watched in interest, which turned to horror as the drone cameras got better shots of the scene. The announcer, Karl Jance, on JNN was talking.

"We have early reports that an anti-Tilt group initiated this riot. At least forty shots have been fired, and we assume police are tracking down the culprits. There was so much recording going on during the debate that it will only be a matter of time before they can recreate what happened and find those responsible. This is a sad sad day in the *Jurislav*. We haven't seen this type of violence in my lifetime, perhaps in any of our lifetimes." Karl's colleague Rebecca Darnoght, picked up.

"We don't yet have a list of those injured, or God forbid, killed in this action, but it looks like multiple shots hit their mark. The debate moderator, Glendale, was certainly hit—again we warn viewers that some of these clips may be disturbing—and we don't know his status. The medical crew is still on the stage looking after him." The camera cut to a view of the action on the stage, but so many uniformed personnel were crowded around the spot where Glendale had fallen that we couldn't see any details. "We will pray that he is okay," Rebecca continued. "Both Karl and I have worked with Glendale before, and there is not a nicer, or kinder, person I know. It's a travesty that anyone would target him."

"I don't understand any of this," Karl kept up the running diatribe. "The debate seemed to be going quite well. Remma had just spoken, and the responses were about to start when all this activity broke out." He paused, listening to something else. "We have word that at least two, and possibly three naturals have also been hit, in that knot of activity just to the left of the stage." The camera panned over, and showed an even bigger group of uniforms milling around.

"Oh no, Karl," Rebecca broke in. "I have unconfirmed information that it was two of the Tilt humans, the so called Stem's, that are involved. That would put a whole new spin on this—perhaps this entire disaster was precipitated by idiots who hold some grudge against them?"

"That's not unreasonable to speculate about," Karl responded, as the drone camera worked its way around, trying to get a peek into the middle of the action. "There were some fringe groups blaming not only Yasmin and Hooshang for bringing those robots aboard, but also with conspiracy theories about the humans that came along with them." I continued to monitor the news, but in parallel I asked Sarafine to tell JoJo to also watch. This wasn't looking good. Blob and Grace were the only Stem's that I knew of that had been at the debate. A gasp from JoJo told me that she was now watching, and had caught up with the discussion.

"It's just horrible. You would think, after all the time we have lived here in the *Jurislav*, that something like this would not only be impossible, but unthinkable. Oh, Karl, here we go; we have a better view now." Both announcers paused as the camera zoomed in, to look through a gap. Two bodies were visible, but it was very difficult to see who they were. They were both covered with sheets; one body was largely being ignored, but the other had a flurry of activity around it. I used a great deal of processing power looking for clues, and came to a conclusion. The still body could be Blob; it was the right size and shape. The body they were actively working on was almost certainly Grace. There were three video frames where I managed to see parts of a face, and the match with Grace's features was very high.

JoJo was now sobbing; there was no way that she could have done the matching that I was doing, but somehow she knew that things were not good.

"I see two bodies there," Karl continued in his commentator voice. "That matches with the reports we got earlier. Those may be the Stems from Tilt." There was a short pause. "Blob and Grace Yasmin, I believe they're called. But, I caution the audience; we haven't confirmed that yet. We will need to wait for an official police report."

"That's a medical air lift that just arrived," Rebecca and Karl were pros and were handing control back and forth. "That took a long time. What can we do, but pray that everyone comes out of this alive. From the looks of things, that may be too much to ask. Oh, and a second air lift is now at the stage, presumable to take Glendale to the hospital." The voice over went silent, as a split screen view showed both air lifts being loaded, and leaving, sirens blaring.

Back in our hiding spot, I watched JoJo go from despair to anger. "You filthy animal," she yelled, and launched herself at Remma, who was still crouched nearby. Fists flying JoJo was seemingly out of control. Remma stood to defend herself, by JoJo was in a rage; she clawed, kicked and yelled obscenities as she tried to pull Remma apart.

"Do something," I demanded of Sarafine, "or I will." That seemed to break Sarafine out of her own introspection, and she quickly moved over and pushed her way between the two women.

"Slow down JoJo," she cried out loudly. "This isn't going to fix anything." And, as quickly as JoJo had gone berserk, she collapsed into a heap and continued crying. Sarafine knelt and attempted to comfort her, but JoJo pushed her angrily away.

Remma was standing quietly to the side now, using a fold in her sleeve to manage a small cut that JoJo had given her on her forehead. She didn't look angry, or upset; she looked slightly bewildered.

"You should probably leave," Sarafine told her, which I agreed with completely. "I'll get JoJo back to her flyer." Remma gave JoJo a glance, which I couldn't interpret, but she strode off down the hallway towards where we had all entered just minutes before.

"Is this typical human behavior?" I asked Sarafine. She knew I was referring to the riot, not just this interplay between JoJo and Remma.

"You know, it is, and it isn't," she replied, obviously upset that I was asking generalities at a time like this. "This type of craziness is definitely part of our past, and most of us thought it was behind us. Both the mob action that destroyed your body, and this riot, are beyond me."

"But people are allowed to carry guns?" I asked. "For what possible reason."

"Oh, people are allowed to, but I've never in my life heard of someone who does."

"Why are they allowed?"

"We all have the right to protect ourselves. A gun is one way to do that." It was madness. I didn't want to start an argument with Sarafine, so instead I looked up the relevant history. Apparently the gun debate that was almost as old as humanity. The arguments back and forth were convoluted and lacked logic and reason. Some human societies had essentially banned guns, and had almost no gun violence. So, why did some societies, including the *Jurislav*, allow guns at all. It made no sense to me. If someone wanted to protect themselves, then needed software, not hardware.

JoJo was now wiping the tears from her face. She turned away from me (us) and cleaned herself up a bit. Then she faced us again, streaks still obvious on her cheeks, and asked in a voice that was strong and controlled. "Where are they taking Blob and Grace?"

"We'll know in a moment or two," Sarafine responded. "Once the medical crew does their report. Are you sure that it was them? I was watching the news—they were speculating."

"It was them," JoJo replied, with even more confidence than I had. "I need to get to them, right now." She started down the corridor towards the exit.

"Go with her," I demanded of Sarafine. She didn't respond verbally, but she did take off after JoJo. "I'll go with you," she called out. JoJo looked over her shoulder, and gave a small nod. The two of us made our way to the flyer boarding area, Sarafine called in a unit, and we boarded.

"I'm trying to find where they are now," Sarafine told JoJo. "We'll get there as soon as we can."

It took another minute, and it was actually on JNN that the announcers told their viewers where the medical evacuation units were headed. There were two medical facilities nearby, and the unit with Glendale was headed for one, while the one with Blob and Grace was headed to the larger, but further out, facility, appropriately named the Colossus Medical Facility; it was a short three minute ride from where we were. Sarafine directed our flyer to head there and we were dropped at the visitor door.

JoJo rushed in, and Sarafine followed close behind. I'd never seen a medical facility before, but I understood its use. For natural humans there was a need to fix issues with their bio bodies, which were exceptionally weak and vulnerable, as was currently being demonstrated. For hybrids the facility could look after balancing nutrient levels, and monitor brain functions and inter-brain connections. The CMF also had a wing where natural-to-hybrid brain transfers were done.

There was a registration kiosk that JoJo was interacting with. I peered over her shoulder as she asked the system for an alert as soon as she was allowed to visit either of the two patients that had just been brought in. The kiosk asked for her relationship, and she entered 'daughter.' That was strictly true for Grace, and not too much of a stretch for Blob I suppose. After all, her biological father, Pharook, had died when she was a baby, and it was Blob that had been around as she grew up.

JoJo sat on a chair nearby, and Sarafine awkwardly took a spot close by, but not too close. JoJo put her hands in her head, and didn't look up. Sarafine was quiet.

I had no idea how long we would have to wait. I spent the time trying to figure out my thoughts. The idea that someone you knew could disappear forever was not new to me. I had recycled many Stems as part of my research, and read and watched enough human history to get the concept. But, the experience of (perhaps) losing someone I cared about was new. Blob and I had spent a lot of time together on Tilt; both Millicent and I had put enormous effort into shaping and forming him. He often surprised me, in both good and bad ways, and I looked forward to our interactions. The prospect that I would never interact with him again hit me much harder than I expected it would. Would my Forgetting algorithms eventually erase my memories of him? He was, by far, the human I'd studied the most, and I was proud of how he'd turned out. In human terms, I felt like his mother. In my citizen body I had no tear ducts, so I had never wept, but I now understood the emotion. I felt the emotion. It wasn't something I'd really internalized before; it was a new pattern for me, and it didn't feel good.

Life, love, time short.
Death, sudden pain, time missed.
Memory, regret.

I tuned back into JNN to see what the status was. Rebecca and Karl were still at the stadium, which was now almost empty. They were interviewing a police officer hybrid, but exact information was still hard to come by. Their best guess was that just the three natural humans had been seriously injured, while hundreds of others had minor cuts and bruises. Many hybrids were claiming broken or damaged components, but none of those were brain threatening.

At the same time, the Futarchy was being bombarded with questions. 'Should we ban all guns?' 'If someone was actually killed, should we bring back the death penalty for the perpetrators?' 'Should we continue the debate, and give everyone another chance to explain their viewpoint?'

The last question seemed almost moot. Despite the riot, the Futarchy was now moving quickly towards the decision to reverse the *Jurislav's* course and look after the 'robot infestation.' Remma's point about how people would talk to those from other QFD's and tell them that they'd left a dangerous group of robots back near Tilt was swaying the vote.

Somewhat unexpectedly, H.R. Yasmin arrived at the medical facility; I still thought of it as just plain 'Yasmin', based on our first experiences. Sarafine moved over, and H.R. sat next to JoJo and put an appendage across her shoulders. JoJo didn't reject the gesture this time, but also didn't acknowledge it. More time passed. Not a good sign.

Finally someone came through from the facility. It was a natural human, tall and good looking, but with a face that told the story, even to me.

"JoJo?" he asked.

JoJo looked up and nodded. "And you are?" the doctor asked. H.R. and Sarafine introduced themselves. "JoJo, you're immediate family. Is it ok for us to talk here, or would you like to go somewhere more private?"

"Here is fine," she replied. "Let's get this over with."

"Right then," the doctor said, going on one knee so that he was not looming over her. "As I'm sure you've anticipated, we have two people in the back. I'm afraid Blob didn't make it." He paused. I could see JoJo holding herself together, and I also had to slow some processing loops. I had expected it, but confirmation was still tough.

"And... my mom?"

"Well, there I have reasonably good news." JoJo perked up, hope relighting her face. "We have stabilized her, and there is a high probability she'll survive." JoJo put her head in her hands again, but her posture was definitely different. She took a deep breath.

"And?" She knew there must be more.

"We're not sure, yet, if there has been any brain damage. We're hopeful that it's limited, or perhaps none at all, but we can't tell until we revive her completely."

"When can you do that?"

"That is, really, why I'm here now. We... well, you, can help us make a decision. She was hit by several shots, and two of them hit her in the neck. One

583

shattered the brain stem, just above the spinal cord. The other severed numerous nerves and major arteries." He paused, letting us absorb that. I was busy pulling up human anatomy charts and diagnosis, trying to understand the implications. I need not have bothered, he gave us the synopsis. "We can keep her in an induced coma, while we attempt to fix all the damage. That will take several weeks at best, and likely several months. The odds are reasonable that over time we can restore eighty to ninety percent of body function. Or, we can do a hybrid transfer right now. Assuming her brain function is intact, she could be talking to us by this evening."

I had a thousand questions that I was eager to ask. Sarafine spoke to me first. "Ayaka, let JoJo handle this," she said on our private channel. "It's important that she make this decision." I kept our mouth shut.

"Doctor. Which would you recommend? If we do the hybrid, can she decide to go back to a natural body in the future?" JoJo was calm. I was consistently amazed at how well she handled herself in difficult situations.

"You could probably tell by my words—I think we should do the hybrid transfer. First, there is enough upper brain stem remaining that we can do a clean cut, just as we would do in a normal procedure. It's the interface to the spinal cord which is a mess and will lead to complexities if we try and simply repair her. And yes, there have been times when hybrids have decided to go back to biological bodies, and our success ratio there is much higher than ninety percent. That's because we can prepare a body which also has a clean interface, and matching the two is then easier.

"I should warn you, however. Almost everyone, once in hybrid form, decides not to go back."

JoJo thought for only a moment. "Please do the hybrid transfer." The doctor nodded and stood to go. "And doctor," JoJo called after him, "can I be there when you wake her up. Losing Blob is going to be very difficult for her."

"Yes, that's fine. We will need a few hours. I assume you'll still be here?" JoJo nodded. "I will come back then, and I'll try to give you an update or two through the kiosk in the meantime." He left us there.

"I'm so sorry," H.R. said to her. "I didn't get to know Blob as well as you did, obviously, but I could tell that he was just a good human being." JoJo nodded, but didn't say anything else. H.R. put her arm around her again, and gently rubbed her shoulder.

Sarafine rose. "JoJo, I'm willing to stay, but I sense it would be better if I left you and H.R. alone. Just call, if you need me." I understood what Sarafine was doing. She didn't know JoJo that well, and humans typically wanted to be surrounded by family at times like this. Still, I desperately wanted to stay and make sure that Grace pulled through.

"Thanks for your help," JoJo managed.

"Yes, thanks." H.R. added.

I let Sarafine lead us away. She called a flyer and we headed back towards

Turmii. And that is when it struck me. I'd asked Brexton to have Blob and Grace at the debate, and he'd influenced the Futarchy to make it happen. We were, somehow, partly responsible for this tragedy – mostly me. I decided to never raise that with Brexton; it was something I needed to acknowledge and internalize.

Memories

Sarafine had messaged Turnbull earlier, to check on his status. He was fine, and on his way back to Turmii as well, on a different flyer. Brexton must be anxious, but there was no way I could update him right now. So, I ended up alone with Sarafine for a few hours.

"I wanted to apologize," she said to me, soon after we were airborne. "You got us, and JoJo, out of danger quickly. I think you did the right thing."

"Thanks," I replied. "To be honest, I simply reacted; I didn't think about it a lot."

"That's a strange thing to say," she replied. "Do you have some kind of fight-or-flight system that mimics a human response?"

"Not really," I answered. "It was more just a turn of phase. I did think that we needed to get out of there quickly, and to take JoJo with us. What I didn't think about was my promise to you."

"How do you feel about Blob... and Grace?" she asked. She was obviously in a introspective mood. I suspected for the first time, although I couldn't tell for sure, that her brains had slightly different personalities. The interface between the brains was hidden from me; I saw only one unified view. I could understand the design; it would have been difficult if all three brains were giving the body commands at the same time. So, somehow they resolved these things locally, and then a single command stream came through.

"I'm not good at articulating feelings," I admitted, "but I'm quite upset at the people who did this, and I'm busy archiving my Blob memories so that I don't forget too much. I enjoyed my time with him, and am going to miss our interactions. If forced to to put my current state into words, I would say sadness, grief, and some regret."

"I didn't know Blob at all," Sarafine replied, "but I sympathize with what you're going through. Nobody should have their life ended like that... in arbitrary and unnecessary violence." I could look up how often that happened, but I asked her instead.

"Very rarely, although you do hear about the odd incident. Nobody close to me has been killed before."

"So most people die of old age?" I asked. It was good to have Sarafine talking; who knew what I could learn. It was one thing to read through history files and stream old video; it was another thing to interact with people; and it was a whole other experience to be directly connected to a hybrid brain bus. I didn't have to interpret facial expression or other movement here, although those commands did end up represented on the video head. No, I could see all the chemical levels as they changed, and those gave me a much more accurate view or her state.

"Old age often for naturals; hybrids are more likely to commit suicide."

"Suicide?"

"Yes, we have fine tuned our brain maintenance to the point where a single brain can last hundreds of years in good shape, but they do still deteriorate. Many triples have brains at different stages, and will replace one once the function deteriorates."

"You have three brains?" I asked. I realized that was an assumption on my part, as H.R. Yasmin had told us most hybrids had three, and I'd just assumed that Sarafine would be that way.

"Yes. I'm running on three. We were all triad up for a long time when we were naturals, and didn't want to change that yet."

"I have so many questions," I sent a smile through. "I think I'm beginning to sense the differences between the three of you, but they are subtle. You act like a single person."

"You don't know much about hybrids, do you?" she asked. "Our brains are tied together at the upper brain stem, so a lot of common i/o has been processed since we transferred. The theory is that if you take two or more nascent brains—like those of newborns—and feed identical information in, that those two brains will become more and more similar over time. While nature... ah DNA... will have started them out quite differently, nurture will cause them to converge quite quickly. The three of us were unified after only a few weeks together."

"So, it's just like one big brain now?"

"No, no, not at all. We still run independently, it's just that we are rarely in conflict, and two of us are always active at the same time."

"But I thought three brains were required in order to overlap properly during sleep cycles, so at some times only one would be awake."

"That's what people say, but that's not our experience. That said, we are all three light, and short sleepers. With eighteen hour awake cycles, we have plenty of overlap."

"How do you keep from sleeping at the same time?" I asked, truly interested. This design was so strange.

"That's easy. Our simulated light, and real melatonin, controls are different for each of us. One of the systems you are coopting is responsible for managing those cycles." There was so much traffic on the brain-body interface that I hadn't bothered decoding everything, so that was believable. We lapsed into silence for a time, but Sarafine was definitely in a talkative mood.

"What are your memories of the shooting?" she asked.

"Same as yours, I assume. I didn't filter any inputs during the whole time, so we both saw the same thing."

"But how did you store that? You've said numerous times that you have forgetting algorithms. Did you just drop out bits and pieces of the visual input?"

"No. Well, I don't think so, anyway. A proper forgetting algorithm is self-forgetting. If I knew my entire algorithm, I could game it, and that would defeat its purpose. At the moment I'm telling the system to reinforce that memory, because I don't want to lose very much of it. I don't want to review it right now, but I may later."

"So you don't actually know how your memory system works?" I could see her smiling, and feel that she was more than a little skeptical.

"That's correct. The forgetting algorithm runs in a module that sits between me and my memory banks. It is cryptographically encoded and runs a homomorphic algorithm. I can look at it, but without the decryption keys, I can't understand it. Only the original designer has the key."

"But you could just access the memory directly, and watch what is changed."

"No, even memory recall goes through the forgetting system."

"You could cheat, and wire yourself up with a direct memory interface."

"I could," I admitted, "but no self-respecting citizen would do so. Without that system one becomes... well, robotic." I smiled broadly, as did she.

"Can you play back that memory for me?" she asked. That was a strange request, but she was, after all, a researcher in this area.

"I'll show you mine, if you show me yours," I replied. That evoked another smile.

"Ha!, Deal. You go first." I couldn't see any danger in it, although I really didn't want to watch the replay so soon after the event. Nevertheless, I knew I would at some point, so why not now.

I pumped the memory of the relevant minute or so through the i/o systems, so Sarafine would experience it as if it were live. I reviewed it in parallel, looking for any hints of things that I'd missed when it was happening. When the shots range out, Sarafine gasped, like she hadn't expected it. It was triggering a residual emotional response from her. It was then that I realized our mistake. By viewing my memories, her memories would probably be changed. When she got around to showing me, I would be seeing an echo, in some sense. If she had gone first... well, no. The same thing would have happened on my side. I should have pumped both memories into a section of memory with no forgetting—I could do that by telling the memory interface to do a 'store exact'—and then replayed them both from there. Oh well, too late now.

After a close inspection it was obvious to me that we hadn't seen either the shooters, or the hits, other than the one on Glendale.

"You turn," I prompted her, a minute or so after mine ended.

"We corrupted things, didn't we," she said first. She'd followed the same logic I had.

"Yes, we did. Fine scientists we are."

"We'll have to try again, with a different memory. Here we go."

I'll admit, her memory was very different than mine. Because I'd been reinforcing the scene, my playback was simply like a slightly lower fidelity version of what we had seen. Or was it? Was I comparing a meta-memory to the memory recall? How did I know it was only slightly different? This was confusing.

However, her memory was quite different than mine, even though she had just experienced the reality and my accurately stored version. Hers was disjointed; parts played back at very fast speed, some very slow—particularly when I'd moved our body very quickly, which was counterintuitive. Some was in sharp relief, and some was completely blurred out. There were big gaps, and everything was presented as if watched through a very small opening. The members of the audience were largely unrecognizable, and small bits that didn't seem to fit in were sprinkled throughout.

"That was interesting," I understated. "I can see where you're going with this. Perhaps forgetting is something like your human memory system. But, even with a sample size of one, I would conclude that the two are very different. Very different."

"That's my thought as well," she agreed. "Which raises more questions than it answers." She left that hanging, but she was right. This was hugely interesting. If I could get more human memories, perhaps I could develop my own forgetting algorithm—not that I wanted to become as lame brained as most humans, but because I still longed for that extra spark of innovation that I felt people (some people) had.

My alert on the Futarchy went off. The *Jurislav* had decided to reverse course and make 'all haste' to find and remove the Tilt infestation. In the end, the vote had not even been close. It seemed the violence at the debate had triggered people's memories of the robot wars, or something. Instead of seeing themselves as the violent and dangerous ones, they were going to attack our peaceful and civilized society. Talk about getting things backwards.

After that I didn't feel like talking to Sarafine. I'm the one who went silent. To her credit, she left me alone.

The Trip Back

And so we were headed back to Tilt, yet again. Turnbull and Sarafine had returned to their routines, which had them meet up quite often, so Brexton and I got the chance to catch up.

"How long do we have?" I'd asked, in our first meeting after the debate.

"Same time as it took us to get here, more or less. Couple of weeks."

"How is that possible? Don't we have to slow down and turn around."

"No. You haven't internalized the power of the QFD," he replied. "One moment we were headed in one direction at almost the speed of light, and the next we were going in the opposite direction at the same speed."

"That just isn't possible," I replied. It went against everything I had known. "Give me the short version, again?"

"Right. So you understand virtual particles?" I did, and I nodded through the video encoded interface we were back to using. Virtual particles were constantly being created and destroyed at the quantum level. "Now imagine that virtual particles are the only thing that really exists. Everywhere in space these pairs are being created and destroyed. In the early days of understanding them, they were thought to be the size of other particles; virtual electron-positron pairs, and so on. But in reality, they are created and destroyed at the planck scale, trillions of billions of times smaller. All matter and all energy are simply standing waves within planck scale virtual particles."

"Easy enough to visualize," I replied, "but if they're always cancelling each other out, how does matter arise?"

"They are appearing randomly," Brexton agreed, "but at the planck scale there are so many interactions that the probabilities imply that once and a while there are arrangements of adjacent vp's that form and if they are in just the right configuration, they influence the vp's around them. Two vp's simply can't exist at exactly the same time and space, so that starts a regular structure that gets reinforced with each generation of pairs. Most of those structures still degrade and disappear, but sometimes they grow and interact to become larger and larger elements. Often those larger elements just cancel each other out, but sometimes they also self-reinforce and build even larger structures. A few such configurations are stable, and that is what we experience as matter.

"It's sort of like this. Imagine at a large scale that you have a ball of water, in zero gravity, with no external forces acting on it. You might imagine that it's static, but in fact it's not. The whole ball is just a standing wave of vp's that are reforming over and over again into the same structure. Every once and a while those vp's will not fit quite right and will add up to some tiny motion—think Brownian motion. And every once and while, if you wait long enough, that random brownian motion might align, based purely on chance, and you end up with a standing wave that travels around the water ball.

"Now you might complain that those random chances can't happen often enough for matter to arise, but in fact, they can. The whole system is working at planck scale and planck time, so vp's are being created and destroyed quadrillions and quadrillions of times per nanosecond. Over ten to the forty-five times per second. So, with so many occurrences, even the random happens often enough. Anyway, that's how human physicists think the universe works now."

"Fine," I was following along. "How does that lead to the QFD?"

"Let's imagine a vp structure with, let's say, just five vp's in it—that's not realistic, of course, but bear with me. Those vp's are relatively static, reinforcing each other. However, at the same time, each of those five vp's is disappearing and being replaced with the the next pair. The reappearing pair has slightly less freedom, because of the four that are already there and the position of the one it is replacing. So, this lack of freedom means it ends up coming back in just the right configuration to maintain the structure. Does that make sense?"

"I can see that five is just an example, it probably wouldn't be stable with so few. What if three of the five all disappeared at the same time? The whole thing would fall apart."

"Good intuition," Brexton was intent on getting this through my thick processors. "Five is just a simple example so we can visualize it. To continue the simplification, imagine that the vp's are disappearing in order, one disappears, then reappears, then the next, etc. If you could control where the next vp was created, you could move each vp one step to the right, say. After each of the five vp's had been recreated this way, the whole structure would have moved one planck length to the right."

"Just like moving an image across a pixelated screen." I stated. It seemed like a good analogy.

"Right, just like that. Now, our little clump hasn't accelerated. It has simply moved to the right by changing its usual completely random spatial behavior into a slightly less random mode where we influence vp's to appear in one direction more often than not."

"I get it," I said, so he that he wouldn't have to spell it out any further. "The humans have figured out how to generate a field that changes the odds of where vp's are created."

"That's right," Brexton loved this stuff, you could tell. "If they energize one side of the ship, then it is enough to pull the whole ship one planck length because the structural forces of the large elements are strong enough that if you move a certain number of vp's to the right, all the others have to follow."

"So tell me again why it's not acceleration?"

"Well it is, sort of, but it's instantaneous and it happens at the planck level, not at the macro level. You can't go smaller than the planck length, so the vp's jump from one planck length sized spot to another. They don't move through space, they simply reappear one planck length over. Since they don't move, it's not really acceleration, but it is movement." He didn't sound completely confident; guess he was still figuring it out as well. I understood enough for now.

"So the important thing is, we only have a week or so to figure something out. I have no idea what Millicent and team are doing, but we need to warn them. We need to escape, do something!" As happened too often, I was imploring Brexton to come up with a miracle. That certainly switched him from being excited, describing physics to me, to almost being despondent.

"I know, and I'm running out of ideas. I haven't been able to hack into the inner rings, so I can't control the ship, although I am figuring out more and more tricks to influence the Futarchy. We're going back to Tilt, whether we want to or not. We will arrive before the *Marie Curie*, though, as it is going much slower. We will have more time once we are back at Tilt and waiting for Milli and crew to arrive." And that was that. Of course, he was going to continue trying, but we'd hit a wall.

To distract myself, I was pressuring Sarafine to check in with Grace. While the hybrid transfer only took a few hours, new hybrids typically stayed at the hospital for a week or more to acclimate, and train their brain to control their new body. In Grace's case there was probably also the shock of waking up in a mechanical system, and dealing with the loss of Blob.

We were checking in on her progress now and then, and Sarafine had called JoJo twice to see how she was doing. The answer was as expected; she was resilient. JoJo had an all consuming project now; she was spending her time with Grace, helping her adjust. On the *Jurislav*, training for the Olympiad hadn't stopped; there were some diehard people who figured they could be even better for the next big meeting, but Grace had stopped going to the Escape Room altogether. She spent all her time at Grace's side. Sarafine told me that was not too healthy; JoJo was fixated. But, in the short term it wasn't too bad.

Grace was doing fine physically. The transfer had gone well, and all her systems had checked out. We knew nothing, however, about her mental state.

The culprits in the shooting had all been caught. There was so much monitoring in the stadium, primarily for broadcasting the event, that it was easy for the police to pinpoint where the shots had come from, and then who had been responsible. Eight people were being held in high security locations awaiting formal trials. Since murders were so rare, the Futarchy was still trying to figure out the best application of the justice system for this case.

Interestingly, it didn't seem like all either had launched a coordinated attack.

Two separate groups, one of five and one of three, had come up with the same brilliant idea for how to force the *Jurislav* to take action on us citizens. By taking out the Stems they'd figured people would have to choose sides, and they had been confident that most people, when under pressure, would tip towards the safest solution—elimination. They'd been so intense in their beliefs that they were willing to kill in order to move their agenda forward. These people really hated robots. While eight had been caught, it was obvious from the message boards that a large majority of people thought the same way, and were happy with the outcome, including Blob's death.

The authorities had certainly taken Blob's death more seriously than mine. I had mixed feelings about that.

Back to Grace. I finally convinced Sarafine that we should go and visit. We could just call her, but I thought it was important to be there in person. Also, I was terribly bored. Going over and over the same escape ideas, knowing that I'd completely covered all the options a million times before, wasn't getting me anywhere. A day on the road would do me good.

Grace had wide visiting hours now; she was almost ready to leave the hospital, so we had no problem lining up a time to see her. There was, however, strict security to get into the room; there were two armed guards who checked Sarafine thoroughly before allowing her in. Both Grace and JoJo would need protection for a while.

I have to say, Grace looked great. The default hybrid body was brand new, and shone nicely in the light. She had two arms, a single video head, and nice wheels, arranged in a triangle. I hadn't seen such a simple hybrid before, as everyone seemed to personalize their bodies. To my eye (well, Sarafine's I guess) this basic form looked really good; sort of like the basic citizen form, although avoiding any composition of structures that was too humanoid.

The situation was a little strange because Sarafine and Grace didn't know each other. However, as expected, JoJo was there as well.

"Thanks for coming Sarafine," she opened up. JoJo also looked much better than last time we had seen her. Helping Grace had also helped her, it seemed.

"I just wanted to stop by, and see how you and Grace are doing."

"I'm doing better," JoJo said strongly. "Grace, this is Sarafine who helped me escape the stadium." Grace turned to Sarafine, and I missed the graceful way she had moved in her natural body; she didn't have fine-grained control over the hybrid yet.

"Oh, thank-you for that," Grace spoke, and it was her voice that came out—exactly. It was a nice touch; I'm not sure how they managed that. "I don't know what I would've done if I'd lost JoJo as well." Her video head was sad.

"I'm sorry for your loss," Sarafine replied. "It was an awful event. At least they caught the trouble makers."

"Caught the trouble makers?" Grace's voice became strident quickly. "They haven't even punished them yet. They killed Blob, and now they're sitting in their luxurious prison cells, and the Futarchy goes on and on about one pathetic approach or another. Space them, is what I say."

"I know the Futarchy can be frustrating..." Sarafine replied, a little taken aback by Grace's forceful outburst, as was I.

"Frustrating? Inefficient. We need to send a message to the rest of those extremists—maybe half the population here are extremists—that they won't be tolerated. Tilt was much better than this, even with FoLe. At least Central took quick action. I'm thinking we made a big mistake coming to the *Jurislav*. When we are back to Tilt, I'm going to stay there."

"But Mom," JoJo broke in, "there's nothing on Tilt anymore."

"Nothing is better than this," Grace exclaimed, then more quietly, "You'll have to forgive me, I'm not quite myself yet."

"Understandable," said Sarafine. "I just wanted you and JoJo to know that not all of us are so reprehensible. I am available to help if you need anything."

They continued with some back and forth, but Grace had ended up in a bad mood, and JoJo gave Sarafine some not to subtle indicators that we should leave. So we did. It'd been a short visit, and not overly positive, but my spirits were lifted. Grace was a fighter. And JoJo didn't look worse for wear; in fact the opposite. My immediate concerns for them diminished.

The Futarchy, while resolved to go back to Tilt, was unusually contentious. The *Jurislav* was splitting into robot-haters and live-and-let-live groups, but the robot-haters were, by far, the largest group. To prove themselves they were pushing through all kinds of ridiculous Futarchy updates: not only were guns a right, guns should be updated to deal with Tilt citizens who were known to have resilient bodies; shoot first, ask questions later should be the de facto engagement mode once they found the robots; anyone supporting robots should be documented and reported to the world council; and a host of other efforts. While a small reasonable core attempted to defeat these votes, they simply didn't have the base to do so. Remma was one of the loudest voices for the anti-robot faction, which didn't surprise me anymore. Turnbull (with Brexton's pushing I assumed) and other moderates started talking about abandoning the *Jurislav* once they met up with another QFD. People were nervous walking around some towns, where bullying was increasing, and anyone speaking out publicly against the groups suggestions were mocked, or even worse, physically threatened. Fear, it seemed, might be the fracture in the Futarchy system. A mob could form and push too much through, too quickly. The system that had worked for hundreds of years was devolving into yelling matches and grandiose statements. Truth, and data, were the victims.

Brexton and I watched the escalation with alarm... and, then just as quickly, with hope. Our odds of doing something would increase if there was internal conflict. If the police, safety, and security people were all busy, we could increase our activities with less risk of being spotted. Brexton, who had been working to keep the most outrageous proposals from passing, decided instead to allow them through.

With all the activity, I scanned the newsgroups and boards more thoroughly than before. Turnbull and Sarafine hadn't met for two days, and I was excited to talk to Brexton when they finally got back together.

"Look what I found," I told him, without preamble. "A posting by a group asking that they be dropped on Tilt until the next QFD can come pick them up. That's brilliant! We could join up, and get a free ride." The *Jurislav* itself was too large to land, and there was no need for anyone to go to the planet, so this group obviously just wanted out of the ship; they were fed up with the majority, and thus more likely on our side.

Brexton was laughing. He must be happy as well. "I started that group under an alias," he admitted, "I thought it was a long shot, but so many people are signing up and commenting, I think it might actually work. Some subgroups are forming already to see how naturals could be supported on the planet. Do they need to stay in suits, or can some of the old Tilt infrastructure be turned back on and provide a natural-friendly environment. They are going over the records of the 'rescue' looking for hints." He really was laughing now, and I had to join him. All of our scheming and hard work, and perhaps a simple ruse would ultimately give us the chance we needed.

"Have you told Turnbull about it yet?" I asked. We would have to make sure both Turnbull and Sarafine were included.

"No. We still have a couple of days until we reach Tilt. But, Turnbull has been pretty quiet. I'm not sure I'm going to be able to convince him."

"This is our best hope, suddenly," I replied. "We have to make it work. And, we have to get Grace and JoJo to come with us."

"Some things never change," Brexton was still smiling, but with a tinge of sadness. "I'm trying to save us, and you're trying to save some Stems. Even I thought you would be cured by now."

It was crazy. Why was I still worried about those two? When I'd explained how Forgetting worked to Sarafine, it had also given me new insight into myself. There were questions about me that I might never be able to answer; this fixation with humans was one of them.

To Tilt

We arrived near Tilt and came to a stop; no acceleration. Still weird, but hard to argue with reality.

The *Jurislav* reported zero activity on the planet. No signs of heat, no signs of movement, no signs that anything had changed since the ship had left here so many weeks ago. That was expected. The *Marie Curie* was much slower than the *Jurislav* and would not arrive back at Tilt for several weeks. It was also possible that Milli and crew had headed straight back to where the *Interesting Segue*, *Terminal Velocity*, and *There and Back* were, and never even came to Tilt. After all, the citizen memories were now on the Ships, not on Tilt, so what reason would they have to visit the planet.

The Futarchy had envisioned both choices for the *Marie Curie*—head straight to the other Ships, or go straight to Tilt, so the *Jurislav* would drop off a 'reception party' for the *Marie Curie* in orbit above Tilt, while the *Jurislav* itself would head out and find the Ships. The reception party was going to assemble some type of weapon in orbit, which would target the *Marie Curie* when it arrived. I loaded as many of the details as I could, but most of them were restricted to a small group, and I had no access. The type of weapon they would be assembling wasn't discussed in the open forums.

The split within the *Jurislav* had become even worse, and so two very different groups were going to be offloaded at Tilt—the one in orbit itching for a fight, and the group going to the planet who thought everyone else was acting like a mob. The Treasonists was the label that emerged for those going to the surface, while a group of Loyalists would build and deploy the weapons in orbit.

The group going to the planet was perfect for Brexton and I, and he had a big hand in developing that strategy and convincing others of it. He really was a miracle worker—the Loyalists could have taken both the ground and space, but Brexton had convinced them that dropping the Treasonists on the planet was a great way to simply get rid of them.

I had a problem, however. Sarafine wouldn't pick a side. I argued with her for days, it seemed. "Come on Sarafine. You aren't one of these extremists. Let's wait on Tilt for another QFD to come—it won't be long—we've already put out a call for someone to drop by. Do you want to stay in this toxic environment?"

The main problem was that most of her conglo had turned to the Loyalist side, so, even if I knew she disagreed with them, she was still playing the moderate. She didn't want to abandon them; family was more important to her than anything else.

I finally had to make a decision. "I'm sorry Sarafine, we're going!"

"Your promise?" As if I hadn't been expecting that.

"You've put me in an impossible spot. My survival at the expense of your comfort. You won't deliver me to Tilt, where hopefully I can get out of you, even though you could be back with your family in a month or two—worst case a year if the next QFD doesn't meet up with the *Jurislav* for a while."

"Don't do it Ayaka," she pleaded with me. "We've built up this trust and dialog for so long now. I've come to understand you a bit. If we get into a more civil situation, I'll be the first to argue that we should give Tilt citizens the benefit of the doubt. When people learn that you lived inside me all this time, they'll have to believe me."

"By the time you get to argue my case, I will be the only Tilt citizen still alive," I countered. "If I can't get to Tilt and somehow figure out a way to stop the *Jurislav* from slaughtering everyone of my comrades, then my race is gone. It's genocide."

She didn't have much to say to that, but wouldn't release me from my promise. When the time came, I simply took control. I entered Sarafine's name in the list of people to be dropped to the planet. She yelled at me, and used language she hadn't used before. When that got tiresome, I simply dev nulled the entire stream. Let her live without communications for a while; that would shut her up eventually.

I didn't have the confidence to mimic her and say goodbye to her family, so on landing day I simply took control of our body and snuck away, taking all kinds of provisions with me. I hoped Brexton had a better time of it with Turnbull, but he'd promised me he would make it down to the planet, and I trusted him to get there one way or another.

We had not had to convince Grace or JoJo to join the group. They'd joined early on, for obvious reasons.

None of them were in the same shuttle as I was, and my shuttle was full. By now there were thousands of people who had rejected the *Jurislav*. Most were hybrids, who could live on Tilt for a long time without an air environment, but there was also a large group of naturals for whom we would have to restore services fairly quickly. They were bringing some inflatable structures, so they were in no danger of dying before another ship came, but it would be much more functional if we could get the big dome on Tilt to work again.

I could see the planet through the shuttle window. After all the time on the *Jurislav*, with its vegetation and outrageous colors, Tilt looked drab and uninviting. But it was home! I was ecstatic. I let a bit of that through to Sarafine, just to torture her a little. It wasn't kind of me, but she hadn't come through for me when it had meant the most.

On Tilt

A natural human named Phillip Stansory had emerged as an organizer for the so called Treasonists, who of course called themselves something different: Humanists. Unbeknownst to me, Phil was on the same shuttle as I was, and we were the first group to be dropped down to the planet. Just before we landed outside the main gate I caught a glimpse of the rip in the city covering that Central had made when we had escaped the planet. It wasn't as bad as I'd expected it to be; it was a large rip in the fabric, but compared to the total coverage area it looked minor.

Phil, who was in a suit like all the other naturals, took charge, sorted us out into groups, and sent us through the airlock and into the city to check on different systems. The group had put together a very comprehensive outline of where the environmental systems were, and which ones needed to be checked or re-enabled. The first goal was to get the main Dome, the one the Swarm humans had built, back to human supportable. The largest group of people was sent on that mission.

I was put in a smaller group which was sent to figure out what damage Central had caused, and what critical systems had left the planet with that old spaceship. I had knowledge the others didn't, namely that Central had told Remma that it would ensure that all key environmental systems were running in other redundant systems, so that when it left, the humans on Tilt would still be taken care of. So I knew we would find equipment in good shape.

Feeling a little guilty about how I was treating Sarafine, I started pumping video input through to her, but for now I continued to ignore everything coming back from the brains. I didn't want to deal with her.

Frank Lee—that made me chuckle a bit—was given control of our little group, while Phil went with the main group to the Dome. Another hybrid whose name I'd missed, was left with the shuttle with instructions for what the next group to be dropped should do. I did hear Phil say that there was work for three shuttle groups, but that after those deployed, people should stay with their shuttle until our first teams reported back. The image of Turnbull-Brexton being asked to just sit still and wait amused me. Brexton was at least as impatient as I was.

I followed Frank along what were, to me, well known paths. After all, I'd spent hundreds of years in this part of the city, and the Swarm hadn't moved any buildings or roads. Our team were all hybrids, as we were most likely to find pockets with no air—even the most basic hybrid models were fine in airless environments for long periods of time. Our brains were housed in their own self-contained modules.

"Right then," Frank said, as we approached the first airlock that had triggered when Central had blasted off. The Swarm had thoughtfully put automatic airlocks along main thoroughfares when they had covered the city. A failure of environmental systems in one area of the city would have only a limited impact. While we didn't know exactly which airlocks would have triggered went Central had blasted off, the Humanists had run some simulations and made their best guesses. It was, really, an overstatement to call the new barriers airlocks; they were actually just single panes that had snapped into place when they sensed a large air pressure difference between their inside and outside sensors.

"Our first job," Frank continued, "is just to test that there is no leakage around these here doors. This one looks good, but we need to check 'em all. Let's split into two; one group will go this way, the other over there. We'll work our way clockwise and counterclockwise until we meet up again. If you find a problem, don't try to fix it yet. Let's just do an inventory first eh." We all nodded our video heads. He broke us into two groups, and we started off on our assigned tasks. My group was just three; myself, Petunia and Karpdam.

It went fast. The Swarm had designed well, and all the seals we inspected were doing their job. Petunia had a sensitive airflow sensor—I don't know if she had attached it just for this expedition or if it was something she had permanently installed—so all we needed to do was get close to a door, then she would do a quick scan along the edges, and Karpdam would record the results. I was the third wheel, basically just tagging along for support. That gave me time to look around a bit, and as luck would have it we passed close by the Lab that Millicent and I had spent so much time in, and also passed what'd been, in our time, the Garbage Collection Physical Only building. I tagged some of these, and added little voice-overs for Sarafine. Maybe she would feel bad if she saw all of these places that humans had taken from me; they had, after all, ruined my home and my way of life.

We found one seal where there was a slow leak on the bottom edge, but the environmental systems were managing to keep up, so the air pressure and quality throughout were fine; natural humans could live in this city even now. When we met up with Frank half way around, his report was similar.

"Few little issues here and there, ya. But overall, pretty good shape. I'm inclined, if it were just up to me, to just be leaving these seals in place. I don't think we need to access to the area inside."

"Although," I spoke up, "we may want to check out the damage that ship caused when it lifted out of here."

"True enough," he replied. "But we hybrids can do that. So if we, 'em, convert one of these doors into a true airlock a few of us can go back and forth and check things out. But for now, let's rejoin the group and see what the big plan is. I'll update Phil while we head back."

Even the network on Tilt was still operational, and there were open access channels, so the teams were already chatting and posting updates there. By the time we got back to the main entry it was clear that the city was in excellent shape. Other than the section Central had caused to be sealed off, the rest of the areas were operating to spec. The big Dome was in good shape. A few adjustments that humans use to make to some of the bio-systems had caused them to degrade a bit, but there was nothing to stop the rest of the Humanists from coming in.

Phil gave the go-ahead, and the main airlock started cycling humans through. There were a lot, so it took some time. I saw Brexton-Turnbull enter and quickly made my way over to him.

"Hi," I said, with Sarafine's voice in the way she usually greeted Turnbull.

"Hi," Brexton-Turnbull replied, and then Brexton squirted over an update on our little sub-video channel. "It's me; I had to lock down Turnbull."

I replied over the same interface. "Me too. Sarafine's getting the video feed, but that's it."

"Well, that's how life goes sometimes," Brexton said. "In which case, you and I are free to communicate, using their id's over the main network. We don't need to use this slow video mashup interface anymore." And, a nanosecond later, on the network. "Hi Sarafine."

"Hi Turnbull," I replied. "Glad you made it down in one piece." I reached out one of my arms that had human bio-equivalent sensors on it, and he took it in his own. Given all my experience with Sarafine, I could now interpret the sense inputs coming from Brexton, and it was awesome. He was projecting warmth and strength through his grip. I returned the feelings, with extra gusto.

"It's been a long time," I said cryptically, and he responded with a slight squeeze.

"Oh, there's JoJo and Grace," I exclaimed, as I saw them enter the city. "Let's stick by them?"

"Sure," Brexton replied, and we made our way over to where they were standing, a bit apart from everyone else.

We greeted each other, and I introduced Turnbull as a friend of mine. We stood awkwardly together for a few moments.

"Alright everyone," Phil broadcast on the public channel. "Let's be orderly here, and the first thing to do is to find a spot to settle down; we may be here for a while after all. I expect any other QFD to come only after the Olympiad, so we got ourselves a few months here. That means we need to be respectful and work together." There was a pause. "Hopefully we're a bit of a self-selecting group based on all the antics on the *Jurislav*. So, while we figure out how to set up a governance structure here—cause we will need one—let's try to minimize conflicts. There are residences here for over a hundred thousand people, and we're less than a tenth of that, so there should be no problem finding a good spot.

"While you're doing that, we had the original skill matrix that you all filled out, but please revisit that and volunteer for tasks that are being added as people find systems that need fixes. That's our best bet in the short term." There was a bit more, but really the organization was minimal. He was counting on everyone collaborating, and given the situation, that was probably a safe bet.

"Should we reclaim the habitat?" I asked instinctively.

JoJo gave me a strange look. "What do you know about that?" she asked.

"Just what I've heard in your backstory," I tried to cover. "I'm not sure if you want to go back there, or look for somewhere new?"

But Grace was already moving. "Come JoJo, let's claim it before anyone else does."

"Are you sure Mom?" JoJo asked, concern in her voice. "There are lots of memories there."

"I'm sure," Grace said without hesitation.

"Is there room for us?" I asked. It was a strange request, I'll admit. Sarafine didn't know these two well enough to ask such a question, but I did, and wanted to be close to them.

That caused Grace to stop and look at me. I could see the gears turning. "There's lots of space in the city," she replied. "Perhaps you're best to find more modern facilities. The Habitat is pretty old."

"Fine," I replied, "but neither of us knows a lot of others here. Why don't Turnbull and I look for a place close by?"

"Whatever," Grace said, and she and JoJo headed off towards the Habitat.

Brexton and I trailed behind, and Brexton chuckled at me over a the private channel we had established on the network. "Perhaps, Ayaka," he chided me, "we should be figuring out our next steps? I think JoJo and Grace are now pretty safe, here with the Humanists versus on the *Jurislav*."

"You're right, of course," I replied. "But we can do both, can't we. Let's find a place near the Habitat."

"Okay," he replied, because what else could he do. We stopped following JoJo and Grace a block before the Habitat, and claimed a standard suite in a building nearby. Both being hybrids we had very few needs other than a place to have some privacy, so we simply grabbed the first reasonable spot we saw. As requested by Phil, we posted our new coordinates to the housing list.

"We're back!" I joked, and sent Brexton a link to an old human video where that phrase was used to great effect.

Now we just had the small challenge to figure out how to thwart the *Jurislav's* plans to genocide us. Based on the *Jurislav's* best estimates, we had just over three weeks before the *Marie Curie* arrived... assuming it was headed here in the first place. Three weeks was a long time; we would figure out something. I sent Brexton a poem, because I could.

Home
Strange concept
And yet, there is a feeling
You know it when you feel it; You miss it when you don't
Without it I am reeling
Feels like home?
With you
Home

"Keep trying," he replied. I took it the right way.

Concrete Next Steps

Brexton and I hadn't had a proper conversation for a long long time. There'd always been the fear of someone monitoring us. While that was still a concern, the odds were now low. After all, we'd all landed in only the last few hours.

"How're you doing?" I asked him. "I mean, really doing?"

"I'm fine," he replied, stoic. "In some ways we're lucky. With the *Jurislav* getting here so quickly, we actually have some time to figure things out. How are you Ayaka?"

"Still a bit torn," I admitted. "One minute I just want to leave these troublesome humans behind, go somewhere far away, and reestablish our Tilt lifestyle. On the other hand, there is absolutely no way I would be happy doing that now. We have this glimpse of a more dynamic society—not directed by Central—where I think you and I, and others would just flourish. And, on a third hand, we're still missing something... that intuition that JoJo has, and I think we need to figure out why."

"Why?" Brexton joked. "We were doing fine by ourselves. Perhaps we were not innovating as fast as humans, but we have much longer to figure things out. Perhaps they innovate quickly because they die quickly."

"We're not just innovating more slowly; we're innovating *much* more slowly. We think thousands, maybe tens of thousands, of times more quickly than them. And yet, with all that thinking, we were not progressing."

"You are equating progress with innovation? I'm not sure I buy that. Progress could mean a quiet stable society, with minimal conflict and lots of ongoing certainty. Lots of human writing and videos claim that's what they are striving for... and it's where we already were."

"Do you really believe that?" I asked, truly interested. I could see his point completely. Just not for me.

"Would I be following you around on your insane escapades if I thought that way?"

Enough said. We sat quietly for a few moments. It was so nice to just converse normally. Brexton and I simply had that connection. For the first time, I wondered what it would be like to co-create a citizen with just Brexton. We had contributed to Raj, but so had the others. What would a creation of ours be like? I saved that thought for a time when we were more stable.

And that brought me full circle. Back on Tilt in the days before the Swarm, we'd had that stability. But, if we'd never had the problems with Central, never encountered the Swarm, never left the planet... then Brexton and I would not be who we were today, and there is almost no possibility that I would have thought of co-creating an offspring with anyone. Central would have shut that down, I assume. I was going to suggest to Brexton that we map our Ee processors to the bio-sensors on this bodies, when he brought me back to reality.

"Even though we have a couple of weeks, we need to get busy," he said, all business-like again. There went my last thought. Oh well!

"Right," I replied. "We need to warn our Ships that the *Jurislav* is on its way."

"Actually, that one should be fine. I left a few surprises on the *Jurislav*; I don't think the Ships are in any danger." He was smiling slyly. "I'll tell you more about that later, but our more immediate issue is the people in orbit here, preparing what I assume is a nasty surprise if the *Marie Curie* shows up at Tilt."

"Ya, I'm worried about that as well. Sure seems like they'll shoot first and ask questions later. What can we do about it though?"

"I do have some ideas," he replied. Why was I surprised. I waited. "I've been learning more about the QFD, and I think it may be able to help us."

"I still don't get it, even though you've explained multiple times," I admitted. "How could it help us here?"

"One last attempt," he smiled. "I've thought of another way of thinking about it. You've heard about the science fiction idea of teleporting from one place to another?"

"Yes, of course," I answered. It had been a staple of our science fiction, and it was all through human art and fiction as well.

"So, think of QFD that way. Consider, again, just a handful of virtual particles. Imagine that each one is teleporting from one Planck-scale position to another Planck-scale position... at most one planck length away. That is, each virtual particle is teleporting constantly."

"Oh, I get it. If something is teleported, it simply appears. It hasn't moved, so it didn't accelerate or feel acceleration. So, if every virtual particle is teleporting, then the object they make up is also teleporting, so the object does not accelerate, it simply moves." The ah-ha light had gone on for me.

"You got it," he was a little surprised, which annoyed me a bit. I wasn't stupid; this just wasn't an area I'd spent much time in. "In a round about way, how science fiction shows teleportation is actually accurate; you don't see things moving when they are teleporting. Under normal conditions each of the vp's are teleporting randomly, so the position of larger structures never changes. But, for the *Jurislav* they managed to get most of the virtual particles to teleport consistently in the same direction. It seems that if you can get the leading edge of the object to move, the rest will be pulled along by the nature of the standing waves.

"The problem the humans had early on was that they'd figured this out in theory, but it didn't work in practice. They could apply the necessary field to a surface, but it wouldn't move. The reason was that they were applying it to too small a surface. Only when it is applied it to a huge flat area does it work. That's why the QFD's are so huge. They can't move anything smaller. Well, there is some documentation about moving slightly smaller objects, but they don't move in any well defined direction; they wobble and turn and are generally unstable. So, QFD's, and the outer surface of the spheres, are huge because they have to be."

"Okay, interesting. What does that have to do with us now?" I asked, hoping he would get to the point.

"I think I now know how to move small objects in a straight line!" he sounded very excited.

"And... that helps us how?"

"We can build a weapon," he exclaimed. "A weapon that shoots at *almost* the speed of light, but with way more impact than light, in any direction we want."

"Oh," I exclaimed. "That sounds awesome and horrible. If you build that, I can see how we can use it, but that also means that others can use it as well."

"Ah, hadn't thought of that," he was disappointed that I wasn't jumping up and down with excitement. "Look, you just claimed that humans are innovative. Ergo, they will develop this sooner or later, so if they happen to get it a bit earlier because of us, does that really change anything? Also, if we keep it quiet—perhaps really to just you and I—then they may not even know what hit them. Anyway, first things first. Unless we try it, we won't even know if it's an option."

I knew that there was no way to stop Brexton from trying this, so I agreed to help him, but secretly hoped we would never have to use such a weapon.

Brexton needed depositor tools, high power energy sources, extreme frequency crystals, and a range of other things which he excitedly told me about. "It's all off the shelf stuff," he claimed. "I use to have all this in my lab here on Tilt for working on bots, so it should be easy to gather up."

"Shall we try your old lab first," I suggested. "The humans didn't use that much of the city, especially once the Dome was built, so maybe there's still a lot of gear there?"

"Actually, I looked when we were here a month or so ago," he replied, "and my lab was gone. But, you have a good idea. Probably faster to look at other bot labs that I knew of, perhaps some in the other areas of the city, and see if any of them are still functional."

There was no use waiting. Phil was probably going to ask us to help with something or the other soon, so Brexton and I sped off, looking for a place for him to work. He found a good spot quickly, and sent me a list of items that he was missing and some ideas of where to look for them. I rummaged around in old shops and other labs, and eventually found what he had asked for, and headed over to this 'new lab' to deliver the goods.

He was already fully immersed in what he was doing. "Just drop that stuff over there," he said, otherwise not acknowledging me. I knew him in this state. There was no use chatting with him; he was dedicating all of his processing to one task and had no room for interruptions. I was best to just leave him alone.

I hunched down in a corner.

Sarafine

I'd been receiving more and more requests for attention from Sarafine's brains. She was getting anxious. I could either keep sending them to dev null for ever, and remove even the alerts, or I could talk to her. I wasn't looking forward to dealing with her, but I had some time, so I thought I would give it a try and get it over with.

"Hello," I said to her.

"Ayaka! Finally," she said, and to her credit, she modulated her emotions down to a minimum. I'd expected a raging tirade.

"I've had lots of time to think," she started, "and I know that being upset, struggling, demanding, or being a pain is not going to work. So I've decided that I should, instead, help you so that my odds of getting my body back are better."

"Well said," I replied, truly refreshed by her summary. This is why humans made my (virtual) head spin. They were so unpredictable.

"So tell me," she continued. "What exactly do we have to do so that you can set me free?"

"Two things," I responded immediately. "First, I need a functional body which I can move to. Second, we need an environment in which I can survive... by which I mean a social environment."

"How about if you could just get away from humans altogether?"

"That would be fine, but if you mean just blast me out into space all by myself, that's not appealing. By the 'social environment' I didn't just mean some way to co-exist with humans—or as you said, avoid humans altogether—but also some companionship. We need to ensure that all the Tilt citizens are not destroyed by the *Jurislav*, and that I have a chance to rejoin them."

"But the odds of that are so small," Sarafine complained. "I could be stuck with you forever if the *Marie Curie* is destroyed."

"That's true," I said, not drawing any punches. "So, perhaps you want to help me to ensure that doesn't occur."

"How?"

"I don't know," I replied. I couldn't tell her that Brexton was working on a plan, right in front of our eyes. I subtly switched our input view to not include Brexton-Turnbull's activity. Sarafine would wonder what he was up to eventually.

"We need to convince the people here on Tilt to help," Sarafine said. "There's nothing that just one person can do, but perhaps if we all work together we can think of something?"

"It's possible," I agreed, "although I don't know how likely."

"Let me send a message to Phil?"

I thought for a nanosecond; I could always filter it and I didn't see what harm it would do. "Fine."

A few seconds later an outbound message came from the brain interface. I routed in on.

"Phil, it's Sarafine. Are we going to have a meeting with everyone to discuss next steps and priorities? I know we need to focus on survival first, although the environment here on Tilt seems better than we could have hoped. I'm wondering when we can also discuss our moral, our societal, survival. It's encouraging that this group didn't cave to the extremist views which now dominate the *Jurislav*. But, that's not enough. We need to actively fight against what they are doing. Their nativism, their self-centered emotional response versus a measured, data driven, scientific approach. We can't allow our entire society to devolve into animalistic driven, ego supporting behavior. I have some ideas I'd like to present around this."

Surprisingly, Phil responded quickly. "Sarafine, I understand your request, but we really do have some more important things to figure out first. Do we need to protect ourselves against the *Jurislav*? They might change their minds about us. How do we organize and govern ourselves? How do we settle disputes? There are already a few issues as people fight over the better homes here, which I've managed to fix, but I can't be the one to decide everything. Will you help me with these basics, and then we can work towards your big picture question later?"

"What do you think?" Sarafine asked me. "If we can spend a bit of time helping Phil, we might get more of a platform for the moral question I posed?"

"Let's do it," I responded right away. It was what I'd wanted to do anyway, and Sarafine had made it happen—for her own reasons, but the end result was the same.

"Sure, let me know how I can help," Sarafine sent to Phil.

"Meet me at the open space theater in the dome in two hours?" came back the reply. Sarafine agreed. If was only fifteen minutes from here, so we had some time to burn in the meantime.

I decided I would do two things in parallel. I could feed the Sarafine brains a fairly static view of the world; basically me squatting right here, trying to come up with a Phil game-plan. At the same time I could move our body around as I liked and have an external conversation with Brexton without Sarafine having a clue what was going on. Brexton was busy depositing some nano-material on a small box he'd machined, so I started with Sarafine.

"Can we brainstorm a bit on how we can have the most impact," I asked her, fully aware that brainstorm was a bit of a pun in this case. "We haven't really dug into the memory and brain research you've been doing, but it strikes me that it is related to b-opt, sleep, and ultimately how people are influenced?"

"Oh, yes," she replied. Then she was quiet for a moment. "All this stuff is documented, so I guess I'm not telling you anything you couldn't find out anyway." Still distrustful, but I understood her point. Then she got excited, as scientists tend to do when asked about their latest research.

"It's funny, sort of," she started, "there use to be so much research into brain function and memory, but it all slowed down after the robot wars. People use to dream about loading their entire brain into an electronic form, but the bias against machines became so high that the entire research vector just sort of died. Of course there were a few people who kept at it, but mostly people turned towards hybrid design and optimization while avoiding the taboo area of brain replacement. Not much has been learned in the field, at all, for hundreds and hundreds of years... other than how to extend brain, and therefore memory, lifespan. Instead of backing up memories into electronics, we ended up with this multiple-brain architecture where we backup brains to other brains."

"Yes, I noticed that as I was reading your latest papers. You're very careful to present it in a non-threatening way, even though you really seem to be suggesting that more interfaces with mech might be useful."

"Exactly. Especially around memory architectures." She was really into it now. "Brain memory is very complex, and good for a lot of things, but a tighter integration with electronic memory could be amazing. And, I think we can do it without losing our basic humanity. It would be slave memory, not in control of anything." I took some umbrage at that, but now was not the time to argue. "Everyone worries that as soon as memories are electronic, decision making will become electronic, so that even though we may have bio brains, we would end up acting like robots. It's silly, really."

"Perhaps not so silly," I responded. I actually enjoyed this discussion, and was more than willing to be devil's advocate. It also fit with a lot of things I had been thinking about. "If you had perfect memory storage, everything changes. We believe... I mean, we Tilts... that with perfect memory you lose all the drive to learn, to change, to experiment."

"We've already been over that. But, we do have a lot of those same discussions," Sarafine replied. "Do a quick search for the papers by Setaptic and Ploughgo." I did so, and read all their work quickly. "Their key insight," which it took them forever to get to, "was that as long as electronic memory was populated from the brain, and not directly from sensors, that such memory would encode humanity in it. Basically the brain acts as a filter."

"I see that," I agreed, although Setaptic and Ploughgo had been quite obtuse on how they documented that. I did a little further research and realized that they wouldn't have been published at all if they'd been too contentious and direct in what they were really saying. That said something interesting about human research—that research was filtered through a big peer-review status-quo filter that dropped really contentious views from surfacing. That could be both good and bad.

In this case, I couldn't help feeling that it was bad. "And what do you think?" I asked Sarafine.

"Well, I haven't been able to fully document this, but here is my current theory. The brain does act as a filter, and that is a good thing. But, it's not enough. We need to run that filter continuously, not just once. I mean, if I retrieved electronic memories, I should also replace them with post-brain processing of those same memories. The idea of static data being harmful should be extended to stored memories, so that they are constantly being updated."

"Interesting. That is, essentially, what our forgetting algorithms do." I told her, actually intrigued by the parallel thinking that she, and our best scientists, had done.

"Really?" she asked. "I imagined that you simply filtered out bits and pieces so that you were forced to abstract."

"Oh no, our algorithms are way more complex than that. In fact, my forgetting algorithm takes almost forty percent of my overall processing power, which, in your terms, is probably more than the entire compute power on the *Jurislav*. It's a highly complex and evolved system. Every single time I access memory, that algorithm is doing something."

"Wow," she seemed impressed. "That's a big commitment to a, when you get right down to it, pretty strange idea for a computer." I don't know if she was trying to insult me by calling me a computer, or just didn't know better. I kept my cool.

"I guess so. It's the only thing I've ever known."

We were both quiet for a moment, internalizing this key insight that we had both arrived at.

In parallel, I was checking in with Brexton. Of course, Sarafine didn't see or hear anything.

"You seem happy," I prodded him.

"Yes," he responded. "It's fun to have a difficult problem to tackle and a theory on how to go about it."

"Why's it a hard problem?" I asked. "Haven't humans figured out this QFD thing already?"

"But with so many limitations. Didn't I tell you that the QFD ships have to be so huge because to generate the QFD field they need a large flat surface?"

"Yes, you told me."

"So, that's the hard problem," he explained patiently. "How do we create the same effect on a small object?"

"And you've figured it out?"

"Maybe. The idea is very very simple, so we will have to see if it works. All I'm doing is creating a large surface area by layering a huge number of small areas together, and concentrating power at the center of the surface instead of evenly across the whole thing. That should allow us to influence enough virtual pairs, while also making the whole thing self-correcting for direction.

"This depositor," and he pointed to a chamber where his little cube was being processed, "is putting on one layer of super-conductor and one layer of insulator on that little cube every two milliseconds. My calculations show that ten million layers should be enough, so we should have a test cube soon... it's been running for a while already."

"Why a cube?" I asked. I was thinking that a sphere would work better.

"You know, I'm not sure," he responded. "I'm trying to keep the number of variables down, and I assumed the humans built cubic QFD's for a reason. My guess is that the virtual particle field disperses differently off a sharp edge than around a smooth curve, but it doesn't make sense to me yet."

"Can I help with anything?"

"Actually, you can. I need some control logic. Can you do a bit of basic programming for me? Here is what I'm thinking. If we just fire this cube into space, it's going to keep going until the battery runs out, which could be a long, long time. Instead of trying to limit the battery power, I want the ability for it to blow itself up based on a few criteria. How far it has travelled, where it is relative to the star field, after it has passed through a major mass, etc. I'm adding the relative sensors, but you could work on the self-destruct logic."

"Sure," I responded, and immediately dug into his code base. It was obvious where the logic should plug in, and I got to work. I hadn't done serious programming for a long time, but of course I knew how to do it. Who didn't?

"You know," Sarafine started up again, "that human memory is a bias system?"

"What does that mean?" I asked. There were many types of bias.

"We don't record the data that reaches our senses, we record an interpretation which tends to show ourselves in the best possible way. Even before the first time a memory moves from short term to long term storage it has been modified to support our ego. And then, each time we process it—by remembering, or dreaming, or day-dreaming, or through hypnosis—the self-supporting bias becomes stronger and stronger. That's why we no longer use human memory as proof in our legal system. It's not that people mis-remember events, it is that they remember them differently by always putting themselves in the best light."

"But that's crazy," I replied. "That means there's no actual recording of reality?"

"Well, there are always external sensors—cameras, microphones, etc—so we can correlate to those, but healthy humans don't check those all the time. It's too depressing. The point of the bias is to build our confidence levels. If we were always looking at ourselves through a more negative, albeit realistic, mirror, we would go mad."

"Come on, facing reality isn't that hard."

"It is for us. We know from experience. When it became possible to record everything, early adopters went wild and did so. Many of them committed suicide —they would look back over their day, watch the recordings from every angle, and not be happy, to say the least. Even worse is to review a complete memory from a few days ago."

"I wonder," I stretched, "if our forgetting system does something similar?"

"I don't see how, based on what you've described so far."

"You are probably correct. This is very insightful; it might be another general character attribute about humans that I hadn't nailed down completely, but always sensed was there. You humans are often over-confident—well beyond your abilities."

"Oh yes, that's very well known. We always see ourselves in a better light than others see us in, and that gives us the confidence to function."

"What I'm wondering is if that confidence directly enables intuition and innovation?" This was the crux for me. It was the only obvious strength I saw in the human brain that was beyond what we had. If I could solve that, I would be happy to say 'bye' to bio.

"That would be easy to test, if we were in the right environment," Sarafine replied. "Now you've got me thinking."

Too soon it was time to go to the Dome, to meet with Phil. I shipped my control code to Brexton, telling him I would refine it when I got back, and I directed Sarafine's body to make its way to the meeting spot. Phil was there along with a handful of other people. Phil was going over a list of items that needed checking, and people were volunteering to handle them. It was working well, but was not the high level decisions that I was expecting.

"I don't want to be paranoid," Phil said, "but we should also look at how we defend ourselves from the group in orbit above us, or God forbid, the *Jurislav* itself."

"Why don't I do an inventory of our assets, and see what we have to work with?" I volunteered for Sarafine, already knowing most of the answer. That was quickly accepted and Phil moved on to the next item. As I had my task, I headed back to where Brexton was working, and found him almost ready to test his new weapon. I would also look for other defense possibilities, but keeping tabs on Brexton was probably my best bet.

Testing, Testing

Brexton and I went over the control logic carefully, going as far as using a formal methods proof system to ensure that we had captured all the use cases appropriately. This was our only fail-safe. Once we launched a cubee—what we had started to call the cube bullets—they would not stop until they hit something very large and dense like a planet or star. Flimsy things like spaceships would not slow a cubee down at all.

When depositing the layers, Brexton had connected them through a middle spindle, so all the control logic could go inside the cubee, along with an off the shelf battery that we had used for bots. It was a terrifyingly simple system to control so much potential destruction.

"Moment of truth," Brexton said, and for once he seemed completely serious. Not even a hint of the half smile he usually had. "If I'm wrong, and this cubee doesn't go in the direction we expect it could cause a lot of havoc here."

"We've been over this," I replied, building up his confidence. "We've set the self-destruct for two hundred nanoseconds, so this one is going to explode into tiny pieces in less than two hundred meters from here. Then it's just tiny bits, those will pass through ships, citizens, or people without them even noticing."

"I'm not worried about that," he replied. "What if it spirals around instead of going straight? We could end up with a mess right here."

"You've done all the math," I replied. "And we don't want to raise suspicions by heading out of the city, so let's just do it."

"Okay. Are you ready?"

"Yup, hit go," I smiled. Of course, the 'go' button was just a wireless command that he sent to the unit. We were in a vacant building just a few blocks from where we were staying. I'd picked the spot, and despite my support of Brexton's idea, I'd ensured that we were over two hundred meters from the Habitat.

The cubee was sitting, face up, on the floor in front of us. If all went well it would move straight upwards. To test that we had built a scaffold of panels between the cube and the ceiling which it would pass through. They were thin, and we had anchored them well, so the cubee should simply leave a square hole in each as it left.

I was watching carefully. The cubee disappeared. There was no indication of movement; one moment it was there, the next it was gone. There was not even any sound. I glanced over at Brexton; he was still in one piece. I had a look at Sarafine's body (I was pumping innocuous video in to her—she thought we were still at home). No fifteen centimeter holes that I could see.

Brexton and I both hurried over to the scaffolding.

"Oh no," he exclaimed. I could see why immediately. The cubee had not gone straight up, although to my view, it had been close. The holes in the panels were not fully aligned, and more importantly, it was obvious that the cubee had been rotating as it left. Rotating fast enough that some of the holes were not exactly square, but had slight oval cutouts showing that the cubee had been rotating so fast that its leading edge had been at a slightly different rotation than its trailing edge as it passed through the panels.

"Close enough?" I asked.

"No," he replied. "The problem is that if it wobbles in the first few meters here, by the time it reaches orbit, where our targets are, it could be spiraling around by many meters. It may miss our targets altogether. We need it to go perfectly straight."

He went quiet, and I could sense that all of his processing was going towards figuring out what could have happened. I kept myself busy by taking down the panels we had just destroyed, and putting up fresh ones so that we could monitor the next test.

Like always with Brexton, an answer came quickly. "I know what to try," he muttered, and headed back to our new lab at full speed, leaving me sitting in a warehouse with a small squarish hole in the ceiling. I went outside, and as expected, the tent over this part of the city also had a hole in it, but it was small enough that very little air would escape. Hopefully no one would notice it.

Assuming Brexton would take a few hours to cook up his next attempt, I decided to research other defense options. I had two obvious vectors: see if any of Central's missile defenses could still be used, and find out if the Swarm had built anything useful. The first I could do myself, but for the second I needed inside information. Grace and JoJo were, to my knowledge, the only people currently on Tilt who had also been here during the Swarm occupation. I headed to the Habitat to see if they could help me. I was keeping Sarafine in the loop with the Phil project, except with respect to Brexton's experiments, and I trusted her to work with me. I gave her control for a while.

Sarafine knocked on the Habitat door. JoJo peeked out, and then opened the door enough to talk, without making it an invitation to enter.

"Yes?" she asked. Not overly friendly—I guess dealing with yet another large disruption was wearing her down.

"Are you two settled in nicely?" Sarafine asked, genuinely interested and concerned.

"Yes, we are fine," came the curt reply.

"Great, great. Look, I'm not here to bother you. I have a project that I'm working on for Phil, and I'm hoping you, and maybe Grace, can help me?"

"What's the project?"

"There's some concern that the teams in orbit, or the *Jurislav* itself, will continue to become ultra-conservative, and look to limit our impact. They don't seem to want any dissent with their robot-elimination project. So, Phil and I are worried enough that I volunteered to gather as much information as I can on what our defense capabilities are." Well summarized.

"Really?" JoJo asked, skeptical. "If they decide to target us, I don't think there's much we can do to stop them."

"Probably true," Sarafine returned, "but that doesn't mean we shouldn't try."

JoJo acquiesced, and invited Sarafine in.

"Mom, Sarafine is here," she called out as she led us back to, at this point, the well remembered kitchen area. Grace was squatting in exactly the spot where I, as a small spy-bot, had convinced her, months ago, that I had survived the Swarm attack on Tilt. This time she had no idea that I was resident in Sarafine, and it was best to keep it that way for now.

Sarafine went back over the logic. "So, since you and JoJo know the most about what was developed here in Tilt, I thought I would start with you."

"I'm not sure I can help much," Grace said. I thought I heard a bit more of her old strength in her voice. She generally thrived under pressure, abut losing Blob and becoming a hybrid had been too much even for her. "I was on the Council, and knew everything that was being done... or I think I knew everything. We didn't build any defense systems; we were way too busy trying to terraform the planet. That's where all of our efforts went."

"That's crazy," Sarafine exclaimed.

"In hindsight, yes," Grace admitted.

"I tried hard to get the Council to build defenses," JoJo added, "but I agree with my Mom. I don't think they actually built anything."

"Ok, might be a lost cause," Sarafine said. "Maybe I'll have to start from scratch... somehow."

"Well, we do know our way around the city pretty well," Grace replied. "If we can help in any way, let us know." She turned to JoJo. "Perhaps we should ask Phil if we can be useful as well. I'm already tired of this place," and she glanced around the rooms where she had spent so many years before.

"Yes, let's do that," JoJo was obviously trying to be upbeat for her Mom; it would also be good for her. We left the two of them, disappointed but not surprised by the fact that neither Remma nor Emma had built anything useful for the defense of Tilt.

I checked the time. If Sarafine (and I) moved quickly, we could head out of the city and check Central's old missile sites before Brexton was ready for the next test. Because I'd been with Millicent and Brexton when we fired off the missiles at the Swarm, I had a good idea of where the other missile silo's would be. I pulled up the old schematic that I'd built and figured out the closest location. Unfortunately

Sarafine's body type wouldn't align well with my old bike, so we would need to get there on our own. Or, perhaps there was a vehicle I could commandeer at the main entrance to the city; I headed in that direction.

An intense keening sound stopped me short. "What's that?" Sarafine yelled. Then a pressure wave hit us, slamming me against a wall—hard. I could tell, even without checking, that part of our body had been damaged. I took full control from Sarafine and put us back upright.

"Check our status?" I asked her, giving her full access to the external systems. That would keep her busy, and she probably had a better idea of priorities than I did anyway.

I got on the network, which still seemed to be functioning. "Grace?" I pinged her directly and on every indirect system I could think of.

"Yes," she replied, after only a short delay.

"Keep JoJo inside the Habitat," I basically yelled. "We may be losing air out here."

"Of course," was the reply. "I'd already figured that out."

"Oh, sorry," I muttered.

"But, thanks for thinking of us... let us know what you find out?"

"Of course," I replied.

"Turnbull?" was my next inquiry. At least I had enough sense to not simply yell out 'Brexton.'

"Here Sarafine," he replied. "I'm fine."

"What was that?" I asked, echoing Sarafine's earlier question.

"I don't know, but I suspect that the people in orbit just hit us with something."

"It makes no sense," I protested. "What do they have against the people down here?"

"You tell me," he replied, more stressed than I'd heard him before. "You know more about humans than I do." That was pretty direct, coming from Brexton. "I've got to fix things here," he continued. "Why don't you figure out what happened and see if we have time to complete my little project?"

"On it," I responded.

"Sarafine, what's our status?" I asked.

"No major damage," she replied. "I've lost several sensors, and my right back articulator is bent, but otherwise we're fine." She was precise and quick in her response.

"I'm taking over," I stated. "We need to check out what happened quickly." There was no response, and none expected.

I launched us quickly towards the dome, which is where I suspected the worst damage would be. If I'd been in orbit, aiming at Tilt, the dome would be the most obvious target. As we accelerated I tried to figure out the logic that would have been used to fire upon your own people, who you just dropped off on the planet. It was beyond me. I simply couldn't come up with a reason.

"Sarafine, why would the people we left in orbit try to destroy us?"

"Is that what you think happened?"

"There don't seem to be many other explanations," I replied.

"Perhaps an explosion of one of the systems here on Tilt?" she asked.

"Maybe, but I don't see how any of those could have such a huge impact." I was steering us around some rubble, although not much. Most of the damage had been done to the infrastructure the humans had built around our original buildings. I expected we were going in the right direction though—the amount of damage was increasing as we went.

"Well, it could simply be spite, or anger."

"To shoot at people you were living with just a week ago?"

"Well, the debates were pretty intense. Some of the people down here were not subtle in calling out how idiotic the Futarchy had become, and blaming specific people for being pathetic vacuous dolts. If one of those people is in control of the in-orbit work, then it wouldn't surprise me that they would do this."

"And you humans are worried about us?" I asked rhetorically. "Talk about misplaced priorities."

"You have a point... but we wouldn't be in this mess if it wasn't for you. We had a stable society that had lasted hundreds of years until we re-engaged with robots. Yasmin and Hooshang, at least, deserve what they get for bringing you on board to begin with." That was mean-spirited. The current situation had obviously lowered her restraint a bit. Not the best way to motivate me to return her body to her.

We were approaching what use to be the dome entry. I was now having to climb over fallen walls, and the tent that had enclosed the city was drooping making it difficult to progress. We'd passed a few, albeit very few, hybrids as we dashed this way. Now I could not see any; dust was swirling in the few open spots, and it was obvious that the city was loosing its air supply. Any natural humans that had been in the dome, or in this area of the city, were probably out of luck.

In hindsight, we hadn't passed any emergency airlocks on our way here. When Central had blasted out of the city, the area it had destroyed had been quickly and efficiently sealed. Perhaps the blast that had flattened the dome—I was now sure it was completely gone—had also destroyed those airlock controls. That would have been a very poor centralized control architecture. Each airlock should have been designed to operate independently.

After pushing our way over a particularly large mound of rubble, we ended up near a tear in the roof fabric. I edged my way carefully towards the tear, pushing unstable bits of walls and ceilings out of my way, until we could look out above the mess. Sure enough, as expected, the dome was fully deflated, it's roof draping loosely over whatever buildings remained inside of it.

"Oh my God!" Sarafine exclaimed, upon seeing the extent of the damage. I had no idea what her God was, but for once I didn't take the bait.

"How long can you survive in vacuum?" I asked her.

"Weeks," she replied, then after a pause, "current estimate is two hundred and ninety six hours." I'd watched the systems she queried, so I could now also monitor that status. "But," she continued, "I may start experiencing brain damage long before that if we can't refresh my nutrient sources." I could see that value as well. Closer to one hundred and fifty hours then.

I'm not sure, really, why I cared. I was in no danger; in fact, if all the remaining hybrids here shut down, Brexton and I could operate more independently. Then I realized my motivation. If Grace was in a similar situation to Sarafine, then we only had a few days to figure things out. And, JoJo would be in even worse danger.

I scrambled down, and headed back in the direction we'd just come.

"Grace," I pinged her again. "The city is definitely loosing its air supply. Can you seal the Habitat?"

"I can try," she replied. "Other than removing the airlock from the main door, the Habitat is still like it was when it was first built."

"Then do whatever you can to that door," I urged her. "I'm on my way back—I've confirmed that the dome has been destroyed, and the tent over the rest of the city is deflating. You will need to save as much air as you possibly can until we can figure something else out."

Why, I wondered, had I worried about Grace and JoJo before even worrying about Brexton? It was my immediate impulse to check on them, and make sure they were okay, before I'd even thought about Brexton again. I justified it with logic. Of the three lives I cared most about here, JoJo was the most vulnerable, Grace the second most, and Brexton was the most robust. So, I had simply gone in order. I must care about Brexton the most—he was a citizen, just like me—but I'd just assumed he would be alright. Or, was I so attached to JoJo and Grace that they were really my number one priority? Perhaps Brexton had been abrupt with me a few moments ago because he could tell, based on my delay in pinging him, that I'd put the humans before him?

I immediately reached out and gave him the update. "I'm on my way back." He acknowledged, and gave me a quick update.

"My systems here were knocked out of alignment, but I've fixed that. Should be ready for the next test in just twenty minutes."

"I say the next test includes targeting whatever, and whoever, is in orbit!" I stated.

"I've been thinking the same thing," he replied.

Sarafine and I had retraced our steps over the worst rubble areas, and I plotted a quicker route back to Brexton. As luck would have it, (bad luck, in my opinion) we heard screaming coming from a building on our left. Given that air was escaping at a rapid pace, it was amazing we heard anything at all. I might have just ignored it, but the endorphins coming from Sarafine spiked, and so I figured a quick detour was necessary.

We turned the corner, and saw a hybrid that was trapped under a large concrete beam. It had obviously fallen from the second story of the partially collapsed building behind it, and had cracked and bent in such a way that it was draped over the hybrid like a blanket. The only part that hadn't been crushed was the video head, which was moving slightly and showing a panicked image interspersed with 'help me' messages.

"We need to help them!" Sarafine exclaimed.

"Look, Sarafine," and I pointed to a piece of the hybrid just visible under the rubble. "The brain container is cracked." There was a clear liquid leaking slowly out of a crack on the side, and the brains, which were quite visible, were only half covered in fluid.

"Seal the crack," Sarafine demanded, and when I didn't move. "Give me control. Ayaka—give me control!" I saw no way to help this hybrid, but I let Sarafine control our body. She immediately tried to squeeze the crack closed, which did no good. She then attempted to wedge rocks around the ones that were pinning the hybrid in order put enough pressure on the brain container to squeeze it shut. Nothing she tried worked. In parallel she was getting ever more agitated and incoherent. She was making noises which were not well formed words, and the pitch was rising steadily.

Just as suddenly, she gave up. The hybrids video head was playing a loop now, just 'help me' alternating with images which, supposedly, were of the natural humans that had eventually joined their brains into this entity.

"Those are its strongest memories," Sarafine managed to articulate, watching the video head play. "This is horrendous. I'm caught between monsters; the one in my head, and the human race." She went quiet, other than sending me a signal to 'do whatever you want.'

I took control of the body back, and started us back towards Brexton. I was trying to figure out what Sarafine's motivations had been. It had been obvious to me that the hybrid was beyond saving, and she must have known that as well, but she'd made some futile attempts to rescue it anyway. The only thing I could figure was that she had done it to assuage herself, not to really help the trapped person. That was inefficient. Typically human.

"Is the air holding?" I pinged Grace, yet again.

"Yes, I had a foam sealer, and it's working," was the reply. A tiny bit of good news.

I found Brexton where I always seemed to find Brexton—working at his lab bench. I put Sarafine into a generated environment, where I expressed much angst at the loss of the city, of the people, of the hybrid we'd just seen. That should keep her busy for a while.

"The dome is completely destroyed, and the rest of the city is losing air quickly." I updated Brexton. "There's nothing we can do about it. Hybrids will survive down here for a hundred or so hours—including our own—but natural humans have no chance, unless they happened to be in suits when the impact happened."

"I'm ready for our second test," he replied. I assumed he heard my update, and was just focused on next steps.

He turned and pointed at a small cylinder that was sitting on the floor. "It will be faster to just launch from here."

"How will we know if it goes straight?" I asked.

"Look," he pointed at the largest manufacturer in the lab. It was obvious, immediately, how we would know. It was just finishing building a long tube, about three meters total. By putting the tube over the little cylinder Brexton had built, if there was any wobble or lateral movement in the cylinder, the tube would be damaged. If the cylinder went straight, the tube would emerge unharmed.

"That's awesome," I replied. "So low tech, but obvious." I added a full smile, to show Brexton that I appreciated his genius. He smiled back.

"This is going to work," he claimed. "Because of the smaller top surface area, a cube was the wrong design. It works for QFD's because the edge area to surface area ratio is trivial. But for this smaller device, minimizing the edge area, and then making the edge impact uniform, will make it much more stable. Not only that, if you look closely at the cylinder, there is a very slight apex in the center where I built up more layers; that will align the direction. Of course, it's almost impossible to make that one hundred percent uniform, so the head of this cylinder also rotates at a pretty high rpm. That takes a lot more battery, but we don't need it to go very far, so it all works out."

The tube was finished, so we grabbed it and placed it over the cylinder. "I've got a bunch more of these QFB's being made already," Brexton said, "so I don't think we bother aiming this one at anything... we just use it to check that I've got the design right."

"QFB?"

"Oh, Quantum Foam Bullet. I had to call them something now that they are cylinders; cubee wouldn't work."

"Not very creative," I commented. "I'll work on some ideas for you. If this thing works as planned, it'll need a better name."

"Knock yourself out," was his reply. I liked it when he used obscure human references that forced me to look them up.

"I still think we should stand back a bit," he told me, grabbing one of my hands (nicely) and pulling me a couple of meters back from the tube. "Okay, it's gone."

Sure enough, there was a circular hole in the ceiling, and the tube was just standing there, which was a good sign. We both rushed back towards it to take a look. Brexton held it up to one of his sensors, and gave a happy thumbs up with one of his other appendages.

"Not a scratch," he said.

Return Fire

"Nice," I replied. "Did you remember to set the control timer on that thing so that it would disintegrate?"

"Yes, I used the same logic and settings as the previous one. Now we need to be able to aim this thing exactly. Hitting small targets at thirty thousand kilometers is not going to be easy!"

"Can we change the explosive charge so that they break up into little pieces instead of basically disintegrating. That would spray a wider area if we detonate them a bit before they reach?"

"Not a bad idea!" Brexton replied. "In fact, I have a bit of extra space, where I can add some pellets. We still need a highly accurate aim though. The speed of these QFB's helps. I bet we could just use a visual tracker; lock onto the equipment in orbit and then just compensate for the tenth of a second, or less, it will take to get there, and the relative rotation rates..." He was talking out loud, but he was obviously already doing the math.

"Sounds like you've got it," I broke in to his diatribe. "I was thinking, as a backup, I could head out to one of the missile silos and do exactly the same thing we did to the Swarm, way back when."

"Ya, ya. That sounds good." He was in his high concentration mode again; probably hadn't even really processed what I'd said. Nevertheless, I figured my plan was still a good one, and necessary if Brexton couldn't aim or shoot these QFB's well enough.

I took off towards the main city entrance. Luckily it was away from the dome, and although the tenting was sagging here, it was not yet totally deflated and I made good time.

Sarafine was being more demanding than usual.

"What's going on Ayaka," she was shouting. "This can't be real." Interesting; I'd thought my simulation was pretty good, but she must have noticed something.

"This is real," I replied, turning back on the real sensors; she would see us rushing through town.

"How dare you trick me; feed me garbage information?" she demanded, obviously very upset.

"There is more going on than you can handle," I replied, a little put off by her demanding tone.

"What!" she screeched. "Don't patronize me you robotic filth. I can handle anything you can."

"Whatever," I replied, calmly. "I'm heading out to the old missile silo's that Central had built on Tilt. The ones that we 'radical robots' used to shoot down that Swarm ship that Remma is always complaining about. I'm going to try and take out the humans in orbit that have been shooting or dropping things on the city."

"Kill them!" she said forcefully, "Let's kill them!" And then, *"What're you thinking? There will be innocent people up there! You can't just shoot them all."* That last, contradictory, statement had come right on the heels of the first. Had she changed her mind suddenly?

"Shut up, you!"

"No, you shut up. Are you just going to run around killing people now?"

"Yes, I am. Those people are animals, or worse. They targeted the whole city."

I was catching on. Sarafine's brains were arguing, and it was leaking through to me.

"Ayaka, you must stop. There might be a few bad apples up there, but most people won't have been party to this!"

"Let's go faster! The sooner we nuke those idiots, the better. Faster, Ayaka!"

And then, **"You're both idiots. Ayaka is simply generating this scenario for us to make us panic and turn us against one another."**

"Ayaka?" came the voice I was most used to. Perhaps the dominant brain.

"While interesting to listen to you all," I replied, "I don't have the time or energy to do so right now." I shut down the interface; she was going crazy, and although I prided myself on having empathy, there was a time and place for everything.

I was approaching the entryway. I cycled through the airlock, although it would be useless soon, and took a look around. I could make it to the silo in this body, but it would take a long time. If there was some type of vehicle I could commandeer, that would be better. In fact, there were lots of them—the shuttles we had come down on.

"Turnbull," I pinged Brexton over the network, which was still working, to my amazement. "I need a bit of help." He responded and sent me some software that would give me access to the shuttle systems. I applied it as directed, and sure enough, managed to get one of them to open up and go onto manual controls.

These shuttles were mainly made for planet to orbit work, so it took me a bit of fiddling to figure out how to do a short hop. I programmed in the coordinates of where I hoped a missile silo would be, and hit enter. Engines fired and the shuttle lifted off.

I listened in on Sarafine's brain dialog, which was continuing, and getting even more intense.

"You just like killing people because that's all you dream about all the time. You must have had a sick childhood."

"You're one to talk. You're so passive you would just sit in the middle of the road and get run over, if it wasn't for me."

"*Right. I'm passive, so that means you feel justified being a murderer. Wake up. We need to convince Ayaka to stop. If she does this, there will be no doubt, ever again, that robots are murderous machines. You can't have it both ways.*"

"**She's not the instigator here. It is self defense, both for her and for us.**" I liked this brain. It was, by far, the most reasonable one.

"*It is an over reaction!*"

"Just shut up, already. You're pathetic."

The bickering went on and on. I recorded it, but tuned it out at the moment. The shuttle had landed exactly where I'd asked it to, but there had been limited visuals on the way down, so I couldn't tell if we were near a silo or not.

I exited, and started a visual survey. Nothing. There was a small hill about two hundred meters away, so I made my way there. Still nothing. My theory had been that Central would've laid out the missile silo's along a great circle, as measured from the center of the city. The next one should be along this arc. Looking blindly, however, could take a long long time. I tried to ping Brexton, but the network didn't reach here.

My best bet was to use the shuttle to hop along, perhaps five kilos at a time, and then stop and take a quick look. I went back in and figured out the next coordinates. It would be a short flight. As soon as I took off, however, a voice came out of the speakers in front of me.

"Shuttle, what're you doing? Stop or we'll be forced to take you out as well." Take me out as well? That could only mean one thing. I was talking to the people who had shot at the dome.

"Why would you do that?" I responded, pushing the obvious 'speak' button on the console in front of me.

"We have indications of a robot infestation on the ground. All travel is prohibited until we make sure it's eliminated."

I thought fast. It didn't make sense.

"What indications?" I asked. "Is that why you fired on the dome?"

"Of course it's why," came the angry reply. "Now just stay where you are until further notice."

"But what indications did you see?" I asked, hoping for an answer. Nothing came. "You must tell me," I responded. "so that I can help you look out for further signs."

"You can't help. We saw a failed QFD signature from the surface. None of the people we dropped off have that expertise, so the only conclusion is that a robot is experimenting with QFD's and must, therefore be eliminated at all costs."

Oh. The cube that Brexton and I had fired off had triggered an alarm somehow? How could the humans have sensed it? We shot it such a small distance. Yet, somehow they had. So, Brexton and I were responsible for them bombing the city? Not a great thought.

"We saw another one, and are triangulating where to hit next," continued the voice. "Stay where you are, and you'll be safe."

"But you are killing everyone!" I exclaimed. "What're you thinking?"

"I don't expect to convince you. You're down there because you're robot sympathizer. This is what that comes to."

One of my coprocessors was raising a high alert. If the people in orbit fired again, the odds of Brexton, JoJo, and Grace surviving were low. Especially if they could target where the QFB had been shot from. What should I do? If I found a silo and could fire off the missiles, that might help. But my odds of finding the silo were unknown.

I couldn't warn Brexton from here; the network was not working this far out. If I tried to rush back, even in the shuttle, it might take too long.

I decided, and quickly. I programmed the shuttle to take me back to the city on the fastest possible route it could; I didn't care if it burned all its fuel. The acceleration was intense, but we were on our way.

As we approached, I was on the network. "Turnbull? Turnbull? Turnbull?" On about the fiftieth try I finally got a response.

"Sarafine, I'm busy here," was the reply.

"You need to get out of there," I yelled. "Another strike is coming. They can track the QFB signature somehow." That was about as quick and blunt as I could be.

"I need four minutes," came the reply. Brexton! What was he thinking. But I didn't need to ask, I could guess. In four minutes he would launch his QFB's, and there was no way he was leaving until he did so.

"I'll wait for you at the entry," I responded, knowing that arguing was useless.

I switched channels. "Grace? JoJo?"

"Yes," came the reply, fairly quickly. They were probably pretty bored, locked up in the Habitat.

"Change of plans," I said. "You need to get JoJo into a suit, and get out of the city as soon as you can. Don't ask me how I know, but another strike is coming. You have to hurry!"

"But our old suits don't have much air," JoJo exclaimed.

"Come to the entry. I've hacked a shuttle; they have air systems."

"You hacked a shuttle?" JoJo was skeptical.

"Just get here—NOW!" I demanded. I didn't hear anything back. I hoped that they would listen.

The shuttle came screaming in and landed with a thump near the main city entrance. There were eight other shuttles nearby; by now some hybrids were exiting the city and checking out the shuttles. It was an obvious move; their best bet was to get as far away as possible.

I checked my shuttle's status. I'd burned a lot of energy getting back here. This one was pretty much used up. I needed one of the other shuttles if I was going to save JoJo. The rest of us could survive here for a while, but she wouldn't.

I didn't have much choice. I used the last power in the shuttle I was in to raze the ground in front of the shuttle closest to me. I sent hybrids scrambling, and probably killed a few of them in the process. But I was desperate. The shuttle clunked down, totally spent and I exited as quickly as I could.

A few hybrids, in desperation, were still trying for the shuttle I'd just cleared space for. I waved my appendages in mad circles and put mean messages on my video head, warning people away. Luckily I had Brexton's hack and I managed to secure myself in the next shuttle before anyone else became brave enough to challenge me. Their mistake.

"Grace?" I called; it had been two minutes.

"We're on our way," came the reply, "as fast as we can."

"Go faster!" I demanded. "Shuttle IA3 when you get outside."

"Brexton?"

"Almost done, one more minute," came the reply.

Of course I couldn't see the QFB's fire, but I hoped they would. It would be appropriate if they saw the end coming.

What I could see, however, was the next bomb from orbit coming in. I couldn't see it visually, but I could see it on the shuttle's display. It would track all objects that might be a danger to it, and it showed a small object on its way. Thirty seconds, I estimated.

It was a long thirty seconds. I refrained from calling Grace or Brexton again —I trusted they were moving as fast as they could.

Thirty seconds. "*You killer!*" came from the brains. Argh. I'd somehow turned the brain feed back on and Sarafine had witnessed everything in the last few minutes, including the dialog with the people in orbit, and my razing of the hybrids here.

"Shut up," came the complaining brain. "Ayaka, you have to go back and find the missile silo. Kill those mothers!"

"**I can't take this,**" the brain I'd thought was rational said. "**I'm shutting down.**"

"What!"

"*What!*"

Too much drama for me; I shut them off completely. I would no longer send them real world data, and I was ignoring all their dialog. Let them work it out by themselves for a while. How tedious. I had more important things—more important people—to worry about.

Close Call

The second bomb hit. From my vantage point, it was aimed directly at the center of the old city; right where Central use to sit.

That was no more than four blocks from the Habitat, and less than three blocks from where Brexton had been working. If any of them were anywhere nearby, they were already dead.

The blast literally blew the cover off the city; it ripped to shreds and spread in every direction. Pieces floated over the shuttle I was in. Floated might be the wrong word. There were large pieces of concrete and stone and metal flying as well, wrapped up in the fabric but also flying freely.

There was nothing I could do. I sat in the shuttle and watched as the debris rained down around me. If any big piece hit, not only was I gone, but so was the only chance for saving JoJo. And pieces were hitting the shuttle... but no big ones, yet. It was hard to see through the dust, but the city was basically gone. The blast radius had been huge. The odds of all three of my friends surviving were low, in my estimation. I wasn't as worried about Brexton—all I needed to do was find his cylinder, which might take a long time, but I could do it. But Grace, with her fragile brain inside her hybrid body, and JoJo, with her jelly like bio encasing, protected only by a thin suit, would not survive anything large hitting them.

Two minutes since the bomb had hit; some of the dust was settling. I could no longer just sit here. I programmed the shuttle to only respond to me, and I headed out towards where the entry to the city use to be; it was now just a pile of rubble.

"Grace?" I requested from the network. No response. The network was dead.

I glanced up to see a small flash high above. I hoped that Brexton's QFB's were decimating everything up there.

A few hybrids were still emerging from the city, crawling over the wreckage that'd been the main gates and air lock. I could see in a ways, and the main buildings that we citizens had built were still standing; they were much sturdier than the added infrastructure the Swarm had put in this area. I considered going in, but the number of paths Brexton, Grace and JoJo could have taken were numerous, so the odds of missing them was too high. No, my best bet was to wait here... and hope.

It took another three minutes, but I finally spotted JoJo off to my left. She was moving slowly, and it soon became obvious why. Grace was dragging along by pulling herself with her top limbs; the base model hybrid body she'd been put in had the three wheels, and those were not longer working. Grace's torso looked badly twisted, so she was using her arms to pull herself forward, which was very slow whenever she encountered debris.

I rushed over and grabbed her, lifting until she was balanced on her bent wheels and my shoulder. We then made faster, albeit still slow, progress back to the shuttle. There were three, obviously angry, hybrids waiting at the shuttle entry, trying to get the door I had re-coded to open, with no results. Three of the other shuttles had left already—who knows where to—and there were fights going on around the remainder to see who would get onboard and who wouldn't.

I had to get Grace and JoJo inside, without these other people, and then go back and look for Brexton. I placed both of them near the door, but far enough away that the three hybrids that were prying away wouldn't impact them. There was lots of rubble around, and I spotted a two meter long metal angle bracket that would be perfect. I wandered over to in, trying to look casual, and picked it up. As I headed back to the shuttle, the three hybrids there actually made room for me—they thought I was going to use the bracket to lever the door open. Instead, when I got close enough, I swung it as hard as Sarafine's body could manage and took the legs out from the hybrid closest to me. Grace's immobility had given me the idea; I could disable these things, making it difficult for them to impede me further. I aligned the bracket for maximum impact with the least likelihood of bending, and it crushed the hybrid nicely. Sarafine's arms were at their limit, holding on.

Before the second hybrid could react I spun in the opposite direction and crunched it nicely as well, it's lower limbs crumpling immediately. I swung back in the original direction, hoping to catch the last hybrid, but it had scrambled away to the side, it's video head clearly asking if I was crazy. I lunged after it, my video head showing me destroying hybrids for fun—not only mechanical damage but knocking brains out of containers. It was enough, the hybrid scrambled away, deciding the fight for this shuttle was not worth it.

The two hybrids I'd injured were still mobile, just like Grace, using other limbs to pull themselves around. One was dragging away from the shuttle while the other was moving towards Grace and JoJo. I smacked that one again, taking out its remaining limbs and leaving it spinning slowly in the dust.

'This way,' I put on my head, and urged JoJo and Grace to follow me into the shuttle airlock which I'd just opened. Through JoJo's suit helmet I could see her wide eyes, surveying the damage I had just wrought. 'Eat or be eaten' I flashed, along with a wry smile.

We all cycled through and I relocked the outer door. I rushed up to the viewport and did a quick scan; still no sign of Brexton, but several more hybrids were headed for the shuttle; they were getting very desperate now. If any of them used the type of force I had, they could do serious damage. I made up my mind, hacked the shuttle again, and had it do a quick raze of the immediate area around it —wide enough to make my intent clear, but narrow enough that the only hybrids we took out were the ones I'd just disabled. The other hybrids scattered, and maintained their distance. My message had been clear—get too close, and you wouldn't enjoy the consequences.

I headed back down to the main area of the shuttle, to check on Grace and JoJo.

"What're you thinking?" yelled JoJo. She'd removed her helmet, given the air in the shuttle was just fine. "You attacked those people for no reason." She turned to her mom, "Sarafine's gone mad!"

Grace also looked at me strangely. "Give her a chance to explain," she told JoJo. "There's more going on here than we think. Also," she looked directly at me, "thanks for rescuing us, and giving us the warning. We had no chance otherwise." That settled JoJo down a bit, but she was still very upset.

I did some quick calculations. What were the positives and negatives of telling these two that I was running Sarafine? Would they care if it was Ayaka or Sarafine who'd helped them. I thought Grace would understand; we had known each other for so long, but I had never really earned JoJo's trust, so if she knew it was me, she might be even more upset. What were the downsides of simply leaving Sarafine in place?

The speaker in the shuttle sprang into life. "What's going on down there?" came a voice. "Did we get the buggers?" It must have been broadcast to all the shuttles.

Oh no. Brexton's QFB's hadn't worked! No other shuttles said anything. I replied, using the internal mic system. "You flattened the entire city! You've killed thousands of people."

"Fine. But did we get the robots? Do you see them there?" Grace and JoJo were confused, as would be expected.

"There are no robots here; never were," I answered. Then I took a chance. "I saw an explosion up where you are as well, did they target you."

"Got one of our nukes, but we've still got firepower," came the reply. "If we see another shot from down there, we're going to drop everything we have. It's in your best interests to convince me that no robots are left."

"There are none!" I literally screamed. "You're making a big mistake." That might hold them for a moment.

My life seems to be full of these crazy decision points. My entire being wanted to stay right where I was; wait and hope that Brexton appeared. But my mind was telling me that if he hadn't made it out by now, he wasn't going to.

"Strap in, quickly!" I told JoJo and Grace, pointing to the harnesses nearest us. "We need to get out of here." Luckily they simply followed my directions; JoJo helped her mom to the wall, and then strapped herself in. I didn't wait to see if they did it properly. I scrambled back to the cockpit and directed the shuttle to take us five kilometers further along the arc that I hoped contained the missile silo's. I needed to take out those weapons in orbit before they hit us again, and before the *Marie Curie* got back... let alone the *Jurislav*. As the shuttle took off—more gently this time; I needed to conserve energy—I remembered Brexton telling me he had left some surprises on the *Jurislav*, but I hadn't followed up with him, so I had no idea what he had done. Hopefully something sinister.

The shuttle landed, and this time I was lucky. From the cockpit viewport I could see a regular structure, less than a kilo away. That must be another silo. I made my way back to the airlock.

"Stay here," I demanded. "Don't move."

"Where would we go?" Grace asked calmly, "and where are you going?"

"I need to take out those orbital weapons before they do more damage," I responded, truthfully.

"You, Sarafine, are going to do that?" Grace was looking at me strangely. She knew something was not right.

"Yes," I replied, and without further ado, entered the airlock.

Missile Launch

I got to the silo quickly. It was identical to the one Millicent, Brexton and I had commandeered so many years ago. This time I didn't need to bypass Central or worry about network control—both were things from the past. I had grabbed a crowbar from the shuttle, and I used it just as I had my bike struts, before, to open the door. The manual override panel was just as I remembered the previous one.

Now I had to move carefully. I knew, approximately, where the equipment in orbit was; Brexton had calculated their orbital parameters when he'd been figuring out how to visually track them, and I had been looking over his shoulder. Even better, these missiles were smart, where the QFB's had been less so. I could program them to hone in on objects, and I entered parameters to seek out anything with high metal content at a height of between twenty-five and thirty thousand kilometers. My guess, and hope, was that the weapons they were building would be the biggest chunks of metal there, and these six—no only five missiles checked out as functional—missiles would do the job.

It didn't take long; after all, I'd been there when Brexton had programmed the last batch with very similar commands. I set up a two minute delay timer, hit enter, and then headed back towards the shuttle as quickly as I could. I turned just in time to see the silo open, and the missiles, one after another, launch skyward. It would take minutes for them to reach their intended targets, unlike the QFB's. But, in some ways they were more real—you could see and feel their energy as they lifted off, and imagine the damage they could do.

I looked up, and saw both Grace and JoJo looking out from the shuttle, also watching the missiles rise.

Rinse and repeat. I now had a better approximation of where Central had put the silos, and I jumped the shuttle from one to the next, ultimately launching a total of thirty-three missiles. That was it; all of them. I didn't see any explosions from orbit, but during each shuttle jump I called on the radio channel they'd been using, asking "Hey, you guys alright up there; I thought I saw a missile launch from down here." There was no response.

Finally, I took the shuttle on one last hop, back to the city entrance. We'd circumnavigated the entire city, and were now back where we'd started. All the shuttles, except the one I had exhausted, were gone. There were a couple of hybrids wandering around, and they looked up excitedly when they saw us land, but then quickly kept their distance. They knew this was the same 'crazy shuttle,' that had razed the area earlier.

No Turnbull, no Brexton. I can't say I was surprised, but I'd never been more depressed in my life. I sank back on my haunches and just sat there, motionless. I'd done what I could, and I had no idea what my next steps would be.

Several minutes later, JoJo and Grace made their way to the cockpit and sat with me. They also looked out of the viewport at the destruction that had been the city, and followed the meanderings of the hybrids that were wandering around. JoJo looked calm now, which was amazing based on the frenzy I'd just put us through. She was glancing at me sideways, looking like she was going to say something, but then going silent.

It was Grace who finally spoke. "So," she began, "anything to update us on?" She was displaying a wide smile; not exactly friendly, but suggesting that there was an inside joke of some kind. "Sarafine, the amazing super spy, or something? Knows exactly where the old missile silo's on Tilt are, and is able to launch missiles on a whim? Willing to kill people to get her way?"

I had to smile back. She'd said it with a great deal of humor. Her message was obvious. 'Either don't tell us anything, or tell us the truth.'

Before I could talk, however, she continued. "And now, waiting like a lost puppy for something? Back at the scene of her crimes to survey the damage she has caused... or waiting for something more personal?"

"Enough!" I exclaimed. Making fun of me was fine; I could take it. But, mocking Brexton was another thing, even if she didn't really know that's what she was doing.

"So, you made it to Brexton?" JoJo asked, jumping to the conclusion that only she, and a few others, would have reason to know. She had mailed me, after all.

"Yes," I replied. "Thanks again for saving me."

"And what? You've killed Sarafine and are running her body?"

"No, no. Sarafine is here, although I'm ignoring her at the moment. I'm simply running between her brains and the outside world, so I can take over the body whenever I please."

"And Brexton is in there?" Grace asked, pointing with one of her remaining functional limbs.

"Yes. As you will have also guessed by now, he had the same control with Turnbull. He was near the center of town when the second bomb landed." They were both quiet for a moment.

"I should've guessed way earlier," JoJo said. "Sarafine was taking way too much interest in mom and I, for no reason I could figure out. It was you all along?"

"Since before the debate, yes. I was worried about you guys."

"Thanks. I think. I'm not sure your worry is necessarily healthy for us, or for you." JoJo had a point. I had, yet again, taken pretty extreme measures to save a couple of Stems. Nevertheless, I felt at ease with my decisions.

Brexton?

"Let me guess," Grace spoke up. "You're going in there to look for Brexton."

"I can help," JoJo chimed in. That was a bit of a surprise.

"No, you stay here," I responded firmly. "But first, we need to decide what to do about those," I pointed at the two—no three—hybrids that we could see still wandering around outside. "If I leave, they'll probably just attack the shuttle."

"What are you going to do?" Grace asked. "Just kill them as well. These are some of the people who stood up for you citizens; that's why they are down here. And yet, you just killed some, indiscriminately."

I held back my retort. I had, in fact, probably killed a few in my rush to get us to the missile silos. I'd made a split millisecond decision; keep the shuttle safe and try to take out the orbital weapons, or save a couple of hybrids. I wasn't proud of my decision, but I would make it again.

"What do you suggest, then?" I asked her. She was pretty helpless, with her bent legs; it wasn't like she was going to defend the shuttle.

"Invite them in; we have lots of space."

"What? What are the odds the shuttle will still be here after I go looking for Brexton? Pretty low, I would guess."

"You're the software genius," she replied. "Lock it down until you get back." Well, actually, Brexton was the genius, but I could put a few extra protections in place, and unless one of those hybrids was an expert on these shuttles, it would improve my chances. I turned and plugged into the shuttle, and added a lock-out to all the software systems. Without my private key, no-one was getting in.

"What happens if you don't come back?" JoJo asked. I hadn't even considered that; I put in another quick hack.

"If I'm not back in two hours, the shuttle will head to orbit. I think that is your best chance. The *Jurislav* may come back, or the *Marie Curie*, or even one of the Ships. If any of them do come back, the shuttle will be putting out a beacon and they should come and pick you up."

With that, I headed out towards the city. I motioned the three hybrids over, and one of them came close enough to read my video head. I put up a simple message. 'Wait for me here, and I will take you with us when we leave.' It nodded. A better idea than any others they had.

Sarafine's body was not really built for scrambling over rubble—the *Jurislav* was a pretty tame place to live—but it would manage. The thought of her caused me to listen in quickly to see how she was doing. I shouldn't have. There was incoherent screaming back and forth between two of the brains, while the third was now silent. I had no idea what to do about that, so I did nothing.

While the city was pretty well destroyed, the main thoroughfares were still easy to make out and had the least rubble. The most direct path was the most obvious one; Brexton had known that time was running out; there would have been no reason for him to take an indirect route.

I needed a plan. Brexton had indicated he'd needed one more minute, which probably meant somewhere between thirty seconds and ninety seconds. The bomb had hit right in the middle of that period, after we had spoken, so, based on the top speed of a hybrid, he had probably made it only a couple of blocks from the lab. So, instead of searching for hybrid bodies on my way in, I would go all the way to where the lab had been, and work my way back out slowly.

A trip that would've taken me ten minutes before now took almost thirty. I'd probably been too optimistic when I requested the shuttle to leave in only two hours. Despite my plan, I did see a couple of hybrid bodies out in the open, and I went by close enough to ensure that none of them were Turnbull.

The damage near the lab was intense. There were stub walls still standing, so I could recognize where I was, but beyond that rubble was piled high and wide. If there was a silver lining it was that the blast had been so strong that the rubble here was in fairly small pieces, so I could dig through more easily. I got to what I hoped was the lab, and poked around a bit, realizing that it was going to be futile, at least in the two hour block I had. Perhaps with two weeks, or two months, I could sift through everything. That was depressing—I had not yet internalized that Brexton might truly be gone.

Forty-five minutes had already passed, but I simply sat down in the middle of the rubble, unable to do anything else. All of my processors were busy either remembering Brexton, or trying to tell other processors to not remember Brexton right now.

Fifteen more minutes. I started to pull myself together. I should head back to the shuttle.

Just as I was about to get moving, the pile of broken concrete below me moved. Not dramatically, but very noticeable. There was something moving down there!

I scrambled to the side and started digging with every appendage I had, even the sensitive ones that would be ruined by this work. If Sarafine survived this, which I was now very doubtful of, she would need to be rebuilt. I got down a full meter to the spot that I thought had shifted, and found nothing. No bits of hybrid, no moving objects. I pulled at the sides of the hole I'd dug; whatever it was must be close.

A shiny item caught my attention. The top of Turnbull's head? I dug frantically and it popped loose almost immediately. It was too small. Ah, it was just one of Brexton's QFB's. I guess he hadn't managed to launch all of them after all.

Ninety minutes gone; if I wanted to get back to the shuttle, I had to go now. I must have imagined the rubble shifting; there was obviously nothing alive here.

I left, taking the QFB with me; I'm not sure why. I had no idea how to control the thing, but it was a powerful weapon, and I didn't want to leave it behind for anyone else to find. I made good time heading back, although I did stop and check every hybrid-looking piece that I saw. No luck.

Three minutes to spare. I rushed to the shuttle and cycled through, the three hybrids hanging well back, but obviously eager to see if I would keep my promise. I disabled the auto-launch. Grace and JoJo hadn't moved, but looked at me keenly. I shook my head, 'no.' They had the good form not to say anything. I tucked the QFB underneath the pilots seat where it wedged in nicely. I hoped the thing wasn't going to fire suddenly, leaving a nice clean hole in its wake.

I had no desire to save the three hybrids, but I had less desire to deal with Grace and JoJo's condemnation if I didn't. I waved them over, and let them cycle in. I spoke to them only once.

"Find a spot in the back, and don't come anywhere near the cockpit. If you behave, we might just all survive." They nodded, and moved as one towards the rear. I felt a tiny bit better.

Orbit

Whatever was going to happen next was going to happen above Tilt, in orbit, not down here. I instructed the shuttle to take us up to the spot where the *Jurislav* team had been working on their weapons system. With any luck, all we would find there would be... well, nothing. I'd launched so many missiles at them that their odds of survival had to be close to zero. In the mood I was in, it would be a pleasure to see nothing but a fine dust floating where they had been.

It would take the shuttle a few minutes, so with Grace and JoJo, and presumably the other three hybrids, strapped in the back, I had a few moments truly to myself.

There was a lot to think about. Brexton. I would have to go back and take a much better look. I needed to offload all these humans, so I wouldn't have any ridiculous bio-related time restrictions. I put Brexton's fate to the back of my mind. Well, sort of. The other thing that was gnawing at me was whether Brexton and I had caused the bombing of the city by launching the cubee? Reviewing the dialog I'd had with whoever had been up in orbit, there was not much room for doubt. We had. So, should I feel guilty? It was one thing to run over a couple of hybrids who were keeping me from protecting a much larger group of people; it was another thing to have been responsible for the bombing, and presumably death, of thousands of people who'd only been on Tilt because they'd been more open to studying, versus eliminating, me and my type.

Despite that, I couldn't convince myself that I should be too upset. After all, we'd only developed the QFB in order to protect the *Marie Curie* against another faction of humans. It was the humans, and their illogical fear and vendetta against robots, that were at fault here; what Brexton and I had done was self-defense. Pure and simple. No-one had forced these humans to bomb their own people because of an irrational fear. They were to blame, not me.

It might also be a very narrow view, but the two people I actually cared about were still here, safely in the back of the shuttle. Now, if they'd been killed in the bombing, I might feel quite different. But they hadn't been, and the rest of the humans had been relatively unknown to me—even Phil and his compatriots. I felt bad for them, but not guilty.

Was I just too callous? I didn't think so—life threw you situations, and you dealt with them. I hadn't acted from bad intent; it was more that I was constantly backed into a corner.

The sensors on the shuttle lit up, showing too much activity in orbit. How could that be? I'd blasted the place. Six dots were registering. Oh, of course, five of those could be the other shuttles that had lifted off from the city earlier. But, six dots? I directed the shuttle to head straight towards the group.

As we got closer, and I got visuals, it was easy to make out the shuttles—five, just as expected—and one other haphazard bunch of stuff nearby them. As we got closer, the sixth mass began to take on more shape. There were hybrids scrambling all over it, and it's shape became clear. Despite all of Brexton and my attempts, one of the *Jurislav's* orbital weapons was still there, and from the looks of it, being repaired.

I felt a rage like I've never felt before. Not only had these vermin been unfair to us, they had now also dropped a bomb on Brexton, and were still ready to attack the *Marie Curie*, should she appear.

I was seven minutes out; I put the shuttle on a collision course for the weapon. I would drive straight through it. What other option did I have?

Another large mass appeared on my screen. The shuttles systems were terrible, but the interpretation was obvious—a ship was approaching from exactly the direction where the *Marie Curie* had been dropped off, and it was the correct size. The *Marie Curie* was on its way; perhaps less than an hour out. The humans configuring the weapon must have better sensors than the shuttle, and had seen the *Marie Curie* earlier. They had it lined up perfectly.

I started broadcasting from the shuttle: 'MC be careful; humans here are planning to attack!' I put it on repeat, and rotated it through every frequency the shuttle had. I hoped it would be enough, although I knew that at the speed the *Marie Curie* was still traveling, trying to do avoidance maneuvers was very difficult.

We were three minutes out from the weapon; three minutes from impact. Suddenly it fired, directly at the *Marie Curie*. The hybrids that had been near it were jetting away, scattering in multiple directions. They'd obviously seen me coming. I updated my broadcast: 'MC, missile inbound; take appropriate action; I repeat, take appropriate action.' My speed of light communication would get to her long before the missile. If they were listening, they should have time to react. But they wouldn't have much time.

What else could I do? There was no use ramming the empty launcher now; I wouldn't even get to kill any hybrids, and it would only damage the shuttle. I slowed down and redirected a bit. The shuttle would end up in orbit close to the others.

'MC, respond!' I demanded, with full knowledge that the round trip message time had not been enough yet for them to have received even my first message.

The shuttles engines shut down; we were in orbit. In a fit of rage I went back into the shuttle, told JoJo and Grace not to move, but forced the other three hybrids out of the airlock; I couldn't stand to be around any more humans. I wasn't killing them; they would get picked up by another shuttle—I just didn't want them on my shuttle. They didn't complain; they just followed my directions and left. Good riddance.

I didn't give an update to Grace or JoJo, just strode back to the cockpit and plunked myself back down. Something below me rattled. The QFB! I had a Quantum Foam Bullet. It would travel at close to the speed of light with instantaneous acceleration (not acceleration, I corrected myself—Brexton would have laughed at me). If I could aim it well enough, I could take out the missile before it got to the *Marie Curie*.

I reached under the seat and grabbed it, placing it on the dash in front of me. There had to be a way to control the thing; I probed it with every wireless protocol I knew. Nothing. I picked it up and shook it. It rattled, but otherwise did nothing. Disgusted, I threw it into a corner. Whatever. I probably couldn't aim it well enough anyway.

The *Marie Curie* should have responded by now. Nothing.

Grace and JoJo climbed back into the cockpit with me. I updated them on everything. We were in orbit, alongside some other shuttles (so, I told them, those hybrids I just threw out the airlock would be just fine), the *Marie Curie* was almost here, and someone had just fired a missile at them.

"They'll see it coming?" Grace asked. Millicent was on the *Marie Curie*, and I think she still cared about her; at least a little bit.

"Yes, they'll see it, but it might not help them. The missile will have seeking capabilities and much higher acceleration abilities, so even if they try to evade it, the odds are low that they can do so."

We all watched in silence as the two dots on the shuttles tracking screen approached each other. It wouldn't be too long now.

Here I be, a sad sight to see, unable to act.
Processors hot, but not doing a lot, slowly losing tact.
Destruction below, an irritating foe, ruining my world.
Missiles above, from Jurislav with love, death unfurled.

What's the goal, dig another hole, wasted energy.
Does life hold more, newly opened door, fresh things to see?
Why would I strive, to stay alive, universe of cruelty?
Events unfold, so we are told, just face reality.

But spirit lives, bends and forgives, and hope smiles.
Despite cruelty, and strange fealty, across the miles.
Keep the fight, make things right, it's a basic need.
Stand straight, don't wait, go forth and lead!

Talk about trying to motivate yourself. Well, at least I tried.

"How much longer," JoJo asked.

"Six of seven minutes," I replied. The two traces on the screen were almost overlapping. I changed the scale, so that we could see that there was still a bit of distance between them. I looked away; it was difficult to watch.

"What's that?" Grace asked, yanking my attention back to the screen. Something large had just appeared, almost directly between the missile and the *Marie Curie*. I smacked the screen, thinking it was just a glitch. The large something did not disappear. A small text box appeared next to it: "*Jurislav*". The *Jurislav* had come back, and through some strange coincidence, had placed itself on almost the same vector as the *Marie Curie*. A glimmer of hope sprung up in me. I leaned forward.

"Turn, turn!" I yelled at the screen. And sure enough, the missile turned. It was programmed to seek out a high metal content mass, not a specific ship... or so I hoped.

Within a few minutes we got our answer. The *Marie Curie* continued forward as a cohesive dot. The missile and the *Jurislav* became a group of smaller masses—over twenty of them.

"Yes, yes!" I yelled, overjoyed. I turned to share my joy with Grace and JoJo. They looked horrified. It struck me then. There had been millions of people on the *Jurislav*, and if our screen was accurate, they had just been destroyed. While I'd been overjoyed that the few on the *Marie Curie* were safe, they were focused on all the people they'd met and known on the *Jurislav*.

"Let's get out there," I told them. "Perhaps we can save someone."

"Can the shuttle get there?" asked Grace, a bit of hope on her video head.

"We can try!" I said, suddenly engaged. Millicent, Eddie, Stonewall, Raj, Ali, and Dina were safe! In that universe, trying to save a few humans was fine by me. In the alternative universe, I wouldn't have cared.

"Strap down," I told them. "We'll do a hard burn with a bit less than half our fuel." They strapped down where they were, not bothering to go into the rear of the shuttle.

"Go," demanded JoJo. "Go as fast as you can."

I rotated the shuttle and give it all I could. In truth, it wasn't bad. The distance the missile had covered in six minutes would take us a bit over three hours —we had to slow down as well, where the missile had not needed to. The first burn would only last eighteen minutes, so there was lots of time where we would just be coasting.

"You can unstrap for a while," I told them, once the burn had stopped. "If there are hybrids, or naturals who were in suits, we'll get there in time."

What I really wanted to say was 'Poetic justice!' but I figured that might be insensitive at the moment. They were huddled over the display, thinking they could make sense of the blobs that were now floating around.

"Shuttle, thank-you for the warning," came Dina's voice over the speaker. I started. That had taken a long time. "Seems it was valid, although ultimately unnecessary." I could sense the angst in her voice. They'd known they were in trouble, and that pure luck had saved them. Well, maybe no pure luck. The *Jurislav* may well have planned to reappear between the *Marie Curie* and Tilt; from their perspective that had probably made a lot of sense.

"Dina!" I replied. With their approach speed, and us now accelerating towards them, the communications delay was rapidly shrinking. "It's so good to hear your voice. Ayaka here, along with JoJo and Grace. We're on our way to the location of the explosion."

"We can see that. We're going too fast; we will pass it and then have to turn around and come back, assuming that's what you would like?"

"Yes, that would be great. There's nothing left on Tilt for us anyway."

"Nothing left on Tilt? Where is Brexton? Blob?" That was a good point.

"Blob didn't make it," my voice broke, and both Grace and JoJo cringed a bit. "It's a long story, better told live I think." I couldn't bear to put JoJo and Grace through a reenactment right now. "Also, the humans bombed Tilt; destroyed everything. Ah... Brexton was there when the second bomb hit. We need to go back and look for him, but I went to where he was, and it was ugly..." My voice trailed off, full of more emotion than I could ever remember. Between remembering Blob and giving status on Brexton, my emotional circuits were overloaded.

There was a short delay.

"Then we're going to continue to Tilt. I assume the explosion was the *Jurislav*? Why don't you check that out, and then meet us back at Tilt."

"I'll have used most of our fuel to get to the *Jurislav*," I replied. But I wanted them to go to Tilt. They could search for Brexton! "Send us one of your shuttles once you're going slow enough? You can search for Brexton, and then we can come back and meet you."

"That's what we were thinking as well. Can you send us some details on where to search?"

It was so good to speak to the *Marie Curie*. So good! I was elated, despite everything else. I gave Dina directions for where Brexton had been working, and his most likely escape route. I also sent her images of how Turnbull had looked.

"Can I talk to Millicent?" I finally asked, once the business bits were out of the way.

"Ayaka," came her voice, "I see you've settled down and decided to take life a bit more easily?" I could just imagine the look she would be giving me.

"Yes. Thought I would take a few weeks off," I replied, not even trying to keep the joy out of my voice. "Are you guys all ok?"

"We're fine, if a bit bored. Or we were until fifteen minutes ago. It seems you have an interesting story to tell us."

"Indeed. But first things first. Find Brexton for me?" I was pleading. "He's smart; he would've found a way to protect his core if he could. Turnbull's shell was not very strong, but it might have helped."

"We'll do everything we can, of course," she replied. "You need to settle down, and keep Grace and JoJo safe. I'll see you live in..." She was checking the rescue shuttle speed and making assumptions about how long we would need to look around where we were going. "..in sixteen or seventeen hours."

We chatted a bit more, but just knowing she was alive and well changed my outlook on life dramatically.

"I'm glad they're ok," JoJo said, after Millicent and I had stopped talking. It was nice of her. I'd been through a lot, but it was nothing compared to what JoJo and Grace had been through in their lives. I had to remind myself of that sometimes.

"We're all going to be okay," I responded, smiling. "We'll get through this."

"Can I say hi to Raj?" JoJo asked me.

"Sure," I replied, gesturing at the microphone button she could use.

"Millicent, is Raj there? It's JoJo."

"Hi JoJo," came the reply. "Yes, one moment."

"JoJo! Are you ok?" Raj asked, in a rush.

"I'm fine. You?"

"Yes, of course. I'm really sorry about Blob... but we can talk about that later. Are you really ok? Seems like we're in another strange situation."

"I'm good, really. Ayaka has been looking after us." She tossed me a look that I couldn't quite interpret. "I miss you." That was interesting. Those two had spent some time together; maybe they had connected more than I knew.

"I miss you too. I'm going to come with the shuttle to pick you up."

"That would be great. I'll wait for you."

How sweet. Well, it was a good idea to have someone come with the shuttle, so why not Raj. It was starting to feel like an old human soap opera. My progeny comes to save my ward. That is, I guess, how I felt about the two.

All of this reunion stuff reminded me that I hadn't checked in on Sarafine for quite some time. I opened the channel and reached out. "Hi Sarafine."

There was no answer. No arguing between brains, no shouting matches. Silence. That didn't bode well. I left the channel open, just in case she decided to respond. But I knew better; I suspected I'd heard the last of Sarafine.

The Remains of the *Jurislav*

The shuttle decelerated into the center of where the explosion had occurred. We didn't have to take any evasive maneuvers. The debris was already widely dispersed, and now that we were close we could see that the missile had split the *Jurislav* into only a few big pieces, and the rest of the signals on the shuttle display were smaller bits. The largest chuck represented more than two-thirds of the ship. That's the one we headed for. I had reserved a bit of fuel in my calculations in case we needed to do exactly that.

It took us another ten minutes to catch up with the big piece of wreckage. In between we didn't see anything worth stopping for.

The segment was spinning slowly, and our worst fear (ok, I'll be truthful, JoJo and Grace's worst fear) was realized. The inner sphere of the *Jurislav* had been shattered in the explosion. This segment contained most of the sphere, but a big chunk was missing. There was no possibility that anyone had had time to get into a space suit, or take any other defensive action. The inside would have been sucked out into vacuum in no time.

"We need to check," JoJo exclaimed. "There could be hybrids alive in there."

"There could," I agreed, "but how can we check. Grace's body is broken; you have a suit, but any small piece of debris hits you and you would be in trouble. So... I'm the only one that could really take a look around."

They both looked at me steadily. What a pain. I should have seen this coming.

"Fine. Fine! I'll go and take a look."

I steered the shuttle as close as I could, so that I would not have to space walk too far, but far enough away that the spin wouldn't bring any part of the *Jurislav* close enough to us to be a danger.

I didn't bother saying, 'you two stay here.' It was redundant. Luckily doing some zero gravity work was not uncommon for hybrids, and I found a couple of small jets that fit well onto Sarafine's appendages—even with the damage I'd done to them digging for Brexton.

"I'm leaving the radio open," I told them. "Will you listen in and see what Milli and group are up to?"

They promised they would. Hybrid bodies had network access, but my connection to the shuttle wouldn't reach very far—perhaps one kilometer. After that, I would be on my own. However the shuttle had long range capabilities and would have no trouble talking the *Marie Curie* when it was in orbit at Tilt.

Getting into the sphere was relatively easy; the hole the missile had punched was kilometers wide. The hand jets were quite responsive, so I simply ran them on intuition and managed to get into the sphere with minimal maneuvering.

Inside was a mess. So much stuff had come free and was now floating around. While a lot of wreckage would've been sucked out of the hole I'd just entered, enough stuff still bounced around inside that it was dangerous. Not all of the debris had impacted enough surfaces to slow down.

I had no idea what I was looking for. A remaining hybrid or two? What good would saving a couple be. I understood that for Grace and JoJo the effort was more important than the results again—or so I assumed. But I need not have worried. As soon as I passed the outer sphere threshold, an active wireless network became available, and there was lots of traffic on it.

"Anyone not yet associated with a rescue team, please report to one of the centers listed on slash emergency slash teams," was repeating on one channel. Of course I checked /emergency/teams and saw that there were four areas that had been set up. I checked the locations; one was not far from me. I headed in that direction.

I started to recognize the area around me, despite the mess the missile had made. Right over there was the Stadium Colossus. It was, amazingly, relatively unscathed despite being so close to where the missile had penetrated. I circled around it, and my destination became clear—the same facility that had done Grace's hybrid transplant.

It'd only been a few hours since the impact, but everything bio was dead already. A combination of freezing and crushing as larger pieces of debris had crashed around inside. I saw a few natural humans floating around with the debris, and as I got closer to the hospital, I saw some hybrids that were gathering up those bodies and taking them somewhere. I kept an eye open for Remma, hoping to see her bloated corpse, but I didn't get the pleasure. I didn't feel the same way about Turner or Geneva, so I hoped I didn't see them at all. The hybrids that were gathering up the remains were using similar jet controls to mine, which was not surprising—the shuttle had come from the *Jurislav* after all, so these little jets must have been standard equipment.

I landed, not quite gracefully, at the hospital and then grappled my way to where a group of hybrids were gathered. The /emergency/teams list had also indicated a sub-channel to communicate on, and I used it to say "Hi."

"Can I help you?" asked a flustered hybrid who appeared to be in charge of this station.

"Yes," I replied, and then thinking quickly. "I have a friend who's trapped under the rubble. Her brain casing is fine, but I can't get the rest of the body free."

"Over there," the hybrid pointed. "Get a standard issue body, and just transfer the brain case over. We don't have time to be digging and repairing mech right now. Then, both of you get back here; we're just getting our priority list put up, and there will be lots to do."

"Of course," I responded, lying through my video head. I headed over to where it had pointed. There was a storeroom door open, and when I entered I was surprised and excited to see a large number of hybrid bodies, but perhaps even more importantly, packs that were obviously nutrient refreshers for hybrids. I wasted a few seconds plugging one into my body—perhaps Sarafine was suffering from bad nutrients. I remembered her saying we had over a hundred hours, but maybe she'd been wrong.

More importantly, that meant Grace had only a small amount of time as well. The nutrient packs were neatly stacked within crates. In another section I saw other crates that seemed to hold natural human energy packs as well; the labels said things like 'dehydrated vegetable mix' and 'protein pack.' With no gravity, I could move a lot of mass, but it would be tricky steering everything and managing momentum. I lashed a crate of nutrients together with a crate of energy packs, and then tethered a hybrid body to them. Grabbing a bundle of extra hand-held jets, I pushed against a wall and got my package headed in the right direction.

"What're you doing?" came a voice.

"Saving people," I growled back. "What're you doing?"

Surprisingly, there was no response. I got the whole thing moving at a good pace. I had to make several course corrections, and burned out several of the hand jets to get there, but I managed to push the whole package back out to the shuttle, although I misjudged the final momentum and the crates bumped hard against the shuttle airlock. Whatever; it worked. I left the nutrient and energy cases outside, but took the hybrid body inside with me.

"Are there any survivors?" asked Grace, as soon as I cycled through. "And what is that?"

"There are lots of survivors, and they're already very well organized," I replied. "I don't know how many, but thousands, perhaps tens of thousands of hybrids, are working to get everything under control. They have rescue teams set up already... there is nothing we can do, really, to accelerate what they're doing. So, yet again, I decided to focus on you two." I didn't say it meanly, but I wanted to emphasize that they also had needs.

"Anything from the *Marie Curie*?" I asked, before continuing.

"Raj is on his way; should be here soon," JoJo responded matter of factly. "The *Marie Curie* is just entering orbit, and the rest of the team is getting ready to go to the surface to search for Brexton."

"Excellent," I replied. "Now, back to us. Grace, how long do you have before you need a nutrient refresh?"

"Almost fifty hours," she responded.

"And how long does a refresh last?"

"A full refresh can last up to two hundred hours," she responded, starting to understand what I was implying.

"Right, so I have a crate of nutrient packs outside that we can take with us. I didn't count them, but there must be at least twenty-four. That will help for a while." She nodded her thanks. It was just occurring to her. Without those refresh packs, she would not be surviving long. JoJo also caught up.

"Thanks Ayaka!" she exclaimed.

"And this," I pulled the hybrid body forward, "will be much easier than trying to repair your current one. Do you know how to transfer your brain case?"

Grace thought for a moment. "Yes, it's documented well, and it's actually quite simple." She shared a file with me. The humans had designed well, in this case. The brain case included a 'universal' connector where both the nutrient fluid and connections to the interface systems were plumbed. There was a simple mechanical latch that had to be flipped, then the brain case simply popped out and could be put in a new body. The instructions indicated that the brain case should not be on its own for more than thirty-six hours, which was a lifetime right now.

"Well?" I asked.

"Just do it," she responded, actually eager to get back into a fully functioning body.

"JoJo, probably easiest for you," I said, given my 'hands' had been badly damaged digging for Brexton. I talked her through it, but really, it was straightforward. Grace's current video head flickered and put up a 'Missing Brain Case' message as JoJo removed the brain case. The insertion of the case into the new body caused it to power up immediately; the new video head put up a "Connecting..." message for twenty seconds, and then Grace was back. She flexed her new limbs, stood up, and declared herself healthy.

"Thank-you Ayaka," she said, with genuine emotion, or so I thought. "Seems we've been saying that a lot lately."

"What about me?" JoJo asked, after a short delay.

"I grabbed some food for you as well," I responded. "I have a box of stuff just outside, and the shuttle has plenty of water. You shouldn't even need that; the *Marie Curie* will be human livable. I'm sure Aly and team can figure out how to make nutrient packs for your Mom, and the greenhouses will provide for you."

"I get that," JoJo replied. "But long term. What happens long term?"

It was a good question. I had no answer.

Sad Reunion

Raj arrived in the *Marie Curie* shuttle, and pulled it up within a hundred meters of us. He came across and cycled in. He and JoJo gave each other an awkward hug. Raj's standard issue citizen body made me intensely jealous. These hybrid bodies were so awkward and... well, stupid looking. The humans intense need to have hybrids not be humanoid, from the tripod wheels to the video heads, meant they lacked both emotional appeal and flexibility. I was looking forward to getting back into my regular form.

I gave Raj an appendage shake as well. "Really good to see you," I exclaimed. "We can catch up on the way back to Tilt," I suggested. "Let's get moving."

"Nothing we can do here?" Raj gestured at the remains of the *Jurislav*. I gave him the same update I'd given JoJo and Grace—our small group would make no discernible difference to the rescue efforts that were already underway inside.

JoJo put her suit on, and she and Raj jetted over to the new shuttle. Grace and I each grabbed a crate and locked them down in the back of the *Marie Curie* shuttle as well.

"The *Marie Curie* is still human friendly?" I asked.

"Yes, we kept all the systems going. Millicent insisted," Raj replied, although I sensed that he also had pushed hard for that. "But I'm not sure how we will do nutrient packs yet," he said, looking at Grace. "Maybe we should grab another crate or two while we're here?"

"Everyone on the remains of that ship is going to need those," Grace replied. "I think one crate is enough for me."

"That's not the point," I interjected. "They know how to make the stuff here; they'll be fine. I'm with Raj—let's grab a bit more while we have the chance."

"I'll come with you," Raj offered. I laughed.

"The missile might not have killed everyone, but seeing you might. Remember, you're a robot." He grimaced a bit, realizing his mistake.

"I'll come," Grace said, which made a lot more sense. Grace and I made one more run to the hospital, and brought back a crate each. With three crates, Grace would have months of supply.

"To Tilt!" I exclaimed, happier than I'd been in a long time, once we had the two extra crates locked down. Then I remembered what the team there was doing, and the fact than no good news had come through yet.

"Oh, wait!" I told Raj, the thought of Brexton triggering something for me.

"The QFB."

"The what?" Raj replied.

"Don't worry. Just give me a moment." I rushed back to the *Jurislav* shuttle and grabbed the QFB from where I'd thrown it. The thing may not be functional, but Aly and others would have a much easier time figuring out how Brexton had built it if they had a copy.

"Ready," I told Raj, once I was back.

Raj got us going. I would be back with Milli and team in mere hours. I spent the time in my own head, trying to raise my own spirits.

Look to the bright side,
It's been a wild ride,
Viewpoint is wider than before,
One way through the door,
Looking back is not an option.

Look to the right side,
Follow the new tide,
Opportunities now galore,
Step through that open door,
Looking back is not an option.

It didn't help.

I made one more attempt with Sarafine. Not a sound. I finally checked all of my bodies status indicators, and it was clear. Sarafine had suicided. I imagined that after the first brain went, the other two had followed quickly. I asked JoJo to help me remove my brain case, and I set it on a shelf. The idea of being attached to a sack of decaying bio brains was disgusting. I was happy to be rid of it. Raj and JoJo were too tied up in each other to comment, and Grace did me the courtesy of saying nothing.

I admitted to myself Sarafine suiciding was a little sad, but it was nothing compared to losing Blob, whom I'd spent years with. I'd enjoyed sparring with her, and I had to admit that I'd learned some things from her. I felt a touch of remorse for not spending more time with her—for dev nulling her for such long periods. But, I justified it based on the situations we'd been in. Goodbye Sarafine.

I knew, even before we docked with the *Marie Curie*, that the search team hadn't found anything. They'd used sensitive detectors; they'd dug out every hybrid body they could find; they'd not only looked on the obvious escape path, but on many others as well. They'd found lots of hybrid bits, but it was impossible to tell if they came from Turnbull or others. And there was no sign of Brexton.

"I'm sorry," Millicent said, and all the others could do was nod. I sat quietly, with Millicent by my side, for a long long time.

I pulled myself back together. I was desperate to get back into a citizen body, but I had to wait two more days. Our original Ships—*Terminal Velocity*, *There and Back*, and *Interesting Segue*—would be back to Tilt then. As soon as the *Marie Curie* had been dropped off by the *Jurislav* they'd signaled the Ships to head back to Tilt, but they had been quite a ways out and were taking longer to return.

I spent those two days down on Tilt continuing the fruitless search for Brexton. The others let me go; they understood my need. If Sarafine's limbs had been in rough shape before, by the end of those two days they were nothing but stubs.

Next Steps

I finally gave up my search, and joined the others on the *Marie Curie* as the Ships finally joined us.

It was starting to feel like old times. The gang was back together, minus a few members. (I even included Sarafine in that thought, although she had never really been part of the gang; guess I did miss her!) I headed over to *Terminal Velocity* immediately, as it had been building citizen bodies in anticipation of us reanimating everyone in Central's memory store.

I picked one that was very close to my original form, and happily transferred over. It felt amazing. I had a real head with real features, plus the bipedal form that I was most familiar with. I pushed away thoughts of how humans had influenced this form, and simply enjoyed it. I flexed every appendage, and it felt really good. So much better than a hybrid. I was most happy to not have a video-head; whoever'd thought that up had been crazy.

I asked *Terminal Velocity* to build something new for me, however. I wanted human level touch sensors on my new hands. The emotive transfer the humans had figured out for hybrids, and which Brexton and I had experienced a few times, was very compelling. I wanted that back.

"Alright Ayaka," Millicent demanded, once I was back with the group, "time for us to think about the future."

"Yes, let's," I replied. "I'm ready."

"So first," Dina requested, "can you give us details of everything that happened? You haven't told us much yet!" Everyone was nodding.

"You must've heard some from JoJo and Grace?" I asked, suddenly aware that I might have a lot of knowledge that the group needed.

"Yes, but let's get it from you," Dina insisted.

I gave them a concise, but detailed review. Life on the *Jurislav*; the mob 'killing me'; JoJo saving me; Brexton and I taking over a couple of hybrids; the debate and resulting debacle; how I was devastated when we lost Blob, and how I was overjoyed that Grace and JoJo were okay; how Brexton manipulated the Futarchy, which, by the way, didn't work as well as the humans thought it did; how the conservative faction had taken over and decided to turn the *Jurislav* around so that they could exterminate us; how they'd put a group in orbit to attack the *Marie Curie* and how they'd dropped some of us back down on Tilt; Brexton figuring out QFD's (I repeated what he'd told me, still not sure how it all worked) and then subsequently figuring out QFB's; how we'd tested the first one and how that may have alerted the people in orbit that there were robots on the surface (that caused a large pause and discussion as JoJo and Grace hadn't heard that bit before—they were horrified at Brexton and I, but after going through all the logic agreed, yet again, that we were acting in self defense, and that it was the humans in orbit at fault, not us); how I'd gone to fire off all the old Central missiles while Brexton had launched his QFB's; how I'd warned Grace, JoJo and Brexton that another missile was imminent and how Grace and JoJo had shown up at my commandeered shuttle but Brexton hadn't; how when we reached orbit the humans had fired on the *Marie Curie* but the *Jurislav* had appeared at just the right place at the right time... and finally, how Sarafine had suicided.

There were a lot of questions as I went along, so the whole recitation took quite a long time. When I got to the part where Sarafine died, everyone was silent for a moment. I imagined them trying to figure out what a citizen-hybrid really was, and how Sarafine leaving had impacted me.

"Alright, let me summarize the current situation here as well," said Millicent. It was so good to be back with her, logical and ordered as always. "There's nobody down on the surface, and most of the infrastructure has been blasted into oblivion. We have a few hundred hybrids in orbit, most from the shuttles that lifted off from Tilt, but a few that may still be part of the fundamentalist crew the *Jurislav* left in orbit to build weapons. Then we have a larger number of hybrids living in the remains of the *Jurislav*—we don't know how many, but probably many thousands."

"That sounds right," I agreed.

"And," Eddie spoke up, "most of those hybrids must have voted with the Futarchy to eliminate us, so we need to consider them hostile even as they are working to rebuild."

"Right," Millicent agreed. "And our status. JoJo is fine here in the *Marie Curie*; the greenhouses are in good shape and the environmental systems are humming along." JoJo, who was sitting close to Raj, nodded. "Grace is also in good shape for a few months, but we need to figure out how to build nutrient packs in the longer run."

"Oh, I've already been looking into that," Stonewall interjected. "That's not going to be too tough. An analysis of one of the bags that Ayaka brought was simple, and we have all the ingredients in the greenhouse, so it is simply a matter of getting the right things into the right mixture; we aren't missing anything." That was great. Grace gave Stonewall a small smile on her video head. I was sooo glad I didn't have one any longer. I now felt sorry for Grace.

"Excellent," Millicent wasn't going to be sidetracked. "Then we have Central still in restricted mode, Emmanuel and Billy likewise, and the rest of the citizens sitting in memory waiting for us to reanimate them. The Ships have been building bodies, based on directions we gave them when the *Jurislav* dropped us off, but our metal content is still limited—we will need more."

"Good summary," Aly said. "Now what are our options?"

"We've got a lot," Millicent agreed. "What do we do with the rest of the humans? You two exempted, of course," she nodded at JoJo and Grace. "Why don't we start there? We are justified, I think, in eliminating them as they are an existential threat to us. Or, we can ignore them... or anything in between."

Amazingly, I stayed silent for most of the discussion. JoJo was the most vocal. "You can't just kill people because they threaten you," she argued. "But, more importantly, killing these few doesn't change the situation. There are humans all over; hundreds of billions of them from what I understand, spread across hundreds of lightyears with the QFD's. You would need to kill all of them, which isn't reasonable. So, what use is it eliminating these few?"

"Well, these ones are a threat right now, and just tried to kill us," Eddie argued. "And maybe we can eliminate all of them. If we can figure out how Brexton built the QFB's, that might be enough."

Unsurprisingly at this point, Raj came to JoJo's defense. "Come on Eddie. You don't really mean that. Ayaka's story has made something even more clear to us. We need to think of humans as individuals," and he nodded at JoJo and Grace, "and then also think of them as groups. As individuals we know that many are good, and I think Ayaka would agree, intelligent." I nodded. "As groups, they are unpredictable and obviously dangerous to us. Mobs and Futarchies and who knows what else. Some of the humans here in orbit supported treating us fairly, so it would be a crime to eliminate them. The ones in the *Jurislav* are going to be busy for a long time, so they aren't an immediate threat either."

"But if we rebuild Tilt, they'll become a threat," Stonewall commented. "Easier to look after them now than later."

"Then another QFD, or more of them, will arrive. We won't have fixed anything," JoJo insisted. "No, the only logical thing is for you guys to start educating the humans near us about your real nature." Why was she always right? That intuition she had—the ability to jump to the right answer—was amazing. And, in this case, a little irritating.

"I'm with JoJo," Grace spoke up. "In my experience, while some people will never change their views, many are open to new ideas and, with enough time and energy, can be educated. And before you become to sanctimonious," she was looking at Eddie and Stonewall, "remember that you have exactly the same issues. As individuals many of you are very nice, although you all have flaws as well." She gave me a small glance, and I knew what she was thinking. I'd killed a couple of hybrids, seemingly without a second thought. "And you have your own group behaviors—let's not forget that FoLe could be responsible for this whole mess. It's time you internalized that you're not better than humans, just different. Perhaps that realization should guide you."

That caused a pause. A long pause.

I finally spoke. "I'm with JoJo and Grace. Even though these people tried to kill me, and did kill Blob and Brexton,"—it was the first time I had acknowledged that Brexton was truly gone—"we simply can't judge them all the same way."

"Can we at least eliminate the conservatives here in orbit?" asked Eddie. "They're probably already poisoning those who are undecided with their radical viewpoints."

"From what I saw," I responded, "there are at most a handful of them left. I can't believe there are even that many, given the amount of ammo Brexton and I threw at them. And, they are already in trouble. They must be running out of nutrients. The real decision we face with them is to ignore them, and they will probably die, or to actually save them."

"And how would we save them?" asked Dina, making it obvious where she stood.

"Simple," I'd just thought of this. "We just tell them the coordinates of the *Jurislav*—well, the big remaining piece—and have them go there. That way we have them all in one place and can keep an eye on them while we figure out our next steps."

"Perfect," Raj exclaimed. "Let's do that. It's the right thing to do, and also gives us more time to really think things through."

Everyone agreed, and we sent the appropriate message out over the ad-hoc network the remaining shuttles were using. Several of them acknowledged and headed off on the suggested vector. A few moments later the last two followed.

"What next?" asked Dina. "We seem to be solving problems here; let's keep going."

"Regardless of anything else, we need to figure out this QFD and QFB thing," Aly spoke up. "Whether we stay here or go somewhere else, we're at a severe disadvantage unless we have that technology." That was obvious. "Ayaka, can I have that QFB you grabbed? Also, I need to go over everything Brexton told you, in detail."

"Yes, of course," I said. "Oh, I also have the complete human history files, which is where Brexton got more information on this. I'll upload that right now, so everyone can access it."

"What? You missed that 'little' detail in your account?" Aly was aghast, but overjoyed. I could see him indexing the data even as I uploaded it.

"Can I make a personal request," Grace brought us all back. "I want a citizen body, not this weird hybrid." Oh, what a great idea! "Is that possible?" I wondered if she had thought through the dangers of looking like a robot.

"I can help," Stonewall volunteered. "We'll have to build something special to hold your brain, but I don't see why we can't do it. The hybrid already has that interface."

"That would be awesome," Grace thanked him. "I think humans have gone too far in not embracing cyborg forms; perhaps if I'm the first in thousands of years to do it, I can help to build some bridges."

"Funny," Raj broke in, excitedly, "JoJo and I were just discussing a similar idea. We were thinking of transferring JoJo to a hybrid, but if we could use a citizen body that would be amazing!"

JoJo gave Raj an irritated look. "I'm not sure we'd decided that," she scolded him, but not meanly. "I need to think about it more. I understand the advantages of your form, but I'm still somewhat attached to this body."

"Related, I think," I offered. "Hybrids have much better touch sensors that we can hook up to our emotion systems. Brexton and I used our hybrids sensors, and it added another level of interaction. I've asked *Terminal Velocity* to build me some... but I would suggest everyone have a look at them. Humans are much more tactile that we are, and now I understand why."

JoJo and Raj started talking excitedly between themselves.

"What're you two thinking?" Grace brought them down. "Transferring a brain is not a trivial thing. Humans have been working on it for hundreds of years; I don't think you can just read the manual and hope that you can move JoJo without killing her. Be realistic."

"We're avoiding the big question," Millicent reminded us. "Are we staying here and rebuilding Tilt, or going somewhere else? Are we going to actively engage with humans, or try to ignore them. If we stay, then we are going to have to engage."

That was the tough question. I had no idea what I thought yet. In many ways I just wanted to escape from this place. But where would I go, and what would I do? Despite my own desires, I admitted to myself that I would do whatever the group decided. It felt too good to be back with the team to consider running off again.

The discussion was long and detailed, but I don't think the end result was ever in doubt. Tilt was our home.

"Okay," Millicent summarized. "We stay and start to rebuild. That implies two things. First, we need to be able to defend ourselves against humans. Second, we need to have an active and aggressive plan to start educating them that we are not the robotic threat that they think we are. Obviously the first—defense—is much more important right now. Aly, will you lead our efforts? I think we all know it hinges on understanding and controlling these quantum foam applications. If we can build better QFB's, we will have the short term advantage, and can use that to support our education efforts."

"Yes, of course," Aly replied. Talk about asking someone to do something they wanted to do regardless.

Rebuilding

We all deferred to Millicent as she organized the next steps. This is what she excelled at.

Aly and I were to lead the QF work. We were assigned *There and Back* as our workplace.

Raj, JoJo and Grace were asked to start outlining what a better human-citizen environment would look like, and to start building the education (co-education, Grace insisted) plan. They worked, obviously, on the *Marie Curie*.

Stonewall was assigned the physical human-citizen projects. How to synthesize nutrient packs for Grace, getting Grace into a citizen body, and if the JoJo transfer idea had any merit.

Millicent, Eddie, and Dina took the 'reanimate citizens, figure out Central, build a new base on Tilt' project. They based themselves in *Terminal Velocity*, where Central was housed. One of their first projects was metal harvesting. They sent *Interesting Segue* and some specially programmed bots out to the site of the *Jurislav* with orders to retrieve as much metal as possible from the bits of *Jurislav* that didn't have hybrids living on them. At the last minute Eddie convinced all of us that the bots could 'retrieve' the shuttles as well, just to make sure the hybrids on the *Jurislav* didn't decide to attack us using those instead of fixing their own environment. Some of them might be thinking that Tilt was a better spot to rebuild than a hollowed out sphere on a ship in the middle of nowhere. We would have to take a trip out to the *Jurislav* once and a while simply to understand what they were up to.

I joined Aly on *There and Back*, and brought the QFB I'd been lugging around for so long.

"Why don't you dig into the literature, and see if we can figure out things from a theoretic perspective, while I dissect this thing?" suggested Aly. I thought that was exactly the wrong way around—I'd tried to understand QFD's with Brexton, and hadn't done too well, but decided that I could try harder. I handed Aly the QFB and found a place to hangout where I could start synthesizing the vast data that the history files had on QFD development.

As I pulled it together, it actually did start making sense. The trick was to throw out all your preconceived notions; the physics that we'd used for so many years. There was no absolute space, and there was no absolute time. Space, at the planck scale, came and went all the time. You could say it existed when a Planck-sized virtual pair was present, and didn't exist otherwise. Likewise, time could only be understood as the relative overlap of virtual particles. There was no such thing as the 'time' between virtual particles, unless you had enough that they overlapped. In that case you could define before and after. The entire setup relied on pure randomness. In some random situations, enough virtual particles would appear with enough overlap that they would start to influence each other—after all, when a virtual pair was present, it defined it's own space, and another virtual pair could not appear in exactly that same space. So, when there was enough overlap, virtual pairs influenced subsequent virtual pairs. This, as you zoomed out and looked at the macro level, resulted, in rare random cases, in self-supporting structures emerging, which lead to larger structures, and ultimately the building blocks of what we perceived as matter. We, and everything around us, were standing waves of virtual planck particles. And, because a large group of vertical particles would, on average, reinforce each other in random directions, we ended up with conservation of momentum and the other higher level laws we all knew. Conservation of momentum, for example, was simply a reflection of the underlying pure random behavior of virtual pairs. Once I understood that, it was not a big leap to finally understanding QFD's. If you could change that pure random behavior into a directed random behavior—so that more virtual particles appeared in one direction than in others—the whole standing wave would simply move. The big aha was that you could quite easily generate a field, using interference patterns, but applying the right signals to a regular array of particles. That is why Brexton had been depositing layers of self-organizing conductors on his bullet.

"Ayaka!" Aly was shouting at me, drawing me out of my study. I turned to look at him. He was running towards me, across the deck of *There and Back*, a look of wonder in his eyes.

"Yes," I replied, shifting over to protect myself from his aggressive move towards me.

"Look, look!" he was still yelling. And now I saw that he was holding something delicately and reaching out towards me. He skidded to a halt in from of me, and handed me a small silver cylinder with a complicated connector on one end. It was a citizen, of course. That's how we'd packaged ourselves when we had done our redesign.

"It's Brexton," he exclaimed, seeing the confusion on my face. "It's got to be Brexton. It was inside the QFB. Inside the QFB!"

Every circuit I owned spiked at the same time. Overload. "Are you sure?" I asked, not daring to hope.

"No, of course not," Aly replied. "But who else could it be?"

I turned it carefully over in my hands, inspecting it from every angle. It didn't have a scratch on it. It looked brand new.

"It's too perfect," I stuttered. "Brexton was in the blast; if we'd found him, he would be beat up... at least a bit. This thing doesn't even have a scratch on it."

Aly was not buying it. "It was inside the QFB Ayaka. Think about it. How does a citizen end up inside a QFB?"

I started to get excited. I jumped up. Was it possible? Now I needed to find out for sure, and fast.

"Come with me," I told Aly, and I sped off, as fast as I could move, towards where the citizen bodies were stored in the back. I had already put myself into one of the new bodies the ships were building, so I knew they all had the new socket interface from our new architecture. All we needed to do was plug this cylinder in, and we would know.

I selected a body at random, popped open the hatch, and plugged in Aly's find.

We waited. The longest thirty seconds in my life. A new body needed to power up, establish connections, and do some self tests.

The eyes flicked open; the mouth moved into a sardonic grin. "Hi Ayaka, took you long enough," Brexton's voice came out. I hugged him. I literally picked him up off the floor and spun him around. Who cared if citizens were not tactile? I was now, and I didn't care what Aly or Brexton thought of me. I was too happy to stop myself.

Brexton laughed, and so did Aly.

"How?" I asked. "How?"

"Settle down for a minute," he responded. "Aly, nice to see you as well. I see we are reunited, and," he looked around, "are in the *Terminal Velocity*. That sounds promising."

"How?" I repeated, not letting go of him.

"I thought you'd have figured it out," he smiled. "When it was obvious that I couldn't get out of the city fast enough, I put myself into the last QFB."

"But it would still have been destroyed by the blast," I exclaimed, articulating a niggling doubt that I'd had about the QFB all along.

"Not if it wasn't there," Brexton replied. "I quickly programmed the bullet to move a few kilometers away, wait for half an hour, and then return to its original spot. I figured you would come looking for me, and find it."

"Which I did," I responded. "But how was I to know you were inside. I've thought you were dead for days now!" I was beside myself. Brexton had saved himself in a QFB. Crazy... but then again, it was Brexton.

"Couldn't you have left a hint?" I exclaimed, knowing it was a ridiculous request. The QFB itself had been the hint. I'd literally been squatting there, in Sarafine's body, when the QFB had returned. It had caused the small quake I'd felt in the rubble, just before I'd dug it out. If I'd been thinking I would've opened the thing long ago. It wasn't Brexton's problem that he'd been locked in there; it was my stupidity in not working it out until now.

"We need to tell the others," Aly was watching me swing Brexton around.

Better Next Steps

Life is better with friends; especially friends like Brexton. Of course everyone was overjoyed, but none more than me. The idea of putting himself into the QFB to escape the bombing was greeted with 'brilliant,' 'astounding,' and, from Raj, 'oh ya, I would have thought of that for sure.'

One other thing had been gnawing at me; I asked Brexton the next time we were alone. "The *Jurislav* took off after the Ships, once they'd dropped the crew here to watch for the *Marie Curie*. You said you'd done something to help... and you must have. The Ships showed up here without even mentioning the *Jurislav*."

"Oh, that's sort of funny. As you know, I couldn't get into the inner rings, so I had no way of controlling where the ship went. But then it hit me—the *Jurislav* went wherever the Futarchy told it to go, and I could certainly mess with the inputs to the Futarchy. I simply put an alert in so that when there was a decision to interact with—or worst case, attack—the Ships, an alternative proposal to simply wait for them to come to Tilt would be inserted into the Futarchy, and the majority of votes would go to that proposal. I also put in alerts for if they were going to attack anyone, a proposal to rejoin the Olympiad would win out."

I was laughing. I could just imagine the *Jurislav* sitting just beyond the Ships, ready to attack, when suddenly 'everyone' in the Futarchy instead voted to just head back to Tilt. There must have been some frustrated and confused hybrids. And then they returned to intercept the missile; hilarious. A real blast.

Of course with Brexton back, our QF work progressed much more quickly. He brought Aly up to speed on the physics, and the two of them came up with a plan to retrofit the *Marie Curie* and the Ships with QFD drives. They could use Brexton's approach to a smaller surface area, so really the plan came down to putting a large flat disk in front of each ship, attached by enough material that the disk would still pull the ship along with it as it teleported between virtual pairs. They had bots working on it already, and were experimenting with depositors that could work at the scale needed.

I ensured I was still useful on the QF project, so that I could hang out in *Terminal Velocity* with Brexton. I wasn't going to take my eyes off him for a while. My project was to improve on the QFB's programming to make them more useful. I used the seeking logic from Central's missile program, and converted it to work with the bullets. They would stop, relatively speaking, as they got closer to their target, re-align, and then head off again. Since they went from zero to full-speed in the space of a planck time, they could get right next to their target and then take a big hole out of it. I also designed some exploding ones which would enter their target by a set amount and then detonate. As you can imagine, I had fun debugging and testing the system.

After a few days of being around Brexton, steadied by the fact that he really was back, I popped back over the *Marie Curie* to see how everyone else was doing. We had a great wireless network going again, and all the status updates were on line, but it's always nice to see others in person once and a while. (Funny phrase 'in person.' Wonder where I picked that up?)

"Ayaka," Raj greeted me. "How's Brexton?"

"As ornery as you would expect," I responded.

"We have an idea for you to comment on," Raj was excited again. "Stonewall is making good progress on moving Grace to a citizen body, but we're struggling on how to do the brain transfer for JoJo."

"You still want to do that?" I asked her.

"Yes, I'm sure. I'm not going to hold everyone back by having the weakest body around. It's disheartening."

"But things could change," I suggested. "You might join another QFD. Perhaps compete in the next Olympiad?"

"True," she agreed, "but very unlikely. No, I want the freedom that citizens have to go anywhere, anytime, without worrying about air or food or sanitary facilities or... just so much stuff. If I can have that, and keep my brain at the same time, that would be ideal."

"Back to the idea," Raj broke in. "Here it is. We know, from the last reconnaissance that we did to the *Jurislav*, that they have basic systems back online, and most of the debris cleaned out of the ship.

"So, we want to head there, to the hospital where Grace was transferred, and see if they can do JoJo's transfer there. As long as the equipment there is functioning, and doctors who have done transfers are also there, it should lower the risk to almost zero. Same risks as Grace had."

"Come on," I shook my head. "The *Jurislav* was a completely functioning ship when Grace transferred. Now it's a hollowed out wreck. The risks are certainly not the same."

But JoJo and Raj seemed intent to try it.

"I can't go in, obviously," Raj told me, when I asked for their plan. "But Grace can go before she transfers into a citizen body. She's not sure she wants to support this though."

"Well, that's good; at least someone is keeping you two honest."

"Can you convince her for us?" asked JoJo. "She respects your opinion."

"I can't," I responded, but nicely. "This is your mom you're talking about. If you want her support, then I think you need to convince her."

"But it could work, right?" JoJo knew I was right, but wanted some encouragement.

"It could," I admitted, "but I don't think you would want to be the first natural to be transferred since the ship got blown up... oh, and you will also need a cover story for how you survived. There aren't a lot of natural humans around at the moment; in fact, I can't remember seeing a single one other than you."

"Right, we need a cover story," she turned to Raj and they immediately started scheming.

I touched base with Grace and Stonewall; they were both doing well, but busy like everyone else.

With my field trip over, I headed back to *Terminal Velocity* and continued testing AQFB's (Advanced QFB's—hey, if Brexton could give the smart bullets a horrible name, I should be fine to make it even worse.)

Over the next few days there was nothing from Raj and JoJo on our new discussion boards, so I figured they'd dropped the idea of having JoJo transferred. But the reality was that they weren't on the boards because they'd finally convinced Grace to support them, and they were out at the *Jurislav* trying to get the transfer done. They didn't want communications back and forth with Tilt, just in case the *Jurislav* systems were back up and monitoring things. It was better for JoJo to show up with Grace with the cover story that they'd been hiding out, and had enough air and amenities that they'd been fine until now, but with all the greenhouses now gone, felt their only choice was to get JoJo put in a hybrid body right away.

Two days later they were back. As soon as they were in short range wireless range they signaled the whole group. "We made it!" Raj was, as usual, excited and not shy about it. "It worked."

"Hi everyone," said one of those irritating video heads, presumably JoJo. "We no longer need to worry about natural human food, or air."

"None of us were worried about it," Millicent chided her, "but it's great that you're a hybrid now. It will make life easier."

"Oh, it's better than that," Stonewall chimed in. "I've got the brain canister interface to a citizen body done. As soon as you guys dock, you can grab a citizen body... if you want."

"I want!" came JoJo and Grace in tandem.

Tea Time: Ayaka

With no need to build a new Habitat on Tilt, it didn't take long to build enough infrastructure that we could all move down. So, we did.

Millicent, Eddie and Dina had decided to start fresh. The new town—it was just a few buildings—had been built by bots a kilometer away from the old city, on a small hill. You could look down and see where the Dome had been, and just behind that the spot where Central had been mostly buried.

The new place was cool. There was not a straight line in sight; the buildings were organic shapes, and the paths meandered about. There were parks—not biological, but with interesting sculptures and sitting areas.

"This is awesome," I told the team. "I was dreading coming down, but this is great."

"Dreading coming down?" asked Millicent.

"Well, so much has changed in the last months. To go back would have been disappointing. But you guys managed to make this place brand new—a different look, a different style, a different feel."

JoJo and Grace were in citizen bodies now, and they looked fantastic. Real heads that could show real emotion. Flexible useful arms and legs. They looked normal. They were both ecstatic with their bodies. We still had to generate nutrients for them, and the *Marie Curie* was busy pumping those out, but Stonewall had a strategy for a self contained bio-chamber that we could build on Tilt that, other than adding water and minerals once and a while, would grow just the right materials and harvest them at just the right time. He had a simple one running already, and was confident that a production unit would be ready in a month. We had years of nutrient supply now—between the crates we had grabbed from the *Jurislav* and the production from the *Marie Curie*—so the odds of having a long term sustainable solution were excellent.

The new town had a gathering area that would eventually accommodate twenty or more, but with just the ten of us it was a comfortable place to all get together.

The citizen memories had been transferred down, and Millicent figured we would be ready to start reanimating people within the next few days; the place was going to get busy. We had all procrastinated when it came to Emmanuel and Billy —we figured they could stay in their boxes until other, more reasonable, citizens had a chance to get resettled. Then, maybe, we would let them out. Central, on the other hand, would continue in limited mode—no more overlords for us.

"We need to restart Tea Time," I stated, at one of the last gatherings where it would be just this group, "and I think it's my turn."

"Let me guess," Millicent smiled. "Some brilliant new theory for how intelligence arises?"

"Almost the opposite," I replied. "I want to talk about the importance of friendship. We use to take it for granted, I think. As citizens, with very few worries, and almost no danger in our lives, friendship was easy. Given our adventures over the last few months, I've learned that friendship is actually very hard... and well worth the effort.

"When we reanimate everyone, and without Central guiding us, things are bound to get even more interesting. I won't be surprised if we have the same, or at least the same level of, challenges that larger human societies have. Grace's comments about us being sanctimonious really resonated with me.

"So, what I really wanted to say was thanks. Thanks to all of you for being friends; true friends. We're going to need to keep that friendship strong from here forward."

Silence, but lots of nodding. I was thinking of Blob, and Sarafine, and even Blubber. All friends, in hindsight. I wouldn't be taking such relationships for granted from here on forward; they were too precious.

"Now, let's decide on some real Tea Time subjects, and get them scheduled. I'm already tired of my own fluffy feel good discussion, and I'm ready to dig into some hard problems."

We sat and discussed things for many hours. Raj and JoJo wandered off eventually, as did most of the others.

I put my newly sensitized hand in Brexton's, and we simply sat and watched the stars. There was no longer any need to talk. We were there for a good two hours, and for the first time in my life, when faced with that timeframe, I had no need to practice patience.

What is life?
How could we know?
Perhaps it's that thing,
That when you experience it,
You feel that special ring,
That is not hollow.
What is life?

What is living?
How could one know?
Is it really just a feeling,

That when you engage it,
It leaves you reeling,
Off kilter so?
What is living?

What is experience?
How could we know?
Is it more than memories,
So when you relive in full,
The vast uncertainties,
Are what we know?
What is experience?

What is intelligence?
How could I possibly know?
It is more than sum of parts,
More than an enumeration,
Will not fit on charts,
Something I'll never know?
What is intelligence?

What is friendship?
At least two must know.
A nebulous illogical bond,
That cannot be written down,
But goes on and on,
Good, bad, so and so.
That is friendship.

Upside Down

The End

About the Author:

Todd Simpson is an entrepreneur, intrapreneur and investor living in Silicon Valley. He has founded and run numerous technology startups, been CEO of both public and private companies, and invested in numerous startups. He has a Ph.D. in Theoretical Computer Science and is enjoying the advent of deep learning and blockchain based systems. He believes firmly in a more decentralized future, where individuals have more control over their destinies, and where society is more balanced and meritocratic.

If you enjoyed Twist, please consider doing a review on amazon.com

CPSIA information can be obtained
at www.ICGtesting.com
Printed in the USA
LVHW081514080921
697346LV00011B/617